Riven

The Arinthian Line: Book Two

SEVER BRONNY

This book is a work of fiction. Names, characters, places and incidents either are the product of the author's imagination or are used fictitiously, and any similarity to actual persons, living or deceased, establishments of any kind, events, or locales is entirely coincidental.

Library and Archives Canada Cataloguing in Publication

Bronny, Sever, 1979-, author
Riven / Sever Bronny.

(The Arinthian line ; bk. 2)

Issued in print and electronic formats.
ISBN 978-0-9937676-2-3 (pbk.).—
ISBN 978-0-9937676-3-0 (epub)

I. Title.

PS8603.R652R59 2015 C813'.6

C2015-901205-8
C2015-901206-6

Version 1.2

Map and cover by author using creative commons and commercial licensing. "Riven" cover font by Steve Deffeyes, deffeyes.com.

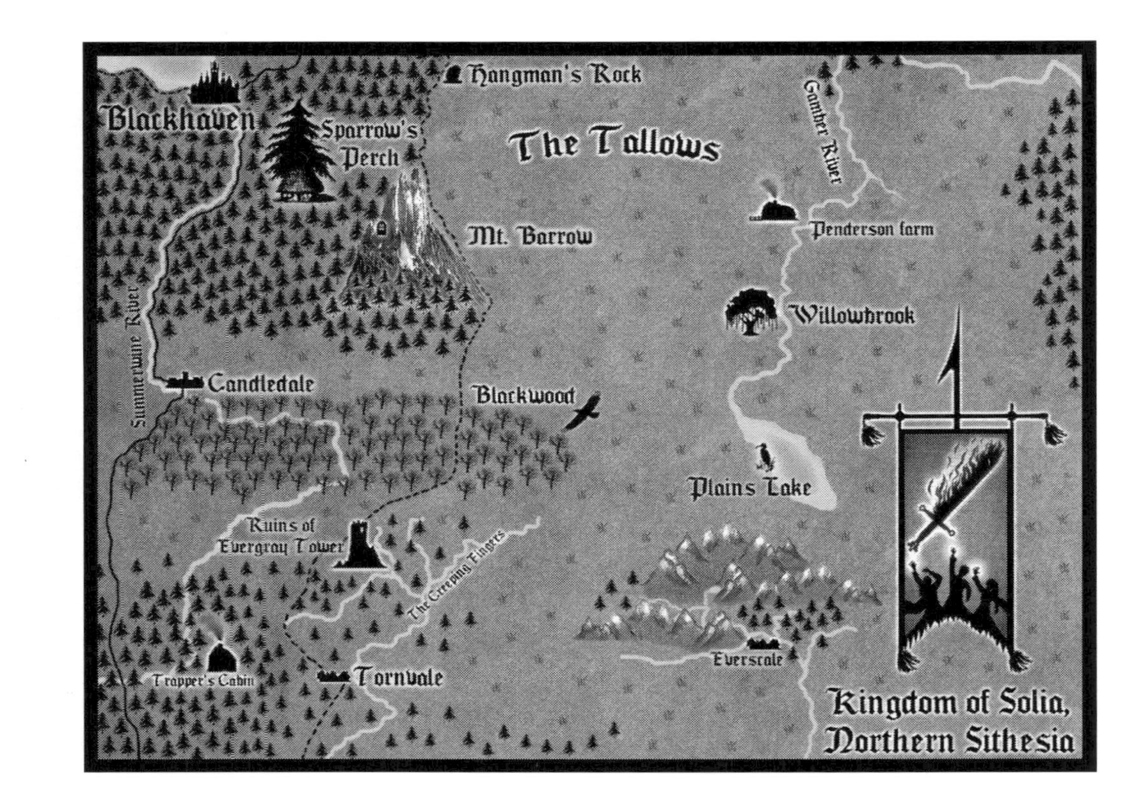
Blackhaven
Hangman's Rock
Sparrow's Perch
The Tallows
Gamber River
Penderson farm
Mt. Barrow
Willowbrook
Summerwine River
Candledale
Blackwood
Plains Lake
Ruins of Evergray Tower
The Creeping Fingers
Everscale
Trapper's Cabin
Tornvale
Kingdom of Solia, Northern Sithesia

LEY

There was murder in the sand here, Augum Stone thought, sweeping the horizon with parchment-dry eyes. Ley stretched in every direction, a blistering, dusty wasteland squashed by fast-moving clouds. Something about the place made him feel as if he was walking over graves. He imagined entire armies buried just beneath the orange desert. Armies from some ancient era, long forgotten. Armies that met a slow end, where the land choked their thoughts until they turned on each other in a barbaric bloodbath.

"Leera—" he said. Leera Jones trundled just ahead, shoulder-length raven hair sashaying with hypnotic rhythm. How irritating—she was ignoring him again. She and Bridget were supposed to be his good friends, except friendship felt like a distant echo in this harsh land.

"Lee—" but he tripped over something. His heart stopped.

It was a soldier's hand.

No, it was a rock, stop seeing things. He rubbed his eyes and continued on. How many times had *that* happened? Too many visions that mirrored his fears.

"Leera—" Was it so hard to answer him? They had explored Castle Arinthian and achieved their 1st degree together, she specializing in the water element, Bridget in earth, and he in lightning. They had saved each other's lives and witnessed so much, and now she was … now she was ignoring him!

A particularly strong gust whipped the hood off his head. For the umpteenth time he jerked the scratchy wool back over his tangle of short umber hair, cracked hands aching.

The march was wearying. His limbs throbbed as if each had an extra heart. His thigh was bruised from the slap of his sword, the Dreadnought blade Burden's Edge. Then there were his tender feet, numb and sore.

What he wouldn't do for a quiet night in a soft bed, sheltered from the wind. It had been ten days since he and five others had stepped through a portal linking Castle Arinthian to Ley. Yet, with the exception of a memorial ceremony on the first day, all they had done since was drag themselves through this barren landscape.

Days were unusually long in Ley, the sun never rising more than a third of the way up the sky, as if too tired to finish the journey. It would shine for twenty hours of every day before surrendering to an icy tempest of night that made restful sleep a luxury of the past.

Flopping one foot before the other, his thoughts drifted to the Kingdom of Solia. He had never stepped outside its borders before. He missed the smell of a cedar campfire, the crisp stillness of the forests, the pristine snow. He missed the castle, abandoned for the last two hundred years and now surely swarming with Legion soldiers. He even missed the rustic confines of Mrs. Stone's cave, long collapsed. Above all, he missed the almost carefree joy he had felt, at least in comparison to this dreary march of an existence in which every thought seemed tainted by an unexplainable dread.

Maybe someone else will talk to him. He glanced to the front of the line where his great-grandmother and mentor, the legendary lightning warlock Anna Atticus Stone, shuffled along in the lead, white robe billowing in the wind. Her shriveled frame bent over a gnarled walking stick, silver ponytail dangling past her waist. But even she had been particularly terse of late. Just that morning, she snapped at him for not paying attention to some long-winded speech about staying close together.

Bridget Burns hiked behind her, wearing the same burgundy apprentice robe as Augum. She had a small pert nose and long cinnamon hair she habitually swept away from hazel eyes. A Dreadnought piercing dagger named Blackbite hung from her belt. She probably missed Solia as much as he did, if not more. Then again, after everything that had happened, maybe not …

She'd probably ignore him too. None of them got along lately. Even Bridget, the most thoughtful person he knew, had yelled at Sydo for breathing too loudly. That led to a big argument that required Mrs. Stone's intervention.

Prince Sydo Ridian the Fourth, heir to the Kingdom of Solia, slouched along next, his close-cropped fiery hair in disarray, the once-pristine royal doublet dusty and unkempt. Augum had never met a more spoiled brat, their acquaintance strained by the fact his father murdered Sydo's. As it were, just watching the way Sydo's back labored like a dog annoyed him, just as everything seemed to be bothersome of late, from the sand that crept into his clothes to the long silences between conversations.

"Pssst Leera," he hissed. "Leera—!"

She barely turned her head, voice raspy. "What, damn it!"

He finally had her attention, but forgot what he wanted to say. "I'm worried about Mya, she still hasn't spoken," he blurted.

Leera gave a derisive snort.

"You don't care?"

She didn't reply.

"Fine, don't say anything." When she still didn't respond, he had to fight the urge to shout at her. He really wanted to talk about all the things going on in his head, all the worries and fears. If anyone could understand, it should be her.

Instead, he turned his attention to Mya's dragging footsteps behind him. Mya hadn't spoken since the memorial ceremony days ago. Even when the prince addressed her—whom she was sworn to obey—she gave no response. She had not been the same since witnessing the death of her fellow servants.

Augum stole a glance at her, sure that seeing her porcelain face would lift his spirits. But instead of a tall beauty with a warm smile, he saw a hunched girl plodding along as if carrying a great weight. Her once silky jet hair was lanky and uncombed. Her almond eyes, usually brilliant emerald, were downcast and dull. Her plain black servant dress would have been the picture of cleanliness back in the castle, but now it was dusty and torn.

He turned back lest the image burn itself into his mind. Despite being five years his senior, he thought her the most beautiful girl he had ever seen. He wanted to tell her everything would be okay, that soon they'd find plenty of food, water and shelter, yet he just couldn't bring himself to say it. Perhaps he was too afraid of making a fool of himself, like the time he had opened a door in Castle Arinthian and found her standing there wanting entry. Instead of moving aside, he gaped like a fool while Bridget and Leera snickered.

Had they snickered, or was that a malicious twist of memory? This place … this place gave him a bad feeling. Maybe Mya had a remedy for the dark thoughts. She was, after all, a non-arcane traditional healer. He tried to think of ways to approach her on the subject, but his mind drifted with the ever-changing dunes. He imagined her suddenly grabbing him and tearfully apologizing for being so cold, so distant, so—

Mrs. Stone abruptly stopped and turned around. Everyone gathered near, hair and robes whipping in the wind like dry grass.

"It should not be far now," she said in a wheezy voice.

"The same story she fed us yesterday," Prince Sydo said under his breath. "I wager she really could teleport us there, she just wants to teach us some inane lesson."

Bridget's face darkened. "Mrs. Stone already told you that Ley blocks certain spells to prevent a quick attack from armies. You know she'd never—"

Sydo's face twisted. "Unnameable gods, must you prattle—"

Mrs. Stone held up a withered hand, instantly quelling them. "Sit. Down."

They collapsed where they stood while she reached into her robe, withdrawing a small crystal orb.

"Mercy, your endless bickering is getting quite tiresome of late. I need to depart to scavenge more food. Comport yourselves until my return."

Augum stared at the scion with undiminished fascination. He still had a hard time believing the Leyans forged this highly sought-after artifact over fifteen hundred years ago. How his ancestors managed to keep it in the family from one generation to the next, stretching all the way back to Atrius Arinthian, was a complete mystery to him. He had an even harder time believing that little orb was what all this trouble was about. His father, the Lord of the Legion, wanted all seven to complete his Great Quest. He supposedly possessed two thus far—what would happen if he attained them all?

He checked over his shoulder, half-expecting to see the murderous man astride his deathly horse, golden armor gleaming in the bleak sun. He only saw a wind-blasted orange emptiness.

When he turned back to his great-grandmother, the scion hovered before her, emitting a quiet hum. She whispered arcane words and imploded into nothingness with a percussive THWOMP.

"That's what she should be teaching us," the prince said with a sneer.

For once, Augum agreed, never mind that Teleport was a 9th degree spell.

Leera sneered. "Yeah, and you certainly have the talent for it, *Your Highness*." She closed her eyes and fell backwards onto the dirt.

"Your sarcasm is as dull as your wit, peasant girl."

Usually Leera would not let that slide, but in this case, she only sighed deeply, probably as exhausted as Augum was. He stole a sidelong glance at Mya, who sat with glazed eyes.

Bridget placed a hand on Leera's arm. "Don't worry, I'm sure we're almost there."

Leera did not respond, letting her tongue loll out from her mouth like a lazy snail.

Bridget frowned and turned her attention to the group. "Maybe we should all tell stories, or practice arcanery, do something … constructive. You know, stay busy and positive?"

Sydo massaged his temples. "Ughh … why have I been condemned to the company of commoners?"

Sydo had obviously forgotten he was only here because they had *saved* him from a most untimely end. Augum leaned forward to deliver a few terse words but caught a look from Bridget. She seemed determined to keep it civil, and he relented.

"The legendary Land of the Ley. What a jape," Sydo went on, head now resting on his knees. "I should be in Blackhaven on my father's throne, commanding a kingdom and attended to by royal subjects. Instead, I am surrounded by fools in this miserable desert—"

"Oh, shut *up* already!" Leera said without opening her eyes.

Sydo's face went purple. "How. Dare. You. You, whose parents, like my own, were slaughtered by this one's villainous father!" He stabbed a thumb at Augum, who felt his blood begin to boil.

Leera shot up, voice a deadly whisper. "Don't you dare bring that up—"

"The only difference," Sydo continued, speaking through gritted teeth, "is yours *deserved* to die."

For a moment, they all stared at him. Even he appeared stunned by what he said, his mouth hanging open. "I … I didn't mean—"

Leera shot forward, grabbing him by the throat. Sydo gasped and flailed.

"Stop it, both of you!" Bridget desperately tried to pry them apart while Mya sat watching as if they were nothing more than two quibbling hens in a coop. "Augum, help me—"

Augum, who was still trying to understand *why* Sydo had said that, sprang to help. It took both of them to uncurl Leera's fingers from the prince's throat and wrestle her back. She stumbled and fell to the dirt, raven hair sticking to her forehead, looking like a freckled bull about to charge. Instead, she scowled, dusted herself off, and turned away.

"Are ... are you all right, Your Highness?" Bridget asked, panting.

Augum felt his temper rise—Sydo had just said her parents *deserved* to die and she was calling him *Your Highness*?

The prince coughed, rubbing his neck, face a patchwork of loathing. He slowly turned his gaze to Bridget. "How could you let her maul me? You believe yourself worthy of *my* company? You are a miserable, unbecoming—do not presume to touch me—!"

Bridget recoiled as if bitten, eyes immediately tearing up.

For a moment, there was only the sound of robes flapping in the wind, until Sydo gave Augum a disgusted look.

"What are *you* looking at?" Augum asked, fighting the urge to punch the snotling in his face.

Suddenly Bridget turned back to them, wiping her face with her sleeve. "Fine! *Great!* Just kill each other, see if I care!" She fell to her knees, weeping into her hands. "I can't do this anymore ..."

Augum watched his friend heave with sobs and felt his heart tighten. What was happening to them? Why were they so angry, so emotional? "I'm ... I'm sorry, I don't know what—"

"—my mother told me about this place," Mya said, voice almost lost to the wind, hair flailing like a tangle of snakes.

Everyone froze. It was the most she had spoken in days.

"We shall claw each other's eyes out then lie down and starve to death."

Bridget took Mya's porcelain hands in her own. "Can you tell us more?"

Mya wiped a tear from Bridget's face, and looked off into the distance.

"You need not bother with her," Sydo said, waving dismissively. "She is as useless as a mule without legs."

Augum's fists instantly curled, but Bridget noticed and lunged in between, holding his gaze, the compassion in her eyes disarming his anger.

"Just let that fiend finish the job already! After all, it runs in the *family*—"

Bridget's head whipped around. "What's the matter with you! Have you no sense of decency? Have you turned into an *animal*?"

Sydo's gaze faltered under Bridget's glare.

"What if Mya's right?" Leera asked. "I mean, what if we keep walking until we're driven mad? What if we don't find the Leyans in time? Or what if they're all dead, or even worse, only myth, and this whole place is nothing but stupid, endless desert—"

"Control yourself," Bridget said. "We'll be fine. We have Mrs. Stone."

Sydo made a sound like air flapping through loose bellows. "Oh, yes, and what great good that has done us here. Do you truly believe we can continue this death march on berries and leaves and so little water? We should be dead in a day if this continues—"

"—will you just stop it, you're not helping." Bridget's voice shook. "We'll be fine, you'll see."

Augum glanced at their tracks, concerned Mya might be right. He watched the wind slowly eat away at them. By the morning, they'll have disappeared.

Bridget wiped her sandy face with her sleeve and drew her robe tighter. "Please, let's all just get some sleep. Who knows when Mrs. Stone will return."

Augum tightened his hood to keep the sand from stinging his face and tried to catch some sleep. But his dark thoughts just wouldn't let him. Everything that ever went wrong in his life paraded across his mind in a never-ending cavalcade of torment—the first time his foster parents beat him; Dap's fist connecting with his face; being chased by a gaggle of boys in Willowbrook; watching the village burn from the safety of the Tallows while he anxiously curled the yellow grass around his fingers ...

THOMAS

The day steadily dimmed as the clouds picked up their pace. The wind blew at a cold roar, stinging any exposed flesh and forcing them to huddle together. Nobody seemed to catch a wink of sleep. Prince Sydo's teeth chattered as he sat in the middle of the group, a spot that afforded the most shelter. Lamenting the lack of blankets, Augum shivered in the front, taking the brunt of the wind.

As night descended, Augum felt as if he was trying to think through a fog. He stopped caring about his painfully cracked hands, his aching feet, the gnawing hollowness in his stomach, whether or not Mrs. Stone would return. He even forgot about all the terrible memories of his past. When he sat up, squinting at the palest of lines on the horizon, he let his hood fall away from his face, exposing it to the raking wind. The sting was numbing, yet he did nothing to correct it. He glanced skyward with the expression of a dull child, marveling at the moving masses of black cloud that seemed within reaching distance.

Glancing to his right, he was strangely unsurprised to see Bridget's silhouette standing apart from the group. She faced the wind, hair streaming behind her, robe flapping violently. She took a step into the wind, stopped, took another step, and stopped again, repeating this motion, slowly walking further and further away.

He observed with neither fascination nor fear, only the subtlest feeling that something wasn't right. He watched until Bridget's form disappeared into the night, and when she was completely gone, he kept his eyes on the blackness still.

Suddenly there was a loud THWOMP. The area flooded with the light from a hovering pumpkin-sized sphere of lightning. It brought Mrs. Stone's creased face into sharp relief, gnarled stick gripped tight in her hands, a sack slung over her shoulder. Augum, usually impressed by her ability to cast the 1st degree Shine spell in a different form, found himself observing with nothing short of banal apathy.

Her eyes took quick account of them. "Where is Bridget?"

No one stirred. Augum struggled to understand what she wanted. He knew the words, just not their significance. His head turned to the darkness where he last saw a familiar form. Mrs. Stone's eyes followed his gaze. She immediately strode off in that direction, the globe of light trailing. He watched it weave about, shrinking down to the size of a firefly. The motion was oddly calming, the peace of it a soothing, mesmerizing balm.

He awoke on the ground, unaware of having even fallen asleep.

Mrs. Stone stood near, holding a shivering Bridget by the elbow. "I daresay you have been gripped by the song, girl. Sit."

Bridget, pale and shivering, did not respond. Mrs. Stone's lips pressed together and she gently pushed her into a sitting position beside Augum. Then she unslung her sack, withdrawing vaguely familiar fruits, vegetables, and a skin of water. No one reached out for them or even so much as blinked.

"I see. It is as I feared." She removed something from her robe and soon a smaller globe was floating alongside the larger, this one flashing with silent lightning. Augum began to feel better. Meanwhile, Mrs. Stone placed what looked like purple pears into their listless hands.

Augum glanced up at his great-grandmother. She made a motion akin to eating. He stared at the strange fruit before biting into it. Mrs. Stone nodded and moved on to the others. Augum felt better still as he ate, though his thoughts remained as murky as the sky.

When they had all finished eating and drinking, Mrs. Stone sat amongst them, the two mismatching globes floating lazily around her, unhampered by the wind. Augum struggled with his thoughts until finally, in what must have been the thick of night, he felt himself conscious enough to ask a question.

"Nana, what … what happened?"

Mrs. Stone, who seemed to have been dozing, startled awake. "Hmm? Ah, yes … I fear I am to blame—I was gone too long and, without the protective influence of the scion, you succumbed to the Song of the Wastes."

"The Song …?"

"An ancient enchantment meant to turn invading armies against each other, implemented in the time of Occulus. The effect seems to have become rather strong, however, and the weather—well, last I visited, let us say it was quite peaceful."

"You've been here before, Mrs. Stone—?" Bridget asked in a groggy tone.

Mrs. Stone sighed. "Yes, a long time ago. But enough of that. Is everyone feeling well enough to walk?" They gave unsure nods. "Good. Let us go on then. We shall rest soon enough."

One by one they stood, readying to depart—except for Mya, who gaped into the darkness with half-closed eyes.

Mrs. Stone shuffled over to her and waved a hand before her face. "Bridget, Augum—drag her if you must. I want everyone to walk alongside me and watch each other. No one is to drift off on their own, am I understood?"

"Yes, Mrs. Stone," Bridget said, grabbing one of Mya's hands. Augum grabbed the other, distinctly conscious of wrapping his fingers around hers. If this moment were to be his last, he would not mind in the least. He looked up at her, trying to draw her back to them with a look of empathy, willing her to understand how much he cared about her … but she did not meet his eyes, dazedly letting herself be guided along.

Augum caught an annoyed look from Leera. Was he walking too slowly again? He quickened his pace a little.

Mrs. Stone held stride, keeping a close eye, globe lighting the way. After what felt like hours of ambling, she abruptly stopped, peering ahead into the darkness. At the edge of her light stood a hairless man dressed in nothing but sandals and baggy black pants that rippled violently in the wind. He possessed a square jaw, bald head, and a bronze muscle-sculpted upper body. His eyes were what captured Augum's attention though—solid black, blacker than coal, blacker than the night. Unnameable gods, they had run across a demon and he was going to—

"I think it's a Leyan," Bridget whispered.

Mrs. Stone took a step forward. "Thomas."

"Anna," the man replied in a deep voice that cut through the wind. "You have returned."

"For the time being."

"You have aged, my wife."

Everyone but Mya exchanged looks. Augum felt goosebumps rise on his skin. His great-grandfather was a Leyan! But how could this be? The man looked nothing more than thirty years of age!

"The teachings can still reverse the course of time on the flesh, Anna," Thomas continued. "You have not accepted the invitation as of yet."

"My duties to the mortal world bind me there. Forgive me, but I must condemn you to this loneliness still."

"I have the company of the sand, the wind, the clouds."

Mrs. Stone stared at him a moment before giving a pained smile. "You still return to the same spot."

"It is as good as any other."

"It took some time to find it again. My memory is not as it once was."

Augum looked around. There was nothing to distinguish this place from any other.

"All things pass," Thomas said.

"So they do indeed ..."

Thomas' unblinking ebony eyes seemed to focus on the hovering scion. It flickered with silent lightning, emitting that quiet hum.

"Yes, I still have it." Mrs. Stone hid it within her robe. The hum immediately died.

Watching it disappear, Augum suddenly felt himself grow very tired, as if all the hours of sleeplessness had finally taken their toll. He really wanted to lie down.

"This is your great-grandson, Augum Stone."

Augum stared at his strange great-grandfather. His grip on Mya's hand tightened.

Thomas only stood there, letting the wind flow over his body like water over rock, his face expressionless. "My great-grandson."

A windy silence passed before Mrs. Stone spoke again. "I bring grave tidings from Solia. Our grandson, Lividius, has become the Lord of the Legion. He calls himself Sparkstone now and seeks the seven scions. Also, I fear, he treads the necromantic path. His ambition knows no bounds."

"It is as it is, and cannot be otherwise."

Mrs. Stone took a deep breath. "The ancient Song of the Wastes has affected the young."

"As per its nature—the childlings are uninvited."

"Yes, well, I could hardly have left them behind now, could I?" Mrs. Stone adjusted her robe. "Forgive me. I do not recall the song being so potent. Even I do not feel quite myself."

"You have always come bearing the scion, though it is true the song has changed of late. I do not know why, I simply, along with the others, stand to witness change."

"And the skies?"

"There is much debate amongst us on this matter."

"I see. The young need sanctuary."

"Very well." Thomas swept over them with his night eyes. "I shall break the Vow for you, Anna. I will build sanctuary and make light for the uninvited." His right arm flared to life with bands of fire and the ground started shaking. Clay beds rose from the dirt around them, with moss growing into pillows and blankets. When the rumbling stopped, he made a simple gesture to the beds. Everybody but Mrs. Stone chose one and lay down, while he continued his arcanery.

As Augum struggled to keep his eyes open, trees rose from the ground, making a large protective grove. The last thing he saw before sleep overtook him was his great-grandfather, arm burning bright, raising an earthen table the color of rust.

A VOTE OF LIFE AND DEATH

Augum awoke to the rustling of leaves and creaking of trunks, feeling as if he had slept for a month. Somewhere out of view, his great-grandmother spoke to her husband in low tones.

He paid no attention. It was snugly warm under the moss blanket, from where he watched orange-tinged clouds race by, until his great-grandmother's head swam into view.

"Breakfast, Augum."

He smiled for the first time since arriving in Ley. "Yes, Nana." He sat up, stretched, yawned, and glanced about.

They were in a grass clearing surrounded by twisting oaks. Braziers burned on simple pedestals. Moss beds lay strewn about. Earthen stone benches sandwiched an earthen table, on top of which were an assortment of Leyan fruits and vegetables in rough wooden bowls.

The others stirred in their beds. When Augum saw Mya, she smiled. He felt his face grow hot and turned away.

Bridget prodded her mossy pillow. "I thought this was all a dream."

Mrs. Stone strolled to the table. "Thomas has placed a sanctuary enchantment on this grove. You should feel completely normal by now, and if not, I promise you will after breakfast."

Prince Sydo moseyed up to Thomas and inspected him. "You have an unusual quality to your skin. And I remember … that you are Mrs. Stone's husband, is that not so?"

"It is so, Sydo Ridian." He stood calm, hands idly by his sides, eyes unfathomable.

"Are you a Leyan?"

"A Leyan I am."

"Yet you know the element of fire. I saw you build all this … I saw your arm."

"It is as you have observed."

"How many stripes do you have?"

"That is quite enough, young prince," Mrs. Stone said. "Please join us at the table."

The prince hesitated, made a face, and took a seat opposite Mrs. Stone. Bridget, Leera and Augum took a seat to her left, Mya and Thomas to her right.

Mrs. Stone gestured to the food. "Well it won't eat itself now, will it?"

All hands but those of the Leyan reached forward.

"That was a very strange night," Leera said, inspecting red fruit in the shape of a star.

Mya's cheeks reddened. "I apologize for being so—"

"—it's all right," Augum said a little too quickly. Bridget and Leera snickered into their hands while he shrank.

"No apologies necessary, young lady," Mrs. Stone said, glancing over at her husband. "My word, Thomas, time has certainly dulled your tongue."

"Time is meaningless. The moment is real."

Mrs. Stone grunted, pulling out a black apple from a bowl.

"Mrs. Stone," Bridget began, cheeks pink, "if you'll forgive me, but, how did you and Mr. Stone meet?"

"That was a very long time ago now, young lady. It happened back when we were in the academy together—and yes, even I was a schoolgirl once."

The girls, including Mya, exchanged warm looks.

Mrs. Stone looked off into a brazier and smiled to herself before clearing her throat and dabbing at her lips with a cloth. "But I shall not bore you with tales." She turned to her husband, ignoring the dramatized groans from the girls. "Where are the others?"

"They stand observing change."

"Has change observed them?"

"All things change."

Mrs. Stone nodded slowly.

"Thomas—err—Mr. Stone," Augum said, unable to resist the question any longer. "Um, how are you so young if you're my great-grandfather?"

Everyone stopped eating to listen.

"That, Augum Stone, only a Leyan may discover."

"Has my royal father ever come here?" Prince Sydo asked while Mya peeled a pink banana for him.

"That I do not know."

"But are you not supposed to know *everything*?"

"I find I know very little."

Sydo rolled his eyes as he took the banana from Mya. "So what *do* you know then?"

"Manners, young prince," Mrs. Stone said.

Sydo turned away and silently mimicked her.

"Are we going to train here?" Bridget asked.

"For a time," Mrs. Stone replied. "Thomas will train you while I investigate what is happening to Ley."

Augum shifted in his seat, barely able to contain his excitement. They were going to train with a real Leyan! To think of all the ancient arcanery the man knew—and how much of it was off-the-books?

"Begging your pardon, m'lord," Mya began, folding her hands neatly, "I cannot help but wonder what would happen if the Lord of the Legion acquired all seven scions."

The group quieted down. Augum felt a prickle at the mention of his father.

"Thomas, the vow—"

"—has already been broken, Anna."

And what was all this vow business about?

"Fifteen-hundred years ago," Thomas continued, bronze skin shining in the brazier light, "in the time when Leyans mingled with the mortal world, seven scions were forged and distributed to seven warlocks, for the purpose of defeating a necromancer by the name of Occulus."

Augum exchanged knowing glances with Bridget and Leera. One of those scions was gifted to Atrius Arinthian, his great ancestor and the one who ended up slaying Occulus.

"When Occulus was vanquished, we let mortals keep the scions as gifts. Yet we suspected a day would come when one would covet all, seeking to bathe in frothing shores of never-ending influence. Thus, precautions were taken."

Mrs. Stone folded her cloth napkin. "Precautions. And what, pray tell, were these precautions?"

Thomas fixed his black eyes on his wife. "Possession of all seven scions results in self-destruction."

The fire from the braziers fluttered as Mrs. Stone's face darkened. "Do you mean to tell me, Thomas Stone, that if Lividius finds the other six, I need only give him the seventh to vanquish him?"

"Perhaps. The future is as yet unwritten."

"Surely there must be another way—"

"That is conceivable."

"With only two scions, Lividius will most certainly annihilate all of Solia and every kingdom beyond in search of the rest."

"The path of the river of time is as yet unwritten. We cannot know what is unknowable. That is for the Seers."

Mrs. Stone stared at her husband, tapping the table with a bony finger. "You have given us much to think on."

The group ate on in silence. Only Thomas did not eat. The clouds grew dark and the wind picked up, forcing them to bundle in their robes and draw their hoods. The great oaks creaked, leaves rustling softly. Mrs. Stone dabbed at her lip with a cloth, cleared her throat, and stood.

"I am going to leave you all under Thomas' care for the day. I should return in the evening. I expect all of you," she eyed the prince in particular, "to behave accordingly."

The prince smoothed his fiery hair, which did not appear to be cooperating. Augum had the impression Sydo was not coping well without his daily royal bath and flock of servants attending to his every need.

Thomas stood. "Then let it be so. Mya Liaxh, Sydo Ridian, Leera Jones, Bridget Burns, Augum Stone—please follow me."

Augum wondered how Thomas knew their last names. Had Mrs. Stone told him?

Mya Liaxh. Even her surname was pretty.

Thomas led them to a small clearing apart from the beds and table. As they gathered round, Mrs. Stone vanished with a loud THWOMP. Thomas stood there observing the swaying oaks, pants fluttering in the breeze. He did this for so long that Sydo plopped on the ground and started fiddling with the grass.

"Your Highness, that is unbecoming of you," Mya said out of the corner of her mouth.

Sydo glared up at her slender frame. "Do not presume to lecture me, servant—I am still your prince!"

Mya curtsied. "As you say, Your Highness."

" 'As you say, Your Highness,' " Sydo mocked under his breath. "Gods—listen to her drivel … pathetic."

Augum was about to say something vicious to Sydo when—

" 'Gods—listen to her drivel,' " mocked a *second* Prince Sydo, striding from between the oaks. He was dressed in a similar royal doublet, but finer and in impeccable condition. He had makeup on, as if attended to by the King's own artist, and his velvet pants were unblemished and without creases. His hair even appeared redder and parted perfectly down the middle. He held his arms behind his back, his twisted expression reserved solely for the real Sydo.

Sydo sprang to his feet. "What dark trickery is this—?"

"What a shame," the imposter said, shaking his head. "Look at this cheap, royal imitation. I have witnessed rats with better grooming."

"How dare you—I am not the imposter, you are!"

" 'How dare you,' " the imposter mimicked, exaggerating the whine and making a gesture as if crying. Leera snorted, quickly silenced by an elbow from Bridget.

Sydo looked upon Thomas with frantic eyes. "This is not humorous! I demand that you stop this at once!"

Thomas' face remained a bronze mask.

"Oh, did nobody bother to tell you—?" the imposter continued. "Allow me to speak in simple terms, so even *you* can understand." He gesticulated as if talking to a very stupid boy. "You—are—being—re—placed—by—me!"

Sydo blanched. "No …"

"Oh, indeed yes. Why have a filthy, obtuse, overindulged, and inferior prince when you can have a brilliant, witty, funny, and caring one?" The imposter made a graceful gesture at himself. "Oh, and did I mention I am much *friendlier* too?" He bowed to the group, winking at the real Sydo. "That is quite right, my silly little pretender—if they want, they may have me by their side, and there is nothing you can do about it."

Sydo shook his head. "This surely must be a … a jest … a farce!"

"I am afraid not, my dear halfwit prince. There is going to be a vote, the most ultimate, final, *delicious* vote."

"A vote?" Mya's face scrunched with worry. Her almond eyes flicked between the princes.

"Quite right—a vote," the imposter repeated in a whisper. "Think of it—you would never be treated poorly again, but rather with respect and courtesy, as befits your many excellent years of service."

Mya swallowed while the imposter turned to Leera, whose brows rose.

"And you, dear companion. Could you not imagine someone kind by your side, even helpful, as opposed to a spoiled little brat—?"

Leera took one look at the sorry state the real prince was in, and Augum could just see all those terrible things he had said to her running through her mind. "Well, now that you mention it—"

Bridget gave her a scandalized look before the imposter turned to her.

"And you, dear Bridget—could you not imagine me actually *returning* your affections instead of throwing them to the dogs?" He took her hand in his and kissed it.

Bridget went redder than a summer apple.

The imposter next turned to Augum, but the real prince intervened.

"Wait—! Please, I beg of you, before you vote to replace me, hear me speak—"

"Ah, the piglet wants to squeal." The imposter crossed his arms. "This shall be amusing. Make it quick then. I have training to do with my new companions."

Sydo dropped to his knees. "Augum, I beg of you, I am … I am sorry for … for being a brat, I really am! Please do not vote for him, *please* …"

The imposter shook his head. "They do not believe you, Your Royal Highness. Now stop groveling, it is beneath your station and you are making us *both* look quite beastly."

Sydo did not appear to hear. He crawled over to Bridget with clasped hands, further dirtying his pants. "Dear, beautiful, kind, merciful Bridget … I am so sorry, I … I did not know! I shall promise to treat you right from here on. Please, *please*—do not vote for this … imposter."

Bridget could only stand there, mouth hidden behind her fist. Finally, she reached out to help him stand, but he was already crawling over to Leera.

"Still begging," the imposter sang.

This time Sydo seemed to realize what he was doing and quickly got up, trying to dust off his doublet and smooth his hair. "Leera—" he began, hands splayed in welcome.

Leera raised an eyebrow and folded her arms. She looked like she was enjoying this.

"Leera …" Sydo repeated, looking her square in the eye. "I apologize to you. I apologize for being a brat, and for the things I called you. I'm sorry for what I said about your parents, I know they didn't deserve to die, I'm so sorry for that. If you give me a second chance, I promise I'll do better."

Although he was saying the right things, Augum noted the tone sounded flat.

After a long pause, Leera's face softened and she unfolded her arms.

"I would make this last plea impeccable," the imposter said as Sydo moved on to Mya. "For they might be the last words you ever utter."

"Mya …" Sydo began, grasping her porcelain hands. She towered over him, blushing. The trees groaned in a particularly strong gust. "My loyal servant, I have treated you unkindly over the years. Of everyone here, I am least deserving of your vote. I should apologize—"

"All right, enough of your whining," the imposter said, stepping between them. "Hark! It is time to vote! Now who will it be—a better, smarter, wiser, *kinder* Prince, or a foul, useless, spoiled brat? Come now, step beside the one who wins your vote."

The two princes stood apart, one with a victorious grin, the other trembling.

Mya was the first to the real prince's side, placing a supple hand on his shoulder. He closed his eyes and stiffened. Bridget was next, standing beside Mya. Augum glanced at Thomas, who stood serenely by. What he felt from his great-grandfather was not judgment, but compassion. He stepped to Bridget's side.

"You can turn the tide, dear Leera," the imposter said, hands outstretched as if ready to give a great hug. "All I need is *one* vote."

"*One* vote? Well then I hope the changes you promise are genuine."

"Oh, yes, they truly are," the imposter replied, smile widening.

"I wasn't talking to you," Leera said, stepping to the real prince's side.

When the imposter realized what she had done, he screamed and flailed like a little child. His cries soon morphed into loud cracking as the color drained from his face and clothing. He grayed and stiffened, until finally he was nothing more than a stone statue.

Sydo fell to his knees, clutching his chest. Mya and Bridget attended to him as Leera fixed Augum with an impish grin.

"He's just lucky I didn't vote first."

Prince Sydo wiped his face with a cloth, staring at the imposter now permanently frozen in a tantrum. Thomas stood beside him, studying the statue dispassionately. For a while, there was only the sound of swaying oaks, hissing braziers, and the gentle flapping of robes.

"Witness before you a reflection of that which could have been," Thomas said at last.

Sydo felt the stone buttons of the imposter's doublet. "Was … was the choice real?"

"It was real, as is the karma we carry."

Sydo breathed a slow sigh of relief.

Leera elbowed Augum, whispering, "Not even a thank you."

That was some spell, Augum thought. He bet it was off-the-books. Probably ancient and high degree too.

After a time of quiet reflection, he decided to ask his great-grandfather a nagging question. "Um, Mr. Stone, what do you know of Dreadnoughts?"

"Dreadnoughts are an ancient race of smiths and warriors. Legend says they are the lion children of Treyus, the God of War—"

"—Mr. Stone!" Mya cried, a hand over her mouth. "You mustn't speak the name of the Unnameables. It brings ill tidings."

"That is a belief shared by many, not just the common folk. Yet is it a true one?"

Augum, who also had been brought up to never speak the names of the Unnameables, could hardly believe Thomas would risk being wrong. It must be because he was a Leyan, or perhaps Ley itself allowed him sanctuary from ill tidings.

"As it is," Thomas continued, "legend says the Dreadnoughts are the God of War's children, and that it was He who trained them in the arts of war, as well as how to forge superior weapons and armor. One day, the children rose against the father, and so he cast a powerful curse on them—they were to serve a master, and when no master was there to be served, they were to sleep until a new one emerged to command them."

Leera's brows rose. "Dreadnoughts are evil?"

"They reflect their master, nothing more."

"So how do you become the Lord of Dreadnoughts anyway?" she pressed, quickly adding, "not that I'm interested in becoming their master, of course."

"Occulus slew the previous Dreadnought lord and took his place. The one before him did the same. It has been this way for eons. Once in a long while, however, the heir to the Dreadnought throne forsakes power for peace."

"My ancestor …" Augum whispered. The pieces were falling into place.

"Atrius Arinthian was indeed such a man. He had the choice, upon slaying Occulus, of becoming the Lord of Dreadnoughts. He abdicated and they went to sleep. He was thus the last to see one for some time … until now."

"Until now?" Mya asked.

"Yes. The Dreadnoughts are waking to a new lord."

"Unnameable gods," Bridget murmured, placing her gaze on Augum.

"What? What is it?" he asked, feeling a cold prickle. When she did not reply, it hit him. "Sparkstone …"

"Yes," Thomas said. "The Lord of the Legion has also become the Lord of Dreadnoughts."

Augum placed a hand to his forehead. He did not need to know much about the Dreadnoughts to know that Sparkstone becoming the master of a race of superior weapon and armor makers was dire news for Solia … for all of Sithesia.

"Mr. Stone, forgive me, but, how do you know for sure?" Bridget asked.

Thomas glanced skyward at the racing clouds. "Although we Leyans have withdrawn from your world, we nonetheless keep watch through arcane means."

Sydo's brows furrowed. "What about Augum and Bridget's Dreadnought blades, are they not *evil* then?"

"A child is not born with the sins of its parents."

Bridget began pacing back and forth. "We have to tell Mrs. Stone."

"But I don't understand something," Augum said. A thousand things, really. "How could Sparkstone gain control of the Dreadnoughts?"

"Through the bones of Atrius Arinthian."

Bridget stopped pacing as Augum gaped.

"He's going to *raise* my ancestor from the dead?"

Firelight reflected in Thomas' black eyes. "It has already been done."

"Gods ..." Prince Sydo mumbled, playing with the buttons on his doublet while staring at his statue.

Augum remembered the beautiful tomb his ancestor rested in and shivered at the idea of it ripped open. "Does this mean he'll raise more of my ancestors from the castle crypt?"

"The future is as yet unwritten, Augum Stone."

Augum exchanged looks with Bridget and Leera. So his father's ambitions were even greater than they had feared.

"Let us move on to your training," Thomas said after giving them time to digest this new information. "Mya Liaxh—certain herbs and plants are growing amongst the trees before you. Gather as many as you can and we shall then confer together."

"Yes, m'lord." Mya curtsied and walked off to the encircling forest, already searching the ground. Augum watched her depart with a tinge of disappointment.

"Augum Stone, Sydo Ridian, Bridget Burns, Leera Jones—I am going to teach you the ancient forgotten spell of Centarro."

Augum felt a shiver race up his spine—they were going to study an off-the-books spell after all!

"Centarro is a difficult spell. You must allow yourselves patience. It predates the Founding, its name and incantation unchanged for thousands of years. Many generations ago, we Leyans shared it with humans, its use now lost to time."

Leera crinkled her nose. "What does it do, Mr. Stone?"

"It enhances focus."

Her face fell. "Oh, that's all? So it'll just help me study better?"

"Centarro has many uses. It will sharpen your senses, your reflexes, your concentration, and heighten your perception, allowing a brief time of clarity. However, one must be prepared for the spell's side effects—headaches, lack of concentration, sluggishness, confusion, nausea, and even memory loss. Thus, one must carefully choose the timing and place of casting, for the spell can be very dangerous if ill-timed. Let us begin with observation. Walk with me."

Thomas turned on his heel and led them to the forest, stopping at the base of one of the massive oaks. The foursome lined up to watch. Sydo was actually making a serious effort at paying attention, nodding his head whenever Thomas spoke, not interrupting or making faces.

"Study the bark and tell me what you see."

They crowded around the oak.

Leera shrugged. "It's just bark."

Thomas stood unmoved.

"It appears to have deep grooves," the prince said, looking to Thomas for approval.

Augum peeled off a long sliver. "It flakes."

Bridget glanced at a nearby brazier. "It would burn if we lit it on fire."

"All true indeed, and it is the application of said potential that we concern ourselves with. Depending on one's mastery of the spell, Centarro allows a glimpse of the many hidden possibilities one is usually not privy to in everyday life."

Bridget and Sydo nodded along while Leera and Augum frowned, straining to understand.

"Let us discuss potential. Bridget Burns—you have stated the bark could be lit on fire. This is potential." Thomas fell silent, face as smooth as glass.

"Oh, and you could make armor from it—" Leera blurted.

Bridget gave her a look.

"What, I've heard of druids making armor from bark."

"I beg to differ—there are no druids," Sydo said in a strained tone. "Those are tales for children."

Leera glared at him a moment but swallowed what she was going to say.

Bridget raised her hand. "You could make bark tea—"

"Or stew," Augum added. It sounded plausible, though he hadn't heard of such a concoction.

"Yes, these are indeed examples of potential. Let us situation together." Thomas peered beyond them and raised his arm. It flared with bands of fire. This time Augum was able to count seventeen rings in all—seventeen stripes to his one. Sydo's lips moved as well. For a moment the two caught each other's eyes before promptly looking away. It made Augum uncomfortable knowing he had done the same thing as the prince.

Where Thomas pointed, a bark-covered wooden dummy appeared in the clearing. It had a tree trunk body, thin log legs, branch arms, and twig fingers. The dummy stood upright, reminding Augum of one Sir Tobias Westwood built for sword practice. How many hours had Augum hacked at that dummy with the wooden sword Sir Westwood had fashioned for him?

Thomas turned back to the group.

"That is absolutely astounding, sir," the prince said. "Your powers are exceptional."

Leera rolled her eyes.

"Let us situation an attack on our wooden friend," Thomas continued. "Augum Stone—please demonstrate."

Augum looked to the group, hesitantly drew Burden's Edge, and approached the dummy. He raised his blade and with one clean swoop sliced off an arm.

Leera gave a snicker. "Aww, how could you?"

"As you have witnessed, Augum Stone did what he thought best—he struck the arm. Augum Stone—please tell us in detail what you observed upon approach."

Augum felt the eyes of the group on him. "Um, what I observed ..." He thought back to what he noticed when approaching the dummy and shrugged. "I think I looked at its feet, then maybe its head?"

Thomas gave a brief nod. "Let us situation together anew."

"Hope this is going somewhere," Leera muttered as Augum returned to the group, sheathing Burden's Edge.

Thomas looked to the dummy and raised his arm. It instantly sprang to life, picked up its hacked-off arm, and re-attached it. It then swayed in eager anticipation.

"It moves like that dented scrap heap from the castle," Sydo said, cocking his head.

Leera grimaced. "You mean Fentwick."

Sydo's nose rose a little. "Quite correct, my lady."

"Gods," Leera mumbled, turning away from the prince.

Thomas placed his gaze upon Bridget. "Bridget Burns—please attack our wooden friend."

Bridget withdrew Blackbite and charged at the dummy. It easily dodged out of the way.

"Bridget Burns—please describe what you focused on upon approach."

"Oh, that's easy—its torso," Bridget replied, sheathing Blackbite and returning to the group.

"We shall now example Centarro. In this circumstance, I will cast the spell on one of you so that you may see the effect for yourselves. Later, each of you will have a turn."

Augum rubbed his hands together. What will it be like to try an ancient spell?

"The word for Centarro is, like the spell, quite old and may be difficult to pronounce at first." Thomas raised his arm at the prince and rings of flame once again leapt to life, curling around his bronze skin. "Centeratoraye xao xen."

Sydo immediately took one long look around, as if seeing everything for the first time. "Beautiful," he whispered, staring up at the clouds.

"How does it feel?" Bridget asked.

Sydo looked at her, eyes wide. He did not respond, instead looking at his hands and tracing the lines of his palm with a finger. He then dropped to his knees and began inspecting the grass.

"Sydo Ridian—if I may direct you to attack our wooden friend."

Sydo glanced up at the swaying dummy. Augum wondered what in the world was going through his brain. He was behaving like some sort of wild animal. Maybe the spell wasn't working as it should—

Suddenly the prince sprinted forward and to the right, close to the ground. As the dummy turned along with the prince, Sydo tacked left. Just as the two were at arm's length, Sydo rolled underneath the dummy's flailing arms and tore off the bark from one of the legs. As the dummy twisted around, Sydo, still on the ground, whipped about and kicked the bare leg. Weakened from the lack of bark, the leg broke and the dummy fell.

"Sydo Ridian, please describe your focus upon approach."

The prince gracefully stood up, the dummy motionless at his feet. "First I examined my hands and realized their potential," he said in an awed voice, "I then witnessed the slipperiness of the grass and its particular texture."

Even the way he spoke sounded different.

"As I approached, I watched the movement of my adversary, who tended to keep his arms at a certain height. Remembering the texture and feel of the bark of the tree, I calculated the weakest point to be its leg. I came up with the idea of stripping the bark off the leg, which needed to be done with speed and direction—and then breaking it with a kick, which relied on the particular texture of the grass and my momentum. I also needed my adversary to be off balance to minimize its reach. I therefore changed my approach near the end. From then on it was a matter of following through with the motions."

Augum and Leera stood gaping while Bridget smiled and gave a proud nod.

"Nuance, awareness, assertiveness, forethought, creativity. Let us situation together again and witness the side effects. Sydo Ridian—please prepare to attack once more."

Sydo strolled back to the group, eyes still roving about as if reborn. The dummy got up off the ground, re-attached its leg and the torn-off bark, and resumed its defensive dance.

"I shall now discard the enchantment." Thomas raised his arm, rings of fire bursting to life. A glazed look came over Sydo's face. Thomas made a graceful gesture towards the dummy and Sydo ambled forth. As he came within striking distance, he raised his fist and went for a straight-on punch. It was clumsy and the dummy effortlessly dodged out of the way, raising its own stumpy hands in a move to smack the prince on the back of the head. Thomas, however, raised a palm and the dummy froze.

"Sydo Ridian—please recount your thoughts upon approach."

Sydo's eyes crossed a little. "Uh …" but his brain seemed to have slowed down to the pace of a snail. Eventually he just stumbled back to the group, completely forgetting about the question. He stood with a simple look on his face, staring off into the distance.

Leera waved a hand before his eyes. He didn't even blink. "I think you've improved him."

"Leera—" Bridget said as Augum suppressed a snicker.

Thomas raised his palm and Sydo seemed to snap out of it. "At first, you will only be able to cast Centarro for a very short time. As you develop in skill, however, the duration will lengthen and the side-effects will shorten."

"That was incredible, yet … strange," Sydo said, absently smoothing his hair. "Let me do it again."

"In due course, Sydo Ridian. Let us now learn the pronunciation and application of Centarro."

The group studied the rest of the morning, Thomas lecturing with examples. When one of them could not pronounce a word, he would say it aloud in their *own* voice back to them, over and over, until they got it. When he asked a question, he remained silent until one of them came up with a satisfactory answer.

Augum understood that the spell would take tremendous practice, far more than the others he had learned. However, out of all the spells they did know, this one was by far the neatest. The creativity aspect alone was incredible—when Bridget took a run at the dummy, she faked slashing it with Blackbite, tossed the blade above the dummy's head, and entangled its arms into a knot—all while its focus was still on the dagger. It was a feat he'd have pronounced impossible if he hadn't seen it with his own eyes. As for his turn, he had sprinted forward, somersaulting over the dummy while grabbing its head, snapping its neck. Long after the effects wore off, he could hardly believe he had accomplished such a thing.

Leera took the prize for creativity though. She performed a snake-like dance in which the dummy became distracted by her waving hands. She somehow hypnotized it to pay more attention to her left arm by waving it about a certain way. She then kicked out with her right foot—the dummy's blind side—and used the momentum to rip out its arm, clubbing the dummy with it until it was still. Augum, Bridget and even Sydo clapped.

As successful as they were with the spell, it was most amusing to watch someone trying to perform the same tricks after the effects had worn off. When Bridget tried, she tossed her dagger away and told the dummy to jump in a fire, before sitting down cross-legged, staring at it with a dull yet satisfied look on her face. Augum fared no better, running into the dummy head-on, almost skewering himself. Later he swore he had a plan but simply forgot it. Leera, on the other hand, ended up hypnotizing herself and getting all confused, somehow managing to kick *and* punch herself simultaneously. Even Mya, who happened to have been watching from the oaks, found that funny.

"The practical applications are limitless," Thomas explained after the group had a chance to see and try both the spell and its after-effects. "And not just for combat—the spell can be used in any situation needing focus and concentration, especially when one is completely out of ideas. But beware, for many have died using it, accomplishing an astounding feat only to be slaughtered when their wits slowed after. I therefore advise you plan for the side effects while *under* the influence of the spell."

Augum made a point of engraving that into his brain.

Thomas continued lecturing, the group hanging onto his every word, though there were more than a few foggy looks exchanged when he delved into too much detail, or said things like, "Learn to use the parts of your mind within." He would often leave them with practice tasks that involved tedious observation while he took a turn training Mya on herbs.

By the end of that morning, although no one had yet successfully cast Centarro, they were at least able to pronounce it, and were so exhausted no one complained when they broke for lunch.

STORIES

The tightly-packed clumps of cloud darkened as the group gathered for lunch at the earthen table. The winds had strengthened by then, bending the oak canopies and making the braziers flicker.

Thomas, much like Mrs. Stone, arcanely set the table. Except, instead of popping things into existence out of thin air, he simply gestured to the trees. What appeared to be burgundy carrots and blue potatoes pulled themselves from the ground. Purple peaches and white pears flew in from who knew where, landing in rough wooden bowls. Augum wondered if Mrs. Stone could do that, or if it was another lost spell from eons ago.

They peeled the carrots with Blackbite and skewered the potatoes over a brazier with sticks, discussing what they had learned that morning.

"Mr. Stone," Augum said near the end of the meal, "why did you go to Ley without Nana?" He couldn't bring himself to address the Leyan as great-grandfather.

Thomas observed him with a serene expression. "In the river of time, paths often diverge."

Augum scratched his head. Must the man always be so cryptic? Fine, might as well ask about Nana, since she's not here. "Can you tell me a little bit about, um, your wife? How did she grow up? What made her, you know … *her*?"

"The past is a mirage. The future is a haze. The difference is the moment." Thomas glanced skyward. The tone of his voice softened. "I recall what it was like to be a father, a husband. I recall words we would exchange. 'The children need feeding.' 'Fetch me some goat milk from the market.' 'I love you'. I recall stories people would tell, stories Anna would tell. Anna was born in a village named River's End. Anna's father was a most respected and wise warlock. Anna loved studying his spell books when he thought her studying the written word, or arithmetic. Anna was young, perhaps only ten when she cast her first spell."

They exchanged incredulous looks.

"Ten?" Leera mouthed.

"Your return reminds me of what it was like to be mortal. To speak that way. To … taste things. Feel things." Those coal eyes settled on Augum. "Anna's father possessed an ancient spell book, one that, combined with her great aptitude, allowed her to learn spells far beyond her capability. There were accidents, experiments, but Anna prevailed. Anna's sister, Dradeya, who was older, became jealous of her talents and tormented her. Anna supposed Dradeya worried the scion would pass to Anna because of her talent.

"At thirteen years of age, the Academy of Arcane Arts accepted Anna. She was the most advanced student in the academy's history, though Anna hardly used her powers for personal gain. Unfortunately, at the end of Anna's first year, her father, the most important person in her life, became sick from necrotic plague."

"I've heard of that plague," Leera said. "My grandfather said his grandfather died from it. It was a plague made by a necromancer, wasn't it?"

"That it was, Leera Jones. Anna rushed to see her dying father. It was then that he bestowed her with the family scion before passing away."

"How did her sister react?" Augum asked.

"Dradeya did not take it well. She demanded the scion, calling it rightfully hers."

"That's what *my* father says about the scion. He calls it rightfully his too."

"So what happened next?" Leera asked.

"There was a duel, Leera Jones. Anna bested her older sister, but tried doing it without causing harm. Yet Dradeya's ego would not let her yield. She kept attacking, until Anna unintentionally used the scion for the first time and slew her sister."

"How awful ..." Bridget mumbled.

"That is *her* version," Prince Sydo muttered.

The trio gave him a hard look.

Sydo straightened. "I mean, I am sure she had no other choice."

"Imagine attending the academy after that," Augum said. Imagine being burdened with the scion at that age. Imagine killing your own sister ...

"She did in fact attend, though it was a very difficult time for her."

Augum was amazed he told them all this. Would Nana even be all right with them knowing it? He decided *not* to ask her.

They sat in silence for a while until Bridget cleared her throat lightly. "Mr. Stone, why did the Leyans retreat from the world so long ago?"

"After Occulus, we chose to stop communicating with the great many, for envy resulted in unnecessary war. Over time, we became legend—a children's tale—and no one believed enough to seek us. Instead, we invited those that were ready to join us in secret."

"A secret society," Leera muttered, pushing away a bowl full of pits. "So how many of you are there?"

"There are no less nor more than sixty-seven."

Sydo almost choked on a golden plum. "Sixty-seven—? Is that all?"

"That is all."

The table fell silent. Augum rubbed his forehead. Any hopes of mounting a Leyan army against the Legion were smothered.

"Excuse me, m'lord," Mya said, folding her hands neatly, "but were there not more of you once?"

"For eons our numbers were great. Since the creation of the scions, however, we have only dwindled. Some among us say we passed too much of our strength into the scions. Others say it is because we have withdrawn from the world. Still others argue it is because of reasons we have yet to fathom, for there is much we still do not understand. There is considerable debate amongst us at this time."

"You debate?" Sydo asked, raising a fiery eyebrow. "I mean … sir."

"We discuss, hypothesize, challenge, commune, and yes, even debate, Sydo Ridian."

Leera's hands splayed open. "But sir, can you not simply invite more people to become Leyan?"

"Invitations are scarce, a consequence of our withdrawal. Those that believe in our existence are few in number. Those that believe in our existence and also strive to be among us number even fewer, for we only choose those that are ready, those that seek enlightenment."

"Enlightenment?" Sydo looked around. "What exactly is there to do out here?"

"We practice old ways and share old knowledge passed down to us from those before. We practice the arts of silence, awareness, and peace, watching and listening to the countless subtleties of existence." Thomas made a slow sweep with his hand. "The unfolding beauty before us keeps us enthralled. Other times we watch your world through arcane eyes, chronicling its history, searching for those that are ready to join us."

Sydo shrugged. "Well I guess you *do* get to live for a long time."

Augum peered at Leera, who had a look as if being Leyan sounded like the most boring thing in the world. He had to agree. He couldn't possibly fathom sitting out in a great desert and simply … listening.

"Do Leyans live in groves like this, Mr. Stone?" Bridget asked.

"We live in the winds of the desert. In ages past, we lived in a great underground city. We have not felt that need for much time. Some of us still visit, however."

The clouds dropped, almost rolling just above the treetops. The wind increased once again, and Mya glanced upward.

Augum snuck a sidelong look at her, studying her long jet hair as it rippled in the breeze. When her gaze returned to the table, he hurriedly looked away, only to find Leera watching him. She did not look upset, but there was something in her eyes that made him feel guilty.

Bridget reached for dessert, consisting of green strawberries and a comb of dark honey. "Mr. Stone, where has Mrs. Stone gone to? Is she exploring the old city?"

"Anna seeks the other portals."

Bridget froze with a strawberry at her lips. "Other portals, sir?"

"Before the knowledge was forgotten, those possessing a scion had the power to create a portal to Ley. Four portals are known to have been built, one you already know of."

"Castle Arinthian," Augum said, thinking of the stone fountain with the figure of a hairless Leyan. He recalled Mrs. Stone using her scion to unlock it.

"Another has long since been destroyed. But there are yet two others. I have told Anna where to find them."

"Does she want to destroy all of them?" Leera asked, scraping the honeycomb with a fingernail.

"This I do not know, Leera Jones."

"Oh, I get it," Leera said, waving a honeyed finger around, dripping everywhere and drawing a look from Bridget and Sydo. "She wants to prevent Sparkstone from entering using the other scions."

"A correct conclusion, Leera Jones. A portal can only be opened with the scion that created it."

Augum wondered if destroying the remaining portals would really prevent Sparkstone's entrance. Obviously, the Leyans themselves traveled to Solia using other means. If it was possible for Sparkstone to use the same method, Augum was sure his father would find it. After all, if there was a trait the man certainly did not lack, it was determination.

A glint came into Sydo's eye. "Sir, will you be teaching us other ancient spells?"

"As per Anna's instructions, I will not, Sydo Ridian. However, Anna has asked me to continue your training with standard spells. Sydo Ridian, you will practice the 1st degree with me. Mya Liaxh, you will continue your training with herbs. Bridget Burns, Augum Stone, Leera Jones—you will begin your 2nd degree training with Oba Sassone. He will be here soon."

Augum exchanged a look with Leera and Bridget, excited they were going to meet another Leyan. Would he look anything like Thomas?

The trio finished eating in thoughtful silence, on the lookout for Oba Sassone. They did not have to wait long before a tall Leyan emerged from the trees.

OBA SASSONE

Oba Sassone possessed the same kind of solid black eyes as Thomas and appeared just as young and hairless. But unlike Thomas, his physique was that of a seasoned gladiator, skin dark metallic, muscles rippling with veins. He wore brown pants and a tattered long-sleeved shirt the color of red wine, unbuttoned. Two curved blades hung from his hip, one on each side.

"You have come, Oba Sassone," Thomas said.

"Come has Oba," the man replied in a thick accent, night eyes sweeping over Augum and the others. "Vow you break for childlings?"

"Yes."

Oba grunted.

"I believe the time has come for us to share our knowledge with the mortal world once again."

Oba raised his chin. "Invited young Oba to Ley Thomas Stone has. Trust his wisdom Oba does. Consequences Oba accepts."

Thomas nodded slowly. "So be it."

"It be so." Oba Sassone turned his broad back on them and sauntered over to a clearing, not far from Sydo's statue. This, evidently, was the signal for them to begin training again. Augum, Bridget and Leera followed Oba, Sydo went with Thomas, and Mya returned to her collection of herbs and plants.

"He talks funny," Leera whispered.

"And what did he mean by 'consequences'?" Augum replied before Bridget gave them a silencing look.

Oba Sassone stood waiting, hands resting loosely on the pommels of his blades. Augum kept his distance, reminding himself he still knew very little of the land of the Ley and its people.

The man's eyes narrowed as they lined up before him. "You know? Hmm? How much?"

The trio exchanged cagey looks.

"Push, Disarm, Shield? Hmm?"

The words were hard to make out with his accent, but Bridget finally raised a meek hand. "We don't know any of those spells, sir."

Oba crouched to her height, pushing his face into hers. "Know you two degree?"

"We only just earned our 1st degree."

Oba straightened. "Stripes you show Oba."

The trio extended and flexed their right arms. A shimmering ring of water appeared around Leera's arm, an ivy ring around Bridget's, and a bolt of lightning around Augum's.

Oba Sassone grunted. "Childlings tell Oba names."

"I'm Augum Stone, and these are my friends, Bridget Burns and Leera Jones."

"Augum Stone, Bridget Burns, Leera Jones. What from kingdom?"

"We come from Solia," Leera replied, teetering on her toes.

Oba's eyes enlarged to the size of plums. "Craven kingdom, Solia—full of craven men!" He slammed a fist into his chest and four leafy rings erupted around his arm. The trio took a step back. "Solia not Nodia. Oba Sassone proud Nodian warrior. Oba meet few brave Solians. Sacrifice for no one, Solians. Know greed better than honor." He pointed at each of them as he spoke. "Below Oba you stand until brave you prove."

"Sir, how do we prove we are brave?" Leera asked.

"Leera Jones, Bridget Burns, Augum Stone—prove brave by listen, learn, sacrifice."

"Great, we're back in class again," Leera muttered, clearing her throat the moment Oba glanced at her.

"Dark times in Solia," Oba continued, the sinews in his neck bulging. "Thomas Stone ask Oba help train so childlings help craven kingdom. Oba not happy break vow for cowards. No brave warriors in Solia. No Speedswords. No honor. Hide behind metal skin Solians do. Mountain monks of north ignore craven kingdom and Solia king die like goat under necromancer blade."

Augum looked down at his feet, wondering if he should mention who his father is.

"Why Augum Stone sulk? He afraid training?"

Augum looked up. "Sparkstone, The Lord of the Legion … he's my father. He murdered the king and …" He wanted to say he murdered a great many more. He wanted to say his father murdered Bridget and Leera's parents—

"Defend father does Augum Stone?"

"No, I mean—"

"Follow path of father does Augum Stone?"

"No, of course not, I—"

"Is heart of father heart of Augum Stone!"

"NO—!" Augum found himself breathing hard, fists clenched.

Oba Sassone studied him. "Carry weakness of craven kingdom you do. Overcome weakness you must. Much sacrifice need. From birth, Nodian warriors train. Solians coddled, pampered with feathered pillows." He turned his black eyes to Bridget and Leera. "Solian women weak, defenseless. Solians made weak by weak kings, weak warriors. Now, Solian necromancer conquering weak people like lion conquers mice."

Leera held up a finger. "Excuse me, sir, but is Nodia the kingdom to the south east?"

Oba looked her up and down as if deciding which limb to slice off first. His voice was deadly quiet. "Leera Jones not know where mighty Nodia lies?"

Leera's hands travelled behind her. "Well I *have* heard of it."

"Foolish childling—name kingdoms for Oba!"

"I know Tiberra is to the east ... and Canterra to the south—"

"—and Sierra to the south of Canterra," Bridget added.

"And north of Solia what is?" Oba asked.

Leera winced. "Mountains?"

"Northern Peaks belong Ohm kingdom, home of mountain monks and Seers!"

"Oh, right."

"Solians arrogant. Think Solia center of world, when it tiny north kingdom. Abrandia only kingdom more tiny, far west of Solia. Nodia is kingdom of four tribes, watching over Sunburnt Plains, southeast to Solia, and twice size. Moonclaw. Jadefire. Wolfhowl. Oba Sassone is Warblade." He gave a bullish snort. "Now begin training we will. Oba's time you will not waste. We start two degree spell Shield."

Augum stole a sidelong glance at Sydo, who was working on Telekinesis with Thomas. The prince was trying to get a rock to jump to his hand. All that royalty around him all his life and he was still bumbling around with the most basic spell. Then he remembered his own futile attempts at making a rock move while Mrs. Stone watched and felt a creep of shame.

"Augum Stone—waste time with idle thoughts you will not. Concentrate you will!"

"Yes, sir. Sorry, sir—"

"Augum Stone, your sword you will draw."

Now he'd done it. He hesitantly drew Burden's Edge. The blade began lightly crackling.

"Oba you will attack."

Augum glanced to Leera, then Bridget.

"Them not—Oba!"

Augum raised Burden's Edge and half-heartedly swung at Oba, who did not move, letting the blade hit the ground, making it painfully obvious Augum had not intended to strike true.

"No! When Nodian invites attack, dishonor him you will not with weakness! Again you will try!"

Augum, forehead prickling with sweat, swung his sword with all his might.

Oba lazily raised his arm and a moss-covered wooden shield appeared, deflecting the blow before disappearing. He nodded for Augum to step back in line.

"Many years warlocks fight. Before scions, before Founding, warlocks fight. Fight they will long still. Old spell Shield is. Block arrows, sword, spear, arcane attack. Difficult spell to master. Size, shape, texture you learn control." Oba stepped away from the group and turned to Thomas, who patiently stood watching Sydo reach out to a rock that would not come. "Thomas Stone—fireball."

Thomas turned as if expecting to do this very thing, arm bursting to life with flaming rings. He moved as if throwing a rock at Oba, instead hurling a massive fireball that hissed through the air.

Oba only had a moment to raise both hands in a defensive gesture, summoning a large green shield of interwoven wet leaves and sticks, stretching from his feet to his head. The fireball smashed against it, expanding with explosive force. The flames licked around the edges, torching the grass. It evaporated quickly, Oba's shield along with it. The grass continued burning as Oba paced back to the group, breathing a little quicker.

"Sometimes two hands need you will. Art, Shield spell is. Remember Oba's shield—Oba use water to fight fire. Adapt you must or die. Learn this you will."

Bridget raised her hand. "Sir, is there an arcane word for this spell?"

"Non-verbal, this spell. Oba now teach."

For the next while, Oba explained how to conjure the shield. They were to use their left forearms as their right hands were to be free for spell casting or sword wielding. Augum found the method similar to the repair spell, especially the part about imagining the final shape, texture, and size—except it had to be cast reflexively, which made the spell far more difficult.

"Childlings ready to cast Shield?" Oba asked after one last example.

They nodded. The Leyan sauntered over to the oaks and picked up a stick. When he came back, his opaque eyes fell upon Augum, who barely had time to raise his forearm to block the stick from smashing his head. It crunched into his arm with a sickening crack. Augum cried out involuntarily and fell to his knees, gripping his throbbing forearm. Bridget and Leera gasped as Sydo peeked from behind Thomas.

"No. Again," Oba said, shooing Bridget and Leera off.

Augum bit his lip and stood up. He felt his anger rising.

"Augum Stone concentrate."

SMACK!

Augum fell to the ground again, trying not to utter a sound, the sting travelling up his arm and radiating throughout his body.

Bridget helped him stand. "Sir, this isn't right, this isn't how we train at school—"

"Bridget Burns next. Prepare she will."

Bridget and Leera threw pleading looks at Thomas.

"Anna requested the ancient way of training," Thomas said. "It is the way of suffering, but rapid advancement. Anna believes it may save your lives." He turned back to the prince, who strained to keep watching.

The trio exchanged resigned looks.

SMACK!

Bridget now fell to the ground, clutching her forearm. Leera and Augum immediately helped her stand.

"No! You no coddle. Let sting. You Solians weak. You not know pain. Not know sacrifice. Hide too much behind metal skin. Lesson you will learn. Leera Jones. Prepare."

Leera stood up, breathing heavily, fists clenched.

SMACK!

Leera fell, writhing in pain. This time when Bridget came to her aid, Oba whacked her hand with the stick. She sprang backwards with a cry, the stick pointed at her face.

"No coddle or Oba give Nodian smile." He made a slicing gesture across his throat with a finger. "Understand?"

Bridget nodded quickly.

"I'm all right," Leera said through gritted teeth. "I'm all right. Let me … let me try again."

Oba surveyed her with those eyes. His metallic muscles flexed.

SMACK!

Leera cried out and once again fell to the ground, clutching her forearm, groaning.

Oba grunted and turned to Augum.

"Wait—!" Leera said, climbing to her feet, tears of pain streaming down her freckled cheeks. "Again."

Oba's hairless brows rose up his shiny forehead. He surveyed her a moment before the stick rose into the air. This time Leera gave a kind of war cry as a small round shield of pond leaves coalesced on her forearm. The stick smashed into it. She fell to the ground from the force of the blow, the shield gone as quick as it had appeared.

"Leera, you did it—!" Augum said, resisting the urge to help her stand.

A panting Leera stared defiantly at Oba.

"Good teacher pain is," Oba said, extending his hand to her. She took it. "Ancient learning way this is. When war come, many need train fast. Harsh it feel to soft Solians. From birth Nodians feel sting."

From that moment on, they did a little better. It was still painful, but by suppertime, Bridget managed to cast Shield twice, Leera four times. Augum had the most trouble. He just couldn't figure out how to harden his shield. He had successfully spawned a tiny one from lightning, but it didn't stopped the stick.

Oba had only shaken his head, saying, "Imagination you have not, Augum Stone."

The group finally sat down to supper, exhausted and bruised. The table was once again full of a wide assortment of colorful fruits and vegetables, but Augum was in too much pain to care. "Mya Liaxh," Thomas said, "after supper, you will apply what you have learned. Balm of Sable."

Mya nodded gravely. "Of course, m'lord."

Leera glanced over at Augum's forearm with a look of worry. He tried to cover it with his sleeve but it was too tender for the scratchy burgundy.

"You're going to have to think of a way to harden your shield," she whispered. "It'll have to be something lightning related though—it's not like you can use rock or wood or anything like that."

He shrugged. "I'll think of something ..."

The prince's eyes fell upon Bridget's bruised arm. He opened his mouth to say something but froze. Instead, he turned to Thomas. "Sir, is this appropriate, this method of teaching?"

"All things have purpose, Sydo Ridian."

"But surely the Leyan way cannot allow such ... barbarity."

Oba cocked his great head at Sydo. "I am Oba Sassone of Warblade. We no need pampered princes. We no need kings. We no need false priests. We have Grand Raven. We have War Chief. We have elder council. We have Nanukin, God of the Hunt; Konkorra, God of War; Anwama, Goddess of love. We no need high degree. Nodian childlings learn pain young. Learn sacrifice young. You weak and cowardly. You not know true strength. Coddled you are. Need much pain to learn. Need sacrifice."

Sydo reddened. His eyes travelled to the two curved blades as he swallowed.

"Oba Sassone has been Leyan for over ten years," Thomas said. "He is a young Leyan, as am I, relatively. Learning is a lifelong path. Some Leyans live over a millennium. We young Leyans listen to the knowledge of the old. Oba Sassone was a Nodian warrior before his invitation to Ley. He is a Nodian warrior still."

Bridget gave Sydo a sympathetic smile before filling her wooden bowl with green ginger, burgundy carrots, and pink banana. The others joined her and they ate in silence. Thomas and Oba merely observed, hardly moving.

After supper, Prince Sydo continued his training with Thomas, while Mya bade Augum, Bridget and Leera to wait for her as she ran to the forest, jet hair dancing. She soon returned with a woven grass bag full of herbs, leaves and bark. She pulled out a stone mortar and pestle, splashed a little water in along with an orange mushroom, a leaf and some bark, and ground the contents into a paste. After finishing the Balm of Sable, her almond-shaped eyes searched the trio. "All right, my young lords and ladies—who is first?"

Augum stuck out his arm a little too quickly, cuffing Leera on the side of the head. "Sorry," he mumbled, ignoring the look she gave him.

Mya took hold of Augum's black and blue arm and applied the cool balm. He hoped she couldn't feel his pulse racing.

"Um, thanks," he said when she finished. She gave a radiant smile before moving on to Leera, who still glared at Augum with narrowed eyes.

Oba grunted. "Leave injuries alone to heal, Nodians do. Proud of scars we are."

Augum felt the scars on his back he had received from Mr. Penderson prickle. He had never shown them to anyone, nor could he imagine feeling proud to do so. He would never reveal them if he could help it.

Mya soon finished with Leera and Bridget, departing with a kind smile. Augum watched her go with a twinge. He was hoping to strike up a conversation, but couldn't find anything meaningful to say.

"Until sleep, training we continue," Oba said.

"Have you finally thought of what you're going to make your Shield out of?" Leera asked out of the side of her mouth as they walked to the clearing.

Augum silently cursed himself. "No, I forgot about that ..."

"What about solid lightning or something?"

"Solid lightning? How does that even work?"

"I don't know. I know it's a stretch, but—" at that moment Oba Sassone turned around and began a harsh lecture on the importance of having a sturdy shield, which seemed primarily directed at Augum.

"… and so begin we will with Augum Stone," Oba finished, raising the stick.

Of course we will. Augum gritted his teeth and planted his feet.

SMACK!

He found himself on the ground yet again, writhing.

"No! Imagination you have not, Augum Stone. Again!"

Since he was out of ideas, he decided to try Leera's suggestion. As the stick rose into the air, he mustered every ounce of concentration, picturing a woven bolt of hard lightning curled in on itself much like a rope. He felt something tingle in his left arm just before the stick smashed against curled black lightning, looking a little like dirty ice.

The girls immediately threw up a cheer. Oba only gave a nod. Augum flashed Leera a grateful smile.

They took turns like this until thoroughly exhausted, but at least mildly proficient with the spell. As much as it hurt, Augum had to admit the big Leyan was right—pain *was* a good motivator. There was no way they would have learned so quickly otherwise.

After lessons and a snack, in the darkening evening, he and the others collapsed onto their clay and moss beds, nauseous, heads pounding, arms sore. Thomas extinguished the braziers with a flick of his wrist, leaving only a thin band of dull light shining on the horizon, highlighting the tops of the oaks purple.

Augum stared up at the swiftly moving clouds. He gathered the moss blanket around him. In Solia, it would have been pitch-black long ago, except maybe for star or moon light. He lay there a long time as the others slept, thinking about what a strange place this was, when he heard a distant THWOMP.

"Welcome, Anna," Thomas said. Augum could not see them in the darkness, and could just barely hear what they were saying.

"Thank you, Thomas."

"This is Oba Sassone. He breaks the Vow with me. I brought him to train the childlings in the ancient way."

"Greetings, Anna Stone."

"Greetings to you, Oba, and I am grateful for your help. How do they fare?"

"Struggle they do. Soft they are."

"I expected as much. Time is short and I fear the old way is the only way. Yet it is nothing to what they will feel should they ever get captured." She sighed. "Forgive me but I am weary, it has been a trying day. I have managed to find and seal the remaining portals, but I left the one to Castle Arinthian. I hesitate to destroy the last remaining connection to Ley until absolutely necessary." She sighed. "The sky seems to have worsened since I left. What say the elders?"

"We have not discussed the matter or sought council yet," Thomas replied.

"The Dreadnoughts have woken," Mrs. Stone said as if it was nothing out of the ordinary. Augum wondered how she found this stuff out.

"It is as I feared," she continued. "Lividius has successfully revived Atrius Arinthian. Our grandson's necromantic powers grow. As for the Dreadnoughts, he will use them to outfit his army. His quest for the scions will plunge the entire world into war."

"The scions are a means to an end, Anna."

"They are indeed. He promises eternal life to his subjects, though his true motivations are somewhat of a mystery to me."

"This we Leyans have encountered before."

"Yes—Occulus, but he was not aided by scions. I fear kingdoms will fall to the burning sword of his ambitions, and perhaps even join the Legion as the living dead."

"Are our grandson's necromantic powers that great?"

"Not yet …"

"Permit this Nodia will not."

"All things change, Oba Sassone," Thomas said. "Kingdoms rise and fall, people come and go, knowledge passes. That is the way of it."

"But how many must die needlessly?" Mrs. Stone asked. "I have given much thought to your earlier words, and I am not convinced handing over the scion is the way. I request to convene the millennials. I must hear the wisdom of the elders."

"Convene council a mortal cannot."

"This is true, but I daresay Thomas can."

"The council has not convened in some time, Anna."

"This is no trivial matter. It is of dire importance."

A silence passed. "I will think on it with the wind, Wife, and return an answer in the morning light."

"So be it." Mrs. Stone shuffled to bed while Augum lay awake, ruminating over what had been said.

THE MILLENNIALS

First thing in the morning, Augum whispered to Bridget and Leera all he had overheard from the night before.

"She must fear torture or something if we're captured," Bridget said.

"But we don't know anything," Leera said.

"Maybe." Bridget turned to Augum. "You think the council will be convened?"

"Based on what I heard, yes."

"He's her husband after all," Leera added.

"He's also Leyan," Bridget said. "They're subject to their own wisdom. Come on, let's eat."

Everyone else was already sitting by the time the trio joined the table. As Augum took his place, he glanced skyward. The weather seemed to have worsened overnight, now a churning maelstrom of black and red clouds. As thick as the grove was, braziers, robes, and hair fluttered in winds that broke through the sentinel of oaks. Was it just a storm, or was something happening?

Breakfast dragged on without a word about the elders. Augum didn't want to ask because he felt it inappropriate he had overheard their conversation in the first place. At its conclusion, Mrs. Stone glanced to Thomas.

"Let it be so," he only said.

She stood up and cleared her throat. "At midday today we shall convene with the millennials. Until then, you are to train."

"Yes, Mrs. Stone," they chorused.

She glanced skyward as everyone stood, her wrinkles deepening.

"Why is the sky like that, Nana?"

"A question I shall pose to the elders. Come, you are in need of training. I fear dark times ahead."

Augum, Bridget and Leera glanced at each other before following.

"Thomas has spoken of your previous lessons," Mrs. Stone went on as they joined her husband in the windy clearing. "Consider yourselves very lucky. Centarro is a difficult and rare 3rd degree spell. Not even I know it. I trust you will do your utmost to learn it."

Augum shared a grin with Leera—3rd degree, off-the-books, and not even Mrs. Stone knew it.

"We will, Mrs. Stone," Bridget replied with a polite nod.

"This morning you will continue practicing Centarro with Thomas, while Oba Sassone trains with the prince and Mya."

"But I also wish to practice Centarro," the prince said in a voice tinged with petulance.

"Solian prince want his feathered pillow. Maybe Oba tie him to statue."

Sydo glanced over to his frozen effigy and blanched.

Thomas' black eyes fell upon the prince. "Our greatest fight is always with ourselves, Sydo Ridian. It is our choices that make us who we are, that determine our fate."

The prince slowly nodded, still staring at the imposter.

Mya reached for his hand. "Come, Your Highness, we shall endure together."

Her touching his hand made Augum's heart constrict. He turned away only to catch Bridget staring at Mya and Sydo too. She flashed a hesitant smile and pretended to be busy fixing her robe.

Mrs. Stone stepped apart from the group, invoked arcane words, and imploded with a mighty THWOMP. Augum wondered where she was off to now.

The trio turned to Thomas, who started by going over what they had learned yesterday. He then went on to show examples of the use of Centarro in situations other than combat, such as jumping onto an exact spot; focusing and remembering details such as clothing, surroundings, and words; accomplishing complex tasks like throwing something and having it rebound a certain way; running from pursuers, and a host of other creative uses. He also spent a lot of time explaining how to deal with the after-effects.

Although at first they had failed to cast the spell on their own, Thomas would say, "Let us situation together," and cast it on them for the experience. It was the most fun they ever had learning a spell, but it was also very challenging, for Thomas pushed them to concentrate unlike ever before. The after-effects of the spell were particularly draining, fogging and slowing the mind and reflexes. The trio soon came to understand just how dangerous those effects could be.

When Augum was running from a mock pursuer, he slammed into a tree. In that stupid state, if it had been a cliff there, he was sure he would have run straight off it. Even just walking around, he would trip and get tangled, not to mention the countless times he got lost—a remarkable accomplishment in such a small area.

They also went over the pronunciation again. Centeratoraye xao xen—a difficult phrase to utter under any circumstance, let alone in the heat of battle.

Nonetheless, by the end of that morning, with Thomas' efficient teaching methods, Augum became the first to successfully cast Centarro on his own. The duration was short but felt much longer. Leera and Bridget congratulated him, even asking for pointers. He was more than happy to explain how he did it.

Thomas reminded them that with diligent practice, they could learn to minimize the side effects, extend the duration, and increase the focus. "… nuance, awareness, assertiveness, forethought, and creativity," he said, hands loosely by his side, "that is the key to this spell."

The morning passed quickly, and at midday Mrs. Stone materialized with a loud THWOMP, gnarled walking stick in hand.

"Welcome, Anna," Thomas said.

Mrs. Stone gave her much younger-looking husband a curt nod. "Thomas."

Watching the way they greeted each other, with neither warmth nor affection, made Augum wonder if there were any feelings left between the old married couple. Perhaps the fact that Thomas was Leyan prohibited it, or perhaps the years simply washed those affections away. In any case, they appeared to be mere acquaintances now. Yet Augum hoped that that would never happen to him. If he was ever going to get married, he wanted to be with his love forever.

Mya appeared from the woods carrying a handful of different-colored leaves, while Sydo stopped his training with Oba and approached, cheeks red, hair askew. Earlier, he had made the mistake of whining to Oba, receiving quite the rebuke in turn, something to the effect of donkey droppings having more courage.

Mrs. Stone straightened. "The time has come to speak with the millennials." Her eyes flicked between the trio. "You are to be silent and civil. Are we clear?"

"Yes, Mrs. Stone," they chorused.

Thomas gestured at the swaying oaks. "As custom demands, we shall walk. Prepare yourselves—the Song of the Wastes is as strong as the wind." He led them through the forest and out into the open where a ripping gale raked bare skin with sand. The visibility was almost nil. Those that had hoods drew them. Sydo hid his face in the crook of his elbow. Thomas and Oba were the only ones seemingly unaffected by the blasting, not even closing their eyes.

Mrs. Stone let the young pass, taking the rear with Oba. As Augum put one foot in front of the other, he felt his thoughts slowly darken. Why couldn't Thomas arcane something up to block the wind, or even teleport them there? Why did they always have to do things the hard way? Why why why …

So immersed was he in shadowy ruminations he tripped over something.

"Watch yourself, peasant!" the prince shouted, standing and brushing himself off. "You blind clod—did you not seen me stumble?"

Augum felt his anger rise. "Well I *was* going to apologize—"

"Take that apology and—"

"Why are you two always fighting!" Bridget yelled above the din, turning on them. "I'm so sick of it!"

"What are you talking about," Augum began, "I—"

Leera grabbed her head. "Ugh, why don't you all just shut up—"

"Enough!" Mrs. Stone said, waving her stick to shoo them along. "Keep walking and think of good tidings, we dare not dally." She removed the scion from within her robe and released it to hover around her. "This should help," she said before returning to the rear of the line.

"Lowly commoner," Sydo muttered as the group resumed the march.

Augum restrained himself from replying and followed, but his eyes kept returning to Sydo, bumbling along just ahead. That stupid doublet, the nasty hair—he hasn't changed one bit. It just went to show that even a Leyan's ancient arcanery couldn't change a brat.

He simmered like this for a while, until eventually his thoughts boiled over and he "accidentally" stepped on the prince's heel.

Sydo whirled about, face purple. "How dare you step on the royal heel, you insolent bumpkin cur, you base bastard of the lowest breeding, you gutterborn—"

Augum saw the Penderson brats dancing around the tree he took cover in, calling him names, throwing things until he fell. He listened to poor old Meli's pulse fade and disappear beneath him. He felt Dap's fist buckle his innards and drain his breath. He saw Robin Scarson leading an entire village with laughter …

He did not feel the single lightning ring form around his wrist. What he did feel was a gratifying electrical surge rage up his body, discharge through his arm, and strike Sydo square in the stomach. The prince shot backward as if hit by a battering ram, plowing into Bridget and Leera, toppling them.

For a moment, Augum didn't know where he was. He expected all those villains he saw laying in a heap, yet there was only Sydo, Bridget and Leera, along with the brief scent of burnt flesh.

Mrs. Stone ran past him. "In the name of all that is good, child, what have you done—" Mya ran from the front of the line to help too. He saw her face and his stomach plummeted. Please not her. Someone stop her from seeing this—

A dark metallic hand gripped his shoulder and swung him around. "Cowardly dog …" A curved blade loosened from a belt.

Augum collapsed to his knees, eyes unfocused.

"He's hurt something awful!" Mya called from behind, a voice whose sweetness would never be directed at him again, not after what he had just done.

"Oh, no no no—" he heard Bridget say.

Oba's curved blade rose into the air. "Such treachery never has Oba seen. Death Augum Stone deserves!"

Augum closed his eyes, heart beating like a war drum, ready for the slash that would end his miserable and guilty existence—

"Oba Sassone, the childling has fallen prey to the Song of the Wastes." It was the deep voice of his great-grandfather.

"Thomas Stone, to death he must be put for such betrayal—"

"Oba Sassone also listens to the song," Thomas replied, voice as cool as the wind.

Augum opened his eyes to see Mrs. Stone standing over him alongside Oba, her face livid, eyes full of terrible disappointment.

"Nana, I … I don't know what … I didn't mean for—"

"You have the madness of your father. I was a fool to accept you as my apprentice."

"No, please, you don't mean that—"

"Oh, I *do*, Augum Stone, I do. You are no longer my great-grandson! I hereby disown you and cast you out!" The scion floated near him, darkening with a silent storm, the hum sounding like a thousand angry wasps.

"Kill him!" shrieked a girl's voice. Augum turned to find Bridget's face contorted with a wild fury he had never seen before.

"It's your fault!" Leera said, pointing a finger in his face. "You killed my parents, you killed everyone!"

"Not you too," he whispered.

Mrs. Stone's eyes flashed as she readied to smite him into oblivion. "Anna—" Thomas placed a bronze hand on her raised arm. "Enough. Something has changed. Not even the scion protects you as before. Allow me."

She turned to look at him. He smiled before moving on to touch each of them in turn, until they were all watching him. "Let us focus together. Examine yourselves outside of your thoughts, in this moment, and nothing more. You have succumbed to the Song of the Wastes. Do not listen to it. Instead, listen to my voice as we walk."

He extended a bronze hand to Augum and helped him to his feet. What Augum saw in those night-black eyes was nothing short of pure compassion.

"Walk with me, as we pass through the winds." His pants fluttered ceaselessly.

Even Oba followed. When the big warrior came upon Sydo's body, he put away his blade and picked him up.

"We walk knowing dark thoughts plead for our attention," Thomas continued, a shepherd herding sheep, "knowing that we mean ourselves no harm. We walk with calm spirits, the winds of anxiety doing us no injury …" His voice was melodic, piercing the wind and the darkness. "… knowing each step brings us closer to our destination, conscious of the eternal moment in which we dwell …"

Something was near, a series of stones.

"… we move unhindered by our emotions, unfazed by our fears, and unafraid of the great unknown …"

The wind faded to a dull background roar. Augum rubbed his eyes. They seemed to have walked into a calm spot in the middle of the orange desert. What he mistook for a series of stones was in fact nine Leyans, each one different in clothing and skin color. Four were men, five women. Most were hairless, metallic-skinned, gray-eyed instead of black, and wrinkled as if having spent years soaking in water.

Oba Sassone lowered the prince to the ground. When Augum spotted the large burn mark on his doublet, his heart skipped a beat. Neither Bridget, Leera, Mya, nor his great-grandmother would meet his eyes. What had he done? Was the prince … he dare not finish the thought.

Thomas bowed to the nine millennials. "Wise elders—greetings. If I may begin by asking for the healing of this boy."

"Ancient vow Thomas Stone and Oba Sassone break," an old woman wearing deer hide said. She had a wild accent, her skin was the color of wood, and antlers sprouted from her head. "Life for uninvited childling mortal Thomas Stone now asks. Elders—life do we give this boy?" She turned to the others, each of them quietly returning her gaze, as if speaking in thoughts. She nodded, shuffled to the stricken prince, and held out a withered hand that began glowing. Augum watched the wound shrink until disappearing altogether. The glow faded away and her hand withdrew, only to make a final quick gesture. Sydo jolted to life, coughing and gasping for air, hair frazzled.

Augum quickly stepped forward and offered a hand. "I … I'm so sorry …" he managed to say. He felt terrible, like one of the bullies he thought he had smote.

Sydo refused his hand and stood up on his own, an obstinate look on his face, eyes narrow. He said nothing.

"Augum, I'm sorry too," Leera said as the antlered millennial moved back to the others, her back as crooked as a scythe. "I—I don't know what I was saying … I don't know what happened out there …"

"Yes, overcome by song was Oba." Oba bowed his hairless head. "Forgiveness Oba asks. Much to learn he still has."

"We all have much to learn, Oba Sassone," Thomas replied.

Mrs. Stone cleared her throat. "I apologize for my words, Great-grandson. I did not mean what I said. It appears I, too, was overcome by the song."

Augum gave his great-grandmother a heartfelt look. He wanted to hug her but held back—she wasn't exactly the hugging type.

"Change has quickened in our land," an elder Leyan man said with dark citron skin. He wore a tattered ochre shawl painted with leaves and held a simple wooden staff. "We break our Vow of Isolation for mortals entering with a scion. Two kin break this vow to train the mortals, who seek council. We will hold this council on behalf of one Thomas Stone, who shall reap penance."

Augum's stomach tightened. What did they mean by "penance"?

Mrs. Stone stepped forward and bowed. "Great elders, forgive our intrusion and our mortal follies. We come by necessity. We come with questions."

"Speak your piece," the antlered woman said.

"I am grateful. My first question is of the wastes. Why has the Song become so deadly?"

"Never has one held more than two before," replied a withered old man in sealskin, bent so far forward he was shorter than Leera. His skin was as white as snow, a bone stuck through his nose, and there was a thick black line tattooed down the middle of his bald head.

"The elder refers to the scions—" Mrs. Stone said.

"That is so."

"Then Lividius has at least three now."

Augum exchanged looks with Bridget and Leera. That's not good.

"Do the scions have power over Ley?" Mrs. Stone continued after a thoughtful pause.

The snow-skinned man looked to his right. "I petition to hear from the oldest among us, one who has not spoken in many a year. Krakatos the Ancient, will you break your silence to speak on the subject at hand?"

All eyes turned to an extremely wrinkled man with dark bronze skin wearing a simple white loincloth. Perched on his bulbous nose were square spectacles with pink lenses. The man stared at Mrs. Stone for so long Augum thought he had chosen to remain silent, until quite suddenly he began speaking in a rapid sharp accent.

"The aforementioned scions are symbiotically linked to Ley, yet we can only scrutinize the observable effects of said link. Apropos, we failed to anticipate the inherent attachment upon forging. Incongruously, we foresaw the seven could fall under the influence of a single mind, and thus took appropriate precautions. You may be under the impression possibilities are as invisible to us as they are inversely visible to the Seers. Let us agree that in this era we Leyans endeavor to occupy the moment and must accept the consequence of an opaque future.

"In addendum, and you will forgive my alliteration, the scions appertain to an epoch prior to the covenant, wherein the dissemination of Leyan sapience was the norm, from which you are the unwitting benefit. As a stalwart weed begets an entire field, so you stand as the latest harvest of countless procreations, yet perhaps only the middling step of a super process in search of the singularity.

"The first concurrent summary is therefore a question—was withdrawal beneficial to the whole? Upon examination, I judge the answer inconclusive, though you must factor my limitations of practicality. The second concurrent summary is a statement you may find vacuous—the link is real, the outcomes and subsurface effects unknown, at least to this base body. I therefore conclude advising skepticism and humbly beg forgiveness for the capricious traipsing of an impertinent mind eternally sizzling under the Leyan sun."

Guests and Leyans stirred alike. Augum blinked, trying to understand a single phrase. Might as well have been spoken in Nodian though. There was one thing he did understand, however—Krakatos was very old. Maybe even so old that he might have been around when Atrius Arinthian became a Leyan. He might have even known him! The thought made his blood flow a little quicker.

"You have my thanks, Krakatos the Ancient," Mrs. Stone said at last. "Though I admit it will take me much time to digest your thoughts. Now, my husband, Thomas Stone, suggests the only way to destroy one who yields multiple scions is to let him have them all. Can I assume this is what you meant by 'precautions'?"

"That is so," answered an ancient man with almond shaped eyes, not unlike Mya's. He wore a simple scarlet robe that hid his entire body, except for his bronze colored head.

"I know my grandson. He will butcher half the world in the process of acquiring the scions. Surely there must be another way—"

"There may be, but we are unaware of it."

"For that you must seek the wisdom of the Seers—" said a pink-skinned woman in a servant's outfit.

"—past the Northern Peaks—" continued an ivory-skinned woman wearing a queenly gown.

"—in the Kingdom of Ohm," finished another ancient woman with avocado skin and sunken eyes, wearing a puffy-sleeved wide-skirt dress fringed with elegant ruffles.

"I will think on this. I know he will not stop until his goals have been achieved, and many would die in the mean …"

"The future is as yet unwritten," said an old woman with pale skin, the only one with milky eyes. Her hair was tangled and black as night. A tattered raven cloak hung loosely around her neck, a triangle with a black dot at the tip of each point emblazoned on the chest. The sharpness of her somehow reminded Augum of the claw at Hangman's Rock.

"He lusts for the powers of Ley, particularly eternal life," Mrs. Stone said.

"The eternal can only come to those with peace in their hearts," the avocado-skinned woman said.

"My grandson has become the Lord of the Legion and the Lord of Dreadnoughts. He seeks Occulus' old throne as the Lord of Death, and now wishes to become the Lord of Scions as well. Perhaps … perhaps there is a way his heart could be mended."

Krakatos the Ancient, his gray eyes an echo of time itself, tilted his head ever slightly. "The Lord of Death is by title an elevated evil, his deeds extolled to allegorical proportions. He is not the first, nor will he be the last. On the whole of history, the subsequent idiom can be said to be veritable: those we dread we hesitate to fathom. Yet we can deduce the Lord of Death is mortal, with mortal failings." His eyes fell upon Augum. "Let the following stand exemplar: I purport he desires the company of his son."

Augum blinked. No way was he going to join his father, if that's what Krakatos meant.

On the other hand, what if it would save the world from war?

Mrs. Stone nodded slowly. "Yes … this I know."

"You are as yet quite young, Anna Stone," said the scarlet-robed man with almond-shaped eyes. "A long time ago in an age long past, while besieging a castle holding his son hostage, Atylla the Mighty thus spoke: 'Return me mine son and I shall henceforth unburden thy kingdom of mine wrath and leave thy lands to their woe. Relinquish mine boy and I shall free thy common folk to sow seeds of corn and barley, unchain thy taverns so ale may flow, and free ye daughters and sons of thy flesh, for all such are but trivial wisps of smoke in balance to mine heir.

" 'However, should ye durst linger but a day on mine warning, hark! For I shall erelong smite all ye begat with burning blades, carve thy sons and daughters with mine knife, and cut ye to the quick, for I have become the Lord of Death, leveler of castles, executioner of children, and incarnate woe to mine enemies. I have laid waste to every land and slain every creature known, and yet the wretches follow me still, an endless army of the fallen. I beseech thee—heed mine words and return mine flesh, and be the only to walk in peace.' "

"—I shall not sacrifice my great-grandson!"

The hair on the back of Augum's neck rose—who said anything about sacrifice?

A silence passed before the man with dark citron skin and tattered shawl spoke up. "So be it, the question has been answered."

"As Krakatos the Ancient has said," began the snow-skinned man with the tattooed pate, "your grandson is not the first Lord of Death, nor will he be the last. Many have come before, their stories lost to mortal time. And so thus he travels a path familiar to us, for he is as he is and no other."

Mrs. Stone closed her eyes and pinched her nose. "Then my decision is to seek counsel from the Seers in the Kingdom of Ohm." She swept the line of elders with a determined look. "I am grateful for your wisdom." She bowed and stepped back.

Oba Sassone took her place. "Great Elders, Oba see quick change in Ley, want know what Leyans do."

Krakatos looked up at fast-moving dark clouds that reflected off his pink lenses. Everyone followed his gaze. "The nebular skies give testament and exhort circumspection. I hereby adduce we seek shelter in Absalon."

The millennials glanced at each other.

"So be it," said the avocado-skinned woman.

Oba bowed, as did Thomas and Mrs. Stone. Augum, Bridget, Leera, Sydo and Mya awkwardly did the same.

The antlered woman stepped forward. "Broken the covenant has been. Penance shall be passed." She reached out a glowing hand and there was a fierce and sudden wind followed by a teleportation jolt.

DEPARTURE

Back in the swaying grove, Augum dragged Leera and Bridget aside. "Just imagine … Krakatos might have been around in the time of my ancestor, Atrius Arinthian! Think of the stories he could tell, the questions we could ask him—maybe he even knows how to defeat Sparkstone—!"

"Augum, he's a *millennial,* and the oldest one at that," Bridget said. "We can't just *talk* to him as we please. Anyway, we've got more important things to worry about—you need to ask Mrs. Stone what happened to Attyla and his son, maybe the millennials were giving us some kind of warning there."

"I will. I've got a whole bunch of questions for her actually." What was all that about the Lord of Death, especially the stuff about sacrifice? What does Absalon look like? What did they mean by "penance"? What is the Leyan Vow? And then there was that phrase. *Return me mine son and I shall henceforth unburden thy kingdom of mine wrath …*

Now he just needed an opportunity to ask.

Bridget glanced skyward. "This place feels dangerous now, like it's going to collapse in on us any moment. I hope we leave soon."

"Yeah, but I want to explore Absalon," Leera said, "so we can't leave *too* soon." Her eyes drifted past Augum. "Though we might not have a choice. Look—I think they're up to something."

Augum turned to see Mrs. Stone quietly conversing with Oba and Thomas. "Wonder if it has anything to do with that penance thing."

"I have a bad feeling about that," Bridget said.

Augum began to chew his nail. "Me too ..."

"He's still angry with you," Leera said, nodding at the prince, who sat beside Mya at the table.

Augum glanced at Sydo, whose eyes narrowed upon spotting him. "Think I should apologize again?"

Leera shrugged. "Will it do any good?"

"Of course it will," Bridget said.

When Mrs. Stone concluded the conversation, Thomas and Oba departed the grove without another word.

"Let's find out what's going on," Leera said.

They joined Sydo and Mya at the table, now full of food again. When Mrs. Stone sat down, she only stared at the overflowing bowls—obviously something was on her mind. Augum decided to give her a moment and addressed Sydo instead.

"Just want to apologize again for ... for what I did back there. I really wasn't thinking clearly."

The prince gave him a cold look.

Mya leaned closer to him. "Your Highness, perhaps—"

Sydo cut her off with a hissing whisper. "I do not require your advice on the matter, *servant*."

Augum held his tongue. If Sydo wanted to play it that way, *fine*—what did he care anyway? He turned back to Mrs.

Stone, who had not taken notice of them. There was a lot to go over, so he thought it best to start simple.

"Nana, what became of Attyla the Mighty, did the besieged castle return him his son?"

"Hmm …?"

"Attyla's son, did they—"

"—no, they did not return him his son."

"So … how was Attyla defeated in the end?"

"Legend says by the love and sacrifice of his wife." She glanced at him. "You need not concern yourself, Great-grandson, I shall not hand you over to your father in hopes it would pacify him. Nor will I hand over the scion, for it would mean death on a scale we have yet not seen. Maybe even the end of Ley."

All right, she wasn't going to give him or the scion up. He felt a wave of cool relief. "And how old is Krakatos? Is he at least fifteen hundred years old?"

"I believe so. It is said he is the oldest millennial ever to have lived."

The oldest millennial to have ever lived. Augum suddenly thought his next question was rather tripe and barely mumbled it. "I just thought maybe we can ask him how Atrius defeated Occulus … or something."

"What's the point?" Leera muttered. "Couldn't understand a single word he said back there. It'd be like conversing with a textbook."

Mya looked up at the roiling clouds, her delicate features contorting with worry. "Mrs. Stone, when will we be departing for the Northern Peaks to meet the Seers?"

"I must go alone."

There were audible gasps. Augum promptly forgot about all the other questions he had for her.

"The journey is too dangerous," she added.

"But, Mrs. Stone, how long will you be gone?" Bridget asked.

Mrs. Stone filled her bowl with exotic fruits. "That I do not know."

"But ... can you not just teleport there and back?"

"Teleport only works to places you have already been. Further, it does not allow cross-plane travel. It will mostly have to be a journey on foot."

"When will you depart?" Leera asked.

"As soon as possible, child." She gestured skyward. "As you can plainly see, the question of how to defeat Sparkstone cannot wait. The more scions he gains, the greater the danger for all." She then peered around at them, her brows crossing. "Oh for mercy's sakes—it is not the end of the world. You will see me again. Now *eat*."

But to Augum those clouds certainly *looked* like the end of the world.

The group reluctantly started pawing at their food. Augum played with something akin to a blue pomegranate a while before deciding he wasn't very hungry. "What're we going to do while you're gone, Nana?"

"Continue training with Thomas and Oba. They will be your guardians."

"What about this penance thing they keep talking about?"

Mrs. Stone arranged her bowl a moment. "If I am not mistaken, Leyan penance is usually nothing more than meditation."

"That doesn't sound too bad," Leera mumbled.

"Be mindful, for Thomas and Oba broke the vow for you. Train and work hard. Practice every day. You must learn to protect yourselves. I will leave you the blue book on arcaneology—use it well. I expect that upon my return you will have a thorough understanding of the 2nd degree." She sighed, imparting a ghost of a smile. "Above all, look out for each other."

They only nodded. For a time nobody said anything.

"Mrs. Stone, how will you leave Ley?" Bridget asked finally. "All the exits are now blocked, except for Castle Arinthian, and the Legion might still be there."

"I will not be returning through the castle. Thomas will be of assistance."

"Please allow me to get this straight," Sydo began, taking a juicy bite of a purple peach, seemingly the only one unconcerned she was leaving. "You are departing to ask the Seers if there is *another* way to kill the Lord of the Legion, other than giving up Augum and the scion?"

The group froze as Mrs. Stone surveyed the prince. Augum thought Sydo was in for the tongue-lashing of his life. Instead, all she said was, "A question of that nature, yes."

"And what if the Seers said there *was* no other way—"

Mya leaned toward the prince. "Your Highness—"

"How many times must I tell you to be quiet! You are nothing but a servant dog in need of a good whip—" Sydo stopped himself, realizing everyone was glaring at him. "Uh … I seem to have once again fallen prey to the Song of the Wastes."

Just then, Thomas emerged from the trees holding something small in his fist. "Anna. I have it. It is best we depart immediately."

Mrs. Stone pondered the prince a moment. "Prepare yourselves, for you shall accompany Thomas to the underground city." Her eyes lingered on him before she left the table.

Bridget gave the prince a look.

Sydo smoothed his hair. "What? It was the song, I say."

"Excuse me—" and she went to prepare the rucksack.

Leera scoffed and left to help Bridget. Mya stood, curtsied quickly, and went to gather her herb pouch.

Sydo watched them a moment before fixing his gaze on Augum. His lip curled. "If I were you, I would give myself up to my father to save everyone."

Augum opened his mouth to return a blistering rebuke, but instead found himself just gaping.

"That's all he wants, isn't it? You and that stupid scion." When Augum still did not respond, Sydo shook his head, stood up, and left to join the others, leaving Augum sitting alone, thoughts broiling. The question was inescapable—what if he was meant to find his father and somehow talk him out of the destructive path he was on? Isn't that what the millennials were getting at with their story? Or something like that? If only there was more time to think things over, to ask more questions … and actually get some answers.

Leera returned. "The brat hasn't changed one bit, has he?" She gave Augum a playful punch on the shoulder. "Hey, you all right?"

"Yeah … 'course."

"Come on then, time to go."

The group gathered around Thomas while Mrs. Stone stood apart. She took a long moment glancing at each of them in turn.

Bridget suddenly dashed forward and wrapped her arms around her.

"Goodness me—"

Leera soon joined, followed by Augum and Mya.

"Now now, that is quite enough." Mrs. Stone gently pushed them away. "I will see you in good time." Reluctantly, they padded back to Thomas. Mrs. Stone took a deep breath before giving her husband a grave look. "Thomas, should the penance come to pass in the traditional way—"

"—I will do what will have to be done, Anna." They stared at each other for a moment, eternally young husband

and his old wife. Thomas finally opened his palm, revealing an engraved metallic cube. He then began speaking arcane words that repeated and elevated in volume. A strong wind kicked up as a bright light began emanating from the object, so bright they had to shield their eyes with their hands. Suddenly there was an implosive crunch. When things died down, Mrs. Stone was gone.

Augum stared at the vacant spot where his great-grandmother had stood a moment before, wondering if he will ever see her again.

ABSALON

"Augum Stone, Mya Liaxh, Sydo Ridian, Leera Jones, Bridget Burns—listen to my voice as you walk with me. Prepare yourselves." Thomas' arm flared with fire. He pointed it at the grove, which started sinking back into the ground with a loud grinding noise. The grass disappeared first, forcing them to hold each other for balance, replaced by desert sand and rocks. The table and beds followed, then the braziers, and lastly the great oaks sank as if in quicksand. Without the protection of the trees, the wind was soon upon them, scratching at bare skin. Augum, Bridget and Leera hid in the hoods of their robes, while Sydo and Mya had to make do with holding their arms over their faces.

Thomas immediately started with his sermon that somehow kept the Song of the Wastes at bay. "… knowing that we mean no harm, our spirits calm, the winds of anxiety doing us no injury …" He carried on as they walked, until the sound of the wind changed. Augum peeked out from his hood and spotted a massive boulder, not unlike the size of Hangman's Rock, directly ahead. Thomas led them right to it before stopping. He placed both hands on its face and the surface instantly disappeared, revealing a staircase descending into darkness.

They piled in after him, the entrance closing after the last person, engulfing them in darkness. Thomas cast a small floating fireball, illuminating a dusty tunnel crudely hewn from solid rock, the steps worn down from use. The wind roared outside the rock, muted and distant. It was as if they were listening to a hurricane, but they were safe in some ancient shelter. Thomas wordlessly began descending, everyone hurrying to catch up.

"Shyneo," Bridget said, echoed by Augum and Leera. Their palms lit up with their respective glows.

"Shyneo," the prince said, face contorting in concentration. His hand lit up with a tiny fire. Suddenly Bridget blew it out, giggling.

"What is the meaning of—oh, you jest with me. Most amusing." He gave a nervous chortle.

"Aww, you didn't have many friends back in Blackhaven, did you?" Bridget asked, mindful of her steps.

Leera turned to roll her eyes at Augum.

Sydo scoffed. "I had plenty, thank you. Excuse me now … Shyneo!" but his palm failed to light. "I say, turn around and stop staring, this is hard enough as it is. And I shall have you know the court held me in high esteem."

Augum was baffled. Sydo was being rude to Bridget, had been rude to all of them—and there she was laughing with the brat! He poked Leera and they shared a look that said *Could you believe her?*

"You *were* the prince," Bridget said. "What else were they going to do? But I mean, how many close friends did you have?"

"Well, I …" but he fell silent.

"Oh, I am just awful! I apologize, Your Highness, I did not mean to pry. I'm sure you had plenty of close friends—"

Leera put a finger in her mouth and pretended to gag.

Sydo cleared his throat most properly. "Bridget …"

"Yes, Your Highness?"

"I find you … acceptable."

"Um, thank you, Your Highness," Bridget replied in a halting manner.

Augum had to turn away from the comically horrified look Leera flashed him.

When everyone quieted down and the only sound was the gentle echo of their footsteps, Augum decided to ask a question that had been on his mind for a while now.

"Great-grandfather …"

"Yes, Augum Stone?"

"Can you tell us about the Vow of Isolation?"

"I can. The Vow of Isolation is an ancient promise that took form after the creation of the scions. It was a pledge of abstinence from mortal affairs, put in place so the mortal world would not covet our powers, as had happened with Occulus and many before him. All swear this vow upon becoming Leyan. Since the time of the vow, we have become minders of mortal knowledge, and nothing more."

"But the vow has not stopped my father from wanting Leyan powers."

"Most accurate, Augum Stone, and what is a library for if the books cannot be read? This is why I break the vow—I do not believe it wise for Leyans to continue down the same path if the results are no different than before."

"Sir, how old is Krakatos?" Leera blurted.

"He is … very old, some say eternal."

Augum couldn't resist. "So he knew Atrius Arinthian!"

"He did."

"Great-grandfather … do you think we can speak with him?"

"This I cannot know. Krakatos the Ancient is not one for idle conversation."

They descended for quite some time, the passage always straight, unchanging. At last, the stairs stopped in a room with a stone arch at the other end. The floor was made up of great slabs, each square as long and wide as a man was tall.

"Welcome to Absalon," Thomas said.

Mya pointed at the apex of the arch. "M'lord, if I may ask, what is that symbol there?"

Augum had to look closely to make out a circle with a pair of overlapping ovals inside, a dot at the center.

"That is the Helix, the ancient symbol of Ley. It represents the eternal moment within which we dwell." Thomas let the thought settle before walking on.

The stone slabs sprawled out beyond the arch into darkness. Augum sensed a great space, as if they were in a massive cavern, the ceiling and walls too far to see. The air smelled very old, reminding him of castle Arinthian's crypt.

"Where are the others?" Leera asked.

Sixty-seven, no less nor more, Augum recalled.

"Some are already here, others have yet to come," Thomas replied, his floating fire a beacon in a sea of darkness.

They arrived at a very wide set of long and shallow steps, so wide its edges were lost to darkness. The stairs led them to a plateau, where they finally spotted buildings across from each other, forming an alley in between. They were simple ghostly works of functional stone, unadorned and uncolored, two-storied, windowless.

"So this is it?" Leera asked slowly. "*This* is the ancient city of Absalon?"

"It is, Leera Jones."

"Not what I expected at all. Kind of … drab."

Augum had to agree with her. He thought it would be much … grander.

"Sir, where are we going?" Sydo asked, his fire sputtering.

"To a home better suited for mortals, Sydo Ridian."

They soon stopped at a windowless two-story home with a slanted shingled roof. There was a plain wooden door with a bronze doorknob, flanked by a pair of stone pots, ancient remnants of soil still inside.

"If you'll forgive me, m'lord, but why do the other buildings not have a roof?" Mya asked.

Looking around, Augum realized she was right—the other buildings were completely open to the air.

"Roofs are unnecessary here, but it has been observed having a roof eases the transition for mortals."

"So does having windows," Leera muttered.

Thomas gestured with an open palm and the door swung open. "Please enter."

Inside, the floor was made of polished obsidian slabs, the walls smooth gray stone, broken only by rod-shaped ebony and bronze sconces. To the left was a spartan common area furnished with a polished stone table and square block chairs. The bare kitchen had a stone wash basin and shelves lined with earthen tableware.

Straight ahead from the entrance was a black marble staircase that presumably led to the bedrooms. To the right of it was a bathing room with copper taps in the shape of tree limbs. The polished black stone tub appeared very comfortable. Seeing it, Augum realized he couldn't even remember the last time he took a bath.

"The fixtures here were constructed for the non-arcane, long ago," Thomas said, walking over to a wall with an ebony rod in a bronze sconce, one of many strewn about the room. With a wave of a finger, his floating globe of fire extinguished itself, darkening the room. He pressed an engraved Helix at the base of the rod and it emitted a small flame. "The taps and fireplace work the same way. I hope you find the accommodations comfortable."

"This is incredible," Leera mumbled, pressing a tap in the bathing room. "Oh, yuck—the water's brown!"

"It has not been used for some time."

"Ooo, it's turning clear … and hot!"

Bridget squealed and ran over, testing the water.

Mya followed right behind and daintily placed her hand underneath the tap. "What witchery is this?" she whispered.

"You mean Ancient arcanery," Bridget replied.

"Food will be provided and the water here is good to drink," Thomas said. "Oba will bring you fresh linens and provisions. I shall return later when you are settled." He departed, but they were too caught up to notice.

Bridget grinned. "We can wash our clothes here!"

Sydo shrugged. "I daresay it is not like what I am used to … but it will do."

Augum's eyes dropped to the burn mark on the prince's doublet. "Hey, let me apologize one more time for striking you with lightning. I'll ask Great-grandfather if he can spare some new clothes … or something."

Sydo gave him a cool look. "No need to bother, I shall have Mya prepare me a new one."

Augum had to bite his tongue as the girls piled out of the bathing room, giggling like schoolchildren.

"All right everybody—race for your rooms!" Leera said, lunging for the stairs along with Bridget and lastly Mya, who avoided the race but did skip a step or two. Soon Leera's voice came echoing down the stairs. "Me and Bridge pick this one—!"

Sydo made a sound rather like that of a donkey. "Stupid peasants …"

Augum sighed and walked upstairs, lighting the corridor torches along the way. He stepped into the last room on the right, extinguished his palm, and stood in the partial darkness, listening to the distant exclamations of the girls. He pressed the engraved Helix on a torch and closed the door.

The windowless room lit up in a gentle amber glow. It had a dresser, a small wardrobe, a wooden cot, and a writing table with a spindled chair, all carved with the helix and crafted by patient hands—not a joint out of place, not a single uneven line. The pillow and linens on the cot had long rotted away.

There was a knock at the door. "Pardon me, Augum," Mya said when he opened it, almond eyes peering about his room. "But m'ladies Bridget and Leera insist we take a peek at your room."

We? To his disappointment, Bridget and Leera giggled, completely ruining any chance of him having a private conversation with Mya.

"Um, of course," he stammered, getting out of the girls' way as they piled in.

"Looks identical to ours," Leera said, opening the dresser drawers.

"Does it—?" he mumbled absently, watching the play of torchlight on Mya's delicate features as she padded about the room.

"Oh, stop your snooping, Lee," Bridget said, opening his wardrobe.

Another knock came, this time from below, and much louder.

"That must be Oba with the linens!" Bridget yelled, swooping out of the room. Mya and Leera followed, Augum trudging along behind.

Sydo had already allowed Oba entry by the time they crashed downstairs. The brawny Leyan held two large woven baskets, each overstuffed with items. "Solians spoiled." He dropped the baskets to the ground with a derisive snort before taking his leave.

"Sir—" Leera called after him, but Oba Sassone had already gone.

Bridget fished out a fresh white towel and squealed. "Oooo … look!"

"And soap—!" Mya held up a bundle of multi-colored bars like a prized hen.

Soon everyone was greedily rooting around, even the prince, deprived for so long of his luxuries. In the first basket, they found an ornate silver comb and hand mirror that appeared to have come from an age long past; nightgowns embroidered with the Helix; an assortment of scented oils; white towels; blankets and silk sheets. The other basket held Leyan food, though there were some additional goodies, namely two jars of dark jam and two bars of what appeared to be chocolate.

Mya stood up with a meek expression. "Would m'ladies care to take a bath first?"

"You go ahead," Bridget said idly.

"Oh, thank you—"

Sydo's head shot up but Bridget gave him an imploring look. "If you must," he muttered. Mya flashed Bridget a secretly grateful smile before excusing herself with a curtsy.

Sydo gathered a great many of the goods and slithered to his room.

"Did you want the wash basins too?" Leera called after him. "Take some chairs while you're at it. Ugh, I hate him."

"He's had a difficult upbringing," Bridget said, adjusting her hair in the mirror. "Give him some leeway."

"He's got so much leeway there's no room for anyone else." Leera picked out a nightgown. "Hey, remember when Tyeon tried one of these on?"

Bridget burst with a laugh. "Only he could get away with stuff like that."

They fell silent.

Augum sat down beside Leera. "Miss him, don't you?"

They nodded.

"You would have really liked him, Aug," Leera said quietly.

He recalled Tyeon's clever and friendly wit. Then he recalled the boy taking a spear through the gut for his grandfather and crumpling at the man's feet. "I *know* I would have."

Sydo came down the steps, taking a seat across from Bridget at the table. "What is the matter with you lot? Why so glum?"

Bridget shrugged. "Nothing."

"Do not keep secrets from your prince."

"I suppose it's fair to tell you, since you don't know."

"Tell me what?"

Bridget folded and refolded a blanket. "The Legion burned down Sparrow's Perch, mine and Leera's home."

Sydo gave Augum a knowing look. "I see. Were there casualties?"

Bridget only nodded.

Augum felt his heart constrict. "My father murdered their parents."

There was a fleeting look of triumph on Sydo's face before he caught himself. "So they suffered the same fate as my father."

"And what of your mother?" Bridget cut in.

"She died of coughing sickness when I was but a boy," Sydo replied.

Suddenly it hit Augum—they were all orphans, every single one of them, all but him—and it was solely his father's fault. "I wish I could make it all better somehow," he blurted, remembering that words were just that … words.

Sydo stood up. "You can—turn yourself over to your father!"

Bridget and Leera gasped.

Sydo flipped his hand. "What? It was not I who said it—the millennials themselves are of the same mind. Think about it—it would *heal* Lord Sparkstone's heart and stop the madness. Is that not what they hinted with their story? Search your souls, you know it to be true!"

Bridget's voice dropped to a hurt whisper. "How could you say such a thing?"

"It—was—not—I—who—said—it! You tell me you have not thought the same …"

Bridget abruptly stood and took a step back from the table, staring at the prince as if for the first time. She looked to Augum and hesitated. That moment of hesitation was all it took. Just as she opened her mouth to say something, Augum said, "Save it—" and stormed upstairs to his room, slamming the door. He threw himself down on his cot, not bothering to light a torch. His skin burned with anger and his heart panged with hurt.

So it was true—they agreed he should turn himself over to his father! And if he didn't, they'd blame him for everything that happened from here on—every single murder his father perpetrated was going to be on his hands! And they'd be right—if he had the power to stop his father, he *had* to … A sick feeling surged through him. Suddenly he understood what his great-grandmother meant by *sacrifice*.

He took a deep breath. He knew what he had to do.

MAGUA

"Augum—?" came Leera's quiet voice from the other side of the door.

"What!" Augum shot back.

"Augum I—"

"—I don't want to hear it."

"Well, I'm coming in anyway—" The door opened and closed before he could say anything else. He gave an exasperated sigh and turned away. The cot depressed slightly as she sat beside him.

"Aug, you have to know Bridget's very upset. She doesn't for one moment believe you should turn yourself over to your father."

He didn't reply, too afraid he'd say something mean. He wished she would just go away and leave him alone.

"—and neither do I," Leera continued. "We don't believe you going to Sparkstone would do any good. He'd just try to corrupt you and continue with his plans anyway. Please, Aug, you *must* believe me."

He felt conflicted. Part of him desperately wanted to believe her, but another said it was now his duty to join his father. How many lives would that save? Damn well not enough. Wouldn't bring Bridget and Leera's parents back. Wouldn't bring Sir Westwood back either.

A small knock came at the door. "Augum ...?" It was Bridget.

Leera got up. "I'm going to let her in, okay?"

He shrugged as the door opened.

Bridget padded up to the cot, sniffling. "Aug—please know I'd never, *ever* want you to go to join your father—"

Hearing her troubled voice made him feel like a bratty baby. But why *couldn't* he be the bratty baby for once? He should just tell them he was going and leave it at that.

"Augum? Talk to me ... *please*."

He wanted to say something, but couldn't get any words out. Bridget immediately sobbed and stormed out of the room.

Leera sighed. "I better go see to her." She gave Augum's shoulder a squeeze, and quietly closed the door, once again leaving him in darkness.

He returned to lying on his back. Nice one, why not upset Mya too while you're at it. Idiot.

He lay there for some time, trying to figure out how to get out of Ley and join his father. Maybe he could make a special petition or something, ask to be teleported to the Black Castle directly.

The best thing to do was to slip out without the girls noticing. He didn't think he could bear seeing Bridget, Leera and Mya again. Wait—the fountain! But how could he pass through the portal without the scion, and how would he find it again in the desert?

Another knock at the door. "M'lord, it is your turn at the bath." It was Mya, and she sounded … normal, as if nothing was going on. He really wished she had called him by his proper name.

"Um, okay thanks," he said, trying to sound completely normal too. He listened to the fading sound of her footsteps, heart aching.

No, he *had* to face them, he couldn't just slip out like some weasel! He really *was* acting like a brat …

He got up, deciding to take a bath and think things over more. As he passed through the living area, he surreptitiously checked the dining table. Bridget, Leera and Mya sat together, obviously talking about him because they went quiet as he walked by. He strolled on into the bathing room, closing the door behind him. There he stripped off his old robe, stepped into the black stone tub and took his time washing up.

He tried hard to enjoy the luxuries of hot water and soap, but it proved impossible because of a certain phrase that kept circling in his head—*Return me mine son and I shall henceforth unburden thy kingdom of mine wrath …*

Was that the intention, or was there another message in the speech? He ran through people's opinions to help weigh on the matter. Nana fiercely objected him rejoining his father, yet the millennials seemed to suggest otherwise. After some honest reflection, he came to believe Bridget and Leera didn't want him to join his father either. Sydo certainly made it plain where he stood. As for Mya … well, he only hoped she wanted him around too.

Now if Sir Westwood were here, he would make a big speech about how it was Augum's *duty* to do the right thing—which in this case probably meant joining his father and trying to talk him out of … out of what, being a necromancer?

The more he thought about it, the sillier the idea seemed. What could he, a 1st degree warlock, possibly say or do to stop the Lord of the Legion, a man he did not know except through his atrocities? Most likely he'd be held for ransom for the family scion …

Return me mine son and I shall henceforth unburden thy kingdom of mine wrath …

But even if there *was* a tiny chance, was it not worth taking for the sake of so many lives?

He struggled on with his thoughts as he washed his hair. After the bath, he glanced at himself in the mirror over the washbasin. His scruffy umber hair dropped down to his sharply arched brows now, a touch long for his taste. Maybe he could convince Mya to give it a trim. The thought made his chest constrict. He wanted to stay, but he *needed* to go. He had to be strong. Tough. He sighed, adjusted his robe one last time, and made his exit.

The table once again fell quiet as Augum approached. He noticed Sydo was sitting amongst them now. The girls gave the prince urging looks. He finally stood up and cleared his throat.

"Err … I apologize for having said that you should go to your father," the prince said in forced tones. There was a frantic whisper and he added, "And I hope you will forgive me as I have forgiven you … for striking me with lightning and almost killing me like your fa—OW! How dare—STOP IT!" but he fell silent after the second kick under the table.

Augum frowned. When had Sydo forgiven him? He was certain he'd have remembered *that* happening. "I accept your apology," he nonetheless said, unable to bring himself to argue right now.

Bridget smiled. "Come on, Aug, have some fruit."

His eyes travelled to Mya, who stood tall, shiny jet hair streaming down her front. She smiled. He felt his face grow hot.

A knock came at the door.

"I'll get it—" Augum said quickly, expecting to see Thomas, but after opening it, he was surprised to find a millennial instead. It was the withered old woman with milky eyes, disheveled hair, and triangular symbol on her cloak.

She pointed a crooked finger at him. "You are the heir to the Lord of Death, are you not?"

Augum took a step back. "I really hope not ... but where's Thomas Stone?"

She grunted and shuffled inside, bent so far forward she only came up to his chest. The others, still at the table, stood upon seeing her.

Her head shook uncontrollably as she spoke. "Thomas Stone is readying for judgment and penance."

"M'lady—" Mya began, stepping forward and curtseying, "forgive my impertinence, but, what exactly is Mr. Stone doing penance for?"

"I am no lady! My name is Magua. Remember it well, childling. As for Thomas Stone, he will serve penance for breaking the vow. He is young and foolish, much like that wife of his—too quick to act, too slow to contemplate. It is forbidden to harbor the uninvited. It is forbidden to train them. It is forbidden to pass on secret knowledge. And it is forbidden to perform an unsanctioned Karma."

Sydo's face lit up with recognition. " 'Unsactioned karma'? Your Eldership means the statue trick—!" His tone seemed to suggest Thomas had done him great wrong.

Magua fixed her eyes upon the prince. "A Karma is a grave thing. It is not to be used lightly. We Leyans took the Vow of Isolation—we are not to interfere in the happenings of mortals. Even your being here is an affront to the sacred oath."

"But is it not so that Leyans were once far more involved with the world?" Bridget asked.

"That is so, and so it was once, but no more can it be, for learned we have become." Magua glanced at Augum's apprentice robe and grunted. "You wear history with little concern, childlings. You were permitted to come to Absalon only because old bonds are hard to break. Thomas' judgment is clouded by his attachments to the world—by the way of husband and wife."

"His judgment isn't clouded—" Augum said, stepping away. "He believes Leyans need to help us mortals again—and I think he's right! We need Leyan help defeating my father."

Magua scoffed. "Helping mortals is no longer our way. Our way is long and quiet. It is the way of peace and the keeping of ancient knowledge."

Was it just him or was that disdain in her voice? "But what's the point if there's no one to share the knowledge with?"

The millennial studied him a moment with those milky eyes. "The Lord of Death has much the same argument, only he goes further still, coveting long life for his devoted followers."

"And what if you're wrong? I mean, what if Leyans were *meant* to help us ordinary mortals? Since you've withdrawn from the world, your numbers have only shrunk—"

"—Great Elder Magua," Sydo interrupted in a sweet voice, "is it not your opinion that the best possible course of action would be for Augum to join his heinous father—to prevent war of course?"

Mya gasped. "Your Highness—"

Leera turned purple while Bridget just closed her eyes and shook her head. Augum, on the other hand, was hardly surprised.

The old woman made a hissing noise. "What are ears for if not for listening? I have taken the vow. I cannot advise your course. The vow is in place to protect the mortal world from itself. You have already gained knowledge that breaks the vow."

"You mean the Centarro spell?" Bridget said.

"There is that indeed, but graver is the knowledge that possession of all seven scions would destroy the possessor. This knowledge breaks the vow, for you have gained it from a Leyan."

"But we won't tell anyone, promise—" Leera said.

The millennial smirked. "Is that so?"

"What about the Lord of Death?" Augum asked. "What if he finds a way into Ley? Wouldn't that destroy you? Why won't you help us mortals prevent that like once before?"

Magua paused before replying. "You have seen the darkening skies. Ley suffers from that error. We should have let events unfold. Besides, now there are only two means for the Lord of Death to gain entry. The first is using a scion to build a portal to Ley. That knowledge is extinct among mortals and solely resides with the ancient father, Krakatos." Her tone seemed to suggest it impossible to wrest it from the man.

"The second is finding an ancient recipe that creates a portal *without* using a scion." Her milky eyes wandered over them, eventually fixing onto Sydo, whose fiery brows rose up his forehead. "And that recipe is long thought lost to mortals. So you see, there is no need for Leyan involvement."

"Wait," Augum said, "aren't you breaking the vow just by telling us this?"

She made an impatient wave. "It matters little."

His neck prickled. "Why not?"

There was a tint of malice in her voice. "Because our judgments are always sound." She turned her back on them. "The elders have much to discuss," and departed, Bridget closing the door after her.

Augum couldn't shake the anxious feeling he had about Magua. What was even the point of her visit? Why did she tell them things they weren't supposed to know or talk about? He plopped down at the table. Mya sat across from him, porcelain features wrinkled in thought.

Bridget's robe swished as she began pacing. "Hmm, remember the last thing Mrs. Stone said to her husband?"

Leera took a seat beside Augum. "Something about judgment in the old way."

"Exactly. Well, what if Thomas isn't the only one being judged—what if we are too?"

Leera opened a jar of dark jam and smelled the contents, only to make a revolted face. "Relax, Bridge, we're only waiting for Mrs. Stone. When she comes back, we'll be gone and they can go back to …" she swatted idly, "whatever it is they do around here."

Bridget stopped midstride, voice a conspiratorial whisper. "Did anyone else find it strange Magua told us about the ways the Lord of Death could enter Ley?"

"I did," Augum said immediately.

Leera shrugged. "Sparkstone would have done it by now if he knew how to make a gate, or portal, or whatever—"

"Yeah, but what I'm saying is—" Bridget's voice dropped even lower, "I think that old woman was hinting Sparkstone *could* make a portal with our involvement somehow."

"Now that is quite preposterous," the prince said, taking a seat beside Mya. "I hardly think we could influence the Lord of the Legion with regards to such a thing."

"And you—" Leera began, pointing a jam-covered finger in his face. "I can't believe you backstabbed Augum like that!"

"I merely asked what needed to be asked. What is wrong with the lot of you? Do you not understand the elders' meaning? If we give Augum over to his father, we can avoid war and murder and … and return the throne to someone more … moderate."

Leera's fists clenched and unclenched. "Give. Augum. Over? You just want the throne!"

"You fault me for wanting what is rightfully mine? Besides, I am sure that to save the kingdom from ruin, Augum would *want* to turn himself over." He gave Augum a sanctimonious look. "How did that line go again?"

" 'Return me mine son and I shall henceforth unburden thy kingdom of mine wrath'," Augum said, deflating in his chair. "He's right. I have to try, don't I? If there was only the smallest chance, wouldn't it be worth taking?" He glanced between the girls. "I mean, what if I could prevent what happened to your parents from happening to other people?"

Leera, whose mouth hung open, slowly turned to the prince. Suddenly she lunged across the table and tackled him, the pair falling backwards. "This is your fault, you nasty, spoiled brat! If Augum goes, I'll—"

Bridget and Mya sprang into action trying to claw the two of them apart, while Augum sighed, picked up what looked like a blue Leyan orange, and left to go upstairs.

"You wretched gutterborn," Sydo said to Leera mid-struggle, "it is not as if his father would *kill* him!"

Augum closed the door to his room and pressed the Helix on a torch. He sat on his cot and began mindlessly peeling the odd fruit. His shoulders felt heavy. What he needed was to find a way out of Ley … or maybe what he needed was to wait for Mrs. Stone. Besides, even the thought of leaving the girls made him light-headed.

Yet, if he truly could stop his father, change his mind, or turn his heart … would it not be the right thing to do?

He tore off a slice, but his hand froze in mid air.

No, he *had* to try. As unpleasant and dangerous as the task was, he might just be the only person in all of Sithesia that could potentially reach his father's soul. He got up and reached for the door handle.

"M'lord Augum—?" came Mya's soft voice from the other side.

"Mya—" he managed to stammer after a moment, quickly swallowing the orange slice.

"M'lord, despair is not the solution, nor is going to your father. Do not concern yourself, Mrs. Stone will find another way."

"And how many must die in the meantime? I should go, I *need* to go and try. How can the Leyans be wrong?" He turned his back on the door, angry with her for … for … he did not know for what, truth be told. Oh, if only he were her age …

"M'lord …" her voice was even softer. "Please, come downstairs and talk."

But he didn't feel like talking. There really wasn't much to say, was there? It would just cause more heartache all around. He had decided to leave, and that was that. Why couldn't they just leave him alone?

He straightened his robe and opened the door.

Mya stood there smiling at him with those almond emerald eyes. The vision of her almost broke his resolve. He desperately wanted to stay and be near her … but he knew he couldn't, he had to do the right thing.

"Come drink and eat something, m'lord, you must be ravishing with hunger."

He held up the blue orange. "I have this …"

She laughed, the musical sound making his heart thump and his cheeks burn. "I'll come down," he said at last, "but can you please do something for me?"

"Anything, m'lord."

"Please stop calling me *m'lord*. Just Augum is fine."

She smiled. "As you wish, *Augum*," and led him downstairs, where Bridget and Leera sat at the table with sullen expressions. Sydo stood off to the side, arms folded close to his chest. He turned away upon spotting Augum. Bridget and Leera gave him painful smiles as he sat down across from them.

Bridget's lip stiffened. "You can't go, Aug."

Leera nodded along. "Yeah, you *better* not, or I'll—" She blinked rapidly. "Don't worry, we'll find another way to stop your father … or Mrs. Stone will at least."

Augum smiled half-heartedly. "I've decided to leave."

Leera winced and looked away.

"I have to try … it's the right thing to do."

Suddenly the front door opened. In stepped Oba Sassone carrying a large torch, his metallic muscles rippling.

"With me you come. Now."

"We'll talk about this later," Bridget whispered as they got up. "Where are we going? Should we take anything with us?" She asked Oba.

Oba merely scowled and turned his back, leaving them to scurry after him. He marched off through dark alleys, curved swords clinking. No one dared light their palm.

After turning a corner, they saw a great circle of torch-bearers standing in the vast square of Absalon.

Augum's hands went clammy as they descended wide stairs, coming to a stop in a gap evidently left for them. As they lined up, he recognized the elders on the opposite side. He searched for his great-grandfather, but torches obscured many of the faces. Their metallic bodies and dark eyes gave the Leyans a demonic appearance in that torchlight. There was a skin color for every shade known, and some unknown, along with a wide variety of exotic dress.

Magua shuffled forward. "We gather in our ancient ancestral home of Absalon to hide from angry skies above. Change has come." She stepped back into the circle as a pink-skinned elder stepped forward.

"We come to assign penance and answer a question." Her gray eyes fell on Augum and the others. "What are we to do with these uninvited mortal childlings, testaments to the broken vow?"

The Leyans muttered amongst themselves as she stepped back.

"I propose we train the childlings," a voice boomed. It was Thomas—he had stepped forward on the far right.

There were many mutterings of disagreement and shaking of heads.

Thomas raised his bronze hands to appease them. "I further propose the time has come for us to put aside the vow."

The crowd grew louder, some hissing in displeasure.

Magua stepped forward again, calming the crowd with a single withered hand. "Thomas Stone speaks from the heart, but it is his heart that breaks our vow. The Vow is the balance we have strived to maintain for over fifteen hundred years. It is holy. It is sacred. What Thomas Stone proposes is nothing short of blasphemy." She paused before continuing in a louder voice. "I move to banish the childlings from our land and wipe their minds of the time spent here."

This time the crowd murmured with agreement. Augum turned to Bridget and Leera, sharing silent expressions of alarm. He could barely breathe, wondering what it would be like to remember nothing.

"They should have gone with Anna Stone, why did she not take them?" called a young woman in a forest-colored cloak.

"Yes, why did she not take them?" asked a voice from the left.

"Wipe their minds!" said another.

"Anna embarked on a quest to consult the Seers in the north," Thomas said. "A quest too dangerous for the childlings. The Legion searches for her, for the childlings, and for the scion in Anna's possession. Villages and towns have posters painted of their faces with a coin reward and a promise of eternal life. She could not take them with her."

The old scarlet-robed man with almond eyes stepped forward. "It is not for us to judge or interfere. We have already broken the vow giving council on your behalf, young Thomas Stone. Amends must be made. I am aligned with Magua as to the penance."

The crowd rumbled in agreement.

Thomas once again stepped forward, sweeping the circle with his black eyes until all fell silent. "Our words and our deeds have lost their way. The time of the vow is over. We must include ourselves in mortal affairs again. Choosing not to would be disastrous for many, Leyans and mortals alike. A millennium and a half ago we were part of the mortal world. We shared our knowledge and there were thousands of us. We prospered. Mortals prospered. And since the vow, we have declined. There are only sixty-seven of us left. And we, the keepers of history, know that mortal arcane and non-arcane knowledge has also declined. Mortals know only the bare minimum, and no more." Thomas sighed deeply. "I say the vow will only bring about our destruction, for if the Lord of Death, fortified by the strength of scions and Dreadnought armor comes, we will be woefully unprepared, with no champions to fight on our behalf. We are but legend to the world, spoken of in tales around the fire."

His words caused quite a stir, even amongst the elders, who looked to each other as if communicating wordlessly, all but Krakatos, who stood as still as a pond on a windless day.

Thomas pressed on, his voice rising, the most emotion Augum has seen from the man. "I ask you all, for who do we keep our knowledge? For ourselves? It is time we face the fact that this is most selfish of us. I refuse to believe history entrusted us with ancient secrets only to hoard them—and to what end? Until only one of us remains? To whom would we pass on the knowledge then? The ancient library stands dusty and quiet. It is time to admit the vow has failed in its aim, for the mortals barely know of our existence and yet they *still* covet our powers—something the vow was supposed to prevent."

This time there were many conceding whispers and nods as Thomas stepped back into the circle.

"Thomas Stone again speaks from the heart," answered the old woman with the ivory skin and queenly gown. Heads turned in her direction. "But what he asks we cannot do, for we have sworn a sacred vow—sacred and holy. The Unnameables watch us and judge, for we are their chosen few. No, Thomas Stone must give proper penance. Let us leave the mortals to their fate."

The crowd stirred but stayed silent.

"Even if that fate brings our destruction—?" Thomas countered, late in stepping forward. "Where has the ancient Leyan wisdom gone? Has the vow left us senseless and unable to adapt? We forged the scions in our defense, knowing all too well the coveting ways of mortals. Moreover, what did we do? We gifted the scions to them to save ourselves. So why should we turn our backs when their sufferings are our doing?"

Voices rose at Thomas' words, some in apparent agreement.

Magua stepped forward. "Words change nothing! That which has been done cannot be undone! Enough of this. Thomas Stone and Oba Sassone are hereby charged with transgressions against the sacred Vow of Isolation. The charges are as follows—Thomas Stone has accepted uninvited childlings under his care. Thomas Stone and Oba Sassone have helped train the childlings. Thomas Stone has endowed vow-breaking knowledge upon the childlings. I now move for the elders to convene and assign penance."

Augum had enough and stepped forward. Some in the crowd immediately hissed.

"How dare the childling—"

"Most unorthodox—"

"Such impudence—"

"Let him speak—!" said the millennial woman in the ancient servant's outfit.

Augum forced himself to concentrate on his words not his nerves. "We mortals need Leyan help!" he shouted, hearing his voice echo distantly. "I wish to hear from Krakatos the Ancient!"

All eyes turned to the pink-spectacled man with the white loincloth—except he neither moved or acknowledged anyone. Augum's stomach plummeted. If there was anyone who could sway the Leyans …

Magua stepped forward, lips forming into a victorious smile. "I do believe the ancient father has chosen not to speak—" but she was cut off by gasps—Krakatos had taken a single measured step forward. Magua stood a moment longer before making a scowling retreat. Time passed as Krakatos' gaze swept the circle. Augum felt a sense of peace as the Leyan's spectacled eyes passed over him.

"Let us expatiate," the ancient Leyan began in his rapid prose and sharp accent. "It falls to me, an antediluvian and recalcitrant Leyan, to pass more than mere conjecture on the dilemma I myself have been pondering for an inexcusably protracted panorama of time. My vacillation has been a long-suffering malignance, and so I am quite ready for the perfection of verdict and absolution. Probability reasons that you will see my resolution as nothing more than profane sentiment. I anticipate a swift riposte, though you will find me unduly prepared. Now for the crux of my well-seasoned gambit—contrary to our beliefs, we Leyans *can* and *should* fathom beyond the eternal moment in which we dwell."

At this, the crowd stirred uncomfortably, but Krakatos went right on. Augum didn't exactly know what the Leyan meant, but he knew it was significant.

"In fact, let it be known forthwith that I have spent a copious amount of time conceiving of the next move in the grandest of games, and conjointly, of what has transpired. Ergo, I assert the choice is nothing if not clear. On the one hand, we have dogma, a paragon of orthodoxy and preservation. Diametrically, we have the unperceived alien fluidity of change. Let it be known I simply urge the latter."

Magua suddenly stepped forward. "That is blasphemy and treason of the highest kind! Cease speaking immediately!" She turned to the crowd and raised her arms. "I call on the emergency execution of the traitor and seditionist Krakatos! Step forward with me now and protect the sacred Vow of Isolation!"

A great many stepped forward, including, to Augum's shock, Oba Sassone. Once the stragglers realized they were outnumbered, they too stepped forward, leaving behind only a few dissenters, including Thomas Stone.

Magua turned to Krakatos, pointing an accusing finger. "Ancient father—you have hereby been sentenced to die for sedition!"

Krakatos merely turned to face her. Whatever look he gave made her pause a moment. Then he vanished without a sound.

Magua's lips thinned as gasps came from the circle.

"Impossible," someone whispered nearby.

"What of Thomas Stone and the childlings?" asked a voice in the crowd.

Heads turned to Augum and the others.

"Let us discuss," Magua replied, and Leyans stepped back, reforming the circle. Augum and his group stirred uneasily as the remaining elders conferred with nothing but looks.

Augum caught Oba Sassone watching him, metallic face impassive. He wondered what made the Leyan switch sides.

Finally, one by one, the elders gave a nod.

The woman wearing antlers and animal skins stepped forward. "The accusations have been deliberated upon. The decision is … conviction on all counts."

Augum felt his whole body tighten.

The crowd was silent as the old woman with avocado skin replaced the antlered woman. "Oba Sassone, for aiding the training of the childling mortals, you are to meditate in silence without speaking to, being seen, or hearing from another for sixty nights."

Oba bowed. "Oba accepts."

"Thomas Stone," said the old woman wearing the ancient servant's outfit, "for passing sacred knowledge, training, and harboring uninvited mortals, you are to meditate in silence without speaking to, being seen, or hearing from another for three hundred nights."

The girls, the prince, and Augum gasped. They were alone now, stuck among these ancient lunatics.

"So be it," Thomas said in even tones, bowing.

Augum wanted to protest, or at least hear his great-grandfather say something, *anything* else against—

"Childlings—" Magua's milky-eyes fell upon them. "For inhabiting the land of the Ley without invitation, and for learning some of its secrets without earning them, you will hereby be expelled, your mind wiped clean of your time here, upon first light of morning."

"You can't—!" Mya cried.

"It is done, so be it."

"So be it," echoed every Leyan voice around the circle, but Augum barely heard them past the rushing of blood in his ears.

BLIND

Augum could not remember the trip back to the house. When the door closed, he slumped on the black marble steps. "What just happened …?"

"This is all Mrs. Stone's fault," the prince said, plopping down at the table. "If she had only taken us with her …"

Augum was too shocked to argue.

Leera leaned back against the wall by the door, hands rubbing her freckled face. "Ugh … we're about to have our brains cooked by an old hag."

Bridget began pacing again. "I think we just witnessed some kind of historic overthrow. Magua seems to be in charge now."

"They are not nearly as wise as the legends make them out to be," Mya said, sitting down at the table beside the prince.

Augum shot up and went to the door. "It doesn't matter, we have to get out of here—" He tried the door. "It's locked." He leaned against it, expelling a long breath.

"No windows ... we're trapped," Leera said.

Bridget stopped pacing. "Centarro—"

"Wait, m'lady," Mya said. "We have to be careful—they have powers we do not understand, perhaps it is best—"

"Well we've *got* to try something—!" Augum interrupted, sounding harsher than he meant to.

Mya dropped her emerald eyes. "Ideas come few for a humble servant such as myself."

"You're not a servant—" Augum said, cheeks burning. "You're a traditional healer."

Sydo cleared his throat rather loudly. "Let us not forget that you are *my* servant. Need I remind you that you swore an oath to my father?"

Mya nodded. "I remember, Your Highness."

"It doesn't matter!" Bridget said. "Don't you understand—" she made a sweeping gesture at everything. "*None* of this matters! It doesn't matter because tomorrow morning we'll be vegetables in the middle of nowhere, lost and confused, and sure to be captured by the Legion!"

Silence hung in the air.

Augum wondered why his great-grandfather hadn't done anything after their penance was announced. Suddenly he saw movement. Something small and white scurried underneath the front door.

"Look," he said, "a mouse."

Sydo jumped back with a girlish shriek. "Kill it!"

Bridget whirled on him. "Don't you dare—"

"That's not a mouse," Augum said, watching as the little creature skittered toward him. "It's made of parchment!" It scampered up to his foot, rose on hind legs, and made the tiniest squeak. He scooped up the little bundle of crinkles, wondering what to do with it, when he saw writing underneath a flap—and then he understood.

"Sorry, little one," he whispered, unwrapping the message. The mouse gave a contented squeak. They gathered around and read.

Secure all possessions that make noise. Tonight you shall receive a single, quiet knock. Open the door without a word. Take each other's hands in a line, for I shall cast invisibility on all. I shall then lead you away and up the steps. Do not speak. Do not let go. Walk as quiet as mice.

Burn this message once memorized.

TS

A big smile spread across Leera's face as she suddenly embraced him. "You're going to stay with us, right?"

"Guess I have no choice for now ..." and he forced a smile.

Bridget placed her hands on his shoulders, looked him square in the eye. "I lost all of my brothers, but now I have you. *You* are my brother."

He felt his heart warm. "I'll ... I'll try to live up to that."

They memorized the message and put it to the torch. They then secured their possessions as instructed, Augum wrapping Burden's Edge in cloth to muffle the noise, Bridget doing the same with Blackbite. They kept as busy as they could to pass the time, everyone careful to talk about anything but tonight's escape. For a while, he, Bridget and Leera even practiced the spells they knew—Shine, Telekinesis, Repair, Unconceal, Shield, and Centarro, a spell they were almost completely hopeless with.

Meanwhile, the prince napped or sat by himself, looking sullen and bored, occasionally complaining about his burnt doublet and how Mya needed to fix it as soon as they reached civilization. Mya, when not answering Sydo, sorted through her woven bag of herbs, mumbling recipes to herself.

At one point, Bridget whispered something to Leera and Leera turned to look at Augum with a sorrowful look. Later, when he and Leera were sorting the food and the last of the basket items on the table together, he noticed she was being a little aggressive as she threw things into Bridget's rucksack.

He stopped what he was doing, wondering if he should ask if she was okay.

Leera looked up to make sure Bridget, Mya and Sydo were busy before turning to him. "Promise me you'll not search out your father. Promise me you won't leave us—"

His heart twisted into knots. What could he say? How could he promise knowing he might not be able to keep his word? "Leera, I—"

"Promise. Me," she said through gritted teeth.

Staring into those glassy dark eyes, he knew one thing for sure—he didn't want to hurt her any further, even if he had to lie. "I ..." but he couldn't say it, surrendering a nod instead.

Her lip trembled a moment and she looked like she was going to give him a hug. Instead she turned away, hiding her face behind a curtain of raven hair. "Ugh, I'm so pathetic."

He wanted to tell her she wasn't, that she was an amazing and caring friend and he really appreciated her, but instead he kept sorting.

Time flew by and they started getting tired. Everything was packed and ready to go. Now they just had to make it out of there without anyone noticing.

Eventually, Leera faked a yawn and stretched. "Getting late, isn't it?"

"It is, m'lady," Mya replied with an over-dramatized sigh. "Let us sleep."

"Goodnight," Bridget said with a wink, sitting by the door. She had volunteered to take the first watch. They lay on the cold floor, waiting for that all-important knock.

* * *

It was very late when Augum awoke suddenly to a gentle shaking. Almond-shaped emerald eyes swam into view, a finger held over soft lips. He sat up as Mya moved on to gently shake the prince. Augum immediately spotted Thomas, standing by Bridget, his muscled bronze chest glistening in the flicker of a single Leyan torch near the door.

Thomas glanced at the closed door before gesturing for them to form a line. They did so without a word, Leera at the front followed by Bridget, Sydo, Augum and Mya. Augum worried about his sweaty palm as Mya gripped his hand. A familiar fluttering began in his stomach, though it could just as easily have been nerves.

When they were ready, Thomas made sure he had their attention and pressed the Helix on the wall torch, snuffing it out. A moment later, his arm erupted in rings of fire as he whispered a complex string of unknown arcane words, touching each of them on the head as he went along. Those he touched instantly disappeared with a quick sucking sound.

When Augum's turn came, he felt a strange tingling, like when he slept in a funny position and his arm or leg went numb. He glanced down at his body but it was gone! The sensation was so peculiar it actually made him dizzy. He had to focus his gaze on his great-grandfather to keep from stumbling. At last, Thomas put a finger to his lips before turning himself invisible. The light from his arm immediately extinguished, plunging them into pitch darkness.

The front door squeaked. Sydo's hand gave a light tug and the line began moving forward. Augum took small, measured steps so as not to step on the prince's heel. It was a challenge to walk in total darkness, the kind where there was no difference between opening one's eyes and closing them. He wished they had practiced walking like this beforehand.

They wound this way and that. Augum heard nothing other than the quiet padding of their feet, their rapid breathing, and the thunder of his own heart. Sometimes he sensed they were near an object, perhaps the wall of a house. At other times, he sensed great spaces. The group eventually slowed down and Augum felt a squeeze from the prince's hand, which he instinctively passed on to Mya, figuring it had to be a warning of some kind.

The sound of people's feet in front changed. He was trying to figure out why when his foot suddenly stepped into nothing. He stumbled, letting go of Sydo's hand but managing to hold on to Mya's.

The stairs—of course. He tried to get his bearing, but the group's shuffling quickly faded and he was unsure as to which direction they had gone. He stood there, disbelieving they had not waited for them. Why hadn't Sydo informed the others?

Mya squeezed his hand, probably wondering what was happening. He could only squeeze back. It was so quiet even whispering was too dangerous. He slowly descended the rest of the steps. When he reached the bottom he figured the only thing to do was try to walk as straight as possible. With nothing to see, however, that proved difficult, and he walked painfully slow, his free hand groping in the dark.

The pair walked for what felt like far too long a time when Augum suddenly slammed right into a stone pillar. He grunted involuntarily and immediately froze. Somewhere behind them, a red fiery light lit up. It was someone's palm, waving about, coming closer.

Maybe Great-grandfather had finally realized they were missing and was coming for them … but no, the Leyan certainly wouldn't give himself away like that.

Mya gave an urgent tug at his arm as the mysterious figure approached, hand sweeping in wide arcs. Augum nudged Mya to stand behind the pillar, which was just wide enough to conceal them both—as long as one stood behind the other.

The figure was now no more than thirty paces away, advancing quietly. Augum held his breath, not daring to make the slightest movement or noise. He held Mya's hand tightly, a grip she returned, their hands trembling together. As the figure drew even nearer, with the way his arm swept about, Augum had the sudden realization that they were going to be seen.

His mind raced. There was only one chance, and he had to take it. He calmed his breathing and concentrated unlike ever before, knowing he had to get it right the first time.

"Centeratoraye xao xen," he whispered as quietly as possible.

He knew immediately that he had invoked the spell correctly because he felt every nuance of the moment—the location of each of his limbs in space, exactly where Mya was, and the position of the pillar in relation to them and the stranger. He even felt the pulse of Mya's heart through her palm, a rhythm that matched the frantic beating of his own.

With perfect clarity, he focused on the burning palm and the swing of its light. Time seemed to stretch and sharpen, but not enough to plan for the side effects of Centarro, a risk he was painfully aware of. His free hand gripped the stone pillar, feeling its rough, cool texture. So attuned was Augum to every sound that each of the man's steps sounded like a thunderous crash, each breath a windstorm. He had to act very soon. Suddenly, the solution presented itself in the shadow of the pillar, as it moved opposite to the light. There was a slow cadence to it.

He snagged Mya's other hand, squeezing with reassurance. He then started rocking back and forth, guiding her along to the gentle swaying of the shadow, in an almost musical way, so that whenever the person's lit palm swung to the far right, he and Mya danced left, and vice versa, always in the shadow of the pillar, always just in time. Somehow, she understood and followed his lead in this deadly dance. Only a few times did a piece of their clothing snag the light, but he knew they had to keep going, he had to keep concentrating …

And then, as if a fog had descended on his thoughts, things started to get fuzzy. Knowing what was coming, he drew Mya close, freezing in the shadow of the pillar opposite the burning palm. Miraculously, the stranger walked right by, the pair having danced in the pillar's shadow undiscovered.

As the sound of the stranger's steps faded, Augum drifted away. He knew he had to find some people … he let go of Mya and was about to start walking in search of them when she grabbed him and drew him close. The hypnotic distant light, her soft embrace, and the delicate aroma of her scented oil all served to calm him. He rested like this in her arms, lost in the simplest thoughts, the pair waiting …

It felt like a long time before he was able to put things back together in his mind again. Mya still held him in a soothing yet firm embrace, like a favorite blanket on a cold night. His heart raced, sure he'd remember that embrace for the rest of his life. Yet he realized there were pressing concerns. They were lost and the spell had left him arcanely fatigued. Reluctantly, he tapped her side and she loosened her grip, keeping hold of his hand.

He peered around the pillar. The stranger was combing towering rock walls. Suddenly, although very briefly, the

Leyan's light passed over the entranceway. Augum placed one leg forward in its direction and held it there as a marker, waiting for the person with the light to have gone a distance further before continuing forward. They watched the light sway back and forth in wide arcs, a lonely lantern in absolute darkness. At last, he judged the person to be far enough away for them to go on.

The walk was agonizingly slow, the silence magnifying every sound. When at last his hand felt the cool wall of rock, he felt a wave of relief and gave Mya's hand an encouraging squeeze. They walked along the wall until finally finding the stone archway. The pair quietly passed through and began the long ascent up the narrow steps, stopping now and then to listen. He hoped the others had gone up ahead, and tried not to think of them getting caught down below while waiting for him and Mya.

After a long time ascending the worn stone steps, a "Psst—" came from somewhere up ahead. He made the same noise in return, squeezing Mya's hand in delight. At last he managed to find an outstretched hand, which he could only assume was Sydo's. The line promptly continued moving as if nothing at all had happened, still without a word spoken or a light shone.

As they finally neared the exit, a muted low roar increased. At first, Augum thought it was some kind of monster screaming, until the exit door disappeared, revealing a sandstorm and flooding the corridor with light. Thomas stepped outside, everyone following.

Augum flashed Mya a relieved smile and gave one last squeeze of her hand before letting go to draw his hood. He wished he could hold her hand forever.

The challenge to avoid getting lost in the storm was immense—visibility was only a few feet, yet they had to keep an eye out for the person in front while protecting their faces against whipping sand.

They walked until a figure appeared. As they drew close, Augum identified a wine-colored shirt flapping in the wind. A pair of curved blades clanked at the Leyan's hips.

"Oba Sassone," Thomas said, stopping paces away. "The Song of the Wastes calls. We have little time."

"Prepared is Thomas Stone?"

"I am."

"You—you betrayed us!" Leera yelled. "You betrayed Mrs. Stone!"

The metallic-skinned Leyan's black eyes narrowed. "Pretend Oba must, so back he can go."

"There's no time," Thomas said. "I will explain later. Oba, if you please—"

"Prepared Thomas be for consequences?"

"I am."

Oba Sassone reached out a hand and Thomas took it. The two Leyan friends shared a moment before Oba gave a slight nod and let go.

Thomas turned to the group. "Hold on and do not let go! We are about to teleport." He grabbed Augum's hand then Leera's, who was still eyeing Oba with distrust.

They formed a circle as Oba dug out the same small metallic cube that had been used to teleport Mrs. Stone. Augum now recognized the engraving on its sides—it was the Helix.

Oba held it up and began invoking an arcane phrase. The cube started glowing, the light brighter and brighter as he repeated the invocation, eventually shouting the words as loudly as he could, the veins in his great neck bulging, spittle raining from his mouth.

"Hold on tight!" Thomas yelled as a terrible vibration circulated through their arms, threatening to break their grips on each other. When the light built up to a blinding climax, the air ruptured with a deafening tearing sound, yanking them forward at impossible speed. A moment later, they were tumbling along snowy ground, barely missing trees, until finally there was only the quiet of the night and the distant hooting of an owl.

THE TRAPPER

Augum stood up in knee-deep snow, trying to make his head stop spinning. Leera was nearest so he offered her a hand first. "You all right?"

She coughed and nodded.

One by one, the others gained their footing, taking a bewildered look about. They were in a forest of snow-encrusted evergreens. It was a starry night, the moon's crescent points lending just enough light to see. The cold was sharp, frosting their breath.

Augum noticed Thomas was still down on one knee, head bowed low, his breathing labored.

"Are you all right, Great-grandfather?"

"I am fine, but let us speak quietly. We do not know what manner of folk stir in these woods."

Augum helped him stand. As he did so, he noticed the Leyan's skin lacked its bronze luster—it was now pale and prickled with goose bumps. He also saw that his eyes were no longer night black, but rather light gray, with flecks of gold. "Great-grandfather … what's happening to you?"

"Never you mind me—we have other concerns at the moment."

Bridget draped a gray wool blanket around Thomas' shoulders, then handed another one to Sydo, whose burnt doublet least resisted the cold. "That's the last of the blankets," she said. "Knew I should have taken more."

"We need to find proper boots for Mr. Stone, m'lords and ladies," Mya whispered, nodding at his slippers while drawing her servant garment close.

Augum silently agreed and drew his hood. They weren't going to last long unless they found appropriate garb and shelter. "Where are we, Great-grandfather?"

Thomas glanced up at the stars. "We were supposed to teleport to the Northern Peaks, but I am afraid the portal cube is a difficult artifact to wield, especially for a 4th degree warlock such as Oba. I do believe we are somewhere in Solia, though it has been some time since I have navigated by star." He fixed his gaze upon Augum, wrinkles around his eyes apparent for the first time. "The situation is grave. We must find Anna before my time is up. Let us walk."

"Sir—wait, what do you mean?" Bridget asked in a quivering voice.

"And what about your seventeen degrees?" Sydo added, teeth chattering. "Could you not use your arcanery—?"

"My arcanery is no more. I am … less than mortal. I will explain when we find shelter. Come—north is this way."

Augum exchanged an alarmed look with Bridget and Leera before following along, paying close attention to his great-grandfather now. The Leyan's steps were hesitant, as if he had not walked in snow for a long time, and his back hunched as if carrying a heavy load.

Bridget came alongside Thomas. "Sir, can you tell us what happened to the Leyans? Why are they so stubbornly against helping mortals?"

"Much has changed from the Ley of old, the Ley you know from stories and legends." He kept pace while watching the trees, like a man hunted.

He even talks and moves differently, Augum thought, watching his great-grandfather raise his sandaled feet above the snow.

"There are three theories on what is happening," Thomas continued. "The first and the simplest is that Song of the Wastes, a defensive measure implemented after the creation of the scions, has slowly corrupted Ley and Leyans alike over time. The effect of this would be almost imperceptible, occurring over the course of fifteen hundred years or so, as subtly as the influence of water on stone. The second theory is that some Leyans have not relinquished the mortal realm and work to find and support the next Lord of Death, while maintaining to the others that Leyans should stay away from the world."

"Magua ..." Bridget whispered.

"Perhaps. The third theory has to do with the scions, as they are tied to the plane. The nature of those that wield them is thought to reflect back on Ley, changing the land in subtle—and not so subtle—ways. Unfortunately, those that typically possess the scions have great ambition yet little valor, their hearts dark and their souls needy, and so the Leyan landscape twists and corrupts in turn. Now imagine a man of great darkness possessing more than one."

Augum caught up to Thomas on the other side. "So some Leyans are aware of the change then?"

"Yes. The problem is the elders. They have the power but, as you have seen, are quite resistant to change. There was a time when Leyans used the Karma on many a man and woman, changing their lives for the better, using our vast knowledge to help mortals, sharing it with the worthy and deserving. You are not aware of what you are missing. Your ancestors were far better off when we shared our knowledge with them. They were wiser, more informed, and even more powerful.

"The irony is the current Lord of Death promises everyone eternal life, yet back then, because of the knowledge we shared, people *did* live longer. Since the vow, however, our knowledge has been wasted, much of it jealously guarded by the oldest amongst us. Our numbers dwindle and we are but legend to the world." He sighed. "I shudder to think of the future."

"And what about Oba, why did he step forward to support Magua?"

"He must keep up appearances. He will do his penance then return to the Leyan community. He believes as I do—that a time will come when the fate of many, including Leyans, will rest in the hands of a few. Let us stop speaking now, it is quite wearying."

Augum, worried about his great-grandfather, fell in behind him. He was hungry, cold, and tired from lack of sleep. The others mutely trampled along, each wrapped tightly for warmth.

They walked like this until the moon had travelled a good ways across the sky, the forest thickening around them, the cold deepening. Then, in the dead of night, Augum smelled burning cedar. Even just the thought of a fire warmed him. The others smelled it too, for their noses were sniffing this way and that, eagerly searching out the source of that delicious scent.

Thomas stopped, gesturing to huddle close. "You are all wanted by the Legion, so we must take precautions. Let us speak to each other as family. I will play the father, you my children. We are walking north to join my wife—your mother—but along the way, bandits had beset upon us.

Speak as little as possible. Let us walk loudly now so as not to appear unscrupulous."

Everyone nodded, teeth chattering. Soon they were plodding forward again. Augum tightened his hood further, dreaming of a warm bed and fire. Bridget and Leera walked together, heads buried in their hoods. Mya's cheeks and nose were red, jet hair stiff, breathing labored. Sydo was the worst though, visibly shaking even with the gray wool blanket wrapped tightly about his shoulders. His red hair was frosty and askew.

A dog started barking up ahead. The group froze in their tracks.

"What the matter boy?" called a grizzled voice from the darkness in a thick commoner drawl. "Who be out there, huh? You there—declare you self!"

"Just a weary father and his children!" Thomas called back. "We seek shelter and the warmth of a fire."

"You not be no robbing scoundrel then? I have a bow and I'm a mean to feather you—"

"No need, we seek shelter and fire. My children and I are cold. We were robbed and have lost our way."

Augum thought his great-grandfather did a passable job of sounding common.

"Aye, all right then—come forth already."

As they approached, Augum was able to see a short man with a bushy beard and a tremendous nose, dressed in thick brown furs, a wolf cap, tall turned-down hide boots, and a longbow, which he slung over his back once he had a good look at them. A great shaggy mastiff with black and brown fur strained on a leather leash, barking mightily. The pair stood before a log cabin with a pitched roof, just visible in the starlight, smoke huffing from its stone chimney. The cabin sat above the snowline on a platform of wooden planks, its windows shuttered. Iron traps, rope, and skins hung on pegs above barrels. A shed and a small stable stood nearby.

"What in dog's breath you doing out in the middle o' the night in this here weather?" the man asked, blowing great gusts of steam while watching them with close-set brown eyes. "Miracle ye aren't frozen stiff already, the whole bunch o' you." He shook his head, gesturing for them to follow with one hand while dragging the barking mastiff along with the other. He led them to a door made of thick cedar logs, carefully fitted to keep out the cold. As soon as he turned the crude handle, Augum felt a draft of thick hot air. The group eagerly piled inside.

"All right there, Catcher, that a boy … let him sniff your hands, that's it now … you're such a good boy, aren't you?"

They let the dog rub up against them, tail wagging, shoving them about with his great body while they desperately warmed themselves by the hearth. Mya shivered and sneezed. Sydo shook so violently Mya had to brace him. Bridget and Leera's teeth chattered as they rubbed their hands over the flames. Thomas gave a harsh cough that bent him over double. When his fit subsided, Augum noticed wrinkles on the face where there were none before, and there was even a tuft of silver hair protruding from his naked scalp.

"Father, you're looking weary."

Thomas did not respond, keeping his attention on the flames, shivering hands extended like the rest of them.

"So where ye be from? Not from near abouts, I have to say." The man fetched a large battered kettle. "Your smell be mighty peculiar too."

Thomas drew the blanket tighter around himself, preventing a glimpse of his naked chest. "We're travelling north to find my wife, their mother."

"Oh? And you wouldn't be fugitives now from that there Legion? I don't be needing no trouble." After giving a stern eye, he broke out in a grin and waved dismissively. "Bah—but then I don't rightly reckon I care too much. Everybody who running nowadays be running from them brutes. Get one plowing through here every now and then."

"No, as I say, we're only travelling north in search of their mother."

The man grunted. "As you say then."

While Augum's hands warmed up, he peered around the single-roomed cabin. The log walls were crowded with mounted animal heads, skins, snowshoes, hunting bows, and traps. Shadows swayed in rhythm with the crackling fire. The floor was made of dirty wooden planks, partially covered by a black bearskin rug. Near the hearth sat a great pile of cut wood, a saw, and an axe. A copper washbasin and pitcher stood on a washstand nearby. There was a rustic trestle harvest table surrounded by several crude stools, and a ladder going up to a cramped attic sleeping loft.

The man opened the door briefly and filled the kettle with snow. He then pushed past them and set it on the fire, stirring the logs with an iron. The stench of him was foul—it was all Augum could do not to hold his nose, yet he didn't want to offend the man lest they find themselves back out in the freezing cold. Sydo had a harder time of it, scrunching his face in disgust.

"What's the doggone matter with your brother? He sick or somethin'?"

"Been feeling under the weather of late—" Leera replied in an excellent country twang.

"Aye, the weasel not be looking too good there, lass. Best take good care o' him."

Sydo looked mutinous and was readying to deliver a stinging rebuke when Leera dug her elbow into his ribs, sending him into a coughing fit instead. The dog started barking along, making the grizzled man wheeze with laughter.

"You be needing more o' them blankets?" he asked between snorts.

"That would be fine," Mya replied, catching herself curtsying.

The trapper fetched a pile of yellow wool blankets and handed them out. They had holes and the stench of them was awful, but staying warm outweighed any such inconveniences.

"So what news from out yonder?"

Thomas scrunched his brow but did not reply.

"The Legion is burning them villages—" Augum said, taking a shot at the vernacular. He didn't need a look from Leera to know it was terrible.

One of the trapper's thick brows rose. "Aye, I do declare I be hearing the same from Tornvale. That there Legion took all them men, leaving only women, wee children, and old and sick."

"Tornvale? Is that some there village near?" Bridget asked, reddening. Leera had to turn away and place a hand on her mouth to prevent from cracking up—Bridget's spurious drawl was even worse than Augum's.

The man eyed her as if about to laugh. "About a days' walk east. I run and sell me furs there." He clapped his great belly. "They be callin' me Frankie the Trapper."

"I be understanding," Bridget said with a forced chuckle.

Augum instantly knew it was too much. The trapper boomed a laugh. He clapped Thomas on the back with a meaty hand. "Say there, feller, you got yourself some bastards here—" and laughed even harder.

Bridget reddened while Leera had to place both hands over her mouth to stop from laughing along. Even Augum had to pretend to wipe his mouth because otherwise he would have broken up.

"Don't you be worrying now, I hear ye stranger—got me a few o' them bastards tucked away with me country wives,

I do!" His shoulders heaved up and down as great fits of wheezing chuckles escaped like the steam from his giant kettle, which he unhooked and carried over to the trestle table as his snickering subsided.

"M'lord, do you by chance have something to drink?" Mya asked, eyeing two copper tankards on the table.

" 'M'lord'? Why look, now I be a lord! By gods, if you be country folk then I be the Lord o' the Legion, har!" and he went off in another fit, this time joined by howls from the mastiff. The combo was too much for Leera, who simply cracked, falling to the floor heaving with unrestrained laughter. Of course, that was all it took for Augum to lose his composure too. Soon, everyone was in hysterics, even Thomas and Sydo, both laughing as if unfamiliar with such a thing.

"Aye, you not be needing that there twang round me," the trapper gurgled, wiping his face with his sleeve. "Now, lass, to answer your question, all I have is this here ale, but I give you full use of me fire to boil your own water." He snagged the tankards and tipped them up to an oaken cask. "Don't you all be worrying, I also be fixing this here stew." He grabbed the kettle and poured the steaming water into a bucket, stirring it with an iron rod. Satisfied the contents were mixed, he ladled a generous portion into a grimy wooden bowl, before passing it to Mya, who immediately passed it on to Sydo.

Augum studied his great-grandfather, worried about what was happening to the man. The laughter made him sit more at ease, though his forehead had developed wrinkles, along with the corners of the eyes. His chin had grown jowls and his neck sagged. Bridget had noticed it too, and though her face showed alarm, she said nothing.

"What about you, m'lord, have you heard any news of late?" Mya asked, carefully accepting a tankard of ale and taking a sip. She winced and promptly passed it on.

The trapper's face darkened as he pulled up a stool. "Aye, I be hearing things," he said quietly, bringing the tankard to his lips. "I know that there Legion be building a grand ol' army, taking all the men and even some of the wee boys from the villages. They be getting ready for something—word is war. Folks be saying they be dabbling in magic and the like too—demons and spawns o' hell and other unspeakable sort. And they be searching far and wide for some magical artifacts and the like, making this and that promise."

He finished off his ale with one long swig, eyeing them with squinting eyes. He tipped the empty tankard to the cask and refilled it before continuing. "Aye, but you know the common folk be believing everything the Legion be saying, joining up to their causes and the like, eager for war. I can't rightly blame them. Food's tough to come by nowadays, what with the markets closed or burnt to a cinder and all. That there Legion be providing barley and shelter and protection. Word is, if you don't show proper enthusiasm though, they be turning you into a walking corpse, which is just your usual commoner rubbish, if you be asking me."

The trio's eyes met briefly.

"So have you seen the Legion much around here?" Augum asked, barely holding Catcher back, who was trying to get at Bridget's stew.

"Aye, them Black Guard be patrolling here and there, though I be lucky they haven't seen me, or they'd be dragging me out to fight them wars. If there be one thing me pops taught me, it was to hide when I need to hide, and I be hiding well." The trapper raised his tankard. "And you'd be wise to heed that there advice and stay off them roads."

"Would it be possible to stay here a day or two and warm by your fire?" Thomas asked in a voice that seemed to have deepened in the short time since he last spoke.

"You be welcome to stay as long as you can hunt and find your own food. I need me stocks to make it through this here winter, you understand. Tomorrow I be trapping, maybe going to town come dusk—haven't gone in a whiles, you see— but I can lend you a trap if you likes."

"Thank you, that is most kind," Thomas replied, suddenly overcome by a coughing fit.

Bridget pushed the wooden bowl at him. "Perhaps you should have some soup, Father."

Thomas only waved it off and lay himself down on the bearskin rug, near the fire. He wrapped the blanket tightly around himself. Bridget watched him, her face a mask of concern.

The trapper finished his ale. "It be late, I best turn in. You may clean off that there stew, just be sure to feed the fire before you sleep." He climbed the squeaky ladder, soon disappearing from sight. The attic creaked for a while as the big man settled in.

They finished the rich stew. Mya tried to get the prince to have some more but he coughed and only shook his head. They also helped themselves to some of the contents of the rucksack, finishing the jam, a bag of nuts, and a Leyan orange. Augum then stirred the hearth and lay himself down beside the gently crackling fire. He drew his hood and let his great-grandfather's raspy breathing shepherd him to his dreams.

THE SACRIFICE

Augum woke up with a start to Catcher licking his face. He fought off the mastiff and pushed himself up, forehead prickled with sweat. He had dreamed of being chased by some grotesquely thin creature that had mauled everyone but him. He was relieved to find them curled near the hearth.

Catcher whined a little and then settled beside Leera, who sneezed, rolled over, and fell back asleep.

The fire blazed away, recently tended to. The others were still snoozing, all but Bridget, who watched him from within her hood, cinnamon hair splayed out on the bear rug.

"How'd you sleep?" he whispered, stretching. He was grateful for the bearskin, much better than sleeping on bare planks, something he'd had to do a lot back at the Penderson farm.

"Barely did," she said, eyes ringed with dark circles. "Couldn't stop thinking about your great-grandfather. Look at him."

He glanced over and felt a jolt. Thomas' wrinkled head was matted with wisps of gray hair that definitely weren't there before. His neck was heavily lined, the skin saggy and pockmarked, and his breathing was labored, as if his lungs struggled for air.

"He knew this was going to happen," Bridget murmured, eyes glassy. "I don't know how long he'll last ..."

He stared at the frail body of his great-grandfather. Judging by the speed at which he aged, he guessed he might last another day or two. This wasn't how it was supposed to happen at all—they were supposed to be with Nana, training in Ley, Thomas helping. The boards creaked above as the trapper smacked his lips and stretched noisily. Bridget glanced up before gently covering Thomas' head with the blanket, so the trapper would not see what was going on.

Sydo moaned before being seized by a vicious coughing fit.

Bridget felt his forehead. "He's unwell, and I think Mya is coming down with something too. We'll need to keep them warm and give them plenty of soup. What do we have left in the old pantry?"

Augum dragged the rucksack over. Some Leyan potatoes, a couple Leyan pears, and a black apple. "Not much."

"How are we going to find food?"

"I'll have to hunt," he said with a shrug, trying to boost her morale by making it seem like it was no big deal. In reality, he always had trouble hunting in the winter.

Bridget reached out. "I'll make us some soup. Mind melting snow?"

He grabbed a small cauldron, opened the door a bit, and scooped some snow, which had accumulated up to his waist overnight. He set the cauldron over the fire while the trapper waddled his way down the ladder, wheezing.

"Ah, up with the roosters, are ye?" he boomed. Sydo groaned, Mya stirred, while Leera bolted upright, looking about wildly. "Ugh, slept horribly," she said. "Mutt kept licking my face."

The trapper chuckled. "Aye, he likes a lass' face like any other." He poured himself a tankard of ale.

When the trapper turned his back on them and scratched himself, Bridget mouthed to Leera, "Maybe it was him."

A disgusted look came over Leera as she glanced at the trapper, who happened to burp after finishing his ale in one swig.

Bridget snickered while trying to duck away from the pinecone Leera was threatening to throw at her.

"Sir, where exactly are we?" Augum asked.

"Well, like I be saying last night, you be a days' walk west of Tornvale, and about a four day walk north of Wellsguard Keep and the Central Spires."

Augum had heard of the Spires—a treacherous set of sharp peaks that served as the boundary between Canterra and Solia, often patrolled by brigands.

"Now if you be heading north like you be saying, you'd be wise to hike the Summerwine. It's just west o' here and would take you to Candledale in four day and some, though you'd have to walk through Blackwood. And you best be on your guard in the 'wood—doggone haunted, if you ask me, not even Catcher like it in there. So as I says, if you continue yonder up the Summerwine, it'd take you as far up as Blackhaven."

"So we're in southern Solia," Augum muttered. It was a long way from the northern peaks … and a long way from Mrs. Stone.

"What's that, boy?"

"Oh, just wondering if the Summerwine was a road."

The trapper wheezed with laughter. "My bedeviled boots, son—it's a flea-bitten river! You really ain't from these here parts now, are ye?" Catcher hopped up on his hind legs and pawed at the trapper, nearly knocking over his ale. "Whoa there, you be wanting your meat, eh, boy? Eh? Soon, boy, soon." He rubbed up its fur with his hammy hands, before turning back to the group.

"I be sitting in me cot last night thinking of me pops, who once says to me, 'You done share as much as you can, boy, just be sure you save your hide first.' So I reckon I'd let you know I put down the horse a whiles back. Now it might not be your usual fancy fare, but I have a whole heap of meat left over sitting in the barrel outside. It's rightly frozen through and through by now, so you be needing the axe to free it. And don't you worry about it going sour or nothing, I salted the old girl down before stuffing her in there." He boomed a laugh and took another swig.

"Thank you," Bridget mumbled, a horrified look on her face.

Augum, however, knew they might just have to get at that barrel if the hunting goes poorly. He added the potatoes into the boiling water. "Sir, could I borrow one of your bows and some arrows?"

"Fixing to take yourself a rabbit, eh, boy? Rightly so—be the man of the house, as me pop always says. Aye, you may use the ashwood there." He pointed to a small bow hanging by a boar head. "And the quiver and shafts and the like are here." He pointed at a wrapped bundle. "Can you feather arrows, boy?"

"I can, sir." Sir Westwood had taught him how to make arrows even before letting him shoot a bow.

"Good, 'cause you ain't allowed to take me arrows, I be needing them for the long haul, you understand. But you needn't be worrying, 'cause I traded me a white bearskin for a whole heap of arrowheads to them Nodians a whiles back.

And in that there sack you'll find sinew and turkey feathers. Now they ain't free, mind you, I'll make you a deal for the use of them. For every one you make yourself, you have to make one for me."

Augum took the wrapped bundle. "That sounds fair. You wouldn't happen to have an extra fur coat, would you, sir?"

The trapper wheezed a laugh. "Oh, aye, 'cause me bastards love to visit their crooked pop and don me coat in the mean—course I don't have no extra coat! At least none I be willing to part with. I traded all me furs in town for food and the like."

"Ah. Thanks anyway."

The trapper downed his ale and watched Augum for a moment. "Oh, all right then, bunch of sorry lumps you are … here!" and he reached up behind him and dragged down six ragged wolf pelts. "Useless to me anyway, full of them holes and such. You all would have to sew it yourself, mind you."

"I can do that!" Leera said, snagging the pelts from Augum.

"Me too," threw in Bridget, taking three pelts from Leera.

Leera's brow rose smartly. "We're going to make you the best hunting outfit ever, Aug."

"I can help too," he said.

Leera gave him a wry look. "Absolutely not. Since neither of us can hunt, that'll be your job. Besides, you've got arrows to make."

"Yeah, let us do our part, *brother*," Bridget said with a wink.

He couldn't help but smile as he turned to give the potatoes a stir. "What would I do without you two?"

Leera snorted. "Go mad—"

"Get captured—" Bridget said.

"Maybe even starve—" Leera added.

He waved them off with a grin, glad they were in good spirits as there was plenty to worry about.

"Your sisters be taking good care of you, boy, as they rightly should." The trapper donned his massive fur coat and bear cap. "I'm a going to do me rounds with the traps. Mind the old place for me while I'm gone, would ye? Come on there, Catcher, ready to sniff out some game? That's a good boy."

Frankie grabbed a large black bow, a quiver full of arrows, an axe, and herded the barking mastiff out the door, plowing through the snow like an ox.

After searching about, the girls found some needle and thread in a rusted tin and began sewing hunting garments for Augum. Bridget started a coat, Leera a pair of pants. Augum, meanwhile, started on the arrows, a meticulous process that required patience and dexterity. He even contemplated casting Centarro, but considering the side effects, thought better of it. When it came time to size the initial cuts for the garments, there was no end of teasing from the girls, but he took it all in stride, grateful for their efforts. Meanwhile, the watery soup was served alongside chamomile tea snagged from Mya's stash and boiled in the trapper's giant kettle.

When Augum laid eyes on Mya's pale face, he had to resist putting a cloth to it. She was too weak to sit up, feverish, and shivering. Sydo fared worse, unable to stop his teeth from chattering, eyes closed and puffy. The trio bundled them in what blankets they could scrounge and settled them near the fire, which was always kept at a bright burn.

When Thomas finally sat up, the trio stopped what they were doing. What was once the body of a muscled thirty-year-old now appeared to be that of a withered seventy-year-old. Augum offered him a bowl of soup. The Leyan took it with shaking hands.

"Mr. Stone, why are you doing this?" Bridget asked quietly, a pained look on her face. "Why don't you go back to Ley so you can get better?"

"You must all witness what becomes of us should we leave Ley."

Augum took the bowl from him and replaced it with a mug of tea. "I don't understand, you could have just told us that leaving Ley … does this kind of thing."

"I have lived a long time, Augum Stone—borrowed time. I am simply giving it back, in my own way. Telling you is not enough, you must believe it through and through. You must all *see* it with your own eyes."

"You mean to show us that Sparkstone's quest for Leyan eternal life is futile," Bridget said. "That he can't bring it back into this world, that he can't be immortal here!"

"Most astute, Bridget Burns. There are some causes greater than ourselves—" A coughing fit suddenly overtook him. Augum withdrew the tea and replaced it with a cloth. When Thomas put it to his mouth, it came away stained with blood. Bridget and Augum exchanged fearful looks. As the fit subsided, Augum gave his great-grandfather back his tea.

"My life is a tiny price to pay to pass on this knowledge, and mercy knows some sharing is long overdue. It only pains me I am able to give this gift but once."

They fell silent. Even Sydo and Mya, both bundled deep in blankets, ceased their troubled coughing.

"My poor feet," Thomas said, giving them a rub. "Perhaps it was unwise of me to have worn sandals. I take comfort these mortal sufferings are fleeting. This part of being mortal I did not miss."

"Please, Mr. Stone, place them near the fire," Bridget said. She helped the old man shift his position.

Thomas allowed her to help him. "I am aging quicker than I expected. I am sorry, but you will have to manage finding Anna on your own. I will be with you only a short time longer, perhaps a day or so. Please do not be sad, I have lived a long and full life. This is what I want. It is important to me that you all see with your own eyes that the only real things one can take from Ley are gifts bestowed by the Leyans, and knowledge is the most precious of them all."

The morning passed with the trio taking turns caring for Sydo, Mya and Thomas, the former two seeming to get worse by the hour, while the latter aged before their eyes. When they weren't taking care of someone, they were sewing, cooking, or fletching. Mya, being the only healer there, gave instructions when she could on how to best look after them, while Thomas said not to concern themselves with him, instead choosing to spend his time and energies lecturing on the intricacies of the Centarro spell. He also spoke about the Shield spell and the subtle nuances involved in casting it. It was knowledge accumulated from many years of living, condensed into short, powerful phrases in between coughing attacks. As before, Thomas was an excellent teacher. It pained Augum immeasurably knowing these would be his last lessons. He longed for more time together as there was still much to learn, questions to ask.

"… as for your 2nd degree elemental spell, I regret I will not be able to teach it to you as Anna would have wanted. Neither of us foresaw how closed-minded the elders had become."

Augum nodded somberly, wishing he knew some kind of arcanery that would extend his great-grandfather's life a little longer.

As the afternoon came and went, he prepared the last of their food for supper, realizing he would have to go hunting immediately after in order for them to eat something other than horseflesh. Sydo, Mya and Thomas slept while Bridget and Leera neared completion on his hunting outfit.

Meanwhile, he fletched the last of ten arrows, five of which would go to the trapper.

"Done," Bridget said, turning over the coat in her hands, inspecting the seams. "How about you, Lee?"

"Just one … more … there. Try them on," Leera said, throwing the pants to him, needle in her mouth. The girls giggled and looked away so he could pull the pants on under his robe and don the coat.

"The only thing is we didn't have enough hide for mitts," Bridget said when he finished.

"I'll manage. Um, thanks, *sisters.*"

"You're welcome," Bridget and Leera chorused, beaming proudly. He wished one of them could come along, but neither of them knew how to hunt and would only scare away the game. More critically, neither of them had cold-weather garments. That was another thing they'd have to figure out besides the food situation—clothing for the continued journey.

One thing at a time, he told himself.

He looked over to the three stricken people on the floor. His gaze lingered on Thomas the longest. Will he still be alive upon his return? The old Leyan was doing this for them and Augum would not let him die in vain. The thought made him recall the vow he took with Bridget and Leera back in castle Arinthian, their hands clasped over Mrs. Stone's blue book on arcaneology. The words came back as if spoken only moments ago, and something made him whisper them aloud. "I solemnly swear, on the ghosts of my mother, Sir Westwood, and on those that my father has slain, that I will learn the arcane tongue. Their deaths will not have been in vain." He glanced at his two friends, both of whom stood up.

They repeated it together one more time in a quiet whisper, before coming together in a tight embrace.

"I haven't forgotten it," Leera said.

Bridget smiled. "Nor I."

"I never will." Augum let go, attached Burden's Edge to his waist, and slung the bow and quiver of newly-fletched arrows over his shoulders. He felt thoroughly prepared.

"Oh, and we have something for you—" Bridget reached into the rucksack and withdrew their very last item of food—the black Leyan apple. "Catch."

Augum caught it. They were giving him the last of their food. In a year and a few months, he will be sixteen-years-old and a man in the eyes of the world, yet he needed to be one now. He needed to come through. He needed to find game.

Leera punched him on the shoulder. "Get us a big 'un," and with those words, he departed.

STICKS IN THE SNOW

Augum pushed through powdery waist-high snow, periodically stopping to listen. Other than the soft pitter-patter of fat snowflakes, there was the kind of stillness that could only come from a forest entombed in winter. Gray clouds hung low, the cold bitter, freezing his breath. The wolf coat provided excellent protection for all but his hands. He also had to keep his hood off in order to hear, even though his ears stung with frost.

He marched west, taking note of the trees as he passed, remembering the blinding power of the blizzard at Hangman's Rock. What he wanted to spot were deer tracks, but he'd settle for rabbit or even squirrel. Movement was slow and tedious and he found himself wishing there was an arcane way to hunt.

He soon heard the distant ripple of the Summerwine. He pushed on, stumbling across thin gouges in the snow. At first, he thought they were just marks from felled branches, until he spotted the sweeps between each hole, as if sticks had walked by.

He froze, listening to the murmur of the river, concluding that it had to be some kind of tall-legged bird. Upon closer inspection, there was a drag line on top of the snow, as if someone trailed string or a piece of cloth. Maybe it was a heron with a fish?

He followed the meandering tracks northward for a good hour before he heard the sound of clacking. He ducked, unslung his bow, and prowled forward.

The shape of a person moved beyond the branches ahead, wandering as if lost. Back in Willowbrook, he might have called out, but this was southern Solia, unfamiliar land. The longer he watched the way it moved, the more reservations he had. It seemed to sway back and forth, a shadow beyond the trees, like some sort of deranged person.

Suddenly it stopped clacking and froze.

Augum held his breath, hoping whatever it was had not seen him. Snowflakes gently fell, the Summerwine trickled, but all he heard was the thump of his own heart. He watched the shape so long that he began to wonder if he was losing his mind and there was nothing there.

All of a sudden it sprinted for him, crashing through the branches. And then he understood why the thin tracks—the thing was a skeletal corpse! The clacking was its jaws snapping together, and the trailings were pieces of rotten skin and threads of burial cloth.

He fumbled for Burden's Edge but the cadaver was too quick. It slammed into him, burying him in a plume of snow, and began to hammer his chest like a rabid blacksmith. He gasped as if drowning, unprepared for its speed and strength.

He used the last of his breath to shout, "SHYNEO!" and grabbed the squishy ribcage, but it was immune to his shocking touch. There was only one chance—Centarro, but in order to cast it he would need to get this thing off him. He tried to take a breath but only gulped snow. He tried to punch but it was like punching branches. The last thing he could think of was to buck it off, but its position directly over him, in this snow which hampered sidelong movement, gave him no leverage.

What vision remained began to quickly tunnel as the vibrations of each strike rattled his innards like a drum. There was a sickening crack in his ribcage.

This was it. He was going to die.

A final surge of desperation gripped him like fever. He flailed and screamed, as rabid as the thing itself, pushing it back just long enough to raise his head above the snow and grab a quick breath of air, before being pounded back into the suffocating winter ocean.

The black tunnel resumed its inward caving. And then Augum felt something he had not felt in a long while—the slowing of time. The space around him warped as if elastic, while he felt a familiar energy surge to every point of his body, seeking exit, like a wolf testing a fence for holes. Gasping his last breath, he recalled being carried away by a storm so long ago. Felt the sensation of tumbling amongst the clouds, far above the Tallows …

His hair stiffened and he tasted a peculiar tang on his tongue. Suddenly a monstrous bolt of lightning connected him to the sky, blasting through the living cadaver. For a brief instant, he was able to witness its bones vaporize before the walls of his vision collapsed.

* * *

Augum awoke shivering, covered in a layer of snow, a sharp pain in his chest. He sat up, blearily wiping his face. The snow had melted around him in the shape of a large basin. Pieces of bone and rot lay everywhere and there was the distinct smell of burnt flesh. A tunnel punctured the evergreen canopy directly above, as if a fireball had rammed its way through. He gaped at the singed pine needle edges as the memory of what transpired slowly returned.

Nana had warned him about using it, but that was the third time wild arcanery had saved his life.

The pain in his chest intensified as he opened his wolf-hide coat, revealing a bloody stain on his robe. Wincing, he closed it up and stood, the act jarring his ribs sharply. Something had to be broken.

He fixed his gaze on a large bone stuck in the snow. Where had this thing come from? Had his father raised it using necromancy? Or did it crawl out of the ground on its own, like in those nightmare stories they tell children to scare them into behaving.

Studying the sky revealed the sun was to the far west. He must have been out for a while. Lucky there weren't more of those things.

The Summerwine trickled distantly as snow continued to fall, the flakes tumbling lazily. He drew his hood and scavenged for his Leyan apple, taking cold bites with shivering hands. It reminded him that friends waited by a warm fire.

He needed to get back as soon as possible. The longer he stayed out here, the more dangerous it became. He reeked with the scent of blood, and who knew what else might come calling. He had failed his quest for food but at least he was alive, if injured.

"Horsemeat it is," he muttered, throwing the finished core aside. He adjusted Burden's Edge and picked up the bow and quiver, wincing from the sharp grating in his chest. The bow was intact but four arrows had broken in the melee, leaving him with only one. He slung the bow and quiver over his shoulder and began the laborious retreat back to the cabin. Every step sent a stab through his chest, forcing him to hobble at a worm's pace.

He was halfway back to the cabin when he came across a set of prints he *did* recognize—that of a mirko. Mirkos were smaller and slower than deer, but they liked meat, so they could be dangerous to hunt, especially when they were hungry. When it came to mirkos, many a man thought himself the hunter only to find himself the hunted—and it was usually too late by then. Sir Westwood warned him he should never shoot one without being ready to cut it down with his sword, in case he missed. They were notoriously mean-spirited creatures too, sometimes following a man for days, tormenting him, before finally taking him when he tired and fell asleep. Luckily, they were solitary hunters, not pack animals like wolves. Augum studied the tracks and concluded the mirko was likely still near enough to warrant an attempt. The pain in his chest protested, and the cold was only deepening. He knew he could get lost if the clouds remained this thick, or worse, run into a skeleton again, in which case he'd be done for—yet the others desperately needed food, especially Sydo and Mya. He had to try.

He unslung his bow and painstakingly placed his only arrow to the sinew string, hands so numb the task took a dangerously long time to accomplish. The light dwindled as he tracked the mirko on a northeasterly path.

There was a rustle to his left and he froze, bow held in front. Something was slowly slinking his way. Still your mind, he told himself. He focused on his breathing, waiting for the right moment, as a dark shape prowled nearer in his peripheral vision. The bow shook along with his shivering body. He slowly drew the string back as far as it would go, wincing from the grinding pain in his chest. For a moment, he contemplated trying to cast Centarro, but should the spell fail …

There was a sharp snuffling and a scraping sprint. Augum whipped around, spotting dark brown fur and a grizzled snout. He grit his teeth and let his only arrow fly. It speared the mirko through its front quarter. The animal yelped and stumbled, giving him just enough time to draw Burden's Edge. He sliced off its head in one clean swoop.

Sir Westwood would be proud, he thought, watching as the mirko head stained the snow with blood. There was no time to celebrate the kill, however, as the light was fading fast. He buried the head in snow, wiped his blade, slung the carcass over his shoulders, and retraced his steps.

Luckily, the forest allowed him to stumble back to the cabin unscathed.

Bridget opened the door as he dropped the carcass to the planks. "Thank all that is good! It's dark out and we were so worried—"

The excitement of everything that had happened suddenly wore off, leaving only exhaustion and a grating sharp pain that sent him down to one knee.

"You're injured!" Leera said, rushing to his side.

He was so tired he just collapsed into her arms. All the fight had gone out of him.

"Got a … big 'un …" he managed to mumble, coughing and wincing. "Need to … get inside … smell of blood …"

"But what happened—"

"I'll tell you … inside …" He glanced back at the dark forest one last time, half expecting to hear a clacking sound.

Leera and Bridget dragged him in, followed by the mirko carcass. Leera immediately set to removing his coat, gasping when she saw the giant bloodstain on his robe. He only grimaced, head lolling against her shoulder. He felt woozy and tired. All he wanted to do was curl up by the fire and sleep.

The girls removed his coat and his robe, leaving him in his undergarments. But he was too exhausted and in too much pain to be embarrassed.

Mya, forehead glistening, placed a hand to his chest and felt around, a serious look on her face.

"Ow!" he said as she prodded a sharp bone. As painful as it was, he trembled under her soft touch.

"His ribs are broken. They will heal on their own over a half a month's time, unless we find an arcane healer first. He has been exposed to the cold too long. Make sure he gets plenty of water, rest, and warmth."

"We will," Leera said. She washed his bloody hands while Bridget bandaged him up with clean cloth and wrapped him in a blanket.

"Now don't you dare try to get up and help," Bridget said, tucking him in near the fire. "The mirko is in good hands. You did your part, now let us do ours."

He tried to smile, hiding a wince.

Leera attended to the carcass, draining its blood, skinning it ("The hide will be perfect to barter with!"), and then butchering it ("Ugh—disgusting …"), before placing some cuts of meat on the fire. Bridget, meanwhile, made a pot of herbal tea and attended to the stricken foursome.

Neither Thomas nor the prince had woken upon Augum's return. When Augum glanced at his great-grandfather, his heart dropped. The man looked every bit over a hundred years, skin pale and shriveled as if it had been under water for days.

"We chatted with your great-grandfather a bit, m'lord," Mya whispered, suppressing a cough while raising her head.

Augum didn't bother asking her to stop calling him that.

"He spoke of you and Mrs. Stone, of his daughter, and even of your father."

"My father?"

Mya glanced to Bridget and Leera, who had suddenly gone quiet. "He said … that he missed everyone, and he … he asked us to make supper for the family as he was sure they were all returning for the new year's feast."

He covered his shaking hands so they weren't visible. "Anything else?"

"He rambled a bit and … he said … he said he was sorry he could not help us more. Then he asked to be buried in the old way—in fire. He also asked … he asked for us to remember that he was Leyan, and to remember that he died a mortal death."

He nodded slowly as Mya's head returned to the pillow. For a time nobody spoke. Leera attended to the hearth and the mirko meat as Bridget cared for Mya and Sydo, putting damp cloths to their foreheads.

Augum's teeth eventually stopped chattering enough for him to whisper about the encounter with the skeleton and how he slew it with some sort of desperate lightning bolt.

" 'Sticks in the snow,' " Thomas mumbled.

Augum sat up a little. "What's that, Great-grandfather?"

Thomas' voice was barely audible. " 'Sticks in the sand … sticks in the snow … reveal a man … dead long ago …' "

"I remember," Mya said, eyes unfocused. "My mother once told it to me. She said it's a rhyme that goes back to Occulus' era."

"Augum, I worry about this wild arcanery business," Bridget said, handing him a cup of tea.

"It's saved my life three times now."

"He didn't have a choice, Bridge," Leera said.

"I know, I just … I don't want him to use it if he doesn't have to."

"I won't," he said.

They debated on where the walker came from, what the trapper might do once he returned to find one of them injured and others ill, and wondered why he hadn't returned yet.

Leera fed some logs into the fire from the stack then hung the mirko hide outside. Meanwhile, Bridget brought another pot of water to boil and made licorice root, elderflower and mint tea. She then gently woke Sydo up and offered it to him. He was so weak he needed her help to drink. She whispered soothing words, but he only scowled.

Bridget plopped down between Augum and Leera, trying to unknot her hair. "I think we've been spoiled by that Leyan bath. Not looking too pretty anymore, are we, Lee?"

Leera flipped over a sizzling cut of mirko and ran a finger through her already greasy and matted hair. "Well, at least we didn't get the other royal Leyan treatment." She tapped her temple.

Augum chuckled and grimaced. "Don't … make … me laugh."As soon as the meat was ready, Leera portioned it out, a big juicy slice for everyone, largest for Augum. Bridget helped Sydo take small bites while Leera cut up Mya's steak with Blackbite.

Augum shook his great-grandfather until he roused, helped him grip a bowl of meat.

Perhaps it was the fact Augum had hunted it himself, or perhaps because he was very hungry, but when he bit into that fire-roasted mirko meat, he thought it the most delicious thing he had ever eaten. Even Thomas cracked an ancient but weary smile as he slowly ate.

Leera broke out in a wide grin. "I think Mr. Stone just tasted food for the first time since becoming Leyan."

Thomas gave her a blank look. Leera made a show of smiling and pointing at the food, and Mr. Stone nodded and gave a toothy smile, head trembling uncontrollably, reminding Augum of that twisted Leyan elder, Magua.

They quietly savored every morsel. When they finished, everyone relaxed by the fire. Thomas snoozed for a time before suddenly moaning, eyes fluttering open.

"Mr. Stone—would—you—like—some—tea?" Bridget asked loudly. "Oh, he's going deaf," she added upon spotting the expression on Augum's face.

Thomas Stone, looking every bit one hundred years old, feebly rose, throwing off his blanket. He peered right at

Augum, eyes now milk white, and reached out a withered hand.

"I'm here, Great-grandfather, I'm right here," Augum said, realizing the poor man was going blind too. He grasped his hand and gave it a pat. It was cold and coarse to the touch.

"Great-grandson …" Thomas began in a hoarse whisper, pausing between words to take wheezing breaths. "The last Lord of Death … had three kinds of undead servants … the first …" he raised a withered finger, "is the common kind … men called them … *walkers* … old dead returned … fast … vicious … could be … destroyed by fire … Dreadnought steel … and strong arcanery." He paused to take a few labored breaths. "The second kind … are *wraiths* … they are the dead recently raised … can be a bit like … they once were … but not human … sometimes they are grotesquely distorted … and can be as large as … a giant. And the third are … *revenants* … these you must fear … for they have been raised … using the most powerful … and ancient … arcanery."

Augum nodded, swallowing hard, amazed this man was still trying to teach them something. He thought of his ancestor, Atrius Arinthian, and wondered which of the three undead servants he had become.

Thomas suddenly took hold of Augum's shoulder and pulled him close. "One day … you will face … your father … do not … despair … train hard … it will be a mirror … of your fears … it has been this way … for eons … the blood of kin … can …" but he began choking.

"Great-grandfather! Leera, Bridge—something's wrong!"

The veins on Thomas's face bulged. "Tell … Anna … I … love … her …" and with that, his eyes closed and he slumped into Augum's arms.

"Great-grandfather?" He shook him, appalled by the fact his weight was down to that of a child's. "Great-grandfather!" but it was no use. He was gone.

Mya's head fell into her hands, her shoulders heaving. Bridget and Leera quietly wrapped their arms around Augum and his great-grandfather. The prince only watched through a fevered haze.

It was a long time before the girls let go, squeezing Augum's shoulder, leaving him alone.

"I promise I'll tell her, Great-grandpa," Augum whispered, still cradling him, "I promise I'll tell her …"

* * *

The funeral pyre burned bright against the canopy of pines, setting them aglow in a flickering light. For a time the night was pushed away. Mya and Sydo had stayed inside, too sick to do anything, while Augum, Bridget and Leera cleared a spot for the fire and gathered branches and logs from the trapper's shed, eventually building a small platform for Thomas to rest on.

The girls wanted Augum to stay inside but he absolutely insisted on helping, gritting his teeth and fighting through the grating pain. The pile complete, they had carried Thomas out and tenderly placed him on it, folding his hands across his chest. They stood in silence for as long as they dared in the frigid night, before Augum retrieved a flaming stick from inside the cabin. The trio held it together, lighting the platform's corners.

Augum watched the flames dance higher and higher. He did not care at all if the fire attracted anyone, he was too preoccupied wondering why his great-grandfather hadn't remained in Ley and just told them what would happen to him should he leave. The more he thought about it, the more it just didn't make sense. He needlessly threw his life away.

They bore the cold and stood watching until the fire devolved into glowing embers. Then they snuffed it out with snow, scattering the ashes amongst the trees. Augum couldn't think of anywhere more appropriate than a forest for his great-grandfather to rest in, other than Ley.

"Goodbye, Great-grandpa," he whispered, gently pouring the last of his ashes around the trunk of a large pine.

The task complete, they padded back indoors, sitting in silence for a long time. Augum watched the flames, trying to come to grips with feeling abandoned, first by his mother and father, then by his great-grandmother, and now by his great-grandfather. Must be a family tradition. But they left for good reasons, didn't they? Not his father …

He glanced to the empty spot on the bearskin rug Thomas once occupied. This time, there would be no memorial ceremony. He ran his hand across it before laying down in it, feeling the warmth of the fire.

Sleep came quickly that night.

A DANGEROUS TREK

Augum woke to Bridget shaking him awake. "The prince is worse—" she said in a panicked voice. "He won't wake up and his forehead is boiling."

He sat up and peered at Sydo, who lay on his side in a nest of blankets. Mya held a damp cloth to his forehead with one hand, fidgeting with her servant gown with the other. Leera, meanwhile, was trying to start the fire again. They had forgotten to set a fire watch, and the trapper hadn't returned yet. It was cold in the cabin, fogging their breath. Augum plucked stray fibers from the blankets, the bear rug, and his robe. After gathering a handful, he handed them to Leera. "Try this." Sir Westwood had taught him that trick.

"Thanks." Leera gathered it into a pile and began striking flint against a small steel rod.

Augum's eyes searched for Thomas' frame before realizing he would never see his great-grandfather again. The hollow pang in his stomach returned.

Mya brushed Sydo's damp hair away from his forehead. "We need the services of an arcane healer or he will not survive."

For a moment, everyone stopped what they were doing and glanced to the prince and Mya.

"It's a days' walk east to Tornvale," Augum said. "Maybe I can find a healer there."

"Forgive me, m'lo—err, Augum—but healers are very rare," Mya said. "You will not find one in a hamlet or a village—only in a city."

"Not to mention they're expensive," Leera said, intensifying her efforts with the flint. "We could wait for the trapper. He could take Sydo to Tornvale on a sled or something."

Mya glanced down at the wheezing prince. "Pardon, m'lady, but what if the trapper refuses to take him, or does not return for another day? We cannot wait."

"Ugh, I hate that m'lady stuff. You're not my servant."

"My apologies, Leera, it is force of habit."

"I'll go," Augum said.

Concern passed over Bridget's face. "But your ribs—"

He shrugged, forcing himself not to wince.

Leera blew at a spark. "Then I'm coming with you."

"No way," Bridget said. "You'd freeze without a winter garment."

Leera added some twigs to the smoking pile. "Not if I wrap myself in blankets, and not if we make mitts and boots out of more wolf hide."

"We can't just take more hide, the trapper will throw us out—"

"Look, mirko is harder to come by than wolf. We can scrape and clean it, then leave it for him in trade."

"I don't know," Augum said, fearing for Leera but also wanting company.

"Look, it's simple—if you're going, I am too." She blew at the tinder and a tiny flame emerged. "Bridget can stay here with Mya and look after the prince. Mya seems to be getting better anyway, her fever broke this morning."

"It's true," Mya said. "We have the mirko meat, we now have fire again, and we can make water and tea from snow. We'll be fine. And I agree, Augum should have someone with him this time, and I'm still too weak. But we *do* need to make the mitts and boots first."

Bridget looked at them all before reluctantly nodding. "Then we have to start right away if you're to make it to Tornvale by nightfall."

They worked in quiet harmony, roasting mirko then making two pairs of boots and two pairs of mitts from three ragged wolf pelts. The prince, meanwhile, seemed to be getting worse. His coughing came from deep within his chest, his breathing was ragged, and he mumbled deliriously.

They finished in the afternoon. Augum threw on the wolf hide coat and pants, grabbed some roasted mirko meat wrapped in linen, and pulled on the newly made mitts and boots, right over his own leather turnshoes.

"Couldn't buy a better pair if you tried," he said.

"Forgive me but you need to make haste," Mya said, blotting the prince's forehead.

Leera glanced out a snow-encrusted window. "We're already behind. It'll be well past dark by the time we reach Tornvale."

If we even find it, he thought. Travelling during the day was one thing, travelling by night quite another altogether. And in unfamiliar land no less.

Leera pulled on the boots, mitts, gathered a blanket, and punched Augum on the shoulder. "Come on."

"Wait—" Bridget said. "Here, take Blackbite."

Augum waved it off. "We have Burden's Edge."

Leera finished filling a skin of water from the kettle. "If the trapper returns—"

"—we'll tell him you've gone to Tornvale for help," Bridget said.

Augum peered at Mya and Bridget, both of whom stood to give them a farewell hug. When Mya wrapped her long arms around him, he felt a shiver. Things were different now though. There was a sense of urgency. Their *lives* were on the line here. It was more than just a friendly hug—it was an embrace with hopes of survival attached.

She fixed him with those almond eyes. "Be careful and good luck." Then she traded with Bridget to hug Leera.

Bridget gave him a strong squeeze. He grimaced but bore the pain. "Come back to us," she whispered, sweeping long cinnamon hair from her face.

"We will, and I'll try to bring more food. We should be back by nightfall tomorrow."

Bridget glanced back at Sydo. "Just hope he makes it …"

Leera drew her hood and wrapped the blanket around herself like a giant shawl. She grinned. "All right, stop stalling," and the pair exited, waving their last goodbyes as they descended the creaking steps.

Augum's heart grew heavy upon seeing the charred area where they had cremated his great-grandfather. They strode by without a word, the snow crisp underfoot. It was a gray, windy day, the cold bitter and unrelenting. It was difficult keeping direction, though he generally had a good idea of which way was east. It was mostly a matter of paying attention to the trees, as there were signs that helped determine from where the sun usually shone, such as the particular bend of certain bushes, or the abundance of moss on one side of a trunk. He perpetually scanned the surface of the snow, his heart racing with every pockmark or depression. Sticks in the sand, sticks in the snow, reveal a man, dead long ago …

Leera kept right behind him. "We have to push on till we get to the village. Let's not stop too much else we'll freeze out here. This cold is brutal."

"Is the blanket enough?"

"I'm managing ..."

All she wore were wool apprentice robe, linen undergarments, mitts, boots, and a single blanket. He knew that was dangerously inadequate and made a note to watch her. "We'll trade later."

"I'll be fine."

Their pace soon slowed. As the day wore on, the terrain became hilly and the trees shorter and sparser, broken by occasional snowy fields. The pair hardly talked at all, conserving their energies, stopping only once to eat some salted mirko steak. The wind picked up as nightfall approached, throwing snowdrift in their faces. Both their teeth were chattering now, and Augum was no longer able to feel his toes or his face, despite having drawn his hood tight around his head. His chest grated with each step, a ceaseless annoyance he just couldn't get used to. Leera insisted all the while she was fine and refused to trade the blanket for his coat and pants.

It was well past dusk, the sky opaque, when he began to worry. They had yet to stumble across a hunting or merchant trail.

Leera, breathing heavily, stumbled. "Can we stop for a bit?"

They hunkered down by a white birch, barely shielded from the frequent gusts.

He glanced at her. Her skin was pale and her teeth were chattering. "That's it, we're trading."

"No, I'm fine—"

"No, you're not! We're trading and I don't want to hear anymore about it. Now get up."

She groaned but didn't stand. "Can't ... Too cold."

He drew her hood tight around her head for her then removed his wolf coat as fast as he could. He began to stuff it on her when she stopped him.

"No! Not over the blanket—you're taking *that*, at least."

"Fine." He took the blanket from her and finished helping her put on the coat. Then he removed his hide pants and made her step into them, the whole process shooting spasms through his chest and draining his energy. His legs began shaking almost immediately. How in Sithesia had she lasted this long? Why hadn't he been more attentive to her needs? He wrapped the blanket around himself and hunkered down beside her, his own teeth chattering.

"Aug?" she said as he dug for the mirko meat with numb hands.

"Yes?"

She smiled. "Thanks …"

"You're welcome, Miss Stubborn."

Her cheeks colored a little. She glanced at the cloudy skies. "Sun's going down. Have to be careful."

He didn't reply, choosing to save his energy. He ripped a large chunk of mirko meat off and handed it to her.

"Let's keep going," he managed to stammer. Stopping had cooled them down and it was too dangerous to linger in the fading light.

They resumed their eastward plowing, forced to lean into an increasingly bitter wind.

Leera pointed at a spot to their right. "Stop! Tracks …"

Augum's hand reflexively went to Burden's Edge. Upon closer inspection, they turned out to be sled, dog, and human tracks, and from the looks of them, there must have been three or more people.

People were better than sticks—as long as they weren't the Legion, that is.

They followed the tracks eastward, something that became difficult as night descended and the wind gained in strength. And with no stars or moon, it soon became pitch-dark.

Augum stopped, realizing he'd gone off course. "Where're the tracks? Shyneo," but the light of his palm did not penetrate the hide of his mitt.

The wind gusted violently, drowning out Leera's reply.

"What—!"

"Over here!" She was somewhere behind him. Eventually the two found each other using their voices, though it was disturbingly obvious that there was next to zero chance of them going on without a light source. And should they get separated …

"We have to take turns casting Shine." Leera's trembling was now so bad he barely understood her.

He removed his right mitt. "Shyneo," but his hand would not light. He focused, realizing he was stuttering from the cold. "Shyneo. Shyneo!" with the last attempt, his palm finally lit up in an electric-blue glow, though his hand started hurting from the cold almost immediately. Great. His chest was already giving him enough trouble.

Thirsty, hungry, and shivering, they plowed on, following the tracks, Augum's arcanely lit palm illuminating the trees in a way that turned branches into creeping fingers. Unable to see much, he tried not to think about skeletal figures creeping up on them. His ears were hyper-tuned to any sound resembling a clacking.

After a short while, Leera took her turn with Shine, having similar trouble lighting her palm. Luckily, the glowing arcane water didn't freeze like normal water would have.

Meanwhile, Augum carefully stuffed his painfully tingling hand back in its mitt, wondering just how long they could keep this up. Sydo better show some gratitude, he found himself thinking, pushing one numb foot in front of the other. They traded back and forth like this countless times, each also taking a turn at leading.

Suddenly he spotted dark glistening mounds ahead in the snow. He stopped, gestured for Leera to draw Burden's Edge as he did not want to take time to extinguish his palm. She gripped the pommel with her mitts and unsheathed the blade from his hip.

The wind howled through the branches, the trees creaking as they swayed. The duo slowly approached, spotting dogs lying beside a sled filled with casks, snowdrifts piled up against their stiff bodies. A bloodied man lay close by.

"What … happened—?" Leera asked, voice slowed by cold.

He pointed at stick-like tracks. "Walkers. A bunch of them." He examined the man. It wasn't the trapper, maybe a trader though. The blood had well frozen over, and estimating by the pile of snowdrift, he guessed it happened only a few hours ago.

Seeing bodies in the dead of night, in the middle of nowhere made him feel colder. Life was so fragile, so lonely. What a miserable end. Will the trader's family ever know what had happened to him?

"I wouldn't want to die like this," Leera whispered. "Awful."

Augum could only stare at the unmoving mounds. Now what would they do? Wolves might come at any moment, if not the walkers. It was dangerous to remain yet dangerous to continue, since the sled tracks stopped here.

Leera rummaged through the contents of the sled. "Catch!" She threw him a long fur coat. He immediately put it on, placing the blanket around her shoulders. He helped her search.

Hidden in a compartment underneath, they found a small hooded lantern, flint, steel, ten copper coins, and five silvers.

He held up the lantern. "Finally some luck."

"We could use the coin to barter for food in town—"

"—and now we can keep our hands in our mitts." He lit the lantern, no easy task with frozen fingers and a strong wind. Soon it swayed in his hand as the pair searched the area, finding two sets of tracks going in opposite directions.

"Survivors," Leera said.

"But they were chased." He pointed at stick-like tracks. He guessed the second set was only one man with one walker trailing, and so he chose to follow it, hoping the man had run in the direction of town.

The tracks went on and on. It appeared neither the man nor the walker wanted to give up. Augum tried to keep his mind off the cold by pondering if walkers got tired, if they lived forever, why it was they appeared here and now, and who exactly was bringing them back to life. Was it Sparkstone, or were there other necromancers now? The thought of his father so close made his heart thump a little faster.

He knew the Legion was looking for them, so whatever happened in town, it might be best to go under a false name. He thought of the trapper's grizzled face. Did the man know? Was he leading a slew of Black Guard back to the cabin at that moment?

There was faint light ahead, blinking through branches.

"Aug, the lantern—" Leera whispered.

He snuffed it out. She nudged him with the pommel of the Dreadnought blade and he took it back. Hunching down, they carefully made their way towards the light, forgetting about the tracks. As they neared, it became apparent it was a long series of torches ringing a village.

"Tornvale?" Leera mouthed.

Closer still, they heard voices and could just make out the outline of two figures between the torches and the forest. Leera put a finger to her lips as a man's voice spoke in authoritative yet irritated tones.

"... tolerating the failed experiments of the necrophytes—greener at their arts than you are with that crossbow, son."

"Yes, sir," replied a higher-pitched voice. "Perhaps if we—"

"I do not care for your opinion," the deep voice interrupted, sounding bored.

"Yes, sir. Sorry, sir."

"And we are supposed to raise an army of them. An *army*. The sheer logistics. We cannot even get the damn things to keep away from our men. You saw how that one came tearing into here. That lucky sack of ale and flesh barely made it. Gone are the days when honor meant meeting your enemy in the field, sword to sword, or bow to bow. Now we raise our enemies to do the fighting for us. And do not even get me started on warlocks." The man sighed. "All I ask of my great lord is to do my duty—my *duty,* son."

"Sir, duty unto death—"

"Yes, yes. You mark my words—the days of honor and truth are *over.*"

"Yes, sir."

"This is a waste of my time. Keep watch. Stay alert. Expect more."

"Yes, sir!"

With that, the man with the deep voice walked off. Augum gestured for Leera to back off. A distance away, they crouched down and strategized in quiet whispers as the wind rattled the trees.

"... but they might *recognize* us," Leera finished saying.

"You heard what Mya said though—he'll die if not attended to by a healer. He might drive me as crazy as he does you, but what choice do we have? We at least need to ask them for one. Who knows, maybe they're a different sort than the kind we bump into up north."

"Aug, even if they *do* accept, they'd probably just send us some necromancer or something."

"Isn't that better than nothing?"

She gave an exasperated sigh. "If the town wasn't occupied, then maybe, but now it's impossible—they're the *Black Guard*—"

"Not if we come up with a good story. Maybe we can try bribing them using the sled."

"I sense a crazy idea coming."

"You saw it yourself—casks of ale. Look, we can do this, all we have to do is play dumb," and playing dumb was something he had plenty of practice doing at the Penderson farm. "We'll pretend we're brother and sister from a poor family—I'll be Jared and you can be Wyza." Jared and Wyza were the names of two of the Penderson brats. They were the first names that came to mind, as much as he hated them.

"Wyza? Forget it, I'm going to be Jezebel—!"

"Shh. You can't be Jezebel, it's a highborn-sounding name."

She crossed her arms. "Fine, Wyza then.

"All right. We'll tell them we live in a cabin west of here and we can pay for the healer's services with the location of a sled full of ale—"

A twig snapped and they froze. Something was moving nearby in the snow. Suddenly a lantern was uncovered, throwing yellow light on the both of them.

"Don't move or I'll split your head in two with a bolt!" shouted a squeaky voice. The lantern only threw light forward, so the figure was cloaked all in darkness, except for the front of a crossbow, aimed directly at Leera's head. "Got me some runaways here! Send for the commander!"

Augum's heart hammered as he heard voices shout from the village.

"Please, sir—" Leera began, putting her hands together in prayer, but the man took a step forward.

"Quiet you! Don't say nothin' unless I say so."

Augum's mind raced. Even with Centarro, the most potent spell he could cast, that bolt would be through Leera's head before he even finished speaking the arcane words, and his Telekinesis was nowhere near powerful or fast enough to wrench the crossbow from the man's hands.

Commands were issued from the same voice they heard earlier. Soon a slew of black-armored men grabbed them roughly and dragged them by their arms, facedown.

Augum, who had to bite his lip from calling out from the pain in his chest, caught glimpses of dark peat homes, muddy snow-covered yards, and wooden troughs.

They were dragged in through a doorframe and thrown onto a dirty plank floor. The room had a shuttered window on the side with a cabinet underneath, a hearth at the far end. A wooden campaign desk sat in the middle strewn with parchments, quill and ink. Torches flickered in sconces mounted on the log walls.

A man with close-cropped gray hair wearing ornate black armor patiently washed his hands in a basin. He dried off with a cloth, adjusted his black surcoat—belted in the middle and emblazoned with the burning sword of the Legion—and began pacing before them. A crimson cloak trailed the floor, linked by a collar chain that danced against his breast with every step.

He stopped abruptly and fixed them with pale gray eyes. "Search them," in that deep voice they had heard earlier.

"Yes, Commander," replied a pair of burly guardsmen with stern yet youthful faces. Soon Burden's Edge, coins, hooded lantern, flint, steel, and the remains of mirko meat lay before them on the floor. The commander stepped on the meat, making a show of grinding it underfoot.

Augum's heart ached as he recalled Bridget tenderly wrapping it in linen for them. "So it stays fresh longer," she had said with that affectionate smile of hers.

The commander snapped his fingers and one of the guards grabbed the back of Augum and Leera's necks and thrust them forward, noses to the floor. Leera gasped while Augum let out an involuntary grunt from the pain in his chest.

The man casually kicked the rest of the items. "Quite prepared the two of you were."

"Please, m'lord," Leera began in a commoner accent, "our brother's sick—ow!" The guard holding her neck had squeezed.

"Hand me that short blade."

"Commander." The guard that wasn't holding their necks picked up Burden's Edge and passed it over.

"Now what would peasant rats be doing with such a fine blade?" He let that thought linger as he continued pacing, turning the Dreadnought blade over in his hands. "Do you know what we do to thieves?"

"We ain't—" but Augum's words were cut off by a vice-like squeeze on his neck.

"Why would I care about your little brother? Is he old enough to join us? Hmm?"

"He is, sir," Augum said, wincing, "but—"

The commander unsheathed Burden's Edge and tapped Augum's head with it. "Well then, do tell us where he is so we may send our healer along and help the poor child."

Better alive and taken prisoner than dead, Augum reasoned. Now it was his turn to mimic the trapper's twang. "M'lord, me sisters are taking care of me brother in me father's cabin, a days' walk west o' here." A poor impression at best.

The commander stood there a moment before chuckling mirthlessly. "Good, because when we find him, we shall cut off his head for desertion, then put your sisters to work."

"NO!" Augum struggled, but the guard that had him by the neck slammed him into the plank floor. His nose immediately began gushing, the iron taste of blood filling his mouth. Leera started to shout but the other guard kicked her to a coughing and writhing halt.

"Please don't harm them," Augum managed to say, dizzy from the blow. It hardly helped the guard seemed to take pleasure smearing his face into the bloody planks.

The commander crouched down, grabbed Augum's hair and lifted his head. "Then will you kindly explain why else your brother is still in his cabin, if not hiding from his required service?" Those pale gray eyes were as empty as any Augum had ever seen, reminding him of Sir Jayson Quick, the Nightsword.

"Speak up, boy." He shook Augum's head back and forth like a doll, with no thought as to the hair he ripped out. Augum grit his teeth, refusing to cry out despite the pain and nausea.

The commander scowled, released Augum's scalp, and dusted his hands. "I think I know what happened here. Everyone in Solia received the order for men to join the Legion. You simply chose to ignore it, and now your poor little brother is sick. So that peasant rat brain of yours thought, 'By golly, let us have a good jest an' rub one over on the ol' commander—he's too darn stupid to tell the difference!' "

Augum remained silent, fighting to breathe properly.

The commander inspected his fingernails, voice almost a whisper again. "Well, is that not the way of it, boy?"

"I … I don't know." Damn this nausea.

"You don't know." The commander inhaled slowly, before changing his tone into that of a doting grandfather. "This is quite the fine blade you have here, son. Did you inherit it from your father?"

Augum's mind swam through a murky lake trying to concoct a story, or even to hold onto one. "I … I …"

The commander only shook his head. "Bah, you see, Lieutenant? These filthy peasants are all useless. I venture to guess this boy stole this blade, as well as everything else here. Did you steal this blade, boy? Confess it and save yourself some pain."

"No, I—" but the commander suddenly struck him with an open hand, sending his head flying backwards. The world quickly became a foggy blur. Leera cried out until silenced by a sharp jerk of her neck.

"I do not like hurting you, my boy," the commander said in a way that suggested otherwise, "but if there is one thing I cannot stand for besides filth and degradation, it is lies." He sheathed Burden's Edge and put it on his desk, gesturing at the rest of their stuff on the floor. "Confiscate it all and lock the criminals up."

"Yes, sir," replied the guard standing by. He yanked Leera to her feet, while the other guard did the same with Augum, who was fighting a losing battle to stay conscious. Not even his former foster father, Mr. Penderson, had hit him that hard. It was like being struck with a hammer. Blood dribbled down his chin and onto his fur coat.

Just as the guards began dragging the two of them off, someone walked in. All Augum could see was the bottom of the person's robe, decorated with black and red vertical stripes.

"Ah, our talented young necrophyte enters. How did the day's batch go?"

"Miserably, Commander Tridian," replied the boy in whiny tones. "Raised one so fat he could hardly claw a peasant's eyes out. Then had to put him to the torch along with— " He stopped speaking a moment. "Unspeakable gods—I know these two!"

Augum tried to power through his dizziness. That voice … he knew that voice. A sharp tug on his scalp forced his head up. Before him hovered a pinched face he had not seen since the massacre at Sparrow's Perch.

Robin Scarson smiled with victorious glee. "Commander Tridian, this is the one we are looking for. May I introduce Augum Stone, the son of the Lord of the Legion."

ROBIN SCARSON

Augum woke up on a cold stone floor in a small prison cell with iron bars and stone walls, stripped of his newly-made hide garments, though mercifully left with his burgundy robe and worn leather turnshoes.

He groaned trying to sit up, gently touching his throbbing chest. He felt his swollen face, trying to remember what happened after seeing Robin. Blood crusted across the whole of it, down his chin and neck. His nose stung when he touched it.

He stumbled forward, grabbed the bars, and looked around. Prison cells stretched down both sides of the corridor. Hooded candles flickered in the space between every second cell, casting dim light. There was the sound of distant weeping and coughing, broken by occasional moans of pain. Water dripped with a slight echo. A figure lay sleeping in the cell opposite, but it was too dark to see who it was.

"Leera—?" he whispered, unsure if there were guards near.

"Aug, beside you," came the quiet reply.

He tried looking to the right, but it was impossible—the bars were just too close together. "Are you okay, did they hurt you—?"

"I'm all right." A pause. "They sent a party to get Bridget and Mya and the prince."

"I should have kept my damn mouth shut."

"No, you did right playing the odds. Better captured than dead. And they won't kill any of us if they think us valuable." She extended her hand out to him. He grabbed it and they squeezed. "How about you, you all right?"

"I'm fine." He saw her wrist was purple, probably from the way the guards had dragged her. His heart panged at the sight. "Hey, at least they'll save the prince's life." Though the Legion *had* killed Sydo's father, the king. Then he remembered something—Sydo and Robin were friends, going all the way back to Blackhaven! Robin had bragged about it once.

He decided now was not the best time to mention that.

"Are you sure you're all right, Aug? I … I couldn't bear to watch the way they … the way they beat you."

So that's what had happened. "Nothing I can't handle." He had endured far worse beatings from the Pendersons and Dap. "Was it Robin?" He let go, trying to ignore the many jarring pains in his body.

"He sucker-punched you and you fell unconscious. Then he just … went at you. You … you don't remember any of that?"

Augum grit his teeth. "No." Damn it.

"Probably for the best anyway." She reached out again.

"I'm worried about you. I'm worried what they'll *do* to you."

He didn't want to have this kind of conversation. He needed to focus on staying strong, and so did she. He looked away from her purple hand. "Don't worry like that. I'm *fine*. Just … just keep yourself well."

She sighed, withdrawing her hand. "Aug—" her voice dropped as she pressed closer to the bars. "I overheard them talking. They're sending a messenger for your father. Said he should arrive within a couple days' time."

He leaned back against the wall they shared. It was what he had expected. Of course his father would come—he would want to personally question him on Nana's whereabouts. He thought about his earlier determination to join him and somehow talk him out of war. The thought seemed completely ludicrous now. How could he possibly join his father? He hated the man, hated him for slaughtering Bridget and Leera's parents and so many others. He was a cold-blooded murderer and there was no way Augum could change his mind.

Doubt remained, though he resolved to think about it later.

Footsteps rang down the hall. He and Leera recoiled away from the bars as a smirking Robin Scarson appeared. A guardsman stood obediently behind him, spear in hand, face impassive.

Robin leaned in close. "I tried to improve your face for you. Didn't work."

Augum made a sudden movement forward and Robin flinched, but chuckled when he saw how much pain it had caused Augum.

"Do you realize how big of a hero you've made me? Your own father, the Lord of the Legion, is going to be very, *very* grateful." He tilted his head. "But I'm going to give him an even better present. With the help of Commander Tridian, you're going to tell me where that stinking crone went—"

"I'll tell you nothing."

Robin put on a pouting face. "Aw, wooks like the wittle mousie's found some couwage." He shook his head. "I still remember the first day we met, when you cowered in the snow, pissing yourself at the approach of horses. Now listen carefully, gutterborn—you'd do well to speak freely and openly. They don't call him the Blade of Sorrows for nothing. You *are* going to tell me everything—you just don't know it yet."

"I can't believe what you've become, Robin Scarson," Leera said from within her cell, sounding like Bridget.

Robin flashed her a mock smile. "My dear Leera, remember when I asked you to join my gang back in the academy, and you said no? I don't know *what* it is I saw in you. And then there was that song, the one we all sang about you, how did that one go again?"

Leera did not reply.

He leaned in close. "I think you've become ugly, you know that? To me, you'll now always be *The Leer*, staring at people like an idiot, with that stupid freckled face of yours. Stupid, that's what you are, just like your stupid dad—"

Leera lunged forward but Robin took a casual step back.

"And you're boring too, you know that? You're *boring*. You've become insufferably *boring*, Leera. Now let me explain exactly what *I've* become—an honored necrophyte. Do you even know what that means?"

"Why don't you step closer and I'll tell you."

"Gross. You sure you weren't born a boy, Leer? Now where was I? Right—being a necrophyte means training to become a *necromancer*. I also happen to be best of the lot. I can already raise the dead and command them. I can create *walkers*. Bet you regret not hanging with me now, don't you?"

There was something different about him, Augum realized. It wasn't just the Robin he met on his way to

Hangman's Rock—there was a gleam in his eye now, as if anointed by a king.

"Mind you there's still a lot to work out," Robin continued, waving the details aside. "Namely how to get them to do my bidding and such, but I'll figure it out, don't you worry. And now, since I found you lot, the commander said I'll be rewarded with instruction from the Lord of the Legion himself." He paused for effect, eyes flicking back to Augum. "How does that make you feel, peasant breath? Your own father favoring me? Pretty low, huh?"

Augum would have done anything to be within reaching distance. One solid punch to the face. Was that too much to ask?

"Pity you didn't join me when you had the chance, Leer." Robin's lip curled. "Maybe your parents would still be alive if you hadn't been so—"

Leera spat in his face.

Robin recoiled, quickly wiping it off. "Ugh, you filthy little pig! You'll pay for that." He snapped his fingers.

The guardsman banged the butt of his spear against the stone floor. "Honored Necrophyte."

"Hear that? *Honored.* Unlike how it was in that stupid village of yours, I have a future in the Legion—I'm training to become a necromancer, the highest calling for us sorcerers. And you? Look at you—pathetic gutterborn peasants."

"And you're a useless coward, like you've always been," Leera said.

Robin smiled. "Think so, do you? Well, I look forward to proving it otherwise very soon. But never mind that right now. When the Lord of the Legion fulfills his promise of eternal life for the loyal, I'll make sure you're included so you can forever shine my boots as my personal slave!" He gestured at her. "Guard—show her what power means."

The guard raised the butt end of his spear and repeatedly shoved it through the cell. Leera screamed as Augum shot forward, hand clawing madly after Robin, losing all sense and yelling unintelligible profanities. She kept screaming until collapsing into a heap. Robin made a quick gesture to Augum's arm and the guard smashed the spear onto it. Augum howled and fell backwards, gasping and writhing.

Robin clapped as he laughed. "Oh, I'm going to have so much fun with you two." His robe swirled as he turned. "So much fun!" and he rapped the bars while striding off.

Augum listened to the sound of boots fade, fantasizing about wrapping his hands around Robin's neck.

"Oh, ye done made a foul enemy there, boy," said a wheezing voice from the opposite cell. The pile of rags that lay on the ground moved forward, revealing an elderly man with missing teeth and wispy gray hair. "Best not be provoking them like that. It done only make them angry."

Augum bit his lip and crawled toward the corner of the cell closest to Leera. "Lee, you okay? Leera—"

"—I'm fine," Leera finally said through gritted teeth. "I'm fine …" but her breathing came in short bursts.

"Hang in there," he mumbled.

"If ye are to be questioned by the Blade o' Sorrows, may the Unnameables help ye. Best to spill it quick and spill it all, I says."

Augum slumped against the wall while holding his arm. It throbbed in time to his head and chest in a symphony of torment.

"Lots of hustle and bustle because of ye, boy." When Augum didn't reply, the man continued. "They calls me Cled. Used to farm around here. Gave all four o' me sons to the cause."

"So why are you in here?"

"They says I didn't volunteer me boys quick enough."

Augum grimaced from a spasm of pain. "They threw you in here because you didn't give your sons over quickly enough?"

"That's what I says."

"Can't your sons get you out?"

"Reckon they don't even know. Been sent off to some forsaken place in the east, Tigrera, or some such dastardly name."

"Tiberra," Leera said, crawling closer to the bars, voice cut with agony. "Are you saying they're going ... to war with Tiberra?"

The man smacked his gums together and scratched his ear. "Done guess so, they be sending all the young men there. Buts you gots to take what I says with some salt. I only hear them when they be lazy and the like. Been here a whiles now."

Augum closed his eyes and tried breathing deeper, but his chest was having none of it. He ended up coughing and sending more spasms through his body. "Do you know Frankie the trapper?"

"Darn right I knows Frankie, him and his flea-bitten mutt. He done took ye in, didn't he? Well ol' Frankie'll be a sorry fool."

"For taking us in—?"

"Ye done lost him his cabin, boy. They be burning it to the ground, and maybe some o' your friends along with it. Or they be getting' dragged or beaten or—but you don't want to hear that, I see it on your face. If they catch Frankie and that sorry mutt though ..." He took a labored breath. "Ye should have done scurried when ye had the chance."

"What's the trapper's story?" Leera asked.

Cled smacked his gums. "Had himself a daughter. Died in the famine. A son, too. He died—famine. Wife died o' sickness. I figure he done, but he up in that cabin still trading away, taking his licks like the man he be. Just him and that big ol' mutt. A whiles back, we done some trading—"

The man continued talking but Augum couldn't listen anymore. Even the thought of Mya and Bridget dragged by their wrists through the snow and mud made him sick to his stomach.

Cled fell silent and retreated into his cell.

Augum sat there, having no idea what time of day it was as there were no windows in the prison. He closed his eyes and tried to sleep, but the throbbing pain didn't let him. He needed to do something to keep his mind off it, so he decided to practice the art of observance on his surroundings, something his great-grandfather used in preparation for Centarro.

He first inspected the cold floor and walls, the grooves between the cut stones, the rough texture. He then carefully studied the bars—which parts were thinnest, which rusted and flaked. Then the construction of the iron hinges, imagining them squeaking like the ones in Castle Arinthian.

He missed the castle now more than ever—its cozy canopy beds, the stained-glass windows, that ancient castle smell. But above all, he missed the warmth from those large hearths. He even missed the cellar, with its bronze servant plaque and those mysterious gates. Then again, perhaps it would be better to say he missed exploring the cellar with Bridget and Leera. Except the crypt. He didn't miss that. Even imagining his ancestor walking around under his father's command made his muscles tighten. Would Atrius Arinthian come for him now along with his father?

He became aware of Cled watching him and worried about revealing he was a warlock, especially to someone with four sons in the Legion. Yet he had to get out of there before his father came. Not only that, but he had to somehow save the others and then find Mrs. Stone. No, he had to take the risk.

"Ye can't escape, boy," Cled wheezed, smacking his gums. "They'd cut ye down before ye even be seeing the light o' day. Best prepare to be put to the question. You done need an iron mind, boy—an iron mind for an iron room."

Augum tuned the man out, concentrating on the arcane words that would make the spell real. He closed his eyes and breathed in and out a few times in an attempt to still the pain.

"Centeratoraye xao xen," but nothing happened except the throbbing worsened. He was too tired and needed rest.

The old man gripped the bars, eyes glinting. Others in nearby cells stirred too, and Augum realized what he was trying to do was dangerous. He couldn't let them find out what he was capable of, not until he absolutely had to.

"I be doggone. Would that be magic ye be trying to cast there, boy?"

"It's just a prayer—to the Unnameables," Augum replied quickly.

"Is that right," Cled muttered. He faded back into the shadows, watching.

Augum slumped against the wall. He wondered what Mrs. Stone was doing in that moment. Walking through snow? Teleporting from place to place? What degree did he require to learn Teleport? There was still so much he didn't know, so much more to learn …

He pondered the possibilities, until his stray thoughts became confused with real dreams.

THE QUESTIONING

Augum woke to the unusually sharp prodding of Mrs. Stone's staff. "I'm coming, Nana, I'm coming. Let me just sleep a little more." He squirmed to move away from the sharply increasing prods, until one smacked his mouth so hard he thought a tooth loosened.

"Think the boy's pining for his mother or something," a guard said with a chortle, withdrawing the spear.

As Augum spit blood, he felt stone beneath him instead of bedding. How much time had passed? He was in that cell, wasn't he? All the familiar aches and pains returned—chest, nose, arm, head—though the latter two less so.

Keys jingled.

"Unnameables help him. Let's get this over with," said a second guard.

The words jarred him to his senses. He forced himself to pay close attention to his surroundings—the creaking hinges purposefully left unoiled to warn guards of an opening cell;

the long passage and its low ceiling, meant to delay escape; the harsh smell of lamp oil; these details and more he absorbed like a sponge.

As they dragged him limply by Leera's cell, she clutched his arm and squeezed it tightly, withdrawing quickly before one of the guards caught her. "Stay strong, Aug," she whispered, face muddy and hair tangled. She held her side as she stood, giving him the impression she was still injured from the spear attack.

It hurt to see her like that. The guard that had done it was not one of the two, for if he had been, Augum probably would have tried something stupid.

Even when he attempted walking on his own, the guards would not let him, preferring to drag him. He gave up and instead focused on the corridors. A right, a left, up thirty steps, right at a fork, a last right through an iron door. He caught a brief whiff of crisp wintery air—the exit had to be near!

The two guards threw him into a room that was iron top to bottom, its walls and floor wet and caked with rust. Crude iron lanterns burned in each corner, caged in wire. Bolted in the center was a single iron table the size of a small bed. The guards flanked the door, snapping to attention as the Blade of Sorrows strolled in with a placid look on his face, dressed in his polished ornate black armor and surcoat. Robin Scarson followed, smiling with malignant joy. He gestured to the table with a mailed glove. "Sit. Please."

Augum glanced to the door but did as he was told.

The man studied him a moment with those pale eyes. "You know, Augum Stone, I do not believe you understand your father, or what he is trying to accomplish." The commander began pacing, searching for the right words. "He is building an empire, Augum. An *empire.* It will stretch—" he made a sweeping gesture, "—to every corner of Sithesia. There are lands we have not even heard of, awaiting his Lord's arrival. The world has never seen one such as him, *never.* And you—" he placed his mailed hands on Augum's shoulders, "—you are his son, his only … son."

Robin stirred but Augum was careful not to look away, as the commander was studying his reactions.

Tridian let go and began pacing again, sighing as if encumbered by a heavy burden. "You could be there with him, Augum. Side by side. He wants you there, but not—" he stopped and waved a finger as if addressing a naughty child, "—not with half your heart set elsewhere. "Your father, the Lord of the Legion and eventual Emperor of all kingdoms in all lands, wants you only with a loyal and dedicated heart. Now you think about that."

Augum chose to focus on the tang of blood in his mouth than say anything.

Commander Tridian stopped pacing a moment and placed his hands behind his back. "You know, I fought alongside your father when the Legion was but a seed in his eye. The battle for Blackhaven was fierce. Naturally, we had to dispose of the warlocks first, but it was at the academy that your father proved himself to his troops."

He stared off for a moment. "I have never seen such power … *never*." He cleared his throat. "So let me say this—your father is willing to train you and share with you that power, a power you are predisposed to master." He made a dismissive gesture and chuckled. "Your entire bloodline, apparently." He leaned in a little. "But mark my words—if he feels you will not partake in that power as a dutiful son should, he will crush you, utterly and simply, and everyone that you love along with you."

The Blade of Sorrows studied him as the words sank in. Augum thought of Bridget and Leera, of Mya and Mrs. Stone. He wanted to say something stupid and brash, but bit his tongue and glared.

A smile slowly spread across the Blade of Sorrows' face, a smile without warmth or conscience. Abruptly, he turned to Robin. "Now, young apprentice, it is your turn. The Lord of the Legion expects his necrophytes to know the meaning of discipline, especially when it comes to the question. You must be cold as ice and strong as iron. You must be demanding yet conscious of your subjects' weaknesses and strengths. Above all, you must be *smart.* Are you ready, Apprentice?"

The doubt on Robin's face was momentary before a smirk replaced it. "I am, Commander."

"Good." Tridian made a polite gesture at Augum. "Then you may begin." The Blade of Sorrows crossed his arms and leaned against the wall. The two guards stood statue-still in attention beside him, their eyes focused straight ahead.

Robin paced back and forth in a close impression of the commander. "Where is she?"

Commander Tridian rubbed his forehead. "Do not cut to the chase right from the start. Learn to play with your subject first as a cat plays with a mouse. Lull him into a sense of security. The best questioners can do that for days, making friends of their subjects, before springing on them like a lion."

Robin nodded along. "Yes, Commander." He turned back to Augum and gave a gleeful smile.

Tridian sighed as if bored. "Avoid showing your emotions, either eagerness or hatred. Learn to use them as tools instead, Apprentice."

"As you say, Commander." Robin turned back to Augum, trying to control his facial expression. If the situation wasn't so dangerous, Augum would have laughed.

Robin folded his hands behind his back. "Look, your gutterborn piglet friends will be here soon. I can easily get the information from them, but that would ruin the sport of it, wouldn't it?" He took a step closer, his voice dropping. "I want to hear it from *you.* I don't care what it is I have to do to *them,* you understand, but *you* are going to tell me where the old crone went."

The Blade of Sorrows started clapping slowly, the sound ringing off the iron walls. "Well done, Apprentice. Your academy training is starting to show. Our Lord will be pleased, as I will be sure to mention to him how much of a success his program has been so far. When you become a great warlock in the Legion, do not forget about the little people."

The pair chortled together, Robin's cheeks reddening. Even the guards broke out in a reserved chuckle until the Blade of Sorrows silenced them with a look. He then flicked a finger at Robin. "Resume."

"As I understand it—" Robin continued, "you are being *trained* by the crone, is that not true?"

Augum stared defiantly. Robin smirked back. He made to start pacing again when he suddenly smashed his fist into Augum's face. Augum's eyes involuntarily welled with tears as blood spurted from his nose.

"I've wanted to do that since I met you, you disgusting gutterborn scum. Didn't weasel out that time, did you? Want to black out on me again?"

Augum only glared. Never mind that Robin had sucker-punched him twice now. He refused to touch his nose, letting the blood drip down his chin and robe.

"I can see you are developing a taste for pressure," Commander Tridian said, as if commenting on nothing more than the weather. "Very good. Plenty of questioners use the pressure method. Why? Because it works. Incidentally, most of the great commanders in his Lords' army know the pressure method. I am quite fond of it myself. You will be in good company when you become a man, Apprentice. Perhaps it would also be useful for you to train with

Commander Rames, who I believe was the only other person in our great lord's army to be trained by the crone."

"Oh, you haven't heard?" Augum said, unable to restrain himself this time. "Rames is dead. We killed him."

Robin cackled. "You bluff—"

"No, he tells the truth, Apprentice, learn to spot the difference. Now, we want to reward the truth, but in this case, he is being insubordinate, is he not?"

Robin's lip curled. "He most certainly is, Commander."

"So what are you going to do about it?"

Robin reared back and slapped Augum.

Augum made a show of sticking out his chin and taking it. He spat blood on the floor before resuming his glare. "I've been hit harder." It was true—if there was one thing he could thank Dap and the damn Pendersons for, it was conditioning. "Why don't you take me on one-on-one, huh?" All he needed was a fair fight.

"Trying to be smart, eh?" Robin wiped his hand, returning Augum's glare with a hate-filled one of his own. "Can I drag her in, Commander?"

There was a hint of pride in the commander's reply. "Why yes. This is, after all, *your* questioning."

"Guards—bring the girl!"

The guards thumped their spears before marching off.

A wave of nausea came over Augum. Suddenly he was very thirsty. Must be the blood loss or something.

Robin's brow rose. "What's the matter, gutterborn?"

Augum stiffened. "Leave her alone, or I'll tell my father and he'll destroy you both!" he knew it was stupid and futile, but he had to try.

The Blade of Sorrows laughed, Robin quickly joining, though for a moment Augum saw fear in his eyes.

"Was that not worth watching, Apprentice?"

Robin belted out an overzealous laugh while nodding along.

"Wishful thinking, boy," Tridian said. "You do not know your father like I do."

There came the sound of struggle from the corridor. Leera was dragged in and dumped to the floor, clutching her side and wincing. She flashed Robin a dirty look.

Augum stood. "Leera—"

"SIT DOWN!" the Blade of Sorrows roared, the outburst so sudden that every other soul in that room flinched.

Augum, breathing hard, swallowed his pride and sat back down, though he purposefully took his time doing it.

"Did you notice that little act of defiance, Apprentice? The way he sat himself? I will teach you how to rid him of that."

"I look forward to it, sir."

Augum looked at Leera with deep concern. "You all right?"

"I'm fine, don't tell them anything—"

"Aw, how touching," Robin said. "Hey, Leer, want to go to my advancement ceremony as my date? Just kidding! Haylee's coming with me," and he cackled.

Augum remembered Haylee, the blonde with cold blue eyes. Her father, Lord Tennyson, was the one that informed Sparkstone about Augum and Mrs. Stone, costing almost everyone in Sparrow's Perch their life.

Leera tried to wipe the mud off her face with her sleeve. "You've become a real fine monster. Still an idiot though."

Robin walked towards her and she scurried back. He laughed before snapping his fingers. "Guards—hold her against the wall."

She struggled but it was no use. Robin took one of the guards' spears in hand, watching Augum's reaction. "You are going to tell me exactly where the old crone wandered off to, or I will punish *her* for it."

"Don't do it Aug, don't—"

One of the guards clamped a hand over her mouth. She kept struggling, voice muffled. Augum had never felt more powerless in his life. He desperately tried to think of something to do. Even *if* he managed to cast Centarro, he was not foolish enough to think it would work against all four of them. Yet he couldn't tell them where Mrs. Stone had gone either—"

Robin pointed the sharp end of the spear at Leera's stomach, firming his jaw. Something about the way he was looking at her told Augum he had less than a moment to decide.

"STOP!" Augum blurted, palms open. "Don't hurt her. Mrs. Stone has gone to Canterra, to the land of knights and castles."

Robin looked disappointed.

"He is lying, Apprentice. If there is one thing I excel at, Augum Stone, is discovering a lie. I advise you not to test me on it again."

Robin's face lit up like it was his birthday. He smashed the spear against the side of Leera's head. She yelped before slumping to the ground in a silent heap.

That was too much for Augum, who roared and tackled an unprepared Robin, ramming his fist into his face like a battering ram while feeling the beginnings of a murderous electric rage. And just as suddenly, knowing the catastrophic outcome should he continue, he gave a scream of total frustration and went limp, as one of the guards plucked him off.

"I can't do it. I can't get that angry. You don't understand …" They'd kill all his friends if he let his wild arcanery loose, that much he knew, and that's assuming he could even control it.

Robin stood up with a moan, holding a bloody nose and touching a fat lip. Commander Tridian nodded and the guards threw Augum into the corner. He crashed into the wall and fell to the floor. Sharp explosions of pain came from his chest, which grated disgustingly. A fresh wave of nausea threatened to make him vomit. Blood from his own nose seemed to be everywhere.

Tridian handed Robin an embroidered cloth. "Never leave yourself unprotected, Apprentice, especially in the company of a warlock."

Robin dabbed at his nose and lip while giving Augum a look of the purest loathing. "What should I have done instead, Commander?"

"Always secure the subject before applying pressure."

A knock came at the door.

"WHAT!" the Blade of Sorrows barked with such violence everyone but Augum, who slowly raised himself off the floor, flinched again.

"M'lord, we brought the others," came a stuttering voice from the other side.

"Fine. Lock them up, we shall deal with them later."

"Pardon, m'lord, but the boy … the boy is very sick. Should we attend to him?"

"Fine, fine already! Have someone see to him, and stop pestering me!"

"As you say, m'lord."

Well at least the prince would be taken care of, Augum thought. Their suffering better have been worth it. Then another part of him, perhaps the side that came from his great-grandparents, thought, ah, but that is sacrifice, is it not?

Leera stirred, rolled her head, exposing a raw welt. She watched Augum with glassy eyes.

"I'm sorry," Augum mouthed. "You okay?"

She moaned with a nod.

Her guard gave her a violent shake. "Shut it!"

Robin strode over to a teetering Augum. He slapped him in the face again, daring him to do anything. Augum grit his teeth but chose to look away this time.

"You do know that if you weaseled out and went unconscious we'd just work on her, don't you? Why don't you save her the pain and tell us where the crone went."

"Well done, Apprentice. The choice must always be laid out clearly, and that you have achieved."

Robin smiled proudly.

"Aug, don't you—"

"I said shut it!" The guard smacked her with the back of his mailed hand and she yelped again.

Robin leaned in even closer. Augum smelled the rotten stench of the grave off his robe and felt his stomach spasm.

"Well, gutterborn?"

Augum only stood there, fighting to stay conscious from all the blood loss and pain but refusing to speak. He couldn't give Nana up, it'd be the end of them all. He bit his lower lip and glared defiantly at Robin. Blood continued to drip off his chin, splattering Robin's boot.

"I'm going to enjoy this," Robin whispered. "Hold him!"

One of the guards grabbed Augum and slammed him against the wall as Robin marched over to Leera, who lay slumped on the ground, hands protecting her head. He punched her in the face, glancing back at Augum to make sure he saw. She whimpered and her hand shot to her cheek. Augum jerked in the guard's grip. The man grabbed his jaw and held it firmly pointed at Leera.

"Are you going to tell us where the crone went or not?"

When Augum didn't reply, Robin punched her again, even harder. Her head hit the back wall with a sickening thud. Her hands fell away from her bloody face and her eyes wandered the room in a daze. "Aug ..."

"One. Final. Time, gutterborn. Where did the crone go?"

Augum tensed, fighting to keep the dark tunnel of unconsciousness at bay. This wasn't worth it. Just tell them already, you fool!

Robin opened his palm and smiled. "Grab her!"

The other guard took Leera's arms with one hand and bent them back, holding her head with the other.

"Why don't I make that face truly ugly. Shyneo!" Robin's palm burst with fire. Leera kicked out with her feet as his burning palm closed in, the leather of her turnshoes squealing against the iron floor. She unleashed a scream that rang Augum's innards like a giant bell. He struggled violently against the guard's grip, knowing Robin and the Blade of Sorrows would only keep escalating their brutality until he or Leera told them where Mrs. Stone went. He couldn't stay conscious for much longer, and then what would they do to her?

Forgive me, Nana, he thought.

The commander, who had been carefully watching him, straightened a little. "Look, Apprentice."

Robin glanced over, flaming palm near Leera's face. His eyes were full of … could that be joy? Augum suddenly understood exactly what Tridian was really doing here. Leera was right—he was making a *monster*. The thought occurred to him that if he joined his father, it would be *him* standing there alongside the Lord of the Legion …

Tridian made an idle gesture and the guard let go of Augum's jaw with a yank.

"I'm sorry, Lee, I can't let them hurt you." Leera moaned in protest but he returned his gaze to Robin. "Mrs. Stone has gone north to the mountain monks."

It was over, they had won.

"You see there, Apprentice? How his body relaxed like that? The way the eyes fell to the floor in resignation? One, he is telling the truth, and two, now you must press."

Robin was nodding along, absorbing every word like a dutiful son. He studied Augum carefully, no longer like a human being, but as a *thing,* or rather as a *nothing.*

Augum felt as hollow as a cavern. He recalled the torture room in Castle Arinthian, constructed by Narsus, his father's predecessor, and wondered if others folded as quickly as he did, just by the threat of torture of a friend or loved one.

Robin kept his burning palm near Leera as a barrage of questions followed.

"Does she have the scion?"

"Yes."

"Has she trained you with it?"

"No."

"Does she know where you are?"

"No."

The answers came automatically now. Tridian would occasionally point something out to Robin, but Augum didn't care. His only concern was for his suffering friend, whimpering on the floor. Tears rolled down Leera's cheeks, and all he wanted to do was gently take her in his arms and dry them.

"... what kind of opposition does the Legion face in Tiberra?"

"I don't know."

"Does the crone have an army?"

"No."

"Does she have a following of warlocks with her?"

"No."

The questions kept on, mostly about the coming war. He answered truthfully to them all, though he hardly knew much about anything. There weren't many questions involving him and the others either, perhaps because they hadn't suspected a bunch of fourteen-year-olds to have gone to a place called Ley, and Augum certainly wasn't about to volunteer information like that. Though if they had asked him about it, he would have told them that too.

"And now you must reward your subject for being honest, Apprentice."

A malicious smile crept across Robin's face.

"Not that kind of reward."

Robin's face fell.

"Guard," Tridian said. "Take her back to the cell and see that she is fed."

The guard thumped the floor with his spear and dragged a limp Leera out.

Robin leaned in close. "Oh, we're not done with you yet!" and he laughed before suddenly gripping Augum's head and smashing it against the wall.

Augum saw innumerable white-hot lights sweep his vision, barely felt his body hit the floor. He heard Tridian sigh. "Learn when to show restraint, Apprentice," before blacking out.

He came to on a cold stone floor amid cries from Bridget, Mya and Leera, just as the guards slammed his cell door shut and marched off. He couldn't make any sound or move. He lay numb and spent. Well, at least he'd held out long enough. He hadn't told them that should his father ever come to possess all seven scions, he'd be destroyed. Nor had he told them about Ley.

The girls kept trying to get him to say something, but he just couldn't do it. Never had pain and exhaustion mingled in such a sweet brew. Mercy came quickly in the form of sleep.

NERVE

Augum woke once again to the butt end of a spear, this time having no illusions as to what it was or where he was. He was really starting to hate being woken up this way.

"Eat your slop, boy."

He sat up, wincing from the grating in his chest and the countless other aches and throbs, cuts and bruises. The movement immediately caused the tunnel of darkness and nausea to return. When he placed his hand to his blood-caked face, it felt gritty and foreign.

"Eat your slop, I say."

He glanced up at the blurred outline of a guard.

"They sure worked you over good, boy. You as blue as a berry."

Augum dragged himself over to a bowl of congealed soup and a piece of hard bread. The sight of the soup skin turned his stomach. He picked up the wooden spoon and pretended to eat.

The guard grunted and walked on, followed by a man with a cart. A pair of bony hands extended from the cell opposite. "M'lords ... please."

The guard scowled, threatening Cled with a spear. Cled withdrew, though his eyes soon travelled to Augum's bowl. He smacked toothless lips, waiting for the guards to walk a bit further.

"They only feeds me once a day. They says I be too old for more."

Augum wordlessly tossed him the piece of bread and shoved the bowl of soup between them in the corridor. He then collapsed, the effort draining his energy.

Cled snatched the bowl. "Bless your heart, boy."

"Augum—" Leera whispered, her hand extending from her cell and reaching to his. "Are you all right? Oh, Aug ... please, say something!"

He tried to speak but only gasps came out. His tongue felt like a large slug.

"Don't be too hard on yourself. You held out as best you could."

He stared at her grasping hand.

"Hold my hand, just for a little bit ... *please.*"

He moved towards it but a wave of nausea stopped him. Perhaps he should have eaten after all.

"Are you listening to me—? Say something!"

"I'm ... all ... right," he managed to croak finally, barely able to recognize his own voice.

Leera's hand disappeared as she whimpered. "You sound awful," she said, voice shaking. "But I'm glad you're all right—and you don't have to worry about the others. Everyone's okay—Bridget, Mya, the prince, though they took him away somewhere and haven't brought him back since. Mya's in the cell to my right and Bridget's to her right."

Her hand stretched out again, her voice soft. "Please, take my hand, Aug."

He winced reaching for it. When they connected, she squeezed and refused to let go.

"Aug … I'm so sorry."

"Nothing … to … apologize … for …"

"You need a healer. You lost a lot of blood. You—"

"I'm … fine," he lied. "How's … your … head?"

"It smarts, but I've taken worse knocks falling from trees." She tugged him forward a little, voice dropping to an almost inaudible murmur. "Listen, we have to figure something out. We have to get out of here and warn Mrs. Stone."

Warn her? They don't even know how to get to her.

The blackness returned. Sitting up was too difficult. His grip loosened but she refused to let go.

"Aug?"

"Mmm?"

"Do this with me. Let's come up with a plan."

He grunted, doubting he could put together any coherent thought right now.

She gave his hand a final squeeze before letting go, allowing him to slump. "Great—I'll pass on the word."

He lay there until realizing Cled had been watching him the entire time, and probably had heard every word. The old man leaned forward, smiling toothlessly, still holding the bowl of soup, now licked clean.

"I know that look, boy. Ye done want to escape. Well put it out o' your mind 'cause it be barking mad to try. You'd only be killing yourself and your friends. The Blade of Sorrows is no fool, he has them guards posted everywhere like flies on this here soup they be serving—" Cled hushed up as two guards walked by in the relatively narrow corridor, laughing at a jape one of them told.

Leera's hand reappeared when the guards had passed. "Aug—listen," she whispered as Cled retreated to a dark corner of his cell, eyes glinting. "We've been keeping track. The guards patrol steadily, but they take their time during meal breaks. We could use, you know … see."

He blinked, trying to figure out what she meant, before realizing it was the letter C, as in *Centarro*.

"Rest … first."

"Of course, I'm so sorry. Don't rush it. You rest and I'll be right here, all right?"

He groaned, closed his eyes. He lay in that exact position for a long time, drifting in and out of consciousness, until another bowl was shoved in the cell. This time, he dragged himself over and painstakingly ate every last bit of the bitter soup and stale bread.

The effect was like drinking from the Arinthian fountain. He sat up, trying to avoid scratching at his itchy face.

"Lee …"

"I'm right here—"

"Let's use C, but we'll have to practice for the after effects."

Cled shuffled forward. "Use 'See'? That some power ye be talking about, boy? Ye be trying to magic your way out, that it?"

He didn't respond, thinking Cled may be a spy planted there by the Blade of Sorrows to keep an eye on them. Centarro was their only hope right now. He couldn't take the chance of the Legion discovering the spell. For all he knew, they might be forced to teach the Legion how to use it, and such a spell would be disastrous in the wrong hands. He wondered if there was a prisoner to his left that might overhear, yet he hadn't heard anyone stir in that cell, nor had soup been delivered there.

Cled's eyes shifted left and right as his voice dropped to a conspiratorial whisper. "Well, let me tell ye a secret, boy—one o' me own sons is a warlock."

Augum leaned forward. "What?" He could hear Leera do the same.

"That's right, he once be a Legion warlock, until they done killed him for helping the other side."

"I'm sorry," Augum said.

"Now don't go getting me wrong, when he was just a wee one, I tries to beat it out o' him, I did. I tries hard, but it only made him want it more." His eyes dropped. "I be regretting the way I was. I done him no good. I done him no good at all."

Augum had this strange vision of Mr. Penderson before him and had to rub his eyes.

Cled put his toothless mug right up against the bars now, face grave. "Ye listen to me now, boy, and you listen good. What I be saying is, I *understand*. If ye can magic your way out, ye done better do it. Get out. Get out now, boy. And why? Because soon they'll take them girls and put them to work for the war, and you'll never see them again. That's what happens to girls who done the Legion no good."

Augum's heart thundered. Cled was right, and maybe, just maybe, he isn't a spy after all. He felt the blood in his veins roar again as his mind raced to come up with a plan.

"Go on. Get. And I thank ye for the soup and bread, boy, it done saved me life for one more day." Cled retreated into the shadows of his cell, leaving Augum to contemplate. And then an idea came, and it involved study.

"Psst. Leera—" Her hand appeared and he gave it a reassuring squeeze. "Let's begin."

"Damn right. What's the plan?"

"Study your door. See if you can find a weakness using C. If you find one, pass it along, but keep the door closed.

Don't break it or anything or do anything else. Just learn and observe. Oh, and be sure to prepare for the side effects."

"Gotcha."

He returned to Thomas' initial training on Centarro, when his great-grandfather made them carefully examine the bark of a tree. With that lesson in mind, he set himself to inspecting the bars again—every detail, including every one of the four hinges, and especially the lock mechanism. There was nothing apparent, but he knew that wasn't the point. Under the influence of Centarro, he may yet find some use for his observations.

That complete, he studiously planned casting the spell. Leera and Bridget had been a bit less patient than he, casting it almost right away and with little success, yet passing on information they had learned in their trials. Bridget revealed it was best to cast it right after the guards patrolled by, and to face the wall at the back of the cell when it wears off so one's attention is focused on something unexciting.

Leera, on the other hand, managed to pick off a small shard of iron from one of the bars, which could be used as a small tool. She also told him that his calming words helped when the spell had worn off, and that she would return the favor when he tried.

All this information, in addition to what he had observed, he would apply to this trial. When the guards next walked by, he took three deep breaths and closed his eyes.

"Centeratoraye xao xen."

Immediately time seemed to slow as he became aware of every subtlety. Colors enhanced and sharpened; sound boomed and whispered nuances; the rhythm of his heart ebbed and flowed musically.

Cled watched with interest, but Augum paid him no heed.

First, he planned for the after-effects—he was going to turn around and stare at the back wall and spend the time simply thanking his great-grandfather for passing on this knowledge, and that was all. He then pressed forward and explored the bars with his hands, especially the hinges, finding nothing to exploit. He focused on the lock.

"Leera," he whispered, reaching out his hand. "The shard."

She handed it to him and he began exploring the inner working of the lock. The feeling soon came that his time was almost up, but all he needed to do was understand how it worked, and so he fiddled carefully, not trying to open it, just trying to *understand* it.

Suddenly it dawned on him he needed a second shard.

He continued working on the lock right up until a dull fog started to cloud out his thoughts. It was enough. He knew he had something, an understanding of the inner workings of that lock. He dropped the shard and faced the wall, closing his eyes and repeating, "Thank you, Great-grandfather."

Meanwhile, Leera whispered encouraging words: "Good job, Augum. Relax, just sit and relax, there's nothing going on out here, the guards are *not* coming …" She continued speaking this way until his fog cleared. His head throbbed and he felt woozy, but under the circumstances, it was a very successful casting.

"I think I might be able to pick the lock. Just need another shard or something."

"I'll see what I can do." She disappeared to whisper with Mya, reporting they're looking for one now.

A guard patrol sauntered by, unaware of their plans.

Cled leaned into the light. "Mighty brave, boy. They'd whip ye raw or worse if ye get caught. I wish ye luck, though luck not be good as this—" and he produced something from within his rags.

"I found it when they be giving me a whipping for asking about me boys. They never saw me take it. I been hiding it ever since, thinking I might be needing it one day, either for them, or for me own throat." He wheezed a laugh and tossed it to him. It turned out to be the blade of a kitchen knife, missing its handle.

Augum smiled for the first time in what felt like days. "Thank you, it's exactly what I need." He informed Leera, who gave a quiet squeal before passing on the word. Then he waited a while, renewing his arcane energies—just in case.

"Good luck, Aug," she whispered.

The timing of this had to be crucial. "Don't screw this up," he muttered to himself. He gripped the lock, terribly conscious of how exposed his hands were, and went at it, working only when the guards' backs were turned. They passed by twice more without him getting caught, thanks to his lookouts—Cled watched the left, girls the right.

At last, he heard the most satisfying sound in the world—*click*.

The lock had sprung.

Cled's gnarled face pressed against the bars, grinning toothlessly. "By barrel o' ale—ye done did it, boy. Careful now, don't be rushing. Wait till they pass."

He forgot about the pain in his chest as the guards lumbered by. Should they touch his cell door, they would instantly know it was open. Soon as he saw the back of them, he went to push on the door, but Cled's hand shot up.

"Wait, boy. Ye be needing help opening them bars, they be too loud." Cled made a show of coughing like a sick man. Augum winced as he opened the door. Sure enough, it squeaked, but the guards hadn't noticed. It worked. He snuck through unseen and took his first look around, quickly realizing just how dangerous this was. There were two guards patrolling back and forth down a long corridor, currently pacing off to the left. He would not have much time to get back in his cell. The knees of another sentry protruded from the far right. He hoped that sentry had the keys.

For the first time, he saw Bridget and Mya, disheveled but unharmed. Bridget held a hand over her mouth while Mya bit her lip. Both eyed him with great concern, though he wasn't sure if that was from the way his face looked, or the situation, or both. Nonetheless, seeing them buoyed his spirits.

He prowled to the right, finger on his lips. Frightened emaciated faces watched from the cells between him and the sitting sentry. As he crept past the last three, he was able to see the man scribbling away at a parchment. Thankfully, a ring of keys hung above his shoulder on the wall. Should the man raise his head, should the patrolling guards turn sooner than usual, or should his timing be off even a little—

Augum sharpened his focus, ignoring his many aches and pains. The lives of his friends depended on his next action. There was only one chance—he would have to use Telekinesis in a new way.

His heart raced. He better be ready for what he was about to try.

Sweat prickled his forehead as he raised his arm, envisioning the task, sure it could work. He pointed at the keys and made a confident gesture. They silently lifted off the peg. He took a shallow breath to calm his nerves, letting the keys dangle above the man's head, refusing to think about the two guards somewhere behind him, who only needed to turn around to spot him.

A subtle gesture resumed the journey. The keys hovered past cells of wide-eyed prisoners and into his waiting hand. He immediately smothered them in his robe and scurried back to his cell, ignoring the whispers. Miraculously, the guards at the other end had stopped to argue about some woman, for if they had been patrolling like normal, he would have been late returning to his cell.

He slipped through the door as Cled faked another coughing fit. When he held up his prize, the old man's eyes brightened.

"Done craziest thing I ever seen. Hope ye know what ye be doing, boy."

So did he, but there was no time to dwell on it. The next part was crucial and time was of the essence. What he was about to attempt demanded precision and a large amount of luck. He waited until the two guards patrolled by again. They were still arguing about a woman, yet all they needed to do was look at the spot where the keys once hung and it would be over.

He heard them converse with the sentry. Don't notice the empty peg, don't notice the empty peg!

Thankfully, they continued their patrol without raising the alarm. Almost as soon as they passed back to the left, he gave the signal and Cled started coughing. He readied to open the cell door—

"Shut it, old man!" said one of the guards, making his way back to Cled's cell. "Sick of hearing your hacks. Die already!"

Cled threw a hand over his mouth and nodded, eyes cast to the floor. The glaring guard turned, glanced at Augum—whose white-knuckled hands gripped the bars—scowled, and returned to conversing with his colleague.

The only thing to do now was to wait for a loud noise of some kind. The patrol soon wandered by again, postponing the escape further. Augum felt a bead of sweat roll down his temple. It was only a matter of time until a guard discovered the keys stolen.

A commotion erupted from the right.

His heart sank. That's it, they've been found …

"Attention! The Lord of the Legion arrives!" someone yelled. Many cried in despair, fearing the worst. The two patrolling guards rushed by. "Make sure the report is done before the lord arrives!" one of them said.

"Aug—" Leera whispered from her cell, "all the guards but the sentry are gone now. Hurry—"

"I'm on it—"

After being put to the question, he no longer felt the urge to talk his father out of his ambitions. No, they were getting out of there right then. He opened his cell door just enough to squeeze through, the squeak muffled by the general tumult. He withdrew the iron ring and realized he had no clue which key it was. There must have been hundreds. He stared at them, dumbstruck.

Leera reached out. "Here, let me help—"

He handed the ring to her and she began sorting.

"Look, they have symbols—"

Sure enough, each key had a tiny symbol engraved on it, like a triangle with a dot inside it, or a square within a square, and so on. He found a tiny symbol just above the lock—a circle with a triangle inside—found the respective key, and opened her cell.

"Excellent—" Leera whispered, giving his hand a squeeze before the pair scampered on to Mya's cell. This time Leera helped and they found the key almost immediately. Mya, whose almond eyes had dark circles underneath, flashed a grateful smile that made Augum's stomach flutter.

Bridget's cell was last. By this time, some of the other prisoners began pleading for release, even threatening to raise the alarm if they weren't freed.

Augum made gestures indicating they'd all be freed but to be patient. He ran back to Cled's cell and threw him the keys.

"Boy, ye crazy—!"

Augum inspected the lock. "Your symbol is a circle within a circle. Free as many as you can. Good luck—" and he rushed to his friends who anxiously watched a pair of knees at the end of the corridor. The sentry frantically scribbled away, trying to finish his report, doing his best to ignore all the commotion in the cells.

They had to get past him to escape.

Bridget quickly swept cinnamon hair from her face. "I have an idea—"

To their utter horror, she strolled right up the sitting guard and raised her arm. "SHYNEO!" An ivy ring formed around her wrist just as her palm exploded with writhing vines.

Parchment flew as the guard jumped.

"I am a warlock, and if you so much as move, I will entangle you and squeeze until you suffocate!"

It was a tremendous gamble. Had the guard any knowledge of arcanery, he would have instantly known a warlock with a single degree would not have that power.

The guard froze.

Bridget, never dropping eye contact, gestured for them to run past. The other prisoners begged for release, but they had to be ignored. There was no time.

"How do we get out of here?" Bridget asked as Augum ran by, the tumult in the cells rising.

The guard's eyes shifted about before he stuttered a reply. "You go right twice and then left—"

But Augum remembered the smell of winter from near the interrogation room, which was a right, a left, up thirty steps, and right at a fork.

"He's lying—" he said. "Don't worry, I know where it is. Follow me—"

Bridget scowled and the ivy around her palm seemed to snake faster.

"Please—" began the young guard, dropping to his knees. "Don't kill me, young miss, I didn't mean it, honest … you don't understand what they'll do to me—"

"Lie on the floor face down and stay there—"

The guard did as he was told and they ran off. The hallways flew by in a blur—a right, a left, up thirty steps, the fork. Augum peeked around the corner to the left, where the smell of the outdoors came from. He was distinctly aware of the iron interrogation room just to the right. Bridget, Leera and Mya stood close behind, silent as mice.

"I think they're readying to meet my father," he murmured, watching guards race by through an adjoining corridor that appeared to go outside. Many of them had put on their cloaks or surcoats, trying to look as official as possible. He waited until they were gone and gestured to move. The group scurried past a series of rooms until they stood in an exit corridor.

Augum peeked outside through the rustic door left open by the guards. It looked to be midday, though he couldn't be sure as it was gray and cloudy. Near the center of town, a decent distance away, it appeared all of Commander Tridian's men gathered around a column of caravans and horses.

"Must be around two hundred men or so," Leera whispered.

The entire village seemed to have turned out as well, some with fear on their faces, though many cheering. Mothers held muddy children close. Chickens squawked and dogs ran amok in the filthy snow. Horses whinnied and soldiers raised triumphant shouts.

"We have to find His Royal Highness—" Mya said.

"He's probably in the sick ward," Bridget replied

"What about our stuff?" Leera asked.

Augum gave them a dark look. "Tridian's command post."

They didn't reply. Everyone understood the risks.

"I think I remember where it is," Leera said. "Follow me."

They snuck out of the low gray-stoned keep, darting amongst carts, stacks of hay, peat houses, and torches flickering on iron stands. It would have been difficult to do had there not been such commotion.

"His Eminence has come, His Eminence has come to see us!" cried one peasant woman with only one front tooth, reminding Augum of Cled.

"Blessed are we, soon the receivers of eternal life!" cried another peasant in rough-spun wools.

They continued on, circling the edge of the village, Leera leading. The guards had left their posts to greet the Lord of the Legion, allowing the group to sneak right up to Tridian's quarters. The log house abutted the trees, a single shuttered window visible. They hid behind a stack of barrels, listening for sounds from within.

The crowd hooped and hollered, sending up cheer after cheer, coming closer and closer, until the doors inside Tridian's quarters sprang open. The foursome froze, listening through the gap in the shutters. A gaggle of voices flooded the interior. Floorboards creaked and groaned. There seemed to be some ceremony in how they organized themselves, until Augum heard his father's voice for the first time since the butchering of Sparrow's Perch.

THE LORD OF THE LEGION

"Commander Tridian," the Lord of the Legion began, "your reputation has grown since last we met. Good news comes often written in your hand."

"My lord flatters me."

Sparkstone's voice carried to the crowd gathered inside. "My loyal commander is quite modest, so I am sure he has not yet told you how he has earned the appellation 'the Blade of Sorrows'."

"He indeed has not!"

"Do tell, Great Lord!"

"Let us hear it—"

"It was I that bestowed the title on the man standing before me, and how well deserved it has become. Commander Tridian, who was then, what, a lieutenant—?"

"That is correct, my lord."

"When he was nothing more than a lieutenant, Tridian took hostage the family of the Headmaster of the Academy of Arcane Arts, who had barricaded himself, the pupils, and remaining warlocks inside the academy. The black castle had already fallen, and here was this old fool, refusing to surrender, for the 'children's sake', or some such nonsense.

"Incidentally, some of you may note the headmaster was the successor to my grandmother, who, if you ask my opinion, had more sense in her little finger than this old fool had in totality." There was some strained chuckling. "In any case, Lieutenant Tridian dragged the man's family before the walls of the academy. When the old man refused to surrender, Tridian said—and please help me if I mistake your words, Commander—he said, 'You will find nothing but sorrow on my blade!' Now what did that old fool say back to you again?"

"Something to the effect of, 'You would not murder family, let us battle as men'. "

"So, in full view of the son and daughter and every eye from that academy, Tridian unsheathed his blade and chopped off the wife's head." Sparkstone paused, his voice quiet. "The silence was the loudest I had ever heard. The sight was almost comic in its absurdity. That head bounced along the ground and came to rest at the feet of the fool's daughter. She said nothing, only stood there like a daft cow. Now, guess what the old man did."

"Surrendered!" cried the throng.

"Ah, but you underestimate the resolve of this old fool. He came from a long line of fools—*A*rcaners, what with their silly code and such. The man refused again, begging to resolve the conflict as men, calling us cowards and dogs and unleashing his pale wit at our honor. Now mind you, I had my first scion at the time, so we were quite safe. Nonetheless, it got under Tridian's skin, did it not, the words he had said?"

"A point needed to be made."

"Indeed. Indeed …" Sparkstone paused, the crowd hanging on to every word. "So the lieutenant rips the boy from the hands of his sister and chops off his head too. Let me tell you all, never had I seen such a man capitulate so quickly and weep so hard."

"Motivation is a tricky thing."

"And you are a shining example on its use, my good man. The cause is greater than a child, a wife, a kingdom. You did a good thing that day. The academy needed to be brought to its knees, and you brought it down with only two lives." Sparkstone paused again as Augum exchanged looks with the girls, their faces slack with horror.

"And that is the story behind the Blade of Sorrows."

There were claps and respectful murmurs from the crowd. Augum stiffened as the floorboards creaked close to the window. A bottle was uncorked, the contents poured into many cups.

"A toast—to the Blade of Sorrows!"

"The Blade of Sorrows!"

"Very good. Now let us move this meeting along. A report, dear Commander."

"As my lord commands," Tridian said, a tinge of relief in his voice. "Allow me to dispense of the minutiae first. The men and I stand ready to serve. As for the peasants, the Great Quest is having the desired effect. They long for eternal life and are joining the cause in droves. The only trouble we are having is feeding them. The harvest was poor this season, trade has plummeted, and the roads marred by traitors."

"Revolutions have complications. The food situation will be rectified when we take Tiberra. We shall raid their renowned winter stores like wolves feasting on hare."

The crowd tittered.

"I am humbled by my lord's compliments." Tridian walked near the shuttered window and retrieved something. "Allow me to present my lord with a gift."

"Why, that is the family blade," Sparkstone said in a fond voice. "How appropriate that my son carried it, as his own father had."

Augum felt a hot prickle—he did not want to be compared to this vile man in any way.

"So he is indeed here. I shall see the boy shortly. Thank you, Commander. You have done well. Expect an adequate reward."

"Sire, in ye hand a Dreadnought Blade ye doth hold," said a guttural voice that sounded like two large millstones grinding together.

The crowd stirred.

"Is it now? Well then, the old crone sure loves her secrets!" Laughter rippled among the men. "Tridian, may I introduce Dredius Hestius, my Dreadnought commander. I do believe he is older than all the men in this room put together."

"My lord, it gladdens my heart to hear the stories are true. All hail the Lord of Dreadnoughts!"

"HAIL!"

A Dreadnought, a real Dreadnought—! Augum wished he could see what it he looked like, but dared not take a peek.

"Thank you, dear commander. Dredius, what else can you tell me about this blade?"

"At Master's command I doth serve." The Dreadnought's words came slowly, as if he had all the time in the world. "This ancient blade is thus named Burden's Edge. It hath been forged for one Atrius Arinthian, amidst the wars of the scions."

The crowd stirred as Augum gave the girls a significant look. He had been wielding his ancestor's sword the whole time!

"Thank you, ancient commander," Sparkstone said when the chatter died down. "Amazing, is it not? Dreadnoughts somehow know every single item forged by their kind. The perfect arcaneologists. I shall carry this blade in honor of my legendary ancestor. Pity I had to raise the man and then sacrifice him anew."

Gasps came from the crowd.

"My lord—?" Commander Tridian said.

"You heard me correctly, Commander. It was quite the problem I faced—how to become the Lord of Dreadnoughts when their last master had forsaken them. The answer was remarkably simple if you think about it, though the task actually quite complex—raise the man, sacrifice him, and choose to become their master. Only a necromancer could accomplish such a feat."

Silence followed.

"I assure you the ceremony was the most difficult thing I have ever undertaken, the arcanery well beyond my abilities. Thankfully, three scions did aid in the matter."

The crowd chortled.

"Would you believe it though, that I had to step across the body of none other than Commander Rames to get inside the mausoleum housing Arinthian's bones?"

"Your son confessed to his slaying, my lord," Tridian said.

"Is that right? So the boy was down there. How peculiar. What else did he confess to?"

"Only exactly the information we have been seeking—the location of Anna Atticus Stone. She heads to see the mountain monks."

The crowd murmured approval.

"That is most welcome information indeed, Commander." Sparkstone paced a moment. "There is only one reason for her to journey there—she wishes to see the Seers, probably to ask how to defeat me."

The crowd rumbled with nervous laughter just as the door flew open.

"My great lord!" called a boy's voice from the back of the cabin. Augum felt a flush of anger upon hearing that voice.

"This is the boy I told my lord about," Commander Tridian said, voice bubbling with pride.

"Ah, a young necrophyte. Look here men—witness the future of the Legion. Commander Tridian has already filled me in on your efforts, young man. You have reaped honor upon the cause. I shall reward you with personal instruction."

"My lord, I am extremely grateful." A pause, in which Augum imagined Robin's stupid face bowing down and kissing Sparkstone's boots.

"I come bearing you a gift," Robin continued.

"A gift?"

"Yes. Him."

"You've brought me a boy?"

The crowd chuckled.

"This is Prince Sydo Ridian the fourth. He is a personal friend of mine. I convinced him his father's death was unfortunate but necessary. He is ready to serve the cause and earn the rewards."

Augum glanced at Bridget in alarm. Her face was red, but whether it was from anger, fear, or sadness, he couldn't tell.

"My father was always weak," Prince Sydo said in a pompous voice. "He loved books and council more than anything. He refused to believe in the eternal, but I know the eternal exists, for I have seen the ancient ones for myself. I have been to Ley! I have personally witnessed their arcanery and long life!"

"Impossible …" someone said.

"A fable …"

"The boy curries favor with lies!"

"Oh, do we have nonbelievers here?" Sparkstone asked. "Because if we do …" a tense pause. "You speak of things your little minds barely understand. This boy speaks true, does he not, Commander Tridian?"

"He indeed speaks true, my lord. I have questioned him personally. This boy has been to Ley. He has seen the Leyans."

"Make no mistake," Sparkstone said, "the Leyans are real, and they will give us what we desire. I shall extend the lives of all my loyal followers with their knowledge. We shall all reap the rewards."

"Hear hear!"

"Now, young prince, I am sorry about your father, but know this—he died a noble death, a worthy death. He perished because he believed in neither destiny, providence, nor the might of the Legion. He refused to retire humbly. Above all, he refused to give me his support. Thus, he had to be made example of."

"My father chose the wrong side. I will not make the same mistake. I had to endure the insufferable companionship of rotten, gutterborn—"

The crowd gasped and stirred.

"Begging your pardon, Great One," Sydo blubbered quickly, "I did not mean to infer—"

"—that my own son was gutterborn. No, I do not believe you intended to infer such a thing, for if you had, I would have you quartered this moment."

A deathly silence.

"Now tell me, how did you enter Ley?"

Sydo's voice was meek. "Through the fountain portal in Castle Arinthian, Sire. The crone—excuse me, your grandmother—opened it with her scion."

"Crone is just fine," Sparkstone said, much to the amusement of the crowd.

"Also, the, uh, crone destroyed the other portals. The one in Castle Arinthian is the only one left."

"Then she is a fool for leaving it. You and I have something in common, boy. I am the rightful heir to that scion and you are the rightful heir to the Solian throne. When the time comes, if you continue to show your loyalty, the throne shall return to you. When I become emperor, I will want someone ... loyal ... in the Solian seat."

"Oh, Sire ... that is my only dream—to serve you, I mean."

The crowd laughed a little.

"Ah, but do you not wield any other ambitions?"

"Robin told me what I could become. He says I have great potential. I want to be powerful like him, and one day, maybe even like you."

More chuckling.

"And ... and I do not care to traipse about with minor spells! That is why I wish to become a necrophyte—"

"Is that so?"

"That is so, my lord, and I offer proof of my newfound loyalty—information of even greater value."

Augum barely felt his nails dig into his palms.

"Go on."

"The elders of Ley have said that, should you ever fulfill the Great Quest and come to possess all seven scions, you and the scions would be destroyed—"

Bridget and Leera gasped, immediately clasping their mouths. Luckily, the tumult from within had drowned them out. Bridget sniffed and hid her face in her hands while

Leera held her in comfort. Mya's almond eyes only reflected fear and confusion.

That traitor, Augum thought venomously. Even after they had saved his life … they should have left him behind in that cabin. He'd bet it all that Sydo was too cowardly to tell them the other truth he knew, that taking the powers of long life beyond Ley was impossible. He wished he could stick his head through the window and yell that his great-grandfather died to pass that precious information along. He wished he could run in there and punch both Robin and Sydo in the face.

Sparkstone silenced the crowd. "Are you sure about this, boy? Look at me and say it true."

"It is true, Great Lord."

"Commander?"

"The boy speaks true, my lord."

"I see. Then I will simply have to find a way around this … ancient measure."

"There is more," Sydo continued. "Magua, one of the elders, said there exists a recipe to make a portal to Ley *without* using a scion."

In the deep silence that followed, the huddled foursome exchanged defeated looks. If there had been any doubts where Sydo's loyalties lay …

"That is most interesting. And you say one of the elders, this … Magua … offered this information freely?"

"She did, Great Lord. I was most surprised myself, but then my sharp memory allowed me to remember these kinds of details—"

"Enough," Sparkstone interrupted, pacing. He began speaking in an undertone, as if only to himself. "Some serious research is in order. It would be wise to uncover this alternate method in case my grandmother slithers away again." He paused, resuming in a firm voice. "Your valuable service to the Legion is duly noted. You shall keep your title as prince, and when the time comes, you will be King of Solia."

"A toast to Prince Sydo Ridian the Fourth, heir to Solia!" Commander Tridian said.

"To the heir of Solia!" the crowd chanted.

Glasses clinked and congratulations were expressed.

"Now, we need to find my dear grandmother and lay a trap for her."

A pair of heavy boots stepped close. The foursome froze. The butcher of Sparrow's Perch, of Bridget and Leera's families, stood on the other side of those shutters. Scions hummed. Augum envisioned them hovering around golden armor. He expected those shutters to fly open and a golden-mailed hand grab him.

"I have come up with a plan, my lord," Commander Tridian said.

Sparkstone stepped away from the window. "Good, you can tell me all about it later, right now I want to see my son. We have much to do together—" but he was interrupted by someone bursting in through the doors.

"Begging your pardon, my lords, my liege—" a panting guard said. "The prisoners—they're loose. All of them!"

Augum exchanged a wild look with the girls. Cled!

A flurry of activity started immediately, with commands issued and calls thrown up. A moment later, Tridian's quarters were empty.

"That swine brat pile of dung heap," Leera muttered, still holding Bridget, whose shoulder heaved. "Knew he was no good."

"I'm going in," Augum said, opening the shutters.

Leera grabbed his arm. "Are you mad—?"

"Trust me."

She hesitantly let go. "Just be careful."

He nodded and slipped inside, doing his best to ignore the grinding bones in his chest. The floorboards creaked and he stopped. There were shouts outside but no one entered. He glanced around.

Glasses of wine lay strewn about, some broken in the rush to exit. He tiptoed over to Tridian's ornate campaign desk, where he found Blackbite, Mrs. Stone's blue book on arcaneology, and a small leather bag of coins. There was also a sheepskin map covered with military figurines. He yanked it with great satisfaction before realizing he should have at least studied where the figurines sat.

He spotted their rucksack in the corner and hurriedly stuffed the items inside.

The shouts from outside grew louder so he scuttled back through the window, reaching into the rucksack and withdrawing Blackbite. "Here, this should cheer you up."

Bridget smiled weakly.

"My father took Burden's Edge, but I got Mrs. Stone's book, a map, and coins. Now let's get out of here—"

"Wait—" Leera said. "We'll never survive out there without winter clothing and food."

"What about the trapper's cabin?"

"They burnt it down," Bridget replied, drying her eyes. "Besides, it's the first place they'll look."

Leera peeked around the barrels. "We have to hurry, it's mayhem out there."

"We could steal some horses," he said.

"M'lady Bridget," Mya began, "one of the first things we saw on the way into town was a stable."

"We did, didn't we? Come on, this way."

Bridget led them prowling through the surrounding woods. The village was in chaos—peasants were mistaken for prisoners and beaten; animals ran loose from their pens; groups of black-armored soldiers raided homes, kicking down the doors. The remaining guards fanned out. The group ducked behind a snowy bush as soldiers ran past into the forest chasing a hapless peasant.

They finally spotted the stable, the last building on the edge of the village. Two horses remained, both palfreys—one chestnut brown, the other cloud gray. Unfortunately, there was also a group of armed Black Guards headed straight for them.

The foursome huddled in the forest across from the stables.

"We need those horses," Augum said, mind racing.

"I have an idea," Mya whispered. "I will distract them. You get the horses and go."

Bridget's brows crossed. "And how do you plan to catch up with us?"

Mya gave her a grave look. As they protested, she shook her head. "It is our only chance! Besides, I would only slow you down. They do not want or need me." Her brilliant eyes fell upon him. "They want you, Augum."

"Mya—" he began, his breath catching.

"I will be fine. Good luck, my dear lord and ladies," and before anyone could grab her, she shot out from their hiding spot.

Just like that, she was gone.

He was about to call after her when Leera slammed her hand over his mouth. He quickly nodded, agreeing it would have been stupid. They simply had to take the chance Mya afforded them.

He watched with a knotted stomach as the most beautiful girl he had ever seen ran past the guards, yelling something to the trees opposite, as if there was someone there. Whatever she said worked because the guards immediately gave chase, all but one of them, a big soldier with a double-sided axe.

"I know what to do," Leera suddenly said. She crouched down, as if waiting to sprint, the look of a tiger in her eye. "Centeratoraye xao xen." Her head dropped in readiness. "Get the horses!" A heartbeat after, she set off racing through the snow. Her movements were fluid like a cat, and the last thing the axe-wielding guardsman seemed to expect was an attack from a young girl. Leera pounced on the man with such momentum she knocked him to the ground.

Meanwhile, Augum and Bridget sprinted for the horses. He jumped onto the gray horse, ribs screaming from the abrupt movement. Bridget mounted the chestnut. The horses whinnied, drawing the attention of some of the guards who had run after Mya, the rest having disappeared in the trees.

He glanced back to witness Leera jump away from the guard and face one of the soldiers that had turned towards her, a wiry man with a crossbow. Augum shouted out a warning but Leera just stood there, poised with confidence. The soldier aimed carefully and let loose a bolt. Augum's heart jammed in his throat, but Leera summoned an arcane shield made of pond leaves and the bolt ricocheted off.

They sprinted toward her as the man fumbled to reload. She wobbled where she stood—Centarro was wearing off. Luckily, she still had the wherewithal to jump onto Bridget's horse, barely hanging on to the saddle. Bridget helped her up and they galloped away.

They were riding through the forest with no sense of direction, leaving obvious tracks—it was just a matter of time until the Legion rounded up more horses and gave chase. "Hold on to her!" Augum shouted, raising a hand to ward off low-hanging branches. Plumes of snow exploded with each strike.

His thoughts drifted to Mya's brave sacrifice, and he almost turned the horse around, wanting to use Centarro to save her. His heart lurched thinking of not being able to look into those emerald eyes again.

EVERGRAY TOWER

"I'll miss her," Leera mumbled, shivering, breath fogging.

"She was like a big sister," Bridget said through chattering teeth.

Leera nodded. "She was kind of quiet, but I never thought she could be so brave …"

Augum said nothing, feeling hollow and, strangely, like he had been left behind.

They had stopped in a shallow valley, lightly wooded and quiet. The clouds were darkening overhead as an ominous black mass approached from the east.

He worried they would be caught in a storm, which in this cold, meant certain death. Trying not to think about it too much, or Mya, he withdrew Tridian's map and splayed it across the chestnut's flank.

"Where do you think we are?" Bridget asked, rubbing her arms, lips trembling.

He fingered the map. "There's Tornvale. Nearest town is Candledale." He glanced to the east again. "But that storm will overtake us well before we get there."

Leera squinted up. "Yeah, but if we made it, we could purchase food and board with the coin."

He took a good look at the girls. Their burgundy apprentice robes were quite worn now, hair unkempt, faces dirty, hands bruised. The red welt on the side of Leera's head ran all the way down her cheek. On top of that, they were hungry, cold, tired, without shelter and, like him, lacked appropriate winter clothing.

In fact, ever since Mrs. Stone had left the group, everything had gone wrong—his great-grandfather had died, they had suffered imprisonment, and now Mya had most certainly been captured. Even Burden's Edge was gone. Their possessions consisted of Blackbite, a bag of coin, the blue book on arcaneology, a rucksack, and two palfreys. The only thing they had accomplished was spilling secrets and saving the life of the prince, only to have him turn traitor. Now, they were probably going to freeze to death in a storm, and even *if* they didn't freeze to death, the Legion would likely catch up to them, and if not the Legion, maybe some undead walker—

"Stop it, Aug," Leera said, voice slowed by the cold.

"Stop what?"

"You're worrying. I can see it on your face." She gave him a light punch on the shoulder. "Mya's a big girl and can take care of herself. She was always too old for you anyway."

"And if they put her to the question?"

"Don't think of that. Besides, she's right, she doesn't know anything."

"That doesn't mean they won't try."

Leera sighed. "Hold still, I'm tired of staring at all that crusty blood on your face." She took a bit of snow and gently wiped his face with her sleeve.

He winced. His nose was still tender.

She smiled. "Much better. How's your chest?"

"Trying to be Mya now?"

A hurt look passed over her face and she turned away.

Bridget flashed him a stern look that said he should probably apologize.

"I'm sorry, I didn't mean that."

Leera shrugged. "I know."

"How's your side doing?" he asked, remembering that awful moment the guard shoved his spear at her.

She didn't meet his eyes. "Better."

The one word answer. She was mad. "Um …" Apologies were hard. "Sorry. For being a jerk and all."

Leera glanced back but Augum had returned to the map, not wanting to confront the strange butterfly feeling in his stomach.

"We have to find shelter. I think we're here." He stabbed a lightly wooded and hilly area. Northeast from that spot was a series of branched rivers titled *The Creeping Fingers.* North of the Fingers stood Blackwood, inked with bony trees, and far north of Blackwood stood Mt. Barrow.

"We need to lose our trail and find shelter," he continued, tracing the river branches. "We could ride along the river to here." He tapped a small dot titled *The Ruins of Evergray Tower*.

Leera stood silently observing him before smirking. "Ruins, eh? Sounds exciting." There was warmth in her dark eyes.

"Let's do it then," Bridget said, "but we have to hurry. Those clouds don't look right."

The trio was soon underway again, trotting through a gently rolling wood that eventually gave way to a snowy plain dotted with wiry shrubs. By the time they came upon the river, a biting wind had kicked up. They dismounted to let the palfreys drink.

"I'm going to call her Spirit," Bridget said, watching her horse slurp.

"I'm not naming mine," he said, remembering lying atop old Meli while she slowly died.

"Why not?"

"Because it'll be harder to let him go."

Leera gave him a playful elbow. "You growing up on us now? Don't be so serious."

He shrugged, marveling how carefree she could be under the circumstances. Perhaps she was right though. The weight of all that had happened made him feel older and more responsible, but he was still only fourteen. Well, almost fifteen actually, one year short of becoming a man, but still ...

"Let's follow the river," he said. "It'll obscure our tracks."

"Let me take the reins, Bridge," Leera said. "You rest up."

They mounted, trotting close to the bank. His stomach gurgled. He hadn't eaten a proper meal in ages. His thoughts drifted to all the exquisite dishes he ate with Sir Westwood. Plum sauce with chicken, roast leg of lamb, buttered and seasoned potatoes, salt beef, wheels of cheese, even broccoli soup seemed appealing right now. He was torturing himself with these visions, practically tasting each dish on his tongue, when a jagged outline began to take shape across the river. Plumes of snow blew off it in the wind.

The ruins of Evergray Tower loomed silent and abandoned. Snow piled up against the lipped base. Dead vines clung to crumbling stone. The tower itself appeared smashed as if by some giant fist, the top half completely exposed to the sky. Windows gaped like mouths screaming in agony.

"Not a very cozy-looking place, is it?" Leera said.

The storm approached relentlessly, Augum noted with a glance. At least it would obscure their tracks. He led his palfrey across the shallow water, wondering how they would feed themselves and the horses. They paced by the iced remains of a ruined dock and on to the base of the tower.

"Shyneo," he said, lighting up his palm.

Leera pointed. "Is that a gate?"

What he had mistaken for a wall of dead vines was indeed the remains of a rather large rusted iron gate. If they could get it open, they may even be able to hide the horses inside.

They dismounted and tied up the palfreys. Beyond the gate was a cobbled stone room full of rubble and broken barrels. Augum directed his palm to the gate lock. It was a crude mechanism long rusted over.

"Hmm, think Repair would work on this?" he asked, plucking at the brown mass.

"Worth a try," Leera said, holding shivering hands around the lock.

Bridget suddenly grabbed her arm. "Wait a moment—we don't want to *repair* it, we want to *smash* it. After all, we don't have the key."

"Good point." He reached for a large rock. "Watch out." The girls stood back as he repeatedly slammed it on the lock, distinctly conscious how every hit echoed around the chamber and out across the river. With each strike, the lock weakened, until finally snapping off.

He dropped the rock, panting and holding his sides, the grating in his chest causing shooting pains. Maybe that wasn't such a good idea with broken ribs.

Leera placed a hand on his shoulder. "You all right?"

He winced. "Fine," and pulled on the gate, as if to show her he wasn't hurting, when he so obviously was—and it wasn't just a dull pain either, it was so acute it made him jerk suddenly, letting go of the gate.

Leera cocked her head and gave him a playful smile. "You don't always need to play the hero, you know."

But he barely heard her past the pain. Yup, he needed a healer.

The iron hinges were so rusted over that it eventually took all three of them to jar the gate loose. The girls then led the palfreys inside while he used an evergreen branch to clean up their tracks, all the way to the river, just in case. The wind was soon gusting with such violence he almost felt sorry for anyone tailing them.

As he returned to the girls, Leera waved him over. "Look at this. I think there're unopened barrels under this rubble."

They looked at each other and chorused, "Telekinesis?"

Bridget quickly joined in, reminding him of the time they cleared the doorway of Castle Arinthian. Soon rocks were flying everywhere, revealing a series of unopened oaken barrels banded with rusted iron.

"They had to have been meant for market once," Bridget said, breathing hard from the exertion. "Must have been abandoned by a merchant."

The first barrel was tightly sealed. They had to wedge the lid open with Blackbite. Inside were rectangular objects, wrapped in boiled linen.

"What could these be?" he asked, unwrapping one. Inside was a hard brown chunk, like solidified dirt.

Leera crinkled her nose. "Is that dung?"

"Gah!" He dropped it, moved on to the next barrel.

Bridget picked it up and nibbled on one corner.

Leera gagged. "Bridge, are you—"

"I don't believe it. You know what this is—?"

They gaped at her in revulsion.

"It's biscuit beef!" Bridget tore a chunk off with her teeth. "Must be ancient though."

Leera picked one up and inspected it. "Wouldn't it be bad by now?"

"Not biscuit beef, it's specially made to last through long merchant journeys. I tried it on one of my father's trade missions to Antioc, though it was much softer. This stuff is *really* expensive."

Augum tried biting into one. "I think rocks are softer."

"It's frozen," Bridget replied. "Soften it by chewing on it."

Leera offered a few pieces to the horses. They bit into them immediately. "I think they're hungry."

Augum shrugged. "Well, you stick anything in front of a horse's mouth when it's starved ..."

Leera returned to the barrel. "Enough here to last us a lifetime." She took another small nip of the one she had started. "Though I think it'll take me that long to eat just one," adding with a mutter, "and it still looks like dung."

The wind howled outside, whistling through cracks in the stone. The last remnants of light faded and they had to use Shine to see. They cleared more debris and opened four other barrels, though the remains of two were fruit that had long rotted away. One had nothing but axe handles. The last held colorful striped wool blankets, probably once destined for some rich linen shop. They quickly wrapped themselves up, sat cross-legged in a circle, and gorged on the beef while going over the days' events. Outside, the storm turned into a raging blizzard.

When Augum brought up Sydo, Bridget fell silent. When Leera brought up Mya, Augum fell silent. When anyone brought up how to reach Mrs. Stone before the Legion did, everyone fell silent.

"Oh, come on, let's just talk," Leera said through chattering teeth, freckled cheeks shining in the watery-blue glow of her palm. "It'll keep us distracted from the cold. Got nothing better to do anyway."

Bridget rested her head on her palm. "I thought if I could just *show* him kindness …"

Leera unwrapped another chunk. "Bridge, if a Leyan Karma didn't work on him …"

"Yeah," Augum said, "and thanks to his traitorous big mouth, my father now knows acquiring all the scions would destroy him. So we don't even have *that* as an option anymore."

Leera waved her beef chunk around as she spoke. "Not to mention your father now also knows there's a recipe that can build him a portal without a scion."

"I know, I know," Bridget said. "I'm just … disappointed."

"And he's supposed to be our next king," Leera muttered. "Great."

Augum unwrapped his second chunk. "Imagine if the Seers advised Nana to give Sparkstone the scion, but he figures out a way to keep all seven?"

"I think the Seers would *see* that, wouldn't they?" Leera said. "I mean, isn't that what they do?"

"Yeah, and wouldn't they see that he saw—" He blinked. "Forget it. I'm not even going to try."

"Mrs. Stone is going to ask the Seers how to defeat your father," Bridget said. "It's what she told us before she left."

"Right," he said. "Otherwise I was supposed to join him and talk him out of it."

Leera scoffed. "Yeah, *that* would have worked."

They finished their beef, each lost in thought.

"All right, I have to do some exploring or I'll freeze to death," Leera said.

Bridget nodded. "Agreed. Besides, Mrs. Stone told us to practice our spells every day. Pretty sure she meant all of them. Let's go look for things to cast them on."

They left everything but Bridget's Dreadnought dagger behind. Palms lighting their way, the trio searched the area and found a black oaken door with vertical iron strapping. Strangely, it appeared to have no handle or lock. There was no way to open it, not even using Blackbite as a wedge.

"Think it's arcane?" Augum asked.

"Maybe you have to perform some kind of secret knock or something," Leera said, examining the frame. They joined her, pawing at the wall for any buttons or hidden levers like the secret passageways in Castle Arinthian.

Bridget finally stepped back with an exasperated sigh. "I'm trying Unconceal." She splayed her hands out while Augum and Leera shone their palms at the door for her. After a time of silent concentration, she said, "Un vun deo," and stood there a moment, before letting her hand guide her to a portion of the wall.

"There's something hidden here."

They gathered closely as Bridget pushed on a stone. It collapsed inwards into the wall and the door sprung open with a click.

"Nice one." Leera pulled at the door. The iron hinges shrieked in complaint, the sound reminding Augum of the Legion's prison.

A spiral staircase hugged the wall of the tower. Strangely, it was muggy and smelled a little like a farmyard. The tower groaned in the muffled roar of the wind.

Leera peered around the cobwebbed steps. "All right, castle know-it-all—what was this place used for?"

"I don't know, maybe a watchtower or something," he said.

"Not some foul warlock's home?"

"Could be ..."

"Shyneo." Bridget's hand lit up with glowing ivy.

"All right, down or up?" he asked.

"Up," the girls chorused immediately.

He nodded and led the way, slowly traversing the steps.

They came upon another oaken door embedded in the center portion of the tower. This time there was a simple bronze handle, which Augum turned. The door squeaked as it opened inwards, revealing a spacious round room, the contents of which had completely burned, walls blackened with soot. The only thing visibly undamaged was a massive chandelier in the shape of a caravan wheel, hanging from a high ceiling.

"What a waste of books," Bridget said, picking up the crispy remains of a leather tome. "Wait—it's in the arcane tongue." She and Augum gave Leera an eerie look—perhaps it *was* the tower of some foul warlock after all ...

"Let's search the place," he said.

The trio flipped over burnt furniture and kicked aside debris, until at last Bridget picked up a yellow book that had mostly survived the flames.

"This one's in the common tongue." She pawed at the pages, eyes widening. "You're not going to believe this, but it's on the elements!" She began reading a passage. " 'The caster must be aware of the potential backlash when invoking the power of the Snaking Vine, for it can entwine her if she is not mindful.' " She looked up. "It's talking about an Earth spell! Do you know what this means? We can now study our elements!"

"Well, at least some of them," Leera said, picking off a burnt scrap.

"Maybe we can find an unburned copy," Augum said as Bridget passed it to him. It was a leather-bound tome not unlike Mrs. Stone's. The index and the first few introductory pages were missing. Still, it covered all the major elements—earth, fire, water, air, ice, lightning, and healing.

"Mya would have loved the section on healing," Bridget said.

"Can we please stop talking about her?" he said, shoving the book into Leera's hands. He pretended to search for something in the rubble. He didn't know why he had reacted that way and felt stupid for doing it.

"Sorry, Augum, I didn't mean to bring her up. I know how much you cared—"

"—it doesn't matter, all right? She's gone, probably being tortured as we speak, and I didn't even *try* going back to get her."

"That would have been suicide, and you know it," Leera said.

"We should have never tried to save that traitor in the first place." He turned away.

"You're too hard on yourself," Leera said quietly. "You've done so much. Let it go."

He didn't reply.

"Let's just keep exploring," Bridget said in a shaky voice, storming past him.

Leera sighed. She gave him an *Everything will turn out fine* look before grabbing his sleeve. "Come on."

They mutely climbed the steps one more level, coming upon another door. Bridget gave Leera a furtive look, cheeks red, patently avoiding Augum's gaze.

"Fine, I'll go first." Leera pushed past Bridget and turned the handle. There was a click and then a strange gurgling sound. Lying on the ground just ahead was a scattering of bones that immediately began joining together.

Leera started backing away. "What in the—RUN!" and run they did, as fast as they could, right back down the steps, Augum fully expecting something to snap at his heels. They finally zoomed through the ground level door, slamming it shut behind them and bracing themselves against it.

The palfreys nickered, retreating a few steps.

"I don't hear anything—" Leera whispered, only to be shushed by a frowning Bridget. Soon there was a distinctive creaking shuffle that stopped just on the other side of the door.

"It's right there," mouthed Leera, pointing at the door.

They held their breath.

"We can't hold it forever," Leera whispered finally.

"Maybe it's only waiting until we let go," Bridget said.

Augum glanced to Bridget. She averted her eyes.

"Why don't we come up with a plan?" he asked.

She only shrugged.

Leera glanced between the two of them. "Look, why don't we quietly back away from the door, one at a time? Maybe it doesn't even know how to open it, or maybe it's not allowed to go beyond the tower. Besides, we can arm ourselves with sticks—" she nodded toward the rubble pile by the barrels.

Bridget thought about it a moment. "All right, I'll go first." She detached herself from the door and picked up Blackbite.

Augum and Leera braced, listening.

Nothing.

He reached for his hip before realizing Burden's Edge was with his father. Damn …

Leera edged away from the door next and picked up a barrel slat.

Still nothing.

At last, Augum stepped away. They waited expecting the door to blow open any moment. When it did not, he exchanged relieved looks with Leera. Bridget still wouldn't make eye contact. Maybe it was what he had said about Sydo, how they should never have tried to save him.

Meanwhile, the walls creaked and groaned in the storm. The air was cooling rapidly, a sharp frost that burned their throats.

Leera tossed the slat aside. "It's going to be a hard sleep tonight. We'll need to set watch and start a fire somehow."

Bridget dropped Blackbite onto the rucksack. "I'm going to look around and see if I can find some lamp oil or flint in one of those barrels. Maybe we can start a fire."

Leera handed her a blue and red striped wool blanket. "Here, take one of these."

Bridget wrapped it around herself and stalked off.

Leera delicately touched the welt on her head. "She's mad at you."

"I know, but I don't know what to do about it." He began gathering kindling to start a fire.

"Well, you can wait it out, or … you can just apologize."

"Think I'll just wait it out then."

Leera calmly unwrapped a chunk of biscuit beef. "Your funeral."

"What do you mean? You just said I could wait it out—"

"Yeah, but I didn't say it was the *right* thing to do."

"Oh. Fine, I'll apologize …"

"Look, I know you don't want us talking about her, but she was our friend too. You've got to stop taking it out on us."

He slowly rubbed his forehead. "You're right. I'm sorry."

She punched him on the shoulder and smiled. "All we have is each other. Now let me help."

They gathered wood and kindling for the fire while the cold kept deepening, frost crunching underfoot. It soon became so bad that Bridget returned and curled up in another blanket, trying to warm herself, her expedition a failure.

Augum thought anyone caught in these freezing winds was done for. He was confident they were safe for now, at least from the Legion. The primary threat tonight was the cold.

They built the fire and sat wrapped in blankets. Now they just needed to light it.

"This is bad," he mumbled through chattering teeth, trying to see if the tiny lightning from his Shine spell would set kindling on fire—it couldn't. Even the horses stamped their feet trying to stay warm, their nostrils sending plumes of fog into the crisp air. Bridget mercifully threw a couple blankets on each of them.

"We're going to freeze to death without fire," Leera said. She glanced to the door. He followed her gaze. Then they looked at each other.

"Worth a try," he said.

"Definitely."

Leera drew her hood tighter around her head. "But how are we going to do it?"

"Centarro. It's the only way. Maybe two of us cast it while the third keeps watch and makes sure we don't wander off and do something stupid."

She peered at Bridget, enclosed within a pile of blankets. "We should cast it while Bridget keeps watch. She's the responsible one, after all."

"Agreed, we have to do something about this," Bridget said. "Sleep's impossible. It's just too cold."

Leera and Augum put aside their blankets, allowing the cold to seep right into their bones, and armed themselves with slats.

They had to be very quick.

Bridget positioned herself by the concealed button that opened the door, palm lit, Blackbite in her other hand. Leera and Augum took some time preparing to cast Centarro. He noted the dirty stone floor, the feel of the slat in his hand, and a myriad of other details that may or may not become useful. He ran through the list of other spells he knew—Telekinesis, Shine, Unconceal, Shield, and Repair. As for the side effects of the spell, he was thinking of just sitting down and relaxing.

Shivering, he turned to Leera. "Ready?"

She gave a stiff nod.

"Centeratoraye xao xen!" the pair chorused as Bridget punched the button. The world slowed as he watched the door swing open. The skeleton was indeed right there, shooting forward the moment the door revealed them to its hollow eyes.

Augum noted its awkward steps, judging the best place to strike would be low on the shins. Leera, meanwhile, veered away to the right. He gave cover by raising his arms to attract the skeleton's attention. He absorbed every nuance—how it placed its feet; the sound of the bones grinding together much like his ribs; the sturdy feel of the slat in his grip; and the rapid beat of his own heart.

As the skeleton drew close, reaching for his throat, he ducked and deftly swung the slat at one of its shins. It smashed through the bone, breaking the skeletons' leg. He rolled forward, just in time to see Leera smack the skeleton on the back of its head. Pieces of skull flew in slow motion as the thing tumbled, veering towards the horses. Spirit neighed and rose up on hind quarters. The skeleton fell right underneath as the palfrey slammed its hooves on its ribcage, trampling it to pieces.

The trio threw up a shout of victory, embracing each other in a warm hug.

A few moments later the spell waned, and Augum felt a cloud descend upon his thinking. He was vaguely aware of Bridget placing a blanket around his shoulders, though he was still so cold he had an urge to get away and get warm. In some reptilian recess of his brain, he equated descent with warmth. He was barely aware that Bridget chased after Leera, who seemed to be doing the opposite—trying to go outside.

He let the blanket slip from his shoulders, stumbled through the black oaken door, and fumbled down the steps. With a complacent smile on his face, he followed the simple curved wall. The warmth increased and so he continued, forgetting the world above and his place in it. His fingers stroked the roughly hewn stone, guiding him further and further down into pitch darkness …

It wasn't long until his mind started to sharpen and focus. The dull side effects, like clouds clearing to let the sun shine through, waned and then disappeared altogether.

He froze, the hairs on his neck standing on end.

Where in Sithesia was he? His movements caused an echo that reverberated like in a cavern. The silence seemed to ebb and flow hypnotically. Something was before him, some kind of vast space. He felt its maw open invitingly, like a beast anxious for prey.

Was it alive? Was something there? Best not cast Shine. As his senses sharpened further, he realized there was a pattern to the sound of the darkness—a low, rhythmic heaviness to it, almost like …

Breathing!

ERIKA

After much hesitation, Augum finally scrounged the courage to move. Ever so slowly, he retreated up the spiral steps, back hugging the stone. He let the tower guide him in reverse, the sound of breathing fading … fading …

Bridget snatched his arm the moment he slipped through the door, making him jump. "Augum Stone, where did you go! I was so worried—"

"Shh! There's something down there. I heard it breathing …"

She took a hesitant step into the dark passage but he grabbed her wrist.

"Don't. Trust me on this one."

She paled, nodded. "Of course." Then she smacked his arm with the back of her hand. "But you gave me the worst fright. Don't you *ever* do that again."

"I'm sorry, it was the side effects—"

"You didn't prepare enough for them!" She looked to Leera, who huddled in three blankets looking very frozen and very guilty. "And neither did you!"

Bridget marched to grab some more blankets. She angrily threw him one and wrapped the other one around her shoulders. "I'm going up," and strode through the black door without another word.

Leera tried not to smile. "So you went down to the cellar, eh?"

"Yup. You?"

"Drank snow. Thought it was warm milk."

He couldn't help but snort a laugh before extending his hand. "Let's catch up to her."

"Yeah, before she gets even madder."

They lit their palms and quickly caught up to Bridget, who pointedly ignored them as she crept up the steps. Together they prowled past the burned-out level and on to the room the skeleton had come from.

Leera squeezed past a gaping Bridget. "What in the—it's like some sort of round royal bedroom …"

There was a blue velvet canopy bedstead in the middle, a banded trunk at its foot. A pair of ornate dressers stood side-by-side against the right wall, four bookcases against the left. A curved desk rested underneath a deep window opposite. Iron braziers sat on stands and an iron wheel chandelier hung from a high ceiling.

It reminded Augum of Castle Arinthian. It was odd to see a room so well decorated and unstained by time in a tower where the lock to the front gate had long rusted over. Nonetheless, the trio began searching it immediately. Bridget went for the bookshelves, filled with old tomes and crystals, Leera for the two dressers, and Augum for the trunk—only to discover it locked. A moment later, there was a zapping sound.

"OUCH!" Bridget had sprung back. "The books *shocked* me!"

"And I can't get these drawers to open—" Leera said, straining.

"And this trunk is locked," Augum added, seeing a pattern emerge. "Looks like whoever used to live here really didn't like people snooping."

"But I want to snoop," Leera whined.

Bridget extinguished her palm. "I'm going to try Unconceal."

Leera kicked the trunk. "Why don't the both of you try, I'll light for you."

Augum snuffed his palm. "Sure," and after a few moments of concentration, "Un vun deo." He scanned about with his open palm, hoping to feel that very subtle pull. After some time, still feeling nothing, his concentration broke and the spell failed. The same happened with Bridget.

"Nothing," he said.

Bridget began pacing. "This doesn't make sense …" Suddenly she stopped. "I think I know why, Mrs. Stone said it herself …"

Leera frowned. "Said what?"

"That Unconceal won't help you find stuff that's been arcanely hidden!"

"Oh. Right."

Bridget turned back to the shelves, tapping her lips with a finger. "For that, we'd need to know the Reveal spell …"

"Might as well keep exploring then," Augum said. "Shyneo." His palm crackled to life and he made his way over to the desk.

Leera let herself fall onto the bed, sighing, while Bridget mumbled to herself, poring over the bookshelves with her eyes. Meanwhile, he tried the drawers on the desk, all to no avail. Lacking anything better to do, he dropped to his knees and searched underneath the desk. His hand closed around something cold and thin. When he drew it out, he could scarcely believe his eyes.

"A key—!" Leera said. "But … how? You tried Unconceal!"

He raised a brow and gave a smart expression. "My powers are constantly growing."

Bridget rolled her eyes. "Please, it probably just fell under the desk. Remember, Mrs. Stone said the *intent* had to be there to hide something, and if it was arcanely hidden you probably wouldn't just come across it like that."

Leera sat up. "You know he was joking, right?"

Bridget turned a shade of pink. "Of course."

He saw his chance. "Look, I'm sorry for being such an oaf earlier." He winced. "So … think you can stop snapping at me?"

"Oh, that's some apology, how big of you." She snatched the key from his hand and stomped to the trunk. He appealed to Leera with a questioning look but she only shook her head, mouthing, "Nice one."

He scampered after Bridget. "Wait, I really—" but the words stuck in his throat after spotting what Bridget had found inside the trunk—a pumpkin-sized crystal globe on a tasseled pillow.

Leera saw their slack expressions and rushed over. "What. Is. That?"

"Probably some type of arcane orb," Bridget said.

He chuckled. "Oh, it's not a children's ball?"

She gave him a look and just scowled.

Leera shook her head, making a digging gesture.

"Sorry," he mumbled, wondering how many times he had apologized today.

"I bet Mrs. Stone would know what it does," Leera said, reaching for the orb.

Bridget grabbed her arm. "Better not. You know, just in case …"

All three of them leaned in and peered closer.

He squinted. "Ever get the feeling that you're being—"

Suddenly a giant blue eye opened within the orb. The trio screamed, slammed the lid shut, and scurried back.

Leera drew her blankets closer. "All right, who was that?"

"Maybe the person whose place this is," Bridget whispered.

"Well, whoever it was knows we're here now," Augum said, realizing they couldn't leave even if they wanted to as the storm would kill them.

Sure enough, there was a loud THWOMP, and before them materialized a woman in a red robe fringed with black fur. She looked middle-aged, had pale skin, a large crooked nose, and a face caked with too much makeup. Curly auburn hair spiraled past an elaborate crystal necklace.

Upon laying eyes on them, she crossed her arms and snorted. "You're just kids—!" Large pearl earrings jingled with each bob of her head.

"Uh, hi," Leera said. "Who are you?"

"Erika, and this happens to be my tower the three of you rabble are trying to loot. And who might you be, freckles?"

"We're not trying to *loot* anything—" Leera said, before suddenly sneezing. She curled the blankets around her more. "We're only trying to find a way to make a fire and get warm."

"Oh, you want to burn the place down too, is that it, sweetie?"

"No, I mean—"

"Relax, freckles, I'm only kidding." She gave them a saucy look and waved a languid hand. "The Unnameables know someone already tried." She paced to the braziers, lighting each one with a flick of her wrist.

The trio immediately crowded around one, warming themselves.

Erika placed her hands on her hips. "Like pigs in mud. So, how did you manage to open the chest, my little darlings?"

Augum rubbed his hands above the fire. "I found the key underneath your desk."

"So that's where it went—" she sauntered over and stuck out her palm, raising an arched brow. Bridget dutifully handed over the key. Augum got a whiff of some noxious flowery perfume.

"Thank you, missy, and you really shouldn't snoop around people's things."

Bridget stiffened. "We *weren't* snooping. This tower isn't even yours, you moved in just like a squatter."

Erika ground her jaw, marched over, and slapped Bridget—hard. Augum and Leera stood in shock. Bridget gasped, placed a shaking hand to her cheek, and looked away.

Erika's voice was a quiet hiss. "How *dare* you compare me to a common squatter, you little derelict. You have no idea who I am or what I am capable of, so shut your mouth and don't be rude." She straightened. "Now do the right thing and apologize to me."

Bridget stood there a moment and made to leave, but Erika grabbed her by the elbow and twisted her around. "Apologize. Now!"

"Don't you touch her—" Augum said, reaching for Erika's arm just as it exploded with ten rings of fire.

"I'm sorry—" Bridget said quickly.

"What was that? I couldn't hear you, dear child. Speak up."

"I'm sorry!"

Erika let go of Bridget and extinguished her arm. "There, that wasn't so hard now, was it, sugar?" Her voice was light and sweet. She yanked a cloth from a pocket and wiped her hands, giving Bridget a mirthless smile. She then strutted over to her desk, muttering some arcane word. A drawer popped open and she dropped the key inside, removing a silver hand mirror. She made an idle gesture and the drawer shut.

"What's with kids these days anyway?" she asked no one in particular, turning back to them. "No respect at all. Even the way they talk is improper and offensive."

Augum and Leera exchanged the same look. This woman was nuts.

"I bet you're from the academy. Runaways by the look of your rags, though if I didn't know any better, I'd swear those were traditional apprentice robes under all that dirt." She shook her head. "Filthy, icky children …" She began inspecting her makeup in the mirror, paying particular attention to her nose. Her ice blue eyes flicked over to them now and then, as if to make sure they weren't getting any ideas.

"Definitely apprentice robes. Haven't seen them in some time. Damn ugly, if you ask me."

Leera put an arm around Bridget, who kept her eyes averted, hands shaking over the brazier. Augum was trying to think of how to respond, since he didn't want to let on exactly who they were and where they were going. The woman was obviously a strong warlock, so they had to be very careful.

Erika lowered the mirror, tapping it idly against her thigh. "So how many stripes then, hmm? You *are* aware revealing your degree is a point of honor amongst us warlocks, are you not?" They only stared. "How about showing a bit of gratitude then, hmm? I could have easily kicked you out into that storm." Leera opened her mouth to say something but Erika blithely carried on. "I'd guess you have a maximum of two rings, for if you had three, you would have known about the skeleton door trap."

"We each have one stripe," Augum said, figuring it was best to say something truthful. He lit up his arm with his hard-earned degree.

"Lightning—impressive, though you probably won't make your second ring, kiddo, notoriously dangerous element and all that. Yet it has come to symbolize much, hasn't it? What with the Lord of the Legion being a lightning warlock and all—" she said it without the slightest hint of irony, signifying to him she had no idea he was Sparkstone's son.

Erika drummed the dresser with her fingers, earrings jingling away, stopping only to sing, "And I bet that—" (more drumming with her fingers) "—you are running—" (a final fast tapping flourish) "—from the Legion!" she belted out the last words as if announcing a prize they had won. "I really should have been a singer," she muttered to herself, adjusting her robe.

Augum glanced at Leera, unsure how to reply. Bridget kept her head down, avoiding everybody. He decided to take a risk. "And what if we were, would you help us?"

Erika gave a coy smile. "Why should I, what's in it for me? Hmm? It's no easy thing evading the Legion nowadays."

"You're a fugitive too—?"

"Why of course I am, child! I am a *fugitive* though, not some … *squatter*." She flashed Bridget a repugnant look.

He nodded, trying to play along. "So … why are you a fugitive?"

"Well, sweetie, if there's one thing I despise, it's filth, and the Legion is full of it. Why, as we speak, they have kids your age *raising* the dead, or at least trying to." Erika made a face as if she smelled dung in the room.

Augum immediately thought of Robin.

"Anyhow, it's just so gruesome, if you get my meaning."

"Um, so … about your cellar—"

"—so when I told the local commander," Erika continued on, ignoring him, "oh, who was it now, Commander Rims or something? Anyway, when I *politely* told him I wasn't interested in mentoring some of his witless soldiers, ah, he didn't exactly take it too well." Earrings jingled along to the bobbing of her pasty head. "Yup, I was banished. On the run since. Now look at me, in some ancient tower trying to live decently, though truth be told, I'm better off than many of my noble friends are, put to work doing …" she curled her fingers and frowned, "things of a *ghastly* nature."

A moment of dramatic silence passed. "So what about you, kiddies, what's your story?"

Augum looked to Leera and cleared his throat, trying to come up with one. "Well, we were—"

Erika fake-yawned. "You know what? I don't *actually* give a damn about a bunch of runaways or orphans or whatever gutterborn scum you happen to be, not unless you have a fortune of gold coin hidden amongst those mangy mules you have down there."

"Well, uh, no, we don't …"

"Wait a moment. Are those Dramask—?" Erika marched forward in such a way the trio instinctively recoiled. Her brows arched. "Really now? You can relax, darlings, I'm not your headmistress." She snatched one of the blankets off Leera, who opened her mouth to protest. For once, Augum had to elbow her, masking the noise by clearing his throat.

"What's that, dear—?" Erika asked absently, studying the blue and green striped blanket.

"Oh, I was just about to say that, uh … that I agree, uh, that these are Dramsuck blankets."

Erika gave him a look like he was an idiot. "*Dramask*, honey, and yes, they are indeed. A shame the Legion plans to storm into Tiberra. Dramask is the jewel of the northeast, a truly beautiful city. Puts Blackhaven to shame many times over, let me tell you. Where did you say you got these?"

He was about to reply when she waved her hand. "Never mind already, I don't frankly care. Do you have one with red stripes?"

"Um … we'll have to go check."

" 'We'? What do you mean, 'we', kiddo? I haven't had company here in …" she waved absently then frowned. "Well, all right, I've never had company here really. No one to enjoy my fine china, no one to taste my exquisite cooking, and no one to sit at my glorious ebony dining table. Do you realize how difficult it was importing and getting all this stuff in here with nobody but little old me to do all the arcane dirty work? A lady should never have to lift her own table. Not even arcanely."

"Uh …"

"Exactly—so don't even think about running off, or I'll set my pet on you. I expect courtesy from the lot of you rabble kids. We're going to have a proper, civil supper."

"Your pet …?" So there *was* something in that cellar …

"You're quite the daft one aren't you? Cute, but daft, and I don't have time for daftness. Get me the red blanket and come right back. I'm keeping the missies here. They can help me prepare the feast. We're going upstairs, mind you, so be sure to go through the next door up. Run along now, boy, go, shoo …" she waved her fingers as if chasing away a dirty stray dog.

SERVANTS

Augum raced down the tower stairs, tiptoeing the last portion to avoid waking Erika's pet. He shot through the oaken door and frantically searched through the barrel of remaining blankets. The blizzard roared in full force now, the cold absolutely blistering.

Unfortunately, there were no blankets with red stripes left in the barrel. Frustrated, he began heading back when he spotted one on his palfrey. He snatched it, replacing it with an additional two blankets per horse. He also left them some beef biscuit to chew on. He then concealed the rucksack with their stuff before making his way back upstairs. He had decided, for safety and theft reasons, to leave Blackbite behind. He hoped that decision would not haunt him later.

As instructed, he passed the bedroom they had found the orb in and went into the room above. It was a splendidly decorated round dining room with a crystal chandelier hanging from the ceiling, its many candles flickering. The right wall had a preparation area with a cooking hearth, trestle harvest table, and shelves full of spices, flour, and herbs.

Bridget and Leera were already hard at work baking and cutting, pink aprons strung about their necks, faces tight with anxiety. When Erika wasn't looking, he saw them sneak a few bites.

His mouth watered. He longed for some real food.

In the center of the room, surrounded by eight exquisitely ornate dining chairs with royal blue seats, stood an elaborately carved ebony dining table. Fine silver candelabras sat on top, as well as pearly bone china, gilded flatware, and the finest crystal goblets and tumblers he had ever seen. There was a single velvet-curtained window at the back of the room.

He gaped at all the luxury, wondering if this was what Castle Arinthian looked like before being looted.

"Don't just stand there, boy, put this on—" Erika threw him a fine crimson belted tunic. It looked like it came from a noble. He gladly pulled it over his robe for the added warmth. She herself had disposed of the fur-trimmed red robe in favor of a rose-colored, finely pleated square-necked dress.

Erika pinched his cheek. "Oh, darling, now you look so handsome! You remind me of my dear nephew." She batted her long lashes and dabbed at her eyes as if there were real tears there. "Ugh, I do miss that little brat, I do." She composed herself and grimaced. "Why don't you have a seat and polish my flatware, young man."

She shoved him into the captain's chair at one end of the table and handed him a rag and a particularly lavish set of golden flatware, not unlike the set they saw in Ley. She then hovered over to Bridget and Leera.

"No no no, not like that, you silly little girl." She shoved Bridget out of the way. "Ugh, must I do everything myself?

Shyneo." Her hand burst in flame and she broiled the meat. It served to show her advanced spell knowledge, for no 1st degree warlock could cook with Shine.

"Now don't you dare drop it," she said, handing it to Leera. "Wrap it up. That's it now, that's a good doggie."

"Not your dog," Leera muttered.

"What did you just say?"

"I said I'm not your dog."

Erika stepped back and looked Leera up and down. "I won't have some ugly servant girl talking back to me!" Her hand burst with rings as her voice turned into a low growl. "You'll do the work and you'll do it quietly, or I'll throw you in the oven and have your friend *roast* you."

Leera reddened, nodded quickly, and redoubled her efforts right along with Bridget, not even daring to look at one another.

We have to get out of here, Augum thought just as the window shuddered. Yet it'd be suicide in this blizzard. They'd simply have to wait until it died down.

"Freckles needs an attitude adjustment, wouldn't you agree, dear boy?"

He stayed silent, pretending to be very busy with the last of the flatware. She leaned in close, her flowery perfume clouding his mind and making him want to gag.

"You missed a spot. Here, boy—do it right!" she shoved a butter knife at him, pointing to a hardly visible speck. He polished it away with the cloth as she gracefully took a seat at the head of the table.

"What are you looking at, freckles? Back to work! It's a wonder your mother even kept such an ugly child around. Just look at your nose, ugh, really! You mark my words, girl, no boy will ever like you. You'll forever be somebody's filthy little servant. You're gutterborn ugly with even uglier gutterborn parents, aren't you? I bet your ugly parents are dead. They were so ugly they took their own lives, didn't they? Or did they take their own lives because of how ugly *you* were?"

Silent tears began streaming down Leera's cheeks. She sped up her work.

Erika turned to Augum with a simpering smile. "There should be some kind of rule, you know? Disallowing ugly girls from attending the academy, that is. Though—" she chuckled and leaned back, "I never really got along with girls. They should have all been expelled—except for me of course."

"I think her nose is pretty," Augum mumbled, shrugging.

Leera half-glanced over, beet red.

Erika's eyes narrowed. "Servants are like rats—you don't talk about them. We're going to have a civil, proper supper, and that means the foul bratty missies have to serve and prepare. *You,* my-dear-boy-that-reminds-me-of-my-noble-nephew, are my guest of honor. So—" and she gave him a cold smile, "enjoy yourself. I'm sure you've been thinking this entire time anyway that the girls needed to serve you supper sometime, haven't you, sugar?"

"No, definit—"

"Oh, come now, precious, you can level with Auntie Erika …" She leaned forward, placing her chin on her fists, ears jingling. He was really beginning to detest that sound. "Admit it—you like having the girls wait on you, don't you? It's the first thing a husband should learn, you know—how to put his servants to good use, and how to put them in their place when they step out of line." Her face changed, as if she was reliving something in her past. Bitterness crept into her voice. "Girls *need* to know their place, especially the ugly ones."

All he wanted to do was grab the girls and get out of there. Well, maybe let Leera punch Erika once in the nose, if she could get away with it. Bridget would probably like a turn too, for that matter. He decided the best thing to do for now, though, was to change the subject.

"Would you mind if I asked what happened in the burned room below?" He braced as Erika only stared at him for a moment.

"Very deft, my dear boy, very deft indeed. A conversational pivot worthy of a noble in the king's court. To answer your question, sweetie, it was like that when I got here. Truth be told, I haven't stepped into that room since I laid eyes on it. You understand of course—it's simply filthy." Her head snapped to Bridget and Leera. "How is that soup coming along!"

"Almost done—" Bridget said, while Leera muffled a sniffle. Both girls were frantically working away.

"You are to address me as *m'lady*. Is that understood, my little lowborn squirrel?

Bridget kept on working as she answered. "Yes—I mean, yes, m'lady."

"Good. Just because you think yourself cute with that pert little nose doesn't mean you may take liberties." Erika turned back to Augum, raising an arched brow. "See that, my dear boy? You must command women. Women are put on Sithesia by the gods to be *commanded*. Now you try it. Go on, Nephew, command them to bring the soup here."

"I'm not your nephew, and I won't—"

Erika suddenly shot out of her chair, breaking a crystal goblet on the floor. Rings of fire burst around her arm as her face swelled like a bullfrog. Her head tilted slightly. "Do it. Now."

He swallowed, fearing she was going to torture one of the girls if he didn't. "Please bring me a bowl of soup."

Bridget carried a steaming bowl over giving him a particular look he translated as *just go with it.* Of course, it could also have meant *don't do anything stupid, she's crazy*.

"Here you are, sir," she said, curtseying properly like Mya would have. "And yours is coming right up, m'lady."

Erika's brows rose. She seemed genuinely surprised to find rings around her arm and promptly extinguished them. Then she adjusted her dress, giving a nervous chortle. "Oh, my darling … I forget myself sometimes. You must forgive Auntie Erika. And just look at my silliness, I seem to have broken a goblet." She snapped her fingers sharply a few times.

Bridget bent down and placed her hands over the broken crystal. "Apreyo." The goblet reformed. She polished it and set it back on the table with a curtsy, keeping her eyes low the entire time.

"Now that's more like it. I have to say, it's nice having servants who can actually fix a thing or two around here. I am so oft used to bumbling idiot girls who don't know the simplest cantrip. Now fetch me my soup, girl."

Bridget curtsied, hands in front, and returned to the counter beside Leera.

"Well hurry up already, haven't you learned that a course is supposed to be served at the same time!"

"Yes, m'lady, it's coming." Bridget hurried back with Erika's soup before returning to make the rest of the meal with Leera. He saw her whisper something encouraging to Leera, stopping as soon as Erika raised her head.

"Not bad, though a bit more salt would be prudent. Freckles, did you hear me? SALT!"

Leera jumped and fumbled a fork. It fell to the floor with a clang.

Everyone froze.

Erika smiled kindly. "Oh, you desperately poor thing. It's all right, Auntie Erika won't be mean. Go ahead and pick it up."

Leera slowly picked up the fork, never taking her eyes off Erika.

"Now do be a dear and bring auntie the salt."

Leera promptly brought a silver bowl of salt to the table.

"Well don't just *bring* it here you silly goat, put it in my soup! There now, is that so hard? And don't overdo—THAT'S TOO MUCH!" She suddenly slapped Leera so hard she was sent sprawling to the ground. Augum jumped out of his chair but Leera shot him a halting look, face marked with a new red welt in the shape of a hand. Erika stood glaring, daring her to try anything, arm poised ready to flare up.

Bridget helped Leera pick herself up off the floor, gesturing for Augum to start a conversation or something, anything to get Erika distracted. He actually thought of casting Centarro and doing something crazy, but Erika was too paranoid and dangerous. It was just too risky. He hoped Leera could hang in there and slowly sat back down. His knuckles were white under the table.

"So, uh, what was that orb in your trunk, Auntie Erika?" He had to force a polite tone.

Erika's face hardened. "You mean the orb you tried to steal earlier?"

"No, we were just—"

"Oh, dear young man, you certainly are an easy mark, I was merely jesting! I'm sure it was nothing but young, unadulterated curiosity." She cleared her throat and graciously took her seat again. "Ah, to be young again. You know when I was your age I got into all sorts of trouble. First year at the academy and all that." She sighed, eyes misting over, before glancing back to him. "Sorry, hon, what were we talking about—?"

"The orb, Auntie Erika." He'd rather swim in a rancid sewer than keep calling her that.

"Right you have it, kiddo. It's a seeing orb, kind of like a speaking orb, but *better.* Neat little thing I … discovered once." She flashed a twisted smile, giving him the impression she stole it, and didn't care too much if he knew that.

"It's quite the clever and amusing artifact, really. Set it up anywhere and you can see and hear through it. It's indestructible, locks in place so no one can carry it away, and for fun, you can let the people know you're watching, as you yourselves experienced."

He remembered the way a giant eye opened inside the orb, almost lizard-like.

"I once amused myself by watching a merchant road with an unsavory reputation. Lo and behold, a group of imbecile bandits took interest in the orb. You should have seen it—there was this great big fat oaf that just wouldn't let it go. He tried everything, using sticks, rocks, and even a monstrous cudgel." She tapped at her temple. "Not the sharpest blade in the armory. Anyhoo, the entire time the bandits talked, and I heard every word of their plans. Hours of entertainment I tell you, not to mention a nice payoff in the end."

Bridget served a sliced loaf of hard bread and curtsied, face, hair and apron stained with flour. When Erika spotted the apron, she just shook her head. "Filthy servant squirrel … hey, you know what, dear nephew? That'll be her name—Squirrel. So we have Squirrel and Freckles. How quaint."

Bridget's face reddened. "Will that be all, m'lady?"

"You watch your tone, princess. And no, that will not be all. Fetch me a glass of Titan wine and squeeze out some juice for my waiting nephew here."

"Yes, m'lady." Bridget curtsied and returned to the prep area, before abruptly turning around. "Pardon, m'lady, but, where are the oranges and the wine?"

"Oh, for—oranges in the basket under the table, wine in the corner cabinet!" Erika shook her head, earrings jingling, before turning back to Augum with a sweet smile. "I really have no patience with incompetence, something I'm sure we share, dear nephew." She played with her empty goblet, watching him, while Bridget uncorked a bottle of wine and poured Erika a glass.

The wine made him think of his mother. Before she wed his father, she was Terra Titan of the Titans of Sierra, hot lands of the south. That side of the family made wine from giant grapes and owned a vineyard. One day, he hoped to visit it, see if there were grandparents or cousins he could get to know. Strange how there he was, in the middle of nowhere with some crazy woman, and she drank wine that had a connection to him.

Erika brought out the silver mirror and began fussing with her hair. He wondered if now was a good time to ask which route was best to take on the way to the Northern Peaks, presuming she'd even let them go, something he tried not to think about.

After a while of Augum failing to supply Erika with a steady stream of conversational material, her look soured. She raised the goblet of wine, swished it a while and drained it, gesturing impatiently for Bridget to pour her another. She drained that one too, the veins of her crooked nose reddening along with her cheeks. Her eyes narrowed as she watched Augum.

She began tapping the table. "What's on your mind, cupcake?"

The room went quiet.

"Nothing—I was just thinking about how nice this—this dining table was—"

Erika stopped tapping a moment before her words tumbled forth in a rush. "Don't make a fool of me, boy, I'll flay you raw—!"

"I'm sorry, I didn't mean—"

Erika's chair kicked back as she shot out of it, charging over, pleated dress billowing like her reddening cheeks. She put her face right into his. He held his breath from that ghastly perfume. "You aren't thinking of escaping my little domicile, are you now, sweet nephew?"

"No, it's quite comfortable here …" He was always a terrible liar, and this time was no exception. Erika's face hardened and she slapped him hard, not once, but thrice, each time grabbing his jaw and returning it forward, so he stared into her eyes while she did it again. With each strike, Bridget and Leera gasped. He felt himself getting hot all over as involuntary tears welled from the sting. The beginnings of wild electric arcanery stirred within. He noticed her hair statically stiffen a little. If she had just slapped him one more time, something might have happened, but as it were, she let go of his jaw with a spiteful jerk, took a step back, and crossed her arms.

"So you want to leave, do you? After all the courtesies I've shown you? After everything I've done for you, bringing you in from a murderous storm and *feeding you—?*" She dabbed at her dry eyes with a cloth, batting her lashes. "I hope you know that hurt me more than you. Such ungrateful little brats …"

She made a show of sniffing while he touched his tender cheek, trying to calm down and not say anything that would make things worse. When her gaze returned to him, it was ice cold.

"You listen carefully, kiddos. You—are—not—going—anywhere. You're going to work hard for me, oh, yes you are. I need servants to cater to my needs—the floors need scrubbing, shoes need stitching, china needs cleaning, shelves need dusting, and there's certainly plenty to fix around here. When you're done, this will be a proper noble tower fit for a queen, and I will make proper servants of you, by gods I swear I will."

Her hands straddled the arms of his chair as she leaned into his face.

"Don't think for one moment I'm going to let you just mosey right out of here. Nobody knows you're here, understand me? Nobody! And no one's going to miss you either if you should suddenly, let us say, disappear …"

He stared into those ice eyes, knowing she meant every word of her threat.

Her voice dropped to an almost inaudible whisper. "Now are you going to be a good boy and work hard for Auntie Erika, or will you force your poor aunt to do something she might … later regret?"

He hesitated just a moment before nodding. "I'll work, I'll work—"

She ruffled his hair. "That's a good boy," and slithered back to her chair. If by then Bridget and Leera did not see how dangerous the situation was, they certainly saw it now. He spotted them exchanging looks before hurriedly getting back to preparing the final course.

It was almost worth taking their chances out in the storm. The way she looked at him though, it was as if he was an open book to her. He suspected she could read every traitorous thought that went through his head.

She'd make a fine pairing with the Blade of Sorrows …

Erika gestured for her wine to be refilled, took a swig, and began sipping at her soup. Augum picked up his spoon and mechanically did the same, tasting nothing, mind frantically working away.

Erika finally shoved away the empty bowl. "Next serving, you little wench. Well come on, hurry it up, Freckles!"

Leera, apron as dirty as Bridget's and a welt on her cheek, hurriedly did as she was told. Augum indicated she should take his too, purposefully leaving it half finished so they could have it. Leera saw it and mouthed, "Thank you," before taking the bowl away.

Erika's eyes narrowed as she watched the girls work. Suddenly she raised her arm, pointed it at Bridget, and said, "Flustrato."

Bridget, who happened to be working with a fork, suddenly brought it up before her eyes. "What's this for?"

Leera gave her a look as if she had lost her mind.

Erika slapped her knee and wheezed with laughter.

Bridget turned around and looked at Augum. "Do you know, I think I like pie. I do, I really do. It has to be pumpkin pie and only mother is allowed to make it." She blinked. "But she can't make it right now, she's too busy."

Erika snorted a loud pig-like laugh. She put a hand on her chest and took a few deep breaths. "Now that was exactly what I needed." She waved idly at Bridget, who gave her an odd look, glanced down at herself, and quickly resumed working beside Leera.

"Do you know what I love about the Confusion spell, my handsome nephew? You can control the intensity of the victim's befuddlement. Superbly useful. Sometimes quite hilarious too." She flexed her jaw. "But I suppose you won't enjoy that one until you reach your 4th degree. Too bad, I'd love to watch you confound these little harpies."

He didn't reply, having no idea what he should say to that.

The girls served the main course, featuring arcanely roasted lamb, potatoes and dark gravy, roasted sweet leeks, salted peas and spinach, and buttered mushrooms. As good as the food looked and smelled, he could barely taste it. His cheek still stung, but that was nothing to the pain in his chest, not to mention the buzzing anxiety in his stomach.

His mind kept drifting to the pet in the basement, wondering what it was. If they escaped, they'd have to do it in such a way that the thing couldn't come after them …

Erika's plate sat mostly untouched, her goblet empty. Her cheeks were now apple crimson, eyes glassy. "Squirrel, Freckles—by my side!"

Bridget and Leera scampered to her and curtsied, hands folded before their soiled aprons. "Yes, m'lady?" Bridget said.

"You did well. Take one slice of hard bread, not more. My treat. Now off with you, stand in the corner until you're summoned, and eat *quietly,* understand me?"

"Yes, m'lady." Bridget and Leera curtseyed once again and retreated to the corner, grabbing a slice of stale hard bread in the process.

Augum's heart knotted knowing his two friends had to watch him eat such a luxurious meal. He wished there was something he could do. Centarro ran through his mind once again, yet should it fail, this murderous woman might just kill them all, and her arcane skills easily outmatched them, even with Centarro.

Erika cleared her throat. "Is anyone forgetting anything?" Her crystal goblet sang as she flicked it with a long fingernail.

Bridget immediately brought the wine, mumbling, "I'm sorry, m'lady."

Erika watched her pour with an ever-increasing acid face. "You need to learn to be mindful, my pets. Now put the bread on the floor beside me."

"M'lady?"

"Don't make me repeat myself, Squirrel, or you'll rue the day."

The girls exchanged nervous looks. Bridget gathered their measly slices and placed them on the floor beside Erika.

"Well, what are you waiting for?" Erika asked.

"M'lady—?"

"Eat. It. You too, Freckles. Eat the damn bread off the floor. Now."

Leera shook her head. "No way—"

Erika's arm shot out like a viper. "Dreadus Terrablus."

Bridget dropped to her knees, a look of sheer horror on her face. Her mouth opened wide as she stared at Erika with watering eyes. Suddenly she let loose a blood-curdling scream that raised every single hair on Augum's body.

Leera rushed to Bridget and held her, crying apologies.

"Auntie Erika, stop!" he shouted.

Leera dropped to her knees and began gobbling one of the slices, making sure Erika saw.

Erika gave a nod and made as if swatting a bothersome fly. Bridget fell into Leera's arms, weeping and shaking.

"Shall I eat the other one, m'lady?" Leera asked through grated teeth, tears rolling down her cheeks. She held onto Bridget tightly.

Erika's foot reached out and ground the other slice into the floor. "Yes, Freckles. Please do."

If he had the power to strike someone down then and there …

Leera ate the other slice off the floor while still holding Bridget, eyeing Erika with a loathing he had never seen in a person before.

"And you. You sit."

He hesitantly did so.

Erika gave him a sweet smile. "Eat, Nephew, eat," and took a long sip of wine. "You know, you're lucky I haven't lost my temper yet. I've been known to do some … uncomfortable things. One of my servants … oh, what was the wretched child's name again? Never mind. She had quite the tongue on her. I had her cut it out." Erika watched his expression as she took another sip of wine.

Augum picked up the fork and held it, doing his best to look unperturbed. His mind, however, buzzed with crazier and crazier ideas on how to set them free, yet he was acutely conscious he was dealing with an insane warlock of the 10th degree who was as suspicious as a thief-in-hiding and now probably drunk too.

They'd have to be creative to get out of this bind.

"When you come of age, my darling, you're going to be a very handsome man. I can see these things, you know. I'm sure you'll find yourself some pretty noble woman with a pretty nose and pretty hair. You just make sure she knows her place, sweetie." She glanced at the girls huddled on the floor, who quickly lowered their eyes. "Women need to know their place." She swirled the goblet's contents while glaring at them.

"This wine is quite delicious, my dear boy. Would you like to try some?"

"No, thank you." All wine did was remind him of Mr. Penderson. Besides, he needed his wits.

"A man must learn how to drink, nephew." She sighed. "A pity, but more for me." When she noticed he was still not eating, she made an impatient gesture. "Come, come, we can't let it get cold now, can we?"

He forced himself to eat. After all, he'd need energy for tonight if they were going to attempt an escape. Here and there, he surreptitiously wrapped a portion of his lamb, mushrooms, and potatoes in a finely embroidered serviette, before stuffing the bundle in his pocket. He put away as much as he dared, making sure that when Erika looked up she saw him chewing.

"Mmm, delicious," he said, playing it up during a particularly close call when she happened to glance over at him just as he took his hand from the table. A brief look came over her face, but he managed to distract her by quickly asking where she had acquired her ingredients.

"Oh, dear nephew, you are so naive. Teleport is such a wonderful spell, it really is. When you reach your 9th degree, you'll know exactly what I mean."

He gave an eager nod, thinking he should eat slower, keep her drinking. He hoped she drank so much she passed out, as Mr. Penderson used to. Then they could sneak by her.

Erika was halfway done with her meal when she picked up her glass of wine and leaned back, drumming the table with her other hand. A permanent sneer had attached itself to her face by now, like a foul odor. He decided to keep his head down and concentrate on eating, not daring to put aside any more food.

"You must be quite hungry, my dear nephew."

"I am, Auntie Erika." Her pungent flowery perfume seemed to have somehow strengthened, filling his nostrils and contaminating the taste of the food.

"Squirrel!" she called, not taking her eyes off him.

Bridget instantly appeared by her side, curtseying. "M'lady?"

"Gods, girl, you're filthy! When was the last time you washed that long hair of yours? Never mind, I don't want to hear anymore whining. Put the rest of my food in a bowl for my pet. And fetch dessert, would you?"

Bridget curtseyed and quietly did as she was told.

"Sugared strawberries, dear nephew. Do you know how hard these were to come by?"

"I don't, Auntie Erika."

She watched him continue to fiddle with the last of his supper. "I'm not going to wait around forever to move on to dessert while you chew that cud slower than a cow, child. Squirrel! Take his supper and put it in the bowl for my pet. And don't even *think* about sneaking a bite."

He watched the remainder leave the table with a pang. He was still hungry. Bridget brought a bowl of strawberries. They were sweetly delicious and he even managed to snag a couple for the girls. It was risky as Erika had stopped eating, paying more attention to him and the wine now.

"Let me tell you, my little sugarplum, it sure is nice to have visitors for a change. Sometimes I feel like I'm in a tomb." She sighed, propping her chin with her hand. "Sometimes I don't hear my own voice for days at a time, and now that winter has come it can get quite … boring around here. What sheer luck to have company in such dull times."

He couldn't think of anything to say as he ate the last strawberry on his plate. Leera and Bridget silently watched from the corner. He wondered if they saw him sneak food for them.

The goblet teetered in Erika's hand. She burped, held her chest, and gestured for Bridget to pour another. After staring at her unfinished strawberries for a long time, her head tilted forward a little and her eyes drooped.

Augum stole a hopeful glance at the girls.

Suddenly Erika's head snapped up. "Well, I suppose it's time for the children to go to bed." She licked her lips and flexed her jaw. "Squirrel, Freckles—clear the table."

They quickly followed her orders, being particularly quiet.

"What are you looking at, Squirrel?"

Augum was sure, however, that Bridget was not even looking in her direction.

"Were you just staring at my nose? Think it ugly, do you!"

Bridget took a step back, bowl of strawberries in hand. "M'lady, I wasn't—"

"You dare talk back to me?"

"Auntie Erika, this food really was—"

"—shut it, boy!" She leapt to her feet, the chair tilting back and falling to the ground. Her arm ruptured with rings. She pointed it at Bridget, who hurriedly retreated, bumped into the counter, and dropped the bowl. It smashed on the floor, the strawberries rolling this way and that.

"You little wretch, look what you've done! I could roast you here and now, girl ..."

Leera jumped in front of Bridget. "You'll have to kill us both—"

Erika's eyes glimmered as her hand rose.

"Auntie Erika, please don't—!" Augum blurted in his most innocent voice. She turned to stare at him before suddenly giggling like a schoolgirl, extinguishing her arm. "Stupid, silly girls, I was only jesting! So naive ..."

Bridget stood there, breathing fast, while Leera arcanely repaired the bowl and picked up the strawberries.

Erika shook her head. "Really now, such saps ..." and laughed until she began coughing. She got control of herself, downed the wine, and jovially announced, "Welcome to Evergray Tower, where all the fashionable ladies are banished to!"

When they didn't respond, she scowled and waved her hands dismissively. "Fine, off with you then. I'm taking you upstairs to your room. You're going to bed and that's that. I'm sick of looking at your gutterborn faces. We have a lifetime together anyway. First, we're going to get my orb. Squirrel, Freckles—in front, and leave your aprons. Go. NOW!"

The girls folded their aprons onto the counter. Augum didn't need to be told to do the same with the tunic she had supplied him.

He followed the girls out the door. Erika took up the rear, resentment etched all over her face like a bad painting. When they reached the bedroom, Erika snatched the key from the desk, slamming the drawer shut. She unlocked the chest, kicked it open, and picked up the globe, all the while watching them suspiciously, as if they were going to try anything. He *might* have attempted something if she had been drunk out of her mind. Unfortunately, she was either an accomplished drinker or a good actor, appearing alert and as dangerous as ever. He had absolutely no doubt that she would kill them with the slightest provocation.

No, any attempt at escape had to be well thought out.

Erika herded them up the curving stairs and finally to a hallway door, the other side of which howled with wind. Recalling their approach to the tower, Augum suspected the portion above this section was ruined.

She nodded at the door. "In there." When Leera opened it, they received a blast of freezing wind.

"You want us to sleep in there—?" he asked.

Erika kicked him, sending him tumbling forward into Bridget and Leera. She stood in the doorway, orb in one hand, empty goblet in the other, hair flailing in the wind. "You aren't my nephew, boy, and don't you ever forget it!"

The room was mostly destroyed. A large portion of the far wall was missing, a window into the blizzard. Snowdrifts piled up against rubble. The floor was made of sturdy wood planks, slippery with ice. There were no furnishings or decorations except for an ancient brazier on a rusted iron stand. A small pile of coal and wood sat inside, covered by a layer of frost.

When Augum peeked over the edge, he glimpsed a long sheer drop to a pile of jagged rocks. "We'll die if we sleep here overnight!" he yelled over the wind.

"Yes, and then who'll tend to your dishes and your cleaning?" Bridget added, a note of panic in her voice.

Erika, who had just finished placing the globe on a stone block by the door, glanced around. "Lazy brats. Well, I suppose I can light the brazier for you." She flexed her arm and her rings flared up, even though she did not need to display them—it was done as a reminder. She opened her palm and sprayed the brazier with arcane fire for a while, watching them with distrustful eyes that mirrored the flames.

"I suppose you'll whine if I don't bring you some blankets as well." She drifted to the door. "I'll be watching, so don't even *think* of trying anything. Oh, and just in case you get cheeky, the orb has been fixed in place." She slammed the door, locking it from the other side with a key. The trio quickly huddled around the brazier, breath fogging, wind whipping through their dirty hair and ragged robes.

"Are you all right?" he whispered.

They only nodded, though neither met his eyes.

"I'm sorry for being useless—"

"Nothing you could have done," Bridget said.

"Glad you didn't try," Leera added. "She would have killed us for sure."

Nonetheless, he cursed himself for leaving Blackbite behind, though perhaps it was for the best. An attempt to escape was probably destined to fail.

The door opened and three blankets were tossed in. It slammed shut and the lock clicked. The frozen trio quickly retrieved the blankets and returned to the brazier, backs to the orb.

The wind howled, threatening to blow out the flames. Augum moved to try to block it. It was a constant battle to keep it from getting snuffed.

This was going to be a long night, he thought wearily, suddenly remembering he had food in his pocket for them. Careful to not be seen by the orb, he placed a finger to his lips and unwrapped the serviette, revealing a leg of lamb, lumps of cold potato, mushroom slices, and strawberries.

Apparently neither of them had seen him sneak the food, because they both stared slack-jawed.

"Aug … you daring, brilliant soul," Leera mumbled, licking her lips.

"An awful risk," Bridget said, shaking her head but smiling, unable to take her eyes off the food either. They each took a small portion. He insisted they have it all, however. Now if only he had nicked a tankard or a small pot so they could melt snow over the fire …

As it was, even with the brazier, the situation was perilous. It was even colder here than down with the palfreys, and they had fewer blankets. Peering at the missing wall, he thought they might as well be outside.

They needed to figure something out, and soon.

When the girls finished licking their fingers, the trio discussed the situation, timing their speech to coincide with the occasional loud gust.

"… no way, we'd get killed trying to climb down," he said, teeth chattering. "Besides, there's a blizzard out there. We just have to ride it out and escape when the storm passes."

Leera rocked from foot to foot while rubbing her arms. "Why not try repairing the wall?"

He exchanged a look with Bridget. Why not indeed?

"Did I just have a brilliant idea there?" Leera asked, smirking.

Bridget gave her a wry smile. "Think you did," and the trio got up and huddled near the edge, frozen hands open to the raw freeze of the night. He expected Erika to charge in there any moment, wondering what they were up to. They'd have to hurry.

"Prepare and concentrate!" Bridget said.

It was easy to envision the wall as complete because it was simply a continuation of what was already there. The challenge would come from the biting cold and the size of some of the stones. He remembered the last time they attempted a repair in such conditions, on the front doors of Castle Arinthian. It was a similar circumstance—strong freezing winds preceding a blizzard. Unfortunately, that particular repair failed miserably. Mrs. Stone had to step in to finish it for them, robe billowing, lecturing with words he remembered still: "Cold, hunger, wind, pain, attack—these are all things that you must learn to ignore as you focus. Even a momentary loss of concentration can result in spell failure!"

Luckily, they've had a lot more practice since then.

He steeled his mind.

"Ready?" Bridget asked, hands shaking.

He and Leera nodded.

"APREYO!"

The activity started immediately. The wall reformed before them one stone at a time, the gaping hole shrinking. It was a battle, and despite the raging wind and the painful freezing cold attacking their poor fingers, they managed to repair most of the damage. The remaining barrel-sized portion must have been out of range, probably down below with the remains of the top of the tower.

Upon finishing, they collapsed.

Augum's head pounded and his stomach roiled nauseously. The spell had taken every ounce of his energy, leaving him gasping as if he had run for leagues. If the repair had failed, they would have been too tired and cold to attempt another.

He coughed, the action sending sharp pain through his broken ribs. Still dizzy, he helped Bridget and Leera stand. The wind mostly gone, it was much easier to get warm huddling around the brazier.

After a good long rest, they once again gathered to perform arcanery, this time using Telekinesis on the brazier. They took it off its iron stand and placed it on the ground. Then they lay down around it, keeping as close to each other as they could to preserve warmth.

As Augum fell asleep, he only hoped the brazier didn't go out.

THE ATTEMPT

Augum heard a distinctive jingling in his dream before someone's cry of pain suddenly woke him. Erika loomed over them, looking pale, wearing a red winter robe finely embroidered with roses. Bridget was writhing at her feet from an apparent kick.

Leera quickly came to her aid. "You okay, Bridge?"

"She's fine, she's just exaggerating. Now get up, you lousy wenches, and make breakfast for me and my nephew."

Augum winced, having slept badly on the cold stone floor. His ribs throbbed and he felt like an icicle. A thin shaft of pale sunlight filtered in through the remaining hole in the wall, piercing their foggy breath. At least the blizzard had died. Now if they could only escape somehow …

Erika folded her arms. "Aw, quite proud of ourselves, aren't we? I watched it all, you know, and let me tell you, it was superbly amusing. You three are no end of entertainment. I'm glad you stumbled on my little doorstep." She sauntered over to the wall and inspected it closer. "Since you're so determined to repair the tower, why stop here? You can start on the rest after breakfast. I could use some more room."

She herded them downstairs, humming to herself all the while.

"Start on the bread, Squirrel," Erika said upon entering the dining room. "I'll show you how to finish it quickly using the arcane method. Freckles, I want you making porridge. Well, hop to it you nasty little things and stop leering at me like lost deer." Erika threw the pink aprons in Bridget and Leera's faces, gesturing impatiently to don them.

The girls were soon hard at work while Augum had to wash and polish dishes, no talking allowed. Meanwhile, Erika hummed obliviously, painting her nails. They worked for some time, breakfast almost ready, when suddenly there came a loud banging from below.

"Who in the—" Erika began, before focusing on the trio, "Were you followed? Tell me!"

"We don't know—!" Bridget said, raising her hands defensively as Erika's arm rippled to life with flaming rings.

"Get. Up. Stairs," she said through gritted teeth. The trio didn't need telling twice. They zoomed up the steps, Erika marching right behind while the banging grew louder down below. She locked the door behind them, warning, "I'll be watching."

Bridget angrily ripped off her apron and threw it aside, followed quickly by Leera. The trio wrapped themselves in blankets and sat silently around the still-smoking brazier, its coals extinguished, trying to ignore the orb.

Augum hoped it was his great-grandmother downstairs, or even Cled with an army of former prisoners here to return the favor of freedom.

Their breath fogged in the morning cold as they squirmed to catch the shaft of sunlight coming in through the hole. Time passed. What was happening down there? Who had come?

Suddenly Leera froze. "You hear that?"

Augum perked up. "Hear what? I don't—"

"Shh! Listen …"

They sat listening. Sure enough, there *was* some kind of sound, some kind of tinny, quiet echo.

"I think it's coming from the orb—" Bridget stood and cautiously approached it.

"Wait, what are you doing—?" he asked while she put her ear up to it. Her mouth fell open and she gestured for them to hurry over, a finger to her lips. When he placed his own ear against it, he was astonished to hear conversation. It was a bit distant and echoed, but he could distinctly make out Erika's voice.

"—oh no, my dear lord, this is all for me," she said in sugar sweet tones, finishing with a girlish laugh. Her ears jingled loudly in comparison to other sounds. He deduced from those sounds that a slew of other people had to be there, and by the creaking armor, some had to be soldiers.

"No—? And what about the horses, are they both yours as well, my dear?" asked a deep skeptical voice Augum instantly recognized. Flashes of an iron room paraded across his mind as his heart threatened to hammer a hole in his chest.

"Oh, aren't you a suspicious thing … why, yes of course they're mine, sugar." Erika's voice was much louder than Commander Tridian's. She had to be wearing whatever it was that allowed communication with the orb.

"A lady of my stature requires variety, you understand. Now please, will you and your men not join me for a most delicious breakfast?"

"That would be fine, we shall speak over breakfast then," Commander Tridian replied. Augum had the distinct impression the Blade of Sorrows was just playing a game. He knew exactly what was going on, likely even that the trio were hiding upstairs.

"Sergeant, inform our young necrophyte he may join us."

"Yes, Commander."

That had to be Robin they referred to …

There were some fussing noises that sounded like she was in the kitchen. "Please, noble sirs, sit. Why, just look how handsome you all are in that shiny armor. Now come come, do sit now, I have a fine table and chairs that don't bite."

Chairs squeaked as large men sat down.

"Let me, uh … just fix the bread here …" Erika said, humming a little quickly, the soldiers sitting silent in the background. Augum imagined the soldiers staring at her from her own table.

He wondered if she knew they were listening to her. Perhaps she was too distracted to look through the orb, or maybe it takes concentration, much like a spell. He wished they could see too, just to see her sweat …

"That is quite a lot of food for a lady all by her lonesome," Tridian said.

Erika gave a nervous chortle. "Blizzards always do make me hungry the next day—so what brings you fine bunch of gallant men this way?" and gave a girlish giggle.

"Deserters."

There was the sound of something clanging to the floor. "Oh, dear me, I'm such a klutz, you must forgive me, good sirs." She picked it up, trying to get back to a humming rhythm, though now the hum turned into a kind of nervous gurgle.

Augum wondered if the stirrings in the background were the soldiers covering their ears. He imagined them wincing and exchanging disgusted looks.

"Ah, our honored necrophyte joins us."

A silence, followed by, "Auntie! What are you—"

"Unnameables … my sweet, dear, wonderful nephew!" Erika swept forth and no doubt embraced him, as there was a tremendous scuffling and squishing noise. "Oh my darling, *darling* Robin, how good it is to see you again—!"

Robin Scarson was her nephew? Augum exchanged incredulous looks with the girls. He couldn't believe she had mistaken him for that evil snot.

"But Auntie Erika, I thought you were, um, you know, on leave from the, um, academy …"

"Oh. Oh yes! Yes indeed, my dear nephew. I am on leave to, uh … to investigate the, uh … the surrounding wilds and, uh … and confer back with my report."

Even Augum cringed with how badly this was going.

"So, my young apprentice … this is your Aunt?"

Augum would have done anything to see Robin and Erika's faces there.

Robin cleared his throat lightly. "She is, Commander."

There was an awkward pause. "Perhaps my lady would like to serve some tea?"

Now Augum had no doubt whatsoever that the Blade of Sorrows, a master questioner, had seen right through Erika's measly little attempt to obfuscate the fact she herself was a deserter. The question now was, when pressed, would she turn the trio over or attempt to keep them for herself and deny their existence here? If Tridian or Robin told her the trio's importance, he hadn't a doubt as to what she would do, especially if there was a reward attached.

"Not good," Leera mouthed with a shake of her head.

He silently agreed, wishing he had trained harder and knew more spells. On the other hand, what seems impossible may only appear unlikely under the influence of Centarro ...

There were noises he interpreted as taking the kettle off the fire, which Bridget had set earlier, and the sound of water being poured.

"This tea is quite ... unusual," Commander Tridian said. "I do not think I have had the pleasure of tasting it before."

"Isn't it simply divine? I got it from a merchant who travels regularly to Dramask."

"Is my lady aware that the Legion has cut all trade with Dramask?"

"Oh, uh, yes I am, I acquired the tea beforehand though. But enough about me—let me hear about my precious nephew!"

"Auntie, I've become an honored necrophyte!"

"So I hear, dear nephew, so I hear." A nervous chuckle. "This is most ... fantastic and wonderful. I have nothing but respect for the Legion and where it's going."

"And I used my new necromantic spells to help capture escaped prisoners in Tornvale!"

"Really now? You were always so brave, my precious little—" there was a sound like hair being ruffled.

"Oh, yes Auntie, those filthy prisoners were set loose on the poor population of the town, killing and maiming at will. I made sure they suffered for their crimes though."

"Now now, apprentice, it is unbecoming of an honored necrophyte to gloat," Commander Tridian said in a fatherly way.

"Yes, Commander. Oh, and Auntie, guess what?"

"What is it, honey pie?"

He guffawed. "For my efforts I was awarded my own healer! Sure, she has zero arcane talent but she can get the job done. I have her with me at all times, mostly in chains."

Augum thought he was going to throw up. The snot had to be talking about Mya! He instantly knew he had to save her. Bridget and Leera were looking at him, as if trying to guess what he would do. He stared back at them and mouthed, "Mya," then the word, "rescue."

Leera exchanged a look with Bridget, but Augum couldn't decipher what it meant and frankly didn't care—he was concentrating on what they were saying below.

"—and you deserve many more servants at your beck and call, Nephipoo." Erika prolonged a chortle, earrings jingling.

"Aw, Auntie, stop that." Augum imagined Erika pinching Robin's cheek. Then there was the sound of an embrace. "And don't call me that right now," Robin added in a whisper.

There was the sound of a glass placed on the table. Tridian cleared his throat. "Let us talk plainly, my lady. The Lord of the Legion is not in a good mood, and if my great lord is not in a good mood, I am not in a good mood. Do you happen to know *why* the Lord of the Legion is ill-tempered at the moment?"

A high-pitched giggle. "Oh, my sweet lord, I'm sure I haven't the faintest clue ...!"

"Well let me make it clear." Augum imagined him giving her a perfunctory smile. "The great lord is angry because it has come to his attention that should he achieve the goals of his Great Quest—that is, attain all seven scions—he would destroy himself in the process. Now, that isn't to say our lord is not trying to find a way around this ... *limitation* ... but as you can imagine, it is not a pleasant turn of events."

"Oh, yes of course, I understand." Erika sounded relieved.

"I am afraid that is not all ..." There was a pause as someone tapped the table rhythmically. "The Lord of the Legion is also unnerved by additional news supplied to him. This news, or rather knowledge, shall we say, is dangerous and contrary to the cause. Would you happen to know what news I am referring to, my dear?"

Erika clucked like a hen, a laugh not shared by anyone else. "I'm sure I don't, my dear commander."

"Let me say this, my lady—a Leyan man left the plane of Ley recently—"

"—oh, but we don't really believe in children's tales now, do we my lord?"

"I'm sure what my aunt is trying to say is—"

"—as I was saying," cut in Commander Tridian in a voice rapidly losing patience, "a Leyan man had departed Ley with four youths and one healer. Now as it turns out, one of the boys in this motley gang turned out to be none other than the son of the Lord of the Legion." The finger drumming increased in loudness. "The Lord of the Legion's son. Could you believe such a thing?"

Erika swallowed. "My sweet lord—"

"—Commander," Tridian corrected.

"—of course, forgive me, Commander." Erika's voice wavered. "It's just that the news is so incredible I seem to have lost my composure." There was a hurried wafting sound Augum interpreted as Erika fanning herself with her hand.

"And that is not even the treasonous, undermining knowledge I speak of," Commander Tridian continued in a quiet voice. "You are fully aware, I am sure, of the Great Quest, in which our lord promises eternal life to those that serve him, are you not?"

"Of course, my sweet—err, commander. Why, every woman knows of the Great Quest and her duties for the cause."

"Do they now?" A pause. "You see, the crux of the matter is the Leyan that came with the children died. He did not die in battle, or from some disease, or from falling off some cursed cliff. No, he died simply *because* he left Ley. You can see the implications if this kind of knowledge became known to the common peasant, do you not?"

"Commander, you should not have told me this, oh please, I did not hear you say such a thing, it is *treasonous*."

"But that is precisely the point, my dear. It is treasonous and a LIE!" The Blade of Sorrows' voice suddenly roared across the room accented by a fist being slammed on the table. "You already *know* this knowledge though, do you not! You harbor the Lord of the Legion's son and two others that will dare to spread these treasonous lies to the common folk!"

The room fell silent as the trio shared anxious looks. They had to find a way out of there, yet Augum simply couldn't tear himself away from the globe.

"Oh, Unnameable gods, please, I'm innocent, I swear!" Erika began weeping. This time, Augum suspected the tears real.

Tridian's voice became soft and soothing once again. "My young apprentice, I do believe now would be an adequate time to practice what you have been training."

"Commander, please, I can't, she's my Auntie—"

"The path that you wish to tread, Apprentice, requires fortitude, discipline, and commitment."

A silence passed.

"Yes, Commander," Robin finally said in a resigned voice.

Erika sniffed. "I'm sorry, I'm sure I don't understand—"

"My lady, if you will forgive our indulgence, we must put you to the question. I am sure, since you are perfectly innocent, you will have no objection."

"I ... I ..."

Augum could almost see the look of struggle on Erika's overly painted face.

"Surely my lady would not mind helping her young nephew train in the artful, though necessary skills, of the questioner by presenting herself as a willing subject—"

"My lord, I hardly think—"

The Blade of Sorrows slammed his fist on the table so suddenly everyone jumped, including Augum and the girls.

"That's *Commander*! I will not correct you again." Then Tridian once more switched to a pleasant tone. "Now, my lady, if you will please sit …"

Erika cleared her throat ever so lightly. "Well, if it should help my beloved nephew …"

A chair creaked as she sat down. Augum imagined her sitting opposite Tridian with his soldiers standing guard behind her. The man would have it no other way, he thought, remembering the way the Blade of Sorrows had manipulated and questioned him. And Robin would be pacing in front, though this time, it would be his own Auntie he would have to question.

"Now I turn over the reins to my young apprentice. Please begin." Someone slurped tea.

"Auntie—"

"—she is not your Aunt at the moment, Apprentice. Do not address her by name or title. If you do need to address her, use a demeaning title or name."

"Right …"

Erika summoned her sweetest chortle. "My dear sir—forgive me, I mean Commander—is this really necessary?"

"I am afraid it is, my *dear* lady."

"But I hardly think it appropriate for a little boy to—"

"Silence!" Robin shouted suddenly.

Erika's ears jingled as Augum imagined her recoiling.

"Excellent, Apprentice. It is important to establish control, especially when the subject shows an *unwillingness* to cooperate."

"I most certainly am willing to coop—"

"Quiet—" Robin said in a pleading voice. "Now Aun—I mean—woman, tell me what you know."

"Oh, my sweet, beloved nephew, I'm at a complete loss here, though it's quite pleasant to see you again I must say. Please give your father my regards when you next see him."

"Yes, of course Aun—I mean woman—"

"Not specific enough, Apprentice! And you cannot let your subject manipulate you like some common boy. You are to be cold, firm and hard as iron, regardless of who is before you. Use tricks of the mind if you must. There are *ways* to stick to your principles. Think of wrongs committed by the subject against you, for example."

"Well, my Aunt never did give me very large gifts for my birthday ..."

"Why *Nephew*—" Erika said in a deeply wounded voice.

"SHUT UP WOMAN!" This time, Robin's voice was filled with real rage. The room was completely silent, and Augum knew then that the commander had won. They needed to stop listening and concentrate on getting out of there. He almost felt sorry for Erika. Had to be quite humiliating to be questioned in such a manner by one's own nephew, especially for a lady who considered herself in such ... high esteem.

He unstuck his ear from the orb and beckoned the girls to join him in a huddle.

"What are you doing?" Leera whispered. "I want to see that evil witch squirm—"

"Look, I went through that, it's only a matter of time until Erika spills the grain and tells them we're here, maybe even moments. We have to get out of here, and the only thing I could think of is Centarro. It's the only spell she hasn't prepared for."

The girls nodded.

"All right," Leera said. "We can try the door. If that fails—" she looked to the hole in the wall. The suicide route.

"Let's go then," Bridget said.

They quietly made their way over and began preparing to cast Centarro, agreeing Bridget would perform the spell this time while Leera and Augum kept watch, reasoning two people suffering from the side effects of Centarro was far too risky.

"Centeratoraye xao xen," Bridget said, kneeling before the door. She took a deep breath before her hands began exploring it, particularly the keyhole. She tried various things, from peering into it, picking it with a small iron shard they had ripped from the brazier, to even stuffing it with ice.

Nothing worked.

"I can't …" she said at last, eyes already glazing over.

"Spell's wearing off," Leera said, taking her by the hand and leading her away from the orb. Bridget was soon gazing about the room like a dull child, a silly grin on her face. She pointed at the orb and was about to say something when Leera clamped a hand over her mouth, shaking her head firmly.

Meanwhile, conscious that time was quickly running out, Augum tried the Unconceal spell, hoping to find something hidden, some key or secret door or something else to pick the lock with—but there was nothing.

He caught a shaft of sunlight in the face, emanating from the barrel-sized hole in the wall they had repaired. He paced over to it and glanced outside. A sharp wind waved his hair about his forehead. The trees swayed below, shedding plumes of snow. Everything was covered by a thick fresh powdery snowfall, sparkling in the sun.

Well, this was their only hope now …

He glanced down. It was a straight drop, maybe a hundred feet, with nothing but jagged rocks below. His breath quickened. It looked like certain death to even attempt going out there.

When Centarro's side effects dissipated, the girls appeared by his side.

Bridget looked pale. "You're not seriously thinking ..."

He stepped aside. "Just have a look for yourselves, see what you think."

Bridget vigorously shook her head and retreated.

Leera stuck hers out immediately. "Here—hold on to me." She leaned out further almost before they could catch her arm. She then looked up and down the outside of the tower, hair whipping about in the wind.

"Pull me in!" They did so. "All right, I have an idea. I think there might be a way to climb *up*."

Bridget gave her a look as if she had completely lost her mind. "*What*? Why in all of Sithesia—"

"Keep your voice down," Leera said, giving the orb a sidelong look.

Augum wondered how the interrogation was going. He hoped that, as with him, Tridian was drawing it out.

"Look, trust me on this," she continued, "there're these holes in the walls above this spot. We could use them as handholds. We climb to the ruins above then make our way down, sneaking by the guards. Come on, it'll be easy, like climbing a tree."

"—and rescue Mya of course," Augum added.

"Sure," Leera said quickly.

Bridget glanced to the hole and any remaining color drained from her face.

To Augum's thinking though, they really didn't have a choice. The way down was smooth stone, and no matter how clever they were under the influence of the Centarro spell, it was simply *not* possible to live through a fall from this height. They had to risk it, the alternative too grim to consider.

He inspected the outside of the tower and confirmed Leera's theory. "Bridge, we can do this—"

Bridget took one quick look down from the lip and recoiled backwards. "No way, not doing it, no chance …" She kept shaking her head. "You two *know* I have a fear of heights …"

He rubbed his forehead. He would have suggested Bridget cast Centarro again but since she just cast it, it was too risky. If the spell wore off, or worse, failed midway up the climb … the thought was too horrible to finish.

Bridget took another step back, rubbing her arms, still shaking her head. "You two go ahead, I'll stay here and wait."

"No way, Bridge," Leera said, giving her a firm hug. "You're coming." She glanced to Augum, face etched with worry. What do you think, Aug, can she use Centarro again so soon?"

"Already thought about it—way too risky. What if the spell wore off before she got to safety? I'm even worried about us using it. It could expire before we got to the top."

"Wait, what if me and you climbed first *without* Centarro, while Bridget watched where we placed our hands and mimicked us?"

They turned to Bridget, who took a step back, endlessly shaking her head.

"Bridge, please, this is the only way." Leera took her hands in her own. "It would work as long as you didn't look down."

"You can do it, Bridge," Augum chimed in.

After a tense moment, Bridget forced a nod. He and Leera expelled a long breath.

"All right, you'll have to watch very carefully, Bridge," he said, tossing his blanket aside. He couldn't afford to get tangled up in it on the ascent. "And whatever you do, don't look down, okay? It's just like climbing a tree—"

"But I've never climbed a tree before."

Augum and Leera exchanged looks.

"Never mind that," Leera said, dragging her to the edge. "It'll be easy, trust me."

"Oh, I don't know if I can do this ..." Bridget said, glimpsing the great white expanse beyond. A wind whipped her cinnamon hair across her face. She didn't bother sweeping it aside, instead holding her hands close to herself and trying to step away from the edge, but Leera wouldn't let her.

"Look, I'll go first," he said. "Stop looking down, would you? Only look up."

Bridget nodded stiffly, still trying to squirm away from the edge. Leera took over talking to her, calmly explaining what it was she needed to do—they both need to do in fact—and that was to pay attention to where Augum was finding his handgrips.

As he swung outside the tower, dangling over a drop that would certainly kill him, the entirety of his insides felt as if they had climbed up into his throat. He clutched the wall like a spooked cat and took some time to examine the area above.

The good news was that he could see the lip of the top of the tower. The bad news was the wind and cold would be dangerous foes during the climb. Although he had climbed plenty of trees when he was younger, especially when running away from the Penderson brats, this was something wholly different. He had never climbed a wall like this before, especially not in such vicious conditions.

He reached for the first hole in the stone just above him, wincing from the stabbing in his chest, but discovered he had to scrape off the ice first. The next grip was a tiny outcrop of stone, also ice-encrusted, the one after a groove between two blocks, and so it went. It wasn't long before he developed a rhythm, scraping off a purchase with numb fingers before gripping it. He tried as best he could to let the girls see what he was grasping onto, sometimes shouting an instruction or two about which stones and holes were safest. At one point, however, a strong gust made him lose his grip and he swung out like a loose sail. Luckily, his remaining hand held, though calming Bridget down was another story.

At long last, with frozen and bleeding fingers and nerves strung thin as winter grass, he pulled himself over an icy lip caked with snow. The climb was the most foolhardy thing he had ever attempted, and he had barely made it. He took a brief look around before crouching over the lip to help guide the next person, trying to ignore the horrible buzzing anxiety his entire body felt.

As it turned out, Leera made the call to send Bridget, which he thought was wise, as they could throw encouragement from above and below. If she had gone last, there was a good chance she would not have come at all.

This could actually work, he thought, until seeing Bridget swing out, frantically clawing at the wall like a petrified rabbit. He held his breath, yet somehow she just managed to hold on.

Her small frame, juxtaposed against a long fall ending in sharp rock, was enough to make him sweat, even in this frigid cold.

"Remember, Bridge, don't look down!" Leera called from below.

"Focus on me and every handhold!" Augum called from above.

Slowly, very slowly, Bridget pawed at the next handhold, looking straight at Augum, tears rolling down her cheeks. He had never seen her so scared. "Come on, you can do it Bridge, that's it, take your time ..." he said, even though time was not exactly something they had an abundance of. He expected soldiers to storm up any moment, and then what would happen?

Yet what came next was infinitely worse. Bridget was halfway up, fingers trembling on a tentative grip, when a powerful gust swooped in. For the briefest moment, he locked eyes with her and they shared a look of surprise, before she was ripped off the tower.

Augum and Leera screamed.

THE SEEING ORB

It was a moment Augum would never forget for as long as he lived—a life flashing before his eyes, the entire sequence ending in the death of one of his best friends. Yet at the end of that visual play, where he relived every moment they shared as friends, one particular scene stood out—the time they gathered near a fire in Castle Arinthian and placed their hands on Mrs. Stone's blue book.

He remembered his words well in that sacred moment: "I solemnly swear, on the ghosts of my mother, Sir Westwood, and on those that my father has slain, that I will learn the arcane tongue. Their deaths will not have been in vain."

I will learn the arcane tongue …

A jolt of recognition.

He shot his arm out and beckoned, summoning and applying everything he had learned with Telekinesis, every ounce of arcane strength he possessed—and then reaching beyond, into the arcane unknown. Unconsciously, his 1st degree ring erupted around his forearm, a miniature bolt of lightning spiraling brighter than it had ever before.

He knew it was possible, though at a much higher degree, to move people. He *knew it.* Yet could he himself conjure that power well before he was ready?

He willed Bridget to stop falling and float to him. He felt his arcanery grip her, and amazingly, her fall slowed—but not nearly enough.

"Leera—help!" he called through gritted teeth, for he was arcanely *holding* Bridget, and if he wasn't careful, she would rip him right off the ledge. She kept falling, screaming, pulling at him like a sack of potatoes on an invisible rope.

Leera, without even having to look up, reached out and beckoned, groaning from the strain, a band of watery light vibrantly coming to life around her forearm.

Miraculously, Bridget's fall arrested—*and reversed.*

The concentration and energy required, however, was so much beyond what he had ever attempted, he felt death loom its voracious head in the frantic beating of his heart. The pain of this arcane push was scorching, as if a hot brand was being applied to his very being, but he forced himself to endure its searing sting.

His head felt like it was going to explode, every pulse a vicious hammer blow to the brain. Yet if he so much as blinked, Bridget would fall, and there was no way he would have the strength to try the spell again.

She slowly hovered toward him, wide-eyed and gasping, until at last she was within arms' reach, and just in time too, for he sensed he only had one last precious moment of concentration left. He simultaneously let go of the spell while snatching her out of thin air. They fell backwards onto snow-covered stone, the wind sweeping over them in cool waves.

The consequences of pushing his arcane limits were immediate. Bridget was saying something but he couldn't hear through the hissing rush of blood in his head. The pain was piercing, like an icicle through his skull. He couldn't help but scream and hold his head.

He tasted the iron tang of blood on his tongue, felt it drip from his nose. The pain built to an excruciating climax—he considered flinging himself off the tower to end it. Mercifully, the walls of blackness, the final defense against such blinding agony, closed in, enveloping him in deep unconsciousness.

* * *

When he came to, Bridget was holding him in her arms, gently stroking his hair. Leera sat beside her, face pale, nose bloody.

Bridget put a finger to her lips when she saw him open his eyes, gesturing that someone was coming.

For a moment, he didn't know where they were, thinking they must have gone outside Castle Arinthian to hide from Mrs. Stone or something. The fog in his brain refused him context. The thought seemed perfectly plausible until he heard the growling voice of a man, just to the other side of the ruined heap of wall they hid behind.

Then it slowly came back—the tower, Erika, Bridget falling … the voice had to be a Black Guardsman searching for them.

The tracks—did someone cover their tracks? He tried to raise his head but Bridget held him firm, pleading with her eyes.

"I can tell you they certainly aren't up here!" said the voice before making its way down, the sound of creaking armor following.

At last, she let go. He winced as he raised his throbbing head, and peeked around the corner. The tracks had been swept—maybe by Bridget or maybe by the wind. In any case, there was zero evidence of them walking, or in his case, dragging their way across the snow.

"I tossed our aprons and blankets down to get them off us," Leera murmured when he had scuttled back. She held her head and kept her eyes closed.

Bridget gripped his arm, eyes moist. "Aug—"

"—I know." He smiled and squeezed her hand. "I'm just glad you're all right."

"You saved my life. Both of you. It was … unbelievable …" Suddenly she drew them into a tight hug. His ribs ground against each other, but he ignored the pain. It was nothing like what he had experienced earlier anyway.

Bridget sniffled before letting go. "Thought for sure I was going to die. How did you do it though? To move an actual person around with Telekinesis … I mean, who knows what degree level that even is—"

They shrugged. He sat beside Leera, grimacing. "Guess the motivation was there." He thought about what happens to him when he gets cornered, how a wild lightning charge sometimes coalesces and erupts, and wondered if it was the same principle. He now understood how someone could die performing arcanery. If he had pushed himself like that with his element as opposed to a standard spell, somehow he doubted he would have lived.

The trio took time to recuperate, cleaning blood off with snow, catching their breath, and waiting things out.

Meanwhile, plenty of distant yelling came from within the tower, mostly about the trio and where they were. Did Erika lie? Did she have them hidden? Was she thinking of cashing them in to Sparkstone herself to get some kind of reward? Was she aiding the insurgents? These questions and more were barked into her face from both her precious nephew and, more dangerously, from the Blade of Sorrows, who was utterly incensed, promising a joyful stay at the Tornvale prison.

Augum didn't feel one bit sorry for her as she was dragged shouting and weeping down the steps by guards.

Although he somehow wasn't surprised, he wondered why she didn't just use her arcanery to teleport away.

Commands were thrown out to continue searching the place and look for a trail outside. The trio judged it best to stay in their little hiding spot for now, tucked behind a partially destroyed wall and a pile of rubble. Despite the sun being out for a change, it was still very cold and windy, so they couldn't stay here for more than a couple hours at most. Then they would have to make their move, and it was for that that they planned.

"Why don't we sneak back down," Augum began in a whisper, "to the room we had been imprisoned in? They wouldn't think of going back there."

"No, the orb's probably still there," Leera said.

Bridget glanced to the edge. "Well we're definitely not climbing down." This drew quiet chuckles.

"We could charge down the stairs and barrel over anyone in our way," Leera said, still holding her head and wincing in pain.

He smiled. Saving Bridget made the world seem a lot easier to deal with, knowing she was by their side to enjoy it with them, and that they were capable enough to save her from falling to her death.

A reflective hour passed with no consensus reached as to what to do. Luckily, the throbbing had at least diminished to a manageable level.

I'm going to scout a little," he said.

"No, it's too dangerous—" Bridget said.

"Let him go, Bridge. We have to get out of the cold eventually."

Bridget gave a reluctant nod. "Just please be careful."

"I will, promise."

He crept downstairs as quiet as a mouse, ready to bolt back up at the slightest noise. The door to the room that once confined them was ajar, while the door leading to the lower portion of the tower was closed.

He peeked around the doorframe and saw that the orb now sat in the middle of the room. For a horrifying moment, he imagined himself spotted, until he thought about it some more. The orb was away from its original spot, almost as if it had broken free of its mooring and rolled in that direction. This was odd because Erika had arcanely locked it in place.

So did it mean the orb was 'off'?

Trusting his instincts, he tiptoed up to it. It appeared cold and dead. He poked it, yet no eye opened from within. Finally, he picked it up. It was stone heavy. He carried it back to the girls, who almost jumped out of their skin.

"*Augum Stone,* have you completely lost all sense?" Bridget asked.

"You sound like Nana." He thought he'd have some fun and shook it.

The girls gasped.

"I think its link with Erika is broken or something." He put his ear to it. "Can't hear anything."

"What if it's only turned off for now?"

He hadn't thought about that part. "Um, well, don't think it is, but I suppose that's possible."

Even Leera, who usually had his back in these kinds of things, was looking at him as if he had lost his mind.

He groaned. "Fine, I'll go put it back …"

"Wait—" Bridget ran both hands through her hair. "Maybe … maybe we could use it. If we can figure out how to tap into its power somehow, it could be useful."

"I think it's worth trying," he said. "And honestly, I don't think it's off temporarily or anything like that."

Leera took it from him. "I command you to, um, to meld with me."

He raised his brows. " 'Meld with me'?"

She ignored him. "I command you to be my eyes—"

"Oh, give me that—" Bridget said. She gave the orb a hug, to which both Augum and Leera had to hold back from laughing. It just looked so weird. After she tried a bunch of different variations, all to do with hugging for some reason, she gave up and returned it to him.

He watched it, grimacing.

"Trying to win a staring contest?" Leera asked.

"No … I'm thinking. Just give me a moment."

She folded her arms and sat back to watch, a smug look on her face.

He thought he'd try something neither of the girls had—arcanery. Although his head still hurt from earlier, he was nonetheless able to perform the spells at a basic level. First, he tried the Unconceal spell, though that didn't do a thing, the globe looking as dull as ever. Next, he tried Telekinesis, bobbing it up and down in the air, which also didn't do anything except maybe make his head hurt more and widen Leera's smirk. Then he tried Repair, but as Bridget casually pointed out, "It doesn't look broken to me …"

"Only one possible spell left. Shyneo." He placed his lit palm directly onto the globe—and it instantly lit up. On top of that, he was able to *see* through it for a moment, though the glimpse was as brief as blinking.

"Whoa—" Bridget edged away from it. "You did that, right? I thought I saw an eye open for a moment there."

"I think that was me, yeah." He extinguished his palm. Now, how to see through it?

A genuine smile replaced Leera's smirk. "All right, you win. Good job." She picked it up. "Hey, why isn't it locked in place?"

"I think I have to lock it down or something."

She revolved it in her hands. "It should come with a parchment of instructions. Can you see through it now?"

"Nope."

Bridget shivered and drew her robe tighter. "Maybe it needs some kind of command word."

"Again, instructions ..."

Although it was warmer than the day before due to the sun, they were slowly freezing, and the only real alternative to Mrs. Stone miraculously showing up out of the blue to snatch them to safety (as Leera hoped would happen) was to descend the stairs and somehow sneak by the guards.

When he peeked over the edge of the tower earlier, there were a slew of Black Guards searching for them. He peeked again, this time hoping to catch a glimpse of Mya, whom he was still planning on rescuing. Only about a dozen milled below now, chatting idly as if taking a break. A little ways off in the forest, he spotted men on horseback searching the ground.

He retreated from the edge, disappointed he had not seen Mya. "They're still there."

Bridget blew on her hands. "We're freezing. I say we go down."

He grabbed the globe. "I'm ready."

They followed him to the stairway door just below their former prison room. He placed his hand on the handle and his ear against the door, hearing nothing. Was there no one left in the tower? There were three rooms below this level—Erika's dining room, Erika's bedroom, and that burned-out room, but it was possible someone could be in any of them without him hearing. There could even be guards on the other side of this very door. If that was the case, they were most likely doomed.

He went with his instincts again and twisted the handle.

The passage was clear.

They descended quietly. When he was sure the dining room was just around the bend, he stopped and listened.

Nothing.

He took his first step toward the dining room when the screech of a chair had them freeze to the spot.

"Ugh, I'm so sick of waiting for the search party." It was Robin's voice. "I'm telling you, we should be out there practicing our craft. It's so stupid that we have to sit here with nothing better to do than stare at each other."

"What, am I not pretty enough to look at?"

And that was Haylee's voice!

The trio exchanged looks. Haylee Tennyson had been their enemy back in Sparrow's Perch. Her grandfather had been the central figure in orchestrating the whole raid by the Legion in the first place, a raid that took the lives of Bridget and Leera's families and friends.

Augum remembered Haylee well—long-haired blonde with cold blue eyes and a small pointed nose, walking around the village like she owned the place, a clique of girls and boys (Robin included) always in tow.

"You know what I meant," Robin said.

Haylee breathed an exasperated sigh. "Better to be warm in here than freeze out there."

"Guard, what say you?" Robin said. "Think we can go soon? Obviously the lowborn rats have escaped."

"I do not know, my lord, but we have orders to keep you here until relieved by the commander."

Robin drummed the table.

"Stop that already—" Haylee said. "You've been driving us crazy with that for hours now."

He stopped, making a sound like he was sucking on his teeth.

"Really, Robin, you can be so crass sometimes. Anyway, you were *supposed* to be teaching me about the fundamentals of being a necrophyte. I mean, that's why I'm here, right? Practical experience in the field and all that?"

"Yeah yeah, I don't feel like it right now, okay? Maybe later."

Haylee sighed loudly. A chair screeched as someone rose. "Ugh, this place is so gross, how did your Aunt survive living alone in these … conditions?"

When Robin didn't bother to respond, there was the sound of pacing. "So you think she was telling the truth? Were they really here?"

Robin smacked the table. "I told you I don't know! Auntie Erika was a black sheep in the family."

"Oh? Why was that?"

"Well, for one, she was almost expelled from the academy when she was our age."

"For what?"

"Theft. They said she stole some ancient artifact. It was a real scandal. The family leaned on the council and they reinstated her, not that they had any real proof she stole it. Anyway, she wasn't here alone all this time, she's had that nasty little pet of hers to keep her company."

"Not hers anymore."

"Whatever, I don't care. If the gutterborns were ever here, they're long gone now. The hounds will track them down eventually. The Legion always gets its way, and I'm learning from the best when it comes to the art of the question. Did you know I questioned five people over the last few days? *Five*."

"Five whole people," Haylee said, sounding bored.

"Yeah, seriously. First there was that idiot trapper, who had to be put down for desertion and impudence—so what if I accidentally lit his mutt on fire? It was only a stupid *dog*—"

Augum exchanged another look with the girls. So *that's* what happened to poor Frankie the Trapper and his loveable hound!

"Don't be harming any more animals, Robin Scarson."

"Are you deaf? I *told* you it was an accident—"

"And the kitten at the academy?"

"That wasn't my fault! Anyway, then there was that foul stinking rat that doesn't deserve to be our great lord's son—can't wait to get my hands on him again. Next time I'll make him suffer so much his dead mother will hear the screams.

"Then I had the pleasure of putting my new healer to the question. I assure you she won't be trying to escape. Should have seen her bawl. Easier to break than a twig—"

Augum felt his blood boil. Even imagining Mya in that iron room with Robin made him want to rush in there and deliver a Dap-style beating. Almost as if knowing his thoughts, he felt Leera's hand on his shoulder, giving it a squeeze.

"Then I trained a little on this complete moron farmer that supposedly freed all the prisoners, though how he could have done that is beyond me. Man was as thick as an oak. Probably did it by accident if anything. The only reason he still lives is his sons have signed up to the cause." He paused. "How many is that now?"

"Don't know."

"Oh yeah, and now would you believe I've had to put my own aunt to the question? Huh?"

"Huh," Haylee echoed in dull tones, still pacing the room.

Robin chuckled. "Truthfully though it was kind of fun. I don't really feel sorry for her. She's always been stingy with presents."

"The commander says your aunt's lying, you know. I think he's planning on having her flayed or something."

"Yeah well the Blade of Sorrows thinks everyone is lying half the time ..."

"Careful what you say, people might get the wrong impression."

"You threatening me—?"

"Don't be paranoid."

Robin sighed. "Haven't been seeing much success with raising walkers yet, and I don't want to return to the academy without spawning at least one wraith."

"That's way beyond your degree."

"We'll see. All I've managed to do was raise a bunch of old fogeys at some cemetery, and they were useless, running off almost immediately. One day though, one day I'll raise them like Lord Sparkstone does."

Augum wondered if it was one of Robin's walkers he had run into by the trapper's cabin.

"The great lord himself is going to instruct you when he gets back from capturing the crone. You should feel honored."

"Mind your tone."

Haylee stopped pacing. "Excuse me?"

"You heard me, girl."

"I'm not your 'girl', nor am I one of your slaves, Robin Scarson. I'm a highborn—"

"Why don't you just shut up—"

"How *dare*—"

"You heard me. Shut. Up."

A tense silence passed as the trio exchanged looks.

"I suppose you're right," Robin continued as if nothing had happened, "he *did* reward me with my own healer after all. I'm going to drag her back to the academy and make her carry all my books. Wish I brought her along today, she could have made me lunch. Probably better company too." He cackled like a vulture.

Augum felt queasy. Robin had left Mya behind in Tornvale. Worse still, she was going to be his personal slave.

Suddenly there was the sound of boots on the stairs, ascending quickly. He and the girls barely had time to meld back in the shadows, hoping the soldiers did not advance beyond the room.

"My lord, Commander Tridian found some tracks he thinks might belong to the fugitives. You are instructed to come at once."

"Finally! Come on, Hayles, let's get out of this miserable dump." The sound of movement. "Well, you coming, girl? Silent treatment, huh? Whatever, you can stay here and rot for all I care."

He blew by with a gang of guards. At last, Haylee followed, sniffling quietly.

THE CHASE

"Here—have one of these." Leera handed Augum a piece of buttered bread, the remains of the food the Legion had not confiscated or eaten.

He took it and stared at it dully, envisioning sweeping back to Tornvale and rescuing Mya from the Legion's clutches.

"How are you feeling, Aug, ready to press on?" Bridget asked, riffling through a cupboard. The girls had been searching the kitchen trying to find anything they could take for the coming journey. So far they had found two loaves of journey bread, raisins, nuts, sunflower seeds, dried cherries, two winter apples, and some dried strips of salmon. All he had done was slump in one of the ebony chairs.

Bridget sat down across from him, leaning forward while he played with the chunk of bread. "Aug, I'm really sorry about Mya, I really am, but you know we can't go back. We have to find Mrs. Stone. Don't be sad. Now come help us find food for the journey." She gave Leera a look.

Leera strode over and slapped him on the back. "Come on, you warlock, we could use your help here."

He sighed and took a bite of the bread, knowing the girls were right. They couldn't go back to get Mya, it'd be foolish and dangerous, not to mention it'd send them even further away from Mrs. Stone, and if there was anyone who could save Mya now, it was Nana.

He finished his bread and half-heartedly helped search the place. After some more rummaging, the trio found flint and steel, but nothing else of use. Bridget and Leera then tried using Unconceal. Strangely, both were guided to the same spot underneath the table.

Leera dropped to her knees and crawled under. "Oh, it's just one of Erika's earrings …"

"Maybe it's valuable and we can sell or trade it," he said.

She tossed it to Bridget, who raised it to the light of the candelabra.

Augum, who at that moment happened to glance at Erika's seeing orb resting on a chair, saw an eye open within. He recoiled away. "I think Erika just saw us …"

"Oh no …" Leera whispered.

"Wait a moment," Bridget said. "I just saw *you*, Aug, but from down low, almost as if I was looking *through* the orb."

"Well, I just saw an eye open in the orb …"

There was a communal sigh of relief.

"The earring must be the key then!" Leera said. "She must have hidden it so the Legion wouldn't confiscate it. She probably thought she could get it back later!"

"It's kind of easy to use too. Here, you try it." Bridget handed the pearl earring over to Leera. A moment later, an eye opened inside the orb.

Leera inspected the earring closer. She popped the pearl out of its clipping. "Hey, look at that—she had it mounted on an earring to conceal it. Clever …"

"Now all we have to do is figure out how to see through it without the eye showing up in the orb," Bridget said.

"And how to lock it into place," he said, receiving it from Leera. It was finely engraved, much like ivory carvings he had seen at the village market. He practiced watching through the orb. It was bizarre to see from a wholly different location that had nothing to do with his body. The actual visual was kind of like closing one eye and viewing through curved glass. He couldn't look through his own eyes and the orb at the same time either—it had to be one or the other, which explained why Erika had not checked in on them. She was too busy paying attention to her questioning.

Then he realized something. "We just have to remember that when we use the orb to snoop, someone can listen in on us."

Bridget began gathering the supplies into a tablecloth. "We'll just have to be careful then."

Leera covered her eyes with her hand. "Okay, I can't watch your eye anymore, Aug. It's kind of freaky."

"How about now?"

"That's better, it's gone."

"But I can still see you!" He said, thinking he may have just figured out one of the mysteries.

"What? How?" She inspected the orb.

"Hi!" he yelled, opening his eye at the same time.

She shrieked. "Ugh, you foul—" and punched him hard on the shoulder.

"Come on, it was funny," he said, rubbing his arm.

"Anyway, how did you do it?"

"Best way I can describe it is I just thought the word 'hide' while still watching through the orb."

"Oh, that's all? So I suppose in order to lock it you just have to think the word 'lock'?"

"Let's find out. Try and pick it up." While peering through the pearl, he thought of the orb being locked.

She groaned trying to pick it up. "Locked. Hmm, I wonder if …" She kicked the chair out from underneath. The orb hung in mid-air, unmovable.

Bridget stopped gathering supplies. "Good job, you two. Now I hate to spoil the fun, but we should probably get going. The Legion will be back when they realize whatever tracks they're following aren't ours."

Augum and Leera agreed. It was afternoon already and they had to put some distance between themselves and the Legion before nightfall, preferably without being followed.

"Let's hope they didn't find our stuff," he said, grateful he had hidden the rucksack.

They wandered downstairs, briefly listening at the ground level door before walking through.

"Of course they took the horses …" he muttered upon spotting the empty spot where their palfreys had been.

His father would surely get to Mrs. Stone first now.

Losing the horses was one thing, but what about the rucksack? He searched for it while Bridget and Leera went for the barrels of blankets and biscuit beef.

"Found it," he said, immediately checking the contents. Luckily, everything was still there—the Dreadnought dagger Blackbite, Tridian's sheepskin map, a small leather bag of coins, Mrs. Stone's blue book on arcaneology, and the yellow book on elements. Additionally, he packed in the orb and the supplies Bridget had wrapped in a tablecloth.

The girls rescued nine Dramask blankets and enough linen-wrapped biscuit beef to last them at least seven days. They turned him around and stuffed the beef chunks and three blankets into the rucksack. It bulged, straps already digging into his shoulders, exacerbating the pain in his chest.

The warmth was worth it, he told himself.

The trio then hurried to the iron gate, the girls burdened with three folded blankets each. They soon spotted a group of seven soldiers patrolling the outskirts of the ruins, black armor glinting in the sun. The soldiers seemed more preoccupied with a conversation they were having than being on the lookout, something Augum planned to take full advantage of.

"Leera, mind grabbing the map out?" he asked quietly, kneeling by the gate. She tugged at the rucksack and produced the sheepskin, splaying it out before them.

He traced with a finger. "All right, here's what I'm thinking—we follow the river east a bit then head up north and cut through Blackwood here." He tapped the bony trees.

Leera bit her lip. "I wish there was a way to arcanely message Mrs. Stone ..."

"Must be possible," Bridget said. "Although ... I've never seen a warlock deliver a message arcanely. Come to think of it, they all used messengers or heralds."

"Yeah and they didn't mention anything at the academy about it," Leera said. She nodded at the patrolling soldiers. "Let's just steal their horses."

"I think that's too dangerous," Bridget said.

"But we can't race his father to Mrs. Stone without them."

The girls turned to him.

"It *is* risky to steal their horses," he began, "but the way I see it, it's only a matter of time until the Blade of Sorrows returns with the dogs. I think we need to put as much distance between them and us as possible. That means horses. And for sure there's no way we'd catch up to my father, who already has a head start, without them. Besides, we can take the river."

"I suppose taking the river *would* eliminate our scent," Bridget said. "Make it hard for the dogs. All right … let's do it."

Leera rolled up the map and stuffed it back into the rucksack. "Now we just have to find where they tied up their horses."

They waited until the soldiers passed from sight behind the ruins before sneaking around the opposite side of Evergray Tower, using tracks made by the guards.

The sun warmed Augum's face, something he had missed in Ley. Every branch on every tree wore thick coats of snow. Other than the trickle of the river and a very light breeze, it was winter quiet.

There behind the tower, they spotted the soldiers tending to their horses. They waited until the soldiers returned to their patrol back around the opposite side of the tower. As soon as the soldiers were out of sight, he and the girls crept up on the horses, some of which whinnied.

"Relax and stare at the ground," he said to the girls. He made calm sounds, trying to appear unconcerned, something Sir Westwood had taught him. There were nine horses in all, two of which were the chestnut Bridget named Spirit and the gray he had ridden. The rest were warhorses, powerful chargers that overshadowed the two palfreys. They decided to ride as before, the girls on Spirit, Augum on the cloud-gray.

They snagged a nearby sack of oats and a waterskin and tied each to one of the palfreys, before quietly leading them away from the chargers, who still whinnied. For a moment, Augum contemplated shooing the warhorses away before realizing how stupid of an idea that was. The horses wouldn't go far and were likely trained enough to be called by their owners. As it was, it wouldn't be long before the soldiers returned.

He climbed atop his horse, adjusting the rucksack. The girls secured the blankets and mounted their palfrey, Leera taking the reins, Bridget holding her waist.

They cantered down to the river, but it immediately became clear walking along the edge was impossible. The blizzard had frozen the water almost up to the center. If they tried navigating that narrow watery chasm, they risked freezing to death in its depths.

Suddenly a distant cry of alarm went up.

"They're on to us—" Leera said. "Go—go—go!"

He kicked the flanks of his horse and jolted forward. It was now a race to get out of there. He only hoped the palfreys were faster, though he knew the chargers probably had better stamina.

"We're too slow, cut through the trees!" Leera called.

He turned left over the bank and into a sparsely wooded plain, pushing the palfrey to a full gallop, something that was dangerous in snow this high. The horse could stumble and send him flying.

"They're cutting across!" Bridget yelled.

He glanced over his shoulder and spotted the Black Guard soldiers darting between the trees at full gallop, plumes of snow billowing behind them. He counted six, the seventh probably sent after the Blade of Sorrows' party. Their powerful chargers had the advantage in deep snow and were gaining fast.

The strap of the rucksack cut deeper into his shoulder with every bounce. Branches scratched at his face as he ducked under trees rather than going around them, hoping the size of the warhorses prevented such strategy. It proved beneficial, knocking one Black Guardsman off his horse in a spectacular explosion of snow. Five still kept pace about thirty horse-lengths behind. One in particular, a man standing on his stirrups with a long-handled double-edged axe on his back, gained rapidly, leaving the rest struggling to catch up.

"Faster, Spirit!" Bridget called. "Faster—!"

Augum looked back beyond the flailing hair of the girls. The soldier was furiously whipping his horse with his reins. The rider was doing a sprint, something he and the girls could not afford, needing the palfreys to go long distance.

Twenty horse lengths.

Ten.

Five.

The charger foamed at the mouth, looking as mad as its rider.

Augum ducked under a particularly low-hanging series of branches, hoping the soldier would have to go around. Unfortunately, it accomplished nothing except knocking the man's helmet off, releasing long graying hair surrounding a large bald spot.

The Legionnaire threw up a battle cry and unsheathed his axe.

"Faster, Leera!" Bridget squealed.

Augum slowed his horse and let Spirit overtake. The soldier was now only one horse-length behind, still standing in his stirrups, axe raised.

"Die, insurgent!" The soldier swung his axe with a grunt.

Augum raised his arm just in time. The axe smashed into a coiled lightning shield that disappeared almost immediately. The impact almost knocked him off his horse and caused the soldier to lose a few paces.

"I'm okay, keep going!" Augum shouted as Bridget turned back, terror on her face.

The pack of riders fell further and further behind. If he could only knock this soldier off, they might have a chance …

The rider roared again and pushed forward, his poor charger flaring its nostrils, gushing rapid-fire plumes of steam.

Augum didn't know if he could summon the Shield a second time—he had to think of something else.

He cut the rider off, forcing him to his right side. "SHYNEO!" he called, simultaneously summoning his 1st degree lightning ring.

"A single ring, ha!" called the soldier.

"It isn't for you—" Augum replied, pointing his electrified palm at the charger, who instantly veered aside. The balding Legionnaire flew forward with a yelp, sending up a blast of snow.

Bridget and Leera shouted a cry of victory as Augum raced to catch up.

SCHOOL ON HORSEBACK

The soldiers were now well behind and slowing, probably betting on the stamina of the chargers. The trio reduced speed to a canter only after passing a creek that, along with the other streams and rivers, made up the Creeping Fingers. As the day wore on and the soldiers disappeared out of view, the trio slowed to a trot and rode side-by side.

"Spirit's tired," Bridget said, patting the horse's flank.

"We can't stop to give them a rest," Leera said.

"I know … poor thing."

"Anyone hungry?" Augum asked, removing his rucksack and handing out biscuit beef, dried cherries and journey bread.

After eating, they each wrapped themselves in a layer of blankets. Augum wished he still had the wolf hide coat the girls made for him. His hands were already freezing on the reins and his turnshoes barely provided any protection.

The trees thinned and soon disappeared altogether as they found themselves crossing a gently rolling snow-covered plain, lit up by late-afternoon winter sun. The sky yielded only a smattering of clouds. He felt lucky there was only a breeze, as Solian plains tended to rake the land with howling gales.

"That has to be Blackwood," he said, eyeing a gangly forest in the distance. He dug out the map and double-checked their position, planning to enter the forest's east end. He still hoped to lose their tail in the wood, though they had yet to think of a clever way to do this. The snow was just too deep to cover their tracks.

"What do you think Mrs. Stone is doing right now?" Bridget asked, head resting on Leera's shoulder.

"Probably reading by a hearth, or snoozing," he replied. The idea of a cozy fire appealed greatly at that moment.

"Hey, Aug, mind digging out that yellow book on elements for me?" Bridget asked. He withdrew it from the rucksack and handed it over. Bridget started flipping through the burnt pages. "Hmm, looks like it's only on the lesser elemental spells."

Augum went through the spell levels in his mind. The first five degrees were called lesser spells, the next five mid-range spells, the five after that greater spells, and the last five were Spells of Legend. Mrs. Stone knew all twenty degrees, whereas the trio only toiled on their second.

Bridget started repeatedly lighting up her palm with Shine, the glowing green ivy curling around her fingers and wrist.

"What're you up to?" Leera asked.

"Says here I can latch onto things with my vine. Would have been useful to know hanging outside a certain tower."

"So it's kind of like when I shock something with my Shine spell—" he said.

"It says it's called an 'extension'."

Leera lit her palm, inspecting the watery blue light. "Extension. Hmm, wonder what mine does ..."

"Let me check." Bridget flipped through the pages. "Sorry, Lee—burned away."

"Bah ..." Leera extinguished her hand while Bridget relit hers, trying to manipulate it in various ways.

"All right, this is hard," she conceded after multiple failed attempts to entwine the reins.

"You have to practice," he said, remembering how hard Mrs. Stone drove him to succeed and how hard he had to drive himself.

"Now you know why you're supposed to be paired up with an experienced warlock in your element," Bridget said. "It's what the whole apprenticeship thing is based on."

"Does it say anything else about mine?" he asked.

"Nothing you don't already know—it can administer a small shock, and when you attain a high level, you can create a floating sphere of Shine that follows you. Though it does say, 'There may be uses as yet undiscovered depending on the warlock wielding the spell.' "

"Probably have to attain mastery or something to do that," Leera said. "Like Mrs. Stone."

"What about the 2nd degree," he pressed, "what elemental spell are we supposed to learn next?"

"Sorry, Aug, I keep forgetting you hadn't gone to the academy. The Slam spell."

Leera swatted idly. "You didn't miss much. Just think of a whole bunch more kids like Haylee and Robin running around. But yeah, I remember the Slam spell. It's awesome."

"What kind of spell is it?" he asked.

Leera shifted in the saddle. "It's this huge noise, different for each element. For mine, it's the sound of water crashing. The better you get at it, the louder and scarier and more real it becomes."

"Mine is the sound of a huge tree breaking," Bridget said, face buried in the book.

"What's mine?" he asked.

Leera's brow rose. "Well, isn't it obvious?"

"Is it … thunder?"

"Yes," Bridget said, "and if done right, it's deafening."

"I remember the arcane word to be very guttural, kind of like a growl," Leera said. "Bridge, remember that one time when that second year kid got down on all fours and pretended to be a wolf while trying the spell, as if howling it would work?"

Bridget chortled. "Yeah, he was weird. Hey, remember how that one kid—what was his name, Don or something?"

"The quiet good-looking one with the nice smile?" A dreamy look passed over Leera's face.

"Him, yes. Remember how he would try to perform this spell even though we were strictly not allowed to try it?"

"Yeah I do, and he got suspended and did the spell anyway on his way out the door, this massive sound of exploding fire—"

"—teachers ran for it thinking the building was going to go …"

The girls giggled then sighed.

"Ah, whatever happened to him anyway?" Leera asked. "He didn't join us at Sparrow's Perch."

Bridget turned somber. "Don't know …"

"You miss the academy?" Augum asked, wishing he'd had a chance to go, even if just for a few months like the girls.

Bridget returned to the book. "Sometimes, but not really."

"I kind of like harrowing death-defying adventure," Leera said. "Seriously though, I'd rather be stuck here with the two of you rascals instead of being forced to study necromancy in the academy. Though I'd have probably run away ..."

Bridget gave a wry smile. "Or flunked."

"Hey—"

"Kidding. Anyway, you two want to start learning the second elemental spell or not? It's not going to be easy learning it from a book, but I think we should at least try."

"We did promise Nana we'd study every day," he said. "It'll be a classroom on horseback."

"Except we're the teachers," Bridget added.

"And the lesson might mean the difference between life and death," Leera chimed in.

The first thing they practiced was the pronunciation: "Grau", similar to "growl", minus the last letter, spoken gutturally. To Augum, it was embarrassing and funny at the same time—embarrassing when he tried it, funny when the girls did.

"Aww, you're like a playful kitten trying to sound ferocious," Leera remarked upon Bridget's attempt.

Bridget only frowned. "Anyway, the book says you're supposed to concentrate on the air snapping, whatever that means ..."

It was a line that could have used the explanation of a mentor, a luxury they didn't have and so had to interpret. Even if they managed to understand a paragraph or two, they stumbled on wordy portions like: *The pupil is instructed to discuss these three unimpeachable points with her mentor in order to deduce the substantive application of the spell and its ramifications on arcane stamina.*

Leera made a face as if smelling a most rank odor. "What ...?"

"I think it means we're supposed to talk about the spell with our mentor and understand how it affects our arcane stamina," Bridget said.

Leera flashed Augum a *she's such a bookworm* look.

Bridget smacked Leera's arm with the book. "Hey, I saw that—"

"Careful or I'll fall and you'll get detention." Leera's voice took the tone of a snobbish teacher. "Mr. Stone, you're going to have to discipline this unbridled student here, this is just not acceptable."

"I am in full agreement with Ms. Jones," he said in a nasal voice. "I am duly sorry, Ms. Burns, but we do not permit such barbarous behavior in our fine Travelling School on Horseback."

After the chuckling died down, they continued studying, flipping to each chapter—or what was left of it—pertaining to their particular element, and reading it aloud, discussing the points. Some of the concepts were very complex and obviously meant for the mentor to read and interpret for the student. In those instances, they did what they could, but mostly ended up ignoring or skipping over the section, hoping to work it out later.

As the sun began to set and the cold chipped away at their morale, they traded studying for food, stopping quickly to feed the horses and munch on salted salmon and dried apple.

"Think there's anything in those woods?" Leera asked, stroking Spirit's neck.

Augum looked to the twisted forest ahead. "Don't know."

Bridget placed a hand above her eyes and glanced across the vast snowy plain behind them. "We need to figure out a way to lose the Black Guards following us."

"You can see them?"

"No, but I doubt they just gave up."

"I bet the Blade of Sorrows has been alerted by now." He withdrew the map, splaying it across the flank of his horse. The girls gathered near. "All right, I'm guessing we're right about here." He thumbed the southeast corner of

Blackwood. "They're expecting us to ride straight north to Mt. Barrow, but what if we lost them in the wood and took a detour, say like east through the plain, or west and up the Summerwine?"

"We'd lose a lot of time," Leera said, "and we need to get to Mrs. Stone as soon as possible."

Bridget gave a nod. "I agree. I think we should just go straight north, pick up the pace if anything."

He tapped his chin with his thumb. "If we don't lose them in this wood we'll have to ride through the night. Otherwise they might catch up to us."

Leera curled strands of raven hair around her finger. "I think we should ride through the night anyway, it's something they won't be expecting. They probably think we're little brats that can't push ourselves. Besides, unless we find some unmarked river or another blizzard comes, we won't be able to just make our tracks—" she made an explosive gesture, "*poof*, disappear."

They traded daring looks.

"Really up for this?" Bridget asked.

"Definitely."

"Yes."

"Let's do it then."

He had never stayed up all night before. He put the map away and passed around a few chunks of biscuit beef.

They were going to need all the energy they could get.

BLACKWOOD

By the time they entered Blackwood, the sun had set, leaving a reddish line on the horizon. The forest was eerily similar to its depiction on the map—gnarled and dreary, consisting mostly of rotting white birches. Branches were bare but for snaking caps of snow. The silence amplified every sound.

Be wary of a quiet forest, Sir Westwood used to say. Well, there certainly was something not quite right about this particular wood. Even the smell was off, reminding Augum of the crypt in Castle Arinthian. He made sure to keep an eye on the snow for tracks, especially really thin ones.

"This isn't a forest, it's a tomb," Leera whispered. "If there was a place I'd peg as the spawning ground for walkers …"

"Gives me the creeps," Bridget murmured.

They wound their way along at a cautious gait, Bridget holding Leera with one hand and Blackbite with the other. Augum, meanwhile, entertained second thoughts about the whole plan. Travelling through a forest like this during the day was bad enough. At night, it just seemed crazy.

Clouds soon obscured the twinkling stars. Exhausted, nerves strained from the constant vigilance, he had a difficult time lighting up his palm.

"Shyneo," he said for the third time. It sputtered to life at last, distorting the forest with bony fingers of moving shadow. They bundled in their blankets, Leera resting her head on Bridget's shoulder, trying to sneak some rest. The girls traded places every hour, taking the reins and keeping watch, with Augum volunteering to lead. They also took turns lighting Shine, hoping it didn't draw anything to them.

"What's that smell?" Bridget asked.

Augum took a whiff. "Stinks like something really rotten."

"Death," Leera said. "That's the stink of death."

They stopped the horses, listening to the night's stillness.

"You sure?" Bridget whispered, covering her nose.

Leera watched the trees as she spoke. "Back in Blackhaven, Mum and I went to bring a very old neighbor carrot cake. When mum opened the door, it smelled exactly like that. She told me to fetch dad and wouldn't let me come in. I only found out later she had died. No one had come visit her for so long …"

"That's sad …"

Augum pointed at a black birch to their left. "Is that tree burned over there?"

"I don't know if I want to investigate," Bridget said. "Maybe we should just keep going."

They glanced at each other.

"Why don't I take a quick look?" he said.

"Oh no, you're not leaving us behind in this place," Leera said, tightening the reins.

He nudged the gray forward, suddenly fully aware of the darkness. His horse nickered and stopped. "Come on, boy, forward," yet the palfrey refused.

"Spirit won't go either," Leera said.

"Let's forget this and keep going," Bridget whispered.

He studied the dark forest ahead. "There's something on the ground there."

Bridget made a quiet squeak. "I can't look. Is it … is it moving?"

"No. It's a black area." He smelled burnt wood, too, and suddenly recalled seeing Willowbrook burn. The hair on his neck stood on end. "The Legion …"

He dismounted.

Bridget's voice was full of panic. "Aug, please don't—"

"I have to see what happened." What if there was someone who needed help? He handed Leera the reins.

"Aug, I don't know about this—" she said.

"I'll be quick." He waded through the waist-high snow, sweeping slow arcs with his lit palm. Every bone in his body screamed to turn back.

He froze as out of the darkness loomed black sticks with hanging sinewy strips.

Sticks in the sand, sticks in the snow, reveal a man, dead long ago …

He calmed his breathing, realizing they were burnt tent poles, the strips merely torched canvas. A note hung from the tallest one, gently dancing in the breeze. He swallowed hard and plodded forward, determined to read it.

It was written in blood, long dried, with a shaky hand.

I returned from the hunt to find my wife and three young daughters dead. We thought we'd be safe here, so far from Blackhaven. We were so very wrong. The Legion found us. They slaughtered everyone—the entire village—and burnt their bodies. All that I loved is gone. May the Unnameables have mercy on my soul, for madness awaits.

He left the note be and turned back, only to step on something squishy in the snow. He hurried back to the horses, telling himself it was probably nothing …

"You all right, Aug?" Leera asked. "You look awful."

"I'm fine," he lied, feeling sweat prickle his neck. He mounted his palfrey, gripping the reins with white-knuckled hands. "Let's get out of here."

"What did you see?" Bridget asked in a small voice as they resumed the journey.

"The Legion, they …" He gave them a certain look.

Bridget put a hand over her mouth and glanced in the direction of the razed encampment. Nothing more was said. He was glad they didn't ask him for details. They knew firsthand anyway of the horrors the Legion brought.

The palfreys steadily plowed through the snow, piled so high in these parts the trio had to keep their feet raised or risk frostbite on their toes. The cold deepened with the late hour and it became increasingly difficult to remain alert. It went on this way, league after league, hour after hour, until the night passed.

Dawn came harsh and frozen, the eastern sun lighting up a crisp blue sky. Even the morning was dead quiet in Blackwood. Not an animal stirred, nor a bird chirped—a winter silence that seemed to amplify the cold, quickly freezing exposed skin and fogging breath into a hoary frost.

Exhausted, they finally stopped to eat and feed the horses.

"Here." Bridget handed Augum some nuts, raisins, sunflower seeds, and a chunk of biscuit beef. He accepted it, barely feeling hungry, dreaming of a warm bed.

Leera rubbed darkly circled eyes. "The waterskins are frozen."

That's a problem, he thought, too tired to voice it aloud.

"Think the Legion slept or rode through the night?" she asked.

"Slept," Bridget said. "I hope …"

The weariness that came with staying up kept the trio quietly huddled together between the horses, bundled in all nine blankets. Teeth chattered between bites.

"We're almost clear of the forest," he said. "Maybe we should take turns sleeping on the horses." He tightened his hood around his head, exposing only his mouth. Like the girls, he'd long forsaken awareness for warmth, doing anything to avoid exposure to the brutal cold.

"Fine," Bridget replied from within her blanket castle. "Lee, you held the reins longer than I, you sleep first …"

Leera's blanket mountain gave a stiff nod.

"Why don't the both of you try to sleep?" he said. "Just tie Spirit to me."

"You sure? You haven't slept a wink yet."

"Yeah, it's fine." Despite his utter exhaustion, he wanted to push his boundaries. His former master used to say people were capable of far more than they gave themselves credit for, and always urged him to explore the outer reaches of potential.

"All right, but you have to promise to wake me up if you get tired," Bridget said.

He nodded, determined to stay awake as long as possible.

They set out after eating. The palfreys had noticeably slowed and he wondered how much longer they could be pushed.

He checked the map. They had over a days' journey ahead crossing the Tallows. He recalled almost dying trying to cross those plains. On the other side of the Tallows sat Mt. Barrow and the ruins of Sparrow's Perch. The question was would it be wise to go through there …

He tied Spirit's reins to the back of his saddle and gently prodded his horse forward, plowing steadily through the snow. Soon the girls were asleep, nestled in a large blanket bundle, Bridget leaning forward in the saddle, Leera propped against her back.

A warm sun greeted them upon leaving Blackwood. He raised his hood a little, allowing his face to absorb the kind rays. Lack of sleep, having dulled his senses before, now heightened them. He took note of the rugged yellow grass of the Tallows poking through sparkling snow; the crisp feel of a fresh morning breeze on his cheek; the snort and whicker of his palfrey.

He could just make out the hazy outline of Mt. Barrow in the far distance. Hopes raised, he smiled to himself, remembering the many fond memories of Mrs. Stone's cave. He ignored the fact she had collapsed it. He ignored the fact Sparrow's perch had been razed, its citizens murdered. Instead, he chose to remember the cave in its former splendor—a warm fire crackling in the hearth; shelves filled with books, scrolls, and odd artifacts. He remembered the delicious food, the training, meeting Bridget and Leera for the first time, the naming ceremony … His thoughts drifted to the night he fought off the claw in the tent, sliding down Hangman's Rock, the snowball fight …

Lids heavy, he found himself cheating by closing his eyes for short lengths of time, and thus didn't notice crossing the subtle boundary to the world of dreams.

ONE EYE

Augum was jolted awake by the sensation of falling and crashing into snow. Shocked by the sudden cold, he jumped up, coughing. He had fallen asleep, he realized, brushing himself off.

The palfrey glanced at him with sunken eyes.

"I know, boy, you must be tired. I'm sorry."

It was silent and windless. The sun was past the midway point in the cloudless sky, gently warming his face. The vast ocean of snow sparkled from horizon to horizon. Cursing himself for his lack of discipline, he turned to Leera and Bridget to apologize for dozing off—

Except the girls and Spirit were not there.

His heart skipped a beat. He spun around searching the horizon, but the plain only stretched on. All he saw was the dim outline of Mt. Barrow in one direction and the dark line of Blackwood in the other.

"Bridget! Leera!" He shouted in every direction.

But there was only the brilliant stillness of snow.

Cursing himself anew, he jumped back on his horse and doubled-back on his tracks, frantically searching the ground for any signs, heart hammering in his chest. The tie holding the horses had to have come undone, he reasoned, and the girls, blithely sleeping, were left behind. Terrible visions of what could have happened flashed across his mind—captured by the Legion, or attacked by walkers, or lost and freezing …

This was all his fault. If he hadn't been so bullheaded about challenging himself …

At last he came upon a diverging set of tracks meandering westward. He immediately gave chase, as fast as the tired horse would go, which was just a canter.

The land began to gently roll. He scanned the horizon from every crest, but there was still no sign of them. He rode on, following the trail, until spotting a thin line of smoke a few hills over.

Strange, but they did have the rucksack and the flint and steel. Maybe they started a fire …

He dismounted just before the last crest and peeked over the hill. He spotted a throng of people milling about a colorful caravan of wagons, horses, supplies, and even cows, trailing in the rear. The caravan was led by a team of gigantic oxen, attended to by a group of men. Some wore armor, swords by their sides.

The caravan looked to be headed south and probably just stopped to refresh the animals. He squinted, trying to see through the snow glare, until at last he spotted Spirit, tied at the very back of the caravan to a blue, yellow and orange wagon resembling a small house. A bedraggled man in a thick woolen coat stood by feeding the palfrey.

They had to have taken Bridget and Leera captive. The girls probably sat tied up in that last wagon, which might be some kind of prison on wheels. He was trying to come up with a daring rescue plan when the side door of the wagon opened and Leera popped out, quickly followed by Bridget. The two giggled and nodded to the interior, before pointing in Augum's direction. Next, a frail old man with a very long beard and a cane came to the door, bidding the man by the horse to come closer. He then gave instructions as the girls stood by, almost giddy with excitement.

Augum couldn't make sense of what was going on. Were they under some kind of spell? Who were they with? What was happening? The man in the thick coat mounted a dark horse and began riding in his direction. Meanwhile, Bridget and Leera turned to go back inside with the old man.

Augum, now very curious as to what was happening, threw aside caution and stood up, calling out, "Bridget! Leera! Over here!"

The girls turned and started waving, beckoning him to come over. The man on the black horse stopped in his tracks, looked between them, shrugged, and turned back to the caravan. Augum hopped on his palfrey and rode down to them, full of questions, ready to bolt should anyone make a move for him. The people were dressed in furs, leather tunics and winter coats. Many looked to be servants of some kind, others laborers. There was even a family with small dirty children running around in the snow. Some people glanced his way but most didn't seem to care, going on about their business.

"Aug—!" Bridget called, grabbing hold of the gray horse. "Thank all that is good that you're all right! We were just sending someone to find you—"

"What's going on?" he asked, dismounting. "Who are these people?"

"Oh, it's amazing, come see." Leera grabbed him by the arm and pulled him along while Bridget tied his horse up next to Spirit.

"What is this?" he asked as she led him to the colorful wagon. Bells tinkled as she opened the door. "Wait a moment, just explain—" but he stopped mid-sentence when he saw the interior of the wagon. It was some kind of overstuffed general goods shop, but impossibly larger than the exterior. Trifles, ornaments and wares hung from every surface. There must have been thousands and thousands of shiny things clinking about. Trinkets of all sorts spilled from cracks and crammed every surface. Overcrowded shelves towered all the way to the fifteen-foot ceiling. Some leaned precariously, threatening to collapse. Others twisted and wound in odd shapes. Wooden ladders ascended here and there, various oddities hanging from the rungs.

Amongst it all stood the frail old man with a long beard and gnarled wooden cane, dressed in a silk sapphire vest. The top of his head was bald, one eye milky white. Due to his extreme hunch, he was shorter than Augum.

"Ah, you must be the young man the young ladies were talking about." The old man beckoned to him. "Well come forth and let ol' One Eye have a look at you."

Augum flashed Leera a wary look. She gave an encouraging nod and he approached, letting One Eye grab his sleeve with shaking fingers. He tried not to stare at the man's milky eye, which reminded him of Magua.

"When is the day of your birth?"

Augum glanced at Leera, who only smiled. "Um, I was born on the second day of the second month, in the year 3326."

"Fourteen ..." One Eye let go of Augum and scratched his beard. "Interesting. You share the same birthday as Dordan the Great, Meridius the Fallen, and Atrius Arinthian. You have quite the familiar face, boy, you certainly do ..." He turned toward a counter littered with scrolls and parchment, quills and spilled ink bottles, as well as a multitude of colored drying sands.

"After you pass this birthday, my boy, you will have only but a year until you will be a man—to the eyes of the world, that is. As to yourself, that is another matter altogether. Do you know what a Nodian boy has to do on his sixteenth birthday to become a man?"

Augum remembered Oba Sassone but could not recall ever discussing the subject with him. "No, I don't, sir."

"He has to hunt down and kill a red bear." One Eye watched him as if expecting some kind of reaction.

Augum nodded trying to pretend that nugget of information was interesting. Behind him, bells tinkled as Bridget stepped inside.

"Ugh, so cold out there," she mumbled.

"Hey, nice job leaving us behind by the way," Leera said, face twisting in mock anger.

"Oh, I'm really, *really* sorry about that. I fell asleep—"

"—it's all right, forget about it. Wouldn't have come across this caravan otherwise. It was just odd waking up to the sound of mooing. Not exactly sure *why* Spirit came here though."

"Now don't be daft, young girl," the old man said. "She came searching for a mate."

Leera reddened.

Bridget cleared her throat politely. "So, um, what do you think, Augum?"

"I don't know, what is this place?"

"One Eye's Travelling Shop of Wonders. He's a travelling famous merchant."

"That's just what *he* says," Leera said under her breath as One Eye grabbed a battered ear trumpet.

"What's that now? Speak up, young saplings!"

"We were talking about your shop!" Bridget said while Leera mollified him with a smile.

"Oh yes, is it not grand? A lifetime of collecting. I'm quite famous for my trinkets, I'll have you know. I started back in the academy, when I stumbled upon—"

"—academy?" Bridget interrupted. "Sir, you went to the Academy of Arcane Arts?"

"I sure did, young lady, and I was good, quite good, actually. Did you go to the academy too?"

"Yes, for a very short while that is, until the Legion …" She forced a pained smile, not wanting to finish.

He gave a knowing nod. "Which element are you studying?"

"Earth."

"Ah, how marvelous! That happens to be my element as well. Now come let us be proper and show our stripes in the old way." He boldly faced Bridget and let his right arm explode in sixteen bracelets of green ivy.

Bridget showed hers, bidding Augum and Leera to do the same.

"Very good, very good indeed." One Eye extinguished his arm. "Well met, and what is your name, young lady?"

"Bridget, sir, and this is Leera and Augum."

"What's that now?"

"Bridget, and that's Leera and Augum!"

The old man's eyes briefly flitted over Augum's lightning ring.

Augum extinguished his arm. "Sir, did you happen to know a Mrs. Stone at the academy?"

"Mrs. Stone? You mean Anna Atticus Stone?"

"Yes, exactly—"

One Eye smiled fondly as a twinkle came into his eye. "Oh, I certainly knew Anna. We were friends, in fact. That was a very long time ago now."

"Friends, sir?"

One Eye waved his cane, forcing Augum to take a step back. "Oh yes, we were very good friends. Got into all sorts of trouble. Constantly in the Headmaster's office. We were quite the fearsome trio. There was Jordan Winters, the wickedest prankster you would ever have the displeasure of meeting; Anna, the most talented sorceress of our time; and I of course, the most brilliant plotter ever born in all of Solia, if I do say so myself. That's right, back then I was known as William Smith the Plotter. I'm sure you've heard of me."

"Uh …"

"Of course you have. Now, how about some bellcandy?" The old man hobbled to a bowl of sweets, drew out three pink and blue candies in the shapes of bells, and handed them out.

They popped them in their mouths.

"Good, isn't it?"

The trio nodded, Leera's eyes already back on the bowl.

"Know where it comes from? City of the Iron Feather. There's a sweetshop there that'll make your teeth jump out of your skull."

"I have a new goal in life," Leera mumbled.

"Not to mention the city has the best Canterran food. That's where my caravan's headed."

Augum found himself intrigued by this strange man, a man from the time of his great-grandmother. "Sir, did you also know a Thomas Stone?"

One Eye's face suddenly went cold. He waved his cane dismissively. "Thomas? No, I don't think I recall a Thomas … never heard of him." Suddenly his good eye narrowed in suspicion. "Why are you asking all these questions anyway? Are you a Legion spy?"

"Oh, no, sir—far from it. Anna Stone is … she's my great-grandmother, actually."

The old man sputtered, nearly dropping his cane. "Dear me, I knew there was something familiar about you." He drew close to Augum to inspect him anew. "Yes, yes, I can certainly see the resemblance now." He shook his head.

"You would have been my great-grandson if that no-good fool hadn't gotten in the way … I would have named you Brett, after my late brother."

"You mean my great-grandfather, Thomas? But I thought you said—"

"Never mind what I said—!" One Eye turned his back and shuffled off, leaning against the counter and expelling a long breath. "You wouldn't understand. It was … it was a very, very long time ago, Brett."

"My name is—"

"What? What's that?" One Eye fumbled for his ear trumpet.

"Sir, we're actually trying to get to Mrs. Stone right now," Bridget said. "The Legion is racing ahead. They want to lay a trap for her. If she's—"

One Eye snorted. "Someone's always been after her, or rather, after that darn globe of hers."

"You mean the scion?" Leera asked, chewing on a second piece of candy she had somehow acquired.

"Quite right, my dear Stephanie, quite right indeed."

Leera stopped her chewing. "It's Leer—"

"—Jordan and I were the only ones she told," One Eye continued, idly fingering something hidden around his neck. "We were best friends, you see, but people still found out. After all, the Arinthian line goes back a very long way. That is how we got into so much trouble most of the time—we were simply defending the scion. Jordan and I were just beginning to understand the arcane way, but Anna … Anna excelled even the teachers. Her knowledge and acumen was vast. She was brilliant, just brilliant. We called her the 'Arcane Artist'. Should have seen what she could do with the Chameleon spell—certainly gave Jordan plenty of ideas."

"Sir, please, will you help us find her?" Augum asked. "The Legion is following us, and we've still got a long way to go."

"A very long way," Bridget added. "We're going to the Northern Peaks, to—"

"—to seek the mountain monks of the north, or more likely, the Seers." One Eye looked to the trinket-infested ceiling and tugged on his beard.

"How … how did you know?" Bridget asked.

"You are conversing with an old adventurer, young lady. There would be no other reason for Anna to travel there. She seeks wisdom, wisdom only the Seers could provide. That can only mean she has a big question on her mind. Everyone is allowed to ask the Seers one question—one precious question per lifetime, and no more."

"Did you ask a question of the Seers?" Augum asked.

"I did. Darn wasted it though. I asked them if I was allowed to get comfortable before asking my question."

Leera snorted, spattering bits of candy, before pretending to cough.

One Eye frowned at her then turned to Bridget. "So you say the Legion is following you, is that it?"

"Yes. Can you help us?"

"We're very tired as are our horses," Augum said. "We've left a trail anyone could follow, and if we don't find some other way to reach Nana before my … before the Lord of the Legion does—"

But One Eye was already shaking his head. "I cannot teleport you to the Northern Peaks, not even individually. I am too old, too weak, and it is too far. I am also one degree short of attaining the Group Teleport spell. To be perfectly honest, I am surprised I had not hit my ceiling earlier. Though I suppose you could use a scroll."

"Scroll, sir?"

"Yes, if you could get your hands on a Group Teleport scroll, you can get yourselves there, Brett. I'm afraid that's the only way I know of."

"It's Augum, sir. Maybe we can find a scroll for you—"

"—'find a scroll', the boy says." One Eye turned his milky eye on him. "You can't just 'find' a Group Teleport scroll, young man. Do you know how much trouble it is to make one of those, how much time is involved? Do you even have the slightest idea just how much it would cost? Hmm? Or how you would get into town in the first place, with those Legion crooks prowling the streets?" He waved a dismissive hand. "You might as well forget it, Brett."

"Sir, which town do you mean?" Augum said, giving up on correcting the old man about his name.

"Candledale, but like I said, you need a lot of gold to buy something that expensive."

The trio exchanged determined looks. They were definitely going to give it a shot. Gold or no gold, they were going to get their hands on that scroll.

"I see that look. Foolish kids, you have no idea what you are doing, do you? Are you aware that all unsanctioned spell scrolls have been declared forbidden? Even being caught with a lesser scroll could mean death, let alone a Spell of Legend … No, I can't let you go on this errand. If anything …" One Eye shook his head in a manner suggesting he couldn't believe what he was going to do next. He wandered back behind his counter to retrieve a piece of parchment, dipped a large peacock feather into a tiny ink bottle, and began scribbling as the trio exchanged curious looks.

When he finished, he banged the wagon wall with his cane. Soon the bells jingled and in came the man with the woolen winter coat. He had scruffy black hair and a round face with the beginnings of a beard. His breath stank of strong spirits.

"M'lord?"

"Bartholomew here is my most trusted, able servant." He turned to the pudgy man. "You are going on a merchant run."

Augum wondered if Bartholomew was his real name, or if he too had given up on correcting the old man.

"But m'lord, we're still leagues from Iron Feather—"

"Yes yes, I know, this is a special case, however." One Eye handed Bartholomew the piece of parchment, giving him a moment to read it.

"M'lord! This is sheer lunacy, should I get caught—"

"I am quite aware of the consequences on this trade, Bartholomew. It will be your choice."

Bartholomew took a good long look at the note and sighed. "What will m'lord be giving up in trade?"

One Eye turned to the trio. "Oh, I won't be giving up a thing."

Taking the hint, the trio dug out everything they owned in search of something worth trading for a forbidden Group Teleport scroll. The contents of their rucksack lay strewn about on the well-worn wooden floor.

"Dramask blankets—very nice, very nice indeed," One Eye said, pawing at the fine wool. "But not nearly adequate enough. Oh, what do we have here? Is that—? Surely it cannot be ..." He gently picked up the orb, face lighting up.

"That's just a seeing orb," Leera said. "It comes with a pearl that allows—"

"—'just a seeing orb'? My dear child, this is not 'just a seeing orb'. This is, why I cannot believe you do not know your history, what are they teaching kids these days up at the academy—?"

When One Eye spotted the vacant looks the trio gave him, he scoffed.

"Unnameable gods be good, they do not know. This is *the* Orb of Orion, gifted to the Academy of Arcane Arts a thousand years ago upon its grand opening. But how could you possibly have come to possess this artifact?"

"Actually it's a bit of a long story," Augum mumbled.

One Eye raised his trumpet to his ear.

"We rescued it from an evil sorceress!" Leera said.

"Well, you cannot trade this, not for anything. This has to be returned to the academy, but not until the Legion have been well cleared out of there. If they got a hold of this it would just be a tremendous disgrace on the institution of honorable arcanery."

"Sir, why is it so special?" Bridget asked. "We have already discovered its powers, you can look through it and listen—"

"—oh, no, no, no! It's about the story!" He shook his head. "It's just tragic how little you know. Yes yes, it is an orb of seeing, sure, but legend has it that the Orb of Orion can summon *dragons*."

Leera snickered, composing herself after noticing the looks she was getting. "Sir, dragons are tales for children," she said more politely.

One Eye nodded with a knowing smile. He retrieved an amulet that hung around his neck, obscured by his sapphire vest. "See this?" He dangled what appeared to be a giant black tooth before them. "I retrieved this myself—with a bit of help from Anna and Jordan that is—from an ancient abandoned mine called Shaftspur. Dragons once lived, my dear child, they once lived …"

One Eye removed the amulet to let the trio inspect the tooth. It was large, sure, but Augum thought it looked exactly like a bear tooth. Leera also seemed skeptical, rolling her eyes and passing it on. Bridget studied it carefully before returning it to One Eye with reverence.

"Anna once tried having a go at it, you know," One Eye said, gesturing at the Orb of Orion. "Believe it or not, I once *acquired* the orb myself, as a prank of course. Did we get in trouble for that one—almost got expelled, all three of us. Detention for a whole year. Broke an academy record. Anyway, when Anna saw it, after the tongue lashing she gave me, she simply had to try unlocking its secrets.

Ambitious, that one, I tell you. Once she saw something she did not understand, she could not help but try to figure it out. She tried everything she could think of. Studied it for days on end ..." He chuckled to himself, eyes focused on some distant adventure in the past.

"Well, sir, did she figure it out—?" Augum asked.

"Of course not, my dear boy! Warlocks and arcaneologists have been studying it for a thousand years. *No one* has cracked its secret. Jordan—bless his dark-skinned soul—thought the whole dragon thing was an ancient prank made up by the warlocks that gifted the object. After all, they were from a rival school. I know better though, and finding this tooth was the proof."

Augum and Leera exchanged skeptical glances.

"Um, well, we'll be sure to return the Orb of Orion to the academy as soon as the Legion is gone," Augum said, thinking One Eye lost a few of his marbles in that mine. He made a mental note to ask Mrs. Stone about him when they next met—*if* they met—they had to beat Sparkstone to her first. The thought brought him back to their stuff, splayed out on the floor.

"Sir, is there not anything else we can trade for the scroll?"

One Eye blinked. "Oh, right, the scroll. Let us have a look. Hmm ... I am sorry but I see nothing else here."

The trio's faces fell.

"Wait—what is that on your hip there, Grundvelda? Show it to me ..."

Bridget looked around before realizing One Eye was addressing her. She hesitated a moment before handing Blackbite over.

" 'Grundvelda'?" Leera mouthed to Augum.

"If I did not know any better, I would swear this is a Dreadnought Blade," One Eye muttered, inspecting the dagger with shaking hands. "Yes yes, it has the telltale signs of master forging—the steel, the weight … but is it arcane?" He looked to Bridget, expecting her to answer that very question.

"Its name is Blackbite, and it is a Dreadnought piercing blade." She sounded hesitant. Augum realized she had probably become fond of the blade, as he had with Burden's Edge.

One Eye gave a stiff nod. "Yes, I do believe this will more than suffice."

"Is that all right with you, Bridge?" Leera asked.

Bridget gave the Dreadnought Blade a longing look then pursed her lips. "Of course it is. I'd give up a thousand of those to see Mrs. Stone safe."

One Eye handed the jeweled blade over to Bartholomew. "Use this as barter and keep any profit for yourself for the risks."

Bartholomew's eyes lit up upon receiving the fine dagger. "Most kind of you, m'lord, most kind." He turned the dagger over in his hands, smiling to himself.

"Be sure to give that to Jeremiah the merchant and no other. Tell him he owes me one."

"Of course, m'lord. When should I depart?"

"Immediately. I want you to take the fastest horse and return as soon as you can."

"As you wish, m'lord."

"Good, Bartholomew—away with you then." One Eye waved him off with his cane. The bells jingled as he stepped outside.

"If the job can be done, Bartholomew can do it. You can trust him."

Bridget forced a smile as Augum placed a hand on her shoulder. "Thanks Bridge, that was noble."

Leera gave her a quick hug. "Don't worry, we'll find you another one in some other castle, and you too, Aug. And then we can find me one."

He waved the thought aside. "We've had our turn. Yours is next."

One Eye yawned. "I do believe it is about time for my afternoon nap." He poked at Augum's robe with his cane. "I happen to have a fine bath wagon with a competent attendant. Perhaps you three would like to enjoy it?"

"Oh, that would be most grand, sir," Bridget said.

One Eye filled out another piece of parchment. "It is settled then. Take this to Marta the bath attendant. Let us convene again for supper."

The trio took the note, gathered their things, and trooped out of the colorful wagon, checking for any sign of the Legion. They did notice a guard stationed at the crest of the hill, acting as a scout. Satisfied, they trundled along in search of Marta the bath attendant.

COMFORTS

The bath wagon sported four side-by-side wooden tubs separated by elegant semi-translucent screens. Just like the shop wagon, it was far larger on the inside than seemed possible, an arcane room that perplexed the mind. In the center stood a series of stone hearths to keep the room warm. On the other side of the divide were booths fitted with sconce candles and vanity dressers.

They met Marta, a heavyset woman with tan skin. She took one look at the note, nodded, and told them to undress in the private booths, assigning each a soft white robe. Soon they were relaxing in steaming tubs while she washed their clothing and blankets. The scars on Augum's back from the Penderson farm tingled in the hot water.

"You very lucky," Marta said in her thick eastern accent. "Youth is best time to be warlock. Before joining caravan, I go Dramask academy. Stop at 3rd degree."

"What's your element?" Bridget asked.

"Fire. I go back to Tiberra when make money for family." She squeezed their laundry through a drying roller.

"What's Tiberra like? I've never been there."

"Is beautiful place. You see blankets? Is that beautiful. Bright color everywhere. Color, color, color. You come visit. Then you taste spices, have tea ceremony, buy from market. I miss Tiberran men. I miss dance. Husband die sick. Solia no place for me. People too cold, think war too much. Caravan dancers and singers here no good. And it not smell right here. Smell like tree and fire and snow. There, it smell like food and spices and laughter and family."

"But it's north enough you get snow too, don't you?"

"Oh, ya, we have snow too. But it … different. Me know not how explain."

Augum quickly averted his eyes from Leera's vague form in the booth next door as she began lathering her hair. "How did One Eye get these wagons to be so big inside?"

"He hire great warlock." Marta squeezed their robes through a drying roller. "They work on wagons long time. Cost too much gold."

"Is there any news about the coming war?"

"Please you no talk about war here. I sick of war."

"Oh, I'm sorry." Of course she didn't want to talk about it—her family was there! He decided to ask about something light-hearted. "So this caravan has dancers and singers too?"

"Oh, ya ya ya. But they no good. Tiberran better. Much better. Full of soul. Here they weep. One Eye come to villages and put on arcane show, sell trinkets. He good man. We happy have jobs. We safe. He barter to keep us safe. But he old man. Very, very old man. I worry he sick. I worry he die. Too many people hungry. Legion take too many for war. Is no good. Solia hungry and sick."

Yes it is, Augum thought, it certainly is …

"So what's with the name thing?" Leera asked. "Why does One Eye get our names wrong?"

"If look like someone he know from when he young, he think name is same." Marta's forearm lit up with three rings of fire. "Shyneo," and began drying their laundry with her fiery palm. "He remember some people names, but people must be … how you say … memorable? Ya, memorable. This is because that old fool try new memory spell but it not work. He hurt his brain. Shop was clean, now mess. He no want help. He fussy old man."

Marta finished drying their things and instructed them to rinse off. They stepped out of the tubs, wrapping themselves in soft bathrobes, while Marta wiped her hands on her apron and excused herself.

Leera turned to Bridget. "Hair?"

"Definitely."

In no time at all the girls were in one of the booths braiding each other's hair and trying the many exotic scented oils and powders. They giggled and shared stories and babbled on about the caravan. Augum, meanwhile, sniffed Dramask, Iron Feather, Sweetbow, and Heartfire scents in a separate booth. He found most to be too strange or strong for him, but did enjoy the Heartfire, which had a subtle cedar aroma to it, reminding him of a cozy fire.

Staring into the mirror, he noticed his hair had reached his brows, and decided to give it a trim. He found a silver knife in a drawer and began slicing away.

After some time, the trio met in the central divide, ready to put on their now dry and freshly washed robes. When Augum spotted the girls, his mouth fell open—they looked stunning, particularly Leera, with her raven braids, shiny freckles, and dark eyes. Yet when she spotted him, her face went slack.

"Aug, what have you done!"

"What? What do you mean—?"

"Your hair! Ugh, here, let me fix it—" She grabbed his hand and dragged him back into his booth, pushing him down on the seat before the mirror. "You're not allowed to cut your own hair ever again."

"But I've always cut it myself—"

"Yeah, well, it's a wonder you didn't get flogged for it."

He made no comment. He *did* get flogged—by Mr. Penderson and Dap and his cronies multiple times. He wondered how much his appearance had to do with it. No, it was probably the whole gutterborn thing. There was only one thing worse than being lowborn—being gutterborn, and Dap loved having someone worse off than him.

As Leera worked away, twisting his head this way and that, he felt his stomach go very light and tingly. A girl had never done anything like this for him.

"Oh my, somebody found a pleasant scent." She sniffed his collar.

"Gah—Leera!" He laughed and wriggled away, but the truth was he wanted to say she wore a very nice scent as well, some kind of exotic berry. He avoided looking at her in the mirror, his cheeks burning.

"Stop squirming or I'll cut off your ear!"

"What's all this giggling about?" Bridget made an appearance holding a jar of cream. "What are you doing to our poor boy, Lee?"

"Fixing. He's not allowed to cut his own hair anymore."

Bridget laughed. "You're acting like my mother." She pinched his cheek, voice suddenly deep. "So handsome."

"All right, that's enough already," he said, trying to stand, but Leera immediately shoved him back down.

"Wait, you little worm," she said, biting her lower lip in concentration. "Just … one … more … there! Done! Take a peek."

He looked in the mirror, feeling his well-groomed hair. "Wow, that's actually … nice, thanks."

Leera did a kind of curtsy. "You're welcome."

He stood up and gestured at the chair. "All right, my turn to do some cutting—" but before he was even able to finish, the girls squealed and scurried out of there, giggling.

"Ah, such beautiful girls!" Marta said upon re-entering. "Make boys very jealous."

The girls giggled some more.

"And such a handsome boy! Will make ladies swoon."

Augum shuffled his feet.

"Okay, you clean, blankets clean, robes clean. Happy?"

"Very," they said, nodding.

"Good. You change and have fun."

They finished up and reluctantly departed, still teasing each other, wearing freshly-washed robes and carrying freshly-washed Dramask blankets.

They soon joined One Eye in the red and orange supper wagon. The inside was grand, with elaborate gilt-accents and a long empire table down the middle. There were enough seats to entertain a king's host, reminding Augum of Castle Arinthian's dining room. It was just the four of them, attended to by three plain-dressed servants running back and forth from a partitioned section in the back of the wagon, which Augum assumed was some sort of arcane kitchen.

One Eye greeted them by names from his past—Brett for Augum, Stephanie for Leera, and Grundvelda for Bridget. Leera definitely didn't think she looked anything like a Stephanie, though jokingly said Grundvelda was a most appropriate name for Bridget, who promptly flashed a sour look.

The food was simply divine—assorted exotic cheeses, smoked oysters, boar's ribs, slow-roast chicken breast, hot-buttered garlic soft bread, salted salmon steak seasoned with dill and lime, creamed potato, and a wide array of vegetables and even some fruit. Beverages consisted of freshly squeezed sugared root juice for the trio and exotic Odemai red wine for One Eye.

Bridget cleared her throat politely. "Sir, I'm having trouble with the extension to the Shine spell."

"Is that so, my dear? Do tell."

"I'm unable to figure out how to grab things with my vine."

"That spell is a peach of a thing. You must concentrate on …" One Eye frowned.

"Sir …?"

"Huh?"

"Concentrate on what, sir?"

"What?"

"We were talking about my Shine extension."

"Right, of course we were, you think me daft?"

"No, sir, I just—"

"Right, well, make an effort to pay attention, Grundvelda."

They sat there, One Eye smacking his lips, until Bridget again cleared her throat politely.

"What!"

"The extension, sir—?"

"Right!" He squeezed two bony fingers together and drew a line in midair. "The spell requires finesse. Watch." He made a graceful motion with his hand and entwined a wine glass, then an entire chair.

"Wouldn't he make the perfect mentor for her?" Augum whispered into Leera's ear as One Eye lectured on the details.

Leera hid her grin behind her hand. "It's the only chance she's got of him ever getting her name right."

"Now you try it," the old man said.

It took Bridget many failed attempts, One Eye commentating on what she was doing wrong, before she was able to entwine a spoon.

Bridget's face brightened. "Did you see that?"

Augum and Leera nodded dutifully.

"So what kind of uses does the extension have?" Bridget asked, beaming.

One Eye set a crystal goblet of wine down onto the table with a shaking hand. "Why Grundvelda, I would have thought you could figure that out. It is in fact useful for many a thing. On more than one occasion, I found myself entwining an attacker's arm, or climbing up a difficult surface. It is also perfect for reaching into tight spaces. Eventually you will learn how to extend and manipulate your vine as if it were your own hand. Granted, there are higher degrees involved, what with other spells that further build on the extension, but I have no doubt a clever young lady such as yourself will eventually get there."

Bridget examined her vine-lit palm anew.

"Shyneo." Leera frowned at her own palm. "Sir, is there some fancy trick I can do with my Shine spell? Augum can shock, Bridget can entwine things—so what can I do?"

One Eye gave her a lost look.

"Oh, right—I mean *Brett* can shock and, um, *Grundvelda* can wrap things with her vine—so what is it that I can do?"

He scratched his beard while considering Leera's light with his good eye. The water glistened as it slowly revolved around her hand and wrist, as if perpetually trickling downhill. "To be perfectly honest, I do not remember, though you must understand it is not my element."

Leera extinguished her hand, a sour look on her face.

"My stableman, Fargswabe, has some training in the water element. Perhaps you should inquire with him."

"Farzwabay?" Leera repeated.

Augum could tell she was skeptical about the name. He was too—it sounded made up.

"Quite right, quite right." He raised his goblet to his lips, cheeks as red as the wine now. "I do say we could use a bit of music here. Do you three like music? I personally fancy the flute. Odo, please fetch that fine instrument of yours."

A thin dark-haired servant with a pointy nose and a resigned look on his face bowed and left, returning shortly with an ebony flute. He stood at the far end of the table and played calm melodies. One Eye relaxed in his chair, pouring himself another cup of wine. He stuck in his ear trumpet.

"Such a wonderful talent should be playing in one of the great concert halls."

Judging by the look on Odo's face, that exact thought appeared to be running through his mind.

One Eye swished his goblet. "War is coming, you know. That is why we travel south, though I suspect there shan't be a place far enough to hide from Lord Sparkstone's ambitions."

"You mean war with Tiberra," Augum said.

"I fear Tiberra is but the beginning. Lord Sparkstone strikes east to test his armies, build up his forces. The Blackhaven Herald reports nothing, but rumor says he has Dreadnoughts at his command now. If that be true, they will have already begun forging the finest weapons and armor."

"It *is* true, sir," Bridget said, sweeping a braided lock from her eyes. "A Dreadnought came along with Sparkstone to Tornvale. We were listening in through the window of Commander Tridian's headquarters. We heard him speak but didn't see him."

One Eye chuckled and took a sip of wine. "Now that is quite bold. You remind me of my younger days." He sighed wistfully. "Commander Tridian—or the Blade of Sorrows as he has come to be known. I dealt with him before, you know. A very tough bargainer. He has no arcane talent but is one of the most ruthless men I have ever had the misfortune to stumble across."

"Sir?" Augum hoped to get One Eye to elaborate. Funny how the man could remember certain details about people but completely forget others.

"Well, last we met, I talked my way out of him taking my men for the Legion's cause, arguing that Lord Sparkstone encourages and needs people like me and that I am a vital trading link between the cities. I told him I bring in precious supplies and emphasized the fact there is a famine in some parts of Solia. He said I was, what did he say now, ah yes—he said I was merely an 'entertainer'. Cost a fortune in wines and ale just to keep him on my good side. I hope to never lay my good eye on him again."

Odo played on as the other two servants cleared the table and brought in dessert, which consisted of lemon sugar pie and candied ginger. Barely able to take another bite, Augum nonetheless forced himself to eat a whole slice and a piece of ginger. At the Penderson farm, he had picked up the habit of eating quickly, perpetually unsure of when he would next eat a proper meal.

He lay back in his chair with a groan, content but bloated. Bridget and Leera had not eaten nearly as much, having left most of their food on the plate. Now they slowly picked away at dessert, enjoying it bite by bite.

"One of my wagons is a private quarter for guests," One Eye said after taking only one bite of pie. "Truth be told, it is really for bribes. In any case, I will have someone prepare it for you. Feel free to mill around camp until Bartholomew returns, just be sure to keep your ears open for a call from the watch. You did, after all, leave quite an easy trail to follow. Should a call arise, it would be most wise to hide."

The trio thanked One Eye for the delicious meal and staggered to the door, leaving him to his music and wine. At the last moment, Augum turned around with an idea. One Eye reached for his ear trumpet.

"Sir, we've been trying this new spell and, um, I was thinking maybe we could get your help with it. It's kind of difficult to do without a mentor."

One Eye smacked his lips, bleary-eyed with wine. "And which spell might that be, young sapling?"

"The Slam spell, sir."

"Ah, another elemental spell ..." His face brightened, though it could have been from the wine. "I suppose I could give you a few pointers, though I cannot even remember the last time I mentored someone." He gestured to one of his servants. "Strong coffee if you please, Norda, and take the wine."

Norda, face impassive, cleared the wine and left.

"Come see me after my coffee then."

The trio understood themselves dismissed, thanked One Eye once again, and left.

"That was a good idea to ask, Aug," Bridget said. "We need the help."

Leera looked around. "So where is this Fardabie, anyway?"

"It's *Fargswabe,*" Bridget said.

"Whatever, I bet you it's not even his real name. Anyway, let's find him." Leera walked past wagon after wagon, asking servants and workmen where Fargswabe was, constantly getting the name wrong. She received amused looks, leaving Augum to wonder if this person even existed. At last, an older man pointed them to a wagon that appeared to be a stable on wheels, full of horses and hay, with drop-ramps across one side. A tall youth a few years older than them was tending to a large stallion. He had close-cropped black hair filled with bits of hay, a small face, and wore loose trousers. He looked bored mechanically brushing the horse.

"Um, excuse us but, we're looking for Fazabie," Leera said, checking with Bridget if she got the name right. Bridget just shook her head, not bothering to correct her anymore. Leera reddened as the youth frowned.

"Curse that white-eyed lunatic, still thinking I'm someone I'm not. It's *Justinius*, not Fargswabe."

"Oh, um, sorry, didn't mean offence. If it makes you feel any better, he mixes ours up too."

"It doesn't, actually."

Leera chuckled anxiously. "So, um, why is he calling you by that name?"

Leera's acting funny, Augum thought.

Justinius shrugged. "Some old Sierran stableman of his I apparently remind him of. I don't care, I don't exactly plan to stick around long. So what do you want anyway? And I know I'm supposed to be tending to your horses. I've sent a boy to retrieve them already.

"Oh … no, it's … it's nothing like that. We're just—well it's really me that is, um, that needs, well … you know—" She played with her hair, trying to find the right words, a silly expression on her face that annoyed Augum for some reason.

Justinius wiped his hands on a dirty cloth. "Spit it out already, I don't have all day."

"She needs help with the Shine spell," Bridget said, a small smirk playing across her lips. Leera gave her a quieting look before turning back to Justinius, forcing a toothy smile.

Justinius snorted. "Forget it, freckles, I hate performing any kind of arcanery. I'm destined to become the finest soldier in all of Solia. Besides, I don't train babies." He turned back to his horse.

Leera stood gaping.

"Forget it, Lee," Bridget said, taking her arm. "Guess he doesn't need the money—"

"Whoa there, you didn't say anything about money—"

Bridget took her time rummaging through the rucksack, flashing Augum an *are you all right with this?* look. He shrugged. She paused a moment, brow raised, before he assented a reluctant nod.

"How much?" Justinius asked, eyeing the pouch Augum had snagged from Tridian's quarters.

Bridget turned her back on him and counted out the coins—15 silver, 29 copper in total. "Ten silver?"

Justinius scoffed. "I'm not going to train some little girl the Shine spell for ten measly silvers."

Leera looked like she was either going to slap him or cry, Augum was unsure which. "I don't need training on the *entire* Shine spell," she said. "I just want to learn the extension, that's all. I already know the main part. Shyneo!" Her palm lit up, the gesture coming across as rather rude.

"Just the extension, huh?" He took the silver. "Fine, but I don't have much time. The water element extension for Shine is simple—you can extend the light from your palm into a small body of water."

Leera's mouth hung open.

"Trying to catch mosquitoes in winter?"

"What—?"

"Never mind."

"No, I mean … that's it? I can extend light to water? That's useless—!"

Justinius shrugged. "To be honest, it kind of is. I've never even used it except to show off for a girl."

"Aww, can't be that bad, Lee," Augum said, trying to keep a straight face. "I'm sure it'd be a neat trick to do for celebrations … or something."

Leera's eyes narrowed. "That's exactly my point. It's just a stupid trick! It's like plain magic—totally useless."

Augum, annoyed she had been giving this rude youth so much attention, turned back to Justinius. "So why do you hate performing arcanery, anyway?" He wondered how anybody could possibly hate spell casting. To him, it was the most awesome thing in the world.

"Father forced me to go to the academy but I hit the ceiling at the 2nd degree and dropped out. It was a big embarrassment, but Father never understood that all I ever wanted was to become a swordsman, not some weak warlock like him."

"You talk like you're from the city," Bridget said. "How did you end up here?"

Justinius' eyes flicked to the pouch again. "I'm from Blackhaven. My father was a stablemaster. Convinced One Eye to take me on as stableman, though I don't think he needed much convincing—soon as he saw me he thought I was this Fargswabe person and asked me where I've been all these years. Nothing I said or did could convince him otherwise. Anyway, Father figured that if I joined the caravan, it would get me out of the Legion's army. Been right so far, though to be honest, I think I'd have rather joined up. Bored to death here."

Bridget glanced up from putting away the pouch. "How can you say that? The Legion is a bunch of murderers, they killed our families—"

"I'm sure it was just a terrible misunderstanding. Lord Sparkstone is a leader with vision. One day I'm going to track down a scion just so I can personally give it to him."

The trio gaped at him.

"This life sucks. I hate this stupid caravan and I hate that old fool. I need a sword in my hand and a cause to fight for." Justinius' eyes wandered to the horizon. "The Legion is glorious. Duty unto death. That's me, that's what I should be doing. Fighting the good fight, helping forge an empire."

"Are. You. Serious?" Leera asked.

"The eternal life thing is a lie," Augum blurted, trying to keep calm in the face of this brainwashed young man.

"You're just ignorant. Of course it's true, there's already been one example—Lord Sparkstone himself paraded the man who liberated the third scion through the streets of Blackhaven. It was in the Blackhaven Herald even. He's first in line to receive eternity. Our great lord argues we should all have the right to live forever. Eternal life shouldn't be just for the gods. And I would be careful if I were you, your kind of talk is treasonous."

Leera's face went from cherry red to purple. " 'Our great lord'? What, did you already sign up—?"

"You know what? I don't think I'm going to show you how to cast the extension after all, you little brat."

"Then you can give us back our money—!"

"I don't think I will. I don't deal with traitorous runaways."

"What! You thieving—"

"Thanks, but we have to go now—" Augum grabbed the girls' arms and practically dragged them away. "Let it go, you two. We have to keep quiet until Bartholomew returns. If the Legion came by asking questions …

Leera glanced back with a venomous look. "The nerve of that thieving barn boy …"

"Ugh, if there was ever a time I wanted to—" Bridget made the motion to strangle someone.

Leera and Augum gave her a look—it took a lot to get Bridget that upset.

"Sorry about the money," Leera mumbled.

He waved it off. "Forget it. Come on, let's go see if One Eye is finished his coffee."

When they returned to the red and orange supper wagon, One Eye was using a loupe and meticulously inspecting a piece of parchment with a large black splotch on it. Upon closer inspection, however, the black blob turned out to be tiny writing.

Without looking up, the old man took a shaky sip from a nearly empty mug of black coffee. “Welcome back, saplings. Did Fargwabe tell you what you need to know?”

“Sort of,” Augum replied, taking a seat at the table and giving Bridget and Leera a sidelong look. Bridget pulled up an elaborate chair and sat smoldering, while Leera angrily cleared her throat. “Sir, did you realize Justi—um, I mean Fungusabwe—wants to join the Legion?”

One Eye jerked so suddenly he dropped his loupe to the floor, which Odo the flutist promptly picked up as if used to doing so. For a moment, Augum thought One Eye was choking, before realizing he was actually laughing.

“Don’t be absurd, Stephanie. Fargswabe would never do such a thing. He is a noble young man.”

“I wouldn’t be so sure of that,” Leera muttered.

One Eye reached for his ear trumpet. “What’s that now? Speak up girl—”

“She—a—greed!” Odo shouted into the battered ear trumpet.

One Eye jumped and dropped the thing. Odo sighed, picked it up and placed it on the table, a fresh dent on its rim.

The old man grunted, returning to the blotchy parchment. “Now then, I have just been studying up on Slam, and find myself delighted to rediscover the intricacies of this complex little spell.” He looked up from the parchment, the loupe still stuck to his eye, giving him the appearance of a deranged owl. “Did you know that the spell was originally thought up during a thunderstorm? Makes it quite adequate for a lightning warlock, does it not?”

Augum pressed his lips together into a smile.

“So, let us begin then!” One Eye stood, the loupe tumbling to the floor, quickly tracked down by a resigned Odo. The trio stood as well, awaiting instruction as he paced while tugging his beard.

"Let me see here … first off, why don't the three of you stand together so I can see you better …"

The trio stood in line as if Mrs. Stone herself was addressing them. Augum caught Odo rolling his eyes.

"Good, now then …" One Eye resumed his pacing, stopping abruptly to raise a finger as the trio waited with baited breath. He stood frozen in place like that.

Augum cleared his throat politely. "Sir—?"

One Eye seemed to catch himself and frowned. "I cannot concentrate in here, let us go to my shop. Odo, join us please, and bring the parchment," and so they filed out of the spacious dining wagon and piled into the cramped and messy shop wagon. One Eye bade them to stand in a line again and quickly resumed his pacing, while Odo stood by the counter, parchment in one hand, loupe in the other.

"All right I have it now!" One Eye said suddenly, chuckling to himself. "It is about—" He paused to wait until he was sure they were paying strict attention. "It is about CON—CEN—TRA—TION!"

Leera groaned.

One Eye, undeterred by their lack of enthusiasm, blathered on with mounting excitement.

"Yes. When attempting to cast the Slam spell, one must adhere to the founding principles of the arcane element one stems from. It is about devotion to the sheer knowledge and profound wisdom one attains during the trials and tribulations of the discovery of the nature of one's element. For example, the Shine spell …"

As One Eye droned on, Leera's eyes glazed over while Bridget furrowed her brows in an impressive attempt to understand every word, though even her attention wandered after a while. Augum just nodded, trying not to look like One Eye's sermon was an incoherent ramble. Meanwhile, Odo sat behind the counter and placed his head on folded arms.

"… if one merely attempts to assimilate the patterns that are interwoven into the fabric of the elementary tract one stems from, it would not nearly be enough. No, one needs a complete understanding and belief in the very nature of the spell, which is to crack the air." To make his point, One Eye suddenly whacked his cane into the side of a towering bookcase, breaking the cane clean in two and startling everyone, especially Odo, who fell off his stool. One Eye blinked, studying the broken end.

"Dear me. Do you mind, Odo?"

Odo picked himself off the floor, dusted himself off, fetched the cane, and returned it to One Eye.

"Apreyo," One Eye said, and the cane repaired itself. He swung it about then leaned on it with a nod. "Now, where was I—?"

"Sir, would you mind if we just studied the parchment for ourselves?" Bridget asked.

One Eye gaped a moment before reaching for his ear trumpet. When he stuck it in his ear, Odo shouted into it, "They—want—to—read—the—parchment!"

"No need to shout, dear boy, I am not *that* deaf!" One Eye tried to whack Odo on the shins, but Odo dodged behind the counter. He returned his attention to the trio and sighed. "This spell is far more than mere words. Listen."

For a moment, Augum thought One Eye had lost it completely, standing like that as if in a trance. Suddenly the old man made a gesture as if throwing something to the ground. "GRAU!" he shouted in a guttural voice. There was a monstrous wooden cracking sound as if the entire wagon was splitting in two. It was so loud it shook the shelves, sending an avalanche of knick-knacks tumbling to the planks. The trio dove for cover, Augum expecting a giant rift to appear in the floor.

When the chaos subsided, Odo glanced at the mess and deflated with a groan. He seemed to resign himself to picking things up.

The old man's good eye twinkled. "You see now? Notice my utter concentration and the gesture I used?"

The trio stood, brushing themselves off.

"Now I want each of you to try it, starting with you, Grundvelda."

Bridget flicked dried snakeskin from her robe. "Sir, I don't think we're ready yet—"

"Nonsense, girl, give it a try."

"All right ..." Bridget made a throwing gesture to the ground, face scrunched as if sneezing. "GRAU!"

Nothing happened.

"It was a worthy try but it was obvious to me you were not paying any attention whatsoever, Grundvelda. When I said, 'there should not be a division between the aforementioned desire to break the flowing structure of the air and to actually break the air', what is it you think I meant?"

Bridget was saved from answering by an urgent and authoritative pounding at the door.

"The Legion!" Bridget mouthed, going ashen.

One Eye waved for them to disappear. "Coming, coming! Please be patient, I am an old man—"

They hid behind a large pile of bent scrap metal by the corner.

"Well what a pleasant surprise this is!" One Eye said upon opening the door. "What an honor it is to receive you again, Commander Tridian."

FOES

The planks groaned as many pairs of boots stomped inside. Armor creaked, straps jingled and swords were drawn.

"No need to be rude now," the Blade of Sorrows said. Swords were returned to scabbards. "You can spare me that clever tongue of yours, One Eye, I am not in the mood. You know perfectly well why I am here. Tell me where the rats are and I will spare the caravan."

"I'm sorry, Commander, but they have moved on. Candledale, I believe." In the silence that followed, Augum visualized Tridian staring at One Eye with pale empty eyes, evaluating him, toying with him. He'd see through One Eye as if he was nothing more than a pane of cheap glass.

"Apprentice?"

"He's lying, sir," came Robin's reply.

"And how can you tell?"

"I … my instinct says so."

"You must learn to know, not just feel, Apprentice. It is not just about instinct. There are signs. The direction the eyes follow—or in this case, the eye—" Tridian paused to let his soldiers chortle. "There is the subtle play of the hands, the nod of the head, the coloring of the cheeks … all taken together give you a thorough understanding of whether or not the subject is being truthful."

"Pardon me, Commander," One Eye began in a jovial manner, "but is this about the three men attempting to sell me a scroll of Greater Repair? I assure you we did not trade. My worthy assistant can attest to that fact."

"What are you talking about, old man?"

"Allow me to explain. Three men on horseback came through here in the morning. They came only to see me, knowing my … if you will forgive me … my previous reputation. They tried to sell a series of rare spell scrolls for a very good price. Of course, as profitable as this trade would have been, I regret to say I had to decline, informing them that the scroll trade is now forbidden—"

"That is quite enough drivel, thank you." Tridian expelled a long breath. "Your shop is looking a little worse for wear, One Eye."

"Yes it has seen better days, I am afraid."

"But what was that sound earlier?" Haylee asked in a voice oozing with suspicion.

"That sound? Oh, you mean the Slam spell. I was demonstrating to my faithful assistant how it should be performed. He is just learning, young Atricia."

"My name is Haylee."

"No need to play tricks on me, Atricia. I know perfectly well who you are."

The trio exchanged looks as a silent moment passed.

"He's lost his marbles!" Robin called out finally, joined by a chorus of laughter from the soldiers. "Look, he's laughing along with us. Daft codger," Robin added, throwing up a new round of laughter.

Augum wondered if One Eye really thought Haylee was Atricia or was just using that as cover.

"Now, now, Apprentice, mind your manners. You are still addressing an elder. Just because the man has lost a part of his feeble mind, does not give you the right to treat him that way." They all hooted with laughter upon hearing the sarcasm in Tridian's voice.

Augum didn't think it possible to achieve a higher level of loathing.

"Sergeant, get out there and start searching the caravan for any sign of them," Tridian ordered after the laughter died down.

Augum's stomach took a dive. It was now only a matter of time until they discovered their horses.

"The rest of you—search this dump."

There was the sound of boots dispersing in all directions as the trio tried to shrink further behind the pile of scrap, though all it would take was someone peeking around and it was over.

"Search over there, Hayles, I'll get this section," Robin said over the sound of things being rifled through. They were getting closer and closer to the trio, and Augum had no idea what to do.

"Don't wander off too far, old man," Tridian said.

"Forgive me, Commander. Like you say, I am an old man and I have a hard time hearing. Allow me to retrieve my ear trumpet."

One Eye soon appeared near the pile of scrap. He gave the tiniest gesture for them to stay still. His beard moved as if speaking to someone, hand making subtle gestures.

Augum realized he was casting a spell!

Suddenly Robin's pinched face appeared directly between the pile of scrap and One Eye.

Augum held his breath and crouched absolutely still, feeling like a deer staring at a nocked bow.

"Shyneo," Robin said. His palm lit with a strong fire. Amazingly, he stared right through the trio. One Eye's spell had to be working!

A piece of metal fell from the pile and tumbled behind him. Robin's brows furrowed and he took a step forward—

"—Robin, over here!" Haylee called, and he disappeared.

Augum breathed a tremendous sigh of relief. One of the girls quietly gasped behind him. He turned and realized he was now completely visible, though the girls were not. As he looked closer, however, he could see something was not quite right in the space they sat, almost like the things behind them were mirrored forward, chameleon-like.

He turned back to the opening, hoping to see One Eye's beard still there, only to be disappointed.

"What is it?" Robin asked from just the other side of the scrap pile.

"No idea, let me ask. Hey, excuse me, sir—!"

"Stop sucking up to the old bumpkin."

"Don't be rude, Robin. He's still our elder. Sir, what is this thing?"

"That, young saplings, is a destiny stone. A very rare artifact."

"What's a destiny stone?" Robin asked.

"A stone enchanted with ancient arcanery long lost to mortals. It lubricates action and causality to help achieve one's desired destiny, as opposed to one's true destiny."

"Uh, what? Speak normal, you old windbag."

"Robin!" A pause. "That sounds really neat, sir, thank you."

"My destiny is to become one of the most powerful necromancers of all time," Robin said. "Are you saying this will help me achieve that goal?"

"It will help you achieve your destiny, young man."

"Pfft, I hate it when old people jabber in riddles. Mind if I take it?" Robin asked in a way suggesting it wasn't really a question.

"Consider it my gift to you, young man, but be warned—the stone is karma-balanced and thus exacts a price—although it skews circumstance in favor of your primary goal in life, it may at times undermine that which may benefit you but you do not seek, the degree of which is measured by your own ambition."

"You saying it's broken? You trying to give me a broken gift?"

"Far from it, dear boy. The stone begs the following question—how important is your primary goal in life?"

There was a sudden feeble moan and the crash of a body shoved into shelves. Trinkets tumbled to the planks.

"Robin, how could you—!" Haylee cried. "Oh, I am so sorry, sir. Please, allow me to help you stand."

One Eye wheezed before responding. "Oh, dear me …" He coughed. "Thank you, my dear Atricia. Most kind of you. My cane, if you will."

"You listen here, you sniveling old piece of fungus," Robin said through gritted teeth. "I *will* become one of the most powerful necromancers of all time."

One Eye caught his breath. "Then the stone is most appropriate in your hands, dear boy."

The door burst open and boots shuffled in.

"Commander, we found the horses, and this boy here has information."

"I ain't no boy! I'm a man grown, now let go of me!" Justinius said.

Uh oh, Augum thought. The brainwashed stableman … they were done for.

"Ah, I see you've found my trusted stable hand, Fargswabe."

"Stop calling me that, you old fool, my name is Justinius. JUS—TIN—IUS! Get it through that feeble brain of yours already—"

Robin cackled. "I like him."

"How could you say such things to me, Fargswabe? You wound me, dear boy."

"Excuse me, sir, I wish to join the Legion," Justinius said.

Augum managed to find a tiny hole in the scrap metal pile to peek through. He actually laid eyes on Haylee for the first time since Sparrow's Perch. She wore the same black and red vertically striped necrophyte robe as Robin. The Blade of Sorrows wore his ornate battle armor and woolen surcoat emblazoned with the burning sword.

"So you wish to join, do you?" Tridian asked, pacing around Justinius. "How old are you?"

"I will be turning eighteen on the 17th day of the 5th month."

"Commander."

"Right, um—Commander."

"You have no idea who I am, do you?"

"No, sir, I don't, but I want to join. I want to be part of the cause."

"Why haven't you joined earlier?"

"I've been prevented by this meddling old man and my father."

"Fathers don't always know best, do they now?"

"I agree, sir, wholeheartedly."

"Eager young buck. Good ... very good. We could always use men like you. I believe this caravan has held the men hostage long enough, anyway."

"But we had a deal, my dear commander," One Eye said. "I got to keep my men for—"

"Yes, yes, I remember the deal very well, and I am a man of my word." The Blade of Sorrows stopped before Justinius, placing hands on his shoulders. "That is, unless there is some new information that changes said deal."

Justinius didn't blink. "They're here. I just spoke to them—"

"You mean the younglings, the three wanted younglings of the Legion?" Tridian asked in a mild voice, as if he had been expecting this outcome all along.

"Yes, all three of them, though when I first spoke to them I didn't know they were the three the Legion was searching for."

Augum turned to the girls, now completely visible. Bridget stared at the floor, not bothering to push aside a braid that had fallen across her eyes. Leera just scowled and shook her head. He nodded and raised a finger for them to hold on, trusting his instincts that the time wasn't right just yet. He returned to the peephole.

"What do you have to say about all this, old man? Do you not perhaps agree the circumstances have changed?"

One Eye's shoulders drooped. "The circumstances have indeed changed, Commander. Though I am afraid you are too late. I have already teleported them away. They are safe and sound as we speak, no doubt wondering what has happened to the funny little caravan they stumbled across. The game is up. You may have my men."

"He's lying."

The voice took Augum by surprise. It came from beside the counter, from a spot he could not see. It took a moment for him to realize it was Odo that had spoken.

Robin marched over and dragged Odo forward by the wrist. "Explain yourself!"

"I, too, wish to join the Legion. Not as a prisoner, but as a soldier sounding the trumpet as my fellow troops surge into glorious battle." Odo's voice shook yet had a tone of defiance. "I'm sick of being the old man's lackey. One Eye doesn't have the knowledge to cast Group Teleport.

However, he did send his most *trusted* mule to retrieve a scroll of that very spell from Candledale." There was resentment in Odo's voice.

"You are a traitorous cur," One Eye said, shaking. "If I was a lesser man, I would strike you down where you stood."

Odo's jaw only stiffened, eyes poised on the Commander.

"And now for the finishing touch," Tridian said in a sing-song voice, face-to-face with Odo. "So, my new friend … where are they?"

"They're right here, inside this wagon." Odo pointed to the scrap pile. "Behind there."

Suddenly One Eye began laughing. He threw his cane aside and cracked his hands together, stepping between the scrap pile and everyone else. "You know, I haven't been in a proper battle in a good while. You did not really believe I would simply go along to some dungeon and die under the lash without showing you what these old bones were made of, did you? I am a 16th degree Arcaner, my dear man! Now, Commander, in the old way—show your stripes."

But One Eye *knew* Tridian had no arcane skill, Augum thought wryly.

Sixteen rings of glowing ivy coiled around the old man's arm. Everyone took a step back except for Commander Tridian, who merely folded his arms.

"So your wheezing ways have been a ploy all along. Clever and impressive, all things considering. And an Arcaner! I must confess I did suspect this. Nonetheless, I believe by your own ancient code, it is unbefitting to contest without arcane or steel provocation."

One Eye rubbed his beard as Augum wondered what this Arcaner code business was all about. "Upon reflection, I find you in the right, Commander. To be honest, I am surprised by your knowledge of the arcane arts, especially seeing as you have, if you forgive me for saying so, no talent in the art itself."

"I consider it my duty to study my enemies. That includes the Code of the Arcaner. A most noble set of laws. If only some of my own soldiers understood such discipline and virtue."

"So we find ourselves in a bit of a stalemate," One Eye said. "In any case, I see no point keeping the young saplings hidden. Come forth, all three of you!"

They stepped out. Augum only hoped the old man had a plan. He thought One Eye might be able to take the soldiers all on at such a high degree. Perhaps he was concerned about the safety of the men, women, and children of the caravan.

The two groups eyed each other as the trio approached. The Legion, along with Justinius and Odo, stood in the corner by the door. In between stood One Eye, back hunched, arm rippling with arcane energy. Many eyes flicked between that shining arm and the trio.

Tridian, the only one at ease in his group, watched Augum for a time before his steely gaze settled on the old man. "You know, throughout history, it has often been said the downfall of the noble Arcaner has been his code. That is why there are so few of you left alive today."

"That may be so, Legionnaire, and although I have succumbed to being nothing more than a lowly merchant, hobbled by his beggarly infatuations with things, I have not forgotten my oath."

"We are not as different as you think, you and I. Sure, we may fight for different causes, but we do have a sense of honor. Duty unto death, if you will."

"Is that so? From what I hear, you are a cold-blooded, ruthless murderer. A servant to the lowest depravations. Something tells me those are not mere rumors."

The Blade of Sorrows massaged his neck, glanced to the towering shelves full of countless trinkets, and smiled. "We are all servants to our pleasures."

Robin scowled. "Commander, we have plenty of men outside, let's just take them—" Tridian flashed him a silencing look.

Robin stepped back and swallowed.

"Forgive the boy, he has much to learn about honor. Though he is correct—we *do* have a lot more men out there. We could overwhelm you and the caravan. Besides, all it would take is a single unaccounted for crossbow bolt and one of those traitorous younglings dies."

"Indeed, but if you truly thought it would be that easy, you would have done it by now, Commander. Since you are knowledgeable in the arcane way, you must be aware of the potential of a 16th degree Arcaner. Further, you must surely account for the many rare off-the-book spells I happen to have learned on my travels."

"I think I see where you are going with this, old man. I was wrong about you. You are not really an entertainer, you are a bargainer, and just as before, you wish to bargain, like the merchant you are. It fits perfectly with the code, does it not?"

"As it so happens, it does."

"Then let it be so. Once we bargained for the keeping of your men. Now let us bargain for the lives of the three younglings by your side, three wanted fugitives, one of whom happens to be the Lord of the Legion's son. Are you aware of that, old man? Are you aware that the lightning boy standing beside you is the Lord of the Legion's own son? Are you aware of his *value*?"

Bridget and Leera shifted beside Augum.

One Eye did not even turn. "As it so happens, I am, my dear commander."

So he knew all along …

"Then allow me to ask a question and appeal to the clever merchant standing before me. Why bother defending him? Turning him over would make you richer than any man known. The Lord of the Legion would reward you with eternal life and riches you could only dream of."

Tridian glanced around the shop and slowly shook his head. "You could stop living in filth. Think of it—a castle of your own, with men to command and do your every deed. Is that not your dream?"

Augum looked to One Eye, who slowly stroked his beard, and realized the Blade of Sorrows had struck a chord. "Except it's a lie—!" he blurted. "My father can't give eternal life!"

"Those words are treason!" Robin shouted, eyes burning with patriotic fervor.

"No, it's true!" Leera said, glancing to every face. "We saw the proof with our own eyes, we—"

"ENOUGH!" the Blade of Sorrows shouted, the color rising to his face. "Spare us your brainwashed antics. Your answer, bargainer."

One Eye glanced to the trio as if calculating if they were telling the truth, or perhaps estimating their worth. Then he winked before turning back to Tridian.

"It is a most tempting and alluring offer, Commander. You are a clever man, not to be underestimated. Appealing to the merchant in me would usually work, except there is something you are quite unaware of."

The Blade of Sorrows raised an eyebrow. "And what would that be, old man?"

"I was once friend, and consider myself still a friend, to Anna Atticus Stone, and beside me, shining the light of a blissful memory for an old man such as I, stands her great-grandson. Do you honestly believe I would entertain any riches and paltry baubles as trade for his life, or for that matter, for his friends? Do you not realize that as one gets older those riches and baubles become less and less valuable?"

"No, I suppose you would not, for that would most surely break your precious code." Tridian rubbed his wrist, contemplating his next move. The soldiers stirred behind him while Robin only glared at Augum. Haylee, on the other hand, wrung her hands, a troubled look on her face.

Tridian crossed his arms. "Very well then, offer your terms."

"You may have my caravan, all my artifacts, and my men," One Eye replied immediately. "For that, we are to have a days' head start and horses."

"You, the fugitives, and a days' travel?" Tridian's pale eyes swept over the shelves. "For this junk? Surely you jest."

One Eye's face crinkled with a smile. "Ah, I did not think you would like that offer much. Very well then, let us up the stakes. Caravan and men confiscated. The three younglings on their own, half a days' lead on horseback. I stay behind to insure you do not follow. Once time expires, I disappear and you may give chase."

Tridian's lips thinned with a smile of his own. "Not quite. Allow me to counter. Caravan. Men. Fugitives have a third of a days' head start on horseback, but—" and Tridian raised a finger indicating the crux of the matter was at hand, "the two necrophytes get to give chase after one hour, and you turn yourself in after a third of a day expires."

"No—" Bridget said. "You let One Eye go and it's a deal, otherwise forget it."

Tridian chuckled and shook his head in patronizing fashion.

One Eye glanced to the trio.

"Don't do it, sir," Augum said.

"Not unless you are allowed to get away," Leera added.

The old man's good eye locked on each of them before turning back to the Blade of Sorrows. For a moment, the two just stared at each other, as if communicating silently.

"Let it be so then," One Eye said.

"NO!" the trio chorused together.

Tridian stepped forward and offered his hand. "Give me your word on the ancient Code of the Arcaner."

One Eye took it. "You have my word as a merchant and by the laws set down by the Code of the Arcaner. On my honor."

"We'll be outside waiting." Tridian snapped his fingers and his entire gang, including Odo and Justinius, dutifully filed out of the caravan, leaving the trio alone with One Eye. Robin smirked as he left while Haylee seemed to flash a sympathetic look.

RIVALRY

"Are they going to let you go?" Augum asked when the wagon door shut behind Haylee. One Eye did not respond, allowing his arm to expire, darkening the room a touch. He tried to pick up his cane from the floor. Bridget helped, handing it to him, eyes moist.

The old man gave no response, instead shuffling over to the counter. He picked up the loupe and the parchment of tiny scrawl detailing the Slam spell. He pushed both into Bridget's hands, his voice quiet. "Please take this."

Bridget sniffed, rolled up the parchment, and buried it in the rucksack along with the loupe.

One Eye reached into his shirt, removed the alleged dragon tooth amulet, and placed it around Augum's neck. "I want you to have this, young man, for courage."

Augum fingered its jagged edges. He hesitated to speak, swallowing hard instead.

"Sir, please—" Bridget began, but One Eye raised his hand and she fell silent. He glanced at them all with his remaining good eye.

"I am older than you think. This world tires me. When you see Anna, tell her …" He took a breath before continuing. "Tell her William Smith is grateful, and that … and that he is sorry."

Augum could only nod, feeling unworthy and hollow. Yet another message to take to Nana, the first being the final words of his great-grandfather.

The old man raised his chin. "This is your chance. Ride west, find Bartholomew before they do, and read the scroll. Get to Anna as quick as you can. Think you can handle the necrophytes?"

Leera's face went hard. "Yes, sir."

"Good, come then." One Eye led them to the door, taking one last look around his shop. He smiled, nodded, and opened the door.

Around thirty Black Guard soldiers stood outside in the snow, weapons sheathed. The Blade of Sorrows stood in front, Haylee and Robin nearby. Other soldiers were rounding up the personnel of the caravan.

"William, what is happen to us?" Marta asked, holding her apron while stepping away from a spear-wielding soldier.

One Eye turned to her, face heavy. "I am sorry about this, Marta. You will be all right though, I assure you. Please give my blessings to your family."

Tridian turned to the crowd. The women quietly wept while the men looked on with anxious faces. "You are going to be taken into custody. Some of you will see service on the front. Others will work in smithies, in stables, in officer's quarters as servants. Some of you may even go free. In any case, you need not concern yourselves. You will be fed and you will have a roof over your heads. You will work, and you will even be paid. My officers will see to the details."

Tridian waved dismissively and the crowd was pushed to march southward in the direction of Tornvale. Augum watched the haggard faces as they passed. He sincerely hoped these poor people wouldn't end up in the same prison the trio had escaped. He wished there was something he could do to help them.

Haylee watched them shuffle by, her face turned away from Robin and the soldiers, a hand over her mouth.

One Eye stood nearby, hands shaking on his cane, watching his people go.

"Your filthy beasts—" Justinius said, throwing the gray palfrey's reins to Augum, Spirit's to the girls.

Augum made sure the blankets and rucksack were secured before mounting his horse. He glanced at the many youthful faces of the soldiers. They glared as if he were a criminal getting away, all except Justinius, who smirked. Those men truly believed in the Legion cause, but just what was that cause about? War? The Great Quest? Eternal life for all? Or was it about taking orders, fitting in, doing what you were told? The question echoed in his brain as he watched the backs of the people bobbing along southward, struggling for footing in the snow.

Robin gave him a wolfish grin. "Catch up to you soon."

Augum squared his jaw. "Looking forward to it."

One of the soldiers brought forth a wooden box. He opened it and reached inside, retrieving a large golden hourglass with purple sand inside.

Tridian strolled over and flipped the hourglass. The sand started trickling. "You have one hour."

One Eye raised a frail hand. "Good luck."

Bridget mounted Spirit behind Leera, wiping her face with her sleeve. "Goodbye, sir. We'll never forget—" but she couldn't finish, burying her head into Leera's back.

Leera turned Spirit. "We promise to tell Mrs. Stone what you said."

Augum fingered the black tooth around his neck. "Goodbye, sir, and … thank you."

The old man's face crinkled with a warm smile.

The winter sun had begun to set as the three galloped away, Leera and Bridget leading on Spirit, Augum just behind. He tried not to think about what would happen to the amiable old man. One Eye, follower of the Code of the Arcaner, once known as William Smith the Plotter, had, like many others, sacrificed himself for them.

They followed the tracks from Bartholomew's horse, keeping an eye on the horizon for any sign of him. Augum occasionally glanced astern, watching the caravan quickly shrink in the distance, now only visible from the crests of gently rolling hills.

"Robin and Haylee must be after us by now," Bridget called.

Leera scoffed. "Only if the Blade of Sorrows kept his word and hasn't loosed all his men."

As stars began twinkling overhead, Spirit slowed.

Augum craned his neck. "What's going on, Bridge, you two see anything ahead?"

"No, we don't … we think something's wrong with Spirit …"

His own palfrey began to whinny and cough. When he looked closer, he noticed white foam around his mouth. "What's wrong, boy?"

Spirit suddenly collapsed under the girls. The gray followed immediately. Both had plopped down into a sitting position before falling to their sides, allowing the trio to step off without harm.

"I think they've been poisoned," Augum said, petting the gray's flank. It nickered anxiously.

Bridget dropped to her knees and flung her arms around Spirit's neck. "No ..."

Leera tried to get Spirit to stand by tugging on her reins, but the palfrey's breath was rapid and wheezy, eyes half-closed. "Damn them ..."

Augum watched as the rising and falling of the horses' flanks slowed, until they were completely still. He remembered Meli dying in a similar way. That old beloved mule, his only friend for so long ...

He kneeled by his poor horse and gently stroked its mane. "I'm sorry, boy," he whispered. "I'm sorry ..."

If they did this to the palfreys, what would they do to those people? To One Eye?

He untied the rucksack and stuffed his blanket in. They'd have to leave the other six blankets behind, the weight would only slow them down. He slung the rucksack over his shoulder and glanced about. They were in a shallow valley between two gentle hills. A shrill wind blew around them, bringing with it a frosty bite and wisps of curling powder snow.

He stood up. "We have to keep going. We have to leave them ..."

Bridget's shoulders heaved, still holding the animal's neck. "Oh, Spirit," she kept whispering.

Leera cradled Bridget, pushing her braided locks out of her eyes. "Bridge ... there's nothing we can do. Come on, we have to go ..."

"We'll have to take their horses, it's the only way," Augum said in a distant voice, already envisioning the coming struggle.

Leera nodded, tenderly stroking Bridget's head. "There's only two of them, we'll have the advantage."

But they've got horses, he thought, glancing at the still animals, the wind already pushing snow onto their flanks. The poison had come on so suddenly. He should have seen this kind of treachery coming. After all, they were dealing with people that butchered and burnt entire villages. That should be the emblem on their banner—burning homes, burning animals, and burning people, instead of a burning sword. He clenched his jaw.

Leera dragged Bridget to her feet.

"Spirit was so innocent," Bridget mumbled. "What did she do?" She struggled in Leera's grip. "What did she do!" before going limp. "Just like mother and father ..."

Leera rubbed Bridget's back. "She didn't do anything, Bridge. *They* didn't do anything ... Come on, we have to keep going."

Bridget let go suddenly. She looked at the palfreys, sniffed, and began marching. Augum and Leera exchanged glances before following.

The trio pushed on through the waist-high snow, following Bartholomew's horse tracks. The going felt agonizingly slow compared to the pace of the palfreys. The wind blew into their faces, making the trek even more difficult. Scattered cloud zoomed overhead, leaving enormous swaths of star-filled sky.

"Here they come," Leera said, nodding at a pair of distant plumes.

Augum's heart began racing. There was still no sign of Bartholomew. They would have to face Robin and Haylee and take their horses. It was the only way ...

He ran through a mental list of spells in his head—Shine, Telekinesis, Repair, Unconceal, Centarro, and Shield, the last still hit and miss, though Shine had that shock extension. He wished he knew the Slam spell, or for that matter, an actual offensive spell, like a lightning bolt or something.

They had no weapons to speak of—Sparkstone had confiscated Burden's Edge, and Blackbite was now probably sitting in some merchant's case, a prized possession to be sold at a ghastly price. They did, however, posses the Orb of Orion, whatever good that would do them in a fight.

"They're gaining," Leera said, breathing rapid bursts of steam. "Let's make a stand at the top of the hill."

The trio reached the crest and turned around, shoulder to shoulder.

Leera placed a hand on Bridget. "You ready?"

Bridget only nodded, face hard as stone.

"We can take them, we've faced worse," he said, thinking of the skeleton back at Evergray Tower, the walker in the woods, and the hellhounds in Castle Arinthian. He dropped the rucksack to the ground.

Robin and Haylee slowed to a canter, black and red-striped robes billowing.

Augum raised his palm. "Shyneo!" It lit up with crackling lightning.

"Shyneo!" said the girls, palms lighting up the snow with prismatic hues.

"Remember that we have Centarro," he added out of the corner of his mouth. He fingered the dragon tooth amulet around his neck, hoping it really did bestow courage, because he was going to need every ounce of it.

Robin and Haylee reached their crest and stopped a few horse-lengths away, allowing a moment of windy silence to pass between the two adversarial groups.

"I see the nags couldn't cope," he said at last.

Bridget actually spat in his direction. "Because you poisoned them! Proud of that, are you?"

Robin shrugged. "Hey, it wasn't me. You can thank the stable boy for that one. He's real eager to please."

Augum recalled Justinius' smirk and cursed himself for not catching on.

"You're nothing but a vile idiot toad!" Leera yelled. "A nasty, sleazy, repulsive and brainwashed toad!"

Robin cackled. "Hayles, the Leer is calling me a toad, maybe we should go, it's just too awful, too hurtful and wounding!" but Haylee only gave him a cold glance. He didn't even notice.

Augum was anxious to get this over with. "You going to come and fight? Won't get away with cheap shots like you did last time!"

"Stupid fools." Robin glanced at Haylee with a secretive look. "Still think we're going to play on the same level as the gutterborn rats and get dirty." Robin held up a stone, placed two fingers in his mouth, and whistled sharply.

The trio looked about, confused.

"I don't see any army," Augum said, but he was concerned—if they poisoned the horses, who knew what other treacheries they were capable of.

Robin genuinely laughed. "Just wait, gutterborn ..."

A moment passed and they heard a distant cracking and rumbling, like something was digging through the snow.

"There ..." Bridget said, pointing in the direction they had come from, color draining from her face. A mound of snow was furiously ripping toward them, the icy surface cracking forward of it. Whatever it was, it was big.

Rob and Haylee's horses whinnied, but they held firm on the reins. "If only Auntie Erika was here to witness what her precious little pet will do to you ..."

THE BANYAN BEAST

The mound of snow exploded and out jumped what looked like a nine-foot ape, except in place of eyes there was just a monstrous black nose, its two holes opening and closing like tankard lids. It had glossy black fur and giant arms out of proportion to its body.

"Dark hell ..." Leera said, taking a step back as the thing roared in their direction, exposing racks of jagged teeth. It sniffed the air, turned to Robin and Haylee, and roared again, spooking the horses and almost throwing their riders off.

"Whoa there, whoa—" Robin said. "Not us you filthy beast, them—" He pointed at the trio. "And remember, just the females, not the male. Leave him for us!"

The beast made no gesture that it understood, instead continuing to sniff the air for scents.

"Maybe you should try using the stone," Haylee muttered.

"Oh, yeah." Robin palmed the strange rock. He placed it to his lips and spoke into it. The beast immediately turned to the trio and roared again.

"Sorry about that, it's kind of stupid," Robin said to the trio. "It's an arcanely enslaved banyan beast, and it doesn't like being above ground. Anyway, his teeth will be the last thing you two gutterborn wretches will ever feel."

Haylee's head whipped his way, voice cracking. "But you said no one would die—"

"You wouldn't—" Bridget said, retreating another step.

Robin snorted and held the stone to his mouth. "Knock the females down, make them suffer!"

The banyan beast dropped forward on his two powerful front arms and charged, kicking up white plumes. It was all the trio could do to jump out of its way.

Robin laughed at the spectacle.

It uses smell, Augum realized, desperately trying to come up with a plan. If he could just get the stone … but that would mean he'd have to be faster than the horses. It gave him an idea.

"Bridge, Leera—work with me," he said as the trio prepared for another charge. "Stay close—"

He turned his back to Robin and Haylee, pretending he didn't know where they were, all the while backing up towards them. He let his hands traverse the thin unbroken layer of icy snow as he cracked its surface, feeling its rough texture, judging its strength. He carefully watched every movement of the beast, noting how its blindness was its greatest weakness, smell its greatest strength.

"After the next pass, I'll cast Centarro," he whispered out of the corner of his mouth. "You two cast it when mine expires—watch out!"

He dodged the banyan beast's charge just in time, but Bridget wasn't so lucky. It smashed into her, sending her flying and crashing to the snow in a powdery explosion.

"BRIDGET!" Leera screamed, sprinting for her.

Robin guffawed. "Did you see that, Hayles?"

"Robbie, please, you said they wouldn't—"

"You realize I'm just toying with you," Robin said to Augum, ignoring Haylee. "The real fun will be when I give it a kill command."

Augum picked himself up from the snow, ignoring the pain from his ribs, a pain he had almost forgotten about since coming to the caravan. The ground began rumbling, signaling another charge. It was he and Leera now, and if one of them didn't act, they were lost.

"Leera, keep its attention on you," he said, unsure if she heard him in her attempts to find Bridget. He had no time to say it again. The beast charged straight at her. Robin was only ten feet behind and to the right of him. Haylee was further.

Leera had to withstand the next pass, *she had to*.

"Centeratoraye xao xen!" He felt the rush of the spell slow everything down, or perhaps his mind sped up. Every nuance, every texture, every gesture and feeling was clear as the night sky, and visible for what it was. The snow became crystal sharp. The wind flowed over him like an invisible river. Every moment counted, yet this time he would not prepare for the side effects—he needed that time to do the impossible.

He whipped around and raised his palm at the horse. "Shyneo!" He concentrated on brightness, pushing past the boundaries he knew. It had to be brighter. Lightning crackled to life around his hand. He *willed* fear with his stance, the way his arm jutted, his fierce look.

The horse whinnied, rearing up on its hind legs, but his eyes were already fixed upon Robin's arm. When it reached the right angle, at the apex of the horse's rise, he extinguished Shine and switched to Telekinesis, arcanely reaching for the rock in Robin's hand.

The ground began shaking from the banyan beast's charge as a momentary battle arose between his Telekinesis and Robin's grip on the stone. He knew it would have been next to impossible if Robin was paying attention, but at that very moment, Robin was distracted just enough to yank the stone from his hand and send it flying toward Augum.

By the powerful rumbling, he knew he was too late.

Just as he was about to grab it, a mountain hit him, or at least, it felt like a mountain. He hurtled forward, slamming into Robin's horse, knocking the wind out of his lungs and sending Robin falling to the ground.

The pain in his chest exploded, amplified by Centarro. Yet Centarro also allowed him to recover quickly by focusing on that which mattered. Robin was still lying in the snow as Augum began searching for the stone, struggling for breath, chest grating with wave after wave of bone-crunching sharpness. He fought to concentrate through the pain.

Then he stopped, attempting to do something that would have been impossible without Centarro—he went back to the moment he was hit from behind, poring over the minutiae of events.

The stone was just before him ... he was sent hurtling forward ... his eyes reflexively closed from the impact ... and yes, there it was—he remembered feeling the stone hit his chest. It must have tumbled at a particular angle, a particular speed. He recalled the sound only a stone would make as it careened across a thin frozen layer of ice he had already studied.

It could only have gone in one direction. He turned—and there it was, almost invisible behind a clump of snow, not ten paces away. He sprinted, but he was not the only one that had spotted it—Haylee had apparently witnessed the whole thing and was galloping straight for it.

His brain fogged as Centarro expired. "Shyneo!" he called, hoping to blind Haylee's horse, but the spell failed. He dived for the rock, fully expecting Haylee to trample him, but her horse just jumped over him instead. He heard her shout something as the last threads of concentration slipped. He lay stupidly in the snow.

"Command it!" he heard a girl's voice shout. "Tell it to stop! Gods, tell—"

The ground rumbled again.

"Stop? Stop what?" he mumbled, staring groggily at the stone in his hand.

The rumbling ceased. Something growled nearby.

"He has it—!" shouted a male voice.

A frantic female voice shouted a phrase that sounded like gibberish to Augum. He giggled at the funny words. Time passed filled with otherworldly noise as he nestled the stone close to his chest, its smooth texture cozy, safe. His chest tingled like a bug bite. He stared at the starry sky and smiled, enjoying the simplicity of it, the beauty of twinkling stars.

Suddenly the stone was yanked from his hands as a figure hurtled across him. He barely noticed, brain still foggy, senses crawling back snail-like. A vicious struggle ensued nearby too complex for his feeble mind to follow. Something roared very loudly.

And then … silence.

When the fog in his mind finally cleared, he glanced about as if waking from a dream. His chest pulsed sharply, breath shallow.

Then he saw it.

The banyan beast stood over the cowering figures of Haylee and Robin, Leera standing nearby staring at the stone in her hand, a simple expression on her face.

His blood instantly quickened—she's lost to the side effects of Centarro!

He sprang to his feet and ran to her, taking the stone from her hands. Luckily, Robin and Haylee had no knowledge of the Centarro spell and its side effects, else they would have taken the opportunity afforded them and disarmed Leera of the stone.

"Sit, Lee," he whispered, gently pushing her to the snow.

She peered up at him like a lost child, braids falling across her forehead.

"Where's Bridget?" he asked no one in particular, frantically looking about.

Haylee pointed off to his left.

There he found her face-up in the snow, eyes open. He fell to his knees. "Bridge … are you all right? Bridge!" He placed his ear to her chest. There was a faint thumping.

"Bridge, you're alive!"

Her eyes slowly focused on him, but her mouth remained slightly agape. She did not move.

Something was terribly wrong.

He gently shook her. "Get up, Bridge, get up—" but she didn't move. Her eyes stayed on him, pleading and sad.

"Don't worry, everything's going to be okay," he mumbled, not believing a word of it and painfully conscious of just how fearful he must look. They needed an arcane healer, but where would they find one? He'd never even met one before, and they were supposed to be rare and very expensive, not to mention sought after by the Legion.

He sat there in a kind of panicked trance for a while when the banyan beast snorted, snapping him out of it.

"Leera, I need your help!" he called, seeing that she was regaining her senses. He checked to make sure Robin and Haylee weren't trying anything. Robin watched with a smirk on his face while Haylee looked on with—was it pity?

Leera slowly got up, brushed herself off, and lumbered over. When she spotted Bridget, she gasped and fell to the snow, gurgling, "No no no no …"

"It's all right, she's alive, she just can't move," Augum said. "We need an arcane healer."

"It must be her back—" Leera's hands shook as she brushed Bridget's braids from her face. "I've seen something like this before … a boy in Sparrow's Perch fell from a tree once. The elders had him taken to Antioc. They had an arcane healer there, though *damn it,* I can't remember her name …

"Then that's where we must go," he said, readying to pick Bridget up. "Come on, let's get her on the horse—"

Leera grabbed his wrist. "No! Don't touch her, she could die that way. It's really important she remain as still as possible. We have to use Telekinesis and levitate her onto the horse."

"Just the two of us—?" he asked, fully aware how tired they were from the spell casting.

"We *have to try.*"

He nodded and the two stood back.

"Aww, wut is wittle Bridgey-poo hurt?"

Even Haylee gave Robin a horrified look.

Augum, enraged, put the stone to his mouth, daring Robin to say another word.

Robin, thinking Augum was going to command the banyan beast to do something heinous, quickly said, "Please no! I don't want to die!"

Instead, the banyan beast, towering nine feet over Robin, roared down at him, sniffing the air repeatedly over his head. Augum, satisfied the message was delivered, turned his attention back to Bridget. Her eyes followed him, expressing concern and confusion. Seeing her like this was almost more than he could bear.

"Ready?" Leera asked, breathing heavily.

He nodded, steeling himself, trying to ignore his horribly grating chest. The beast's charge had worsened the damage. They reached out together and began Telekinesis, but it was immediately evident their arcane stamina was too low. Bridget didn't even twitch. They tried again, failing the second time as well. Leera, panting, looked away from Bridget, checking the black horizon behind her, as if expecting the Legion to come at any moment.

Augum grimaced, holding his chest. A wave of nausea forced him to sit down.

It was over. They were stuck until the Legion came, and then what? What would happen to Bridget? To Leera?

"Let me help—" Haylee said, standing up despite the banyan beast towering over her.

"What are you doing?" Robin asked, snagging her robe. "Sit back down!"

"It's a trick—" Leera said.

Haylee shook her head. "It's not." She unsuccessfully pushed a long strand of blond hair from her eyes. "I … I didn't want this. This is too much … I'm not a murderer …"

"Hayles, what are you doing? Have you lost your mind? Do you realize what's going to happen to your fam—"

"Stop it! Just STOP IT!" Haylee placed her hands over her ears, tears streaming down her face. "I told you this isn't what I wanted! We were supposed to be in the academy together, not murdering people! We were supposed to be … this isn't what I wanted!"

Robin only blinked, mouth gaping.

"It's a trap, don't listen to her, Augum." Leera was staring at him, but he heard something else in Haylee's voice—sincerity.

He met Leera's gaze. "It's a chance we have to take."

Leera glared at him a moment then looked at Bridget, before finally nodding.

He reached out a hand. "Will you help us then?"

Haylee wearily paced toward them from under the towering figure of the banyan beast, which followed her with its head as if it had eyes, sniffing the air with that giant nose. She stopped a few paces away, hands wringing.

Leera stared at Haylee with undisguised contempt and distrust.

"I'm … I'm sorry this happened to her, I'm sorry about everything …" Haylee's voice was soft, eyes glassy. "I can't live that way anymore. I can't …"

"Look at her—" Leera said. "LOOK AT HER!"

Haylee forced herself to look at Bridget. Her pale hand slowly came to her mouth. She fell to her knees, hair obscuring her face.

Something caught Augum's attention on the horizon. A low white cloud had formed there, lit by the orange glow of torches.

"Are they coming?" he asked, eyes still on the cloud. "Did they break their word?"

Haylee only nodded.

"What's going to happen to One Eye?"

Haylee slowly shook her head.

Augum wiped his forehead with his sleeve. He knew it. He looked square at Haylee. "We have to go. Help us get her on the horse." He was willing to give her a chance. It was the girls she'd have to win over, especially Leera.

Haylee stood and nodded, composing herself. Leera eyed her distrustfully as they raised their arms to begin Telekinesis.

"Don't you dare help them, Haylee," Robin said. "I swear to the Unnameables we'll find you and—"

Augum raised the stone to his lips again and Robin fell silent, glaring. He then turned his attention back to Bridget, throwing every ounce of concentration he had left her way. Remarkably, working together, her body slowly rose, coming to rest on top of Haylee's horse.

Augum and Leera fell to their knees when the spell concluded, both gripping their heads.

"Here, take this, it'll support her back," Haylee said, unsheathing a short sword from her horse and offering it pommel-first to Leera.

She could have killed us instead, Augum thought. Taken the stone …

Leera snatched the blade. "Just don't you touch her!"

Haylee dropped her eyes. "I'm sorry," she mumbled. "For all of this …"

Augum helped secure Bridget to the horse, wrapping her in a Dramask blanket before tying the rucksack near her feet. He was exhausted, cold, his chest bones grated with every movement, and his head throbbed from all the arcane effort.

Haylee stepped away from the horse when they were done, necrophyte robe rippling in the wind. "What are you going to do now?"

Augum mounted Robin's horse, offering a hand to Leera. She sat behind him, hands around his waist. "We're going to find an arcane healer."

Haylee checked the horizon. The cloud had turned into an oncoming plume, with dark specks at the center surrounded by a pulsing orange glow. The Legion was at a full-on gallop, racing to catch up to them.

"I heard you say earlier you were going to Antioc. There's a healer there my family knows. Miralda—don't remember her last name though." She handed him the reins to Bridget's horse, which he passed on to Leera.

"You helped us, but now what's going to happen to you?" he asked.

Haylee looked back at Robin.

"She's going to burn, the disgusting filthy little traitor!" Robin said, frothing spittle, face contorted. "What happened to having my back, huh, Hayles? What about that? You're so fake! I can't wait to see you burn, and everyone you love too—"

The color drained from Haylee's face. She turned back to Augum, her once icy-blue eyes now hollow and dull.

Augum glanced at Leera.

"No, forget it, don't even think about it—"

"If we leave her—"

Leera's nose flared. "I don't care, she murdered our parents! And look what she did to Bridget—!"

Out of loyalty, he almost didn't argue, but another look at Haylee and he knew it wasn't right to just leave her there. "No, you know she didn't. You might hate her for many other things, but she didn't kill your parents—my father did."

Leera glared at him before removing her hands from his waist and crossing them to her chest.

He sighed. This was not going to be easy. He reached out to Haylee. "Hop on."

Haylee looked back at Robin, who was still shouting obscenities at her, then at the approaching Legion, before finally taking Augum's hand and climbing onto the warhorse, easily large and strong enough to support all three of them.

Leera slapped Haylee's hands away when she tried to grab on for support. "Don't touch me!"

"But … I might fall."

"I. Don't. Care!"

Augum, realizing this was as good as it was going to get, raised the stone to his lips.

Leera peeked over his shoulder. "What are you doing?"

"Buying us time."

HAYLEE

Augum loosed the banyan beast on the Legion with a careful set of instructions whispered into the stone. It roared and dove under the snow, burrowing straight at the oncoming cloud. It would be a battle he had no intention of sticking around for.

They promptly left, leaving behind a frothing Robin, shouting obscenities mostly aimed at Haylee, threatening her family. She broke down but didn't reply. Neither Leera nor Augum made any attempt to console her, though each for different reasons—Leera loathed Haylee while Augum didn't want to provoke Leera lest she shoved her off the horse or something. He wondered what they were supposed to do with Haylee now.

They trotted along rather slowly to avoid doing further harm to Bridget. Leera carefully held onto the reins of her horse, keeping a watchful eye on it as it bobbed along beside them. Haylee sat quiet in the back, avoiding any contact with Leera while trying to balance on the horse.

"You keep wincing. How are those ribs?"

"When the banyan beast hit me, I don't know ... something isn't right though ..."

"Don't you even look at her!" Leera screamed at Haylee. "Don't you dare ..."

He decided now might be the time to question Haylee about a couple things on his mind, at least to change the mood a bit.

"Haylee, do you know where my father is right now?"

She cleared her throat delicately. "You're trying to get to the crone—err, to your great-grandmother before he does, right?"

"Yes."

"Your father is way too far ahead for you to overtake him. If you go to Antioc, though, you might still have a chance—if you're quick finding a healer and leaving the city that is."

"So are you done with the Legion now?"

"I've had doubts ever since Sparrow's Perch. To see people killed like that ... And then Tornvale ... after your prison outbreak, they ... they murdered most of them."

"But you helped your grandfather in Sparrow's Perch!" Leera said.

"I didn't even know about any of his plans! I lost friends that day too. But I played along, I played the good girl, supporting the cause. *I was afraid,* all right? I was afraid of what they were going to do to me and my family if I said anything—"

"—you betrayed the village, and you *knew* what was going to happen—"

"—no, I didn't, I swear it!" Haylee broke down crying again, her long blonde locks falling over trembling hands that cupped her face.

"I'm sorry I … made fun of you and … your friends …" Haylee said between sobs. "I'm sorry about that awful song … I just wanted to be popular and … and liked …"

Augum wondered what song she referred to.

Leera scoffed. "Yeah and look how well that worked out for everyone at Sparrow's Perch—"

"Do you have anyone to stay with in Antioc?" he asked. Even though he knew there were a lot of hard feelings that needed sorting between them, he didn't want things to get out of hand. They still might need Haylee's help with Bridget.

"I have an aunt … I could go live with her in hiding … if … if she'll take me."

"She *better* take you," Leera said, "else we're dropping you off at a Legion guard post and you can see what it feels like to be questioned."

Augum thought that rather harsh. He tried to think of a way to get Leera to leave Haylee alone, at least for a little while. Maybe he was being naive, but he believed Haylee didn't have anything to do with the murder of Leera and Bridget's parents. He also believed she was genuinely sorry about it all.

On the other hand, he was not the one that had to put up with Haylee for years, and didn't know what kind of cruel and malicious things had been said and done. As someone once bullied, he perfectly understood where Leera was coming from, yet that still didn't make it feel right.

Though maybe if it was Robin sitting there instead of Haylee, he would have a lot less sympathy …

"I … I liked Robin … I really *liked* him …" Haylee mumbled through her tears. "I didn't know he could be so … so vile …"

"What are you blubbering on about?" Leera asked.

"The Blade of Sorrows is training him in the art of the question … training him to be cold and … and ruthless …

and soon Lord Sparkstone himself will be training him in necromancy. I don't like what he's becoming … he's not the same Robbie I knew …"

"Oh, shut. Up! He was always a mean toad, and you liked him anyway, all because he showered you with attention and compliments. Pathetic."

Haylee sniffed hard but did not reply.

Augum glanced to Bridget, who only stared at the sky, and wondered what she would say right now if she could talk. Would she show mercy or unleash anger along with Leera?

When they reached the crest of another gently rolling hill, he looked back. The distant torch-lit plume of horses had dispersed a little. Perhaps the battle with the banyan beast had begun, though there was no way to be sure. The command stone certainly gave no hints. To all outward appearances it was an ordinary ornamental rock, yet amazingly, this unassuming stone had the power to command that monster. He wondered if necromancy was involved.

"Haylee, do you know anything about the banyan beast, like where it's from?" he asked, keeping his tone level so as not to provoke Leera.

"Nothing, only that it belonged to Robin's aunt and she got it in the south. When that old man at the caravan—"

"—his name was One Eye!" Leera said, whipping about. "He sacrificed himself for us, a concept I'm sure you know nothing about. The least you can do is get his damn name right!"

"I'm sorry … after One Eye made the deal with Commander Tridian, while you all were still inside that wagon, the Blade of Sorrows gave Robin the stone that controlled the beast, with instructions on what to do."

Leera shook her head. "Figures … and those are the kinds of people you chose to be friends with …"

"I'm not friends with them anymore! And you forget, I'm taking a huge risk helping you. You heard him threaten my family—"

"—at least you *have* a family to threaten!"

That silenced Haylee, though Augum had other questions. "Haylee, did Tridian ever talk about the coming war with Tiberra?"

"Yeah, but mostly with his officers and Robin. He ignored me. Robin was his prized pupil, like his own son. All I know is that the Legion is on the march now."

"Do you believe us when we tell you that my father's promise of eternal life for everyone is a lie?"

"I ... I don't know ..."

"Look," Leera began, "we were just *in* Ley. One of those Leyans, who happened to be Augum's great-grandfather, followed us out and *died*. He died, Haylee, to show us that you can't take that eternal life power or whatever out of there."

"You believe us that we were there at least, don't you?" he asked when Haylee hesitated.

"I guess so ..."

"And what about the Dreadnoughts? Know anything about them?"

"Well, I know that the Dreadnoughts have already started forging weapons and armor. It's kind of a slow process though."

"Is the Dreadnought equipment arcane?"

"I don't know, I don't know anything about Dreadnoughts, really. I always used to think they were just ... stories."

"Like Ley?" Leera asked. When Haylee didn't bite, Leera turned her attention to Bridget, gently reining in her horse. "How are you feeling, Bridge?"

Augum glanced over to witness a tear roll down Bridget's cheeks. Leera reached over and brushed it away, voice cracking. "Everything will be fine, Bridge, don't worry. We're taking you to Antioc where you're going to be fixed up by an arcane healer."

Bridget's eyes wandered over to them, her head completely still, tears flowing freely. He only hoped she wasn't in any pain. They desperately needed to find Bartholomew before the Legion caught up to them. Suddenly, he was reminded of Mya and those emerald almond eyes. The question that has been hounding him for so long now sprang to his lips.

"Haylee, um ... do you know where Mya is? Is Robin really going to take her with him?"

"You like her, don't you?" Haylee asked, not in a cheeky manner, just in a matter-of-fact kind of way. "I could tell—"

"Ugh, you just can't help yourself, can you?" Leera's voice was full of venom. "What, going to gossip about this to your friends? It's none of your business who Augum likes!"

Something about the way Leera said it brought butterflies to his stomach. Part of him wished he had not brought Mya up, yet he really wanted to hear news about her ...

"I ... I really didn't mean it that way," Haylee mumbled. "I'm sorry ..."

"Ugh, well, aren't you going to answer his question—?"

"Right ... uh, Mya has been assigned to be Robin's servant, but while he's away, she has to serve the Black Guard with the other servants. As far as I know, yes, he plans on taking her back to the academy with him, though that kind of thing might not be permitted. The Legion may force her to stay behind. I don't know for sure though, I don't follow what the servants do."

"Of course you don't, that would be *beneath* you."

"Would you rather my parents died in Sparrow's Perch too?"

"Yes! YES I WOULD HAVE—!"

Augum felt the horse lighten and running footsteps crunching in the snow.

"That's right, run back to your precious Robbie and the damn Legion, I'm sure they'll take good care of you!" Leera shouted, but as Augum turned his head, he saw that Haylee was not running back to the Legion. Instead, she appeared as if she just wanted to get far away from everyone by running into the bleak nothingness of winter.

The idea suddenly occurred to him she may not care about her own life in that moment. Already the wind was rising, and with no shelter, blankets, or food, it wouldn't take long for a person to freeze out here.

Without a word, he jumped off the horse and chased after Haylee, who ran haphazardly, crying, until tripping and falling to the snow, her golden locks splayed across the icy surface. He heard Leera shout something from behind, but ignored her.

He finally caught up to her, panting, chest burning. "Don't do this. She didn't mean it, she's just … she's very angry right now. Think about it, can you blame her?"

Haylee replied between heaving sobs. "This was a mistake … I'm so stupid … by helping you … I might … I might have killed my parents …"

He felt for her, but he didn't know what to do. He didn't exactly have much experience with girls other than Bridget and Leera. They had to get out of here, yet this was a delicate situation. All he wanted to do was say the right thing to make everything better. He wanted to *fix* it with words, yet he also knew no words would make this just disappear. Besides, it was beyond that. People *sacrificed* themselves for them already, and there was no way of bringing them back. And here was Haylee, a long-time enemy of Bridget and Leera, doing the same thing—placing her family and life at risk to help them …

Again and again the question which he had no answer for came to mind, and that was, *why*? Why had so many sacrificed themselves for them?

"Haylee, we don't have much time. Come on, we can deal with this later—"

"Leave me alone! I just want to sleep, please just leave me alone!"

"I'm going to talk to her, I'll be right back … uh … don't go anywhere." He realized how stupid that was to say. Nonetheless, he raced back to Leera, who stared in the opposite direction with folded arms.

"Leera, um, look … we can't just leave her out here, she'll die …"

Leera maintained an iron stare.

"We don't have time for this, you know that. Besides, Haylee might very well have killed her own parents by helping us … and I *know* you didn't really mean what you said, you're just angry, and I can understand that—"

"Shut up, please, just shut up …" She placed her face into her hands, shook her head and sniffed. "Fine! Whatever. Bring her, see if I care, but don't think for one moment I have to get along with her."

Augum, knowing that was the best he could hope for at this time, raced back to Haylee, ribs grating like rough stones.

"It's all right, Haylee, come on back," but Haylee had curled up into a ball, shoulders twitching. "Look, I know you're not a bad person, I heard you help One Eye when Robin pushed him over. A bad person wouldn't do that."

"You don't know me, I *am* a bad person—"

"You can't stay here, the Legion will find you by your footprints. They'll torture you …"

She began visibly shaking.

"Don't make me carry you because I will, I'll throw you over my shoulder like a sack of potatoes and tie you to the damn horse—"

Haylee burst with a blubbery chortle and Augum knew he had broken through to her.

"Come on, we really need to go." He helped her stand.

"Thank you," she whispered, wiping her red face with the sleeve of her necrophyte robe. He nodded and led her back to the horses, checking the horizon. The cloud was still there, though a bit closer.

The Legion had overcome the banyan beast.

He helped Haylee back on the horse before hopping on, Leera resolutely keeping her arms crossed, refusing to give him a hand like usual. He urged the horse forward, pushing the pace a little bit. At the rate they were going, he estimated less than two hours until the Legion caught up.

His breathing shortened. Bridget was badly hurt and needed arcane attention from a healer, and Bartholomew … where was Bartholomew? Had he sold Blackbite and kept the money for himself? Was One Eye's trust in the man blind? He scanned ahead, desperate for any sign of the man.

They passed hill after hill in silence, Leera keeping a steady eye on Bridget, Haylee a watchful eye on their rear, though more probably to avoid Leera than anything else.

Augum looked up at the cloudless starry night. At least Bridge has a great view, he thought, glancing at her still form.

He shivered at a particularly strong gust of wind. The excitement from the battle had faded, leaving behind a bone-seeping cold and that damn throbbing pain.

Leera removed the other two blankets from the rucksack and draped one over his shoulders.

"Thanks."

She didn't reply, throwing the other one around herself, leaving Haylee to shiver in her necrophyte robe. Haylee's teeth soon began chattering loudly.

"Here, take mine—" he said.

"No! You need it more than she does," Leera said immediately, casting a vicious glance backward.

"She's right—keep it," Haylee said, forcing her teeth to stop.

He didn't want to push things and reluctantly let it go.

Time passed as they traversed more crests and long valleys. The wind kept steady as the stars moved overhead. Meanwhile, the torch-lit cloud steadily gained—they were quickly running out of time.

More hills, and the legion drew closer still, yet the foursome could not go any faster. The wind had picked up slightly, coming at them straight on making the going that much more difficult. They pushed forward, hungry, tired and cold, now able to make out individual dots of fire amongst the approaching plume, at least ten or so. Augum suspected there were more riders, riders without torches galloping along unseen in the dark. He pictured the Blade of Sorrows among them, face twisted in iron determination.

There was still no sign of Bartholomew. If they didn't see him soon, it would be too late, and they still had to learn the scroll. A thought suddenly occurred to him—what if Bartholomew had seen the cloud and was running away in the other direction? If that was the case, they were done for. He checked the ground for fresh return tracks, but there were none.

"You have to send a signal," Haylee said.

Leera scoffed. "Are you stupid? The Legion will see us."

"They already know where we are," Augum said. "They've been following our tracks. It's worth a shot. Shyneo!" His hand lit up as Leera made a disapproving noise. They needed every chance of being seen, and so he concentrated on brightening it again, pushing the boundaries of the spell. It brightened, a small crackling lamp in a desolate snowy landscape. He waved broadly, as if seeing a friend. He hoped, truly hoped, Bartholomew was somewhere out there to see their signal.

"Hellooooo! Bartholomeeeewww!"

There was no response. He shouted again, all the while draining his arcane stamina, yet it just seemed futile. His heart sank. That was it, their last hope. Nothing to do now but wait for the Legion to catch up. His shoulders slumped. This wasn't the way it was supposed to be …

Haylee and Leera had fallen silent, perhaps also appreciating the severity of their predicament. Leera reached out and patted Bridget's still hand. Tears no longer flowed down Bridget's cheeks. She just stared at the stars, a peaceful expression on her face.

Then a feeble light sprouted to life south of them.

"There!" Leera called, pointing. "There, Aug! Go go go!"

He immediately changed direction, pushing the horses a touch faster.

"Hold on, Bridge!" Leera said—something he thought absurd under the circumstance. The light flickered like a distant firefly in the night, urging them on, calling out to them.

Soon they were close enough to identify the man's pudgy form.

"Bartholomew, Bartholomew—!" Augum and Leera kept shouting over the wind.

He was on his horse, waving a small burning stick, extinguishing it as soon as they came near enough. He began digging around in his bag. "I was running from that army there when I saw your light. You're lucky I happened to turn my head at the right moment. Anyway, this is for you." He handed Augum a large scroll secured with a blue ribbon and a red wax seal. "What happened to her?"

Augum dismounted and helped Leera and Haylee off the horse. He didn't want to waste time explaining things. "Injured in a fight."

"Well I'm sure she'll be fine. What news of the caravan?"

Augum hesitated. Bartholomew, seeing his face, nodded. "A pity." He glanced to the approaching cloud of horsemen. "My end of the deal is done. I take my leave."

"Wait—!" Leera called, but he was already gone, charging off into the darkness, leaving them to fend for themselves. Augum wasted no time breaking the seal, untying the ribbon, and unfurling the scroll. When he saw the tremendous amount of writing, he felt his legs weaken.

Leera craned over his shoulder. "No … this is … this is impossible …"

His hopes flickered and died. They were doomed.

Unless …

He crossed his brows sharply. "You two need to work together for the moment, we don't have much time. Leera—you read this part in the middle. Haylee—you read the end. I'll start the first part. Got it?"

The girls nodded, crowding around him to read. There was enough starlight to be able to see the words. He quickly checked the horizon. He could make out the horses and dark outlines of the Black Guard now. They were at a full gallop and would be here very soon.

"Damn it, what is that symbol there?" Leera pointed to an abstract little thing between inscriptions.

"I think that means you need to hold hands," Haylee replied.

"You absolutely sure?"

Haylee shrugged.

"Good enough," he said, not wanting them to get distracted. "Finished my section, ready?"

"Ready," they chorused.

"All right then, mine basically says that we have to have a speaker to precisely say the arcane words, and that person has to concentrate on the location, really see it in their minds. Here's the thing—they have to have *been there* before."

Leera and Haylee actually exchanged a quick look of alarm, before realizing they were communicating and turned away.

"There's a whole other bit of information, but I think we can skip some of the details."

Leera check the horizon. "We'll just have to deal with it then. My section says we need to firmly hold hands else you could end up teleporting to some nether world, or worse, appear inside a mountain. Also, only what you carry teleports with you, like your clothes and rucksack and stuff. The rest I skimmed through …"

The soldiers shouted in the distance now. The legion knew they were close, had probably seen Augum's lit palm, and charged at full speed, quickly nearing the spot the foursome turned southward from.

Haylee went next, speaking as fast as she could. "My section has the arcane words needed, but I can't pronounce them—"

Pronunciation! And they didn't even have Bridget helping them.

"—it also said that the speaker needs to focus arcane energy on the words and that they have to be spoken exactly, evenly, and all in one breath. It really stressed the one breath part. Oh, and the scroll self ignites after the spell is cast. There's more but—"

"That's fine, we're out of time, who reads?" He searched their faces.

"I think you should, Aug. I don't think I could pull this off …"

"But I haven't been to Antioc—"

"I have," Haylee said, "but I can't possibly read this, it's just too complex."

"Aug, just do it, anywhere but here, quick!"

"Fine, I'll try—" He placed the scroll before him on the snow. "All right, grab a hold of Bridget." He took Leera and Haylee's hands. They were both cold and clammy.

"Wait, the rucksack—" Leera rushed to untie it and quickly threw it on. She also grabbed the blanket from her shoulders and the one from Augum's, stuffing them inside. The four of them then held hands, with Bridget still lying on the horse. Augum turned his attention to the scroll and dropped to his knees to read it, never letting go.

Horribly, his mind went completely blank. The page was suddenly indecipherable gibberish, like a bunch of chicken scratchings.

The shouting of men grew louder and louder as a bead of sweat trickled down his forehead.

"Aug, Centarro—!"

"Good idea—" He stilled his mind, not daring to look over his shoulder at the charging army sure to run them down any moment. This was it. He had to concentrate like never before.

"Centeratoraye xao xen!"

He immediately felt the familiar sensation of time slowing down, of the world becoming sharper, simpler. He went straight to the scroll, ignoring the usual step of preparing for the side effects. The writing appeared brilliant and crisp, flowing in beautiful archaic patterns and loops, but most importantly, it was *understandable*—every word. The parchment appeared ornate and soft, beckoning to be read.

The ground thundered and the page shook ever so slightly from the nearing trample of horses. He took the briefest moment to marvel at the particles of snow and ice dancing on the parchment in time to the reverberations, before visualizing the place he wanted to go, the only one that readily and easily came to mind.

Under the influence of Centarro, he judged he still had a precious moment he could spare to think of his great-grandmother and great-grandfather. He imagined Mrs. Stone giving him advice on the pronunciation, especially the intonation. Then he imagined Thomas advising on the actual sound of the letters.

He smiled briefly, remembering his great-grandfather's kind face, his sacrifice for them. He inhaled one last long breath, watching the words, priming them on his tongue, before invoking them aloud.

Perhaps it was the nature of the spell, or the following fog of Centarro, but he would never be able to remember those arcane words. All he knew was that, under normal circumstances, they would have been too complex and otherwise impossible to read on the first go like that. He did not think of the pressure he was under, nor did he think of faltering. He read them as if it was the most natural thing to do, and because of Centarro, the words flowed like honey.

As he neared completion, everything grew bright and hot and windy. He felt his body being pulled in all directions and the air sucked out of his lungs. No matter what though, he squeezed the hands of Haylee and Leera, not daring to let go, passing on courage and strength. As the last word died on his lips, the air crunched and the space seemed to collapse. He looked up just in time to see Bridget's body framed in white light atop the horse.

I'm taking you home, Bridge, I'm taking you home …

THE ASHES OF SPARROW'S PERCH

Augum woke to discover he was laying with his head in Leera's lap, covered by a blanket, her freckled face attentive to a quiet night. She idly stroked his hair, unaware his eyes had opened, her raven braids dangling over his head. For a short time, he just lay there, feeling sheltered and cared for. The air was cold and crisp, tinted by the scent of pine. When his eyes adjusted to the darkness, he noticed burnt branches overhead. Suddenly it dawned on him that the scroll must have worked—and he had simply been unconscious through the side effects of Centarro!

Leera broke out with a smile, leaning close. "You did it. We're safe."

The dull throb of his broken ribs returned as he sat up. "Where's Bridget—?"

"Shh ... right here. Don't worry, she's okay."

He glanced at Bridget's still form. Her eyes met his and he thought he saw relief in them. "Glad you're okay," he whispered.

Haylee sat against a nearby tree. She gave him a pained smile before looking away.

Leera took the blanket from him and folded it up. "I didn't want to go in without you waking up."

"Go in—?"

"Yeah, into Sparrow's Perch—or what's left of it."

"Oh … right." They had to be just on the outskirts.

"Never thought I'd see this place again," Haylee mumbled.

Leera scowled. "Who asked your opinion?"

"Leera, please—"

"Ugh, so you're taking *her* side now?"

"No—I mean … let's just work as a team for now, okay?" She only shrugged, but he knew it was as good as he was going to get from her.

He crawled forward to peek through the brush, unsuccessfully trying to keep his ribs from grating against each other. The stars basked Sparrow's Perch in a cool glow. The towering pines, with their branches acting as roofs for round homes, were now charred skeletons, shadows of their former selves. The burned remains of tables, benches, and other items of village life lay strewn about. Where there should have been a festive fire surrounded by dancing and laughing people, there was only a soot-covered pit.

Leera shoved his blanket into the rucksack. "Well fine, now that you're up, I'm going to take a look around."

Haylee held up a hand. "Wait, I hear something—"

They froze. Indeed, there was a gentle rustling to their left. A shadow moved.

"Someone's over there," Augum whispered, looking around for a stick, instinctively knowing he didn't have the arcane stamina to cast any spells right then.

"Curses, my sword didn't teleport with us," Haylee said.

They watched the shadow slink closer and closer.

"Who's there! Shyneo!" Leera said.

Haylee promptly followed suit, igniting her palm in a somewhat weak ice-blue glow. It was obvious she had not nearly as much practice with Shine as they had. Augum didn't have time to marvel at the neatness of seeing her hand freeze up like that, however, for their palms revealed a short balding man holding a stick. He wore a tattered long-sleeved tunic and round spectacles, one of the lenses cracked. His cheeks were dimpled and part of his scalp was burned.

Leera's arm dropped a little. "Mr. Goss—? Is that really you—?"

Augum recognized Leland's last name. This had to be his father! Leland and his parents were burned by Sparkstone's lightning on that fateful day the Legion razed Sparrow's Perch. Mrs. Stone had saved the Goss', leaving them safely in the woods before returning to the cave where Augum, Bridget and Leera waited.

"Leera Jones—? Do I hear Leera Jones behind that light there?" Mr. Goss asked in a squeaky and hopeful voice, dropping the stick.

"Yes, it's me, Mr. Goss!" Leera ran forward to embrace him.

"And here I was thinking I was going to find tomorrow's supper! Oh, am I ever so glad to see you safe, Leera. Leland will be so happy to see you!"

Leera wiped her face with her sleeve. "You mean Leland's here too? And Mrs. Goss?"

Mr. Goss' face fell upon the mention of his wife. "I am afraid Annie did not make it. She died of burns not long after Mrs. Stone saved us."

"Mr. Goss, I'm so sorry to hear that …" Leera embraced him again, glancing to Bridget, whose cheeks were wet with tears.

Mr. Goss adjusted his cracked spectacles. "Dear me, who else is here with you, Leera?"

"Oh, uh, you remember Augum Stone?"

Augum stepped forward, clearing his throat, wondering how Mr. Goss would react to seeing him. "Hello, sir. I'm really sorry to hear about Mrs. Goss."

Mr. Goss nodded and extended his hand. "That is kind of you to say, and I am glad to see you are well. If Mrs. Stone had not saved us, neither Leland nor I would be here right now. I would like to thank her, where is she?"

"She's not with us, Mr. Goss," Leera replied. "We're actually trying to find her before the Legion does. She's somewhere north in the mountains."

"I see. And who might that be sitting all quiet and lonesome over there? Step forward, do not be shy."

Leera's tone darkened. "That's Haylee Tennyson."

"Haylee ..." Mr. Goss hesitated a moment. "Why that is just splendid ..." He forced a smile and offered his hand to her. She shook lamely, keeping her gaze on the ground.

"Mr. Goss, Bridget's with us too but she's got a bad back injury. We're looking for an arcane healer for her. We were supposed to go to Antioc, but things got a little ... frantic."

Mr. Goss crouched beside Bridget. "Oh, dear, dear me. You poor girl." He placed a hand on her forehead. "Do not worry now, we will find help, you be sure that we will."

Bridget fixed her gaze on Mr. Goss. He removed a small cloth from his tunic and wiped the tears from her cheeks.

"Allow me to retrieve the cart so we can wheel her inside. You all must be hungry and exhausted. I hope you are all right spending the night with us."

"That would be great, thank you very much, Mr. Goss," Leera replied.

"That is just wonderful. Good. I cannot believe I am laying eyes on you again ..." He shook his head before stiffening. "All right already, let me hush up and fetch the cart." Mr. Goss jogged off, quickly returning with a two-wheeled cart normally used for firewood, portions of it charred and one side missing. Leera, Augum, Haylee and

Mr. Goss carefully placed Bridget inside, before wheeling her back to Mr. Goss' hut.

"Managed to save part of the place as you will see, though I have had to be careful, the protective enchantments the elders placed on the village no longer work. Anyone can wander in now."

He fell silent as they passed a dark area in the woods.

"Mr. Goss, everything all right?" Augum asked.

"Oh, um, yes, it is just that … Annie's plot is just over there, as well as, uh … the other plots …" He nodded at the woods.

Augum suddenly realized what he meant. There in the darkness among the lonely pines lay buried the victims of his father's brutal attack, including Leera and Bridget's parents.

Leera's light extinguished. She stopped, staring into that dense night.

Augum almost placed a hand on her shoulder but relented at the last moment. "You okay?" he asked instead.

Her voice was quiet. "Yeah, I'll … I'll see them tomorrow."

They continued, arriving at a round house below a mammoth pine. It was the least burned of the bunch. They followed Mr. Goss through a hole in the wall where there once was a door. The interior, lit by Haylee's palm, featured burnt tables, chairs, and household sundries. The odor of charred wood mingled with the smell of winter.

"I keep it this way to avoid suspicion, in case anyone shows up," Mr. Goss said. "This way." He wheeled the cart into the next room before gently setting it down. "There is a trap door here, though I do not know how we are going to get poor Bridget down there."

"We can levitate her down, Mr. Goss," Augum said, hoping his arcane energies had renewed.

"Is that so? Why, that is just marvelous, you all really must have been working very hard on your craft. It is just a shame I do not have an arcane bone in my body, not one. Neither did Annie, for that matter. Leland has been the, uh ... the ..." Mr. Goss removed his cracked spectacles and began cleaning them with a cloth.

Leera reached out, voice soft. "Mr. Goss, could I repair those for you?"

"You can repair these—? Why, that would indeed be splendid, they have been quite the thorn." He handed them over with shaky hands. She placed them on the ground, splaying her palms over them. "Apreyo." The cracked lens reformed. She gave them a thorough cleaning before handing them back.

"Marvelous, simply marvelous!" Mr. Goss said, putting them on. "If I was only half as useful as you, perhaps things ..." He gave a nervous chortle. "I see you have been working hard. That is just great, really great. Right, now do not let me hold you up any further." He pushed aside a charred carpet and opened a hidden trap door. Beneath was a steep stone staircase. He scampered down the steps and there were moving sounds. "All right, ready—ready indeed!"

Augum, Leera and Haylee took a bit of time preparing before casting Telekinesis. It was grueling work floating Bridget all the way down and onto a rustic kitchen table. The three young warlocks then collapsed, panting and holding their aching heads, while Mr. Goss draped a Dramask blanket over Bridget.

He turned to them and swallowed. "I am nothing short of impressed. Your parents would be very proud. *I* am very proud."

At the mention of parents, Leera glanced over at Haylee who, wincing from the same pain in her head, dropped her eyes.

"I have to warn you, uh, Leland is ... he is not the same boy you once knew. I think out of all three of us, he took it the worst. It was a miracle he even survived." Mr. Goss looked off into nothing.

When Augum's headache resolved to a dull thud, he took a good look around. Although the house above was round, the house underground was rectangular, with plank flooring. The walls were made of orange clay, partitioned to make rooms without doors.

Leera deposited the rucksack against the wall in the kitchen area, where Bridget lay on a harvest table in the center, surrounded by four rustic chairs. There was also a wooden counter, a washing station, a small iron water pump, and shelves filled with pottery and thick ceramic plates. An assortment of hanging ladles, iron pots, and linen towels hung underneath, near a stone hearth. A box of dusty wooden toy animals sat in a corner.

Mr. Goss began preparing bread at the counter. "It is hard living alone like this, cowering from the Legion, but we get by. An old friend comes now and again to give us a hand with supplies, so we manage just fine, yes we do."

A moan came from one of the partitioned rooms.

"I think Leland is up. Would you like to see him?"

"Yes!" Leera and Augum chorused immediately.

"Good, I am sure he will be overjoyed to see you. Just go ahead, it is the second room on the right there." He pointed before resuming his cutting. "Go ahead now, it is all right."

Augum, Leera and Haylee began to walk.

"Not you!" Leera said through gritted teeth, glaring at Haylee with such contempt Augum could hardly believe it was the same Leera.

A hurt look passed over Haylee's face before she retreated to a spindled rocking chair by the hearth. Mr. Goss did not strike up conversation with her as Augum and Leera entered Leland's room.

Inside was a plain dresser and writing table, a beaten stool, and a cot, where Leland hid under woolen covers. A second box of wooden toy animals sat dusty in the corner, and a framed needlework hung above the bed depicting a child playing with a kitten.

Leera sat down on the stool and tugged on the covers. "Little Lee? Hey there, it's me—Leera—and Augum's also here. You remember Augum, don't you?"

The covers tightened. Leera gestured for Augum to say something.

"Oh, hey Leland, it'd be nice to see you there, but you're hiding under the covers …" Leera gave him a perplexed look. He shrugged. Then an idea came to him. "Be right back," he mouthed, and ran off to retrieve a piece of salted biscuit-beef from the rucksack. Haylee still sat rocking by the fire, holding herself, gazing into the flames, while Mr. Goss was finishing up with the bread.

Augum returned to dangle the beef above the bed. "I have a small gift for you, Leland. It's some delicious beef. Brought it all the way from Evergray Tower, the home of an evil witch."

The blanket slowly curled back, exposing a wispy scalp disfigured by fire. It took a lot of self-control for Augum not to react, though Leera's hand shot to her mouth, eyes watering.

"That's it, Little Lee, come on, we know you want it …"

Leland unfurled the blanket the rest of the way, revealing a face that was almost completely burnt, except for a portion of the right cheek, where one of his dimples remained. Linen bandages covered his eyes and arms.

Augum placed the beef into his groping paw. He squeezed it past his disfigured mouth, making a kind of moaning noise Augum translated as being happy.

"Bridget's here too," Augum said, "but she can't see you because the wicked witch cast an evil spell on her. She's paralyzed, and we're on an adventure to cure her."

Leland made a series of moans Augum interpreted as, "Can I come along?"

Leera suddenly scrambled out of the room, muffling her crying with her sleeves.

Augum swallowed the lump in his throat. "Maybe, Leland, maybe …" He carefully tucked the covers around him. "Goodnight, Little Lee, we'll see you tomorrow."

Leland moaned.

Augum gave Leera a long hug in the hallway before slowly guiding her back to the kitchen.

Mr. Goss fiddled with the cutting board, voice wavering. "He, uh, he lost his sight, the ability to speak, and uh, his sense of smell, but, uh, but the healer saved his hearing, so that is good, right?"

Augum returned Mr. Goss' nervous smile with a vigorous nod of his head.

"She said … she said she, uh, she had never seen someone his age burned so badly, and it, uh, it took all her powers to save him—but she managed it in the end, bless her, she managed it in the end …" Mr. Goss's stood quiet a moment. What came next was barely a whisper. "Though sometimes I wish we had been taken along with Annie …"

"Mr. Goss, please, don't say that," Augum said.

Mr. Goss startled and forced a smile. "No, of course … I did not mean it."

Augum gave him a moment. "Was it an arcane healer by chance that saved Leland?"

"Why, yes it was, and I will never forget her name—Miralda Jenkins."

Haylee stopped rocking. "That's the family friend! I … I know her—"

"Oh, that is quite splendid," Mr. Goss mumbled, unconsciously touching the burnt portion of his scalp. "You know, I am expecting Mr. Bawdings to swing by sometime tomorrow, perhaps I can make an inquiry with him to send for her. If I am not mistaken, she does have the arcane knowledge to teleport, does she not?"

"I think she does." Haylee raised her knees back onto the rocker and cradled them. This once popular girl gave Augum the impression she was lost, and probably terrified for her family.

He had an idea.

"Mr. Goss, do you know where Haylee can find some suitable clothes? She's no longer part of the Legion and, um, doesn't need the necrophyte robe anymore."

For a moment, those words just hung in the air. Haylee gave Augum a surprised look, while Leera gave him a furious one. At last, Mr. Goss, who had been standing as if frozen in mid-thought, caught himself and stuttered to life.

"Oh dear, where are my manners? Why … why yes of course, my dear boy, yes of course I do. Haylee, please have a gander in Annie's closet. She was a small woman, some of her dresses might fit you. Just down the hall, the last room on your right."

Haylee quietly stood up, hands folded in front. Then she actually curtsied, albeit awkwardly. "Thank you, sir, that … that would be very welcome." She hurried out of the room, head bowed.

Leera, who had been standing beside Augum, suddenly pushed him away. "Ugh! I can't … I can't … ugh—!"

He held up his hands in surrender. "I'm sorry, I just thought—"

"Just shut up—" Then she looked away and took a long shaky breath. "I'm so sorry, I'm being … I'm just sorry, Aug. I know it's not …"

He was confused. "Not what?"

She shook her head. "Never mind," and plopped down on a chair by Bridget. "A curtsey even ... you believe that, Bridge? That priss *curtsied*."

Mr. Goss, pretending not to have heard a word, began serving bread, butter, salt, and some hard cheese on plates decorated with neat floral patterns. "Augum, if you please ..."

"Thank you, Mr. Goss."

Mr. Goss paced over to the water pump and began working the handle. "How lucky I feel to have lived around warlocks. I find it simply amazing what they can do. For example, Bridget's father put this here pump in place, bless his soul, using nothing but arcanery. Simply marvelous." He glanced to Bridget's still form, beaming sweetly. "And I am sure she will grow up to be a far more accomplished warlock then her father." Then he caught himself and returned to pumping. "But you must forgive my ramblings. Please, tell me all about your journeys."

Leera and Augum recounted what they could, though it soon became apparent just how tired they were. Mr. Goss, evidently quite attentive to these things, promptly decided they should all go to sleep after the meal. He even devised a way to feed Bridget using a large reed straw. Leera was the one to administer the food, patiently helping her through an entire meal.

When Haylee returned, she thanked Mr. Goss for the dress, a simple country linen affair, probably very unlike what she was accustomed to wearing, before taking a seat and eating as meekly as a mouse. Leera paid her no attention whatsoever. Augum said nothing either, not wanting to upset Leera, though when he accidentally made eye contact with Haylee, she did mouth "Thank you" before quickly returning to her food.

A very long day ended quietly. Mr. Goss handed out blankets and pillows then made Bridget as comfortable as possible with two Dramask blankets. Augum and Leera slept near her to keep her company. Haylee, who kept her eyes averted from Leera's hawkish glare, curled up quietly near the hearth. Before long, Mr. Goss blew out the hooded wall lanterns and bid them goodnight before padding away, leaving them to sleepy darkness.

LEERA AND HAYLEE

"Let me tell you about Mr. Goss' place—" Leera said to Bridget over a late breakfast, taking turns with Augum in describing what she couldn't see, even needling her a little for being lazy.

Bridget smiled through her eyes, but Augum could tell she was putting on a brave front for her friends. He was so worried for her, and couldn't imagine how she must be feeling.

"Any news about the Legion?" Augum asked Mr. Goss, who was flipping bacon in a frying pan.

"Mr. Bawdings, a dear old friend who has helped with supplies, will visit again soon, and he's sure to have news. But a few days ago I did do some scouting." He flashed an adventurous look. "Rather scary thing to wander the woods alone, I have to say, but it had to be done. Nonetheless, I spotted a company of two hundred Black Guard soldiers heading east across the Tallows."

"Probably on their way to Tiberra ..."

"I saw something else too. Two large ... *things* ... walking alongside the soldiers."

Haylee poured the root juice into cups. "They could be wraiths, Mr. Goss, made by the Lord of the Legion."

"Wraiths, my dear?"

"Yes, they're ... horrible. The necrophytes at the academy are to start learning how to make them at the 4th degree, even though it's an 8th degree elemental spell. And everyone is forced to forget their primary element and study necromancy."

"How far along is the training?" Augum asked.

"It's only just begun. I don't think there are any necrophytes beyond the 2nd degree—yet."

Augum and Leera exchanged looks. "Then it's only a matter of time," he said.

Mr. Goss shook his head. "What an awful thing to have such an esteemed and ancient institution as the Academy of Arcane Arts corrupted by a necromancer."

"Necrophytes begin training on simple stuff at first," Haylee continued, "like Feign Death and Spoil. Lord Sparkstone is very ambitious though. Necrophytes start training to raise a walker almost immediately, and it's a 3rd degree elemental spell."

"Why would they do such a thing?" Mr. Goss asked.

She glanced around at them all. "Lord Sparkstone is making an elite army of Dreadnought-equipped soldiers that fight alongside trained necromancers."

There was a quiet moment.

"What degree does a necrophyte have to be to become a full-fledged necromancer?" Augum asked.

"That depends on the aptitude and bravery of the necrophyte, but usually at least 5th degree." Haylee stared past them. "It's called the 'Torment Trial'—an evil test administered by a powerful necromancer."

"My father ..."

"It will be your father, yes, since he is the only necromancer around. He's also the one who does most of the training at the academy."

"You mean there are no other necromancers?"

"None that I know of."

"Please, let us not speak of these dark things over breakfast," Mr. Goss said, carrying the steaming pan to the table.

"Of course—sorry, Mr. Goss," Augum said, feeling a sting of shame. Mr. Goss' wife was murdered by his father, and here he was carelessly reminding him of it.

"Not at all, Augum, it is just that I would like to start the day with a good meal and happy thoughts."

They ate quietly, Mr. Goss giving forced cheery grins.

After breakfast, Leera pushed her plate towards Haylee. "I'm going to pay my respects to my murdered parents now. You stay behind and help Mr. Goss clean up."

The old Haylee would have scoffed. Instead, she dropped her eyes and cleared Leera's plate.

Mr. Goss glanced between the two of them with a puzzled look on his face.

Leera still glared at her. "Care to join me, Aug?"

"Okay." Despite the tension, it was the least he could do. His father murdered her parents. He was determined to help in any way he could. This whole thing with Haylee wasn't going to be solved right now anyway. He snagged the Orb of Orion on the way out, figuring he might as well put it to use.

It was a cold and foggy day in Sparrow's Perch. The snow was knee-high, the winter silence broken occasionally by the lonely tweet of a winter bird.

Leera gave him a look. "Why'd you bring that thing?"

"You'll see. Come help me find a good spot."

"Ah ... clever."

They partially buried the globe in a hidden spot where it could look out over the entire village. He then used the pearl Erika once disguised in an earring to lock the orb into place.

"Now if only the fog would clear," he said.

Leera nodded absently, her eyes unfocused in the direction of where her parents lay.

"Let's visit them," he said quietly.

They padded to the burial ground. He noticed Mr. Goss had carved everyone's names into the wooden markers. It must have taken ages to do. They stopped at the foot of Annie Goss' grave. She must have been a sweet woman, and he silently apologized for what happened to her. He spotted the Sharpe family lined up nearby and fondly remembered the amiable and intelligent dark-skinned fellow that was Bridget and Leera's good friend, Tyeon Sharpe—or Tye as they called him. He would have made a fine companion on their journey.

Leera took a deep breath and paced on until she came to Bridget's family—father, mother, two brothers, and her grandmother.

Augum trailed, resting his hand on each marker, silently apologizing for the horrors of his father, not knowing what else to say or do.

When Leera spotted her parents' markers, she began wringing her hands. They wandered over and stood silent for a time.

"Would you mind giving me some time?" she asked in a wavering voice.

He nodded and quietly retreated, leaving her standing at the foot of her mother's grave. He recalled how much of a similarity the mother shared with her daughter—same freckled face, same sharply arched brows, and same black hair, though streaked with gray. He smiled remembering trying her awful but well-intentioned new concoction.

He glanced back at Leera's lonely figure, hoping the memorial ceremony Nana performed back at Castle Arinthian had eased the pain, even if only a little.

Strolling along the foggy village, Augum stopped now and then to listen to the winter quiet, letting his thoughts wander. Part of him wanted to visit the ruins of Mrs. Stone's cave, but he figured it would be too depressing.

"Hi—" Haylee said, making him jump. She had come out of the Goss residence without him noticing. "Sorry, did I scare you?"

"Oh, hi—it's okay." He looked into the fog in Leera's direction. "Maybe I should go to her—"

"Maybe she needs some time to be alone. Let her grieve."

He sighed. "I wish Bridget could see her family's graves ..."

"Maybe she can if the healer comes." Haylee nudged a rock with her foot. "Look, I just ... I wanted to say thanks for everything—"

"—forget it." He didn't want to start a discussion with her, especially not about what had happened.

Haylee gathered her long hair in one hand. "I mean it. I ... I learned a lot this last while." She glanced into the fog and let her hair fall back down. "I know she hates me. I don't blame her, but ... do you think she'll ever forgive me?"

"Don't know. What did you do to her? I mean, I know you hung out with Robin and that gang, but there's obviously more to it, isn't there?"

"I made fun of her nose a lot, and I'm the one who started everyone calling her 'The Leer', because she always used to stare at people. I feel bad about it now. But I guess it started before that, back in the academy when I sniffed out she had a crush on Robin."

"*What*? She had a crush on that toad?" His skin prickled with heat. How could Leera have had a crush on that evil little—

"—yeah, I know, strange, eh? I liked him too, but I guess he didn't like me that much in the end. Once he became a necrophyte, everything changed between us." She paused a moment. "But I did something to Leera that was … that was worse than making fun of her nose and calling her names."

"What did you do?"

She kicked the rock a little harder and it tumbled through the snow. "Well, when we first started going to the academy, I made up a mean song about her and taught the whole class how to sing it. Anyway, the academy had a big assembly and our class was supposed to sing a traditional melody, but instead we sang my song in front of the entire school. Everybody laughed and Leera had a big meltdown and ran off. Took the teachers ages to find her. They sang that song for months afterward. It got pretty bad. I felt terrible about it, but by then it was too late."

He gaped at her. "Wow, Haylee, that's just … I can see why she hates your guts, and now that you told me that, I'm not too sure I can forgive you either."

Haylee's face scrunched. "I knew I shouldn't have said anything … please don't hate me, Augum, please, you're the only one here—"

"I can't believe you did that to her," he continued, undeterred. "I should have left you out there in the snow!" He regretted it as soon as he said it, but was too proud to apologize. He crossed his arms and turned his back on her, feeling stupid, angry, and even hurt for some reason. Haylee stood there a moment before suddenly running off, yet all he could think was, how could Leera possibly have liked that toad?

Unable to come to grips with the idea, he kicked the snow-encrusted rock into the mist before drawing his apprentice robe tighter.

"Hey, watch it—" Leera said, emerging from the fog, face somber. "What was that all about?"

"Nothing."

"Don't lie to me, Aug, you're terrible at it. What did that foul girl tell you?"

He shrugged. Might as well say it. "She told me about the whole song thing that happened."

Leera's eyes narrowed. "She told you about that?"

"Yes," but a different question was on his mind, aching to be asked.

"She's up to no good," Leera went on. "I know it. Did she teach you the words to the song too?"

"Did you really have a crush on Robin—?" he blurted. He knew he was being immature but he wanted to make her feel bad about it, to renounce Robin in every possible way and apologize for ever liking him.

Leera's cheeks reddened as she swallowed. She dropped her eyes and adjusted one of her long black braids, which was slowly coming undone.

"I ..." Then she folded her arms and furrowed her brows. "So? So what if I did! How is that any of *your* business?"

He took a step back, making a rude face. "What? How could—I mean—" He wanted to appear as affronted as possible. This was about her liking Robin, not about him! But the truth was, he didn't know how to answer her question, nor could he explain his feelings. Yet a deep part of him knew that, above all, he wanted her to say that she liked *him* now, not Robin. "I can't believe this—" he finally said instead and stormed off, face hot, heart buzzing.

He crashed through the foggy wood, muttering to himself, trying to get away as quickly as possible. He was angry with her for ever liking Robin, but now he was also angry with himself. As he cooled down, stumbling blindly through the snowy forest, he began to realize how childishly he was acting. Yet he refused to go back and apologize. No, she had to apologize first. But then another part of him thought, apologize? Apologize for what exactly?

This battle raged on in his mind for some time, until he stepped out of the wood onto a rocky slope. The fog had cleared by then, and he found himself gazing up at Mt. Barrow. Not wanting to head back and face Leera just yet, he began the long climb up.

Augum marched purposefully, ignoring the scenery, choosing to indulge in the many angry and hurtful thoughts spiraling around in his brain. The higher he rose, the colder and windier it became, until at last, exhausted, cold and thirsty, he slumped down at the lip of his great-grandmother's ruined cave.

He stared mournfully at the rubble, wondering what Mrs. Stone was up to, before turning his back on the pile and glaring down at Sparrow's Perch. The fog had moved away with the breeze, revealing a charred village.

Suddenly, he spotted movement in the distance. A column of black-armored riders was entering the wood just north of Mt. Barrow, in the direction of Sparrow's Perch.

Heart hammering in his chest, he bolted down the mountain, tumbling a few times, sprinting all the way to the village.

"Leera—" he called quietly. "Haylee—"

He spotted Haylee standing by the graves and ran up to her. She turned around, revealing red eyes and wet cheeks.

He beckoned urgently. "The Legion are coming—"

"Here? Now—?"

"Just hurry—" He grabbed her by the elbow and practically dragged her along until she took up pace beside him.

"Where's Leera?" He asked as they entered the gaping hole in the wall of Mr. Goss' house.

She raised the trap door. "I don't know."

"Well, we can't just leave her—"

The sounds of horses came from the forest.

"There's no time," she said. "She's probably down here already anyway."

"Oh my, what might be going on?" Mr. Goss asked as Haylee quietly closed the trap door above.

She placed a finger to her lips. "The Legion, they're here—"

Mr. Goss paled. He raced up the steps and pulled on a rope. "This draws a carpet over the hatch," he whispered.

Augum looked around the kitchen, eyes passing over Bridget's still form. "Wait, where's Leera—?"

"Dear me, I thought she was with you—"

He felt light-headed suddenly. If it wouldn't put everyone here at risk, he would lunge at that trap door and climb out of there that instant. Instead, he slid to a crumpled sitting position midway up the steps, back against the clay wall, listening.

Mr. Goss kneeled before him, smiling in that kind way of his. "Do not worry, Augum, I am sure Leera found a great hiding spot. Let us not underestimate her prowess."

Augum glanced up at the trap door. "I shouldn't have left her ..."

Haylee padded down the steps as Mr. Goss moved on to the kitchen. She lingered near Augum a moment before moving on. He did not meet her eyes. Not only had she done so many awful things to Leera, but now she was wrong about her being down here.

He caught Bridget staring at him and felt doubly guilty for leaving Leera behind. He tiptoed his way to her and sat in a chair, dropping his head into his hands. "I know, I know, it's all my fault, Bridge, I left her out there—"

"I'm sorry, Augum," Haylee whispered. "I really thought—"

Augum sighed loudly and she fell silent. He wanted to tell her to shut up. He wanted to be mean and vindictive, but couldn't do it with Bridget looking at him.

"I wish you could talk," he mumbled. "I wish none of this had happened."

She only stared at him. A single tear rolled down her cheek, which he wiped with his sleeve.

There was a moan. When he looked up, he saw Leland standing in the hallway.

"Shh … we must stay very quiet, son, the Legion are above."

Leland made a quiet moan before limping over to sit beside Augum, looking up at him with bandaged eyes that could never see again. Augum wished there was some kind of arcane way for Leland to see, when it occurred to him that he had forgotten about the orb—he could watch the Legion in that very moment!

He frantically retrieved the engraved pearl, squeezed it in his fist and closed his eyes. Almost instantly he was peering through the orb, the image distorted by its shape. Nonetheless, he was able to count twelve horses tied up to the trees. Black Guards roamed about, searching for clues. Suddenly one of the guards pointed to the ground.

"Commander, these footprints are fresh."

A black-armored man came into view with curly hair and a portly countenance. He dropped to one knee and peered closer. "Spread out and search the place."

The men scattered.

Augum thought there was something familiar about the man but couldn't figure out what.

The man slowly began retracing their footsteps.

"They're coming," Augum whispered.

The curly-haired man retraced their steps to the Goss home, disappearing from view. Augum withdrew his attention from the orb and placed his finger to his lips, pointing directly above. Everyone anxiously glanced upward, even Leland with his bandaged eyes. A moment later, they heard the thud of heavy boots. There was a strong kick and dust sprinkled down from the ceiling. Their eyes followed the sound of the boots walking across the floor, all the way to the trap door.

A heavy silence descended as everyone froze in place. Augum desperately reviewed all his spells, expecting the trap door to crash open, when there came a distant muted shout and the boots hurried off.

He quickly peered through the orb. The soldiers were running away from the house. Were they after Leera?

He distinctly heard the man shout, "Where? Well go!" and then ordering two men to stay behind as he gave chase with the rest eastward, back in the direction they had come from. Augum kept watching the two guards.

Suddenly he spotted movement in the forest, the curving effect making it look further away than it really was. It happened when the guards' backs were turned and stopped when one of them glanced in that direction. It happened again as soon as the guard turned away. He was sure it was someone sneaking around them, headed towards the Goss house.

His hopes surged. It had to be Leera!

"I see her," he whispered to the others. "She's sneaking around."

There came a particularly daring moment when she darted across the center of the village while the soldiers searched the far side.

"Crazy girl," Augum muttered, barely able to watch as she safely snuck through the gaping doorway. He shoved the pearl back in his pocket and raced up the steps, reaching the top just as a light knock sounded. He yanked at the rope that withdrew the carpet before opening the trap door.

Leera jumped inside, helping him quietly close it behind her, before slumping down on the steps, panting but wearing a giant grin. He sat beside her, wearing an equally big grin. For a moment, they forgot everything and hugged. He was so happy to see her he kissed her cheek.

Leera's eyes magnified.

He reddened like freshly blown coals, in disbelief with what he had just done. "Sorry, I … it was an accident, I didn't mean—uh, good to see you safe—"

He rushed down the steps, almost tripping on the way. Luckily, it appeared no one else had noticed what happened.

Leera, face as red as wine, descended the steps to sit at the table. She idly fixed Bridget's braids while whispering something in her ear.

"Hey, uh, want to peek through the engraved pearl?" Augum asked as casually as possible.

She took it without a word and closed her eyes.

"May I inquire as to what that is?" Mr. Goss asked, nodding at the pearl.

Augum pulled up a chair by Bridget and briefly explained, noticing Haylee watching him. He felt his face grow hot again as he wondered if she had seen the kiss. Whatever, it didn't matter because he was still mad at her. Truthfully though, as angry as he wanted to be with Haylee, he felt horrible for the things he had said to her.

Leera opened her eyes. "They're leaving."

"I strongly believe we should stay down here for a while," Mr. Goss said, "in case the Legion returns."

"So what do we do now?" Augum asked Leera. As long as he continued to act normal, then the kiss didn't mean anything, right? Yet his insides were puddles of anxiety. What if she got the wrong impression? Worse, what if she thought him ugly? He had never experienced these kinds of buzzing feelings before, and tried to hide his wringing hands.

Leera shrugged as her eyes briefly met his. A light blush came to her cheeks. "Well, why don't we study the Slam spell with Bridget?"

"Great idea," he replied a little too quickly. He had to look away from Bridget's funny stare. He cleared his throat a bit. "But, um … how?"

"Like always, silly—except we'll just pretend Bridget doesn't feel like saying anything. She can listen, though, and I have a feeling she wants to learn it as bad as we do, isn't that right, Bridgey-poo?"

Bridget blinked heavily once.

"See? She said yes."

"She hates it when you call her that."

"Yeah, I know, but she can't do anything about it. Wonder if she's ticklish …"

"I could see her rising to kill you for that."

Bridget's eyes flitted over to him. There was a gleam there he could easily interpret. Smirking, he punched Leera in the shoulder.

"Hey, what was that for—?"

"That's from Bridget for trying to take advantage."

Leera snorted a laugh as he rifled through the rucksack, retrieving the magnifying loupe and parchment One Eye had given them. He tried to ignore Haylee, who sat herself down in the rocking chair.

He grabbed a chair by Leera, who helped unfurl the large parchment. Leland felt his way around the table and squeezed in beside her, moaning. Leera pinched his good cheek. "So you want to learn the Slam spell too, do you?"

Leland nodded.

"Fine, I guess we can let you sit in …" The way she said it was an obvious jab at Haylee.

Augum felt even worse and seriously contemplated apologizing to Haylee.

"You're taking too long." Leera stole the loupe from his hand with a roguish grin. "All right, let's see here …"

Haylee kept stealing glances over at them before finally asking, "Do you mind if I learn it with you—?"

Leera replied without looking at her. "Yes, we definitely mind."

Mr. Goss, who was cutting up vegetables for the evening's supper, looked up. "Now that was not very nice, Leera. Why would you not let Haylee learn the spell with you?" He gave her a disappointed father look.

"But—fine then, sit there." She stabbed a finger at a spot near Bridget's feet.

Haylee quietly took her place, straightening her plain dress.

Leera glared at her. If looks could vanquish, Augum knew Haylee would have been dead many times over by now. He gave Leera a gentle nudge.

"Oh, right … let me start reading then."

They began learning the Slam spell, bit by little bit, absorbing and discussing its many nuances, carefully explaining everything to Bridget as they went. Haylee wasn't allowed to involve herself in any way of course, except to sit there and pick up what she could. Only once did she have a question. Augum, in order to not upset Leera, answered only after Mr. Goss turned around with a kind yet mildly reproachful look.

It was obvious it hurt Haylee's feelings to be treated like that, yet she put on a brave face and did her best to appear dignified. Despite what she had done to Leera, Augum continued to feel terrible for what he said to her earlier, and tried to think of a way to apologize without offending Leera.

With the Legion lurking nearby, they dared not test the spell, remembering just how loud it could be, instead going through the motions and thoughts without actually casting. They made sure to give Bridget focus time to go through the concepts in her head, blinking once if she got a concept and twice if she did not. Needless to say, there was a lot of double-blinking going on, for the spell was particularly difficult to learn this way, especially without someone like

Mrs. Stone mentoring. Without the parchment though, learning anything about Slam from the ordinary text book would have been impossible, underscoring just how important apprenticeship was.

They struggled in this manner, exhausting every word of the dense scroll, until Mr. Goss asked them to break for supper.

MR. BAWDINGS

Augum dutifully took a turn helping Bridget eat with the reed straw. His mind drifted to the Legion, wondering if the reason they passed through Sparrow's Perch had anything to do with them. Had the Legion received word from the Blade of Sorrows somehow? It didn't seem likely as Robin would've said they were heading to Antioc. If anything, that's where they should be searching for them ...

As Augum, Leera and Haylee helped Mr. Goss clear the table, there suddenly came a series of taps at the trap door. Everybody froze except Mr. Goss, who smiled broadly while wiping his hands with a cloth.

"Ah, that's Mr. Bawdings' secret knock!" He ascended the steps as Leera looked through the orb just in case, nodding her approval a moment later.

Mr. Goss yanked on the rope and opened the trap door. "Hedrick! How good to see you!"

"Why Albert, you're looking as feisty as a squirrel over nuts," the man wheezed as if out of breath. "Still alive in this little hole?"

"We manage, but I regret to report that you missed a hot supper."

"Well, now I am disturbed." Bawdings huffed his large frame down the steps, dressed in a merchant tunic and turned down boots, a sack over his shoulder. "But how about a touch of whiskey for a weary traveler?" A grimy hand slid through salt and pepper hair that matched his beard.

Mr. Goss closed the trap door and pulled the rope. "Ran out months ago. Would ale suffice?"

"Most certainly." His head swiveled to Augum and the others. "Taking in stragglers?"

"These are friends of Leland."

"Not all of us," Leera muttered, casting an evil eye at Haylee, who squirmed in her seat.

Mr. Bawdings reached into his tunic, pulled out a large silver flask, and took a long pull, letting out a burp after. "Ah … nothing like expelling a wee bit o' air, eh?"

Leera chuckled while Haylee stared with a look of revulsion.

Mr. Goss gestured to a chair. "How was the journey?"

Bawdings let the sack fall to the floor, stole a chair from the dining table as if he had not seen Bridget lying there, and plopped down by the hearth. "Barely avoided bandits upon departing Antioc, not to mention the Legion."

Bawdings' eyes fell upon Bridget at last. He sucked on the flask again, which was starting to sound empty, before scratching the shirt over his large belly. "Girl all right?"

"I am afraid she is not doing so well. She has a back injury and needs the services of an arcane healer."

"Oh." Bawdings placed his flask to his eye and squinted. "Most unfortunate," he muttered, retrieving a second, dirtier flask from his pocket.

"Yes, well, I was really hoping you could help with the matter."

Mr. Bawdings' eyes shifted to Augum and Leera as he fumbled with the cap of his flask. "I don't know, me even being here ..."

Mr. Goss began slicing some bread, voice quiet. "For old friendship's sake, is there nothing you could do? She lost her family here in the massacre, you know ..."

Augum and Leera nodded along, trying to look as pitiful as possible.

Mr. Bawdings stood, turned his back, and ran his fingers through his hair. He expelled a mighty breath as if from a wheezing bellows. "I don't rightly know you realize just what you're asking me to do. All the healers now work for the Legion. I'd almost have to kidnap one from under their noses." He stood up and gripped the stone mantel above the hearth, head hanging between his arms. "It'd be the end of me, I say, the end of me ..."

Augum and Leera both made eye contact with Mr. Goss, imploring him to push. Leland abruptly pawed his way over to Mr. Bawdings, moaning while tugging on his tunic and vigorously pointing at Bridget lying paralyzed on the table.

Mr. Bawdings kneeled down before Leland. "Is that what you also want, little fellow? You want to see ol' Bawdings roasting over a spit so the poor girl can have a healer?"

Leland made a few exaggerated nods.

Bawdings' shoulders slumped. "Kids are going get me killed, I swear it. Well all right then, I'll give it a go."

Augum and Leera thanked him profusely.

"Yeah yeah, save it for my memorial." He picked up the large bag and placed it on the counter. "The supplies you asked for, Albert, plus a little extra."

Mr. Goss suddenly wrapped his thin arms around his friend.

"All right now, easy there, old chum."

Mr. Goss let go and retrieved a bag of coins from his room. He placed it into Mr. Bawdings' hand and enveloped it with both his own. "I wish I could afford to give you more."

"Bah, don't mention it. Just try not to get all mushy on me."

"Mr. Bawdings, is there any news from Antioc?" Haylee asked while Leera stiffened.

Mr. Bawdings pocketed the money and took his seat by the hearth with a groan. "Blackhaven Herald's about as useful as hog dung. Have to get your news by ear. Legion's clamping down on the merchants. Food is scarcer by the day. Even heard them magic scrolls are now forbidden."

"We call it arcanery, sir," Leera said.

"Whatever, I don't trust magicians enough to—" He suddenly glanced at them. "Don't tell me you brats are magicians!"

Leera opened her palms. "We are, but—"

"Unnameables be good, I'm helping a bunch of witches, I am!"

"Sir—" Augum began, trying to form an argument in his head. The last thing he wanted was to offend Mr. Bawdings and have him renege on helping Bridget. "Please, we might be warlocks, but we're fighting for the same cause."

Mr. Bawdings took a swig, eyeing Augum like a watchman eyeing a thief. "Are we now, and what might that cause be?"

"The downfall of the Legion, of course—"

Mr. Bawdings let loose a boisterous laugh that bounced around the clay walls. " 'The downfall of the Legion', the boy says. You mark my words, boy, nothing's going to stop the Legion now, nothing. We'll all be in shackles by spring.

We're just rabbits running loose, and you know what they are?" He leaned forward in his chair, his breath making Augum dizzy. "They're wolves. A pack of hungry, vicious wolves. Why, did you even know that right now they're demanding women produce sons for their future wars? Did you know that, boy? Of course you didn't, because you seem to think there's some kind of *magical* opposition to the Legion!"

Mr. Bawdings took another swig, eyes flashing. "Let me set you real straight now, son. There. Is. No. Op. O. Sition! There is no underground army, there is no one fighting the Legion, there is no nothing! And if you ask me, all this is happening because of magicians and their cursed witchery." He spat into the hearth and leaned back in the chair. "Should've all been hanged back in the day, I says."

This was news to Augum. He was sure there would be armies out there, secretly uniting to fight the Legion. The idea that no one was on their side was … lonely and depressing. He plopped down beside Bridget. She blinked twice. He just stared at her stupidly. She blinked twice again.

"Bridget disagrees," Leera said.

Bawdings scoffed, taking yet another swig from his flask, which was also starting to sound empty. "The girl that can't move or talk disagrees." The chair creaked as he reeled in it, almost falling off. "A shrew's bottom! I fear I've imbibed a bit much and now my tongue's gone and run off. My apologies, Albert, but you know me …"

Mr. Goss nodded but placed a hand on Augum's shoulder, whispering, "There is opposition—I am looking right at it."

Augum spared a weak smile.

Bawdings' speech began to run together a bit. "But don't you worry, kids, I'll try and find your friend a healer. In point of fact, I already have an idea where to find one. The Legion set up a temporary outpost near Hangman's Rock as a kind of in-between supply station, complete with a healer. I know because I had to get around it without being seen. I'll head over there tonight and see if I can bribe my way to seeing the healer, maybe slip her a note or something. Night's best for such a thing as the ones most prone to take coin serve the graveyard shift."

Augum exchanged a dubious look with Bridget.

"I'll need money though," Bawdings said, taking yet another swig from his flask. He scowled after finishing its contents. "How about some of that ale, Alb?"

"I have more than that, my old friend." Mr. Goss served Hedrick a tall glass of ale, a wooden bowl of bread, and a plate of cheese. "Now let me see what I have got left here …" He retrieved a box above the counter hidden amongst jars of grain and handed it to Mr. Bawdings. Bawdings opened it and his face lit up like a child receiving cake.

"My entire savings," Mr. Goss said.

"Mr. Goss, you can't," Leera said. "What about money for food?"

"We will manage, right, Leland?"

Leland moaned with a nod.

Mr. Bawdings began counting. "Hmm, I hate to say it, but this might not be enough."

Augum immediately reached into the rucksack, retrieved the rest of their money, and handed it over.

Mr. Bawdings counted it all out, stuffed it into the same pouch Mr. Goss gave him earlier, and shrugged. "It's enough to try, I suppose. If anything, I'll throw in some of me own then, eh?"

"You are a good man, Hedrick. I will never forget this."

Bawdings raised a wavering glass, ale slopping to the floor. "To being a good man. I'll leave as soon as I finish me ale."

Mr. Goss flashed Augum and Leera a reassuring smile, but Augum, who had been watching Mr. Bawdings' eyes droop lower and lower, was unconvinced of the plan. "Let's follow him," he whispered into Leera's ear. She immediately nodded in agreement.

They sat listening to Mr. Bawdings' stories, which turned into drunken diatribes, mostly about magicians and their foul ways, or the Legion and its foul ways, or thieves and bandits of all sorts and their foul ways. The only magician sort Mr. Bawdings didn't seem to mind were healers, and that was because one once mended a broken arm he received in a tavern fight. Although it was offensive to a warlock to get confused for a magician or wizard, and arcanery to be confused for magic, no one complained, trying to keep Mr. Bawdings on their good side. After all, he could very well pull through for them.

"Perhaps you might like to stay the night and try to find the healer tomorrow, Hedrick," Mr. Goss said after helping Bawdings stand from a most unceremonious chair slip.

"Nonsense, Alb—" he paused to burp loudly and thump his heart. "I'll be swell. I come from northern stock. These here veins can take—" He suddenly stopped, frowned, and his eyes rolled up into his head. He slumped back in his chair, snoring.

Mr. Goss only shook his head. "Oh, my old friend, how little has changed."

"Will he be all right?" Augum asked, taking the empty ale glass from Mr. Bawdings' hand.

"I imagine so. He will sleep it off, wake in a few hours, then go and find Bridget a healer." Mr. Goss beckoned to help him lower the man to the ground. "He has not been the same since his wife died."

Augum placed the big man's arm around his shoulder. "How did she die?"

"Ridge fever, years ago."

Augum had seen ridge fever once. Back in Willowbrook, a girl his age had come down with it. Ridges formed on her skin, especially her face. She fought it off but the fever left her with awful scars, aging her twenty years. She was called names like "Ridge Ogre" or "Goat Horn". The poor girl ended up taking her own life.

Mr. Goss fetched a small cushion and placed it under Mr. Bawdings' head. "He often joked how she was the envy of every man that laid eyes on her, what with her night black skin and fierce orange eyes. They were madly in love. Poor soul hit the bottle and quite lost his composure."

"That's awfully tragic," Haylee said. "Had you ever seen her yourself?"

"Oh, once, and she was indeed beautiful, almost as beautiful as—" but Mr. Goss fell silent. He finished cleaning up, quietly bid them goodnight, and took his leave with Leland.

Leera leaned close to Augum. "We'll pack light and follow Bawdings soon as he goes. Oh, and we're *not* taking her." She thumbed in Haylee's direction.

Haylee sat down in the rocker by the fire. "Why not?"

"Because—wait, how much have you heard? Stop spying—"

"You're going to follow him, and I know what you're thinking, but I won't tell. I'm not like that anymore—"

"You're going to stay behind and mind your own business, is what you're going to do. When Mr. Goss asks where we've gone, you're to say we went scavenging for supplies so he won't worry. We'll tell him everything when we return anyway."

"Leera, please, what's it going to take to make you stop hating me?"

"A miracle—" and she turned back to Augum with a *you believe the nerve of her* look.

"Maybe she could help us—" he whispered, but regretted it immediately. Leera's eyes narrowed and her lips thinned like Mrs. Stone's.

"Never mind," he said quickly. Leera kept staring at him as if he'd broken a cardinal rule of loyalty.

Haylee gave Augum a mournful look before making her bed close to the hearth.

"Snotty princess," Leera muttered as they began making their own beds near the opposite wall. The hooded lanterns were blown out. For a time, there was only the sound of creaking floorboards and the fluffing of pillows.

"I'll take first watch," he whispered, trying not to think about that kiss earlier.

Leera kept tossing and turning, evidently unable to sleep. She looked to him as if about to say something before changing her mind and staring at the ceiling. What was on her mind? Was she thinking about the kiss?

"So, uh," Augum began quietly, noticing her tense up, "we'll take the rucksack, two blankets, the map, flint and steel, and some biscuit beef—but drop everything else."

She instantly relaxed. "And the pearl—"

"Right." So she's forgotten about it already.

"We'll borrow Mr. Goss's mitts too. I'm sure he won't mind."

"Okay." He glanced at the form by the fire. He felt bad about Haylee, and wondered if there was some way he could help resolve the tension between her and Leera. "Hey, look, I've been thinking—"

"—no need, it didn't mean anything to me either."

He felt like a needle had just pierced his heart. "That's not what I was going to say—"

Leera gaped at him a moment. Even in the darkness, he thought he saw her face redden. "Oh."

"But thanks for letting me know," he said quickly, unable to keep the edge from his voice.

Leera swallowed as he snatched at his blanket and forcefully turned away from her, pretending to go to bed, which made no sense at all since he was the one on watch. Whatever, he thought. She can take a turn.

Leera's voice was very quiet. "So, um, what were you going to say then?"

"I was just going to talk about Haylee—"

"I should have known. Why are you always on her side? Why are you so obsessed with her?"

He turned back around. "What? I'm not obsessed—"

"Shh—"

"You know what, forget it." He pulled the blanket over himself again.

"Fine then."

"Fine." He went back to pretending to go to sleep, completely aware of every nuance in the room—the gentle murmur of the fire, the hammering of his heart, and, to his total dismay, Leera's absolute silence.

This lasted for what felt like a very long while.

By the time Mr. Bawdings jolted awake, the fire had dulled to a glowing heap.

"Mr. Bawdings, are you up now?" Leera immediately whispered, giving Augum the impression she had been as wide awake as him. He continued to pretend to be asleep, but kept one eye focused on Mr. Bawdings, who stared at her uncomprehendingly.

"Mr. Bawdings? Are you ready to bring Bridget a healer now?" she said.

Bawdings smacked his lips and pinched the bridge of his nose. "Ugh …"

Leera quietly got up and filled a glass. "Here, have some water."

Mr. Bawdings drank greedily, burping when he finished.

"Please, sir, you'll wake everyone up."

He scratched at his belly. "Where's Albert—?"

"He's asleep, Mr. Bawdings. I'll see you out."

"See me out? Where am I going?"

"You're going to find us a healer for my friend, remember?"

Bawdings cackled like a mischievous little boy. "You should be quiet, there's people sleeping."

"Ugh, that's what—never mind."

Augum winced at the tone of her voice, but Mr. Bawdings didn't seem to notice.

"Right … the healer thingy … all right then, I best be off, no reason to stick around this sty." He stood up, wavered, and stretched. When he yawned, his breath was so rank Augum could smell it all the way on the floor. He had to restrain from covering up, which would have given away that he wasn't asleep. Suddenly, he felt Leera's loose braids fall onto his cheek.

"You can stop pretending to be asleep now and help."

"I wasn't pretending—" He made a show of stretching.

She rolled her eyes. "Is there anything you'll be needing for your journey, Mr. Bawdings?"

Bawdings scratched at his beard, eyeing the empty glass on the counter like a cougar sizing up prey. "Mayhaps a bit of Albert's fine ale, if you don't mind."

"I'm afraid you drank the last of it, Mr. Bawdings."

Augum knew she was lying, but thought it smart to have him as sober as possible. He surreptitiously finished packing the rucksack while she dangled a waterskin before the man. "How about some more water instead?"

Mr. Bawdings expelled a gust of air and waved dismissively. "Bah." He hitched up his trousers, tugged at his boots, and ascended the steps, wheezing every few as if at high altitude. He fumbled with the hatch so much Leera had to come to the rescue, deftly pulling at the rope and allowing him escape. She closed the trap door behind him, even yanking on the carpet for effect, and listened for a moment before scurrying back down. By this time, Augum was ready—he had strapped on the rucksack and fetched the mitts. He glanced at Haylee's form—she seemed to be sound asleep.

"Wish us luck, Bridge," Leera whispered, giving her a gentle hug.

Augum stepped in after and squeezed her hand. Her eyes followed him in the dim light of the lantern. She blinked once. He forced a smile, trying to ignore the butterflies in his stomach.

Leera waited for him at the top of the steps. He caught up and the pair slipped out into the night.

FOLLOWING MR. BAWDINGS

The bitter cold outside stung. Clouds obscured the stars, and it was as if the moon was too frightened to show its face. The only thing in their favor was the absence of wind, though that was a double-edged sword as the lack of sound amplified their crunching footsteps.

"We have to wait," Augum whispered.

"What? Why?"

"Eyes have to adjust to the dark first. Too dangerous to cast Shine."

"Are you trying to torture me or something?"

"What? No, I just want to make sure we don't get lost. Sir Westwood taught me this trick. Takes only the better part of an hour to adjust to a night like this."

He heard her fold her arms. "So you're saying we have to sit around—"

"Shh—I hear something."

"Shut up, I'm not in the mood."

"No, I really thought I heard something." He stood there a moment, thinking the sound came from Mr. Goss' home. It might have been an animal though. They stood in frosty silence for a bit, with only the sound of their quiet breathing.

"Guess it was nothing," he said finally.

"Of course it was nothing, you were just being *dramatic*."

"Huh? Why would I be 'dramatic'?"

"Because."

"Because why?"

She said nothing.

He felt an angry flush and contemplated saying things he knew he'd regret later.

She seemed to sense this. Her voice returned to a calm state. "Well, anyway, how do you want to adjust our eyes then?"

He took his time responding. "Best do it in pitch darkness." Then, without waiting for her to respond, he led them to the charred remains of a hut, where they plopped down to wait for their eyes to adjust.

"This is stupid," she said after a while. "I'm freezing and we'll just end up losing the tracks."

"You can go anytime you want," he said, colder than he meant to.

There was a long silence in which he thought for sure she would get up and leave without him.

"I hurt your feelings," she said instead.

That surprised him and he didn't know how to reply.

"I'm sorry," she added in a quiet voice. "I mean it. I'm sorry."

"Me too," he said at last, allowing a thoughtful pause to pass before asking the question that had been nagging him. "Did it really mean nothing to you?"

She squirmed, taking too long to respond. "N—"

"Let's just forget the whole thing—" he blurted, cursing himself for not being patient enough to let her put together her thoughts.

A pause, followed by a meek "Okay …"

They sat in black silence, getting colder and colder until he began to see dim outlines. "I think we're ready. Come on, let's go."

"Finally."

"Use your peripheral vision, it's better."

"My what now?"

"Oh, um, just look at things slightly off, as if you're looking to the right or left of them, then you'll see them better. Sir Westwood taught me that."

She said nothing, but he could envision her rolling her eyes.

Soon as they left the dark hut, he knew his plan had worked. The barest amount of light shone through the clouds, making visible dark gray snow, the outlines of trees, and most importantly, Bawdings' fresh horse tracks.

"Hey, I think this stuff you learned actually works. I can see better."

After all her complaining, it took all his will not to say *I told you so!*

They kept up a steady march, stopping occasionally to listen to the night. Mr. Bawdings had ambled northeast and finally northward, following the boundary of the forest and the Tallows.

"If we jumped over to the plains, we'd be following the same path I took on the way to Hangman's Rock," Augum whispered, fondly remembering that first journey when he met Bridget, Leland and, unfortunately, Robin and Commander Rames.

"Wish I had gone with them that day."

As annoyed as he was with her, he wished she had too. "How did Bridget get stuck with Robin on that trip anyway?"

"Yeah, that was funny. As part of learning Shine, we were supposed to go in groups to practice in the wild and find uses for it. Sometimes you get stuck with someone you dislike."

He wondered if she'd have rather have been "stuck" with Robin in place of Bridget. After all, she *liked* him. The thought bothered him so much he fell silent.

As the trip wore on, they started feeling the effects of sleep deprivation. While taking a break to snack on biscuit beef, Leera actually dozed off, her head falling onto his shoulder, only to be jolted awake by a distant wolf howl.

"Sorry," she mumbled, rubbing her eyes. Then she gasped as an answering wolf howl filled the night.

"Don't worry, they're far off."

"I'm not scared."

"Never said you were. Biscuit?"

She held up a hand. "I'm fine, let's keep going before we freeze to death."

They returned to plowing through the snow. After a mind-numbing march, the night gave rise to the first blush of dawn. It became easier and easier to follow the tracks, though Augum wondered if this whole staying-up-all-night thing was a good idea. He felt extremely drowsy, had a hard time concentrating, and kept dreaming of a soft bed by a warm fire. Their exhaustion would affect any spell casting, so they would have to be very careful.

Augum noticed the distance between tracks widen, indicating a suddenly faster pace. Soon another set of tracks joined, tracks that looked alarmingly thin.

A tingle crept up his spine. He stopped upon seeing dark drops in the snow. "Look at this—"

Leera tried to focus with dark-circled eyes. Suddenly she gasped. "That's blood!"

"Yeah, and there's a second set of tracks here. I think … can't be sure, but—"

"—but what!"

"I think they belong to a walker."

For a moment, the pair stared at each other.

"I just got gooseflesh," she said.

"Me too."

"Why didn't you say something earlier?"

He shrugged. "Didn't want to alarm you, I guess."

"Well, I'm alarmed."

They stood listening to the forest, every sound magnified.

"I didn't tell you something either," she blurted.

"What—?"

Her voice dropped to a conspiratorial whisper. "Well, at first I thought it was my imagination, you know, the lack of sleep and all, but … I think we're being followed."

"And you were going to tell me when?"

"Didn't want to alarm you—"

"Oh, for the love of—" He looked past her to the trees behind them but saw nothing. "You're just tired."

Leera followed his gaze. "Maybe."

"I mean, we should keep going either way, right?"

They stared at each other as if to tune out the fear.

She crinkled her nose. "Sure. I'll keep an eye out behind, you ahead. Agreed?"

"Agreed."

The number of drops seemed to increase as they trooped along. He judged by the horse tracks that it was at least at a canter, if not a full gallop.

They stopped after finding one of Mr. Bawdings' flasks. The pair exchanged looks before continuing on, Leera shoving the flask into the rucksack.

Soon they came upon more items—a loose mitt, a bloody boot, a scarf … but it was the leather satchel that gave them pause, one of its straps torn. Inside was the pouch with all the money they had given Mr. Bawdings, and then some. For whatever reason, the portly man hadn't stopped to retrieve it, possibly because he hadn't noticed it fall, or he couldn't afford to. It was the latter Augum feared.

They said nothing and continued on until finding two more sets of tracks.

"Maybe we should turn around," Leera mumbled, staring at the tracks. "I don't think he'd follow through on his promise without the money anyway."

"Yeah, but what if we found him and gave it to him? Think he'd do it then?" He realized how unlikely the idea sounded.

"Or even if we did it instead of him? We can't let Bridget down."

"No, we can't let Bridget down."

They continued the march, constantly watchful, breath steaming in the diffused light, the crush of snow magnified by the stillness.

He stopped suddenly, heart in his throat.

"Aug …?"

He stood there, breathing rapidly, focused on the trees ahead.

"Aug, what's the—"

She was cut off by a distant crash ahead. Something very large moved in the forest.

Leera grabbed his elbow with a shaky hand. "I don't know about this …"

Another crash.

The pair took a step back.

"Um, I think we need to run—" but just as he finished, the thing crashed through the trees. They yelped and began sprinting away. Augum, slowed by the rucksack, desperately tried to keep pace. The crashing followed them, closer and closer, while he trailed further and further behind Leera.

Suddenly a figure stepped out from behind a tree, blocking their path. Leera slid to a halt. The person was dressed in the black and red vertically striped robe of a necrophyte.

The noise of the crashing became thunderous, and as Augum and Leera turned to face it, they finally glimpsed what was chasing them. It was then Augum recalled holding his great-grandfather's hand as the dying Leyan spoke of the three kinds of undead commanded by the last Lord of Death:

"The second kind … are *wraiths* … they are the dead recently raised … can be a bit like … they once were … but not human … sometimes they are grotesquely distorted … and can be as large as … a giant."

ARGUMENTS

The wraith was a monstrously disfigured giant skeleton stinking of rot and decay. Black wet rags hung in strips from gnarled limbs too large for its body. It towered over two regular-sized skeletons—walkers—that had caught up from behind. They crept around in its shadow like demon children around their mother, clacking their jaws.

The wraith opened its crooked maw and hissed, drooling black goop.

The pair stood frozen as it slowly raised two mammoth arms, readying to lunge. Augum knew they had moments to live now, but he could think of nothing to do—his brain was stuck and it seemed any spell of theirs would be too feeble against such a behemoth. Strangely, part of him hoped that if he did nothing at all, then neither would the wraith, and they could just stare at each other like this forever.

Suddenly the wraith and the walkers shot forward. At the same time, the necrophyte plowed through Augum and

Leera, knocking them aside, shouting, “Necro dodai! Necro dodai! Adai, adai!” and the skeletons stopped short, watching the necrophyte, whose hood fell back revealing long golden locks.

“Haylee …?” Augum said.

Haylee didn’t acknowledge him or Leera, keeping her attention solely on the wraith hovering above her, drooling black ooze into the snow.

She pointed away. “Necro onto! Necro onto!”

The wraith cocked its misshapen head.

Haylee pointed again, more firmly this time. “Necro onto!”

The wraith made a kind of squeak, much like a string breaking on a lute. It turned, lumbered away a few steps, and stopped, glancing back at them almost longingly.

Haylee’s arm remained fixed. “Necro. Onto!”

The wraith expelled a hissing breath before continuing along, the walkers following. Haylee didn’t turn around until the menace had disappeared from sight.

“What did you say?” Augum asked, standing and brushing himself off.

“I told them to get lost.”

“Well, thanks for, um … thanks for saving our lives.”

“You’re welcome.”

Leera looked like she was going to castigate Haylee for something, but only mumbled, “Thanks,” and turned away, pretending to search the trees for any signs of movement.

Haylee’s face fell slightly.

“Don’t worry, I’m sure she’ll come around,” he whispered.

She nodded, though he saw doubt in her eyes.

“So you were the one following us all this time—why?” he asked.

She shrugged. “I knew I might be able to help if you bumped into the undead. To be perfectly honest though, I …

I didn't think any of the commands would work on a wraith."

"Can you teach us some? Commanding the dead could be very useful."

"Doesn't work that way. You have to be ordained by the Lord of the Dead in an ancient formal ceremony as a necrophyte, and that's even to have a *chance* of having the dead listen to you. You also have to learn to speak the right words, the right tone, and use the right spells. It's a very tough element."

"You mean ordained by my father—"

"Yes, by Lord Sparkstone."

"I'm glad you decided to follow us."

Leera turned to face Haylee suddenly. "Why are you helping us—?"

"What? What do you mean why?"

"You know what I mean. What game are you really playing—?"

" 'Game'—? I'm not playing a 'game'. If I wanted to turn you in, I would have done it back when I was with Robin and you were too weak to lift Bridget. I could have done it in Sparrow's Perch too. I could have even done it now. Don't you understand? I'm done with the Legion!"

Leera just glared.

"Oh, I think I get it—" Haylee continued. "This is about that stupid song, isn't it? Well I'm sorry for that, I really am! What do you want to hear, that I didn't have the courage to make it right? That I crossed a line and it was impossible to go back? We were enemies, all right? But I don't want that anymore, just like I don't want the Legion and necromancy. Do you get it now? I'm sorry, all right! I'm sorry ..."

"Oh, you're 'sorry', are you? You think 'sorry' covers all the humiliation, the shame?"

Haylee bit her lip before replying. "That's partly why I followed you. I ... I want to make it up to you."

"Leera, she saved our lives," Augum said. "She helped us with Bridget—"

Leera immediately turned on him. "You stay out of this—you have no idea what it's been like putting up with all the mean and nasty things she did and said. She could have stopped at any time. She could have shown compassion or friendship then … but no, she plowed on like the little deceitful vermin she is—"

He held up his hands in surrender. "All right, if you insist on being angry with her then that's fine, but at least she's *trying* to make it up to you."

Leera bristled. "You're taking her side again! Why are you constantly defending her—!" She thrust an accusing finger into Haylee's face. "I know what you're up to, and I hate you! Stop trying to steal my friends!" She turned her back on them and marched off.

They watched her go.

"I deserved that," Haylee mumbled. "She's right, there was a lot more that I did to her, and I could have stopped."

He sighed. "I should get her …"

"Yeah …"

He chased after Leera, who resolutely marched northward. "Leera, wait, please, let's talk—" but she only flashed him a despising look.

"Where're you going?"

"I'm going to get that healer from the Legion myself, without your help. Why don't you go and run off with *her*."

"That's crazy, will you not just stop and talk?"

She halted, but kept her back turned and arms crossed.

"Look, you're not thinking this through right now," he began in the most rational, kind voice he could, trying to figure out why she was so mad at him. "Fine, stay angry with Haylee, stay angry with me even—but whatever you do, please, let's stick together and work on this. If you go alone, something terrible might happen and I'd … I'd never forgive myself …"

"And so you shouldn't—"

"I can't do this without you, Lee. Bridget and I need you. Please. Stay angry at me, that's fine, but just come and work on this. I really think Haylee can get a healer. She's dressed like a necrophyte, think about it—"

She waited a moment, breath fogging in short bursts, before turning around, brows furrowed. She stared at him for a bit before glancing at Haylee over his shoulder. "All right, maybe we *could* use her … that's about all she's good for anyway."

He sighed in relief. "Great, let's think of a plan. Come on."

Leera frowned before finally nodding, lagging behind until they returned to Haylee.

"All right," he said, gesturing diplomatically. "Now let's forget our differences and work together to find a healer for Bridget."

"Maybe I could bluff my way in," Haylee said after a tense silence. "I could say that I need the services of a healer. If I strike the right tone, I might be able to convince them to only send one soldier as an escort."

"We could deal with one soldier," he said, nodding encouragingly at Leera. "Right?"

She just stood there, arms crossed, gaze fixed elsewhere.

"I'd have to have a good reason for being out here on my own," Haylee continued, "and a good reason to borrow the healer too."

"Why don't you just snob your way in to their camp and ask the healer directly?" Leera asked.

Haylee just stared, eyes cool as ice. Augum had the distinct impression he was looking at the old Haylee. It was almost as if Leera was determined to bring her enemy back.

"You know what? Maybe I will!"

"Fine then!" Leera gestured in a royal manner for her to lead the way. Haylee briefly glanced at Augum and marched off, followed quickly by Leera, a determined look on both their faces. He sighed and followed, wishing he had a male friend to complain to about girls. If Sydo hadn't turned into a weaseling traitor, maybe they could have had something in common eventually. He blurted out a laugh, realizing how unlikely that was.

Both girls turned around at the same time, chorusing together, "What're *you* laughing at?" Their cheeks went crimson, though they refused to look at each other.

"Nothing, just thinking to myself how I wish I had a male friend so we could talk about how weird girls are."

Leera and Haylee blinked before each cracked the same smile. Haylee turned around first, continuing on, as Leera swept her hair back. Some of the braids had now completely come undone. He had this stupid desire to fix them for her.

She sighed and rubbed her eyes. "Fine, Aug, I'll … I'll try to be nice for … for your sake and Bridget's, okay?"

"Okay." He strolled by her. "Come on then, it can't be far now."

Leera followed close behind as the trio marched on. The day grew darker, even though it was still morning. A small but ever-strengthening wind picked up, reminding him of his struggles trying to cross the Tallows.

As the excitement of their encounter with the wraith wore off, the exhaustion from lack of sleep renewed its grip. His chest began hurting even more. He wondered if the healer could help him too. Then he found himself dreaming of a warm bed and a fire once again, wishing this cursed adventure, which turned out to be a lot more miserable than he thought, would end soon. What lacked here was Bridget's voice of compassion and reason. He was sure that by now she would have already convinced Leera she was being overly dramatic, and would have probably even had her forgiving Haylee, maybe even become good friends. Well, maybe not good friends, that might be pushing it …

As they trundled along in the snow, ever more tired, his thoughts drifted to necromancy. He hoped Leera wouldn't take offence to him asking some questions that had been on his mind for a while now.

"So Haylee, do you actually know any necromantic spells?"

"Yeah, I do, but only one—Feign Death. Want to see it?"

He glanced to Leera. She pursed her lips but raised no objection.

"Definitely," he said.

Haylee made a dramatic show of a fair maiden falling to the snow. A moment passed. He was about to say that anyone could do that when Haylee's face suddenly turned blue, then black, then rotted away, along with her hands. He and Leera gasped and took a step back. Haylee giggled and the effect instantly disappeared.

"All right, I have to say, that was awesome," he said.

Even Leera seemed impressed, begrudging a nod.

"So what happens to your normal element of ice, do you ignore that, or—?"

"Well, the more energy you spend on your old element the less you have for necromancy, so most necrophytes stop training in their old element all together. They're kind of forced to anyway."

She stretched out a hand to him. He took it and helped her up, conscious of Leera looking on. Haylee brushed snow off her robe. "Necromancy's more difficult than ordinary spell casting though. I wasn't very good at it even. I kind of prefer ordinary spell casting."

"You weren't very good at ordinary spell casting at the academy either—" Leera said, trying to make a joke of it and laughing.

Haylee's eyes flashed but she forced a smile. "I'm not planning on learning any more necromancy. I'm going to focus on my element of ice. I just have to find a new mentor."

Leera gave Augum a look that said *No way is it going to be Mrs. Stone.*

Haylee dropped her head. "All I wanted to do was make my mother proud and hang out with—" She gave a furtive glance at Leera. "I need to send my family a message I'm all right and … and to be careful."

"At least you *have* a family to message," Leera muttered, though mercifully, Haylee didn't appear to have heard, and if she had, she pretended otherwise. Augum was tired of seeing them fight, or more accurately, seeing Leera pounce on Haylee at every opportunity.

"Think they'll go after your family?" he asked.

Haylee chewed on a fingernail, a worried look on her face.

He unslung the rucksack. "They in Blackhaven?"

"Near the academy at our old house. I can't ever go back there, not now."

After a sullen silence, they continued following Mr. Bawdings' tracks. It wasn't long until they spotted a dark mass lying in the snow. Augum exchanged ominous looks with Leera as the trio wearily approached.

"It's Mr. Bawdings," Haylee whispered.

Augum took a moment to inspect the tracks. "The walkers caught up to him. Horse must have run off. We have to keep going." He was surprised at how matter-of-fact he sounded around a dead body. Maybe it was because of the sleep deprivation, or maybe because this was what he had expected to find.

"We're just going to leave him?" Haylee asked.

Leera withdrew Mr. Bawdings' flask and some of the other belongings he had dropped along the way. "Well, what do you want to do, bury him? The ground's frozen and he's too heavy to carry. We *have* to leave him." She placed the items on his body, all but his coin purse.

Not even a proper burial, Augum thought, staring at the man's broad back. The blood combining with the cold had stiffened the tunic like frozen ripples in a pond.

"Let's go," he said, and so they left poor Mr. Bawdings behind. For a long time, no one spoke during the walk, until they heard the sound of horses in the distance.

"Must be the outpost," Augum said, changing direction towards the boundary between the forest and the Tallows.

They crept up to some winter shrubbery and peeked over. The wind here was a little stronger, riffling yellow grass that peeked out from the snowy Tallows. A great wave of dark cloud slowly rolled in from the horizon.

A storm was coming.

Nearby, the giant black egg of Hangman's Rock stood stark against the snow, augmented by a wooden watchtower built upon it. Tents, both large and small, fanned out around it. There was a makeshift stable and even a travelling smithy. Men were securing the camp against the increasing winds. Most dressed in thick winter coats, black armor peeking out.

"This is it," Leera said. "What's the plan?"

"You two stay here," Haylee replied, raising her hood. "I have an idea. I'll need the coin."

Leera hesitated before handing the pouch over.

Haylee hid it inside her robe and glanced at Augum, her eyes sunken from lack of sleep. "I promise I'll do my best." She paused. "If something should happen … never mind, just wish me luck."

"Good luck," he said.

She glanced to Leera, hoping for the same, but Leera pretended to be busy with the rucksack. Haylee put on a determined expression and walked to the Legion camp.

"Hope this works," he muttered, watching Haylee's necrophyte robe billow in the wind like forgotten clothes on a drying line.

"She *better* succeed," Leera said.

Haylee walked up to a guard. The pair conversed briefly before disappearing from sight behind a tent. Augum took the opportunity to withdraw the blankets, handing one over to Leera. She grabbed it without a word.

It was difficult sitting there in the snowy shrub, slowly freezing, wondering what was happening in the camp. Was Haylee successful? How would she convince the commander to lend her a healer without raising suspicion? What if the camp had received news of her betrayal and took her prisoner? What if, what if, what if—?

The questions swirled around his head like snowdrift. Leera sat beside him, wrapped up in her blanket, ignoring him with silence colder than the frost. He glanced at her from within his own nest. He could just see her freckled nose peeking out of her hood, occasionally brushed by tangled raven hair blowing around. He had this strange longing to hug her and tell her everything was going to work out somehow. Instead, he couldn't get his mind off Mr. Bawdings' lonely body.

Snow had begun to fall, the flakes adding to the winter accumulation. It became difficult to see the camp except for ever-present wisps of cooking smoke that revealed the strength of the winds. Sometimes he picked up the scent of roasting meat. It made his stomach pang with hunger.

The day darkened by the hour with the oncoming storm. He snacked on some biscuit beef and nuts, hoping this would work, that somehow, through some miracle, Haylee would be successful and they could return to Bridget with help. Leera eventually fell asleep. He thought it best to let her be and maintain watch himself. As time passed though, his eyelids became heavier and heavier. He let them rest just a little bit …

MIRALDA JENKINS

It was late afternoon when Augum felt an urgent shaking. He jerked into consciousness, peeking out from within his blanket nest.

"Who are you?" he asked, alarmed and struggling to ready himself for the unknown.

"Miralda Jenkins," the woman whispered, eyes darting about. "And you must be quiet. We need to move fast, I have horses waiting in the forest."

Right … she was the healer. He oriented himself as they quickly gathered themselves, Leera already up, stuffing her blanket into the rucksack. The weather had worsened since he was last awake, the wind howling, jamming snow into his face.

He brushed himself off and folded his own blanket, getting his first good look at the woman. She was very large, perhaps obese even, with short legs and arms, a kind, wide face with multiple chins, and hard but attentive eyes. She was dressed in a black sheepskin robe trimmed with fur, marked on the breast with the Legion emblem of a burning sword.

"Hurry now," she said, gesturing for them to follow her quick waddling steps.

They reached two brown mares so large he guessed them former plow horses. Ms. Jenkins mounted one while Leera mounted the other, keeping her hood closely drawn. It was only in that moment that he suddenly realized that Haylee was nowhere to be seen.

"Ms. Jenkins, where's—"

"There's no time. Get on the horse and follow me. I'll explain when I can."

Augum, fearing someone may give chase at any moment, mounted Leera's horse, gripping her waist, which stiffened at his touch.

They quickly got underway. After a time, Ms. Jenkins slowed her pace from an easy gallop to a canter. She lit up her palm in a dim white glow, routinely scanning the trees.

"Would you mind riding beside Ms. Jenkins?" Augum asked. Leera wordlessly complied.

"What happened to Haylee, Ms. Jenkins?" he asked when the horses were side-by side.

"Miss Tennyson was taken captive, I'm afraid," she replied, eyes never leaving the forest. "Word had reached the camp through the commander's speaking orb. They seized her, but not before she slipped me a note. I read it and quickly burned it."

"What's going to happen to her?"

"She'll face a trial, if that's what you could call it. If found guilty, with luck she'll only be excommunicated, denounced, and made to do forced labor."

"And if unlucky—?"

Ms. Jenkins' lack of reply sent a shiver up his spine.

"So what about this speaking orb?" Leera asked. "Can they communicate freely with each other?"

"They can with another speaking orb, but the orbs have to be tuned together. They're quite rare, only the commanders receive them, mostly to communicate with each other and the Lord of the Legion."

"So do they know about us?" Leera pressed.

"They received word about your escape, though they weren't expecting any of you to show up here. Upon spotting Miss Tennyson, they knew you must be near. Commander Canes' first guess was Sparrow's Perch, so they'll be mounting a party right away—"

"Commander Canes?" He could hardly believe it. "As in, Dollard Canes?"

"Yes, the Knight of Disgrace—"

"But he's the one—!" He could barely keep from sputtering. "He's the one who—"

"—betrayed you all to the Legion? For that feat, he was rewarded with command of Venga company, all two hundred men, who once took orders from Commander Rames."

So *that's* who he thought looked familiar back in Sparrow's Perch—it was Canes! Even remembering that bulbous nose of his made Augum tense up with loathing.

"We must beat them back to Sparrow's Perch. I may be able to obscure your presence from them, depending on if they send Corrigus along."

"Corrigus—?" Leera said.

"Corrigus is a very high degree Legion sorcerer they're expecting to arrive with a supply caravan. He has the arcane ability to discover enchantments. We can only hope he is delayed by the weather."

"Won't they be looking for you?"

"I told them I was not feeling well, and to let me rest in my tent. When I heard who you were, I knew I had to do everything in my power to help the resistance."

"The resistance?" Augum blurted. "But we're only apprentices!"

"Yes, well, if you'll forgive me, I more meant Mrs. Stone. Though perhaps one day, should you grow strong enough … after all, you are *his* son—"

"Wait, I don't understand—"

"Perhaps you will in due time."

He wanted to ask more questions but Leera was forced to fall in behind Ms. Jenkins' horse as the trees grew denser. They rode on, shivering in the cold wind, trying to stay warm.

"I think she meant for you to become the leader of the resistance or something," Leera said.

"Oh." He was disappointed if that was the case. How could he, a commoner with little arcane knowledge, possibly lead anyone? He wanted to laugh derisively at the idea, but there was something more pressing at the moment—Leera had spoken to him for the first time in hours! "So … you still mad at me?" he asked.

Her reply was as sharp as the cold. "No," and he instinctively knew she was still mad.

"But … I don't understand, what did I—"

"Because …" she cut in, taking time to form the right words. "Because *she* likes you."

He almost fell off the horse. "Um … what?"

"I didn't want her … stealing you from us. What with her pretty golden locks and her evil charms … I know what she's capable of. I know what she's doing."

He just gaped. Part of him was embarrassed yet another part flattered that Leera was so protective of him. "I … I would never leave you two," he managed to finally stammer. "You're my closest and best friends, and … and I don't *like* her like that anyway. She was just a friend, someone who helped us, who I thought had changed and needed …" What was the right word? "Compassion." To accent the point he squeezed Leera's midriff in the manner of a quick hug. She didn't reply but he could tell she was happy to hear it.

"Look, I'm … I'm sorry for being so mean to her," she said. "I hope … I guess I hope things turn out well for her in the end, you know?" Then she snorted a laugh. "But don't worry too much, I bet her parents will buy their way out of this mess—they're rich."

"Yeah," he said half-heartedly, pondering on the fact yet another person had made a sacrifice on their behalf, a recurring pattern he viewed as a curse. He hoped that, wherever she was, Haylee was not in any pain and that for once Leera was right about her—maybe her parents *would* buy her way out of this mess. The thought seemed vain and pathetic somehow.

Although they had managed to get a few hours of sleep earlier, it was hardly enough to sustain them. Augum found himself constantly dozing off, his head lolling onto Leera's shoulder. She kept waking him, insisting that he suffer through this "adventure" with her, emphasizing they would get plenty of time to sleep when they got back. He hoped so, though he was more worried about the Legion showing up and rooting them all out.

As they trotted south, the wind increased in strength. Leera began shivering, so he extended his blanket around her.

The day wore on, melding into night, ever colder, ever windier, until Ms. Jenkins slowed. "Sparrow's Perch is just ahead," she said.

They circumnavigated at a distance, eventually tying the horses up a short ways to the west in a small grove sheltered from the onslaught of the wind.

They rushed back to Sparrow's Perch, practically stumbling through the entranceway to Mr. Goss' burned-out home. As they did so, Ms. Jenkins used Telekinesis in a manner Augum had never thought of—to obscure their tracks by effectively pushing the snow over itself in a wave-like way. It was neat to watch, an advanced trick that, in his exhausted state of mind, seemed impossible to replicate.

Ms. Jenkins stayed outside to cast protective enchantments while Leera opened the trap door. She was immediately greeted by a sleepy-looking Mr. Goss, his spectacled face lighting up with a smile.

"I was worried sick about you all," he said, ushering them inside. Then his expression turned serious. "I would very much like to lecture you for not telling me your plans."

Augum fidgeted with his fingers. "Mr. Goss, we apologize, but we had to make sure Mr. Bawdings succeeded."

Mr. Goss glanced at Bridget. "I understand, but I would have preferred to have been made aware nonetheless." He sighed. "And how is Hedrick? Nursing quite the headache, I imagine?"

Augum exchanged a look with Leera. "Um, no, actually he, um—"

"He didn't make it," Leera said. "We're so sorry, Mr. Goss."

"Oh, I see." He paced to the counter, retrieved a pot, placed it under the iron pump, and filled it with water, hands shaking. "How did it happen?"

Augum recalled the body in the snow. "There was … there was something in the woods—"

Mr. Goss held up a hand, swallowing. "Please do not continue. I … I shall think of him as I saw him last—garrulously drunk with a smile on his face." He hung the pot over the fire and went to prepare mugs.

"We found her though," Augum said. "The healer, Ms. Jenkins. She's up above casting protective spells."

"Ah, I am pleased to hear *some* good tidings. And Haylee? Is she helping Ms. Jenkins?"

Augum took a seat at the table. "Uh, she was captured."

Mr. Goss stopped what he was doing. "Captured?"

Suddenly Augum felt terribly guilty. "She … she saved us, Mr. Goss. She stopped the wraith from killing us. Then … then she went in Mr. Bawdings' place, but somehow they knew. The camp knew about her through some sort of orb, so—"

"So they kept her," Mr. Goss finished in a quiet voice. "That unfortunate, poor, brave girl …"

A knock came at the trap door. Mr. Goss jumped. "That must be Ms. Jenkins," and climbed the steps. "Ah, Ms. Jenkins, I am so pleased to see you in this grim time." He took her hand and helped her down the rest of the clay steps.

"And you, my dear Albert," Ms. Jenkins said, smiling perfunctorily, eyes darting about. "I'm afraid I can only stay but a moment. The Legion are on their way. I placed protective enchantments over the floor above. They should get you through tonight, unless you run into some bad luck that is."

She means Corrigus, Augum thought.

"I suppose you've heard the news about Miss Tennyson?" Ms. Jenkins continued.

Mr. Goss' face grew serious. "Haylee … yes."

"It's most unfortunate, but I'll do what I can, Albert. I promise you that."

"I am most relieved to hear it. Tea?"

"Maybe just a quick sip while I work." She waddled over to Bridget. "How is your little boy?" she asked absent-mindedly while placing her palm on Bridget's stomach. She closed her eyes as her hand began glowing.

"Oh, yes, he is doing very well, Ms. Jenkins, very well. All thanks to you of course. He is asleep now, shall I wake him?"

One of Ms. Jenkins' brows rose as she completed her arcane examination at Bridget's neck. "I'd very much like to continue his treatment, Albert, but due to its length, I'm afraid it will have to wait for another day."

"Yes, of course, time is precious," Mr. Goss replied, wiping his hands and retrieving the pot, which was now boiling. He poured them all steaming ginger tea, pushing a mug onto Ms. Jenkins.

She took one sip and put her mug down. "I need all of you to stand back and stay very quiet. She has a difficult double injury of the back and neck that will require the entirety of my concentration." She gave them a grave look. "I must warn you that should the spell fail, she'll probably never recover."

Augum and Leera exchanged horrified looks. This was not part of the plan. He, and apparently Leera also, hadn't realized there was a chance of spell failure. Seeing Leland should have given him pause, though—the arcane healing element wasn't perfect and carried the same risks as any other element.

Ms. Jenkins took a series of long deep breaths and closed her eyes. Finally, she placed a pudgy hand on Bridget's forehead and started reciting a complex healing spell, taking special care with pronunciation. Her hand began glowing brightly, eventually consuming her entire body in white brilliance. The glow reached a blinding intensity before fading, leaving a burned-in visual image of the scene in Augum's brain.

Ms. Jenkins, huffing and holding her head as if in pain, stumbled about for a seat. Mr. Goss immediately came to her aid, helping her sit down in the rocking chair by the fire, hurriedly retrieving her mug of tea. She grasped it with shaking fingers.

Meanwhile, Augum and Leera rushed over to Bridget's side. Her eyes were open yet she lay as still as ever. Augum's stomach filled with dread. It hadn't worked …

Suddenly Bridget's little pinky finger moved.

Leera gasped. "You can do it, Bridge, come on!" and they cheered her on, movement by movement, until she lifted an arm and even smiled. Leera and Augum hugged each other tightly; then delicately hugged Bridget until she gurgled for them to stop; then hugged Mr. Goss; and finally a weary Ms. Jenkins.

"I should go now," Ms. Jenkins said, rising.

"Ms. Jenkins, wait—" Leera said.

Ms. Jenkins paused at the foot of the steps. "Yes, dear?"

"It's Augum's ribs, they're broken—"

"Oh, it's nothing," he began, not wanting to make a fuss.

"Ms. Jenkins' brows rose. "Come here, child, let me have a look."

He dutifully paced over. Ms. Jenkins' face grew serious as she felt his ribs. He recoiled as bones grated.

"This is no time to be squeamish, my dear," she said, continuing her prodding. "Now hold still." Her hand began glowing, the light spreading to his chest. He felt a soothing sensation that went from cold to warm. When her hand extinguished, she had to take a seat at the steps.

Mr. Goss immediately rushed over with a mug of fresh tea. "Now I must insist you rest a while, Ms. Jenkins. Please." He helped her raise the mug to her lips.

Augum felt his ribs—the pain was gone, all of it! He had gotten so used to it, a stubborn old thorn, and now it was gone! He felt terribly selfish for letting her drain her energies on him. "It doesn't feel like enough, but … thank you."

She glanced at him weakly. "You're … welcome," and beckoned Mr. Goss to help her stand.

"Please, Ms. Jenkins, your tea at the very least—"

"Too dangerous," and she departed into the night, trailed by a grateful group that followed her all the way up the steps, expressing their thanks and wishing her all the luck in the world.

Mr. Goss shut the trap door and pulled on the carpet rope while Augum and Leera rushed back to Bridget to cheer her on as she worked her way from laying to sitting, and finally to a standing position. When she stood up at last, they threw up a cheer and embraced her in a long hug.

"I hate to be a rainy cloud," Mr. Goss began, "but we should try to be quiet in case the Legion do come."

"Yes, Mr. Goss," Augum and Leera chorused. They sat down beside Bridget to whisper the details of their adventure, mercifully leaving out the tension with Haylee. Then they began peppering her with questions.

"What did it feel like?"

"Do you remember everything?"

"Was there any pain?"

"It was frustrating, yes," Bridget finally said, smiling, "but you'll learn about it tomorrow. You two look exhausted. Get some sleep already. I'll take watch with the orb."

Too tired to argue, they spread out blankets and pillows and fell asleep near the fire.

ANCIENT VERSE

Augum awoke to the sound of a sizzling pan. Still drowsy, he rubbed his eyes and yawned, wondering what time of day it was.

"Hey, sleepyhead," Bridget said with a smile, hands on her hips. "The Legion came last night and you two slept through it all. Watched the whole thing through the orb. Scary, but exciting."

"They did?" he muttered groggily. "Why didn't you wake us?"

"At the end of last night, the two of you could barely see straight. Wasn't going to wake you unless I had to. Legion left after a while anyway. Ms. Jenkins' enchantments worked—they hadn't found anything."

It was an immense relief, even the morning after, to know that Bridget was no longer paralyzed, though he couldn't help but wonder how Mya and Haylee were faring.

Mya … he hadn't thought of her in a while. Somehow, the sting had subsided a little. He glanced to Leera, still wrapped in a pile of blankets. Bridget prodded the mound with her foot. Leera covered her head with a blanket and groaned.

Leland groped his way over and gave Bridget a hug, moaning.

"I'm glad I'm all right too," Bridget replied. She then whispered something into his bandaged ear. He squeaked in reply and quietly felt his way over to Leera, immediately pouncing on her.

"Dark hell, what's happening—!" she shouted while everyone snickered.

"Now mind your language, young lady," Augum said in an authoritative voice.

Leera, realizing who it was, enveloped Leland in a blanket hug. "And now I'm going to eat you …!" she said in a mock evil voice, and made gobbling sounds as she gently ruffled Leland up. He squealed in obvious glee, eventually managing to escape and scurry off to his room by feeling the walls.

Augum began folding up the blankets. "Nice bed-head."

"Shut up, you." Leera made a poor attempt at hiding her grin while trying to smooth her hair.

Bridget, who had been watching them like a long-lost loving sister, gave a wistful sigh. "I missed you two …"

"I miss having a comb," Leera mumbled.

"If I may—" Mr. Goss disappeared into his bedroom, returning with a simple hairbrush. "As you can see, I have little hair to use it on," he said with a chortle. He hesitated though, lovingly staring at the brush, before catching himself and handing it over.

Leera gave him a pained smile.

"So how did it feel to be unable to move?" Augum asked.

Bridget rolled her eyes. "Ugh—that's the thing, I didn't actually feel anything, so it really wasn't any fun, especially at first. It was okay after a while, but I became very bored and, if you can believe it, kind of restless. The best part was when you studied the Slam spell with me—I actually learned something! That was about as exciting as it got for me, the rest of the time I saw nothing but ceiling. I was pretty scared that was going to be my view forever."

"Guess we should've pointed you at the fire or something," Augum said.

"Or given me the pearl so I could practice with it. I bet I could have used it even though I was paralyzed."

Leera turned pink. "Oops—that would've been smart." She motioned between herself and Augum. "That's the kind of genius friends you have."

Mr. Goss removed a large frying pan from the fire. "Well, we are very glad you are all right again, Bridget." He began plating breakfast. "Almost ready here …"

The trio helped set the table and sat down as Mr. Goss called on Leland, who found his way back making a silly moan, which Augum interpreted as a giggle. He was starting to differentiate the various noises the boy made.

Bridget recounted the events of the evening over breakfast. Augum and Leera learned that twenty black-armored soldiers swept into the village while they were asleep, led by Commander Canes, something that was not news to them but had been a surprise to Bridget.

"—and you'll never believe it, but the traitor found the Orb of Orion—" Bridget said, though her tone of voice told them it was a funny story and not to worry. "One of his lackeys used the Unconceal spell, but, get this—" she stabbed at the air with her fork, "he didn't know what the orb was! I watched as brute after Legion brute tried dislodging it. Thankfully, when you two placed it in the snow, you locked it too."

"Wait, I don't understand something," Leera said. "Why didn't that Legion warlock find *us* with his Unconceal spell?"

"Well, in order to find someone who's been arcanely hidden, you need to know Reveal, which is an 11th degree spell—"

"—so whoever searched wasn't past their 10th degree," Augum concluded.

"Exactly."

"It was very stormy by the end and they were all tired. Left soon after. Canes was very angry though, saying how he was going to put Haylee to the question for their failure to find us."

Augum had a vision of Haylee in an iron room with the Blade of Sorrows and Robin, crying as her family was dragged in …"

"—oh, and I heard them inform the Blade of Sorrows and his company, so a whole bunch of them are riding north," Bridget added.

Augum felt queasy. He put down his fork and leaned back in the chair.

Bridget fixed him with a concerned look. "You all right?"

He nodded, swallowing hard. "We should go soon, now that you're well again."

"We still need to find a way to reach Mrs. Stone before Sparkstone does," Leera said. "If he hasn't gotten to her already …"

This dampened the mood considerably and they ate on in silence. Augum pondered how long a way it was to the northern peaks. They lacked horses and proper supplies. As far as battling the cold, all they had were blankets, and that wouldn't do for this kind of journey. If they had only been able to teleport to Antioc, they would have stood a chance of keeping pace with his father …

It wasn't a total disaster to be back in Sparrow's Perch, however—he and Bridget were now fully healed and they had a chance to see Leland again. All they needed to do was find Mrs. Stone. Suddenly an idea occurred to him.

"Wait—what about using a speaking orb?"

Bridget began taking everyone's empty plate. "For what?"

He quickly filled her in on what Ms. Jenkins said, about how these orbs were supposed to be very rare, that most of the Legion commanders had one, and that they communicated to each other with them.

"I'm not following you though," Leera said. "How could we communicate with Mrs. Stone when neither she nor us have one?"

Bridget's eyes lit up. "Wait a moment—we kind of *do* have a speaking orb—we can hear through the Orb of Orion, and others can hear us! And didn't Erika say that it *was* a speaking orb, only better?"

Leera threw her hands up. "Yeah, okay, but I still don't see what you're getting at. Let me repeat myself—Mrs. Stone. Does. Not. Have. A. Speaking. Orb."

Bridget sighed as she took the plates to the washstand. "But what if we found someone further up to communicate with, someone closer to Mrs. Stone?"

"Wait, wait, wait …" Augum interrupted. "Ms. Jenkins also said that the orbs have to be tuned together."

Leera crossed her arms with a firm nod. "That's right!"

Mr. Goss chuckled to himself. "I have not heard so much talk of arcanery since Annie and I showed up at the academy to enroll Leland …"

The trio smiled awkwardly. Mr. Goss looked around at them with pride, face glowing. Augum felt awful knowing they had to leave him and his poor son behind in this town full of lonely memories.

"On the subject of these speaking orbs—" Mr. Goss went on, removing his spectacles and rubbing his eyes. "I seem to recall—and mind you I may easily be mistaken as I am not very knowledgeable in the arcane arts—that Lord Tennyson had a collection of scrolls in his basement."

The trio exchanged hopeful looks. Everyone immediately understood the implication—there could be a scroll of teleportation!

"Now mind you, I have tried going down there, but the place burned to the ground, or rather in this case, well below the ground. It is quite treacherous."

"Mr. Goss, do you mind if we go take a look anyway?" Bridget asked in her most polite tone.

"Well, seeing how dangerous it could be, I would rather you not, but I also understand how much reuniting with Mrs. Stone means to you all. Therefore, I shall not stand in your way. Just promise me that you will be extremely careful."

The trio nodded vigorously. "We promise."

They departed as soon as they could.

The day was windy and gray. A blanket of fresh milky snow coated everything, partially obscuring the many Legion footprints.

"It's over here—" Leera said, leading the way through the burned-out buildings.

"What was this?" Augum asked as they passed a particularly large structure, now a mess of torched planks and cracked tiles.

"It was going to be our new school," Bridget replied before catching up to Leera.

He stared at the destroyed building, remembering the joyous moment when he found out he'd been admitted to the village school. What might have been had Tennyson not betrayed the village, he thought, before catching up to the girls.

Bridget stood before a quaint home that had completely collapsed in the fire. "This is—this *was* my home once." She turned to nod at another not too far from Mr. Goss'. "And that one there was Leera's."

"I don't want to look at it," Leera said, voice full of bitterness. She moved along, Bridget and Augum in tow.

Soon they stood before a rather large round home, the once majestic pine tree above it now charred and barren. Inside, part of the floor had collapsed, exposing a gaping snow-covered pit. They climbed down, navigating the sharp debris.

"Shyneo," Augum said, barely noticing his palm crackle to life. He was so used to casting the spell it had become almost subconscious. Leera and Bridget quickly followed suit, lighting up the blackened interior with green and blue light.

He stepped over a large wooden truss that once supported the ceiling.

"Watch your step—" Bridget yelped, grabbing his arm. One of his feet was on a small piece of charred wood that covered a hole.

Leera crouched by the hole and shone her light down it. "There's another floor below us. Might even be more."

"Tennyson was a rich man," Bridget said. "Hired a high-degree earth-element warlock to excavate the clay. Wouldn't dare to have my lowly father do it for him—what would the Scarsons think?"

"Runs in the damn family," Leera added.

Augum picked up the remains of a very fine boot. "If Tennyson was the one that tipped off the Legion, why didn't they save all his stuff?"

Bridget examined a charred bookshelf. "I get the feeling he didn't realize they were going to raze the village. Maybe he thought he would be allowed to stay, have the village to himself or something."

They turned things over, perused piles of charred furniture, and examined anything that had half-survived the fire, of which there was precious little, and certainly nothing of use. Navigating the scorched detritus proved difficult, and the further the trio went, the more they feared the structure would collapse. It creaked and groaned as if pleading to be put out of its misery, the wooden floors threatening to give way any moment. It quickly became apparent Mr. Goss' warning about the place was no overstatement.

"Can't find the stairs anywhere," Augum muttered as they reached the end of the first floor.

"Let's just climb down through a hole," Leera said.

"Are you crazy?" Bridget countered, face smeared with soot. "How would we get back up?"

Leera snickered. "You look like a barbarian. Every time you push your hair aside, you add to it."

"What?"

"Check your fingers, they're black."

"Oh … darn."

"One of these days I'm going to teach you how to curse properly."

Bridget snorted before breaking into a cough. "Let's find the stairs," and she stumbled off.

"Leave her alone, she's trying to blend in," Augum whispered. The two of them suppressed laughter.

Suddenly there was a wooden groaning sound, a shriek, and Leera was gone.

Augum dropped to his knees by the hole while Bridget raced over, but Leera was already laughing.

Bridget scowled. "What's so funny—you almost died!"

"I know, and now I'm stuck!" Leera said between snorts of laughter, jammed to the waist in the floor. "Since my feet are dangling, we can definitely say it keeps going down though!"

Leera finally hauled herself up.

"Wait there, we're going to look for some stairs—" Bridget said in a firm voice, and the two of them went to search for the stairs, locating them under a pile of rubble. When they finally caught up to Leera, she was readying to jump down through yet another hole.

"Why not just use the stairs—?" Bridget asked.

"Because it wouldn't be as exciting," Augum answered on her behalf. Leera pointed at him without looking up. "Exactly, listen to the wise Augum, who thrives on adventure and seeks it at every turn, as do I. You spent too long lying on that table!"

Bridget rolled her eyes. "Spare me. I'm taking the stairs. Aug—?"

He looked between the girls, each with their own expectant look, and shrugged. "Guess I'll take the hole." When Bridget scowled, he added, "What? Someone's got to keep an eye on her, otherwise she might break her neck."

"Fine. You're taking foolish risks, the both of you." Bridget marched off.

He slipped down to where Leera was. She was already hanging from the edge of the hole, dangling like a monkey.

"Ugh, she needs to loosen up," she said before letting go.

He followed, landing with a thud onto clay ground, indicating it was likely the lowest floor. He began searching the area with his lit palm. Suddenly there was a girlish shriek and the sound of something collapsing. They bolted towards Bridget, finding her entombed in a pile of burnt timber—the remains of the stairs. Two white eyes blinked from a soot-black face.

"Don't you dare say anything—" she hissed through gritted teeth as they each offered her a hand. "I can stand up on my own, thank you very much." She calmly used Telekinesis to push aside the charred planks, trying to keep what was left of her dignity.

He and Leera didn't even exchange glances, knowing that if they did, both of them would break out in laughter.

They moved on with their search, navigating a plethora of charred obstacles. Augum saw a small hole behind some debris. Following his intuition, he shoved the largest piece of timber out of the way, revealing a spacious cavity in the wall.

"There's another room here!"

The girls fought their way over as he shone his light inside, observing a curious set of cubbyholes against all the walls, most filled with sheaves of charred parchment.

"This must be it." Leera shoved aside another charred plank. "Look—scrolls! Or what's left of them anyway." She picked up one burned husk and it disintegrated in her hands.

They began searching the cubbyholes. Finally, Leera stuck her arm in one all the way up to her shoulder, carefully extruding an unburned scroll. "Got one!" She immediately began unrolling the parchment.

"Great, another one of these," Augum muttered, eyeing the contents. The script, as with the Group Teleport scroll, was small, detailed and wordy.

Bridget tapped the heading. "Slow Time. Might come in handy."

"We'd have to practice reading it." He recalled how difficult the pronunciation was with Group Teleport. If it hadn't been for Centarro …

Leera pointed to a particular passage. "It only affects one person though. That means careful planning."

After everyone had a good look, she rolled it back up and they finished searching, finding nothing else.

"Wait a moment, let's all try Unconceal," Bridget said.

"I'll keep my light on." He wished he knew how to chronocast. It'd be awesome to cast Unconceal while keeping

Shine going at the same time. Mrs. Stone knew how to do it. He wondered if it was even possible to learn at his degree.

The girls fell silent with concentration while he looked on, unconsciously dimming his light a little.

Bridget glanced up. "Did you just do that—?"

"Do what? I was just standing here."

Leera also stared at him. "I noticed it too—you dimmed your light like Mrs. Stone. How did you do that?"

"Oh, that." He shrugged. "I don't know. I guess I just … did it."

Leera gave him a wry look. "Teach it to us."

Like toddlers finding a shinier object to play with, they forgot about the Unconceal spell and immediately began practicing dimming Shine instead.

As a testament to their adeptness, they were soon dimming and brightening their palms with ease.

"Thanks for that little lesson, Mr. Stone," Bridget said. "Where were we?"

"Unconceal," he replied.

"Right." She closed her eyes for a bit. "Un vun deo."

He lit the way for her, Leera resting and watching from the sidelines. Bridget delicately held her hand before her, fingers spread wide, feeling for the slightest hint of intent to hide something. For a while, she only stood there.

Augum exchanged an unsurprised look with Leera.

Suddenly Bridget began moving towards a burnt bookshelf. "There's something behind here." They immediately pushed the bookshelf out of the way, revealing a small iron door.

"I don't believe it," Leera said. "A secret door …"

Bridget kneeled down and pulled on its inset handle. The door creaked open and they leaned in. "It's another scroll." The parchment was cracked and yellow. She carefully unfurled it and started reading.

Thus leans this wickedest stone
So shall grant the oldest crone
One wish speaketh without fear
Be warned it shall becometh real

So shall ye giveth tooth or bone
Of ancient wings and death reborn
And warned ye be it would be best
If ye followed one Lord of Death

Find thy mark three pointed star
Shout with Shine your wish bizarre
Crush the object against the stone
And prepare to meet the ancient crone

When she finished, they exchanged ominous glances.

"Sounds like a vile curse or something," Leera whispered. "Like necromancy …"

Augum squinted. "There's something else written in the margin."

Bridget twisted the scroll, struggling to read the tiny script aloud. " 'Beware thy wish be true and plain, for in exchange thy soul she'll drain'."

He frowned. "What does *that* mean?"

"It means we can't screw up the wording," Leera replied. "Or she'll swoop in and suck out our guts."

"It has to mean she'll drain our arcane stamina," Bridget said. "So it's particularly important to get the wording right, because otherwise we'll be left defenseless." She traced over the words with her finger. "So what I'm getting from this is—and sorry for the rhymes, but—if you crush a tooth or bone … against a stone … you'd be visited by some old crone … who'd then grant you a wish."

Leera made a sour face. "Sounds like bad poetry."

"So what do you think it means by 'three pointed star'?" he asked.

Bridget bit her lip. "Maybe you have to do this at night, pointing at a particular formation of stars. It's probably some sort of pillar or something. And I think you have to cast Shine while you shout your wish, because it says 'Shout with Shine your wish bizarre' …"

"And obviously you have to be a follower of the Lord of Death," Leera said.

"Well, it just says 'it would be best'." Bridget read the scroll again to herself, lips moving silently. Suddenly she glanced to Augum's chest.

"Why are you looking at me like that?"

Bridget met his gaze. " 'So shall ye giveth tooth or bone of ancient wings and death reborn'…"

Suddenly it dawned on him what she was talking about. He reached down his robe and pulled out the black tooth amulet One Eye had given him, fingering its course edge. "But … this is a bear's tooth. It has to be."

"And what if it isn't?"

For a moment, they just stared at it.

"Well, if it really is a dragon's tooth, this is our chance to find Mrs. Stone," Leera said, voicing aloud what Augum was thinking. "Now all we have to do is find the stone to smash it against."

"Wait, I know what we can try—" he said. "Let's cast Centarro and concentrate on the verses. Maybe something will come to mind."

Bridget glanced about. "This isn't exactly an ideal place to suffer the side effects of that spell."

Leera shrugged. "Maybe just one of us should cast it."

The girls looked at him.

"All right, I'll be the dummy."

"Just be sure to think of what you're going to do when it wears off," Bridget said, smoothing the ancient parchment at his feet. The girls took up sentry at the exit of the little cave-like room, keeping their palms lit so he could read.

He made himself comfortable. "All right, here goes." He drew in a series of long breaths and stilled his mind. Then, as per his great-grandfather's instructions, he took a few moments to note the details of his surroundings—the fine penmanship on the ancient parchment, the creases marring its surface, the soot lines in the palm of his hands …

"Centeratoraye xao xen."

The world sharpened and magnified. Everything became a poem, every concept simple. Time seemed to slow. The parchment shone with clarity, sunshine awaiting shadow, but he was in no rush to begin. He locked eyes with Leera. She was a visual song, the freckles on her cheeks dancing with joy. The soot that covered her. She was night in the form of a girl. He smiled confidently and she smiled back—a strangely sensitive, embarrassed smile. Her cheeks brightened ever so subtly. He knew he was the only one to see that.

Bridget's face expressed concern, which he resolved with a smile. Her hazel eyes communicated compassion and hope for a better future.

He felt a wave of gratitude sweep over him, for their friendship, their companionship, and their belief in him. He let the energies settle and dissipate in the great forever of the moment, before visualizing himself lying down as soon as the effects of the spell wore off, watching the ceiling calmly. The trick was for him not to be disturbed, so he said, "I'm going to lie down after, don't let me see you." Bridget and Leera exchanged perplexed looks, but he knew it was the right thing to say. He smiled harmoniously and turned to the scroll, feeling every beat of his heart and hearing every subtle sound, from the scraping of his boots on the charred ground to their rhythmic breathing.

He read the poem again, first focusing on the three-pointed star. Memories of anything to do with the number three flooded his mind—three shovels propped against the Penderson farmhouse; a three door ironwood wardrobe in Castle Arinthian; three dark ovens, mouths forever gaping; three knights mingling before a bloody room, silhouetted by torchlight and talking in low voices; his great-grandfather speaking of the three kinds of undead; a withered Leyan woman with milky eyes and a faded emblem on her cloak—a triangle with a black dot at the end of each point, *a three pointed star …*

"I know what it is," he whispered as his mind began to fog. Now to complete the plan. He lay back on the ground, watching the ceiling with its greenish-blue light, lit from a nearby source, a source he knew to be friendly, though he could not remember exactly who or what was casting that light.

He did remember garbled thoughts of burnt wood and black soot faces; a gigantic gaping hole in the floor and someone falling … The thoughts twisted into a vile face, staring at him from the abyss. The face loomed larger and larger, until he was but a speck in comparison, terrified of being swallowed, a miniscule fly in an eternal cave.

He heard himself whimper and the light upon the ceiling wavered, like flames coming to life. Suddenly a great raven appeared, ready to peck out his eyes. He called out, covering his face with his hands, pleading for it not to take his sight. He could feel the soot walls creep in on him, making it difficult to breathe. He felt himself expelling air quickly and inhaling more, quicker and quicker and quicker …

* * *

Augum suddenly sat up in a cold sweat, head pounding as if being kicked. His stomach felt inside out and his hands vibrated with weakness.

"You all right?" Bridget asked, worried eyes reflecting the greenish light of her palm.

"I ... I think it was my fault," Leera said, giving him a sudden hug. He coughed involuntarily and she let go. "I stepped forward when you called out. I didn't mean to, but it was too late, you already saw me ... I'm so sorry."

"You were the raven," he said.

"Huh?"

"Nothing, it just ... it turned into a nightmare." He shook out his arms, dispelling that lingering feeling of dread. They gave him a few moments to recuperate.

Bridget brushed the soot off his back. "At the end you said, 'I know what it is'."

"I did say that, didn't I?" He had to work to concentrate through the fog in his mind. Suddenly the memory came flooding back, vivid as a bright cloudless morning—the triangle, each point accented with a sharp black dot.

"Remember Magua from Ley? The one with milky eyes?"

Leera smirked. "How could we forget?"

Bridget's eyes narrowed as her memory jogged. Her face lit up. "The triangle-thingy, with the three dots—it was on her cloak!"

"Yes, I see it now," Leera said, "but what does *she* have to do with all this?"

They took a bit of time, thinking things over, but no answers came forth.

"We still need to find out what stone it refers to, and where it is," he said at last, choosing to change the subject. Perhaps the significance of the triangle will come to them later.

"The verse could refer to a leaning pillar, or maybe a tower," Bridget said.

Leera cracked her knuckles as if preparing for a fight. "That's it, I'm trying Centarro." Upon seeing the look on Bridget's face, she added, "Don't worry so much, Bridge, I promise I won't run off to play in the snow like last time. Anyway, I need the practice." She flashed a cheeky smile.

Augum and Bridget stood back. He lit up his palm, dimming the light just enough so it wouldn't distract Leera. She sat down on her knees before the scroll and read silently, lips moving. She then closed her eyes and took a series of deep breaths.

"Centeratoraye xao xen."

Time passed as she only sat there. "Shine the light in my face when I slide," she finally said, before opening her eyes and focusing on the scroll.

Augum thought he understood what she wanted—to be distracted by their shining palms when the side effects kicked in.

She stared straight ahead. " 'Thus leans this wickedest stone, so shall grant the oldest crone, one wish speaketh without fear, be warned it shall becometh real … Thus leans this wickedest stone … thus leans …' " Recognition dawned on her face. "Hangman's Rock."

He looked to Bridget—of course, the answer should have been obvious. The Rock *leaned*.

When Leera's eyes began glazing over, they shone their palm-light in her face. Leera gazed into the light with a dreamy look.

Eventually she winced, touching her temple. "That was … intense. Head hurts."

Bridget helped her stand. "We should have seen it right away—'leans the wickedest stone'—Aug, remember the claw against the tent?"

He nodded, the memory as fresh as if it had happened the day before. He pictured that black tilted rock, remembering the stories about it. "So now that we know what symbol to look for, where to find it, and what to use—" He held up One Eye's amulet. "All that's left is coming up with a wish."

"And wording it right," Bridget said.

"*And* getting past the Legion," Leera threw in.

They stood silent a moment pondering the enormity of the challenge.

Leera snorted. "Anyone else think it's suicide?"

"Me—" he said.

"Definitely suicide—" Bridget said at the same time, nodding.

They looked at each other.

"So we're going to do it?" Bridget asked.

"Definitely," he and Leera chorused.

Bridget sighed. "I think I'd like to see my parents now."

"Want us to come with you?" Leera asked.

She only shook her head.

REVELATIONS

"Goodness, goodness me—" Mr. Goss said upon laying eyes on Augum and Leera. "You two look as if you have been mining coal—"

"Mr. Goss, we think we found a way to get to Mrs. Stone," Leera said.

"That is all fine and well but we simply must have you wash up. And where is Bridget?"

"Visiting her parent's graves."

Mr. Goss gave a pained smile. "Such things are always best experienced alone." He sighed. "I will fetch the washbasin and warm you up some water." He handed them a cloth for the meantime.

Leera and Augum sat down with tired groans, using the cloth to wipe their hands.

"We need to come up with a plan," Augum said, watching Mr. Goss pump some water and place it over the fire.

"I know." Leera retrieved Mrs. Stone's blue book, plopping it on the table.

Augum read the title of the ornate tome. *On Arcaneology: A Pupil's Encyclopedia of the Arcane Arts*, and fondly thought of Mrs. Stone and Castle Arinthian. Then he recalled one of the last things his great-grandmother said to them before leaving Ley: "Train and work hard. Practice every day. You must learn to protect yourselves. I will leave you the blue book on arcaneology—use it well. I expect that upon my return you will have a thorough understanding of the 2nd degree. Above all, look out for each other."

He sighed. They'd hardly studied from the book.

Leland felt his way into the room.

"Want to help us, Little Lee?" Leera asked.

He nodded.

"Why don't you flip the pages for us—we don't want to get them dirty or wet."

Leland moaned and groped his way to the book, running a scarred finger over its ornate cover.

"Neat, eh?" Augum said, clearing his throat before changing his voice to mimic an old arcaneologist. "Son, what you are feeling there is hundreds of years of hand-written arcane knowledge."

Leera giggled and Mr. Goss gave an appreciative nod.

"It has been passed down from generation to generation," Augum continued. "The ornate foil is made of gold, the tome itself bound in dragon hide. They say, 'All who toucheth this book will find happiness in life …'."

Leland made a sort of giggle moan as he thumbed through the pages, feeling the coarseness of each one.

"Now you have to help us find …" Augum raised an eyebrow at Leera. "Wait, what is it we're looking for?"

"Mrs. Stone wanted us to learn the 2nd degree, remember?" Leera replied. "So I want to find out what we're missing."

"Funny, I was just thinking we needed to play catch-up," he said.

"There! Stop there, Leland." Leera scanned down the page. "Here we are, 2nd degree spells. There's Shield—we sort of know that one, though we could use some more practice with it; Push—we don't know that one yet; and Disarm—definitely don't know that one."

"We also need to practice the Slam spell," he said.

"Water's ready," Mr. Goss announced, retrieving the ceramic washbasin and placing it near the fire. "So, what did you lot find over at old Tennyson's house?"

While Mr. Goss prepared the towels, Augum and Leera recounted the whole adventure, including Bridget's accident with the stairs.

Mr. Goss looked horrified. "But she could have very well been killed—"

"No, but, it was really funny, Mr. Goss," Augum said with fervent nods from Leera. Nonetheless, he quickly proceeded to the part about the Slow Time scroll and the ancient verse.

"... So we think that we can make one wish at Hangman's Rock," he concluded.

Mr. Goss carefully removed the steaming iron pot of water from the fire. "I must say I am more than a little concerned. This arcanery you speak of sounds dangerous." He poured the water into the washbasin.

"But we have to try, Mr. Goss, we have to."

Leland mimic-moaned in agreement, planting his feet and crossing his arms indignantly.

Mr. Goss gave Augum a searching look and slowly nodded. "I know you do." He dropped a couple towels into the steaming water, stirring them with iron pincers. "All this talk of Hangman's Rock reminds me of an old legend about witches being hung from there by superstitious peasants."

"Yeah, we've heard that one," Augum said, exchanging a knowing look with Leera. Robin told that tale to scare Leland the night they encountered the claw at Hangman's Rock.

"Very well then, but did you hear the one about the three candle sacrifice?"

They shook their heads.

"Ah, then allow me to pass on the legend, a favorite for us chandlers." Mr. Goss removed his spectacles, placing them on the table beside the open tome. "Legend has it that a long time ago, before arcanery was even understood, a coven of witches began exploring arcane sacrifice. They tried all manner of animal and creature, but nothing yielded eternal life. Then one day, they placed an innocent girl amongst three tall candles. After uttering their usual curses, one of the witches killed the girl with a sacrificial dagger. It worked and they became immortal.

"However, there was a steep price to pay for this immortality—they were banished to a separate plane of existence, where they could roam eternally. From this plane, they used their newfound powers to snatch all manner of innocent creatures from the mortal world, enslaving and corrupting them for their purposes. Over many eons, they populated that plane full of demons and monsters. Can you guess what name we give that plane now?"

Leera gulped. "Are you speaking of hell, Mr. Goss?"

"Indeed. Hell is one of the oldest words. Superstition was rampant as people disappeared. Arcanery was branded as evil, setting back arcane learning for thousands of years. Women of all kinds were declared witches and hung, hence Hangman's Rock. That tale is called 'The Legend of Three Candles'."

"But why isn't it called something like, 'The Legend of How Witches Began'?" Augum asked.

"It has to do with the arcane number three. Throughout ancient history, the number three has been perceived unlucky and unholy—but also quite powerful. To this day, it is considered very bad luck to come across three candles, especially in triangle formation"

"—wait, a triangle! So that's what that is!" Augum hurriedly unfurled the scroll with the verses on it. "Three pointed star refers to the symbol of the witch! It's what was on Magua's cloak—that's the symbol we have to find on Hangman's Rock!" He read the poem aloud again, every sentence now ringing true.

" 'Thus leans the wickedest stone', which must refer to Hangman's Rock—" He skipped on to the other relevant parts. " 'So shall ye giveth tooth or bone', which means this—" and he showed the supposed dragon tooth amulet. " 'If ye followed one Lord of Death'—"

"—except none of us do," Leera chimed in with a frown.

"We'll worry about that later then. 'Find thy mark three pointed star', which we now know refers to some kind of triangular symbol. 'Shout with Shine your wish bizarre'—"

"Which will be to teleport to Mrs. Stone," Leera said.

"Right, and lastly, 'Crush the object against the stone'—"

"—smash the tooth against Hangman's Rock!" they concluded together in mutual excitement.

Mr. Goss' face grew serious. "Augum, do you mean to say that you will be asking for a favor from a witch in hell?"

"Um, I guess so."

"As desperate as you are to get to Mrs. Stone, I am not sure I approve of this plan."

Augum was having second thoughts too. What if they ended up in hell instead of by Mrs. Stone's side? Yet what choice did they have? His father was well ahead of them and they had already lost valuable time. This was probably their one and only chance to get to her before he did.

The trap door opened and a soot-stained Bridget descended the steps, padding over to sit beside Augum and Leera. Her eyes were red and her shoulders drooped.

Leera gave her a squeeze. "Oh, Bridge …"

Bridget gave a pained smile. "I'll be all right."

"The water should be ready," Mr. Goss said. "Now if you'll excuse Leland and I, we have some wood foraging to do."

They watched father and son quietly depart.

Leera poked Augum. "Go away, you mischievous villain, we're washing up." He excused himself to Leland's room, taking the verses with him, overhearing Leera recount Mr. Goss' story to Bridget in between splashes.

"… So we think it's the witch's mark," Augum called in conclusion from Leland's room. "And that's what we have to find on Hangman's Rock and use Shine on."

Bridget's voice flooded back. "A witch? What if she snatches us to hell?"

"We think it's a risk worth taking. You two done yet?"

"Yeah yeah," Leera grumbled. The girls soon appeared at the door, looking as fresh as pixies.

Augum handed Bridget the verses. "I'm worried about this line here." He pointed to the part that read, *And warned ye be it would be best if ye followed one Lord of Death.*

"Me too, let me think on it."

Augum boiled some more water and took his time washing up, enjoying the rare solitude, the heat of the water, the crackle of the fire.

"So I think I may have a solution," Bridget called from the other room just as Augum finished. He showed up at the doorway, leaning against the frame.

"Solution to what?" Leera asked absently, concentrating on fixing Bridget's hair.

"To the fact none of us follows the Lord of Death."

"Oh, right … so what is it already?"

"Haylee—OW!"

Leera had involuntarily jerked on one of Bridget's braids. Augum realized Bridget was unaware of what happened between Leera and Haylee outside.

"Sorry," Leera mumbled.

"As I was saying," Bridget continued, "if we found a way to rescue her, she could be the one to perform the spell—ouch! Gentle, Lee—"

Leera grunted. "That's a lot on our plate. I mean, we'd have to somehow sneak by the Legion, rescue Haylee, explain everything to her so she did the ritual correctly, and then somehow not get thrown into hell or captured or killed along the way. Couldn't be easier, eh?"

"And don't forget we have to get past the walkers and a giant wraith," Augum added.

"I don't see how there's any other way to get to Mrs. Stone before Sparkstone does," Bridget said, wincing from Leera's handling. "We just have to plan it well and study our spells, that's all."

"Actually, we were already thinking of doing some serious studying today," he said.

"Good. Are we in agreement then? Rescue Haylee and get her to perform the ritual?"

"I'm in," he said.

Leera sighed. "Fine …"

They moved back to the kitchen where Augum withdrew Tridian's map and splayed it on the table. "Haylee placed my father and his men somewhere north of Antioc, here, and since they're on horseback, that means we should still have a day or two to prepare before they reach Nana in the Northern peaks."

"Let's just get as prepared as possible before going on this crazy quest," Bridget said, exchanging the map for One Eye's parchment. "Looking forward to learning Slam properly now that I'm not paralyzed." They began studying the spell, referencing the arcaneology book, the element book from Evergray Tower, and One Eye's intricate Slam scroll, but it didn't take long for them to realize they were in over their heads.

Bridget tossed One Eye's loupe onto the parchment and rubbed her eyes. "It just doesn't replace a mentor. So much I still don't understand."

Leera, who had been trading punches with Augum under the table after losing focus, grunted in agreement.

"We know enough to try the spell though, don't we?" Augum asked.

Leera snorted. "Speak for yourself. And even if we did, we can't do it outside—too loud." Bridget gave Leera a haughty look. "Maybe if you'd actually do some studying and stop fooling around—"

Leera straightened. "What do you think I've been doing! Just because—ugh, give me that." She yanked One Eye's parchment from the table and stood up to pace with it.

Augum and Bridget exchanged a secret smile. It was funny seeing Leera take studying seriously.

Just as Augum was about to jokingly tell her to stop pretending to be Bridget, Leera made a fierce gesture as if flaying the ground with an invisible whip. "GRAU!" They heard an enormous volume of water crash around them, so real everyone, including Leera, dove for cover under the table.

"I don't believe it," Leera said through snorts of laughter. "For once *I* beat you all to it!"

"Well, I feel stupid," Augum said as they crawled out from under the table.

Bridget grabbed Leera by the shoulders. "I. Am. Impressed."

"Whoa, Aug, did you get that? Let the record show that Bridge *actually* paid me a compliment."

"Noted on the record," Augum said with a nod. "Heralds will be sent to all four corners of Sithesia with the news."

"And watch this." Leera strode over to the table, holding her nose exceptionally high. "So a couple things here," she began in a highborn accent, perusing the scroll with a dainty finger, "as we get better with the spell, we can control its source location, volume, and even the sound itself."

"All right, you've made your point, Miss Bragpants," Bridget said with a smile. "Now give us some pointers.

Leera punched both of them in the shoulder at once. "More than happy to."

She turned out to be a surprisingly good teacher. Augum and Bridget went on to successfully cast the spell twice, Leera five times. It was a spell that really required imagination, creativity and concentration, though not as much as Centarro, their favorite spell. Centarro had side effects, however, and Slam did not—other than the usual drain on arcane stamina.

By the time Mr. Goss and Leland returned with handfuls of branches, the trio were sitting around the table, panting.

"Come now, arcane warriors, give Leland and I a show! We heard the ruckus and are nothing short of intrigued. Let us see whose sound is fiercer!"

"You asked for it, Mr. Goss," Leera said with a mischievous smile.

And so they showcased Leera's water crashing, Augum's thunder, and Bridget's tree cracking. With each demonstration, Leland squealed with delight. Mr. Goss looked on with fatherly pride, hands over his ears.

"I think we have a clear winner," he said at last. "Congratulations to Leera!"

Everyone clapped heartily.

"And here's your prize," Augum said, handing her one of Leland's toys, a small wooden duck.

Leera raised it high like a trophy. "I have won the quacking! Hail to me!"

"Hail to Leera!" they shouted with a new round of clapping.

"Now let us break for supper," Mr. Goss said with a chortle after the excitement died down.

The trio, cracking jokes and prodding at each other throughout, helped prepare seasoned rabbit (Mr. Goss had traps set nearby and had caught one), spiced carrot and potato stew, salted and buttered hard bread, and, as a special congratulatory surprise, chocolate and cheese for dessert, courtesy of the late Mr. Bawdings. The merry feast eventually concluded with hot tea and a rosy fire.

LEARNING

After supper, Mr. Goss took Leland to his room to change his bandages and administer lessons in arithmetic and history, subjects that made the boy groan.

Augum glanced through the Orb of Orion. It was quiet above, the treetops glowing crimson in sunset. "Guess we should get back to studying. Push or Disarm?"

Bridget flipped through the arcaneology book. "Hmm … I think learning either spell without a mentor will be really difficult."

"What's it say about Push?"

Bridget skimmed down the page. "It's used to suddenly impact objects and people, very much like Telekinesis, but involving more energy and a trigger word."

"Which is?"

" 'Baka'."

Leera made a face. "Sounds like a chicken squawk."

"Shouldn't be too hard to learn though," Bridget said, flipping pages. "We already understand the principles of Telekinesis, and Disarm is similar in theory except …"

Leera glanced at Augum, mouthing, " 'In theory'."

Bridget finished scanning the page. "… Except there's way more subtlety to the spell. Oh, and it drains more arcane stamina."

"Is there a trigger word?" Augum asked.

" 'Disablo'."

"Push it is then," Leera said

Augum and Bridget agreed and the trio began by reading the chapter silently to themselves. Augum found the language of the book to be quite technical and wordy, and longed for a cheat-scroll like the one One Eye had gifted them, something in common terms with useful tips and tricks written in the margins. Noticing the glazed look on Leera's face, he suspected she wished the same thing.

"All right," Bridget said after finishing, tapping the page with a sigh, "I have a hundred questions, but they're all for Mrs. Stone. Honestly, I don't get half of this."

"I'm finding it a touch difficult too," he said, though truthfully he barely understood a thing.

"Don't look at me," Leera said, expelling a lungful of air. "I can only perform one miracle a day."

Bridget tried reading the tiny script again, but upon completion shook her head. And that is how it went for the next hour—a long slog of trying to comprehend the complex instructions to what appeared to be a simple spell. At one point Leera even joked they might have plateaued; reached their ceiling; come up against an insurmountable obstacle—

"—all right, we get it, Lee!" Bridget said.

Augum's shoulders slumped. "Think I'd rather go back to the iron room."

"Why the glum faces?" Mr. Goss asked, wandering in to put a pot of water over the hearth.

"It's this spell, Mr. Goss," Bridget said, gesturing impatiently at the book. "It's impossible without a mentor."

"Might as well be written in Nodian," Leera muttered.

"Mind if I take a peek at it?"

"Are you sure, Mr. Goss?" Leera asked. "Forgive me, sir, but you're not a warlock."

"Leera Jones—" Bridget said in an undertone.

Mr. Goss chortled. "Of course not, but I do enjoy reading. Perhaps I can help just a little."

Bridget pushed the large tome towards Mr. Goss, who sat down, patiently taking off his spectacles and folding them onto the table. He then placed his finger on the appropriate page and began scanning downward. The trio watched open-mouthed as he raced through the tiny scrawl, occasionally toning out a, "Hmm" or "Yes, indeed now."

"Well, it seems quite straightforward," he said after reaching the end of the page. "Which parts are you stuck on?"

The trio gaped before talking all at once. Mr. Goss held up a hand to still their clucking. "From the beginning, I take it?"

"Yes please," Augum said.

And so began a most unexpected tutelage under Mr. Goss, who was surprisingly adept at navigating the many complex words, being especially helpful with ones they never heard of, such as "onerous", or "ubiquitous", or "discombobulate", words which made important instructions sound like gibberish.

"How did you learn to read so well, Mr. Goss?" Bridget asked.

He leaned back and smiled wistfully. "I loved reading since I was a boy. I tried to get my hands on any book I could find. Alas, my joy of reading did not translate to a profession. I was content to be a chandler along with Annie.

I suppose you can say I did not want my profession spoiling my love of reading." He straightened. "Shall we continue?"

Mr. Goss was informative, modest, and patient. Although he didn't have an arcane bone in his body, his sharp intellect allowed the trio to make progress with Push *and* Disarm. Mr. Goss was so impressed by their determination he stuck with them until well past bedtime.

* * *

The next day the trio woke up early, ate a quick breakfast, and went on to study their entire roster of spells until supper, by which time they suffered from headaches, nausea and nosebleeds from pushing their arcane stamina.

Mr. Goss made supper while they recuperated at the table. Discussion quickly turned to how they'd tackle Hangman's Rock.

"We're out of time, we have to go tonight," Augum said, spooning up beef stew, nerves preventing him from tasting a thing.

And he wasn't the only one—Bridget kept curling strands of hair around her ears while Leera tormented the same potato with her fork.

"I think we should go early in the morning and observe them a while," Bridget said.

"Can we throw snowballs at them?" Leera asked.

Bridget ignored her. "We can use the Orb to watch their patrols, figure out where Haylee is, quietly free her, and tell her what needs to be done."

"If she hasn't been moved yet," Augum said, tapping the table idly. His finger froze in mid-air. "We need a distraction."

"Yes," Mr. Goss said, nodding while wiping his mouth with a cloth. "Send the majority of their force on a fool's errand, allowing you to free Haylee and use Hangman's Rock to make the wish." He delicately touched his burnt scalp before looking up. "I can help."

"But Mr. Goss," Bridget began in a whisper, "should anything happen to you, we'd never—"

"I know, Bridget, thank you." He glanced at his son, who pawed the table looking for his mug of water. Leera pushed it into his outstretched hand.

"I assure you, I will exercise the highest state of caution," Mr. Goss continued, watching his son clumsily drink. "Further, I have an idea. I could start a large lamp oil fire and run before they come. The Unnameables know I have scavenged enough of it."

"But what about the undead that roam the woods?" Leera asked.

"That is a risk we are all going to have to take, is it not? Besides, should anything …" Mr. Goss made sure Leland was occupied with his food before finishing in a whisper, "should anything happen … Miralda will take care of him, I am certain of it."

The trio exchanged a worried look. What if she didn't, or couldn't?

"Are you sure we can't talk you out of it, Mr. Goss?" Bridget asked.

"I am determined to help you whether you like it or not." He gave Bridget's hand a consoling pat. "Let us plan well."

"All right, so we have our distraction," Augum said, counting with his fingers, "we're going to watch the Legion and wait for Mr. Goss' signal, and then we're going to free Haylee and have her perform the ritual. That leaves—"

"—learning the Slow Time scroll," Leera said, glancing to the rucksack. "We're probably going to need it tonight."

"Right. Are we forgetting anything?"

Mr. Goss stood up and went to his room, coming back with two small identical bronze hourglasses, handing one to Bridget. "These were my father's. We can use them to synchronize. One turn is an hour. I suggest we make our way up there together, turning them over just before we separate. When the sand runs out, we turn them over again. At the end of that second hour, I will light the distraction fire. It should give me enough time and distance to build something to burn and then make my getaway."

"What about footprints?" Augum asked.

"One moment." Mr. Goss strode out of the room, returning with a pair of giant feathered snowshoes. "I built them to avoid the Legion. They are a bit slow, but do the job quite nicely."

Leera gave Augum an *is he crazy?* look.

"Oh, you know what? I have something else that would be of use." Mr. Goss paced back to his room, returning with a small brass cylinder-like object.

"What's that?" Augum asked, having never seen such a device before.

"It is a spyglass, made by the same glass maker that fashioned my spectacles. He extended it and handed it to Augum. "Give it a try."

Augum looked through the wide end but only saw a very tiny image. "It's broken."

"Try the other end."

Augum turned it around and saw everything magnified much closer. "Now *that's* a contraption!"

"Let me see—"

He handed it to Leera, who immediately used it in reverse to look at Bridget's forehead. "Whoa, there's a whole other world here—"

"—give me that—!" Bridget said, snatching it from her.

"Is it arcane?" Augum asked.

"Not at all," Mr. Goss replied. "In fact, it is made with nothing but patience."

"Anymore of that patience stuff left over for Bridgey-poo?" Leera mumbled.

"Ugh." Bridget retrieved the Slow Time scroll. "Can we begin please?"

"Just trying to lighten the mood."

"This is serious, Lee. We have to focus and prepare. Lives are at stake here, and you're … you're making jokes!"

Leera dropped her chin. "Sorry."

The trio took great pains in reading the scroll and understanding the instructions. Mr. Goss helped with translation while clearing the table. The spell was written in such a way as to be read quickly by one person, the most complex part being the very words that triggered the effect. They were difficult to pronounce, though not as difficult as the Group Teleport scroll they once had to read. As to who'd be casting the spell, that decision they'd leave until the time came to use it.

Satisfied with the scroll, they moved on to the lengthy task of wording the wish. This part was tricky. The margin-scrawled words, "Beware thy wish be true and plain, for in exchange thy soul she'll drain," reminded them they had to get it right. And who cared if their arcane stamina was drained if they appeared at Mrs. Stone's side?

Augum twirled a quill while reading what they had thus far. "So we agree that we mention Mrs. Stone, name everyone we want teleported, and also say the destination, which is the Northern Peaks."

Leera nodded absently, eyes glazed.

Bridget frowned. "Instead of naming a location, let's just say we want to be teleported right to her. And maybe we should also start on a respectful note. Something like, 'Oh, ancient crone, please allow us to communicate with you—"

"—but what if simply communicating with her turns into our wish?" he countered.

"Hmm, good point."

Augum held up the parchment. "All right, the phrasing we got so far, as if Haylee was saying it. 'We wish you to teleport Bridget, Augum, Leera and myself to Mrs. Stone's side without causing injury to us or anyone else'."

"Change it to Anna Atticus Stone," Mr. Goss said, drying plates with a cloth.

"Good one, Mr. Goss," Augum mumbled, scribbling away on the parchment, the page now filled with their earlier attempts, all scratched out and edited down to this one simple line.

"Maybe we should have her say all our names in full then," Leera said, head lolling on her hands on the table. "You know ... just in case?"

He once again scratched out the last line, writing a new one underneath with their full names present. "Anything else?" They shook their heads. He dropped the quill. "All right then, the wording of the wish is done."

"It would be best if we all rested before departing," Mr. Goss said, putting the last of the dishes away. "Come along, Leland. Let us give them peace."

Leland, who seemed to never tire of extending and collapsing the spyglass, handed it over and allowed himself to be led away. The trio unfurled their Dramask blankets on the floor and tried to catch some sleep. It didn't work. Anxiety about the dangerous quest ahead kept everyone tossing and turning. They ended up going over the plan, as well as their spells.

Mr. Goss strolled in a few hours later, circles under his eyes, face lined. "Are we ready?"

The trio, quietly sitting by the hearth, gave somber nods and folded up their blankets.

Mr. Goss wandered over to his counter. "I have provisions for you all—"

"No, thank you, Mr. Goss," Bridget said.

"Please save it for you and Leland," Leera added.

Augum nodded in agreement. "It's all or nothing on this one, Mr. Goss. We've already discussed it."

Mr. Goss glanced at them and shook his head. "You are good kids." He packed several skins of lamp oil, as many logs as he could fit, some dry tinder, and his special snowshoes, giving him the appearance of a large insect.

"We should depart," he said at last, calling on Leland to come in. The boy stumped in, scratching at his linen bandages.

"I told you many times not to scratch."

Leland moaned as Bridget embraced him in a gentle hug, followed by Leera and finally Augum, who kneeled before the boy.

"Don't worry, Leland, you'll learn arcanery just like the rest of us when you turn fourteen. Maybe the academy will be clear of the Legion by then and we can go to school together."

Leland drew Augum into a tight hug, holding him until Mr. Goss gently pried Leland's tiny hands away.

"Come, son, let me show you where the food is." He placed Leland's hands on the assorted sacks and cupboards, whispering careful instructions at every turn, before taking him to his room. There were more whispers followed by quiet moans and sniffles.

When Mr. Goss re-entered the room again, his eyes were moist. He took a last long look around, gaze settling on a framed embroidery of two hummingbirds. Augum saw that it was initialed A.G., for Annie Goss.

"Let us go," Mr. Goss said finally, and the foursome departed into the cold night.

THE WICKEDEST STONE

Dark clouds trawled overhead like soldiers marching off to war, backlit by starlight and the sliver of a new moon. Snow crunched underfoot. Breath fogged in the crisp, windless air.

Leera took it upon herself to unlock the Orb of Orion and stuff it in the rucksack, the straps already digging into Augum's shoulders. He used the occasion to take a final look around at the ruins of Sparrow's Perch, almost hearing the ghostly echoes of laughing children. He wondered when he'd see the place again—*if* he'd see it again.

Soon they were on their way, quietly passing the graveyard where Leera and Bridget's families were entombed. Augum, taking up the rear, stared into the darkness, recalling scores of twitching bodies as they dangled off the ground, lightning coursing through them. He thought of Leland's sufferings and Mr. Goss' quiet dignity. He thought of the many faces that ceased to be, all a result of the actions of his deranged father.

As their journey progressed, he reflected on the fact that this was his third time traveling to Hangman's Rock, and sure to be the most difficult. Butterflies of anxiety fluttered in his stomach, the same feeling he used to have when one of the Penderson brats wanted to beat him up.

It was the agony of the wait.

He kept going over the plan in his head, finalizing the details, imagining it going off successfully. Mr. Goss sets a distraction fire. They creep into the camp and free Haylee. They explain the ritual to her. Then they all sneak to Hangman's Rock and perform it.

But the more he thought about it, the more ridiculous the plan sounded. So many possible things could go wrong—could they free Haylee and teach her the wish and ritual in time? Would Haylee even be there? Would Mr. Goss light a strong enough diversion fire and safely return to Leland? Would Canes be at the Rock, or Corrigus, the high-degree sorcerer? Would there be protective enchantments that would give them away? Above all, could they do it while avoiding capture or death?

These questions and more buzzed around his brain like mosquitoes, until he found his breathing shallow and his nerves on the point of fraying.

Hours later, in the thick of a cold winter night, there came the distant sound of galloping horses.

Mr. Goss froze, his face a mask of stern awareness. "They are on the Tallows, headed to Hangman's Rock."

"A patrol?" Bridget whispered.

"Larger, I am afraid."

Augum felt a shiver creep up his spine. "It could be the Blade of Sorrows."

Bridget listened to the fading sound. "Canes may have used a speaking orb to warn him when Haylee was captured."

"Great," Leera said. "So there's a chance we'll see Canes, the Blade of Sorrows, and Corrigus all in one place. That should go well."

"We will adapt," Mr. Goss said. "I do suggest we hurry though, as we may need more time observing the camp. Let us not stop to eat."

The trio agreed and they took up a quicker pace. It helped warm them as well as fight the fear. They maintained this march for a long while, until Mr. Goss raised a hand. Everyone stopped as he put a finger to his lips.

"We are close," he whispered.

They quietly veered northeast, the sky now an open field of innumerable stars crowding a knife-like moon. The light made the snow sparkle brilliantly. Soon, they could hear the sounds of a bustling outpost, much like a disturbed beehive—the neigh of horses, the clatter of metal and harness, the sharpening of swords.

They crawled through the powdery snow to the forest edge, hiding underneath a large blue spruce with low-hanging branches. A manned watchtower perched atop Hangman's Rock, a giant banner with the Legion emblem of the burning sword ruffling from its pointy roof. Rows of canvas tents fanned out in concentric rings from the tower. Men in black armor and furs bustled about. Horses stood in long lines, drinking at troughs of water kept thawed with fire. Smoke rose in columns from countless other fires. A smithy worked away even at this late hour. The scent of grilled meat filled their noses.

Augum's palms were sweaty in his mitts. It was supposed to be a sleepy camp they had a chance of sneaking into. As it stood, counting the horses, tents, and parked wagons, he guessed there to be around a hundred men.

Suddenly something large arose from within the camp that sent a chill down his spine. It moved like a monstrous shadow among the tents, the men steering well clear of it.

"It's a wraith …!" Leera whispered, hastily retrieving the spyglass from the rucksack.

The wraith glided through the camp as if hunting for prey, its shiny wet black rags hanging in long strips that occasionally caught a glint of fire light. Those large limbs that seemed out of proportion for its body swung in sweeping arcs, perhaps hoping to catch a soldier unawares. Men held their noses if they came too close.

Mr. Goss' face turned pale. "What a horror …"

"Is that what you encountered in the woods?" Bridget asked in a fearful whisper, as if the thing, although so far away, would hear her.

Augum only nodded, unable to take his eyes away, expecting it to sprint towards them at any moment.

Leera bumped his arm, offering the spyglass. He took it and swept the camp, fixating on a figure wearing ornate black armor and a black surcoat. He instantly recognized the confident gait and the relaxed gestures dispatching men to various tasks.

"Commander Tridian," he whispered, confirming their conjecture that it was he who rode by them earlier. The others stirred. "And Robin," he added. Robin was near the commander, talking to someone ahead. Augum searched with the spyglass.

"Robin's talking to the wraith," he reported. "He's giving it commands or something …" Suddenly the wraith smashed one of the tents with a massive claw-like appendage. Men ran in all directions. Tridian even took a step back, shouting something incomprehensible from this distance. Robin calmed the wraith down, bidding it to sit like a dog. Tridian gave a nod and patted Robin on the back.

Another figure stepped forward, an old man in an ornate black Robe, its edges fringed with brilliant gold. He had a long gray beard and a thin, hard face. Even from this distance, Augum saw eyes as black as coal. Something about the way the man carried himself exuded power.

"Corrigus," he whispered.

"Damn," Leera muttered.

He spotted a portly man with curly hair approach. "And there's Canes … looks like they're having a meeting." He watched the villains make jokes, congratulate Robin. The Blade of Sorrows charged a few men to fix the tent the wraith had destroyed. The men did so hesitantly, never taking their eyes off the sitting monster that watched them.

Augum passed the spyglass to Mr. Goss, who frowned as he looked through it.

"This is going to be a little tricky, but do not lose faith."

"We might have to change our plans," Augum said.

"We have time," Leera said. "Let's just see what they do …"

They waited together, watching like hawks, snacking on biscuit beef and nuts while passing the spyglass around. With all the activity in the camp, it was evident the Legion was gearing up for something. As the glass came to Bridget for the third time, she reacted almost as soon as she put it to her eye.

"I don't believe it—" She glanced to Augum quickly before checking again. "I think it's Mya …"

His heart skipped a beat. Bridget passed over the spyglass. He frantically swept the camp, finally spotting her lithe figure before Robin, who glared at her. She stood wringing her hands, head bowed, wearing a plain red servant dress with the Legion emblem in the center of her chest.

He saw other girls wearing the same outfit, but paid them no heed. When he glimpsed Mya's almond eyes, a surge of electricity passed through him.

"We have to save her," he whispered. No one replied, but he didn't care. Crazy plans of rescue rolled through his head. As Mya disappeared to do Robin's bidding, he felt a sense of loss, and only then did he give up the spyglass.

"If I may, who is this Mya?" Mr. Goss asked, taking the glass from Augum.

"She's Prince Sydo's old servant," Leera said, her tone a little stiff. "Augum has a crush on her."

Augum reddened as Mr. Goss gave him a playful elbow. "She must be very pretty to get your attention, Augum."

"Oh, she's very pretty all right," Leera said. "Just too bad she's five years his elder."

"Ah, but age does not stand in the way of love," Mr. Goss went on, smiling, a faraway look in his eye. "My own mother was seven years my father's elder and they were very happy together."

Leera pursed her lips while Augum thought of ways to change the subject.

"I think that's really cute," Bridget said.

Leera gave her a dirty look before expelling a resigned sigh. "So what are we going to do now? How can we possibly save Haylee *and* Mya *and* still perform the ritual? I mean, the watchtower is directly on top of Hangman's Rock, right in the center of camp ..."

"It would be helpful if we could hear what they were saying," Bridget said. She gave Augum a meaningful look.

"The orb—" they chorused.

He dug it out of the rucksack along with its accompanying pearl, and studied the area between the forest and the tents. The grass was high enough and the snow just low enough that if he crawled, as long as no one happened to stumble across him, he could reach the southwestern-most tent.

"I'll plant the orb at the edge of the camp," he said.

Leera grabbed his arm just as he was getting up. "What if they have detection enchantments of some kind?"

"If there's no one to fear, why bother putting enchantments in place? Anyway, even if they did, wouldn't it be better to find out now?"

"Augum is right," Mr. Goss said. "They are not expecting anyone to sneak in, and it would be immensely helpful to overhear them."

Leera loosened her grip on him. "Just be careful."

Augum nodded, handing Bridget the pearl. "Here, warn me if someone's coming, I'll keep a close ear to the orb." He then crawled forward over a snow bank bordering the spruce, and scuttled into the Tallows.

His nerves jingled crawling up on the camp like that. Should a patrol stumble across him, should there be any protective enchantments, should the man in the watchtower stare too long in his direction—

"Stop—!" a tinny voice whispered from within the orb of Orion.

He froze just as boots approached. Two voices bantered back and forth.

"Imagine the celebration—"

"Ale for all."

"Ale and wenches."

"What do you think the servants have been brought here for?"

They laughed as Augum felt his blood quicken. His resolve strengthened to iron. The boots soon faded.

"You're good to go," Bridget said from within the orb.

He could almost feel the spyglass on him. He was sure she would be able to follow the slight waving of the grass. After all, there was no wind, which in this case was unfortunate because even a slight breeze would have helped mask his movements.

He pushed on, making it to the southwestern-most tent without raising an alarm. It seemed the Legion were too arrogant to cast any detecting enchantments after all. The tent was quiet so he crawled forward between it and the one over, right up to where the grass had been cut. He then very carefully planted the orb at the boundary. He judged that, by the lack of light and the way he sat in the grass, he wouldn't be seen—not unless someone actually walked right up to him and looked straight down.

"All right, lock it," he whispered into the orb, gently obscuring it with some snow. Just then, a familiar voice rang out close by.

"It is most fortunate indeed, Commander," Canes said. "Now all we need is the boy."

"Let us not celebrate yet, Commander," replied the Blade of Sorrows in a bored voice. "The trap has been set, but it still needs to be sprung."

"He knows where she is. He *will* succeed."

"You of all people should know never to underestimate the crone," Tridian said. "Lord Sparkstone understands this well. That is why he has asked you and Corrigus to join him."

"Now—?" Canes asked, voice almost a whine. "But, how can I possibly help our lord? I lack arcane knowledge."

"Lord Sparkstone is quite aware of your limitations. However, you have spent much time with her of late in the castle, and he deems such intelligence … valuable. Though if he had asked my opinion, I would have told him you were as useless as a donkey without legs."

"Perhaps if you had managed the simple task of holding the boy, none of this would have been necessary." Canes spat into the snow. "So where am I to go?"

"Semadon."

"Semadon! But that's—"

"—yes, it is," Commander Tridian said, voice edged with glee. "Corrigus will teleport himself, you, and forty of our best men in stages—if his arcanery lasts that long."

"It will last that long," growled a voice.

"Corrigus—"

It was amusing yet worrying for Augum to hear a note of fear in the Blade of Sorrows' voice.

"Perhaps you should use some of your time training our recruits, rather than sneaking up on the officers."

"If Lord Sparkstone commanded me to spare time in training the weak I would do so without hesitation," Corrigus replied. "As it stands, he deems my time too precious to waste, Tridian."

"*Commander* Tridian," the Blade of Sorrows said slowly.

Corrigus gave an amused grunt. "Lord Sparkstone summons us. We must depart with haste. I will be casting Group Teleport consecutively until all of us have departed. Be sure you do not dally, fallen knight."

"As you wish, Corrigus," Canes replied.

"Oh, it is not my wish, it is Lord Sparkstone's wish, and I know my duty. Get your men ready and meet me by the rock." Corrigus departed with a swish of his robe.

"You know, I do think the old warlock needs the comforts of a wench," Canes said with a half chuckle. When Tridian made no response, he sighed. "And you? What does our great lord have in store for you?"

"I am to find the boy. I will be riding shortly. I think he may be trying to get into the crone's old cave to acquire a Group Teleport scroll."

That would have been smart, Augum thought, realizing that although the cave had collapsed, it *may* have been possible to move the rocks using Telekinesis.

"Right then. Good luck to you, Commander," Canes said mockingly.

"I look forward to hosting you in one of my iron rooms when you slip, Canes," Tridian replied.

Canes snorted, turned on his heel, and began shouting commands to his men.

Augum was glad they despised each other. Now he just needed to find out where they were keeping Haylee and Mya …

"Did you hear all that?" he whispered into the orb.

"Yes," came the tinny reply. "Come back now before they discover you."

"On my way."

He began the return crawl. Midway, the night lit up with a bright flash originating from the camp, instantly followed by an implosive rumble—the first batch of men had been teleported. When he reached the spruce, Leera and Bridget each gave him their blanket to warm up.

"So let me get this straight," Leera began, "Corrigus will take Canes and forty men. A whole bunch more will go south with Tridian to look for us—"

"—and whoever's left we'll split further with Mr. Goss' distraction fire," Bridget said.

"Anyone happen to know where Semadon is?" Augum asked.

Bridget withdrew Tridian's sheepskin map and gave it a long scan. "It's not even on here."

"It is in the Northern Peaks," Mr. Goss said absently, watching with the spyglass. Another bright flash of light lit up the sky, followed by a low concussive rumble. "There goes another batch."

"We need to find out which tent Mya and Haylee are in," Augum said.

Mr. Goss passed the spyglass to Bridget. "Once all the men are gone, including Commander Tridian's attachment south, I shall run north and build a lamp oil fire. As we discussed, we will do two turns of the hourglass. I will start the fire at the end of the second hour. Hopefully it will clear most of the remaining men out of camp."

The trio nodded.

The flashes kept up a steady pace with relatively short intervals between.

Augum was amazed at Corrigus' arcane stamina. Such a complex spell, yet he could cast it repeatedly. It worried him this powerful warlock planned to attack his great-grandmother alongside his father.

"Shh, I think I hear Robin," Bridget whispered, closing her eyes while clutching the pearl. They anxiously waited for her to hear out what he had to say. "That evil little … they're keeping Haylee in chains in a tent on the opposite side of the tower. There's to be a trial when Tridian gets back from the south. Robin was gloating that they'll probably put her to death."

Augum glanced at Leera, who gave a tiny nod as if finally agreeing that they should indeed save Haylee.

"Here, have a look." Bridget passed the spyglass over to him. "The one with the guard outside it."

He found the tent in short order. It sat on the far side of camp, close to the middle and well lit by torches. Were there guards inside also? If not, maybe they could sneak in from the back, free Haylee, explain the spell, then somehow creep unseen to Hangman's Rock, where they would have to quickly look for the triangular witch's mark and perform the ritual. That's going to be the trickiest part.

But how to rescue Mya at the same time?

The more he thought about it the more impossible the plan seemed. There were just too many opportunities to get caught, too many risks …

When the flashes finally ceased, activity began around the horses.

"Commander Tridian's force is departing," Mr. Goss whispered, glancing at the trio with a grave look. "Are you three ready for this?"

They each gave firm nods.

Mr. Goss retrieved his hourglass, Bridget its bronze twin. They turned them over at the same time. To Augum, it was somewhat ceremonial—there was no turning back now.

"All right, you have two hours. I leave you with full confidence in your abilities. Please give Mrs. Stone my best regards and pass on my wish that we meet again."

Augum hardly knew what to say. His throat went dry and there was a hollow feeling in his stomach. Mr. Goss was really leaving them, taking a huge risk on their behalf …

"Mr. Goss, your spyglass—" Bridget said, voice breaking.

"Keep it, you need it more than I do. Goodbye and … good luck." With that, he crawled out from under the blue spruce and disappeared into the night.

"Goodbye, Mr. Goss …" Bridget whispered.

For a time the trio sat in silence, watching the particles of sand dribble down the neck of the hourglass. Augum thought of Leland and hoped Mr. Goss returned to him. He'd never forgive himself otherwise.

"They're departing," Bridget reported.

They began counting the horses together.

"…eighteen … nineteen … twenty."

"Twenty men gone to look for us," Augum said, spotting Commander Tridian among the departing group, but not Robin. "So including Corrigus and Canes, forty-two had gone to trap Nana, which leaves about forty still in camp. Now we wait and see how they react to Mr. Goss' fire."

"Think he has enough time to build it?" Leera asked. "And what about all the snow—won't it be hard to light a fire?

"I don't know," he mumbled. "I just don't know …" He hoped Mr. Goss' plan accounted for that.

They continued their surveillance as the camp settled down. They even spotted Bridget and Leland's healer, Ms. Miralda Jenkins, who appeared to be shooing soldiers to go to bed already.

Augum used the spyglass to check how many stood on watch—a man in the watchtower, a man standing before the prison tent, and one idly patrolling the camp, sometimes stopping to chat with Ms. Jenkins. He wondered why she was still up and what she would do if she spotted them.

"Almost time to turn," Bridget whispered, rubbing her eyes as the last sand particles dropped into the bottom of the bronze hourglass. She turned it over, embedding it carefully back into the snow. The time to act quickly approached. Dawn would soon come, and when Mr. Goss lit the fire, they'd have to move fast.

"All right, let's go over everything one last time," Leera said.

They went over the ancient verses, the Slow Time scroll, and strategized on how they were going to sneak in there, something that depended on how many left the camp to investigate the fire.

With about half of the hourglass left, Augum pressed the spyglass to his eye. Ms. Jenkins was still up, idly pacing the camp. Strangely, she stopped right where the Orb of Orion lay hidden.

"Bridge, you have the pearl in your hand? I think Ms. Jenkins might be signaling something."

She fumbled around for it. "Got it," and closed her eyes.

Ms. Jenkins took a careful look around before making a show of dropping something by accident. When she bent down between the tents, disappearing from his view, Bridget began nodding, eyes still closed.

"Yes, it's us. Uh-huh. No, we're here to save Mya and Haylee and use Hangman's Rock to teleport out of there. We have to find this triangular mark on—" A pause. "Uh-huh. All right. That's great ... no, but in about half an hour Mr. Goss will light a fire to the north, anything you can do to—uh-huh ... perfect, thank you, and what about—"

Augum shifted back and forth between the Bridget and the spyglass. Suddenly he spotted movement. "Guard coming—!"

"Ms. Jenkins, watch out—" was all Bridget had time to say.

He watched as Ms. Jenkins revealed to the patrolling guard the thing she had dropped, then seeming to profess her clumsiness, gesticulating how hard it was to find anything in the snow. The guard chuckled along, adding his own story, and the two moved on.

"All right, she got away with it," Augum said, putting down the spyglass.

"So what did she say?" Leera asked. "And how did she know about the orb?"

Bridget covered the pearl so she would not be overheard on the other end, just like when they were able to overhear Erika speak to the Legion. "Get this—there *were* detecting enchantments around the camp, but guess who placed them there?"

"Ms. Jenkins—" he and Leera chorused.

"Exactly—didn't take her long to figure out who crossed the arcane boundary."

"What's she going to do?" Leera asked.

"Well, she seemed to know about the witch's mark on the Rock and promised to help when the time came. Also, she said she'd try to send as many of the soldiers after the fire when it starts."

"What about Mya—?" Augum asked.

"Don't know. The guard wandered over before I could ask."

Augum checked the hourglass, judging about a third of an hour remained before Mr. Goss was supposed to start the fire. Excitement sharpened his awareness as he looked eastward to the horizon, spotting the first blush of dawn. A cold breeze sprang up, scratching at the branches of the blue spruce and shaking snow loose.

"It's time," he said. "I'll go retrieve the Orb. Let's meet on the other side of camp, closest to Haylee's tent. Don't go in there without me."

"All right, we'll take the rucksack," Bridget said.

He gave her a nod. "See you soon," and began crawling over his previous trail. The wind rustled the hardy grass of the Tallows, helping obscure his movements all the way to the southwestern-most tent, where he stopped to listen.

Someone snored inside. He edged closer and closer, stopping when the guard on patrol sauntered by. The snoring man coughed and the patrolling guard stopped briefly. Soon the rhythm of sleep resumed, as did the bored pacing of the guard. Deeming it safe once again, he slithered his way to the orb.

"All right, unlock it," he whispered, giving it a tug. It didn't give. He repeated the request but it wouldn't budge. He cursed himself for forgetting to tell the girls to unlock it before departure. They simply weren't paying attention to the pearl at that moment, so there was nothing to do but wait. Alternately, he could leave the orb there. The thought was amusing—having the ability to permanently observe the Legion outpost at Hangman's Rock, as absurd as it seemed, was an idea that could come in handy one day, if not here, then somewhere else maybe. After all, the orb was supposed to be indestructible.

He peeked out from the grass. He was stuck between two tents, with another one in front obscuring his view. The sound of footsteps had him frantically tugging at the orb again—but it was still locked. Cursing, he slunk back into the grass.

A shape appeared ahead. It hovered a few moments as if looking directly at him.

"Lose something else, Ms. Jenkins?" called a laughing voice.

"Not at all, Sergeant, I just can't seem to sleep tonight," she replied, walking back.

"Aye, I know how that feels. Miserable cold …"

Augum slithered back to the orb, worried something happened to the girls. "Hey, can you hear me?" he whispered. "Unlock the orb—!"

Finally, he felt it loosen in his hands.

"Sorry!" came a tinny voice from within.

He didn't bother replying, just happy to be able to crawl away. He swung southward in a wide loop, dragging himself across the path Tridian arrived and departed on. Luckily, no one saw him, his movements disappearing amongst the undulations of the grass. Eventually he stumbled upon Bridget and Leera's crawl-tracks.

The sky to the east continued to brighten, the night retreating westward. The stars would soon disappear, leaving the crescent sliver of the new moon, until the sun made its inevitable appearance, outshining everything. He had to get to Bridget and Leera before it became bright enough for the watchtower guard to spot him. Taking a risk, he decided to double-time his crawling, the Orb of Orion secured tightly under his arm.

Suddenly there came a piercing whistle. He froze, only feet from where Bridget and Leera had to be. His heart threatened to punch a hole through his chest. This was it, they had been spotted. He expected the entire camp to be running his way, until someone shouted, "Fire to the north! Fire to the north—!"

AGAINST THE ODDS

It's begun, Augum thought with nervous excitement. He crawled forward the rest of the way, taking advantage of the confusion erupting in the camp, stumbling upon Bridget and Leera nestling behind a black tent. The trio exchanged suspenseful looks as they heard the shouts of commands, the whinny of horses, and the hustle of men rushing to get ready.

"You okay?" Leera mouthed.

He nodded, handing the orb over to Bridget. She stuffed it into the rucksack, retrieving the Slow Time scroll.

Leera peeked around the north corner of the tent. Her head bobbed a bit as she counted the horsemen that rode off to investigate the fire. "Only fifteen gone," she said finally, meaning twenty-five still remained in the camp. Disappointing, since they'd hoped to be left with around ten or so. "There's too many walking around, we can't move yet ..."

Augum had an idea. He slowly lifted the bottom of the back of the tent, peeking inside. "It's empty." He lifted the canvas so the girls could sneak through. Bridget crawled in first followed by Leera, lastly Augum.

Inside was a neat cot, simple folding chair, and a small trunk. A thin layer of hay covered the ground.

Leera rushed to the door flap, taking the tiniest peek. "Ms. Jenkins is out there shooing them along. If we can get to the next tent, the one after is the prison tent. We're going to have to time it," and, without taking her eye off what was going on outside, gestured for them to get ready to dart across.

Augum nodded for Bridget to go. She tiptoed up behind Leera, breath steaming in rapid bursts.

"Hold … hold … ready … and … now!" Leera yanked open the tent flap and Bridget raced forward, braids flying and rucksack bouncing.

"She made it," Leera said, checking for guards.

Augum grabbed the flap. "You go next," and kept a steady watch. Bridget peeked out from the tent opposite, eyes darting rapidly to the left and right. She gave a wink that it was clear from her perspective. He waited another moment until a nearby Black Guardsman with an axe turned his back.

"Now—go."

She bounded across to the other tent. He was just about to jump out to take his turn when two burly men walked by, swords and armor clanking. They entered the next tent over.

"What do you think it is?" asked one.

"Couldn't say," replied the other. "There's nothing there, not even a farm. Strange, isn't it?"

"Probably some deserters lettin' a fire get out of hand."

"Well then it'll be the last thing they ever do."

Augum was forced to wait. It was too risky to go right then. Bridget, whose face peeked out from behind the opposite tent flaps, raised her eyebrows.

"One moment—" he mouthed. The bustle of the camp slowly died down. One particular man who was removing his breastplate headed directly for him. Augum immediately realized he was standing in the man's tent and dived under the cot just in time for the flaps to shoot apart, a weary sigh escaping the man's lips.

Augum held his breath watching the soldier's mud-splattered boots. The man sauntered over to the trunk, threw something inside, slammed it shut, and sat down on the cot. The wooden bed-beams creaked as he proceeded to pull off his boots, throwing them aside. Then he fell back onto the bed, almost crushing Augum's head in the process.

Augum lay motionless underneath, cursing himself for not running to the other tent sooner. He couldn't imagine what Bridget and Leera were thinking just then. There was nothing to do but wait for the man to fall asleep now.

His heart never ceased its pounding as he lay there, feeling stupid. Every time he thought the man was finally asleep, the bed creaked with movement. At last, after what felt like forever, the man settled into the steady breathing of sleep. Augum gently wiggled his way from underneath the cot. The camp had fallen quite silent by then, amplifying every movement.

Just as he was going to pull his legs out, the man suddenly turned on his side, his nose a hair's breath from Augum's. The soldier blearily opened his eyes, looked straight at him, and closed them again.

Augum held his breath. He expected the soldier to bolt upright and sound the alarm, but amazingly, the man's steady breathing returned.

Must have thought he was dreaming …

He waited a little longer before finally mustering up the courage to tiptoe to the tent flap. With one final backward glance, he peeked outside, spotting a relieved Bridget staring at him from the tent opposite. The morning sun brightened her face, having risen in the time he was pinned under the bed. He took the first opportunity to tiptoe across. When he got near, Bridget yanked him inside.

"What happened?" she mouthed. The camp was so quiet now communication was reduced to hand gestures and unspoken words.

"I hid," he mouthed back, making a motion like diving under a bed.

A patrol passed by the tent. They froze, listening to the footsteps fade away, watching each other with wide eyes.

They were now one tent away from Haylee.

He wondered how much time they had. The soldiers that rode to investigate the fire must have reached it by now. The question then was, would the soldiers be on their way back, or had they gone on to search the wood?

The tent the trio stood in was near identical to the last, except there were two trunks and two cots. Augum tiptoed to the far end, lifted the canvas bottom, and peeked out. The prison tent was less than five paces away. To the left were bales of hay, to the right, a wagon filled with oaken barrels. The tower loomed overhead and this time, because the tent they occupied was a lot closer, there was a direct sightline between the guardsman occupying it and their position.

This was going to be tricky. Not only would they have to sneak across unnoticed but also hope there wasn't a guard actually inside the prison tent.

He gestured to the girls about the tower guard then signaled he would go first, hoping they understood. Maybe that's something they should have practiced—hand signals.

The tower guard spent most of his time looking north toward Mr. Goss' fire, using a spyglass like theirs. Augum steeled his nerves, made one final check for anyone walking by, and scurried over to the prison tent. With one swift movement, he lifted the canvas and rolled underneath.

The tent was stuffy and relatively dark, the walls glowing from the diffuse morning sun. There was hay everywhere, along with post after wooden post embedded into the ground, manacles hanging from each. A lone figure hung from one.

Bridget crawled in followed quickly by Leera. Upon seeing what was inside, Leera stiffened, while Bridget put a shaky hand over her mouth.

He made to go to the figure but Leera grabbed his elbow, gesturing a reminder there was a guard standing directly outside the entrance. He nodded and the three of them crept forward.

A voice sounded from outside. It was Ms. Jenkins striking up a conversation with the guard. Did she know they were inside at that very moment? There was no time to dwell on it. As Augum approached the figure, he recognized the long blonde hair and his chest tightened.

Haylee's condition was dire. She was unconscious and scratched all over, her hands manacled above her drooping head. Her bloody feet were bare, her frame covered by a muddy burlap dress, cinched at the waist with rope.

Leera inspected the clunky lock and shook her head. They exchanged an ominous look acknowledging there was going to be no way to open it without using loud brute force or stealing the key, two scenarios almost impossible to pull off successfully under the circumstance.

Bridget placed a hand on Haylee's cheek, pushing aside a lock of muddy blonde hair. Haylee started awake, shriveling away from Bridget's hand, moaning loudly. When her eyes opened though, there was shock and hope there.

Bridget only gave a loving smile and placed a finger to her lips.

"Damn her, always moanin' about this an' that—" said the guard outside. The tent flap wavered and the trio stiffened.

"Oh never mind her," Ms. Jenkins interrupted, evidently staying the guards' hand. "Let me shut her up this time, you've been out here all night."

"That's most kind o' you, my dear."

The tent flap opened and in walked the bulging figure of Ms. Jenkins, her eyes taking in the scene as if it was exactly how she had expected it—the trio huddling near Haylee like rabbits ready to bolt. She walked up to them and started talking in a loud, threatening voice, all the while searching for something within her robe.

"I do not want you making any more noises, girl, or we will send in the brute, is that understood?" Haylee took her cue and moaned a supplicating response. Meanwhile, Ms. Jenkins finally found what she was looking for—a large iron key, promptly handing it to Bridget.

Augum wondered how she got it.

"Good, now keep your mouth shut," Ms. Jenkins concluded with a wink. She turned and walked right back out.

The trio exchanged surprised looks before Bridget readied to unlock the manacles, waiting for the conversation outside to start up again to cover up the noise.

"The prisoner needs to be fed," Ms. Jenkins said to the guard. "Let me send for a girl. I can make sure she brings you something, too."

"That would be fine, Ms. Jenkins, just fine."

Bridget finished unlocking the manacles just as Ms. Jenkins walked away. The lack of outside conversation forced them to be still.

Haylee couldn't stop shaking as she rubbed her wrists. Black circles ringed her eyes, cheeks red as if recently slapped. Suddenly she enveloped Bridget in a hug, shoulders quietly heaving. Bridget squeezed her and patted her on the back. Then she did the same to Augum, who whispered, "We're getting you out of here," into her ear.

Leera, who was edging away, was saved from a hug by a gaggle of footsteps outside. "What a treat," the guard said. A moment later, the tent flap opened and in walked Ms. Jenkins, followed by Mya carrying a tray.

Augum immediately felt a familiar tingle in his chest and gulped. Mya nervously smiled at them—Ms. Jenkins must have told her about their presence.

He kept staring stupidly before Leera elbowed him. Mya bent down and put the tray aside. They were readying to huddle and conspire the next step when a familiar voice crowed outside.

"Guard, I can't sleep, there's too much excitement in the air," Robin said. "I'm going in to talk to my *friend,* practice my skills."

Augum realized Robin was intending to put Haylee to the question. Ms. Jenkins seemed to have arrived at the same conclusion, sprinting for the entrance just as the tent flap rose.

"Now that won't be necessary—" Ms. Jenkins said, catching the flap just in time and stepping outside.

"Excuse me—?"

"The prisoner needs rest."

"Do you know who I am, woman? I am the favored necrophyte, soon to be training *personally* under the tutelage of none other than the Lord of the Legion! As well, I am the Blade of Sorrows' apprentice—Commander Tridian, to you—and that means that I am expected to put prisoners to the question in my spare time to advance my skills—"

"—that is all very well and good, young man, but this camp is responsible to Commander Canes. Further, I am the camp healer and I am afraid my authority in such matters is unquestionable."

There was a spitting sound as Robin marched off.

"What a rude little brat," the guard outside muttered.

"Never mind him, just enjoy the pastry." Ms. Jenkins soon returned, wiping her cheek.

"Another close one," Leera mouthed, reaching for a piece of bread. Bridget gave her a stern look though, staying Leera's hand.

Augum tried to make eye contact with Mya, passing on how good it was to see her, but she was too busy smearing a clear balm on Haylee's puffy face. Then he remembered what he had to ask. He tugged on Ms. Jenkins' fur-trimmed robe and gestured the symbol for a triangle, then held up his hands as if to ask, "Where is it?"

Ms. Jenkins replied with a leaning hand, symbolizing the rock. She pointed to her palm, meaning the symbol had to be on its underside.

He gestured his thanks just as the side of the tent suddenly rose, revealing a malevolent pinched face.

"I knew it—!" Robin said gleefully. Before anyone could react, the canvas dropped. "Guards! They're here, they're here in the tent! Guards, come quick—!"

Ms. Jenkins' arm immediately rippled to life with white rings climbing up just past her elbow. Augum, Bridget and Leera followed suit, each summoning their one and only ring, its light shining around their respective wrists. Haylee, too weak to stand on her own, hung on to Bridget with shaking hands, while Mya stood protectively in front of the pair.

The tent was quickly surrounded, the shadows of soldiers splaying on the canvas walls.

"Trapped—" Leera said.

A huge shadow loomed behind and over the tent, crisply defined by the rays of the morning sun. Long strips hung from two oversized appendages, stretched by the angled light.

The wraith hissed like a monstrous snake and the girls screamed.

Augum, forcing himself to do something—anything—snatched the Slow Time scroll from Bridget, opened it, and began reading aloud. He focused on the words, grateful they had practiced reading the spell, and began speaking them aloud.

Suddenly everything happened at once—Ms. Jenkins cast her own spell, Robin streamed in through the entrance with countless soldiers, and the wraith slammed its giant arms down on the back of the tent, collapsing it on top of them.

"Muerto tempus ideus deo didaeiee!" Augum shouted just as the canvas roof was about to hit him.

Everything slowed dramatically, including sound, which deepened and lengthened. Wood chips from splintered tent supports cartwheeled in slow motion. Dust glittered in bright morning light that streamed in through the rear of the tent. Robin's scowling face froze, shouting something indiscernible at this tempo. Augum looked down in real speed and watched the scroll evaporate, misting into a smoky cloud.

He knew the spell's duration. Under influenced time, he couldn't spare a moment. There was only one thing he needed to do, the only thing that could possibly save them—he needed to get to Hangman's Rock. Without another moment's hesitation, he bolted for the canvas door, pushing by Robin, who seemed to weigh as much as a horse. Robin's eyes tried to follow him, but they were far too slow.

He must appear a blur to them, Augum thought, crawling through a pair of Legion legs as if playing a game of Piggy Run. Everything seemed difficult to move—canvas felt like soft iron; his feet met the hardiest resistance from the smallest piece of snow; edges were unusually sharp and crystalline. Even passing through a cloud of dust was like swimming against a strong current of water.

He easily side-stepped a soldier drawing an enormous double-sided axe, dodged around two more soldiers running after the mob, and sprinted straight for the underside of Hangman's Rock, the watchtower sitting on top like an oversized mantis on the back of a bull.

As he passed a cooking fire, he couldn't help but notice how beautiful and otherworldly the flames appeared when slowed down. In fact, everything seemed strange, twinkling and glittering, vying for his attention.

In his blind rush to reach the Rock before the spell timed out, he made the mistake of thinking he could whip through a line of hanging linen, something that would have been completely normal in any other circumstance. Under the influence of Slow Time, however, the usually soft cloth felt like weighted leather hide, slapping him down to the muddy snow. The ground itself felt hard as steel, gouging into his back.

It cost him a moment to regain his composure, a moment he knew he couldn't spare. Fumbling forward, soldiers slowly turning his way, he jumped between the wooden log scaffolding of the watchtower, bracing himself against the icy surface of Hangman's Rock. There was a thin layer of frost along the entire underside. He thought it'd be nothing to pry the icy crust off with his fingers—until he actually tried, its hardness magnified by the spell.

He began stabbing at it with the only thing he could use—One Eye's tooth amulet. It, too, proved nearly futile, the many particles of ice not even clearing aside fast enough for him to be able to see.

Just as quickly as it started, the sound and movement sped up, and sped up rapidly. Suddenly everything moved along at impossible speed and he felt so slow, even though he knew reality was as it was before. He paid no attention to what was happening around him, returning to stabbing at the icy underbelly. Relative to before, striking the ice now felt powerful, like slicing through butter with a hot knife. A giant sheet gave way, cracking up the middle and falling on him. Almost unconsciously, he summoned his hard lightning shield and the ice plunked off harmlessly.

He looked up to see the witch's mark—a triangle carved into the rock, each point accented with a dot. Soldiers were streaming at him from all sides, almost at the scaffolding now.

In one fluid motion, he snatched a stone at his feet, lit up his palm, held up the tooth against the mark, and smashed it.

Hangman's Rock rippled to life like the surface of water, swallowing the shattered remains of the dragon tooth. For a moment he was afraid it would pull him in. A shadowy, stooped figure emerged just on the other side of that watery wall, emanating a horrible sensation of malice.

Meanwhile, gauntleted hands reached in through the scaffolding.

Damn, what was the wording for the wish? Quick, think of something, anything! "Tell Anna Atticus Stone that they're coming for her and that we're at Hang—"

Suddenly he was tackled from the side, the impact slamming his head against a wooden beam. As he lay crumpled beneath a black-armored Legionnaire, he heard a hissing whisper in his mind. Even as the walls of consciousness closed in, he willed himself to remember the words.

"Your bidding I shall do. A price I shall exact."

THE PRICE

Augum was awoken suddenly by freezing water hurled into his face. He began shivering immediately.

"Wake up, you disloyal traitorous swine—" said a vaguely familiar voice.

He groaned, head pounding with such ferocity he dared not open his eyes. His arms, manacled above his head, throbbed. Every part of him felt drained, every muscle sore.

He heard the sound of a bucket being placed on the ground.

"Fetch the commander, the brat's finally awake," said the voice. Feet rushed and tent flaps parted.

He tried placing that voice, but with every beat of his heart, a fresh spasm of pain shot through his head, smashing concentration.

"Augum, are you all r—"

The sound of a slap and a quick yelp.

"Shut it, missy. The commander does the talking."

Your bidding I shall do. A price I shall exact. That's what the crone said to him. And just as expected, she had drained his arcane stamina so much his head wanted to explode. But had Nana received his message? Would she evade his father's trap? Above all, were his friends all right? How could things have gone so wrong?

It was that cursed Robin …

Augum sensed many people in the room, yet no one spoke. Manacles clanked. The pad of light feet mingled with the subtle crunch of hay as a person adjusted their weight from foot to foot. A particular tension was in the air, a tension he remembered experiencing once before …

Someone with heavy boots entered the tent. Augum steeled himself before attempting to open his eyes, yet just the slightest glimpse of light made him cry out.

"He cries like a baby torn from its mother's grip."

Augum felt a cold wave wash over him. He knew that voice all too well—would *never* forget that voice, forever imprinted in that iron room.

"Justinius, send word to my apprentice."

"Yes, Commander."

There was the squeak of leather as the Blade of Sorrows crouched before Augum, cloak chain jingling against his chest plate.

"You seem to be injured here." The Blade of Sorrows squeezed Augum's head. A white-hot pain forced him to scream in agony.

A girl cried out, only to be silenced by a slap.

Tridian let go and pain ebbed away. "Oh, but that was merely a whisper. You are being sensitive, my boy, the fun has not even begun. You know, I was a little disappointed to have caught you so quickly. It was all … too easy. I was really hoping to drag this out."

Augum felt a strong kick to his gut. His eyes opened involuntarily and the white-hot pain returned. It was so intense he didn't even have time to scream.

Sometime later, he was revived by another sudden splash of frigid water to his face. His whole body seemed to pulse in spasm after rolling spasm. His arms tingled numb above his head. There was the sound of whimpering nearby.

"How far the rat has fallen," Robin said.

Augum, gasping from the cold shock, could visualize the bastard's grin.

"Do not let them know your thoughts, Apprentice," Tridian said in a bored voice.

"Yes, Commander."

Augum knew what was coming—another questioning. What did they want this time?

Robin crouched before him. "Open your eyes and look at me."

Augum ignored him.

"I said—"

"—never repeat yourself," the Blade of Sorrows interrupted. "It makes you appear weak. Instead, make the subject regret his impudence."

Augum heard Robin smile, an exhalation of breath as if he had discovered a new toy.

"Justinius, fill up the bucket."

"As you wish, Honored Necrophyte.".

Robin paced across from him. "Haylee, look at me. Did you enjoy our talk earlier?" He snorted a laugh. "I suppose there wasn't much talking, was there? Did you miss me? Sure you did. I missed you too. But don't worry, we'll be spending a lot of time together. Just like the old days, eh, Hayles?

"Damn you …"

"What did you say to me?" He repeatedly slapped her face, the sounds accented by girlish yelps.

"Don't you ever give me lip."

"Good, Apprentice, very good," the Blade of Sorrows said. "You must always assert your dominance as the superior."

"Thank you, Commander. Now, Hayles, I want you to know something—how that rat over there answers my questions will affect the outcome of your trial. Do you understand? Nod if you do. Good, that's a good girl."

Robin paced over to Augum, forcing Augum's head up by squeezing his jaw. "Look at me."

Augum refused. The pain of it would be too great and the trial was a farce anyway.

Justinius re-entered the tent with a slopping bucket.

Robin let go of Augum's chin with a pinching twist. "Hmm, which one shall we douse? Let's see here …" He began pacing, stopping before each of the candidates. "No, not her, she's got a special surprise awaiting her when our great lord returns. And not her, she's too ugly … Let's make it this one, she could use some cooling. Soak the dog."

There was a splash and a girl gasped for breath. Augum felt his skin rise. *It was Bridget!*

"You damned bastard—" he blurted.

There was a marked silence for a moment. "Oh, such a dirty mouth," Robin said with dramatic flair, as if acting in a play. He crouched.

Augum, who was familiar with the sound of an arm rearing back, flinched just enough to deflect the majority of the blow. Nonetheless, he felt his cheek swell.

"Look at me."

Augum felt the taste of salty iron on his tongue and spat it forward, hoping to hit Robin's face. There was an angry cry and a whirlwind of cheap blows.

"Apprentice," Tridian said in a silky voice.

Robin stopped, panting.

"Try not to let yourself be manipulated so easily."

Augum, barely conscious, was also panting. Nonetheless, he managed to smirk. His aim had been true.

"You'll pay for that," Robin said.

Robin roughly grabbed his chin. "This is what you're going to do—you're going to open your eyes, or that dog of a friend over there is going to get soaked again."

Augum couldn't let that happen. In this cold, another dousing could prove fatal. Yet he hesitated long enough to hear the slop of the bucket.

"All right!" he called just in time to stay Justinius' hand. He steeled himself and forced his eyes open. The light was a thousand daggers at his brain. He instantly closed them, writhing and screaming in agony.

"Stop it—! Don't you see he can't do it!" Leera cried.

Robin stood up. "Did I give you permission to speak, you nasty girl?" and casually kicked her, sending laughter through the soldiers.

Leera groaned.

"Stupid Leer." He kicked her again.

"Why don't you pick on me," Augum spat. "You coward."

Robin ignored him and kicked Leera once more. There was more scattered laughter as she moaned. Then he kicked her yet again. She barely yelped, and this time no one laughed. A silence befell the tent as there were uneasy stirrings.

"Leera?" Augum asked, wanting to throw up. "Leera, you all right—?"

"Good, Apprentice. You are learning well. Leave it there, lest you cause too much injury. Save that for true intransigence. Now you may begin asking the real questions."

Robin paced back over to Augum. This time he didn't crouch. "Yes, I do believe him ready, ready like … like …"

"Roasted rabbit," Tridian finished for him. There was a titter from the soldiers.

"Shut up, you common peasant rabble!" Robin said, but the chuckling went on for a little bit.

"You will make a fine commander one day, Apprentice, but there is much for you to learn on how to lead men."

"Yes, Commander. You there, what are you laughing at!"

Suddenly Leera screamed.

"That'll teach you, you filthy rat."

Augum knew Leera hadn't laughed. It took every ounce of restraint not to hurl the vilest curses he had ever heard.

Robin crouched before him again. "I'll only ask you one time. If you fail to tell us the truth, I'm going to consider that, um, 'true intransigence', and you can say goodbye to that gutterborn wench, the Leer. So … who lit the fire?"

Augum knew he was cornered. He had to answer, yet he couldn't give up Mr. Goss and Leland. "It was Mr. Bawdings."

"Who now?"

"Mr. Hedrick Bawdings, the merchant."

"You mean the very same fat oaf that's been lying dead in the woods gathering snowfall? *That* Mr. Bawdings?"

"Very good, Apprentice, very good," Commander Tridian said, clapping. "Now, how are you going to punish him for such blatant treachery, such … *intransigence*?"

Robin stepped back and drew a blade.

"No, please—" Leera suddenly made terrified muffled sounds as if her mouth was covered. Her feet kicked at the straw ground.

Augum struggled with his manacles. "Don't you even think about it, you—"

"What? What were you going to call me? Say it."

Leera let loose a blood-curdling scream even through Robin's hand.

"Robin, stop it!" Haylee shouted. "For the love of all that was good between us, stop it, please …"

Robin stepped back, Leera whimpering at his feet. "Hey, it was only a scratch. Wait, what am I hearing here? So now you're best friends with these disgusting gutterborns?"

Haylee just wept.

"That's right, cry your bleeding little heart out! And you better beg for me to take you back. Beg!"

"I'll never be by your side again, ever!" she said through sobs.

Robin just stood there a moment. "Wait, I know how this happened—" He dropped before Augum, leaned in, and whispered into his ear. "You took her away from me. For that, I will take them all away from you. I promise you that. Your father only needs you, he doesn't need them." He gave Augum a poke with the blade.

Augum gritted his teeth, breathing hard, trying to restrain himself. His manacles shook as he struggled, though it could have been the shivering.

"A little too eager, my young apprentice," Commander Tridian said as the crowd rustled nervously. "Never threaten the ultimate for such trivial matters. That you save for the *big* questions."

Robin stood up and sheathed his dagger. "Yes, Commander, I … I forget myself sometimes …"

"Don't … tell him … anything, Aug—" Leera said between gasps.

"Are you all right, did he hurt you?" Augum blurted.

"You'll never learn, will you? Justinius."

Leera gasped as she received another soaking, her teeth chattering uncontrollably.

"Hey, you should be thankful, I washed your wound. Oh, and douse her too while you're at it."

Haylee began breathing rapidly.

"Shut up, Traitor," Robin said. "I never really liked you, I only said that because I felt sorry for you."

Another splash and Haylee screamed, immediately descending into fits of shivering.

"M'lord—"

Augum's heart quickened at the sound of Mya's soft voice. He wondered how long she had been there in the tent. Strangely, he felt embarrassed.

"What do you want, servant?"

"M'lord, they will not survive long in such a state. Will you allow me to dry them and place a blanket around their shoulders?" Her voice sounded so sweet and so kind that it hurt Augum to hear it. It was a sharp pain inside his heart, overcoming the one in his head. He imagined those emerald almond eyes trained on him, filled with pity and caring.

Robin snorted. "Stupid peasant. I should have you flayed raw for your impudence." He strolled over to Augum, tossing a cloth in his face. "So if it wasn't Mr. Bawdings that lit the fire, who was it?"

He couldn't give up Mr. Goss and Leland. "I don't know ..."

"Liar. Douse everyone, starting with this one."

Augum barely had time for a breath before freezing water slammed into his face. He coughed and gasped, trying to regain control over his violently shivering body.

It wasn't long before Justinius returned with another full bucket, throwing frigid water in all the girls' faces. They shrieked in turn.

"No no, a full one for each of them," Robin said.

Augum wanted to protest but he was so cold now he actually stopped shivering.

"M'lord, please—"

"Shut up, wench, or I really will have you flayed." Robin sauntered back to Augum, crouching down before him once again. "Who lit the fire?" he asked quietly, almost kindly.

Suddenly Augum noticed something, or rather the absence of something. The mysterious force that usually coalesced within him, that might have once erupted violently in an electrical explosion, wasn't there. It was simply gone.

Your bidding I shall do. A price I shall exact.

The realization of what had really happened, the true price the witch had exacted, instantly snuffed any fight he had left. She had taken his ability to cast spells. This he knew in his bones. He slumped, the fight drained out of him.

"Ha, I think I broke him," Robin said.

"You'll never break him—" Leera spat.

Robin was swifter than a cobra. There was a sickening pulpy sound and audible gasps. Then silence.

"Leera—?" Augum said through trembling lips, but there was no response.

Robin leaned close. "She is on the brink of life and death now. Whether she lives or dies depends entirely on you. The final question that decides her fate. Who. Lit. The. Damn. Fire?"

Augum raised his head, knowing there was only one way to buy more time. Steeling himself with every ounce of courage he had, he squared his face with Robin's and opened his eyes wide. He screamed from the pain, holding them open, begging for unconsciousness to take him.

And it swiftly did.

ROBIN SCARSON THE QUESTIONER

Augum awoke to a quiet tent, a cloth dabbing at his scalp. A blanket lay draped around his body, his arms still manacled to the post above him, numb and useless. At least the pain in his head had subsided to a dull throb.

Testing his vision, he opened his eyes a slit and saw before him the outline of Mya's delicate features. He felt a peculiar lightness in his stomach. She seemed unaware of him watching her.

Candles perched atop wrought-iron stands flooded the tent with pale yellow light. He guessed it to be the evening of the day of their capture.

Something had happened to him, something bad that he didn't want to remember. Whatever it was, even the murky idea of it made him want to leave his body, to fly far, far away …

He began shivering.

"Shh, you're all right," Mya said in a voice as gentle as a spring breeze.

He looked into that caring face.

She gave him a troubled smile. "Close your eyes. You were so brave. Please, don't ever be that brave again."

Her voice calmed his roiling soul. He allowed his lids to rest, welcoming each tender touch of the cloth.

When she at last stood, he was almost in a trance. She moved on to Leera, who hung from the post beside him, unconscious, arms purple above her head. He noticed her chest rise. She was alive! Oh, thank all that was good, Leera was alive!

Bridget hung on the post beside Leera, asleep. Haylee hung on the post opposite him, Ms. Jenkins on a post beside her. The poor woman looked like she had taken a bath in a pool of blood. He wondered how the battle had conspired to capture her—was it the wraith, or one of the soldiers that overtook her?

Whatever happened, it didn't matter much. They had allowed themselves to be captured. Had Nana received his message? Why wasn't she here already if she had? Yet the witch exacted her price, so she *must* have received it.

To test the theory, he tried concentrating on a nearby pebble, hoping to draw it forth using Telekinesis.

The pebble didn't even wobble.

Maybe it was because his arms were tied above his head.

"Shyneo," he said, barely having the strength to look up at his purple arms.

Nothing, not even a spark.

Mya turned in his direction. "Augum, you must be very quiet or—"

The tent flap suddenly opened. He had the good sense to pretend he was still unconscious.

"Haven't you been attending to them enough, wench?" Robin asked.

"I only do as the commander bids me, m'lord."

"Yeah, well, I don't think he intended you to nurse them all night. Go and clean my tent. The peasant fool that it belonged to was a filthy pig." He laughed. "Must be related to you or something."

"Yes, m'lord."

Augum listened to her hurried steps fade. How he wished the plan hadn't failed. If only he'd been smarter, wiser, stronger …

Robin walked over to him and kicked one of Augum's feet.

Sharp pain shot up his spine, exploding his brain anew, but he dared not move.

"Damn," Robin muttered. He patrolled by the others before departing the tent, saying something to the guards outside.

Augum opened one eye to make sure the tent was clear before taking a better look at Leera. Her face was swollen and blue, hair damp and messy. Wrapped around her waist was a Dramask blanket. A blood-soaked linen bandage enveloped her left arm. Was that where Robin had cut her?

"Leera—" he whispered.

She didn't stir.

"Leera—"

Instead, Haylee moved her head. Her face was pale and puffy, one cheek larger than the other. She gazed at him with wandering eyes that were unable to focus, finally closing them, as if having given up on the endeavor.

"Haylee…?"

She didn't move.

He stared at the dim light, grateful for the candles—they needed every source of heat to fight the freezing winter. He just hoped they stayed lit long enough for day to come, or for them to get out of there. But how? He was useless without his arcanery.

"Leera …"

She finally stirred, blue lips trembling. When she saw him, her eyes seemed to enlarge, as if seeing something gruesome.

It had to be his head wound. "I'm fine," he gurgled. Blood had pooled in his mouth again and he hadn't noticed. "I sent a message with the witch. Let's hope it works."

Leera gave a weak smile. She winced before turning her attention to Bridget, who was still unconscious. When Leera turned back to him, she wore an expression of utter defeat.

Then it hit him. The questioning hadn't stopped when he passed out. It continued until they successfully pried the truth of who lit the fire from one of them …

Oh, no … Mr. Goss, Leland …

Robin re-entered the tent too quickly for Augum to pretend he was unconscious. His pinched face lit up with a smile when the pair of them made eye contact. He casually stuck his hands in the pockets of his necrophyte robe and sauntered over, gazing upon him like a hunter eyeing fallen prey.

"So you're finally awake. Quite a day the others had. Shame you deserted them like that, but I guess as father liked to say—once a coward always a coward!" and he laughed at his little joke, giving Augum an idle kick.

Augum bit his lip and grimaced as a new spasm of pain shot up his spine.

"Oh, come now, why so glum? It wasn't your stupid friends who squealed. It was the healer. All it took was threatening her son. You should have seen how quickly she blabbed. Stupid woman. Anyway, the commander rode off to pick up what's left of that nasty pest and his goody-good father." Robin sighed. "I heard the kid's a mess. A 'miracle he survived', she said. Sounds like he's pretty miserable. I'm sure it'll be a favor to end his pain."

Augum wrestled violently with his manacles, desperate to get at Robin, but it was completely useless. Robin seemed to enjoy watching his futile struggles.

"Hey, want to see something neat?" He raised his sleeve. It burst with a single fiery band around his wrist. "That's right, loser, I have my 1st degree. Want to see what I can do with it? Shyneo." He grabbed Augum's ankle.

Augum closed his eyes and beared it, trying not to gag from the smell of his own burning flesh. Instead, he focused on the fact Robin was using his extension, a mirror of Augum's lightning shock.

"I should have never fled with you," Haylee mumbled.

Robin let go to face her, allowing Augum a chance to catch his breath, ankle stinging.

"Well then you would have gone up in flames like the rest of those maggots."

Haylee tried to focus on him with wandering eyes.

"You look so stupid right now. Aww, was the judgment not severe enough for you? We could have another trial, send some more of your dumb relatives to war. Maybe that other precious cousin of yours—?"

"You've changed, and much for the worse, Robin Scarson."

"You're the one who betrayed me! It's *you* that's changed. You've grown soft and weak hanging out with these rats. It's pathetic."

Haylee didn't reply as Robin dug something out of his pocket. It was the destiny stone One Eye had gifted him. "But yes, I have changed—I have grown bolder and smarter. Everything seems … easier."

"You truly are becoming like them. I used to … I used to really like you, Robbie."

A hurt look passed over Robin's face before he straightened. He smirked and strolled near. "Not becoming—*become*. See, what you don't realize is, I don't need you anymore, Hayles. I can have *anyone*, even you if I wanted to. But that's the thing, I don't *want* you anymore. Look at you, you're ugly and disgusting and a traitor now. What boy would ever want you?"

He posed above her and slowly spat on her, watching her reaction. The spit landed on her cheek and dribbled down her chin. She seemed to glaze over, a faraway look in her eyes. He shrugged, placing the stone back in his pocket.

"Hmm. Anyway, you're luckier than you know. If it wasn't for that rich grandfather of yours ..." He left the rest unsaid, turning back to Augum. "And you—now that we have you, all that remains is that crone of yours and the scion. Once the Lord of the Legion collects what is rightfully his, the work in Solia will be complete."

Augum didn't bother hiding the venom from his voice. "What do you mean, the work in Solia?"

" 'What do you mean, the work in Solia?' " Robin mimicked in that old way of his, laughing and turning around as if expecting Haylee to laugh along. For a brief moment, his countenance changed with recognition, but he recovered quickly. When his eyes returned to Augum, they were full of loathing.

"I don't understand how *you* can be his son. You don't deserve such an honor. *I* should have been his son, not you, you stupid little rat. *ME!*" He finished by jabbing a finger into his own chest, face flushed. After a few moments of breathing hard, he sniffed and adjusted his robe.

"Lord Sparkstone seeks to become emperor of the world. It's just that simple. He needs all seven scions to do it, and I can promise you, he *will* possess all seven scions without destruction, he *will* enter the land of the Ley, and he *will* recover their powers for his most loyal servants."

"And someone *will* stop him—" Augum said. He expected retaliation, but Robin only shook his head, smiling.

"You have no idea, do you? Imagine combining the strength of the scions with necromancy, the might of the Dreadnoughts, and the power of Ley. Lord Sparkstone will surpass even the legendary Occulus. It has hardly begun, yet already the other kingdoms beg and bribe for the Legion not to make war on them. Soon all of Sithesia will be groveling at our feet, calling the Lord of the Legion Emperor, and I will be right there alongside the most powerful warlord the world has ever seen."

He snorted. "And to think *you*, the pathetic little rat that you are with your pathetic little piglet friends, are *his* son?" He spat on Augum. "You don't deserve the honor."

"You can have it. He's nothing but a bullying murderer, a cheap coward, just like you are—"

A brutal look passed over Robin's face. "You dare …" He lunged for Augum's throat, choking with the intent to snuff out his life, eyes flashing with murderous zeal. "Die, you damn gutterborn—"

Augum, with his hands manacled, was unable to defend himself. Choking, legs flailing, his vision began to tunnel. Distantly, a girl shouted for help. A burly guard pulled Robin away just as Augum was on the verge of blacking out, leaving him coughing and gasping for breath. Other guards had rushed inside but stood apart, watching with uncertainty.

"Master Robin, you must not run afoul of the Lord Sparkstone's wishes," the soldier said. "The great lord wants his son alive."

Robin struggled in the soldier's arms with a rabid energy, anxious to finish what he started. At last, he relaxed a little and the guard let Robin shrug away from his grip. Robin adjusted his robe, gave Haylee a venomous look, and marched out of the tent. After a moment's stunned silence, the burly Legionnaire gestured to the others and they left.

"Aug, you all right?" Leera asked, vainly tugging at her manacles.

"Just … great …" he croaked, wishing he could rub his raw throat. "When did she … when did Ms. Jenkins tell them … about Leland and Mr. Goss?"

"Early on. Tridian sent a message up to Antioc using a speaking orb. The commander there brought in her son, threatening his life if she didn't talk. Tridian made her hear the boy's cries right through the orb. She resisted, but they put a knife to his throat. She cried but told them everything she knew."

"What's going to happen to her?" he asked, glancing over at her wretched limp form, legs tangled underneath.

"They're giving her another chance to serve the Legion, something about not being able to afford to lose any healers, but they're also going to keep her son hostage."

He turned his aching head to Haylee, who watched them with tired eyes. Her face was paler than ever.

"They're going to send one of my cousins to fight the Tiberrans," she said weakly. "He's only thirteen. Thirteen, Augum. He is … he is the kindest, sweetest …"

He tactfully looked away as her eyes watered.

Haylee blurted a gurgling laugh, her voice softer and softer. "I deserved it … I deserved it …" She closed her eyes, resting her head back against the post.

"Nobody deserves this," Leera mumbled, turning to her right. "Bridge, you okay?"

Bridget stirred and groaned. "So … cold …"

"I know, I know," Leera said, dropping her voice. "Look, do you still have the pearl?"

Bridget nodded. "Think so … can't reach … lower pocket."

"Use Telekinesis."

"I'll … try …" Bridget focused. It took a while, but the pearl floated free at last, landing in Leera's lap. She gasped from the effort and rested her head back against the post.

He decided not to tell them about his lack of arcane powers. Not yet, at least. It would only sap their remaining will.

A hollow feeling opened up inside his heart. Would he be able to watch his friends succeed in the arcane ways while he lingered behind? Would they even still be his friends? He wondered if this was what Bridget had been feeling when paralyzed. No, what she felt was much worse—he could still move at least.

"Pay attention, Aug," Leera whispered before using Telekinesis to guide the pearl up into his awaiting hand. His fingers closed around the engraved object.

"All right," she said, "they don't know what the Orb of Orion is. They think it's just a broken speaking orb. I heard them talking about it outside the tent. Anyway, see what you can find out."

He nodded, swallowing. He squeezed the pearl, closed his eyes, and made a concerted effort to push away the disheartening fact he would never again cast spells, instead focusing on seeing through the orb, praying that he was still able to do that at least.

Almost instantly, he was watching the inside of a black tent through curved glass. There were two beds. Their rucksack rested on one, contents spilled. Based on the perspective, he guessed the orb sat on a dresser, opposite the entrance, where a Black Guard Legionnaire in full shining armor stood somewhat rigidly, speaking to another soldier dressed in dark trousers and a loose linen shirt.

"No, I haven't heard any word yet, Sergeant," said the soldier in the linen shirt. "They should have been back by now though."

"Think something went wrong, Lieutenant?"

"I doubt it, Commander Tridian is most astute." He paused. "Nonetheless, are the men on guard?"

"Every single one of them, sir, and we're expecting Axon Company by morning light. They will bolster our number by another two hundred men."

"Ah, but Axon is scheduled to meet up with the other companies."

"If you don't mind me asking, sir, how many others?"

"Four—Wolfpack, Comborai, Malfease, and Nordika. They're going to form a new battalion. Then they march on Tiberra from the northwest while the Bastards of Black march from the southwest."

"Sir, if you'll excuse me, but, that's what the general named that battalion—the Bastards of Black?"

"Yes—and don't ask me why. I heard Axon's new battalion will be called the Haven Slayers."

The sergeant cleared his throat. "When do you think we'll get our marching orders, sir?"

"I imagine soon, depending on Lord Sparkstone's trap." The Lieutenant sat down on the empty bed and took off his boots.

"I still cannot believe his own grandmother stole the scion from our lord, sir."

The lies they feed these soldiers, Augum thought.

"Yes, well, did you know she is the only known living sorcerer to achieve mastery?"

"I did not, sir."

The two pondered that a moment before the sergeant continued. "How many warlocks do you think the companies have, sir?"

"Not nearly enough, but recruits are being trained in the academy."

"Are they anything like Commander Tridian's brat?"

"I would watch that tongue, Sergeant. That necrophyte is honored by Lord Sparkstone himself."

"I understand, sir. I apologize for any offense—"

The lieutenant waved him off. "Forget it. What we could really use are those Dreadnought blades and armor. Then a company of two hundred could take out a battalion of a thousand."

"Have you, uh, ever seen a Dreadnought in person … sir?"

"Not yet."

"Have they at least begun making the equipment?"

"Yes. Our Lord Sparkstone built a secret forge, but reports say the going is very slow."

"That's too bad, I was really hoping to get my hands on a Dreadnought battleaxe." The sergeant made a swinging motion with his arms. "I'd call it … Headsmasher."

"Yes, well, everything in its time, Sergeant, everything in its time …" The lieutenant lay down on the bed, dismissing the sergeant with a wave of his hand.

"Good night, sir." The sergeant departed, but before Augum returned his focus to the prison tent, he heard the lieutenant mumble, "That boy *is* a brat though …"

"Learn anything?" Leera whispered when he opened his eyes.

"A bit …" he replied, careful to keep the pearl tightly closed in his fist so the lieutenant didn't accidentally overhear. "Mostly a bunch of army stuff—company and battalion names; how they're going to attack Tiberra; that they have a secret Dreadnought forge; oh—and they're worried about Commander Tridian, he's late returning."

Leera crinkled her nose mischievously. "That's good, maybe something's happened. I just hope they failed finding Mr. Goss and Leland."

"Maybe they ran away together …"

One of the guards opened the tent flaps, allowing Mya to enter, her plain red dress billowing slightly with every movement, the mark of the burning sword looking completely out of place on her chest. She carried a small basket of bread and a skin of water.

Augum's gaze followed her.

Leera watched him and sighed. He really didn't want to hear anything about him liking Mya right now. He'd lost his ability to cast spells and he'd failed in bringing Mrs. Stone to their rescue. For all he knew, his father had sprung the trap and had killed her. The thought was enough to make his heart thud in panic.

No, he definitely didn't want to be nagged about Mya right now. Mercifully, Leera stayed her tongue.

Mya crouched silently before Bridget, tearing apart the bread and tenderly feeding her piece by piece.

A silver-haired Black Guard walked in, followed by Robin.

"Remember your orders," Robin said. "Keep a stern eye out."

Mya quickly stood to receive them, head bowed. "M'lord, would it be possible to shackle the prisoners with their arms at their sides? This is most inhumane."

Robin laughed aloud. "What do you think this is, some kind of luxurious manor house? The prince really spoiled you."

"But m'lord—"

Robin held up a hand and she fell quiet.

Augum hated the way she had to address him, hated everything about the situation. If he could only get free from the manacles—

Robin bade the burly guard to follow him as he paced over to Augum. "I'm going to question this prisoner. I command you not to interfere. Is that understood?"

The silver-haired guard unfolded his arms and glanced at the entrance. "Forgive me, Honored Necrophyte, but I do not think this fitting. I best seek out the lieutenant."

"Then go crawling to the lieutenant already!" Robin turned back to Augum, eyes afire. "In the meantime, send Justinius in." Before the guard even turned away, Justinius rushed inside. The older guard flashed Justinius a disgusted look before slapping the tent flaps aside.

Robin glanced between Mya and Augum and gave a salacious grin. "You like her, don't you? You like *my* servant."

Augum felt the blood rush to his head. He better not—

"It's the way you've been looking at her. I'm not stupid, you know. Justinius—seize her."

"NO—!" Augum struggled so hard against his manacles he felt them cut into his flesh.

Justinius snatched Mya by the neck and marched her over. She didn't protest, almond eyes low.

"Look at him struggle. I don't think the gutterborn rat struggled that hard even for the Leer." Robin gave Leera a malicious smile.

Leera's head dropped. Augum felt a horrible pang in his stomach.

"So we know why you all came here," Robin went on, turning briefly to glance at Haylee. "Though I don't know *why* you'd want to save the likes of her—in any case, what we don't know is, who *else* is involved in the insurgency."

Augum gaped at him. "What are you talking about, there *is* no one else!"

"No—? There's no one else, you say?" Robin's voice had a deadly softness to it. "Then tell me, my little rat friend, why is Commander Tridian late returning? Hmm?"

"I have no idea, I really don't—" He looked up at Mya, whose long jet hair still managed to shine, almond eyes cast at her feet. She was a lamb ready for slaughter. It was enough for him to bitterly regret not having the frantic lightning power as a last resort, for he would have smote Robin there and then.

Robin's lip curled as he turned to Justinius. "Apparently he doesn't have any idea. Why don't we *make him* understand."

Justinius seemed to take the unspoken hint and drew a dagger, placing it to Mya's throat. Her chin rose as she yelped, breathing rapidly.

The tent went into uproar. "What are you doing, are you mad—?" Haylee shouted, while Leera threw curses and Bridget tried to alert the guards. Ms. Jenkins, meanwhile, still hung unconscious.

Augum felt every muscle in his body tighten to the point of breaking. The manacles strained.

Robin didn't flinch, patiently awaiting Augum's response.

"There *is* no one else—"

"You lie," Robin said in a tone trying to mimic the Blade of Sorrows.

Justinius adjusted the blade at Mya's neck. She stiffened with a squeak and shut her eyes tight.

"I'm telling the truth, I swear it—! Damn you, I'm telling the truth!"

"I think he's lying, sir," Justinius said.

"Cut her—" Robin said just as the lieutenant with the linen shirt entered, followed by a group of guards, one of them the silver-haired guard.

Justinius immediately lowered the blade from Mya's throat, but kept a firm hold on her neck.

"What is the meaning of this—?" the lieutenant asked.

"What does it look like? I'm *questioning* this prisoner. If it wasn't for your meddling interruption, he would have revealed who else is involved in the insurgency."

"He was about to kill her!" Augum said, unable to control the desperation in his voice.

Robin scoffed, waving the idea aside.

"On whose authority—?" the lieutenant challenged.

"Commander Tridian's, *sir*," Robin replied in a mocking tone.

"Commander Tridian's authority stops with Mizora company. This is Venga company, under the command of Commander Canes. Now—" and the lieutenant casually stepped forward. "Young man, need I remind you that threatening a legion servant is dishonorable and unseemly?"

"And need I remind *you* that she is *my* servant, given to me by the Lord of the Legion himself!" Robin took a step back, his face twisting with an over-dramatized sneer. "Are you aware that I'm the only one in this camp with the power to control that wraith out there? One word from me and you'll all be torn to shreds—"

The lieutenant and guards gave him hard looks.

Robin must have known he had overstepped because he quickly held up a hand in supplication. "But I understand, Lieutenant, how you feel. Corrigus, the Blade of Sorrows, and the Lord of the Legion himself have the utmost confidence in my training, which I have to continue. You see, not only am I going to be the most powerful necromancer—besides Lord Sparkstone of course—but I am also going to be the most adept questioner, even more capable than Commander Tridian himself."

Robin paused a moment to let his little speech sink in. "Now, if you would kindly let me continue my training, I am sure I can overlook this … interference."

Robin had changed a lot, Augum thought. Even his speech was more refined. Then he remembered they were grooming him for command.

He could almost see the thoughts running through the lieutenant's brain—if he stood in the way of this brat now, later, when the brat became powerful, there could be retribution.

The lieutenant rubbed his chin. "The Blade of Sorrows has truly taken you under his wing, hasn't he?" He sighed, his eyes sweeping over Mya with a calculating look. "Well, since she *is* your servant, given by Lord Sparkstone himself, I see no reason not to let the questioning continue."

The tent erupted with all the girls shouting their disagreement, while Mya gasped as Justinius' knife returned to her porcelain throat.

"Leave them be," the lieutenant ordered, and with a gesture, took all the guards with him.

"Now where was I?" Robin asked, fingering something in his pocket.

Augum glowered. "I promise you, if you do anything to her—"

Justinius pressed the knife closer, staying anything else he wanted to say.

"Who else is involved!" Robin shouted.

Augum's mind rushed for some kind of plausible lie.

"I'm tired of waiting for your lies," Robin said, shaking his head. "Cut her."

"My pleasure."

Leera, Haylee and Augum began shouting and screaming, yet something strange had happened—Justinius seemed to struggle to cut her throat, as if an invisible hand was holding the knife back.

"What are you waiting for? I said cut her!"

Justinius' knuckles were white. "I … can't …"

Robin looked around until spotting Bridget, whose brows were furrowed, gaze solely on Justinius. "It's her, she's using Telekinesis—"

He advanced toward her, but what happened next changed everything. A series of concussive, implosive bangs were heard outside, one after another, accompanied by corresponding bright flashes that lit up the outside of the tent like lightning.

The noise culminated in multiple volleys before trickling to a stop. Robin and Justinius hesitated as soldiers bustled outside.

Robin paled. "That's the sound of teleportation …"

All was still in the tent. When the noises ceased, someone shouted, "All hail the Lord of the Legion's return!"

Robin visibly relaxed. Perhaps he'd been afraid the resistance had come.

A moment later, Lord Sparkstone's voice rang clear across the grounds. "The crone knew about the trap—prepare yourselves, for she heads this way!"

KARMA

Robin and Justinius exchanged fearful looks before throwing Mya to the ground and scrambling outside.

"Are … are you all right?" Augum asked.

She brought a trembling hand to her throat and glanced through him. Suddenly the tent flaps flew open as a slew of heavily armored Black Guard rushed inside, followed by the Red Guard—towering crimson-armored warriors holding burning swords, their bloody eyes gleaming through slits cut into great bucket helms. A putrid stench much like rancid meat filled the tent, nauseating the prisoners and some of the guards.

The tent flaps moved aside again, this time of their own accord, and the Lord of the Legion entered, followed by Corrigus, Commander Canes, and Prince Sydo Ridian, wearing a gold-fringed necrophyte robe and a proud look on his face. Robin, Justinius and the lieutenant squeezed in behind. Robin was whispering a question to Sydo, gesturing at his elaborate robe, but Sydo seemed to ignore him, his nose in the air, making a show of paying attention to the Lord of the Legion.

It didn't surprise Augum to see the traitor by his father's side. The Lord of the Legion appeared how he remembered him, wearing golden battle plate with a golden plumed helm. His cloak crackled with lightning, as did his eyes. The shortsword Burden's Edge hung on his hip, looking undersized.

Despite Augum's manacled hands and the loss of his arcane ability, hope flowed. The crone delivered his message and Nana was coming!

Lord Sparkstone fixed his son with a hard stare and exhaled. He paced toward him with regal ease, the plume on his helm so tall it brushed along the tent ceiling. He stopped before Augum and crouched.

A hush befell the tent as he slowly removed his helm and ran a mailed hand through sweaty umber hair. He sniffed sharply, a bull readying to charge, before laying electric eyes on Augum.

"My son, how I regret the way things … turned out."

Augum's voice was flat. "You're a murderer. You burn down villages. You even murdered my mother, your own wife."

Had anyone ever talked to the Lord of the Legion this way before? Judging by how his entourage stiffened, Augum thought not.

Lord Sparkstone's eyes softened only a moment before hardening. "Inflexible and stubborn, much like your mother and great-grandmother. The day will come when you see how necessary all of this was. One must rule with an iron fist to achieve anything these days." Sparkstone stood up. "You're injured."

Augum turned his gaze to Robin, who shrank behind Canes.

"Nothing like a good battle scar," Sparkstone said. "But let us talk of more pressing concerns. The crone stands in the way of our dreams. Perhaps you can speak with her, convince her that giving me what is rightfully mine is for the good of us all. Do you not see, my son? Do you not see what I offer? Eternal life for *everyone*—think on that!"

"That's a lie, and you know it. We came from Ley with great-grandpa Thomas Stone, and leaving Ley killed him—he aged a hundred years right before our eyes." He threw a glare at Sydo. "*He* saw it with his own eyes."

His father surveyed him a moment. "And how was my dear, absent grandfather? Did he apologize for abandoning his wife?" Sparkstone flexed his neck before loosening his shoulders, as if gearing for a fight. "I know about the Leyan curse, Son. I am confident I will find a way around it. Thanks to the prince, I also know about the curse of the seven."

Sydo smoothed his red hair while flashing a smug look at those around him. Few paid him any attention.

"I will find a way around that, too," Sparkstone continued. "I will be the first in all of history to possess all seven scions—but I won't stop there." He clenched his fists close to his golden chest. "How I long to share my grand plans with you. How I *long* for that, Son."

He sighed dramatically and let his arms fall to his side. "But you have not joined me. You have not followed in the footsteps of your own father. Nevertheless, one day you will, and on that day you will hear the reason—" He waved idly at his surroundings, "—for all this. You will hear the reason, and you will understand—and you will agree."

What was he talking about? "You can't make me join you."

The Lord of the Legion slowly glanced at Leera, Bridget, Haylee, even Mya. "Do you really think that true?" he asked softly.

A shiver crept up Augum's spine. Did his father know about Mya? Did Robin say something?

"Do you not see what it is I will be forced to do?" his father continued in mock sorrow.

Augum looked at Leera and Bridget, both watching him with defiant faces, though in their eyes he saw fear. He knew he had to be very careful here. If he protested too much, his father might make an example out of them. He did, after all, slaughter an entire village in front of him, so why would he hesitate now?

An idea came to him. His father wanted something from him, maybe he could use it as leverage to keep them safe …

"Then promise me my friends will come to no harm, Father," Augum blurted in a purposely defeated tone, saying the last word tenderly. "All of them—Ms. Jenkins, Haylee, Leera, Bridget, and Mya. No matter what happens, free them." He was counting on his father being blinded by the longing to share his grand plans with him, at least just enough to yield maneuvering room.

Lord Sparkstone watched him a moment. "If I do, will you cooperate with me in retrieving the scion?"

The question had a taint of cynicism to it, but Augum saw little choice—he had to try to save his friends somehow. Besides, without arcane powers, this was all that came to mind—a lethal cat and mouse game with the Lord of the Legion.

He dropped his head, hiding his eyes. "Yes."

His father nodded slowly. "Take them away," he commanded, "including the servant."

Robin scrambled to the front of the group. "But, Lord Sparkstone … she's mine!" He pointed firmly at Mya. "You gave her to me!"

The Lord of the Legion slowly turned his head and Robin instantly dropped his eyes. Meanwhile, one of the guards began unlocking the manacles. After staring at Robin for a length of time, Sparkstone returned his attention to Augum, idly resting his palm on Burden's Edge. "So how do you think Nana's going to come at me, hmm, Son?"

Augum glanced to his right. Bridget was freed first, so weak she had to be helped up by the silver-haired guard.

"She gave us quite the slip, almost as if someone had warned her. She cannot be working alone."

So his father had no idea it was him that alerted Nana …

"There are obviously others involved in the insurgency," Sparkstone continued. "An insurgency I shall crush as I have crushed all impudence. You know, Son, your great-grandmother has identical ambitions to mine, if you could believe it—" He idly glanced to Leera, now also free from her manacles and held up by a guard. "That's right, she, too, wants to live forever. How do you think she's as old as she is? How many great-grandmothers do you know still walking around performing arcanery with such strength?"

Augum remained silent, trying to keep his face impassive.

"Let me tell you the real reason she wants to keep the scion." He leaned closer. Augum detected the faintest scent of rot. "It's what's allowing her to live so long."

"If she's keeping the scion, it's for a better reason than that," Augum said.

Sparkstone gave him a condescending smile. "Stupid boy, you think her so benevolent as to eventually pass the scion to you? It would mean her death!"

Augum didn't believe him in the slightest. He knew Mrs. Stone wanted to pass him the scion, but was just waiting for the right time—and if the scion truly was keeping her alive, there was no way he would accept it from her. Despite his true feelings on the matter, he decided to let his father think that seed of doubt had been planted, and so he dropped his eyes and acted sullen.

They freed Haylee next, followed by the unconscious Ms. Jenkins. Then the guards dragged them out of the tent, including Mya. The girls gave Augum a longing look, a look that said good luck and goodbye. Something about it made him feel tired and lonely—he hoped they'd be all right, wherever they were being taken.

"Would you get these blasted things off already—" Lord Sparkstone said to the guard, gesturing at Augum's manacles.

The guard hastened to free Augum's hands. When they dropped at last, a stretching pain shot through his shoulders, as if he'd been quartered by horses for days. His arms were swollen, purple and numb. Luckily, no one noticed the engraved pearl still clenched in his fist.

"Stand him up."

Augum was yanked to his feet.

"Lord Sparkstone—!" Canes said, holding up a small speaking orb. The entire crowd turned to the curly-haired man Augum would forever perceive as a traitor.

"What is it—?"

"Forgive me, Great One, but I think it's—I think it's one of the other commanders. He's trying to say something—"

The Lord of the Legion made an impatient sucking sound with his teeth and strode over, the guard dragging Augum right along. Everyone parted out of their way as Sparkstone snatched the speaking orb out of Canes' hand. No one dared move as he listened.

Augum, held right beside his father, was in perfect position to see and hear what was going on. Inside the small orb, he saw a burned face, still smoking, whispering something.

"My liege, who is it?" Canes asked quietly.

Sparkstone's nostrils whistled as he inhaled. "Commander Tridian."

"The Blade of Sorrows," someone mumbled.

The soldiers exchanged anxious looks.

"No, I expect you to survive—!" Sparkstone roared into the orb. "You are to live and suffer your failure!" He shoved the orb back to Canes, who fumbled it in his hairy hands. "That's what the fool gets for refusing to have an accomplished warlock with him. Man hasn't an arcane bone in his body, but I thought he at least had a brain."

Some of the soldiers tittered but Sparkstone shot a glaring look at them and they instantly fell silent. He put on his plumed helm. "She'll be here soon. Prepare yourselves." He made an impatient gesture and everyone but Corrigus, Canes, Robin, Sydo, and the Red Guards vacated the tent.

Augum stood by his father, trying to contain his hope. If the Blade of Sorrows and his men had fallen, it could only mean one thing—Mrs. Stone had saved Leland and Mr. Goss—but how she could have known about them was a mystery.

Sparkstone glanced at his Red Guard, as if communicating silently with them. "Corrigus—prepare defensive enchantments around the camp," he said without taking his eyes off them.

"As you wish, Sire," Corrigus said, dismissing himself.

"Prince Sydo."

Sydo skittered forth with an elaborate bow. "Yes, my gracious lord?"

"You've had enough training with wraiths. Take command of Robin's."

Sydo paled, stuttering, "You mean for a real battle?"

Robin strode forth. "But, my Lord, that's my—"

The Lord of the Legion glanced over at them and they instantly fell silent. Both swallowed, made a short bow, and left.

Canes shifted where he stood, still clutching the speaking orb, his pudgy face sweaty even in the cold.

"A great battle approaches," Sparkstone said softly. "I have been waiting for this a long time." He turned to Augum, the plumed helm making him appear much taller. "Today I prove I am the most powerful warlock alive." He made an idle gesture and out flew three cloudy spheres from a leather pouch in his belt. Each had a light tint to it—one red, one green, one pale blue.

The scions hovered around the Lord of the Legion like attentive bees, humming with ancient, potent arcanery. The space around him warped slightly. Canes swallowed and took a step back.

"Keep the boy close to me at all times," Sparkstone said, leaving the tent, Red Guard in tow.

"Yes, m'lord." Canes grabbed Augum by the arm and dragged him along.

Outside was a hive of activity. Torches burned around the outer perimeter of the camp, where Corrigus paced making complex gestures. Guards ran to and fro. Horses were prepared, armor donned.

The night was dark. Clouds rushed by overhead without a whisper of wind on the ground. Augum searched for the girls. They had to be near, no way would his father give up precious hostages.

"You there," Commander Canes said to a hapless guard. "Sharpen stakes and impale them in the ground there and there."

"She's a warlock, you fool," Lord Sparkstone said.

Canes reddened. "Cancel that order, soldier. As you were." The guard rushed off.

Augum spied Robin hissing something at Sydo, again gesturing at the prince's more elaborate robe, then at the wraith hunkered down behind them. Sydo merely shrugged, and as soon as Sparkstone happened to look his way, he made another elaborate bow. "I am here, My Liege! The wraith is under control and ready to attack."

Robin looked incredulous. "You haven't even given it a proper command—"

"I will not stand for your insufferable attitude. You are to address me as *Prince Sydo,* and you will bow upon doing so."

"You trumped up little bag of snot, I'm the one who gave you—"

Sydo, conscious of the Lord of the Legion looking on, held up a hand right in Robin's face. "You will cease speaking to me immediately and step away. I am in control of the wraith now."

Robin was shaking with fury but, conscious of the Lord of the Legion looking on, stepped away and crossed his arms.

It gave Augum some pleasure watching those two go at it. Both should have been Sparkstone's sons, not him.

They were in a clearing near the middle of the camp. The Lord of the Legion paced back and forth, hands behind his back, scions buzzing. His Red Guards stood near, towering sentries clutching burning blades.

"My Lord," Canes began, constantly glancing about for any sign of Mrs. Stone. "How do you think she will attack us?"

"That I do not know, Commander."

Canes swallowed. "I … I've heard a little of what she can do … back at … back at Castle Arinthian, that is."

"You mean when she folded your arms back?" Augum said, unable to help himself.

Canes gave Augum a murderous look.

"Ah, yes." Sparkstone turned to face Canes, who shrank. "She freed you to deliver me a message. How did that go again … 'Tell Lividius the hole in his heart can't be filled with what he seeks'. Wasn't that it now?"

"I … I think so, my liege."

"And how does it feel to wear the burdensome title of Fallen Knight?"

"I serve you in the only way I know, Sire. I had an opportunity and I took it. The sacrifice was … necessary. Eternal life is worth the price of my honor."

"Precisely why you are one of my commanders. An honor well deserved."

Canes nodded while slowly exhaling.

"Yes, there are indeed quite a few tales of my grandmother's battles," Sparkstone went on, looking off into the horizon. "Apoc's forfeit. The vanquishing of the Desert Destroyer. The Canterran Cobra. The Blacktongue tragedy. The two duels against Ottentus Maledius Anavictus, one of the last living masters." He was rattling them off now, hands animated. "Snix the Speedsword, Sabius the Reaper, Totillus the Turncoat Monk, Endius, Scadius, Trintus, Zodian the Grand, and of course, no one will ever forget Narsus … and I could go on." He paused while Canes adjusted his collar, looking a little peaky.

"She is, uh, quite accomplished, Sire."

"You know I studied every one of those battles, and to this day, I still don't know how she beat her adversaries in half of them." He turned to Canes. "But that's just between us of course."

"—of course, Great lord."

For Augum, it was one thing to hear stories about Mrs. Stone from Bridget, quite another to hear them from the Lord of the Legion.

"You know that when I was a boy," Sparkstone continued wistfully, "I would hear about all these legendary duels, but none of them were real to me, none of them. Today though … today will be real." He nodded to himself. "She is now the only living master. She was my mentor, and I must say, a better one than Narsus."

"Sire, you trained under the great Narsus?" Canes asked.

Sparkstone turned to Augum, ignoring Canes. "Few know that, my son, but it is true. I was Narsus' apprentice."

Augum wondered if Mrs. Stone even knew that.

Canes cleared his beefy throat. "And … and she vanquished him—"

"—below the Academy of Arcane Arts, yes," Sparkstone finished, lightning eyes still on Augum, who only wanted to yell how Nana would also defeat them and walk away unscathed, but he remembered he was pretending to cooperate.

Sparkstone resumed pacing. "You are wondering why the stories of the greatness of our foe, Commander Canes. We must be honest with ourselves in order to succeed. Never underestimate your opponent." He began talking to himself in an undertone now. "I have three scions and she only one. We have Corrigus, the wraith, the Red Guard, and over eighty men at our disposal. But above all, we have *them*." Sparkstone waved idly at Augum, apparently forgetting he had agreed to free his friends. Augum, however, had no illusions as to his father's so-called promises, and it came as no surprise to him. To be fair, he also had no intention of convincing Mrs. Stone to hand over the scion, especially now that he knew it might mean her death. The whole thing was like some strange play they were in, trying to convince each other of their acting abilities.

The question now was how it would end. With no way to cast spells and his only possession the near-useless pearl, the prospect of him doing something meaningful seemed remote.

He hoped Nana had a plan.

Canes, still holding onto Augum's elbow, spoke into his speaking orb before turning to Sparkstone. "My liege, I sent Axon Company a message to double-time their march. If all goes well, they should be here within hours."

"Ah, Rotus Magnavilius—a good man and a good commander."

"Pardon, my liege, but he's a warlock, isn't he?" Canes sounded hopeful.

Sparkstone smiled to himself. "One of the best. He was with me in the beginning, you know. 17th degree fire, a bit of a madman, and a hell of a drinker. Back then, you couldn't just refuse a contest with Rotus. He'd keep after you until you said yes, and then you'd wake up in the morning with the vilest headache. I gave him Axon Company for his service, though I envision him becoming my first general one day. It will be good to have him by my side, but what I really need is necromancers and an army of Dreadnought-equipped soldiers, not just warlocks. Damn, why must everything take so long?" He sighed. "I suppose I should know the arcane way can't be rushed …"

Augum studied him as he paced. If he couldn't use his arcanery, he'd use his wits. Maybe he could exploit his father's fear of Mrs. Stone …

Sparkstone approached the wraith sitting beside Sydo and pet one of its rotten limbs. "Ah, you are quite the triumph, aren't you? Thousands of years of necromantic artistry passed down by my predecessors …"

The wraith cooed like a pigeon.

"He is a marvelous incarnation, Your Eminence," Sydo said as Robin glared from nearby.

The Lord of the Legion ignored him. "Don't worry, my pet, one day you'll have many brothers and sisters to fight alongside you, this I promise. For now, you must do your ancient duty and obey this fledgling necrophyte." Sparkstone glanced between Sydo, Robin and Augum. "The children of the Legion are its future."

For the first time ever, Augum exchanged a look with Robin and Sydo, and all three agreed on one thing—no way did they want anything to do with each other.

"So you just summon the wraiths from the ground?" Augum asked his father, trying to sound casual. "How hard are they to control?"

Robin quietly scoffed.

"Is that interest I hear?" Sparkstone asked, turning away from the wraith. "Does my son secretly wish to become a necromancer?"

For some odd reason, Sydo pranced forward and smacked Augum on the cheek with one of the lamest slaps Augum had ever felt. It barely stung.

"They are not merely *summoned* from the ground, you gutterborn little—" Sydo stopped mid-sentence, suddenly conscious of what he had inferred. He shrank away from the cold look the Lord of the Legion was giving him, speaking very quickly. "My Liege, I did not mean what I said of course, but let me show this … this usurper … anyway let me show him exactly how, err, how much skill is involved in commanding such a beast—" and before anyone could say anything, Sydo whipped around, gesturing for the wraith to stand. "Necro ita! Ita!" but the thing just sat there. "I said, ita, ita! You damn—" He kicked the wraith in its massive shin. It reacted as swiftly as a viper, snatching him in its giant clawed hands and readying to take a great bite out of his skull while he screamed.

"Adai!" Robin said in a firm voice, and the wraith instantly ceased. He gestured over to a rather large pile of horse dung. "Necro sinna ad endo."

"No!" Sydo shouted. "Gods, no—adai! ADAI!" but the wraith shoved him into the pile of horse manure, smearing him in there for good measure, before letting go. For a moment, the prince was completely still. Then he slowly dug himself out, gibbering and whimpering. Everyone, from the Lord of the Legion, to the soldiers, to the lowliest servant, laughed. Even Augum cracked a grin.

Sydo stood up, slopping with manure, lip quivering.

"I think His Highness needs a bath," Robin said, much to the amusement of the crowd.

Sydo took a squishy step toward Robin.

"Oh no, here comes the sewage monster—" Robin called as the crowd roared with laughter. "Everybody run!"

"I ... I will kill you!" Sydo shouted in a shrill voice, running at Robin.

Robin snorted before firmly shoving at the air."Baka!" Sydo was sent flying—right back into the manure pile.

As soldiers doubled over with laughter, Sydo gurgled something.

Robin made a show of placing a hand to his ear. "What's that, Your Royal Highness? Not quite the royal feast you're used to?"

"Uhhnnnghh ..." Sydo stood up, hands shaking, looking around as if lost. "M-m-m-m—" but he couldn't stop stuttering. "M-m-m-m—" Finally, the crowd in hysterics, he tottered off. "M-m-m-m ..."

Augum watched the prince slink away, almost feeling sorry for him. If only the Karma spell had worked on him, maybe that wouldn't have happened.

"It seems our humble prince is not as adept with the wraith as I had hoped," Sparkstone said with a note of amused disdain. When the laughter died down, he turned back to Augum, raising a golden-gloved finger. "Now as I was saying, interest is a gateway. Necromancy is a fascinating element, far more challenging than I had ever imagined—more so than the lightning element even, if you could believe it. There are ... subtleties involved that I cannot explain. And the rewards ..." He shook his head and paced closer, hands travelling behind his back, helmed chin rising, revealing a black leather strap. "The rewards are greater than you could ever imagine. I know what you're thinking, Son, I know it because you are my flesh and blood.

You're thinking, 'How did such an ordinary man accomplish so much?' "

Augum gave a half-shrug, playing along.

Sparkstone swept the grounds with crackling eyes. "You see, I believe a father should be honest with his son. Perhaps I'm not the smartest man. Nor am I the most cunning like, say, Commander Tridian. I'm not the most garrulous, as Rotus, as wise as Corrigus, nor as eloquent as Narsus was. I'm not even the best mentor, like my dear grandmother." He smiled. "But perhaps no one is as talented a mentor as she."

He stopped, focusing on the burning blades of the Red Guard, who watched him with steadfast gazes. "You know what separates me from the common man? Ambition. That's it. Simple, pure, ambition—but it is the greatest ambition known, and I shall change the face of the world with it. Woe to those that stand in my way."

The Lord of the Legion stared at the horizon, the flames reflecting off his golden armor, until Corrigus strode forth.

"My liege, the arcane defenses have been put into place, though I cannot make any guarantees of their strength in relation to—"

"—yes, yes," Sparkstone said. "I understand perfectly. Even you, my most powerful warlock, fear her."

"It would be unwise to underestimate your old mentor, Great One."

"Agreed." Sparkstone glanced up at swiftly moving coal-gray clouds, as if expecting her to come from the sky.

Augum absolutely loathed to admit it, but some distant iota of his heart felt something for his father. He wondered what life would have been like if his father had never dabbled in necromancy—would his mother still be alive, the family together? Would they be visiting Nana, sharing tales around the fire?

"Why?" he asked, staring at his father.

Sparkstone's brows rose behind his helm. "Why what?"

"Why did you kill her? Why did you murder my mother?"

Canes stiffened, but Corrigus remained impassive, while a quiet grin spread across Robin's face, perhaps thinking Augum was finally going to get his comeuppance.

Sparkstone observed Augum with electric eyes before striding forth and delivering a back-handed smack with his mailed hand.

Augum fell to the ground, cheek smarting, eyes watering.

Sparkstone stood over him a moment, adjusting his gauntlets, before pacing away.

Robin's face lit up as Canes dragged Augum to his feet.

"Corrigus—your counsel," Sparkstone said.

Corrigus cleared his throat, black eyes watching Augum with no hint of emotion. "My liege, all precautions have been taken, but we must remain vigilant. The crone is unlikely to attack us head-on. Instead, I would expect her to probe our defenses. She may not be alone, so we must be wary of separation. In the end, your greatest weapon will be the child."

"I should have spent more time practicing with the scions," Sparkstone muttered. "I still feel these cursed things withholding their secrets from me, Corrigus. Yet another damned inconvenience. I am a relative babe when it comes to the use of these ancient artifacts, whereas she has had a lifetime of practice. Curse her stubbornness, her refusal to give me what is rightfully mine—I should have been trained in the scion's use as a child!"

Corrigus' black gaze fell upon the three hovering scions, vibrating with energy. He said nothing.

His father was very impatient, Augum noted, trying not to touch his stinging cheek.

Time passed slowly as the camp stood waiting. Soldiers' necks craned at every sound from the Tallows. He hoped

Nana struck before Axon Company arrived with their two hundred men and 17th degree fire warlock. Just to try something different, he closed his eyes, feigning tiredness, and, using the pearl, glanced through the Orb of Orion into the Lieutenant's tent.

What he saw surprised him. Three black-armored guards, one of which was Justinius, guarded Bridget, Leera, Mya, Haylee, and Ms. Jenkins. Ms. Jenkins lay on one bed attended by Mya. Haylee and Bridget sat on the other with their rucksack. Leera stood in between, staring imploringly at the Orb of Orion as if searching for any sign of Augum.

Since the guards weren't paying much attention to him, he tried making the orb wink, remembering how Erika spooked them by suddenly revealing her eye. Leera's face immediately lit up. It had worked. She promptly nudged Bridget, who in turn nudged Haylee. All three flashed him a hopeful smile before he withdrew to avoid attracting suspicion.

He felt some satisfaction knowing he had at least bolstered their spirits, and, having seen they were all right, his own as well.

Yet they still didn't know the witch had stripped him of his arcane powers …

He sighed, setting himself the task of trying to locate where exactly the lieutenant's tent was. When the man appeared, he followed him with his eyes until the lieutenant entered a tent on the other side of the watchtower. He confirmed the location with a quick peek through the orb.

More time passed. The pudgy Canes had long dumped Augum to the frozen muddy ground, having tired of holding him. Sparkstone paced continuously, occasionally barking a command, while Corrigus merely observed. Soldiers patrolled the camp carrying torches, hands resting on their weapons, eyes constantly watching the horizon.

Robin practiced giving the wraith commands while everyone stayed clear.

Augum, meanwhile, bundled his robe close and waited for the arrival of his great-grandmother.

LEGEND

The more time passed, the quicker Sparkstone paced. His electric eyes roved from the horizon to the trees to the tents and back again. Suddenly he stopped, fixated on the trees.

Canes followed his gaze. "Sire? Is there something—" but he was cut off by a distant rumbling.

The hair on Augum's neck rose as soldiers shouted from outside the camp. Men scurried about, frantically gesturing to each other, preparing for the inevitable attack. The rumbling grew louder.

A Black Guardsman exploded out from the tree line in a plume of snow, waving his arms. "Axon Company approaches!"

The call echoed around camp. Soon soldiers were cheering and congratulating each other as countless horses began crashing through the trees. As the horsemen lined up, one rider cantered forth.

"My benevolent, gracious, and most honorable liege!" said a burly man with an ale gut, dismounting. He wore ornate black leather armor under a brilliant red cloak. His face was as red as his beard, and on his great head rested a thorny steel helm. The man tottered over to Sparkstone and bent a knee before him. "My eternal allegiance, Lord Sparkstone. Axon Company reporting with two hundred and seventeen men at your disposal."

"Commander Rotus Magnavilius!" Sparkstone said. "Rise, my weary friend. Good of you to join us, I am sure you've heard of the expected attack by the crone—?"

"I have indeed, my liege—your speaking orbs are quite useful." Commander Magnavilius nodded quickly to Canes and Corrigus. Only Canes responded in kind.

"Still sore about that duel, eh, Corrigus?"

One of Corrigus' brows rose. "Your use of Immunity was ... interesting."

"All in good fun, old man, all in good fun." Magnavilius glanced around the camp. "Glad I'm not too late for the fight." He turned to a soldier that trailed him. "Lieutenant—merge the men with the patrol squads. I want all hands armed and ready."

"As you wish, Commander," his lieutenant replied, turning his horse to call out commands.

Magnavilius stepped by Augum as if he didn't exist at all, almost crushing his fingers in the process. "Well, I hope you've all been practicing," he bellowed, laughing at his own joke. Others laughed when Sparkstone joined in. Magnavilius clapped Corrigus on the shoulder. "Nothing like a good arcane battle, eh, old chum?"

Corrigus only frowned.

"And who is this now—?" Magnavilius asked, turning beady eyes on Augum, who sat in the muddy snow between the warlocks. "A necrophyte under punishment? Why the old rags then?"

Sparkstone raised his chin. "This is my son."

"Your son? This is Augum Stone?" Magnavilius' red brows trolled up his forehead and he let loose a great steaming laugh. "Do you know that I had you on my lap when you were a wee tot? Sire! What great news to have you reunited with your boy—"

Sparkstone nodded, though there was no emotion in his voice. "Yes, it's quite the occasion."

"My word, I have a lot to catch up on, don't I, Lividius?"

"We shall toast after our victory. Right now, I could use some honest counsel."

Magnavilius gave a grunt as his eyes searched the horizon. "It's late. Is she waiting us out?"

"That's not her style. She can't stop teaching. She'll probably wander in here lecturing us all on our vagrant ways."

The soldiers chortled until a bright flash of light cut short their clucking, followed immediately by a thwacking explosion just to the south of them. The light flared around the camp, making visible an enormous arcane protective dome. It vibrated like a bell before disappearing into invisibility once again.

There were cries of alarm from all corners of the compound as soldiers ducked, before realizing it was safe to stand.

Magnavilius snorted a laugh. "You can stand now, Commander Canes." He flexed his arm and seventeen fiery rings erupted around it.

Canes didn't bother brushing the muddy snow off his haunches. "What was that—?"

"She tripped my outer defense," Corrigus said, his own arm coiling with nineteen rings of ivy.

"At last the wait is over," Sparkstone said quietly, arm raging to life with twenty electric bands shining brightest of all. The three scions began rotating around his plumed helm like a protective halo.

"Is she invisible?" Canes asked, head swiveling about.

Corrigus' brows furrowed together. "She may have doppelganged."

"Why would she bother?" Magnavilius asked.

"She could be ghosting," Sparkstone muttered.

Augum saw an opportunity to cause dissention. "Nana learned some really powerful new spells in Ley, you know," he lied, "and she knows plenty off-the-books spells too. She's also going to—"

"—I'm not as adept at detecting lies as Commander Tridian," Sparkstone replied, lightning eyes sweeping the outskirts of the camp, "but I know when my own son is lying."

"You don't know me, and she's not afraid of any of you at all, not even of the whole camp together—"

Magnavilius smacked the back of Augum's head with his hand. "You try your father's patience at the most inopportune time, boy!"

Augum scowled at the big red-haired man, wishing he could cast Centarro just to use his tongue as a weapon against them. Oh, how he will miss that beautiful spell.

The night sky rumbled and necks immediately craned skyward.

"That thunder sounds peculiar," Canes said.

Sparkstone watched unfazed. "It is her."

The clouds seemed to darken and lower, moving ever swifter in a gargantuan silent whirlpool around the camp. Suddenly, the entire spiral lit up with internal lightning, the accompanying crack rumbling Augum's bones like a drum. Horses neighed and whickered. The soldiers stirred uneasily, some edging nearer to tents.

"Steady now—!" Magnavilius shouted to his men.

Canes paled. "What good are common soldiers against a master warlock?" he muttered, though no one but Augum seemed to hear him.

And then it happened—the sky ruptured with wide bolts of lightning that struck the dome repeatedly in the same spot. Strike after raging strike lit up the shell, sending great ripples across its surface. The sound alone was like standing under a village-sized gong struck by a giant hammer. Soldiers ducked under tables and behind tents. Horses reared up, throwing their riders off.

"It's weakening—!" Canes shouted, dropping to his knees and holding up his hands in a defensive pose, like many of the soldiers.

Sparkstone, Magnavilius and Corrigus remained standing, watching the pummeling with a fixed curiosity. Robin took shelter under the wraith, which stared upwards at the storm as if entranced, its vacant eyes almost mournful. The Red Guard merely stood quiet near their master.

The lightning slowed and finally fizzled, leaving the dome riddled with giant gaping wounds.

"It seems it has withstood the onslaught," Corrigus said, gray brows rising up his forehead.

For a moment, there was only silence, punctuated by the sound of a horse whinny.

"There!" shouted a soldier. "The horizon—!"

Heads turned to the distant east where a tornado made from pure lightning swirled to life, so bright it lit up the Tallows for leagues. It stood in place, growing larger in size, before rushing forth in a crackling rage that tore up everything in its path. Thunder pulsed from it in a steady low roar that shook the ground. Soldiers began backing away, fear written across their faces.

"The dome will absorb it!" Corrigus shouted, holding up his hands. He shouted something else but his voice drowned in the rumbling.

The lightning tornado was upon them, howling and screeching and grinding at the dome. The shell cracked. Giant glass-like chunks began falling. A tent collapsed underneath one nearby. The chunk promptly disappeared, leaving carnage in its wake.

Almost everyone sought shelter, except for the warlocks. Magnavilius cast a red sphere around himself, Corrigus a shimmering armor, while Sparkstone merely stood there, flanked by the Red Guard.

Augum scrambled under a nearby trough that had fallen over, while the tornado settled directly above, allowing a vertigo-inducing glimpse up its cavity—a vast, murderous, rotating tower shining brighter than the sunniest day. Even he hoped the dome would hold, otherwise he'd be sucked up into that maelstrom along with everything else.

He stole a glance at his father. Sweat prickled the Lord of the Legion's face. The plume on his helmet whipped about in the wind. His golden form stood rock still.

"It's failing!" Corrigus mouthed, voice lost to the grinding din, hands waving for everyone to take cover.

The dome suddenly ruptured with a mighty cacophony and dissolved. The winds rapidly increased—tents flapped like laundry in a gale; barrels rolled and splintered; cookware, cots, dressers and chests lifted into the spiral, later destroyed by lightning tentacles snapping from within the vortex.

Soldiers hung on to what they could, a few already flying upward. The ones that remained stared up in horror as their colleagues vaporized.

Augum curled into a ball, hoping death would be quick. The true might of his great-grandmother was on full display, and it made his very bones tremble.

Suddenly the noise and light disappeared, leaving a ringing silence, except for the smash of objects falling back to earth, some of which were bodies.

"The dome is no more," Corrigus said, panting. He flexed his arm and it flared back to life with ivy rings. Magnavilius also rekindled his. Only Sparkstone's arm had not extinguished during the onslaught.

"Your arrogance knows no bounds," Anna Atticus Stone said in a booming voice that seemed to come from everywhere. Heads swiveled, seeking the source, but only the warlocks knew that was a fruitless endeavor, and stared into the black horizon of the Tallows.

Augum's breathing quickened. Somewhere out there in that dense night stood his great-grandmother … and she wasn't here to play games.

"My arrogance?" Sparkstone's voice was equally loud, rumbling across the plains. The non-arcane near him startled from the sudden outburst. "You stole the scion from me. You stole my own son. You lead the resistance against me. And you dare call *me* arrogant? I want that scion. No more lessons, grandmother. Now we battle."

Lightning flared up distantly, too far for the boom to reach the camp.

Mrs. Stone's voice wheezed a sigh, a low hum seeming to fly across eons of time. "Let it be so." The distant lightning raged closer and closer, the many strikes coalescing, finally forming a massive lightning creature with arms and legs like giant tree trunks. It flexed, roared electrically, and charged.

"Lightning elemental!" Corrigus yelled.

"Warlocks, cast your beasts!" Sparkstone called.

Augum watched as Corrigus, Magnavilius and his father cast their own elementals a ways forward of the camp. Their words were long and complex, as were their gestures, but when they finished, it appeared the Tallows had become a massive arena.

Corrigus' elemental was made of earth and rock, ripping up the ground with every step and sending rubble flying. Magnavilius' was made from pure fire, immolating the snow-covered grass. His father's was made of lightning, smaller than Mrs. Stone's, but not by much.

As everyone began cheering for the Legion elementals, Augum noticed his friends for the first time—they stood tied together outside of their tent, Justinius and the guards apparently wanting to keep abreast of what was happening. Only Ms. Jenkins was absent.

The elementals came at each other with tectonic ferocity, each punch and kick rumbling across the plains. Augum stole a glance at the warlocks, who concentrated as if fighting with their mind. It was not long before Mrs. Stone's snuffed Magnavilius' with a great uppercut, sending a stream of curses out of the man's mouth.

Corrigus used the opportunity to flank Mrs. Stone's elemental. He raised his arms to strike, his elemental mimicking his action. Augum saw his chance and dove at the man's waist, knocking him to the ground. Magnavilius immediately yanked him away, but the damage was done—Corrigus' earth elemental hesitated long enough to take a leap kick in the stomach. It collapsed in a heap of rubble.

Corrigus' face twisted with rage. His hand shot out, blasting the ground at Augum's scurrying feet with some kind of hissing venom.

It was merely a warning …

Luckily, his father did not notice what Augum had done.

A monstrous smack brought everyone's attention back to the battle. The mood amongst the camp grew tense as Augum pumped his fist, quietly rooting for his great-grandmother. But it wasn't to be—Mrs. Stone's elemental had taken too many hits, finally exploding in a shower of sparks that set the nearby grass on fire.

The camp erupted in cheers. Sparkstone threw up a fist in acknowledgement, turned to his audience and, with a big twirling flourish of his arm, exploded his elemental in celebration. Soldiers cheered even more, raising their weapons in salute of their leader.

Meanwhile, lightning continued in the plains, still too distant to hear. It wasn't long until everyone was looking ahead, waiting for the next assault.

And then they saw her—she stepped up onto the mound of earth left behind by Corrigus' earth elemental. Framed from behind by the lightning and below by the remnants of the grass fire, Anna Atticus Stone appeared a pathetic figure, a trifle compared to the size of the elementals that fought moments before.

Augum squinted—it appeared she held a new staff and wore a pristine white robe. He would have given anything to have Mr. Goss' spyglass just then.

Magnavilius raised his arm. "Lord Sparkstone—the men are anxious to attack!"

The soldiers threw up a roar.

"My liege—I urge caution," Corrigus said. "Allow me council to—" but the Lord of the Legion held up a hand, staying the old man.

"Commander Magnavilius, Commander Canes—take half of your men and SHOW THE CRONE THE MIGHT OF MY LEGION!" Sparkstone roared the last words arcanely, the sound rolling across the Tallows, shaking the tents.

Every man in the camp threw up a resounding cry, weapons clanging against shields or armor.

Magnavilius and Canes shouted commands. The men mounted their horses and formed into ranks—Canes and his men on one side, Magnavilius and his men on the other.

The two commanders looked back at their master and saluted with outstretched arms. "Hail to the Lord of the Legion! Glory to us all!"

"Hail!"

Sparkstone nodded proudly. The two commanders took this as a sign to attack. The ground rumbled from hooves as soldier after soldier urged his horse into a canter. The soldiers that remained cheered on their comrades. Halfway there, the swarm sprang into a gallop, and finally a sprint.

"And so I watch my brave Legionnaires ride to their extinction," Sparkstone said in a solemn voice, hands behind his back. He shared a look with Augum, and it was then Augum realized no one else had heard but him. His father's face, although partially hidden behind his golden helm, was proud and defiant.

He turned to his men. "Watch as your fellow men fight for the good glory of the Legion! Watch as they give their lives this day, so that one day, you may live eternal!" He screamed now, gesturing grandly. "Heroes! Every last one of them, heroes! I so name this battle, the Battle at Hangman's Rock!"

The men threw up cheer after cheer, a crowd of frothing wolves eager for meat.

Augum suddenly understood what his father was doing—he was creating *martyrs.* He remembered something Sir Westwood had once said— "Behold the martyr, for he lives forever." Even if his father should lose this day, he'd use it to his advantage in the future. Even calling it the Battle at Hangman's Rock served a purpose.

For the first time, he thought he understood one of the driving forces behind the Legion. It wasn't just for eternal life—it was also for *glory*.

Two spyglasses were rushed to Corrigus and Sparkstone. Corrigus began to relay aloud what they were seeing in a flat voice.

"She is making no moves yet. Front ranks nearing."

There were numerous quick flashes.

"First rank triggered a lightning trap—four gone. Now seven frozen in place—some kind of chain paralysis. Make that a dozen. Unknown number fallen off their horses, screaming—I suspect Fear. A few more are wandering off. That would be Confusion—"

The soldiers quieted down, paying close attention to each dispatch while staring at the distant light show. Rumblings and explosions echoed.

"Magnavilius casts darkness—"

Augum saw the mound disappear into the night.

"She evaded. Magnavilius casts fireball—Teleport Evasion. Counter attack. Mass disarm—"

Numerous weapons tumbled through the air, backlit by fire.

"Hold on … looks like … some of ours are attacking each other. Could be mastery level Possession."

Sparkstone and Corrigus exchanged brief glances before resuming their watch.

"Sleep against … looks like ten or so," Corrigus continued. "Magnavilius casts Rain of Fire—her Mystic Armor withstood. Paralyze Group against our own—another seven down, though could be more."

Suddenly there was a rumbling explosion followed by multiple quick bursts of light.

"Simulcast!"

There were audible gasps from the watching soldiers. "That's impossible," someone said.

"It was Forked Lightning and Mass Frenzy—" Corrigus said.

"That one's off-the-books," Sparkstone muttered.

The soldiers behind them fell completely silent. No one could tear their eyes away.

"She has sped up her movements greatly now," Corrigus went on. "Must be Slow Time."

A tremendous flash of light.

"She just Teleported ten from the field—" There was a hint of surprise in Corrigus' voice.

Augum, despite his frayed nerves, couldn't help wondering where those soldiers went.

"Triple Doppelganger—the troops don't know which one to attack. Lightning strike. And again. And yet again. Three down. Speared lightning—" Corrigus shook his head. "Unknown casualties."

Sparkstone adjusted his stance as Corrigus continued.

"Magnavilius' arcane armor has failed. He appears injured. Canes is rallying the troops around the mound. They are having a hard time getting close enough to use their weapons. Magnavilius casts Firebolt—blocked with Shield. Meteor—Teleport Evasion. Blaze—out of range. Lava river—Teleport Evasion *again*." His head shook continually now. "Her endurance ... Magnavilius is losing arcane stamina. Curtain of Fire—immune, probably from Sphere of Protection ..."

The Tallows were a flurry of fire and lightning now.

"Multiple flashes—many blinded. Thunderclap—several stunned. Chain Lightning! Twenty more gone—"

Low gasps from the crowd of soldiers.

"Magnavilius casts Fire Army. She countered with Wall of Lightning. Wait, he has successfully used Push, she's knocked down—!"

Augum's heart leapt to his throat as a cheer went up from the soldiers, but Corrigus raised a hand, silencing them.

"Troops trying to get near—they have fallen through the ground! Unbelievable ... must be an extension of Combat Portal at the master level. She's moving! Now casting Ball Lightning—seven plowed down. Explosive Lightning—four down. Canes has been levitated with Telekinesis ... struck by Flame Lightning ... he is on fire and now thrown against his own troops—two more down."

Augum stole a quick glance at his father—his jaw was tightly clenched.

"She seems to be leaving Magnavilius for last. Remaining soldiers fleeing into the darkness. She's letting them go. Magnavilius standing before her now. He's bleeding. They seem to be just staring at each other …"

A final flash of light.

Corrigus slowly lowered his spyglass. The camp went completely silent.

Augum stared at the distant scene. Thick smoke blew around pockets of fire. Horses meandered or lingered by their fallen riders. A lone figure stood silhouetted against the flames on the mound.

Sparkstone nodded slowly and turned to the soldiers, whose faces were pale as death. "On this day, good, proud, loyal men were sent into the hands of the Unnameables. We mark them as heroes to be remembered for their sacrifice. Commander Dollard Canes. Commander Rotus Magnavilius. Your many fallen comrades. Remember them well, for they shall live on in your hearts and in the eternal glory of the Battle at Hangman's Rock. Hail!"

The soldiers solemnly raised their weapons. "Hail!"

"Glory to the Legion!"

"Glory! Glory! Glory!"

"I shall spare the rest," Mrs. Stone's voice boomed, breathing hard. "If you face me alone, Lividius."

Sparkstone turned back to the Tallows, lightning eyes focusing on the tiny figure on the mound. "How about we trade—the scion in exchange for your great-grandson's friends." He hauled Augum up by the scruff. "Son, it is time for you to fulfill your promise. Your voice shall become arcanely loud. Speak the words of sense that will change her iron mind." He touched Augum's throat with a glowing palm. "This is your moment, Son. If you cannot do it for me, do it for your friends. Their lives rest in your hands."

Augum steeled himself before turning to Mrs. Stone, who stood on that distant hill, looking like the loneliest person in the world. His heart thundered—he was about to communicate with his great-grandmother again.

"Nana ... it's ... it's me, Augum," he began as a test, voice vibrating his innards and rolling across the plain. He knew what he had to say. He simply had to do it. He thought of his friends—Bridget, Leera, Mya, Haylee and Ms. Jenkins—and prayed for their forgiveness.

He took the deepest breath of his life and shouted, "NANA, FINISH THEM—THEY'RE AFRAID!"

THE ATTACK

The moment Augum ceased, his father struck him on the side of the head, sending him to the ground. He drew Burden's Edge, its blade sparking.

This was it, his father was going to murder him …

All of a sudden, something smashed into a nearby tent, capturing the Lord of the Legion's attention. It was the wraith, knocked off its feet by a wagon. Screams and shouts tore the air as ordinary objects began attacking people—a fork impaled a soldier's eye; a trough knocked another off his horse; a wheelbarrow chased after a screaming man who ended up tripping and being repeatedly run over.

"What spell is that—!" someone shouted.

"Master level Telekinesis," Corrigus replied, halting a hovering axe from cleaving a soldier in two.

Augum used the confusion to crawl away as fast as possible. To his right, he caught a glimpse of a Red Guard decapitating a Black Guardsmen, the Legionnaire apparently possessed, having raised his mace against the death knight. To his left, he witnessed his father shoot lightning at nearby tents, ripping them asunder. Ahead, just beyond the tower, he spotted Justinius drawing his blade, about to use it on his struggling, tied-up friends.

Suddenly the tower burst into flames. The watchman screamed and jumped, landing right before Augum in a burning heap. As he scrambled around the corpse, he glimpsed Corrigus levitate a tremendous boulder from the earth, overturning a tent in the process, before hurling it at what appeared to be a very speedy Mrs. Stone. A moment later, he spotted his father zoom by in a blur, equally as fast. He pictured them fighting against each other in that inflexible, slow-motion world he had experienced under the influence of the Slow Time scroll.

Explosions and bolts of lightning began striking the camp, some from the sky, and some from seemingly nowhere. Soldiers were thrown in the air; tents burst into flame; horses scattered. The ground never stopped shaking, making it hard to stand.

He kept crawling as fast as his tired body would let him. He made it around the burning tower just in time to see Leera performing several impressive feats of arcanery—she had somehow freed herself of the rope and disarmed not one but two Black guardsmen. Bridget, for her part, had Justinius on the ground in a headlock.

They'd cast Centarro, he realized, immediately understanding the implications. Then black smoke obscured his view of them.

The ground stopped shaking and he scrambled to his feet. Suddenly an intensely sharp pain stabbed at his right flank. He screamed and buckled.

"Die—!" Robin shouted, withdrawing his dagger in an attempt to strike again.

Augum wilted from the shock, raised his arm to cast Shield, forgetting he had been stripped of his arcanery. The blade caught his palm, piercing it, jolting him with more excruciating pain and robbing him of breath. Robin, his face lit with murderous zeal, yanked the dagger for a third and final strike.

A tremendous wooden cracking began. Augum thought it was the Slam spell until he looked up. He just barely managed to jump aside as the watchtower crashed onto the spot he had been occupying a moment before. He curled into a ball, shielding himself from the rush of flames. The air became white hot, burning his throat.

When he raised his head, fire engulfed everything, including both his sleeves and shoulder. He rolled in the mud to snuff it out. He ducked as a barrel zipped by, followed by a wagon and a spear. Soon more objects flew, aimed at a golden armored man artfully blocking them with a giant lightning shield. When his shield suddenly failed, he picked up the closest thing nearby—a broken trunk lid.

"My supreme lord, in here!" shouted a voice.

Augum looked about to see a disheveled Sydo holding up a tent flap. Half of the tent was on fire, but that didn't seem to bother him.

One of Mrs. Stone's furious telekinetic attacks tore the Lord of the Legion's makeshift shield from his hands.

Sydo gestured inside the tent. "Great One, it's safe in here—" but the Lord of the Legion, suddenly finding himself defenseless against a rabid onslaught, simply picked Sydo up and blocked a broken broom that would have otherwise impaled his face. The broom sliced through Sydo, jamming at the bristles. Sparkstone discarded him without notice, continuing to block Mrs. Stone's advances with other objects until he backed out of sight. Sydo was left twitching on the ground, soon going still.

Augum felt pity for the boy. A sad end to a miserable existence. If he'd only had the courage to change instead of taking the dark path. If he'd only been able to see his own arrogance, his own failings, to appreciate what he had, he might not have lost it all.

"I see you—!" Robin sang from the other side of a burning truss, searching for a way to get at Augum.

Augum tried to scramble to his feet but slipped from the pain. His vision dimmed in time with waves of nausea, like a rough ocean swell. The stabbing had weakened him more than he thought. He needed to get to his friends, but lay bleeding and coughing, the smoke and heat slowly extinguishing his life.

"Augum—!" Leera suddenly leapt from out of the flames, robe ablaze. She grabbed onto him, and with a strength summoned from the arcane unknown, began dragging him.

He blearily saw soldiers rolling and screaming. Horses flailed and galloped nearby. Tents burned, the fires joining together to create miniature flaming tornadoes.

Leera concentrated on the path ahead, completely confident, ignoring her blazing robe. A soldier rushed them but she deftly flung muddy snow into his eyes. He stumbled right by them and into the flames, screaming.

Augum held on with all his remaining strength, feeling his life drain with every drop of blood that stained the muddy slush, melted from the heat.

Another explosion tore the air nearby, sending Leera sprawling—she recovered quickly, and used the roll on the ground to smother the flames that stubbornly clung to her robe. Soot-stained yet determined, she dragged him onward. It was only when she began to slow that he realized the effects of Centarro were wearing off.

"Help!" he called feebly. It was the only thing he could think of—he couldn't cast spells anymore and was too weak to do anything. "Help, please, somebody …"

But there was only the roar of fire.

Leera let go of him and stared down at her hands, a lost child in an inferno. She'd wander off any moment, never to be seen again, and he didn't have the strength to stop her.

"Leera …"

She gave him a blank look before focusing on the flames.

He winced. "Leera, stay with me … Please, look at me …"

She cocked her head, a vacant expression on her face, and took a step toward the fire. She was about to step to her death when someone snagged her hand.

"Gotcha!" Haylee said, her face and hair blackened with soot. She turned away only a moment, keeping a firm grip. "They're over here—Leera and Augum are here!"

Augum coughed, desperately trying to stay conscious, wincing from the sharp pain in his side and hand.

"I got her!" Mya said, emerging from the smoke and taking Leera by the hand.

"And I'll get Augum." Haylee furrowed her blonde brows, grabbed his hands, and dragged him through a haze of black smoke, keeping her eyes tightly shut.

They emerged before a torn tent, coughing. Mya stood in front of it holding a confused Leera. Ms. Jenkins held Bridget nearby. Justinius lay back over a barrel, pierced by his own blade.

"Ms. Jenkins, help—!" Haylee said, collapsing to the ground, gasping.

"I'm okay now," Bridget said, sitting down. "Help them …"

More explosions and sounds of arcane warfare came from within the camp, punctuated by the occasional scream, or shout of command. Augum dazedly wondered how long Mrs. Stone could hold out.

Ms. Jenkins hovered over his form, holding a hand over her mouth to suppress the coughing. Her brow was sweaty, her skin pale. He closed his eyes, about ready to let go—it was just too difficult to stay conscious. He heard soothing words and a cold hand on his forehead, over his heart, then over his wounds—first his side, then his pierced palm. He felt a warm light shining through him, his strength slowly returning.

When Ms. Jenkins finished, she collapsed beside him, wheezing shallow breaths. Bridget stumbled into the tent, emerging a moment later carrying the rucksack. "We have to get out of here, *now*!"

Leera, who seemed to have finally come out of her daze, dropped to her knees by Augum. "Aug, you have to get up and help us. We're spent … you're the … you're the only one that can still cast spells—"

"I can't …" he mumbled between coughs. "Witch … cursed me … can't cast spells …"

Leera, Bridget, Mya and Haylee gaped at him, but it was Ms. Jenkins that caught his eye. She fixed him with a particular look that sent a shiver up his spine. Somehow, perhaps unconsciously, he knew what she was going to do.

"No," he said, "I won't let you. Your son—"

"He will … understand. Let me … do this." She coughed blood, gesturing for the girls to help her sit up. They did so, and she palmed Augum's forehead and heart, beginning a complex arcane recitation that increased in volume as she spoke. He was going to fight her off and cancel the spell, yet it was her face that stopped him—it radiated love and compassion, mercy and joy.

He felt the most bizarre buzzing sensation, as if being filled up with a long-forgotten energy, re-awakening and renewing his strength and vitality.

At the end of the spell, her face was purple. Her eyes steadily closed as she spoke in a fragile whisper. "I know … you won't … waste this." She gave the faintest smile before dying where she sat, in the hands of the girls.

"Oh, Ms. Jenkins …" Bridget whispered.

They were a leaf floating amongst a flaming ocean of chaos—soldiers screamed as they burned; explosions boomed, punctuated by rumblings; arcane missiles tore through the air, maiming anything in their path. Yet all five of them just stared at her still form.

At last, the girls gently laid her down, covering her peaceful face with her own robe.

Watching the body of Miralda Jenkins the healer, now forever at rest and free of her torments, Augum thought of the Lord of the Legion's speech.

We, too, have our glory, Father …

A huge ball of electric fire slammed into a nearby tent, forcing them to hit the ground. It exploded, shooting objects past their heads.

"We have to get out of here!" Augum yelled. "Everybody hold on! We have to run through the fire!" He snatched Mya's hand.

As soon as all five grabbed hold in a chain, he began navigating the maze of fire. He covered his mouth with his sleeve, trying not to breathe in the acrid smoke. The flames seemed to rage everywhere now, consuming every tent, even horses and bodies. The stench was enough to roil his gut and send bile into his throat.

The moment after exiting a cloud of smoke, a looming shadow slammed into him so hard he thought a charging bull had hit him. He flew through the air, plowing into a burning tent and emerging out the other side, rolling in the muddy snow.

He stood up, dazed, seeing a giant black form emerge from the fire. The wet rags on its limbs, hanging in strips, hissed and bubbled in the heat.

"Kill him!" Robin shouted from somewhere. "Kill him now!"

The wraith lowered its skull-like head, vacant eyes watching him. It cooed, growled, and charged.

There was nowhere to go and he wasn't quick enough to move out of its way.

"Nana, help—!" but there simply was no time. He had to save himself.

The wraith reared back, readying to perform some kind of charging claw-punch, a move that would surely end his life.

There was only one possible thing that might work … he placed both forearms before him in a blocking gesture and focused on making a giant shield of hard lightning.

The clawed fist whistled forth just as he felt a white heat on his arms. It smashed into a shied that actually curved over his head slightly. The force of the blow sent him tumbling backward through the mud until he slammed against an overturned barrel of ale. It ruptured, its hoppy smell mingling with the scent of burning flesh and pine.

The wraith threw its head back, snorted, and flexed.

He arcanely shoved the barrel out of his way and stood up, panting.

Damn it was good to have his arcanery back.

"Nana! Can you hear me?" He glanced around, hoping for any sign of her. Black smoke curled into the air in every direction. "Bridget! Leera!" A distant explosion sounded; muffled screams.

The wraith made a guttural roar, lowered its head, and charged, its great claws spanning the length of five men, tearing at burning tents along the way.

If he timed it right, it might work …

Just as it was upon him, he shouted, "Grau!" making a fierce throwing gesture at the ground. A tremendous crack of thunder rumbled the earth, waving the flames and pulsing his bones.

The wraith flinched. Augum used that split moment to jump out of the way of its claws, tumbling aside as it blew past.

"That won't work again!" Robin yelled, emerging from the flames holding Mya, a dagger to her throat. "You move and I give her a Nodian smile."

"Bridget, Leera, Nana—he's got Mya!" Augum called, hoping to get help.

A crooked smile lit up Robin's face. "They're busy fighting. Don't worry, they won't last ..." The wraith emerged from the flames beside him, smoking, watching its master.

"Pick him up."

Augum tried to crawl away from it, but he was too slow. It grabbed him like a doll, holding him by his midriff, cooing as if about to pet a cat.

"Squeeze him."

Augum screamed. It was like being in the grip of a gigantic rotten vice. "Nan—" he tried to say, feeling like he was about to explode from the pressure. Suddenly there was another crack of thunder, this one even louder.

"I told you that wouldn't work—" Robin paled. "No—!"

A giant lightning hand gripped the wraith's arm. It shrieked and let Augum go. He fell to the ground, rolled away, and looked up—it was another lightning elemental. The electric monster gave the wraith a massive uppercut that sent it flying up into the air.

"Nana! Are you here? We're in trouble!" but there was no sign of her.

Meanwhile, the two giants attacked each other like rabid dogs, the earth rumbling with each strike. Then the lightning elemental tackled the wraith and the two creatures rolled off into the flames.

"No, no, NO—!" Robin screamed, spittle shooting out of his mouth. He was breathing rapidly, knuckles white around the dagger at Mya's throat. In his other hand, he held the destiny stone.

Augum stood up, palms spread wide before him. "Let her go, Robin, this is between you and I—"

"You shut up—" Robin pressed the blade against her throat.

Mya whimpered. "Augum …" The fear in her voice squeezed his heart tighter than the wraith had squeezed his body.

"I know you're not a murderer, Robin, let her go and fight me, fight *me*—"

"Don't you tell me who I am!" The hand that held the destiny stone curled into a fist. "You took Haylee away from me, remember? I swore to you I would take from you. You want her? Here, have her, you gutterborn swine—"

He shoved Mya forward, cutting her throat in the process.

"NO—!" Augum screamed, sprinting.

She stumbled to him, gurgling, porcelain hands at her throat. Blood gushed over them and down her Legion servant robe. She fell right into his arms. Behind her, several paces back, stood Robin, dagger covered in blood, eyes wide.

"What've you done—" Augum said, unable to keep the horror from his quivering voice. "What have you done …"

He laid Mya gently on the ground, holding her close. She was dying in his arms, staring at him with those almond eyes, the brilliant green light in them fading. He placed a trembling hand on top of both of hers, hoping it would somehow stop the bleeding. Her face grew whiter and whiter, the skin developing a blue sheen to it.

"Mya, it'll be okay, everything's going to be fine," he mumbled absurdly.

"There. There! Now we're even," he heard Robin say in a shaky voice. "It was your fault anyway—you made me do it. You shouldn't have taken Haylee from me!"

To Augum, the words were a thousand leagues away. Time slowed to a crawl. It was just him and Mya, together at last. She kept staring at him, her light now a sputtering candle.

Every moment he remembered of her swam before his mind—the first time he had laid eyes on her in Castle Arinthian, when she curtsied and smiled; seeing her unconscious on the stairs and shoving oxy into her mouth to save her life; her feverish form in the trapper's cabin; feeling her porcelain hand touch his chest to survey the damage done by the walker; her hair whipping about as she ran to distract the guards, sacrificing herself so the trio could get away; the time he danced with her in the ancient Leyan city of Absalon, holding her close to him, a dance he would never forget as long as he lived …

A single tear rolled down her cheek. She smiled weakly, her hands going limp under his, the blood no longer gushing. Her eyes remained upon him even after that precious light had dimmed to total darkness.

"Mya …" he whispered, holding her gently. "Mya …"

FEATS

Everything was in slow motion when hands began prying Augum from Mya. The voices were distant and muted. Flames leapt nearby, but they were dim, their heat feeble compared to the burning inside his heart.

"Come on, Aug, we have to go!" said a freckled girl he barely recognized.

"You monster!" shouted a cinnamon-haired girl. "What have you done!"

"He's in shock," said a blonde-haired girl. "Take him, go—go now!"

A great shadow appeared nearby, but he could only see it as a blurry figure in the flames.

"It's back—!"

"I'll stay and fight, I might be able to command it—what are you waiting for, take him and go—!"

He felt himself led away from Mya's still form, unable to comprehend what was happening. Was he still holding her?

Had he *ever* held her? Part of him was clear, the part that told him she should be saved—but he didn't even have the fight to run back to her, to save her from the encroaching flames, to give her a proper burial.

Explosions boomed yet he could barely hear past the sound of rushing blood in his head. Fire roared as men moaned and died all around them.

He didn't care. Nothing mattered.

All at once, they were free of it, emerging just west of the camp, stepping over scalded soldiers with bizarre lightning patterns on their flesh, none of whom seemed willing or able to fight. He was dragged to the woods, suddenly hearing an implosive sucking sound.

He turned to his right only to find Corrigus standing there, splattered with blood from his beard to his boots. His gold-fringed robe was torn and his left arm hung limp at his side. A giant gash streaked across his face.

"No, I won't let you, not again—" Augum said through gritted teeth, barely conscious of what he was saying. He broke away from the girls' grip and charged the old warlock, every fiber of his being alive with anger. The girls were screaming behind him but he didn't care—he wouldn't let them kill another of his friends, even if he had to die to prevent it.

Corrigus gurgled a laugh, making a beckoning motion with his good hand, before deteriorating into a bloody coughing fit.

"Centeratoraye xao xen!" Augum spat, never meaning a spell more. The world instantly became profoundly simple. There were less than seven paces between himself and Corrigus. The old man was choking but regaining his composure quickly—too quickly in fact. Augum noticed he wore an ornate dagger at his belt. That was his chance. He was aware Corrigus didn't fear him and would strike him down quicker than he could run. He decided to resort to plain trickery.

Knowing it was Mrs. Stone Corrigus truly feared, he glanced a little past the man and made a grateful face as if seeing a familiar savior.

"The oldest trick in the book," he could hear Sir Westwood say, a straw dangling from his mouth.

This maneuver may not have worked on the Blade of Sorrows, but Corrigus fell for it, turning his head to what he perceived to be the true threat—Mrs. Stone. Augum increased his charge to a full-on sprint, using, with the aid of Centarro, certain pockets in the snow for better footing. As Corrigus' head turned back to him, pronouncing the first words of an incantation, Augum's hand was on the man's dagger. Just as Corrigus finished the spell, Augum buried the dagger in his temple with one graceful motion.

One of the Legion's most powerful warlocks stood gaping, jaw clacking as if stuck on a word, before falling dead.

But Augum's Centarro-laced mind was solely on Mya. Plans formed on how to save her, how to rush back into the flames, pick her up, and somehow bring her back to life. Everything seemed possible in that moment, *everything*.

Yet he just stood there, staring at the bloody corpse of this old man. He wondered what kind of life Corrigus had lived. Did he have friends that would miss him? Did someone love him? Did he ever care about others, or was he just … evil? Did he have sons, daughters, nephews, cousins? Was there a Mya out there somewhere without a father now?

"Aug … I can't believe what you just did," someone said as the fog began to cloud his mind. "What a feat …"

He dully felt himself led away. The stupidity that came along with the side effects of Centarro forbade comprehension. All that he experienced was a series of basic sensations. Hands kept at his back and shoulders, pushing him onwards. He didn't understand what the big rush was. A harsh smell burned his throat. Shapes moved in ways far too complex for his mind. He recognized the basic outlines of trees. They were kind of pretty in the dull darkness, lit by something orange and hot.

When his sense began returning, he found himself sitting in the snow, back against a trunk, hands bloody and shaking. Bridget and Leera conversed in low voices beside him, trying to decide which direction to go next. The smell of wood smoke was in the air. Was there a hearth nearby? Could he sit before it and warm up?

"Where are we?" he mumbled, rubbing his eyes. "Where's Mya? Is she all right?" He knew where she was, he had left her to the flames …

Bridget and Leera exchanged looks before each embraced him.

"Mya's gone," Bridget whispered, refusing to let go even when he tried pushing her away.

"No she's not," he said, haunted by Mya's final smile. "We have to go back and get her." He recalled how cold her hands were. "She's waiting for us right now." The blood from her throat had been warm though … "Why aren't we moving to get her already?" He left her all alone back there.

Leera squeezed harder. "Oh, Aug …"

Why weren't they going back to get Mya? He swallowed, envisioning her lying on the ground, alone, surrounded by flames and a looming shadow that moved.

"I think Mya's in trouble, we should get her," he mumbled through Bridget's hair. Her shoulders were heaving, as were Leera's, and neither of them would let go for some reason. Why wouldn't they let go—didn't they realize they had work to do? What was wrong with them! He tried to pry them off again, but it was in vain—their grip was stronger than his trembling hands.

"Haylee stayed behind to hold off the wraith," Bridget said, finally withdrawing, hands remaining on his shoulders. Her eyes were red, cheeks soot-stained.

"It's just us now," Leera said quietly.

"Just us?"

Leera nodded. "Just us …"

"Where's Nana?"

"I don't know. There was a really big explosion—"

He finally tore away from them to peer around the trunk. The entire Legion camp burned. Black armored bodies lay smoking in the slush. Some figures still hobbled or crawled within the flames, crying out. Horses roamed riderless.

"We have to find Nana—" he said, repeatedly straightening his stained and charred robe.

Bridget's brows knit together as she stood. "Augum, what can we do? We have to get out of here. We have to save ourselves. That's what Mrs. Stone wants."

He looked her in the eye. "I don't expect you to understand, but I have to try to find her." She was the only one who could save Mya. "Find some horses and stay here, I'll be right back—" and without waiting for a response, he raced toward the flames, the girls desperately calling after him.

Find Nana. Save Mya. Find Nana. Save Mya … The mantra repeated in his frantic brain.

He soon reached the outskirts of the burning camp, strewn with bodies. Flames licked around Hangman's Rock, a giant black egg baking in the inferno. He envisioned it cracking and that witch spilling out.

"Nana!" he called, searching the bodies. "Nana—!"

Suddenly a stick shot out from the fires and tumbled in the snow, coming to rest only feet away, smoking and melting through the top layer of frost. Something else, maybe a sack of some sort, also rolled out of the fire.

He gaped stupidly before realizing what the object really was. "Nana—!"

He ran to her, falling by her side, tenderly holding up her bloody head. Her eyes barely opened into weak slits. Her once pristine white robe was charred, torn and frayed.

He felt a nauseating weakness and had to steady himself. "Not you too, Nana, not you too …"

"My … staff …" she said in a barely audible voice. He laid her down gently, turning to the raging fire. Sparkstone laughed triumphantly from within, the sound amplified arcanely, visually reverberating the flames and shaking the ground.

"I'll find it, Nana—" he said, running off to where he saw it sink into the snow.

He stopped as the laughter suddenly sharpened. Without turning around, he knew the Lord of the Legion had emerged from the fire.

"Leaving her behind already, Son?" boomed his father, sounding out of breath.

Augum turned, conscious of the staff only paces away. He pretended not to have seen it and faced his father. Mrs. Stone lay between the two of them.

"Shyneo," Augum said, lighting up his palm and flaring his arm with his only stripe.

Sparkstone smiled. A melted gash tore across his golden chest plate. Besides that, there were only scratches and occasional char marks. The plume of his helmet had burned completely off, as had his cloak and leather pouches, though he himself seemed immune to the flames. The three scions slowly revolved around his head, glinting sentinels humming faintly.

"Congratulations, Son, you have achieved your 1st degree. I am proud of you. Your mother would be proud too, I know it."

"My mother …" Augum said mockingly.

"You have to understand, Son, things were never supposed to happen that way. If I could go back … one day …" Sparkstone stiffened and raised his chin. "You know, I think I am finally getting the feel of these scions. They extend arcane powers and strengthen them, but they can do so much more, I can sense that now. As you are a beginner in the arcane ways, so, too, am I a beginner with these ancient artifacts."

Augum squared his body, splaying his hands in a gesture as if readying to fight. His father didn't seem to care, sighing and pacing toward Mrs. Stone.

He thinks she has the scion in her possession! Augum realized, senses sharpening. He concentrated on the one task he knew he could do at that moment.

"Feel the attraction of the stones", he remembered Mrs. Stone say to him at the beginning of his training. Without another moment's hesitation, he reached out, using Telekinesis to summon her staff. As soon as he felt its sleekness in his shining palm, a powerful surge shot through his heart, quickening it.

"Centeratoraye xao xen!"

The effect of Centarro while holding Mrs. Stone's staff, topped with the family scion, was like being transformed into an arcane bull. The first thing he felt was a fountain of new arcane strength, instantly accessible. He knew the power and duration of his spells were extended by unknown amounts. Additionally, for the first time in his life, he felt certain he could completely control his arcanery.

All this he understood in the time it took for his father to look up. Sparkstone blurted a laugh before seeing something in his son's face, something that made him hesitate. Augum, in Centarric perfection, calmly pointed the staff at his father. He accessed that mysterious and arcanely wild part of him he knew could slow time, and watched in fascination as the flames, leaping tall behind his father, slowed to a calm wavering. Everything began to sparkle, just as when he had been under the influence of the Slow Time spell. He hoped Mrs. Stone had worn the Lord of the Legion down just enough for him to pull this off.

Ever calm, he allowed the lightning to manifest inside him, building and building, until the blue crystal scion shone radiantly. Before his father even blinked, he pointed the staff and discharged the buildup of his arcane strength, like an over-extended crossbow bolt. Even under the influence of Slow Time, the bolt of lightning was instantaneous. For the briefest moment, he glimpsed surprise on his father's face as the bolt smashed into him, sending him flying backward into the fire.

Now came the choice he'd known he would have to face the moment he had gripped the staff—even though Centarro's duration would be extended, it would not be extended enough for him to rush into the fire, find Mya, carry her back, and then do the same for his great-grandmother.

He could save one of them, but not both.

The choice was impossible, but it had to be made. He glanced up at the flames, roaring in one giant inferno.

"I'll always remember you ..."

He pointed the staff at his great-grandmother and effortlessly lifted her with Telekinesis. He then raced back to the girls, Mrs. Stone floating alongside. He had to return before the side effects of Centarro kicked in, and he still had to give Nana back her staff, for if his father was right, she would die without the scion in her control. The thought reawakened the memory of Thomas Stone aging before his eyes.

Augum navigated trees, bodies, horses, and fire as if they were mere puddles, yet when the scion-extended effects of Centarro finally began wearing off, he still had not found his friends.

"Bridget! Leera!" he kept calling out. "Bridget! Leera! Where are you!"

At last, there came a muffled reply. He ran stupidly, every ounce of his concentration dedicated to keeping Mrs. Stone afloat—and stumbled right into Leera's arms, somehow managing to allow Mrs. Stone to float safely to the snowy ground. With the last echo of any rational thought, he thrust the staff into Leera's hand.

"Give … this … to … her…" he said before the familiar nebulous fog overtook him for the second time that night.

REUNION

When Augum regained his senses, he found himself bobbing to the rhythm of a horse. Leera sat behind, holding him tenderly with one hand, reins with the other. They were riding through snowy woods on a black warhorse, Bridget and Mrs. Stone on a chestnut mare beside them. Dramask blankets covered everyone.

Leera was unaware he had woken from his stupor. For a little while, he just let himself feel nothing but the secure sensation of being held in someone's arms.

Suddenly he remembered holding Mya, his hand over both of hers trying to stop the blood flow, her eyes watching him. He bolted upright, searching for her.

"Aug, it's all right, we're safe now," Leera whispered, squeezing his midriff.

Bridget glanced at him, a pained expression on her face.

He wanted to ask about Mya, if she had made it out, but couldn't voice the question. It wouldn't move past his lips.

His heart tightened painfully as he let Leera guide him back into her embrace.

Then he remembered, and the world turned gray and hollow.

"You did good," Leera whispered. "Mrs. Stone is all right, but she'll need lots of bed rest."

He glanced over at the unconscious form of his great-grandmother. The legendary warlock held her staff to her chest, the scion tip gleaming. Perhaps it was his imagination, but it looked like there were more lines on her face.

"We don't know what happened to Haylee though," Bridget said, tugging at the blanket so it covered Mrs. Stone's neck. "She stayed behind to take on Robin and the wraith. I hope she's all right ..."

His thoughts were black. Haylee, too, was gone. What happened to her? Nothing turned out as it should have. He dully watched fields of stars sparkle in the cloudless sky, thinking how miserably his plans had failed.

"You were senseless a long time," Leera said. "Half the night. It was odd."

Augum recalled the lightning striking his father. His voice was distant when he replied. "I used Centarro a second time. The scion made things weird. It made my spells ... stronger. I even used wild arcanery with it ..."

"I think you pushed your arcane stamina beyond its limits." She delicately brushed aside his muddy hair. "We have to clean you up, you're a mess."

As if all the pain needed was a reminder, his ankle began stinging where Robin had scorched it. His head, too, throbbed. He licked his lips, tasting blood.

"Aug, you did ... you did amazing." There was a quiet affection in Leera's voice, but to him, amazing wasn't good enough. In fact, he wished she would curse at him instead.

"I really didn't think we'd survive that one," Bridget said.

"Yeah, neither did I," Leera said. "How'd you get past your father?"

He said the words without emotion. "Centarro and Nana's staff. Got lucky—he was distracted. Blasted him into the fire." What did it matter though? Mya was gone.

"You mean distracted like Corrigus? It's not all luck, you know."

He didn't bother shrugging. Why won't they just leave him alone …

Leera gave him a squeeze. "One day, they'll call you a hero as great as your great-grandmother."

He sat up suddenly, blanket falling from his shoulders. "Stop it! If you were in my place, you would have done the same, probably better even. I failed, all right? Mya's dead, do you understand? She. Is. Dead!"

Leera's hands quickly retreated, dropping the reins. A hurt look passed over her eyes.

"Aug, you did what you could," Bridget said. "We all did what we could …"

He took up the reins, face hot. Not good enough.

Leera placed the blanket back on his shoulders. "I'm sorry," she mumbled.

They rode in silence for some time, Augum hating himself.

"Think your father survived?" Bridget finally asked.

He pondered the matter. His father had been walking through that fire unscathed only moments before he struck him. "Probably." Then he remembered something. "We have to tell Nana about Thomas." How in Sithesia was he going to approach that subject? How does one tell his great-grandmother her husband died? And One Eye made them promise to pass on his message of apology too.

"Better wait until she's well enough. I wonder what the Seers told her …"

He didn't reply, in no mood to talk. Anything he said would probably come out wrong anyway.

They resumed a silent canter.

Eventually, he started feeling terrible for taking his anger out on Leera. She was Mya's friend too. What right did he have to be angry with her? Better to reserve that for Robin and his father. His thoughts turned against him and all this silence was making it worse.

"So where're we going, anyway?" he asked, trying to sound somewhat amiable.

"To retrieve Leland and Mr. Goss," Bridget said. "Mrs. Stone told us she sheltered them in an abandoned cabin somewhere west of Sparrow's Perch."

He felt a warm gladness sweep over him—so Nana *had* saved Leland and Mr. Goss first. He wondered how she knew they would need help.

His thoughts wandered to the selfless acts of the healer, Ms. Jenkins. She had saved him and paid the ultimate price for it. Sacrifice on his behalf was a recurring pattern. Maybe a witch had cast a curse on him when he was a boy …

"I hardly knew Ms. Jenkins," he said. "Are all healers like that?"

"I think most healers have a kindly disposition," Bridget said. "Makes you wonder how many under the Legion's thumb are like her."

"I didn't know they could remove witch curses though."

"Neither did I."

He lit up his wrist with his degree ring, heart filled with gratitude for that greatest of sacrifices, all so he could cast his arcanery once more. The thought was powerful and unnerving—*someone had actually given up their life for him to be able to cast spells again.*

It will not be wasted, that was a promise.

He gave a half-glance back at Leera. She quickly looked away, but not before he had a chance to spot the dark circles under her eyes. She had to be as tired as he was.

"Lee, I'm sorry."

She didn't reply, choosing to fuss with a loose strap hanging from the saddle.

"I didn't mean to hurt your feelings," he continued. "I'm a rotten friend and I got Ms. Jenkins and Mya killed and—"

"Stop it—" Leera said, looking up with watery eyes. "Just … hush."

He turned back around, confused.

"We should go single file," Bridget said, ducking underneath a snow-covered branch. "I'll take lead."

Time passed. The cold deepened as night fell. A hush descended over the snowy forest.

Augum adjusted the blanket, stretching it so that more would be available for Leera. She took it wordlessly, wrapping it snug around the two of them. Suddenly she put her arms around his waist and placed her head on his shoulder. It wasn't long before she slept quietly.

He was confused as to his feelings. He remembered kissing Leera on the cheek and felt a hot flush. Then he remembered Leera's advice to stop torturing himself with Mya—but now Mya was gone. He had watched her die in his arms. It all made little sense and hurt to think about, so he shoved the thoughts aside, choosing to focus on the path, the forest, anything but Mya.

It proved impossible. That look—that final look would never leave him. The fading pulse in her porcelain hands, that shining smile, those almond eyes …

At last, after hours of trotting well into the wee hours of the morning, they arrived at a dilapidated cabin surrounded by frozen overgrowth and towering cedars. The snow here was pristine, only punctured by occasional rabbit tracks.

"Leera," Augum whispered over his shoulder. Leera groaned and readjusted her grip on his waist. "Leera, we're here ..."

She stirred, lifted her head, and opened her eyes. "Already?"

"Yeah, sleepyhead, come on." He helped her dismount. He then took the reins of Bridget and Mrs. Stone's horse, leading it up to the cabin. The rickety door suddenly creaked open and out came a tired-looking Mr. Goss, adjusting his spectacles.

"Mercy, what a wonderful, sooty sight you all are—!" He quickly drew Augum and then Leera into a tight hug.

"And Bridget ... oh, I am just so happy to see you all safe."

"Hello, Mr. Goss," Bridget said in a weary voice. "How is Leland? Is he all right?"

"Oh yes, he is sleeping inside." His eyes then travelled to Mrs. Stone. He gracefully took her hand and kissed it. "My dear Mrs. Stone, this is the second time I find myself thanking you for saving the life of my son ..."

Mrs. Stone stirred, too weak to speak. She patted his hand without opening her eyes.

"Come, let us take her inside," Mr. Goss said.

With a little group effort, they carried her to the dilapidated hut and bundled her in blankets near Leland, who blithely snoozed away, a linen bandage wrapped around his head.

Augum went out to tie up the horses. "Ms. Jenkins didn't make it," he blurted upon his return, closing the door behind him, head low. Her life for his arcanery. He never felt more undeserving.

Mr. Goss, who had been busy helping Bridget remove the rucksack, slowed down. He placed it on the ground and took off his spectacles to clean them. "I ... I see."

"We don't know what happened to Haylee either," Bridget said. "And one of our other companions …" She looked to Augum, whose mouth suddenly went dry. Mr. Goss didn't know Mya, so what was the point of telling him? He looked away. He'd rather not talk about it.

Mr. Goss held the spectacles in his hand while staring at his son lying quietly beside Mrs. Stone. "There has been much loss this day." He slowly glanced around at them. "Yet we live on. Ms. Jenkins saved the life of my boy. I will never forget that. I will never forget her, as I will never forget Mrs. Stone for her efforts. I am a humble chandler with no hope of paying these debts back." He replaced his spectacles. "You all look exhausted. Let us not think on the matter anymore. Get some sleep. There will be plenty of days ahead for rumination."

They washed their faces and hands with snow as Mr. Goss swept the floor and readied blankets. By the time dawn sent thin light streaking in through the shutters, everyone snoozed, breath fogging in the crisp air.

Augum dreamt of Mya. He was holding her as she disappeared before his eyes, like the morning mist after the sun shone upon it. The harder he held, the more she faded, until she was gone, leaving the memory of that final look.

A QUIET FIRE

Little was said the next morning. They packed and washed up. As they were readying to take inventory, Augum realized he had forgotten the Orb of Orion. Luckily, he still had the pearl in one of his pockets.

He had to see. Maybe Mya was there, waiting to be rescued.

When they weren't looking, he closed his eyes and concentrated on seeing through the orb. A moment later he was staring at the remains of two cots, a tent, and a slew of blackened bodies. In the background, between clouds of black smoke, was the hazy outline of Hangman's Rock.

The scene was eerily still.

Suddenly he realized what he was doing—somewhere in that charred mess lay Ms. Jenkins and Mya. He tore away from the orb, gasping for breath. Everything that had happened came rushing back. The fire, the chaos, the desperate struggle for life. He fell to his knees, thinking he was going to retch, pearl rolling from his hand. Mya was gone and he was still here, walking and talking and breathing …

Leera rushed to his side. "Aug, you all right? What happened?"

He only shook his head.

Leera picked up the pearl. "So you still have it. And you looked through it, didn't you? Don't do it again, all right?"

He gazed into her dark eyes, eyes filled with concern. "All right."

After taking some time to comfort him, she shared a look with Bridget. "If the orb survived and the Legion found it—"

"—we could listen in," Bridget said. "We just have to be careful they don't do the same to us."

Meanwhile, he knelt by Mrs. Stone, taking her withered hand in his own. She had definitely aged, though not as fast as her husband—and just how was he supposed to tell her Thomas was gone?

He stared at her pale face, cracked with ancient lines. They looked deeper, more defined. Her hair seemed wispier too, though she still had it braided in a long silver ponytail. He glanced at her charred robe. It was fringed with gold and embroidered with unfamiliar white flowers. Had she received it from the monks?

Her eyes opened a little and she smiled. "You … have … done … well … great … grandson …"

Augum shook his head. "No, I haven't, Nana. I've failed miserably. Mya is … She's …"

"I … know. All … things … pass …"

It was painful to hear. He squeezed her hand. "Please don't speak, Nana, you need rest. I know we've got a lot to talk about, but it can wait."

"We … must … strike … east … Muranians …"

"Muranians?"

"Sounds like a mountain range," Bridget said, retrieving Tridian's sheepskin map. She scanned it with a finger. "They're not on here. Must be further east."

"I know where they are," Mr. Goss said, stepping through the door, face grim. "They are the dividing range between Tiberra and Solia. Such a journey would be perilous at this time as the Legion is moving through there on their way to attack Tiberra.

"Why the Muranians, Nana?"

They all turned to Mrs. Stone, whose eyes were closed. "Occulus' … castle."

"But Mrs. Stone," Bridget began, "Occulus' castle has been lost to time for, for over fifteen hundred years—"

"Must … find … it."

Augum suspected it had something to do with the Seers, but didn't press the issue as he didn't want to weaken her further. She'd explain in due time, he figured.

"We should find another hideout until Mrs. Stone recuperates," Mr. Goss said. "Somewhere safe." He rubbed his chin. "Maybe the Waxmans … old friends of the family who happen to possess a farm on the Gamber."

"That's my old river—" Augum said. "I lived near there."

"Let me see that map please. Ah, yes, here—" Mr. Goss tapped a spot north of Augum's old village of Willowbrook. "Mr. and Mrs. Waxman, their three daughters, and seven sons, I believe. If they are well and able, they will take us in and allow us rest."

Leera hunched over the map with knitted brows. "Mr. Goss, that's at least a four day walk …"

"Yes, I am aware, but I have a small store of food in Sparrow's Perch, and if we find more horses …"

"My father would search Sparrow's Perch first."

"We have no choice," Bridget said. "We need food."

Mrs. Stone beckoned weakly, whispered something into Bridget's ear.

"Mrs. Stone said it'll be safe to enter Sparrow's Perch right now, but we must be quick about it."

Mr. Goss gave a nod. "I believe the vanquished Legionnaires left behind a horse or two there as well."

Augum wondered what had become of the Blade of Sorrows. Would they find the man lying in the snow in the middle of the village?

"Bridget, you take the warhorse with Mrs. Stone," Mr. Goss said. "Leera, you take the chestnut with Leland. Augum and I shall walk."

Thick cloud trawled slowly overhead, the air crisp and dry. Not a sound stirred the forest other than the crunch of snow beneath hoof and foot. Augum's thoughts dwelled on Mya, Ms. Jenkins, and Haylee. The former two had perished, but what happened to Haylee? Could she still be saved? It was torment, not knowing. She deserved her freedom regardless of what she had done in school.

Mr. Goss had them stop outside the village. He made the girls wait with Mrs. Stone, taking Augum with him. Sparrow's Perch was riddled with Legion bodies, but not one was Tridian. While Mr. Goss gathered provisions, Augum quietly searched for a horse, finding a black Legion warhorse nearby. Mr. Goss soon emerged and they returned to the group. "So they left one behind after all," Leera said with a smile.

"And we should have enough food and blankets to last us the journey," Mr. Goss said. "I refilled our skins of water and found us some tents too." He proceeded to feed the horses, starting with the new arrival. "Leland, come ride with your father so the two adventurers can ride together."

Leland moaned, allowing his father to pick him up off the saddle and place him on the new horse.

Augum turned to Leera. "Stuck with me once again."

She sighed dramatically. "Whatever will I do?"

"Take the back."

She smirked. "Forget it. I've got the reins," and reached out a hand.

"Fine ..." He took it and hauled himself up, grabbing her waist.

Soon the group paced east on a course Mr. Goss surmised would take them directly to the Waxman farm, barring any encounters with the Legion. As they rode, the trio recounted the entirety of their adventures to Mrs. Stone, avoiding the subject of her husband and One Eye for now. They also informed her about the three things Sydo passed on to Sparkstone—that if he claimed all seven scions he'd be killed; that all the portals to Ley but the one in Castle Arinthian have been destroyed; and that there existed a recipe to make a portal to Ley without a scion.

"That is unfortunate," Mrs. Stone wheezed at the mention of these last three things, "but perhaps inevitable."

"Hey, whatever happened to that bag of snot anyway?" Leera asked.

Augum realized the girls hadn't witnessed the spectacle. He shook his head. "It all started with Sydo giving me the lamest slap—" and he went on to recount what happened to Sydo Ridian the Fourth, and how he met his most unfortunate end, though the comedic moments were greatly muted by the past evening's events.

"That poor, foolish boy," Bridget said in a broken voice.

"He was a traitor that got what he deserved," Leera said. "Just wish I could have seen him smeared into the manure."

"Don't say that—"

"But he—"

"Stop it. I don't want to hear anymore about it."

They passed through the snowy forest without incident, circumnavigating the southern side of Mt. Barrow before breaking out into the open Tallows. A wind had kicked up as clouds clumped overhead, casting a gray pall over the day. As there was no one around, the trio practiced their arcanery, especially the more difficult spells such as Push, Disarm and Slam, the latter only when they were far enough away from the forest to insure they would not be heard. By the time evening arrived, the trees had all but disappeared behind them, leaving the dim outline of Mt. Barrow, its peak lost in cloud.

Somewhere along that vast empty plain, they stopped to set up camp. After erecting tents and feeding and watering the horses, they bundled in blankets around a cozy fire and ate from their provisions. Mrs. Stone seemed to feel a little better, her eyes remaining open as she watched the curling flames. Finally, during a lull in conversation, Augum thought it a good time to fulfill his promise.

"Nana, I have something to tell you," he said, while Bridget and Leera instinctively stiffened.

Mrs. Stone turned her weary face to him.

"I told you how we had to leave Ley because they were threatening to wipe our memories. Well, what I didn't tell you was … about Great-grandfather … he saved us by leaving Ley with us, and, um—"

"—and he passed," Mrs. Stone finished for him in a gravelly voice, giving the slightest of nods, coughing. She closed her eyes and sighed. "I should have known Thomas would have gone with you. We discussed the possibility—only should something happen, that is. Though I rather had it in mind that he teleport you out of Ley. I told him you were more than capable of taking care of yourselves." She shook her head and smiled. "That old fool and his nonsense …"

"Nana … he … he did it to prove that immortality couldn't be taken beyond the boundary of Ley. Leaving aged him before our eyes. He said it was important we saw eternal life couldn't be taken beyond Ley."

"Knowledge is important. It is like fire—if it is not kept alight, it shall extinguish. Once in a while, a reminder is needed."

"There is more, Nana. He said … he said to tell you that he loved you." He thought of Mya and a lump formed in his throat. Mrs. Stone smiled sweetly and nodded, eyes distant as if remembering something warm and beautiful.

"It is as it was meant to be," she said.

After a reflective time silently watching the fire, Augum began telling her about a strange old man they met named One Eye. He told her about his odd shop; the supper and bathhouse; learning the Slam spell; and the dragon-tooth necklace, which led him to recount what One Eye told them about finding it in an ancient mine. At this last mention, Mrs. Stone surrendered a chortle.

"Indeed I thought your description sounded familiar. I daresay I find myself astounded to hear William is still alive—"

Augum exchanged a glance with the girls. He'd have to tell her about his death too, though he didn't want to break her fond reminiscence.

"I remember that adventure well," Mrs. Stone went on. "We were indeed a fearsome trio—William Smith the Plotter, Jordan Winters the Prankster, and I, Anna Atticus Stone, the young, ambitious warlock. A little too ambitious, perhaps. Yes, we found a supposed dragon tooth, though everyone doubted its authenticity. Dragons, after all, were the stuff of children's tales, and still are."

Augum then told her everything that happened with the witch's poem and Hangman's Rock, including smashing the supposed dragon tooth and passing a message on to her via the witch.

"So doesn't that prove dragons were once real?" he asked.

"I am in the dark in this matter as much as you. Yes, once in a while a mysterious skull would turn up, but it was always dismissed as some sort of ancient creature long extinct, anything but a dragon. Who is to say that this supposed dragon tooth was not itself something even the witch mistook?"

He had to acknowledge she might be right, but it was too tempting to believe the tooth was real.

"Witches are the main reason the common folk fear arcanery," Mrs. Stone continued. "They are the source of much superstition. I shudder to think how many died from false accusations. A good number of spell words are said to have their origin in their ancient tongue, and thus a great amount of knowledge has been exiled from places of learning due to their influence. Legend says that in olden times, witches would snatch unprotected children in the night, dragging them to hell."

"Mother used to scare me with stories like that when I misbehaved," Leera said.

"Didn't seem to work," Bridget said with a sly smile.

"Everyone has heard the tales. Witches communicate with that terrible plane, so far removed from Ley. Necromancy, too, draws its power from the same well, and so we should be wary of any such interactions. Though it is said when Occulus fell, the witches lost a lot of their power and it was safe to travel the night again."

"But witches do exist, just like Ley exists," Augum said. "Does that mean Hell exists too?"

Mrs. Stone paused a moment. "That is a word assigned by millennia of contradictory beliefs, but behind the word lie ancient arcane stories, stories lost to mortal time. All I can definitively say is that, if it exists, there is much we do not understand of Hell, as there is little we understand of Ley."

"So I guess hellhounds actually could come from Hell …" Leera said.

Mrs. Stone fought off a wracking cough. "Mercy, I fear I may be coming down with something."

"I'll make tea," Bridget said, placing snow in a kettle before setting it over the fire.

"Thank you, my dear. Now, in old mythology, all things ugly come from Hell, and all things beautiful from Ley. A rather simplistic view, but that is why it is myth. Whatever kind of plane it is, Hell has always been a great source of power for witches and necromancy. Consider yourself lucky, Augum. Many a man has fallen prey to a misspoken word when performing a witch's spell."

She patted his hand. "Do not concern yourself so, great-grandson. Real or not, what is important is that we are alive and together."

"Not all of us," he blurted.

She watched him a moment. "You have all witnessed more than your fair share of death. I wish it were not so, but we live in turbulent times." She glanced skyward. The clouds snailed along, darkening with the night. "When my strength returns, we shall perform a memorial ceremony."

They sat a little while, watching the flames ebb.

Augum stirred the fire. "I should tell you about what happened to One Eye, Nana," and at last, he recounted the events that unfolded after the Legion had showed up at the caravan. "... and in the end, One Eye sacrificed himself for us. He said ... he said to tell you that he was sorry and ... and grateful."

Mrs. Stone let silence pass before replying. "Sorry and grateful ... well, he is quite forgiven, that I assure you. You see, when we were young—that is, before I met Thomas—we were ... an *item*, if you want to call it that—"

Bridget and Leera exchanged blushing looks.

"—that was all a very long time ago, mind you. Anyhow, many years passed when I received word that William Smith had become an Arcaner. Arcaners are warlocks devoted to the old ways of chivalry and honorable arcane combat, ways that have almost gone extinct with such ruthless foes as Attyla the Mighty, Occulus, Narsus, Lividius, and others throughout history. One could say they are the knight version of the warlock. Unfortunately, there is little room for honor in this day and age. Yes, William was noble, great and honorable. I am content for him. Surely he would have said it was a good death."

After another long silence, Augum finally drew up the courage to ask what's been nagging him for some time. "Nana, why did so many sacrifice themselves for us?"

She coughed again, harder this time. He reached out to steady her but she waved him off. "For hope, Augum, hope. Remember these words—sacrifice for the good of all is the greatest strength of the benevolent—and the greatest enemy of the selfish. No one fights the Legion in Solia—no one. And why is that so? Because the threat comes from *within*. When the Tiberrans invaded hundreds of years ago, the king rallied the common folk to protect Solia. The same happened when the Canterrans and Nodians invaded, and they have invaded scores of times. That is why we have the Spears."

"Spears?" Augum asked.

"Eastspear Castle, now in ruins, erected to defend against Tiberra. Southspear, to defend against Nodia, and so on. Throughout history, there has always been great opposition to foreign powers." She placed her blue-eyed gaze upon him. "People need hope to survive. No one has stood up to the Legion and declared with a loud voice, 'We are sick and tired and cannot take it anymore!' "

"Forgive me, Mrs. Stone," Mr. Goss began, "but what about the might of Tiberra? Or Nodia, or Sierra? Could they not come to our aid?"

"These kingdoms are indeed powerful, Albert, but I fear they are not nearly powerful enough. Warlord necromancers have come and gone through all of history, leaving behind a trail of destruction, and most have not come from Solia. Attyla the Mighty was Canterran, for example. What we are witnessing is but the beginning of an old cycle. As we speak, Lividius builds, albeit slowly, an army enhanced by the might of Dreadnought steel, and once he masters the necromantic path, he will have armies of undead as well—walkers, wraiths, revenants, and creatures we cannot yet fathom. Then of course, there are the scions … artifacts the previous Dreadnought lords did not possess. Yes, I am afraid it has only just begun …"

These words sent everyone into more thoughtful reflection. At last, the fire smoldering low in the crisp air, Bridget perked up. "Mrs. Stone, we also overheard the Lord of the Legion say exactly why he had raised Atrius Arinthian—so that he could kill him again and take the choice to command the Dreadnoughts."

"Ah, of course! Had I the wherewithal to foresee such a thing I would have hidden Arinthian's body." She grimaced. "Hmm, to raise someone that has been dead for fifteen hundred years is quite the feat of necromancy. I daresay Lividius has grown in power. Once he learns how to use the scions, he will be fearsome to behold indeed."

"Father also told me he was once Narsus' apprentice," Augum said.

"I must confess that I have long suspected some kind of secret tutelage. It would account for his knowledge in the necromantic discipline. No book can compare to a competent mentor. I should not be surprised it was with one of my greatest foes."

Bridget handed her a cup of steaming tea. "Mrs. Stone, what happened with the Seers?"

"I did not know what to expect when I first arrived in the mountain city of Semadon. It had been a long journey and I was woefully tired. Having never been there before, I had to undergo the trek by foot and mule, unable to teleport myself further than Antioc. Thankfully, the mountain monks were quite hospitable. They even seemed to know who I was, yet mercifully took little regard.

"After a grand feast, I was guided high up a sacred mountain the monks referred to as Chomolagma, which I believe translates to The Great Mountain in the Sky. Halfway up this enormous mountain—and mind you it indeed was the largest mountain I have ever laid eyes upon—sat the monastery of the Seers, an ancient order of soothsaying mountain monks. After much ceremony, we meditated and fasted in silence for many days on end. After all that, they allowed me to ask a single question. One gets a single question per lifetime, so I took great care in its wording. I expect you already know which question it was that I asked."

"How to defeat my father," Augum replied.

"Quite correct. I received a troubling and cryptic answer to this great question, one that will take me some time to digest—one I will not share," she added after seeing the hopeful looks on their faces. "The Unnameables know you have enough to worry about. I do know we must find Occulus' castle, for inside that castle lies an ancient recipe long thought lost to mortals—"

"—are you talking about the one that builds a portal to Ley without the need of a scion, Mrs. Stone?" Leera asked. "Magua told us about it—"

Mrs. Stone's brows furrowed. "Magua spoke of it, did she?"

"She did, and we all thought it was strange that she said something like that to us. It kind of breaks their vow, doesn't it?"

"Magua …" Mrs. Stone took a sip of tea, brows knotted in thought. "Interesting. Regardless, I am quite certain Lividius was already aware of this recipe's existence. Aside from my scion, that recipe is Lividius' only hope of a bridge to Ley. We must find it before he does. Now incidentally, it was shortly after my meeting with the Seers that I received a most peculiar message—" she glanced to Augum, "—a message from, if I am not mistaken, a witch. I remember her words well. 'A price extracted for a message delivered,' and then I heard your voice, Augum. I departed immediately—and not a moment too soon, for apparently Lividius and his men reached the monastery thereafter. I must confess I am curious as to what price the witch extracted—"

"She took my arcanery," Augum said, watching the flames. "Ms. Jenkins gave it back at the cost of her life." How many was that now that gave their lives for them? Thomas Stone. William One Eye Smith. Ms. Jenkins. Three precious lives. Countless years gone, for what?

"Ms. Jenkins healed our wounds too, Aug," Leera said. "When they took us to the other tent without you."

"Then this Ms. Jenkins was a worthy healer," Mrs. Stone said.

"But how did you know to save Mr. Goss and Leland, Mrs. Stone?" Bridget asked.

"When I came upon the camp at Hangman's Rock, I took it upon myself to conduct surveillance. It was then I overheard that soldiers had ridden south to find Leland and his father. Judging that the encounter between the camp and I could wait, I hastily teleported to Sparrow's Perch."

"Mrs. Stone arrived just in time," Mr. Goss said. "The Blade of Sorrows had captured us, intending on returning to Hangman's Rock—but they certainly were no match for Mrs. Stone's arcanery. What an incredible show of strength, I tell you."

Leland moaned, making a grand explosive gesture.

"Once the villains had been dispatched," Mr. Goss went on, "she kindly escorted us to the abandoned cabin nearby. We are eternally in debt to her, are we not, Leland?"

Leland moaned.

Mrs. Stone gave the Goss' a kind smile. "That is quite a tired boy."

"Yes, I would say it is almost bedtime."

"Then what happened, Mrs. Stone?" Leera asked.

"I returned to confront Lividius and the problem of your confinement." Her eyes wandered over their charred and bloody robes. "The delay was not without a price, but that price was paid triple by Lividius' men."

"You mean Axon Company—" Augum said, remembering the very late arrival of two hundred men, once destined for Tiberra. He wondered if what happened would affect any outcomes in the war.

"I am afraid I am not familiar with the various names of Legion companies and battalions."

"It's just that I overheard them talking about their strategy. Axon company was supposed to go to Tiberra and join up with …" He searched his mind for the names of the other companies. "Wolfpack, Comborai, Malfease, and Nordika …"

"Ah, we have an aspiring general amongst our ranks!" Mr. Goss said, eyes sparkling behind his spectacles.

"When I recover my arcane stamina, I will teleport to Tiberra and pass along the information you have told me. I am sure their generals will find it useful. I must try to help them resist, though I fear they will not take a foreigner's advice with great humor. The Tiberrans, as welcoming and kind as they are, tend to rely on their own intelligence for solutions to great problems. Perhaps as all kingdoms do."

"So you've been to Tiberra, Mrs. Stone?" Bridget asked. "What is it like?"

"Many times. Their people are warm, friendly, and rich with tradition. Their academy is older than ours, but the essential arcanery is the same. More of their commoners read and write than ours. As a result, there are more warlocks."

Augum fingered the bright blanket wrapped around him. "Have you been to Dramask then?"

"Oh, indeed. The first time I went I was but a young warlock fresh out of the academy. It is a market paradise with rich and earthy foods. They make wonderful thread, spices, and love the sea. There are as many flavors of tea as there are grains of sand. One day, perhaps, I will take you all there."

Leera passed around more cups of tea. Augum took a mug, thoughts drifting to Sparrow's Perch.

"What happened to the Blade of Sorrows, Nana?" He wondered if he'd ever see him again. Perhaps, if he was lucky, Commander Tridian lay frozen stiff in the forest …

"I am not sure. Had I known what he put you through beforehand, I might have paid more attention to him at the time. As it was, I recall striking the commander with a bolt of lightning, but that is all. Now, whether he had lived or died—"

"—he lived," Augum said, shoulders slumping. "He sent a message to warn the camp about you, using a speaking orb. And I didn't find him in Sparrow's Perch."

Mrs. Stone sighed, adjusting the gold fringes of her once-white robe. "I have a question for you now, Great-grandson."

He stiffened, fearing a scolding of some kind.

"You mentioned the Orb of Orion was left back at Hangman's Rock—"

"—that was my fault, Mrs. Stone!" Bridget said, lowering her tea. "I could have grabbed it but—"

Mrs. Stone merely held up a hand, staying her protestations. "Allow me to tell you a story. The Orb of Orion was stolen twice in my lifetime. The first time I shall speak of in a moment, the second happened much later, while I was headmistress of the academy. I assure you it was quite the scandal. Suspicion fell on an Erika Scarson, though her family had the wealth to effectively silence the disciplinary council. I always knew she had stolen the orb, though I could not prove it. Thus, with the urging of my peers, I let the matter drop." She gave Augum a piercing look. "Now as I understand it, you have what you call a 'pearl', is that correct?"

"I have it here, Mrs. Stone," Leera said, digging it out of her robe pocket and handing it to her.

Augum wondered if they were in some kind of trouble. One Eye said the orb had been gifted to the Academy of Arcane Arts upon its founding a thousand years ago, and urged its return as soon as possible.

"Remarkable," Mrs. Stone whispered, examining the engraved pearl closely before closing her eyes in concentration. When she opened them again, her withered face creased with sadness. "The scene of battle still smokes. All is quiet."

Augum had a vision of Mya lying in the snow, alone and cold in the night. He hid his face, battling his feelings.

"Now let me tell you about the first time the Orb of Orion was stolen," Mrs. Stone continued. "When I was not much older than you lot, William, or One Eye as you know him, stole it from the academy—"

Augum looked up to share a secret look with Leera and Bridget, remembering this very story told from One Eye's perspective, how Mrs. Stone gave William a tongue-lashing before trying to crack the orb's secrets herself. Later, when they got caught, Mrs. Stone and her two friends received an academy record for the longest detention—almost a whole year.

"—back then the theft caused quite a stir," Mrs. Stone went on, eyes twinkling merrily, "and I feared our expulsion, so naturally I was going to give the orb right back. Before I did, however, I spent a few hours trying to understand its secrets—"

Augum couldn't help but smile knowing—from One Eye's version of the tale—that Mrs. Stone actually spent days with the orb.

"It was fabled that the Orb of Orion had the power to summon dragons, which I and everyone else thought nothing short of myth. So I gave it my all—and you could say that in my day, I was a rather advanced student—yet I failed to penetrate the orb's secrets. I understand now why I failed, but do you?"

She searched their faces, yet Augum and the girls drew blank looks. She smiled and slowly held up the pearl. "I failed because of this. When William stole the orb, he did not know there was a controlling pearl. Interestingly enough, when I became headmistress of the academy, there was no pearl then either. In fact I was not even aware of its existence until today. However, now that we are in possession of it, perhaps I may be able to spend some time studying the orb in detail, though without the orb itself, this may prove difficult. So allow me to consign it back to your care with the following duty—" She ceremoniously handed the ancient pearl back into Leera's reverently cupped hands. "You are to monitor the Legion to our advantage. But be warned—do not let them discover its nature, nor hear you speaking, because, as I now understand it, it is possible to listen through from the other end, is that not so?"

Augum and the girls nodded solemnly.

"Now what is interesting to me," Mrs. Stone began, steepling her fingers and looking scandalously at them all, "is if we did not have the pearl back when I and my friends borrowed the orb, then who did? And did they listen in on us all the while?" Her lips curved in a smile as she let everyone enjoy the little mystery. Discussion ensued as to the possible suspects, from the academy headmaster of the day, to the king, to a powerful sorcerer—or perhaps no one had been listening because the pearl was lost at the time. And just how did Erika come to possess it?

After much talk and reflection, Mrs. Stone's coughing worsened to the point she couldn't hold her cup of tea without spilling it.

"Will you allow me to escort you to bed, Mrs. Stone?" Mr. Goss asked. Mrs. Stone, still coughing, could only nod. "And you too, Leland, come."

The trio bid them goodnight and gathered closer to the fire, a pinprick of light among the black vastness of the Tallows.

"She really doesn't sound good," Bridget said. "I'm worried."

Leera shrugged. "I'm sure she'll be fine. She's the most powerful warlock alive, she's got a scion, and she can heal herself. I wouldn't worry."

"Long day ahead tomorrow," Augum said, idly stirring the flames, not looking forward to the drab journey across the Tallows.

Bridget adjusted a braid. "Lee, can you help me take these out tomorrow?"

"Sure, but you have to help with mine too." She turned to Augum. "Imagine if we actually find Occulus' castle …"

He shrugged. "I miss Castle Arinthian."

"So do I," Bridget said, washing the cups with snow. Then she stopped. "Isn't this the first day of Endyear or something?"

"Don't know, lost track of the days a while ago." Augum thought of the end of year traditions, the feasts, the games, the dancing and singing. He never got to take part in them much, having been ostracized from having friends or family. Sir Westwood had celebrated with him now and then, but it was still … lonely. Regardless, Endyear was a time of joy and peace and families, yet all across Solia, there was only suffering.

"Ten days of holiday celebrations," Bridget said in hollow tones.

After a time of quiet, Leera frowned. "Forget Endyear. Think we'll get our 2nd degree soon?"

"Hope so. Can't wait to show Nana what we've learned." He glanced up at the dark sky. "What an adventure, and somehow, I feel like it's only just begun …"

"Same," Leera said, resting her chin on her knees. Then she snorted.

"What?"

"Can't believe he got dragged through manure."

They chortled together.

Leera eventually sighed. "What your great-grandmother said about the good of all. It was … powerful."

"How did it go again …" Bridget said. " 'Sacrifice for the good of all is the greatest strength of the benevolent—and the greatest enemy of the selfish'."

"That's why they died," Augum said. "So many of them. They didn't just sacrifice themselves for us, they did it for everyone …"

The girls nodded slowly. He glanced at his two friends, their eyes reflecting the low flame, and smiled, grateful for their companionship.

They smiled back. Words were unnecessary. They were together and that was all that mattered.

FOR FANS OF *THE ARINTHIAN LINE*

Sign up to my mailing list and get the next *unreleased* ebook in the series for only 99 cents (and to be kept in the loop about releases). You'll have a window of 24 hours once the book goes live. After that, it'll go back to regular price, so make sure to open that email as soon as you see it.

Go to severbronny.com/contact and subscribe using the link on the page.

BOOKS IN SERIES

Check out severbronny.com for news on the other books in the series.

BE A HERALD—SPREAD THE WORD

Honest reviews are critical in today's highly competitive market. I'd be grateful if you would consider leaving one on Amazon.com and/or Goodreads.com for *Arcane* (or any of the other books in the series).

Word of mouth also helps. It makes a *huge* impact when you share a link to *Arcane's* Amazon page on social media like Facebook, Twitter, etc.

Thank you so much, it really means a lot to me :)

ADVANCE READER TEAM

Want to take things to the next level? Read my books before anyone else does for free? Receive secret special rewards? Apply to join my Advance Reader Team at severbronny.com/team

CONNECT

I *love* hearing from readers. Email me anytime at severbronny@gmail.com — I respond to everyone :)

Website: severbronny.com

Twitter: @SeverBronny

Goodreads: goodreads.com/severbronny

My other passion: Tribal Machine — www.tribalmachine.com

ACKNOWLEDGMENTS

The Arinthian Line has been in the making for years, and I couldn't have done it without the loving support of my amazing wife and editor, Tansy.

A special thank you to my family, friends, my ART team, and my loyal readers for supporting my work.

All my best to you and those you love,

Sever Bronny

ABOUT THE AUTHOR

Sever Bronny is a musician and author living in Victoria, British Columbia, Canada. He has released three albums with his industrial-rock music project Tribal Machine, including the full-length concept album *The Orwellian Night*. One of his songs can be heard in the feature-length film *The Gene Generation*. His love of fantasy began with Dragonlance and continues on with Harry Potter. Connect with him at his website severbronny.com.

Printed in Great Britain
by Amazon